Rebels and Traitors

Also by Lindsey Davis

The Course of Honour

The Falco Series
The Silver Pigs
Shadows in Bronze
Venus in Copper
The Iron Hand of Mars
Poseidon's Gold
Last Act in Palmyra
Time to Depart
A Dying Light in Corduba
Three Hands in the Fountain
Two for the Lions
One Virgin Too Many
Ode to a Banker
A Body in the Bath House
The Jupiter Myth
The Accusers
Scandal Takes a Holiday
See Delphi and Die
Saturnalia
Alexandria

Rebels and Traitors

—◆◆◆—

LINDSEY DAVIS

St Martin's Press   New York

REBELS AND TRAITORS. Copyright © 2009 by Lindsey Davis. All rights reserved. Printed in the United States of America. For information, address St. Martin's Press, 175 Fifth Avenue, New York, N.Y. 10010.

Picture of London from Southwark © Museum of London

www.stmartins.com

Library of Congress Cataloging-in-Publication Data

Davis, Lindsey.
    Rebels and traitors / Lindsey Davis. — 1st U.S. ed.
        p. cm.
    ISBN 978-0-312-59541-8
    1. Great Britain—History—Civil War, 1642–1649—Fiction. I. Title.
    PR6054.A8925R43 2010
    823'.914—dc22

                                                                    2009033708

First published in Great Britain by Century, an imprint of
The Random House Group Limited

First U.S. Edition: January 2010

10 9 8 7 6 5 4 3 2 1

London from Southwark, 17th Century

For Richard
dearest and closest of friends
your favourite book
in memory

SCOTLAND

IRELAND

WALES

Edinburgh
Dunbar ✕
Berwick
R. Tweed
Philiphaugh ✕

Newcastle
Carlisle · Durham

Marston ✕ · York
Moor
Adwalton ✕ Hull
Moor · Pontefract
Preston · Doncaster

Drogheda

Dublin

Chester
✕ Nantwich Newark ✕
Shrewsbury Nottingham
Lichfield · Leicester
Birmingham Coventry Naseby ✕
(Aston, Edgbaston) Daventry · Holmby Newmarket
Worcester · Cambridge
Wexford Tewkesbury ✕ Edgehill Newport Pagnell Colchester
Gloucester Stony Stratford
Oxford · Chalgrove
Pembroke ✕ Wallingford London
Bristol · Roundway Newbury Windsor The
Bath · Down · Reading Cobham Gravesend Downs
Langport ✕ Basing · Maidstone ✕ Dover
Alton
Portsmouth Brighton
Carisbrooke
Lostwithiel ✕ Plymouth Portland Isle of
Fowey Wight

R. Severn
R. Trent

N

miles
0 20 40 60 80 100

Guernsey
Channel Isles
Jersey

Turnham London R. Thames
Green
Putney Southwark Greenwich
Hampton Court

Prologue

Whitehall: 30 January 1649

The King would take his dog for an early morning walk in St James's Park. What could be more civilised?

Its name was Rogue. As the eager spaniel tried to run outside, the soldiers made it go back. Its master strolled on without the dog, going to his execution as if taking daily exercise.

Other deposed monarchs suffered greater brutality. Charles Stuart of Britain was never chained, starved, imprisoned in a bare cell or tortured. People would argue whether his trial was legal, but he did have a trial and it ended abruptly only because he refused to acknowledge the process. Once condemned, generally he continued to be treated with wary good manners. No silent, black-clad assassins would arrive by night to carry out violent orders that could be denied later. King Charles faced no slow neglect in a remote castle dungeon, no thrashing head-down in a wine-butt, no red-hot poker spearing his guts. Variants of all of these tortures had been perpetrated on his subjects during the bloodshed he was charged with causing, yet he remained exempt. His accusers were determined that calling him to account would be open, 'a thing not done in a corner'.

On that bitter January Tuesday, the King was given bread and wine for breakfast. Two of his children were brought for tearful goodbyes. Then he went on his final walk, across the royal park. He had asked for two heavy shirts, in case he shivered in the cold and appeared afraid.

At about ten in the morning, he was taken from St James's Palace to Whitehall Palace fifteen minutes away. An escort of New Model Army halberdiers formed his guard, with colours flying and beating drums, while a few permitted gentlemen walked with him, bare-headed. Regiments of foot soldiers lined the route.

There were no tumbrels. No orchestrated mob spat and shouted abuse. Wearing a tall hat and the embroidered silver Order of the Garter on his dark cloak, King Charles reached the waiting crowds; he was protected by the halberdiers, but the people's mood was sombre, almost curious. Whitehall was packed. Dissidents, any known Royalists, were barred from London, so almost all of the people here were his opponents. When they first sided with Parliament, few had dreamed of an outcome like this. Few of them had sought it. Some were still uneasy.

The guard-party climbed the steps to the Holbein Gate. Its direct access to the old Palace of Whitehall brought the King to private apartments which he had last seen seven years before, when he first fled London as his subjects became rebellious.

Once indoors, he had to endure a delay of several hours. With him was the aged Bishop of London, William Juxon, who, as time went by, persuaded Charles to take some bread and a glass of claret, lest he should falter on the scaffold. Colonel Hacker, a particularly boorish Roundhead, had wanted to place two musketeers in the King's chamber, but had been prevailed upon not to do it.

Apparently, the reason for the delay was that Richard Brandon, the public executioner, had refused to act and his assistant had disappeared. There was also a problem with the execution block; the usual waist-high block could not be found, so a much lower one was brought, which was normally used only for dismembering dead traitors' bodies. However, the execution axe had arrived safely from the Tower of London. Eventually two men agreed to stand in for the executioner and his assistant. They wore masks for anonymity and their identities were kept secret.

At two o'clock in the afternoon, Colonel Hacker knocked discreetly at the door of the private apartment, then rapped again, louder. With Bishop Juxon on one side and Colonel Tomlinson who had personal charge of him on the other, the King was led along a route he knew well into the Banqueting House, created for ceremonial occasions and celebratory masques.

The cold stateroom echoed and smelled of neglect. Motes of dust drifted in the winter light that crept wanly through cracks in the boarding that covered the elegant windows. Tapestries had been looted or officially taken away. Gone were the candelabra that had once filled the great space with warmth and illumination. As he walked past his one-time throne of state, the King's way was lit only by feeble lights carried by soldiers. A crowd of onlookers murmured sympathetically, and some prayed; the soldiers on guard allowed this without annoyance.

Overhead, quite invisible in the gloom, soared the fabulous ceiling paintings by Sir Peter Paul Rubens which Charles had commissioned to promote his belief that he was God's appointed Lieutenant, with a Divine Right to rule. After the panels' installation, no further masques had been performed in the Banqueting House, to prevent smoke from the torches damaging the work. Had King Charles been able to see them, the magnificent paintings must have mocked. They celebrated the union of England and Scotland — personified by Charles himself as a naked infant, beneath the conjoined crowns of the very two kingdoms which in the past decade he had repeatedly set against each other as he scrambled to keep his position and his life. These florid, heavily allegorical pictures extolled his father's successful reign. Peace embraced Plenty. Reason controlled Discord. Wisdom defeated Ignorance and the serpents of Rebellion.

The party measured the length of the dark reception hall then emerged into more light through the tallest doorway at the end — the entrance through which ambassadors, courtiers, actors and musicians had once advanced to pay reverence to this monarch. He was taken out through it onto the stone staircase in the northern annexe. On the landing, a wall had been knocked out around one of the large windows. King Charles stepped outside, emerging onto a scaffold, surrounded by low posts upon which were hung black draperies. Although the swags partly hid proceedings from the street, the roofs of surrounding buildings were crammed with spectators. Down at street level, the scaffold had been lined, and then interlined, with Parliamentarian soldiers. Inevitably, the armed troops were facing the crowd.

Others, official agents, were watching the spectators, alert for any sign of trouble and seeking known faces. In uniform by the Horse Guards Yard stood a fair-haired man, just short of thirty: Gideon Jukes. He had been very busy that day and now kept to himself, shaken and avoiding contact with anyone he knew. Everywhere were soldiers whose faces he recognised. Always rather solitary, he felt himself to be a disengaged observer. Everyone around him seemed lost in the occasion. He was troubled by the event, not because he felt it to be treason, but because he feared the arrangements might go wrong. To Gideon Jukes, what had once been unthinkable was now the only course to take.

When movement caught his eye at the window, he raised his eyes to the scaffold with expectation and relief.

King Charles was met by the disguised executioner and his assistant. Heavy metal staples had been bolted to the scaffold floor in case it was necessary to chain him, but his demeanour remained quiet. Still in attendance, the Bishop of London received the King's cloak and his Order of the Garter, giving him a white silk cap. Charles removed his doublet and stood in his waistcoat. The King attempted to make a speech to the crowd, but the noise was too great. To the bishop he said, 'I go from a corruptible crown to an incorruptible one.' Then to the executioner, who was looking at him anxiously, 'Does my hair trouble you?' The executioner and the bishop together helped position the King's long hair under the cap.

Eyeing the block, the King exclaimed, 'You must set it fast.'

'It is fast, sir,' replied the executioner civilly.

'It might have been a little higher.'

'It can be no higher, sir.'

'I shall say but very short prayers, then when I thrust out my hands this way —'

The King knelt before the block. He spoke a few words to himself, with his eyes uplifted. Stooping down, he laid his head upon the block, with the executioner again tidying his hair. Thinking the man was about to strike, Charles warned, 'Stay for the sign!'

'Yes, I will,' returned the executioner, still patient. 'And it please Your Majesty.'

There was a short pause. The King stretched out his hands. With one blow of the axe, the executioner cut off the King's head.

The assistant held up the head by its hair, to show to the people, exclaiming the traditional words: 'Here is the head of a traitor!' The body was hurriedly removed and laid in a velvet-lined coffin indoors. As was normal at executions, the public were allowed to approach the scaffold and, on paying a fee, to soak handkerchiefs in the dripping blood, either as trophies of their enemy, or in superstition that the King's blood would heal illnesses.

* * *

When the axe fell, a low groan arose from the crowd. Friends to the monarchy would call it a cry of horror. Others, including Gideon Jukes, thought it merely an expression of astonishment that anyone had dared to do this. He too had caught an involuntary breath. *Now*, thought Gideon, *now indeed, is the world turned truly upside down.*

Not far away, the young wife of an exiled Royalist also watched the grim scene. But she believed that the world is not so readily altered. The old order had not been destroyed, the old conflicts still raged. If this was a new beginning, Juliana knew, men like her absent husband would conspire bitterly to make it falter and fail.

After the blow fell, she stood lost among the crowds. To be at the Banqueting House had taken her back to the age of eight, one blissful night when she had been allowed to attend a masque played for the King and Queen. She remembered her entrancement, particularly with the Queen. Four months after the birth of her second son, Henrietta Maria was at that time radiantly returning to court life, a petite vision in silvered tissue, pointed slippers with beribboned rosettes, pearl necklaces and exquisite lace. To a child, this expensive doll-like creature sparkled with magic. Little girls love beautiful princesses and freely forgive heroines who have buck teeth and a lack of formal education. The Queen had brought the slightly raffish sophistication of her French upbringing to the wary English, along with a fixed certainty that a king's authority was absolute. She would never understand her mistake.

Little girls grow up. The brightest of them come to loathe short-sighted policy, based on ignorance and indifference. The child who attended the court masque full of innocence and fun had learned this all too well.

The King was dead. His Queen would mourn. Trapped in the desolate struggles of a widow even though her husband was alive, Juliana wept on a London street. Though she pitied the King and his newly bereaved Queen, she was weeping for herself. She wept because she could no longer pretend: because she knew that the civil war had deprived her of all her hopes in life.

It was time to go. She was plainly dressed because of her poverty, worn by struggles and uncertainties, yet too firm-willed to seem a victim either to pickpockets or government agents. She was confident she could leave the scene quickly and go home without misadventure.

Trying not to attract attention, she slipped down a side street to the river where she hoped to take a boat downstream.

Moments later, mounted soldiers swept through the streets, clearing the crowds. Once the area appeared deserted, a small escort party surreptitiously left the Banqueting House. Gideon Jukes led them, setting the executioner safely on his way home. So as the winter darkness closed in, he too went down the dark side street that led to Whitehall Stairs.

Chapter One

London: 1634

Gideon Jukes first publicly became a rebel when he put on a feathered suit to play a bird.

Few who knew Gideon later would have expected he started his defiance of authority by acting in a royal pageant. As his elder brother cruelly said at the time, the best thing about it was that Third Dotterel's costume included a complete feathered head with a long beak, which hid the boy's erupting acne.

They lived on the verge of political upheaval, but at thirteen adolescence overwhelms everything else. Gideon Jukes in 1634 knew little of national events. He was bursting out of his clothes with uncontrollable spurts of growth. He was obsessed with his ravaged complexion which he was sure repelled girls, his fair hair which at the same time attracted more female attention than he could handle, and the thunderous wrongs done to him by everyone he knew. He was convinced other people had luck in unfair abundance. He believed he himself lacked talent, friends, fortune, looks, likeability – and also that he had been denied any skills to remedy the situation. He was certain this would never change.

That year, he devoted himself to being obnoxious. His worried family railed at him, making his grudges worse. After one particularly loud and pointless family argument he decided to become an actor. His parents would be outraged. Gideon was bound to be found out. But there is no point in rebellion if nobody notices.

The Jukes were tradesmen, hard-working and comfortably off. John Jukes was a member of the Grocers' Company of the City of London. His wife was Parthenope, née Bevan. His elder son was Lambert, his second Gideon, with fifteen years between them. Between Lambert and Gideon, Parthenope Jukes had borne nine other children. After Gideon there had been three more. None survived infancy.

So Gideon Jukes had grown up a younger son, separated by many years from his more fortunate brother. Lambert was also a grocer. As the eldest, he was in the English tradition his father's pride and joy; he was clapped on the back by fellow members of the Grocers' Company; he was greeted with familiar joshing by other grocers. Most importantly, Lambert would one day inherit the family business near Cheapside and their home, a substantial merchant's house in Bread Street.

Lambert had entered into his apprenticeship the year Gideon was born; Gideon never had a chance of sharing and this imbued him with a hatred of unfairness. As soon as Lambert completed his indenture and became a journeyman, he strutted around the family house and shop as if he already owned them. Becoming a master grocer was a particularly smooth process when your family had been in the fraternity for the past two centuries; Lambert seemed fair set to be an alderman before Gideon left puberty.

Lambert was a large character too. London apprentices were rowdy, opinionated youths, who revelled in their uniform of leather apron and short hair. They took to the streets in boisterous crowds whenever there was a chance to demonstrate their opposition to anything. King Charles gave them plenty of opportunity. Lambert had been thrilled by apprenticeship life, and long afterwards, if the lads took to the streets for a riot, he liked to be there.

Lambert Jukes was a big, fair-headed tough, always popular and strong enough to roll a barrel of blue figs one-handed, which he would do all along Cheapside, aiming at butter wenches. He had large numbers of friends. He could have had many lady friends, but being known as a good steady fellow, he cast his eye over the prettiest, then settled for Anne Tydeman. She had stayed on his arm for a long time, but Lambert had now reached twenty-eight and after letting Anne sew her trousseau linen resignedly for years, he declared he was ready to marry her. That was more cause for despair in his younger brother.

In truth, Lambert kicked Gideon around no more than any elder brother would; Lambert had no need to be jealous and he was by nature reasonable. Only a churl would have taken against him. It was pointed out to Gideon at home that he was fortunate. His father encouraged him; his mother excused him; even his brother tolerated him.

Gideon saw none of this, only his own bad luck. As soon as Lambert brought a wife home, Gideon knew, his own position must deteriorate. No chance of being a cuckoo in the nest: he had been tipped over the edge of it while still squirming in his shell.

He was due to leave home in any case. His father was fussing over arrangements for his apprenticeship. It would be with another member of the Grocers' Company, who would take the youth into his home and business for about seven years. In his current irritating phase, Gideon waited until almost the last moment, so that his father was under the greatest possible obligation. Then he refused to do it.

That was bad enough. Soon his great-uncle stepped in and blew up an even greater typhoon by suggesting that Gideon should *not* be a grocer.

The Jukes brothers were moulded by the aromatic trade of their father. As children they had mountaineered over barrels of dates and currants. They bartered for other boys' spinning tops with pieces of crystal sugar – the fine dust that surrounded sugar loaves when they arrived in their chests – and they swapped caraway comfits for conkers. Gideon had been scarred for life by falling off a delivery cart. His memories were dominated by a kitchen redolent with allspice and nutmeg. He was a toddler when he first learned the difference between cinnamon bark and a blade of mace. A good baked pudding would suffuse the whole house, buffeting anyone who opened the front door. It would linger for three days if nothing else was baked – but something always was.

His brother Lambert's very name recalled the moment his mother felt her first birth pang, which had happened most inconveniently when she was moulding the decorations for a Simnel cake.

"There I was, mopping up my waters with a pudding cloth. I knocked the pestle and the ground almonds right off the table – my hands were so oily from the paste, I could not open the door to call for the maid. Now I feel queasy if I ever look at marzipan balls –'

'And how was the cake?' young Gideon would ask gravely.

'Not one of my best. I had quite forgot the zest of orange.'

'And it had squashed balls!' Gideon would mouth at his brother, making this not just obscene but personal. In reply Lambert rarely did worse than throwing a cushion at his head.

They ate well. Generations of Jukes had done so, ever since their first member of the Grocers' Company set up a home and business just off Cheapside. The certainty of good dinners in the Jukes home had attracted Bevan Bevan, Parthenope's uncle, who dined frequently with them while making irritating claims that *he* had organised their marriage. John rejected any idea that he owed his wife to anyone else. Most Jukes men assumed they could win any woman they liked simply by expressing an interest. Historically, they were right.

John groaned every time Bevan visited, but Bevan had promised to be a patron to Gideon. Bevan's will would generally be mentioned about the time in a meal when Parthenope served a quaking pudding or an almond tart. For over a decade, as his great-uncle gorged on the spiced Jukes cuisine, it was expected that Bevan would leave Gideon an inheritance. A bachelor for fifty years, he had had no other heir. Then with no warning he married Elizabeth Keevil, a printer's widow. From the moment they entered the marriage bed – or, as the Jukes always reckoned, from a couple of months beforehand – Bevan began prolifically fathering children of his own.

'Let him dine at his own table from now on!' snarled John, through a mouthful of 'Extraordinary Good Cake'. 'A little more ginger next time . . . ?'

'*I think not!*' retorted Parthenope, tight-lipped. The set of her jaw was just like Gideon's.

Bevan politely kept away, especially after strong words passed between him and Parthenope. But once Gideon started to resist his father's plans, it was Bevan Bevan who added a fuse to the gunpowder by suddenly offering to pay for an apprenticeship with a printer his wife knew. John and Parthenope saw this as the ultimate treachery.

Robert Allibone, the printer, genuinely needed assistance with his business. Gideon was proposed to him by Bevan as a bright, honest boy who was keen to learn and would stay to a task. No mention was made of his troubled behaviour.

Bevan's intervention caused uproar. Gideon, of course, found it exciting to be at the centre of the quarrel. Parthenope had already spoiled two batches of buttered apple pudding, and John accidentally set fire to the house-of-easement in their yard while gloomily taking too many pipes of tobacco as he brooded. The half-built house-of-easement had never been in use, because it was a long-term project of the kind that remains a project. Nonetheless, John had been able to sit in the

roofless structure enjoying quiet philosophy and flaunting at their neighbours, none of whom had one, the fact that the Jukes were constructing
their own dunny. Now they must continue to throw their slops into the
street and to have their nightsoil collected by sinister men with carts
who tramped foul substances into the hall floorboards. John Jukes, who
was only allowed to smoke out of doors, had to sit on an old molasses
barrel, grimly contemplating the burnt ruin as he blamed Bevan for
seducing Gideon to an alien trade.

Gideon complained rudely: 'It is the loss of the project that matters
to you most!'

'You are an ill-mannered boy,' was his father's mild reply. 'Yet you
are mine, dear child, and I must bear my disappointment.'

When Parthenope noticed that John's mole-coloured britches had
been irretrievably singed in the blaze, another tempest started, during
which Gideon stormed out of the house close to tears. That was when
he ran into Richard Overton, a casual acquaintance with a yen for
causing trouble, who told him that bit-parts were being offered in a
court masque.

This was a fine way to offend everyone. The Jukes saw the devil in
theatricals, and royal entertainments were the most perverted. As
respectable traders, they solidly opposed the debauchery and idleness
of courtiers; like many Londoners, they were even starting to oppose
the King himself. These were the years when King Charles struggled
to rule without a Parliament. His methods of financing himself grew
ever more contentious. People in business viewed his ploys as interference. Even at thirteen, Gideon knew this. Royal monopolies were the
sorest point. Whereas once patents had been granted only for new
inventions, now all kinds of commodities were licensed only to royal
favourites, who charged exorbitant prices and grabbed huge profits.
Selling salt and soap had always been the prerogative of the grocers,
so that rankled; beer was a staple and so was coal for Londoners. The
City had also been outraged by Ship Money, the King's hard-hitting
tax for the navy, not least because this tax was devised to finance a war
about bishops, a war they disapproved of. John Jukes declaimed the cry
of one Richard Chambers who had been imprisoned and fined for his
part in a protest strike: 'Merchants are nowhere in the world so screwed
and wrung as in England'.

'Screwed and wrung!' had chanted the Jukes sons, who had an ear for a catch-phrase.

The family also held Independent views in religion. They belonged to one of the puritan churches that lurked down every side street of the City parishes; Gideon was of course taken there every Sunday. John contributed to the fee of a radical weekly lecturer who was frequently in trouble with the Bishop of London for his unorthodox preaching. The Jukes believed in freedom of conscience and freedom of worship. People who never bowed the knee in church were sceptical of a civil ruler who expected his subjects to kneel to him. 'If God does not require ceremony, why should a king?' They feared that Charles Stuart, encouraged by his French wife, was trying to impose Catholic rituals upon them, and they hated it. They homed in on Queen Henrietta Maria as an object of hate because she loved theatre and masques. Theatres, every Londoner was certain (because it was true), were haunts of prostitutes and rakes.

So if there was one thing Gideon could do to upset his family, it was listening to Richard Overton and volunteering to take part in a masque – a masque, moreover, which the lawyers from the Inns of Court were to present to the King and Queen.

He had never acted before. Nevertheless, he came cheap, so he secured a very minor part as one of three dotterels, small quiet birds of the plover family. He was young and naïve enough to be embarrassed when his two acting companions, slightly older boys, made jokes that among dotterels it was the female bird who engaged in displays while the male tended the nest.

Gideon's own sense of humour was more political; he was smiling satirically over the masque's title, which was *The Triumph of Peace*.

Rehearsals were brisk. During them, Gideon soon realised that he was a player in a work of numbing obsequiousness. *The Triumph of Peace* had been written by the popular poet James Shirley. It relied on spectacle rather than a fine script. All anybody wanted from it was flattery for the King, with gasps of delight at the rich costumes and at the complex engineering of the stage machinery.

The best talent in London contributed. The music was by the King's favourite composer William Lawes, his brother Henry Lawes, and Simon Ives, who excelled at glees and part-songs. The indoor stage sets were by the tireless Inigo Jones, architect, painter and emblematic publicist of the Stuart monarchy. The pageant's enormous cost included payment to a French costume-maker, brought out of retirement to stitch bird costumes, plus the cost of many sacks of feathers, acquired by this Frenchwoman at inflated prices from the canny feather-suppliers with whom she had long been in league.

For Gideon and his two companions she had produced padded suits sewn with hundreds of grey, white and russet feathers, costumes which had to be kept pulled up tight under the crotch, to make their legs look as long and thin as possible. The suits were held on by braces over the shoulders and were topped with heavy heads that had to be applied very carefully, or they ended up askew. In his feathered costume, Gideon had a fine, bright-chestnut padded belly marked with a distinctive white bar across his upper chest like a mayoral chain and prominent white eye stripes, joining on the back of the neck; after his headpiece was fixed, he could dip and raise its narrow beak, though at risk of breaking it.

Once inside, visibility was almost nil. He felt hot and claustrophobic, and the bird's head crushed down on his own with disconcerting pressure. Gideon began to experience regrets, but it was too late to back out.

Chapter Two

Whitehall: 2 February 1634

The blur of torchlight first became visible to the waiting crowds at Charing Cross. Spectators made out an occasional twinkle, then ranks of tarry flambeaux bobbed queasily in the darkness, finally filling the broad street with light. The horses and chariots made their slow, noisy way towards Whitehall Palace and the watching lords and ladies. A spectacular cast of players had spent hours preparing themselves in grand private mansions along the Strand and now they advanced towards the Banqueting House. Above the clatter of horses' hooves, a reedy shawm struggled to make its music heard in a hornpipe for frolicking antimasquers, who were to present low-life comedy interludes. They wore coats and caps of yellow taffeta, bedecked with red feathers, and were ushering *Fancy*, the first featured character, in multi-coloured feathers and with big bats' wings attached to his shoulders. This quaint figure led the way for numerous curiosities, who were celebrating a tricky moment in history.

The Triumph of Peace was being presented to a King who certainly ruled without conflict. He had dismissed his truculent Parliament six years before. Now, though, his independence had an end-date for he had made himself penniless. To set the moment in context, that year of 1634 would see the notorious witchcraft trials at Loudun, the first meeting of the *Académie française*, the opening of the Covent Garden piazza in London, and the charter for the Oxford University Press. North America was being colonised with permanent settlements. Europe, from Scandinavia to Spain, was a theatre of blood, rape and pillage in what would come to be known as the Thirty Years War. The previous year, Galileo Galilei had been tried in Rome and forced to recant his opinion that the earth went around the sun; he now languished in the prison where he would die. In London the world revolved around King Charles.

In England, without apparent irony, its ruling couple could be hailed in song by Shirley as

> '. . . great *King and Queen, whose smile*
> *Doth scatter blessings through this Isle . . .'*

The masque celebrated the King's and Queen's recent return from Scotland. There, causing as much offence as he possibly could to his strait-laced and suspicious Scottish subjects, King Charles had been crowned monarch of two kingdoms. He had worn ostentatious robes of white satin and had outraged the fierce Scottish Kirk by using a thoroughly Anglican ritual, conducted by a phalanx of English bishops in jewel-bright robes. This display was not designed to win the hearts of sober Presbyterians. Although always convinced of his personal charm, King Charles saw no reason to show diplomacy to mere subjects. Why should he? He was accustomed to uncritical praise – for instance, the nauscous blandishments he was about to hear in Shirley's masque, calling him *'the happiness of our Kingdom, so blest in the present government . . .'.* Perhaps only lawyers could have endorsed this. Even some of those paying for the masque may have choked on it.

There were three kingdoms, in fact, some more blest than others. It was never thought necessary to have a coronation for the Irish, even to offend them. They were seen as savages, whose best land English monarchs and their favourites greedily plundered – more recently, an investment opportunity even to the well-off English middle classes. The Welsh skulked in a mere rocky principality; they were allowed the traditional honour of their own Prince of the Blood, even though, as was also traditional, they never saw their sovereign's eldest son. The Prince of Wales was not quite four years old and so not allowed to stay up to watch *The Triumph of Peace*. Peace would play little part in his early life.

On returning from Edinburgh, King Charles and his enormous entourage had been ceremonially welcomed back by the Lord Mayor and Aldermen of the City of London. Gideon had gone to watch. Borne in the civic procession was the traditional naked sword – which might be prophetic. The staged welcome, with bare-headed reverence from the leading citizens, colour, vibrancy, noise, and crowds of applauding onlookers penned behind street rails, had similarities to the masque which the flattering lawyers then offered at Whitehall. It may have helped the monarch to believe that life was one great pageant of admiration, with himself its adored centre. But the grudging boy in the dotterel-suit was starting to wonder.

Bulstrode Whitelocke, the go-getting lawyer who had arranged *The Triumph of Peace*, knew what he was about. The royal family lapped up such entertainments, oblivious to the obscene expense. This masque cost twenty thousand pounds, at a time when a well-to-do farmer with his own land might earn two or three hundred pounds a year and a cobbler was paid sixpence a day – but must supply his own thread. Apples were three for a penny and ribbon was ninepence a yard. You could buy a horse for two pounds, or a blind one for half as much. Brought up to know the value of money, Gideon goggled at this extravagance. Twenty thousand pounds lavished on one night's court entertainment could only mean enormous royal favour was expected in return. Would the King understand the bargain?

Gideon began to see why the Queen's love of such theatricals had attracted scabrous comment. As this procession was wending its colourful way along Whitehall to the Banqueting House, everything about it – including its staging on Candlemas, which was a Catholic feast day – looked like deliberate defiance against William Prynne, the puritan author of a fanatical tract called *Histriomastix: the Players' Scourge (or Actor's Tragedy)*. Prynne had an obsessive hatred for the theatre. He denounced the Queen, who had shocked England by importing French actresses to take part in court masques, at a time when women did not appear on the stage. Worse, it was said that Henrietta Maria had scandalously danced in these masques herself.

William Prynne, who was a lawyer, had been tried in the hated Star Chamber, which ruled on censorship. He was sentenced to a ferocious fine, the pillory and prison; he was doggedly continuing his activities from jail and would eventually be tried a second time, have his ears lopped and his forehead branded 'SL' for Seditious Libeller. He was already deprived of his Oxford degree, and expelled from Lincoln's Inn, the very Inn whose more grovelling members had contributed to *The Triumph of Peace*.

Few of the satin-clad lords and ladies probably gave much thought to the imprisoned campaigner as the crowds gasped with delight at '*Jollity* in a flame-coloured suit' and '*Laughter* in a long coat of several colours, with laughing vizards on his breast and back, a cap with two grinning faces, and feathers between'. But as they stamped their cold feet outside in Whitehall, Lambert Jukes and his uncle were discussing Prynne sardonically. Bevan had an intimate connection with literature nowadays. Those who love books love free ones best of all. Through his new wife, the printer's widow, Bevan obtained reading material which – since the widow was extremely well-off – he had leisure to peruse.

'Have you read this *Players' Scourge?*' asked Lambert.

'Nobody has read it,' scoffed Bevan Bevan flatly. 'No man has a life long enough. We use this book to prop up a dilapidated court cupboard that has lost a foot. It is more than a thousand pages of bile! This is a mighty cube of invective, expelled like foul air from the posterior of one who professes never to visit the playhouse –'

'Difficult, when the theatres are closed due to plague.' Lambert sounded pleased to find this flaw.

Bevan eased his bulk, trying to get comfortable on his lame leg. He and Lambert were squeezed into a dark corner opposite the Horse Guards Yard, to which Bevan had led them by a back route up from the river, passing through the woodyard, coalyards, and other palace offices. 'They say Prynne's book is a very conduit of foul-mouthed, narrow-minded, fearsome flame-throwing spite which the crazed author has gathered over seven years –'

'And he calls the Queen a whore?' Lambert was always direct. From their position, they could see the tall windows of the Banqueting House; within its warmth, persons who called themselves quality were pressed against the glass panes, craning out at the spectacle. The King and Queen would be among that richly dressed throng. From time to time a jewel flashed on the white neck of one of the ladies, whose high-waisted gowns with puffed sleeves and snowflake collars were like costumes for fairies in just such a masque as they were preparing to watch.

'A *notorious* whore,' concurred Bevan.

'Not well advised!' Lambert sniggered.

As the torchlit procession continued past them, they watched many strange phenomena. To antique music representing birdsong, came a man-sized owl accompanied by a magpie, a jay, a crow and a kite. Struggling to spot their own bird, Lambert and Bevan made out three satyrs with their own torch-bearers – and finally what they were waiting for: the three dotterels. They expelled a roar of greeting, which they kept up until one of the high-stepping wildfowl turned slowly towards them.

Despite the winter night, inside the dotterel's heavy costume, Gideon had sweat in his eyes. Adolescents like to hide, but this was far too uncomfortable. Striving to keep up with the parade, the young actor momentarily tripped over the long claws of his bird's feet. Bevan's derisive cheer had been unmistakable even through the muffling head-piece. Now he was for it. He knew that his great-uncle and his brother had tracked him down.

Gideon was wary of Bevan. Even the recent offer of a printing appren-ticeship seemed a mysterious ploy of some kind. Gideon always felt there was something unsound about his great-uncle. And he was right. When civil war came, Bevan Bevan would be a Royalist. Bevan was stirring trouble now, even though he always insisted he was supportive of Gideon. The lad's rebellion would be exposed, to become family lore, occasioning many more furious arguments at home.

Third Dotterel was forced to acknowledge that he had been recognised; he lowered his delicate beak in a sad salute. Thoroughly despondent, he flapped his arms like wings and stepped on his way.

'So there he flies; we have done our duty.' *What duty?* Gideon would have roared. 'To a tavern, Lambert!'

'Do we not wait, to fetch our fledgling home?'

'It will be morning before he obtains his release. Let him find his own way.'

Lambert at least was beginning to regret landing the young scamp in more trouble. 'Oh you mean, let him answer to my mother on his own!' Lambert knew Bevan was frightened of Parthenope. 'We need not speak of it –'

'Too good to keep to ourselves!' replied Bevan cruelly.

Thick crowds prevented them from moving off immediately. They saw out the rest of the parade. Immediately after the dotterels tottered a fine mobile windmill, at which a fantastical knight and his squire tilted raggedly while they tried to avoid its whirling sails. Then the proces-sion became more formal. Fourteen trumpeters cantered by with rich banners; next rode the marshal among forty attendants, all tricked out in coats and hose of scarlet, trimmed with silver lace; then a hundred mounted gentlemen passed, two abreast. Finally in the manner of a Roman Triumph, three decorated chariots bore along *Peace, Law* and *Justice,* queenly females all coruscating with stars and silver ornament, thrilling beneath the shadows and light of many torches.

The King and Queen were so impressed, they sent out to request that the entire carnival be led right around the tiltyard at the far end of Whitehall, and brought back again for a second viewing. It was a chilly night and the crowds outside began to lose interest. As soon as they gained space to move, Bevan Bevan and Lambert Jukes took themselves off. They picked their way through the fresh horse-dung along to the Strand, then headed east, back to their own turbulent city parishes where they could enjoy a tankard in a tavern more at ease than here.

The masque participants finally dismounted outside the Banqueting House. Through his costume, Gideon could make out parts of the stark new classical building in three subtle shades of stonework, its harmonious Palladian style a cool contrast to the brightly painted beams and red brick of the rackety old Tudor buildings in Whitehall. Jostled by the other players and afraid his tail would be stepped on, he entered at the level of the Undercroft. The claws of his costume slipped on the stone, as he made his way up the easy flights of a broad stair. A tall doorway brought them into a magnificent two-storeyed hall, purposely designed for state receptions. Heat, braying voices, the stench of sweat and the cloying scent of rosewater assailed them. At the far end stood the King's canopied throne, flanked by the noblest gentlemen and ladies of the court. Lapdogs scampered about at will. Other courtiers, decorated with pockmarks and great pearls, lined the two side aisles, where splendid tapestries covered the tall window niches, pegged back on the street side to allow a view outside. Above, lesser spectators hung over the balcony which ran around the upper storey, including members of the Inns of Court who had fought the Lord Chamberlain for permission to see their own masque. The room, already warm from so many jostling bodies, was ablaze with lights, the glister of silver and gold tissue, and the sparkle of jewels. Only its ceiling was bare. Painted panels had been commissioned from Peter Paul Rubens, but they would not arrive from Holland until the following year.

The King and Queen, diminutive figures enthroned like dolls on their state dais, faced a specially constructed raised stage. During the masque, this would represent variously arbours, streets, a tavern, open country-side and clouds, with all the scene changes and spectacles wrought by cunning machinery.

Gideon was allowed to remove the head of his costume temporarily, and listen to the first scenes. Emerging red-faced, he found the proceed-ings hard to follow. To a grocer's son, it seemed completely alien. The script was tedious: anodyne exchanges which punctuated a strange mixture of clowning and dance. Presentations came and went, in a drama more remarkable for its ingenuity than its content. Moments of burlesque led into banal songs that would never be picked up and hummed on the streets; there were many dances and then a curiously stilted musical drama for *Peace, Law* and *Justice.*

Lacking the vigour of the old Ben Jonson masques which had once been played here, James Shirley's text was unworthy of the fine poet who wrote 'Death the Leveller'. His low-life comedy scenes were more spirited than his solemn allegories, but not much more. Wenches and wanton gamesters went into taverns and emerged drunk; thieves were apprehended by a constable; romping beggars and cripples attempted to cheat gentry, then threw away their crutches and danced. Shirley touched on controversy only with great care: '*Are these the effects of Peace?*' asked *Opinion* (understandably perturbed); '*corruption rather . . .*' It was the only scathing comment. The King and Queen, who were still laughing at the cripples dancing, must have missed it.

Peace, according to this masque, did have the benefit of encouraging English inventiveness. Characters lined up to astonish the audience with fabulous ideas: a jockey brought a bridle that would cool overheated horses; a country fellow had devised a wondrous new threshing machine; a bearded philosopher with a furnace on his head could boil beef in a versatile steamer. There was an underwater chamber which allowed submariners to recover lost treasure from riverbeds, a physician with a hat full of carrots and a rooster on his fist had worked out how to fatten poultry with scraps, and a fortress to be built on Goodwin Sands would melt rocks. In a century where science was to make dramatic advances, this was the crazy side of science.

The three dotterels, Gideon presumed, were intended to illustrate country pleasures during times of plenty. Now they had their moment. Hastily donning his costume head again, Gideon scampered onto the stage. He hardly had time to be nervous. The trio of birds were chased around by three dotterel-catchers, who duly caught them with wires and cages, before they all scampered off to make room for the windmill and its jousting knight. Gideon experienced the gloom of an entertainer who knows the next act is bound to be more popular.

Soon afterwards, accompanied by solemn music, *Peace, Law* and *Justice* descended in gold chariots from stage clouds in the upper flats, three statuesque female deities wearing classical robes of green, purple and white satin. The ladies pronounced compliments to one another in curiously bad poetry before the entire cast moved towards the King and Queen and addressed Their Majesties with sanctimonious song. Gideon was at the back, so could barely glimpse the monarch.

The scene changed. The song changed, though not in quality. A finale was anticipated, yet the dance was interrupted by apparently real stagehands and costume-makers, whose dialogue was significantly more spirited than anything else in the pageant. Backstage, a small girl who was skipping about unattended shrieked with joy. Gideon Jukes had almost fallen over her as she stood below his line of sight, constricted as his vision was through the eyeholes. She pushed him aside, almost sick with excitement as actors playing a painter and a carpenter, a tailor's wife, a feather-maker's wife and an embroiderer's wife exchanged banter on stage. They represented ordinary people from a backstage world to which she had just been introduced by her somewhat frowsty grandmother. *'Juliane! Où es-tu?'* She was eight years old, and had been helping with the costumes, thrilled by the responsibility – but that night she was most entranced that she had seen the Queen.

The scene changed yet again. A representation of *Morning Twilight* glided onstage – a pale girl in a partly see-through costume, with whom Gideon was much taken. This brought the formal entertainment to its end. The Queen did dance with the masquers, proving her indifference to William Prynne's insults and delighting at least one small girl *quite utterly!*

Gideon felt shocked when Her Majesty danced. The rebel in him was out-rebelled. Any idea of running away from home to be a player evaporated. He would have to accept some other career.

So delighted with *The Triumph of Peace* was Henrietta Maria that she ordered it to be played all over again at Merchant Taylors Hall, where its anti-puritan message might reach larger numbers of people, especially the young. Third Dotterel would be forbidden by his parents from acting the second time. The small girl would not attend either, since her grandmother, always a game woman, wanted privacy to encourage a legal man called William Gadd, whom she had met at the first performance.

On that royal night at the Banqueting House, all the players and lawyers were taken afterwards to an enormous feast which lasted until daylight. Gideon was too sleepy to eat much. Next morning, Third Dotterel stumbled home to his mother with his bird's head under his arm, shedding feathers all the way from Ludgate Hill to Cheapside.

Chapter Three

London: 1634–42

Parthenope forgave him.

He was her baby – and she was about to lose him. She thought this was not the best moment to send Gideon half across London to another home. But sometimes it is easier for a youngster to respect strangers.

Gideon almost backed out before he started. His first task was to locate Robert Allibone, his new master, who worked at the sign of the Auger. This, his great-uncle had airily instructed, would be found off Fleet Lane. Brought up in the City, Gideon had to leave the few streets around Cheapside that he knew well, pass through the hubbub of book-sellers around St Paul's and explore westwards beyond the city wall to Ludgate Hill and the busy environs of the Old Bailey. Though only half an hour's walk away, this was unknown territory. He was reluctant to ask directions. He had walked to an area of lawyers and their hangers-on, some visibly seedy. He sensed that his steps were dogged by sneak-thieves; he could hear the drunks raucously tippling in dark taverns and victualling houses. He had come among scriveners, printers, carriage-men and – since the law was so lucrative – goldsmiths and jewellers.

When few side streets had names and no premises had house numbers, wooden signboards swung by almost every door; they were high enough not to decapitate a man on horseback, but were otherwise unregulated. The pictures were crudely drawn and often faded. Few signs had any connection with nearby shops or tradesmen. Wandering about with youthful absence of urgency, Gideon gazed at Cocks and Bulls, Red Lions, White Harts, Swans, Crowns, Turks' Heads, Kings' Heads, Boars' Heads, Crossed Keys and Compasses, Rising Suns and Men in the Moon, Bushes, Bears and Barleycorns. It took him another hour to find the Auger. Welcoming him without complaint, Robert Allibone, a compact sandy-haired man in brown britches and shirtsleeves, admitted that the street board lacked finesse.

Gideon confessed he had not known what an auger was.

'A bodger. A good honest piercing tool. Not to be confused with an au*gur*, who is a pagan prophet or prognosticator, a dabbler in offal and trickery . . .' The printer gazed at the boy. 'I hope you like words.'

'I will try, sir.'

'And how are you with ideas?'

'Do you print ideas?'

'I print words. Remember that. Take no responsibility for ideas. Whoever commissions the printing must take the risks – the publisher!' A firm hand pushed Gideon onto a stool and a book was opened on his knees. 'Show me you can read.' Although few people in the shires were literate, the majority in London could read. Gideon saw at once that his test piece was an extremely dull sermon so he pulled a face; Allibone seemed pleased, either at his quickness or his critical taste.

Bevan Bevan was standing as guardian. Gideon saw Allibone stiffen when his great-uncle walked in, wearing a florid scarlet suit, the outfit in which he had married Elizabeth Keevil. The Jukes family had focused their revulsion upon this wedding suit. The main colour was vivid; the braid which outlined hems, edges and side-seams flashed with spangles. The short cloak, which was worn with a casual flourish on the left shoulder, made Bevan look immensely wide. The outfit came with gloves – one to wear and one to clutch.

Bevan placed his clutching-glove upon a pile of printed pamphlets, while he handed over the fifty pounds agreed as bond money. This was supposed to represent a surety that Gideon came from a good background and would be capable of setting up in business on his own account eventually. Normally a bond would be repaid when a young man completed his apprenticeship; its purpose was to establish him. However, Gideon deduced that Bevan's fifty pounds would remain with Allibone, for it represented some debt the Keevils owed. He sensed rancour between the men. Allibone's voice was pointedly dry: 'You are a fortunate boy, Gideon Jukes. Entry to apprenticeship in the Stationers' Company is regulated strictly!'

Bevan shot Allibone a sorrowful look. Then he took it upon himself to explain the contract of apprenticeship: 'Your indenture – which you must guard with your life – this witnesses: that you, Gideon Jukes, will faithfully serve your master to learn the trade of a printer.' He ran a fat finger down the terms. 'You shall do no damage to your master, nor allow it to be done by others. You shall not waste his goods, nor lend them out unlawfully. You shall not fornicate, nor commit matrimony. You shall not play cards, dice, tables, nor any unlawful games which may cause your master to have any loss. You shall not haunt taverns or *playhouses!*'

Gideon scuffed his feet. Robert Allibone's sharp eyes lingered thoughtfully on this boy who had been promoted to him as so intelligent and keen to learn: a gangly specimen, with a newly cut pudding-bowl of straight tow-coloured hair and vividly pustular skin. Still, he seemed well mannered. Before the irritating uncle arrived, Allibone had warmed to him.

With a wave of his clutching-glove, Bevan fluffed on. 'Well, well, it is all here – not buy or sell goods on your own account, not absent yourself from your master day or night, but behave as a faithful apprentice, et cetera. In consideration, your master shall teach and instruct you in the art and mystery of his trade by the best means he can, while finding you meat, drink, apparel, lodging, and all other necessaries, according to the custom of the City of London.' They were outside the City, but nobody quibbled.

'Thank you,' said Gideon gratefully to the printer. His parents had threatened to throw him out of house and home for his disloyalty. It was probably bluff, but a thirteen-year-old boy needed to feel confident he had not seen his last beef-and-oyster pie.

His great-uncle proposed a drink with Allibone to seal the contract. Gideon was left behind, sitting on a paper bale, gazing rather dolefully at the terrifying equipment. The silent press stood taller than a man. In due course Allibone would explain to him that it was based on the design of olive and wine presses. It had two tall, heavy, upright side-beams, which carried a lighter cross-piece. Down through that ran a big wooden screw. Into its bell-shaped lower terminus was fixed a turning lever, then a flat box containing the paper. Below was a long table, where the form sat, full of mirror-image type to be inked. Around the room Gideon saw a daunting array of boxes which contained letters, large and small, in seeming disarray. On shelves were unbound books and pamphlets awaiting sale.

Allibone, who was not a toper in Bevan's style, soon returned and taught his new apprentice his first lesson: how to make up a truckle bed for himself in the shop.

John Jukes, the careful parent, showed up two days later to inspect the printer.

He found a freckled man of twenty-nine, with a cool eye and a confident air. Jukes had ascertained that Allibone was married with no children. He owned one press, since to possess more caused difficulties with the authorities. He worked from a tiny shop, living above it with his wife. He sold some works himself, but passed out other copies to bookshops and itinerant pedlars.

'I understand there are but twenty licensed printers,' Jukes began pedantically. Allibone listened, sizing up Jukes: a well-fed shopkeeper, probably sent today by his wife. He wore an English cloth suit, with no French, Dutch or Italian accessories, a suit made for him a decade earlier when he was middle-aged and carried more weight. A man who brooded on slights, planned his argument, then came out with it as if reading a sermon. 'You are not troubled by the authorities, Master Allibone?'

'I avoid exciting them . . . There are twenty or so *Master* Printers, licensed by the Stationers' Company and approved by High Commission.' Allibone went back to inking a tray of letters, deftly deploying a wooden tool covered with lambswool. John Jukes sucked his teeth at the mention of the King's Court of High Commission; Allibone shared the moment, then confided more freely, 'We mere yeomen and liverymen strive to stay friends with the company officers, and if we are suitably humble, they duly pass work to us. Always the least profitable work, of course.'

The father began a new tack: 'Sending a boy out to a stranger's trade is a common thing.' Allibone merely nodded. Though a dealer in words, he could be content with silence. Gideon, whose family would yammer on about nothing rather than leave fifty seconds empty, had already noticed the difference. Allibone was to be a strong influence; Gideon Jukes was on his way to becoming a quiet man.

'We are rubbing along,' commented Allibone, who privately thought his young apprentice was quite tough enough. There was no meekness in Gideon. He had a mind of his own but had been polite these past couple of days, a willing learner. Allibone was finding him easy to instruct and if Gideon was making mistakes, it was only because he was trying to rush ahead and do things before he was capable.

John Jukes reluctantly convinced himself that Allibone was reliable. The printer made no attempt to bluster about himself or his trade, and happily no mention of Bevan Bevan. He gave Jukes a moment alone with his son. Allibone had noticed the awkwardness between them, exacerbated by the fact Gideon had suddenly that year grown taller than his father.

'Are you content with your situation?' John was staring at his son's apprentice clothes, old britches of Allibone's, beneath a blue leather apron. Everything Gideon touched seemed to cover him with ink; only his newly cropped hair had escaped. John was not sure whether to laugh at the filthy picture he made, or to deplore it.

Gideon bravely maintained that he was happy; his sceptical father knew any lad would be forlorn after his first two days in strange surroundings. Stepping from childhood into adult work was an ugly shock. Gideon now had to contemplate a lifetime of near drudgery, rising at first light and sticking to a mundane task until dinnertime. 'Well, you have bound yourself, Gideon. Your mother's uncle, for his own reasons, put himself to some trouble to win you this opening.'

'Plenty of apprentices fail to stay their term,' muttered Gideon glumly.

'Not in our family!' John must be forgetting wastrel cousin Tom, Gideon scoffed to himself. Tom Jukes tried a new occupation every year and the only one he ever liked was going to the bad . . . Sympathetically, his father offered, 'You must stay for a month, to try it thoroughly. Then if your heart cries out strongly, you may come and consult me.'

'*A month!*'

The boy had revealed how homesick he was. To overcome the tug on his emotions, Jukes senior summoned back the printer. Allibone gave no sign of his own misgivings. Gideon was the first apprentice he had been able to take on, and he was anxious that things should not go awry. He satisfied John Jukes eventually, soothing him with a free almanac and a proposal that Jukes should compose an encyclopedia of spices for publication. Robert Allibone was a sharp businessman despite his reserved manner; he had recognised in Gideon's father a man of many projects – though perhaps he had not realised how frequently John's projects were left incomplete.

'Well, Gideon, your mother has sent you some jumbles.'

A packet of cinnamon-flavoured pastry twists was handed over and Gideon went back to work. John Jukes made his farewell; Allibone noticed that he brushed away a tear. Gideon, too, wiped his inky nose on his shirtsleeve.

Those first jumbles were hidden away and eaten in secret, but within the month Gideon opened up, so when his mother sent him treats he would share them. Margery Allibone, a brusque woman, older than her husband, whose cooking was merely adequate, once asked if Gideon's mother would pass on the jumbles recipe. The printer went further. Cookery books, herbals and household manuals were favourites with the public; he nagged for Parthenope to compile a *Good Housewife's Closet*, which he could illustrate with woodcuts and sell to anxious brides. But Parthenope was about to acquire a daughter-in-law, Lambert's wife, and felt the need to preserve her position by guarding her knowledge. When the Jukes wanted to be gracious to the Allibones, they sent raisins or Jamaica pepper.

Gideon stayed out his term. For the full seven years of his indenture, he was a typical apprentice: clumsy, scatterbrained and sleepy. He went from delivering parcels to operating the press, learning the tricks and pitfalls. He was taught that typography was critical; for hours he sat at the high compositing desk, mastering fast use of the box of type, with vowels in the middle compartments, frequent consonants next and X, Υ and Z at the outer edges. He learned how to tighten the form so the lines of type were clenched fast, how far to turn the lever to lower the press – first once, then again for the second page – how to regulate the amount of ink on the pad, how long the wet sheets needed to dry. He watched how Allibone negotiated with the Stationers' Company who registered books and controlled publication; how he commissioned work from authors, both professional and amateur; how he extracted debts from dilatory clients; how he organised bookbinders; how he kept a careful list of decent importers of paper, and ink and pen suppliers; how he handled people begging him to print subject matter he disapproved of (which was very little) or knew he could not sell (rather more).

Gideon was paid nothing, but had freedom to read. If he had a fault as a worker, it was his tendency to get caught up in the words. Correctly setting and spacing the text was hard enough, without losing his place as he read on obliviously through the manuscript pages. Many a time Robert Allibone threatened to show him what it was like to have a harsh master who beat him – though, being addicted to reading himself, he never did.

For anyone interested in politics, there would soon be no better trade. However, at first the outlook for printers was poor, and it grew worse before it got better. Censorship prohibited publication of all foreign and domestic news. Then in 1637, three years after Gideon's indentures, the King's Star Chamber issued a draconian *Decree concerning Printing*. This aimed to suppress seditious books, particularly those which did not accord with the High Church ideals of the reforming new Archbishop of Canterbury, William Laud. It insisted on registration of all printed works by the Stationers' Company. Fines for seditious authors were reinforced by fines for their printers; Allibone somehow escaped penalties, but it was an anxious period.

Then, another four years later, when King Charles was forced to call a Parliament, the Star Chamber was abolished. At once, printers began selling books without official registration. Pamphlets and news-sheets immediately flourished; every *Fiery Counterblast* bred a *Witty Riposte*. Anyone with a burning cause could promote his opinions, whether he brazened it out openly, hid under a false name or tantalised with his initials only.

By chance, Gideon Jukes had been positioned right at the heart of this. He finished his apprenticeship, at the age of twenty, the same year that the King would at last summon a Parliament. He had seen the old regime; now he experienced a great rush of excitement at the new.

One of the first decisions Gideon then made as an adult was to join the London Trained Bands.

England had no standing army. Trained Bands had been established by Queen Elizabeth. They were local militias, where men were drilled every summer in the use of pike and musket in order to defend the realm against foreign invasion. Generally viewed as a joke, poorly equipped, badly trained and liable to desert, in most of the shires the Trained Bands were truly inefficient though in London the situation was different. The London Trained Bands were greatly superior.

Gideon's father was an enthusiast; he had been a captain of the Artillery Company, the high-minded theorists of the Trained Bands, for as long as Gideon could remember. Once a month in summer John would put on a buff coat and collect his weapons. He would proudly march off to an enclosed piece of ground on the western edge of Spitalfields, the Artillery Garden, where the company met to practise under the guidance of hired professional soldiers. Jukes and his comrades read up old campaigns and composed passionate military treatises. None had ever fired a shot in anger. All were convinced they were experts. After the thrill of parading, these companionable hobbyists always adjourned to an alehouse. Their feasts were legendary; the utensils, plates and tureens they used for dining were their most tenderly guarded equipment.

Lambert Jukes was an enthusiastic regular of the Trained Bands' Blue Regiment. He too revelled in wearing uniform, firing practice shots, and drinking with comrades after drill. 'You are just weekend warriors!' grumbled Gideon. 'Posturing amateurs. Your bullets have no bite.'

Membership of the Trained Bands was compulsory for householders, though they were allowed to send substitutes and many instructed an apprentice or servant to attend for them. Deep political foreboding made Allibone attend training sessions in person. He was in the Green Regiment, which Gideon began to eye up warily.

London was astir. In 1641 Gideon was released from his indenture, a qualified journeyman printer. Taller and less thickset than his older brother, he was now nonetheless strong – toned by working the press and shouldering paper bales. He had the square features, pale skin and fair hair that ran in his family, suggesting that if Viking raiders had not made their mark in the remote past, at least Swedish or Danish seamen had been spreading joy among the ladies of medieval or Tudor London. Allibone had made him a good all-round printer, although he would never be a perfect compositor. 'Your thoughts wander! What are you dreaming of?'

Calm and good-natured, Gideon merely smiled. He felt diffident of discussing it but was wondering what his future could be, a second son without a patron, passed fit to be a journeyman but with no money to start up in business.

The solution came, though in a sad manner. Robert Allibone's wife died. Gideon's brother Lambert had served his grocery apprenticeship with a master whose wife ordered the lads about, but Margery was no bully and rarely came in the print shop. Gideon had always known that she and his master were devoted. He occasionally overheard what he knew were the sounds of lovemaking; at first a fascinated boy, he came to be a young, frustrated bachelor who covered his ears. Frequently, Fleet Lane would be filled with the slow measure of the Allibones playing musical duets on large and lesser viols which they had owned since they first married.

Once widowed, Robert sought change. He decided to move to new premises in the City and asked Gideon to go with him as his partner. Gideon eagerly accepted. They set up at the top end of Basinghall Street, close to the Guildhall, between Cripplegate and Moorgate. At the north end were fair houses with long gardens, while southwards were smaller premises and closeted alleys. Walking for a few minutes, across Lothbury, with its noisy copper shops, and down Ironmongers Lane, Gideon could reach the Jukes's grocery shop. He had not quite come home to mother, but he was well within reach of Bread Street; he could reacquaint himself with the glory of her Dutch pudding. Nowadays puddings were mixed as a joint effort by Parthenope and Lambert's pretty wife Anne, a dark-eyed, sensible girl from Bishopsgate; as soon as it was seen that she had a light touch with manchet rolls, Anne had fitted in with her mother-in-law. The women worked peacefully together in the kitchen, where John Jukes often nodded on a settle nowadays, dawdling into his senior years with his head as full of schemes as ever. Lambert effortlessly ran the business.

Gideon was welcomed back. Since he would be sharing premises with Allibone, he would cause no ructions with Lambert. His mother took a new look at her returning son, this twenty-year-old with fair hair and a loping stride, who had reached manhood with a scathing view of the world, but was apparently now content with his own place in it. She wondered what other concerns would call him, and whether she would live to see his future. Mothers like to believe their sons are marked for greatness. Parthenope, whose head was filled with musings whenever her hands were busy in a mixing bowl, knew that it mainly led to disappointment. But Lambert, who had never given her a moment's qualm, had also never given her the feeling of potential she experienced with Gideon. So she made him some mock-bacon marzipan – two-tone stripes in a whimsical streaky pattern – while she pretended he was just a troublesome boy again, needing rosewater for his acne. And she waited.

Gideon liked to take Robert home as a guest to dinner. However, it happened infrequently, after a mishap when a piece of skewer was unfortunately left in a veal olive; it splintered into the unwary printer's hard palate.

Gideon had always known that Robert Allibone was sceptical of authority. All through his apprenticeship Gideon had spotted that their shop sold some inflammatory material. The master never involved his apprentice. Seditious 'almanacs' were only ever printed by himself; they were kept in a locked cupboard and were quietly passed to customers who knew in advance what they were buying. Gideon now started reading them.

Once they moved to Basinghall Street, Allibone's yearning for reform became more open. 'Print brings knowledge. What we publish can show the people their rights and liberties.'

He had chosen his new premises deliberately, to bring him amongst others of a like mind. Basinghall Street seemed close to respectability as it wound around the Guildhall and several livery company halls. But Gideon soon realised that their narrow shopfront was less important than their even more ramshackle back door. Behind where he and Allibone worked and civilly served aldermen with tide tables and news-sheets, accessible through adjoining yards and over a wall with convenient footholds, lay Coleman Street. This was a hotbed of radical printers and several extreme religious groups had meeting-places there. This was where the women preachers gathered and gave soaring sermons to their free-thinking sisters, and occasional free-living brothers. Coleman Street also contained the Star Tavern, which was to become famous as a haunt of Parliamentarian conspirators.

Chapter Four

London: 1641–42

Gideon felt he was living at the turn of an extraordinary period. All generations complain about the government, but he felt a distinct tingle that this would be different.

Nobody really intended to start a civil war. Most past wars had been fought against foreign aggressors. Others were to decide who should be king, not whether a ruler was a bad king – though if he *was* a bad king that helped to validate any usurper. In a highly unusual gesture, Scottish King James had acknowledged that he was invited to succeed Queen Elizabeth by his new English subjects. His son Charles never entertained any such concept; Charles believed God had given him authority, which none could question. Puritans and other Independents, who talked to God directly, heard a different message. Why would the Lord have chosen a rickety, ill-educated, devious autocrat, married to a manipulative foreign Catholic, a man who was at once desperate to be loved and yet had an impressive flair for causing offence? While earnest subjects tried to find a compromise, a compromise the King never thought necessary, the nation slipped by a series of shunts and bumps into armed conflict. Since there were neither foreign aggressors nor pretenders to the throne, people called it a war without an enemy.

It was never foreseen that the struggle would turn into a revolution. Everyone was clear that it was treason for subjects to take up arms against the king. On both sides there was horror of the coming bloodshed. On both sides there were many who hoped to preserve the peace.

There was, initially, a 'junto' of aristocrats setting up to challenge the King's authority after he took back their traditional powers and privileges to grant to his own favourites. The earls of Northumberland, Warwick, Bedford, Hertford, Pembroke, Leicester and Essex were men of land and lineage whose ancestors had held great power; they were also backed among others, by lords Saye and Sele, Mandeville and Brooke. These plotted secretly, how to wrest back influence the King had taken from them. They all owned homes in the country where they were out of reach of the court, and also houses in London between which they could flit like sociable moths, right under the King's nose. Their family trees were so interconnected they could scarcely be untangled to draw them on paper, as intricately linked by blood and marriage as lace, with a web of younger brothers, stepsons, sons-in-law, even bastards. They were patrons to others, further down the social chain yet educated and energetic – lawyers, secretaries and men of business – who would eventually be significant in the House of Commons. The junto members were Presbyterians and puritans; they loathed the bishops' influence in secular affairs. They cultivated their own links with foreign states. Some had considered escaping to the New World to form a godly commonwealth more to their liking. But instead they were colluding with friends, and although it was treason to invite a foreign army into England, they formed an alliance with Scotland which would have very long-term consequences.

The King became embroiled in dispute with the Scots. They were to feature frequently and often cynically in events. Back in 1637 in Edinburgh, a kerbside cabbage-seller called Jenny Geddes had flung her stool at the head of the Dean of St Giles Cathedral, bawling in protest when he used the hated new Anglican Book of Common Prayer. Two years later, encouraged by the English earls' junto, the Scots rebelled in arms against the King's imposition of High Anglican bishops. They were pacified. In 1640 they rebelled again.

Desperate for money to finance an army, the King summoned a Parliament for the first time in eleven years. Gideon barely remembered the last time this happened, though he paid attention now. He could not vote. He did not own freehold property.

New members were returned after a hotly contested election. They insisted they would only grant the King funds *after* discussing abuses of royal prerogative. The King testily dismissed this 'Short Parliament' after only three weeks.

The Scots invaded England. The King raised some troops, a rabble who were soundly thrashed. Advancing south, the Scots demanded £850 a day merely to keep a truce. In November the bankrupt King caved in and summoned the 'Long Parliament'. It passed an act that it could sit in perpetuity and it was to last for almost twenty years.

This time members were determined to take control. The King's closest and most hated advisers, the Earl of Strafford and Archbishop Laud, were impeached: accused of treason and thrown into the Tower of London. Other royal supporters fled. Radical members of the House of Lords were imposed as Privy Councillors. Of course there was no way to force the King to follow their advice.

To Gideon, this was a heady period, when it seemed reform could not be stopped. Strafford was tried and executed. Ship Money was declared illegal. The hated Courts of High Commission and Star Chamber were abolished. The seditious pamphleteers, Burton, Bastwick and Prynne (author of *Histriomastix*, the book which had libelled the Queen for performing in masques), were pardoned.

In August the King travelled to Scotland to negotiate peace. In November he set out for home. During his absence, members of the House of Commons had taken a detailed audit of their complaints. An emergent reformer called John Pym compiled a *Grand Remonstrance*, a daunting state-of-the-kingdom review. The Remonstrance would be read out to the King in full by messengers from Parliament; they would need vocal stamina. A bitter compendium of over two hundred clauses listed every possible grievance in church and civil life. Singled out were unjust taxes, with an enormous list of land encroachments, distraints of trade, monopolies and fines. The most impassioned outcry condemned the evils of the Star Chamber, which had organised censorship.

Even while it was in draft, secret copies of the Grand Remonstrance circulated in Coleman Street. In next-door Basinghall Street, Robert Allibone quoted with relish: *"'Subjects have been oppressed by grievous fines, imprisonments, stigmatisings, mutilations, whippings, pillories, gags, confinements, banishments.'"*

Gideon snatched the copy. *"'After so rigid a manner as hath not only deprived men of the society of their friends, exercise of their professions, comfort of books'"* – ho! ho! –'" *"'use of paper or ink, but even violated that near union which God hath established between men and their wives, whereby they have been bereaved of the comfort and conversation one of another for many years together, without hope of relief . . .'"* – Comfort of books – this is excellent for our trade, Robert!'

'We shall see . . .' Allibone was rightly cautious. Printers would soon be summoned to the bar of the House of Commons to account for seditious material, and in coming weeks an order would be given to collect certain books from stationers and burn them. 'The conclusion is good.' Allibone retrieved the paper. '"*That His Majesty may have cause to be in love with good counsel and good men*" . . .'

Gideon pulled a face. 'Why not simply say they hate the cut of his beard?'

Revolts come and go but young men remain the same. At twenty, Gideon Jukes was obsessed with beard and whisker design. With fair hair and equally fair skin-tones, the current fashions made him look from almost any distance as if he had a long upper lip and a pointed chin. He had let his hair grow down to his shoulders, an unsuccessful experiment to show he was no longer an apprentice, but was tormented by whether or not to remain clean-shaven.

Robert had been beardless as long as Gideon had known him, his chestnut hair clean, trimmed and parted centrally. For all the usual reasons, Gideon wanted more dash. He had been brought up to aim for a plain appearance – but, having given much thought to this, he knew women would not be tempted to adventure by a demurely respectable look.

'I saw King Charles once.' Gideon chose not to mention that he had been acting in a masque at the time. (One thing was sure; he could not have a courtier's beard.) 'His Majesty smiles to right and left – but does not see or listen.'

'He must hear this.'

'And if not?'

'I fear he will rue it.'

'And I fear we shall all be hanged,' replied Gideon, the pragmatist. It did not hold him back from supporting the Remonstrance.

When the King arrived home from Scotland, surprisingly, he was received with fervent rejoicing. He entered London in procession and enjoyed a four-course feast in Guildhall. This did not go down well with Robert and Gideon nearby in Basinghall Street. Church bells pealed and the fountains ran with wine. There was divisiveness, however. The King dined in his majesty with the House of Lords; the Lord Mayor and alderman, though his hosts for the event, were allowed only to form an audience in the upper gallery. The House of Commons was snubbed entirely; none was invited.

The Scottish Presbyterians had been pacified, but the Irish Catholics rebelled, fired by resentment towards the many English settlers. Horrific stories of massacre and mutilation circulated.

'Is this true, or invented to arouse passions?' Gideon demanded as he read the details, all eagerly believed by the public, who were appalled and terrified.

'Oh, we must publish and let the people judge,' his partner answered.

Gideon was silent for a moment. He remained an idealist. 'People will believe these stories *because* they are printed.'

A few printers provided reasoned comments but most were selling sensational stories. The King viewed Ireland as a conquered province full of savages. Now came sickening accounts of the revenge taken by these downtrodden people: the Lord Justice forced to hide in a hen-house, a bishop's family found shivering in rags in a snowdrift, an immigrant Englishwoman hanged by her hair from her door, a bulky Scotsman murdered and rendered into candles, allegedly hundreds of thousands killed, pregnant wives and young daughters raped, babies spitted on pikes, children hanged. Official reprisals followed. Horrors carried out by the King's forces were then reported, horrors on a scale that even shocked veterans of the brutal war on the Continent. The soldiers' terrible deeds were cited as illustrations of the King's personal cruelty.

Amidst terror that Irish rebels would cross to England, bringing such atrocities with them, men of conscience carefully read the news-sheets. Many were turned into supporters of Parliament by their revulsion for the royal power that had caused, encouraged, tolerated and apparently remained unmoved by the inhuman events.

The *Grand Remonstrance* was passed in the House of Commons by a majority of only eleven, after a tense all-night sitting. Gideon had begun to take serious notice of what Parliament did. Where Robert had the hard attitude of a man who had been knocked about by life, Gideon was open, fresh and eager to receive new ideas.

People began to issue petitions of their own, many sent from remote parts of the country. All the London apprentices, thirty thousand of them, signed one. They then flocked around Parliament, armed with staves, oars and broomsticks, but were cleared away by the Westminster

Trained Bands, for 'threatening behaviour'. They moved on and mobbed Whitehall Palace. This was when Queen Henrietta Maria was said to have looked out and christened the lads with their short haircuts 'Roundheads'. The apprentices took it up eagerly. Meanwhile staider demonstrators flowed down the Strand to Westminster, members of the lower and middle classes from one shire after another, beseeching Parliament to urge the King to abandon his evil counsellors, as if people believed all the country's ills were the fault of bad men who had bamboozled him.

The abolition of the Star Chamber and official censorship directly affected printers. Robert and Gideon were furiously busy. News-sheets erupted onto London streets, giving reports of Parliamentary debates. They were cheap, and the public devoured them. It was the first time in England that detailed political material was available without crown control. The first tentative pamphlets were followed by a rash of competing *Mercuries*, *Messengers* and *Diurnals*. Many were printed in and around Coleman Street. Robert and Gideon produced their share.

In December, Gideon's brother Lambert made a journey across the river and out to Blackheath. A cavalcade of coaches turned out along the Dover Road, with thousands of well-wishers on foot. Lambert jumped on the back of a carriage and was carried up the short steep hill near Greenwich, arriving just in time on the bare, windy heath that had previously seen Cornish rebels and Jack Cade, and which now witnessed the triumphant return of the convicted pamphleteer Dr John Bastwick from his intended life-imprisonment on the Isles of Scilly. Roaring crowds adorned him with wreaths of rosemary and bay, for remembrance and victory – garlands which hid his missing ears, sliced off as a punishment for sedition on the orders of Archbishop Laud's Star Chamber. Lambert hitched a lift home with an apothecary, who was looking forward to boosting his fortunes with salves for soldiers if there was a war.

A week later, the *Grand Remonstrance* was formally presented to the King at Hampton Court. He loftily said he would reply 'in due course'.

'I cannot imagine His Majesty will miss dinner because he has his nose buried in our two hundred clauses!' Gideon's brief experience as a masquer made him feel an expert on court etiquette.

After a fortnight of royal silence, the *Grand Remonstrance* was printed for the public anyway.

Six days later, significant change came to the Common Council of the City of London. Elections were held and the council was packed with radicals, displacing the traditional conservatives who grovelled to the monarchy. John Jukes was one of the new members. He reported that support for the King was fast declining in the City, although the present Lord Mayor remained loyal to Charles. 'A bombast in greasy ermine, a corporation sultan!' scoffed Robert.

Gideon described how the ermine was passed down through merchant families in an obstinately closed City community that was just as elite as the royal court. 'Dick Whittington and his cat would never find advancement now. Robert, the fat sirs in Guildhall cling together like Thames mud. They win their gold chains because they are on a tight little rota of rich and influential cronies. They hold onto power because they support the King whatever he does.'

Gideon had felt some surprise when his father identified himself as a radical. Parents are supposed to be hidebound, not hotheads. It made him pause. Men of wealth and reputation were necessary for reform, yet he felt some consternation at the involvement of his now elderly father.

'I thought your father was a company man.'

'And his forefathers before him. This is the first time ever that a Jukes was elected to the Common Council.'

The next tussle in London was for control of the Tower of London. The King appointed Sir Thomas Lunsford as Lieutenant, but there was a public outcry and outrage in Parliament; he was replaced only five days later.

'What is this Lunsford's history?'

'Unfit for office.' Robert had the background. 'The man murdered his own cousin. He fled abroad and became a professional soldier – which shows his low quality – was pardoned by the King – which shows *his* – then served in the Bishops' War where he is famous for shooting out of hand two young conscripts he accused of mutiny. He also put out a captain's eye.'

'My father says, if this godless outlaw is in charge of the Tower, where the bullion of the realm is kept and coined, there will be too much anxiety; it will put a stop to trade.'

'*Stop trade!*' cackled Robert satirically. 'Surely merchants are more robust? But to pardon and promote such an outlaw shows what kind of king we have.' Gideon could see that.

On Sunday, the day after Christmas, the Lord Mayor warned the King that the apprentices were on the verge of rioting. London apprentices always loved a rumpus. Their football games led to casualties and damage; they insulted visitors and foreigners; they roamed in gangs on May Day and at St Bartholomew's Fair. Now they came out of the workplace, using their holiday to mobilise. On the Monday, as members reassembled after Christmas, they flocked around the Commons, protesting against the inclusion of bishops in Parliament. On Tuesday, with extra support from crowds of shopkeepers and merchants, they forced the doors of Westminster Abbey, intent on destroying popish relics. On Wednesday evening, the King entertained at a hearty dinner Thomas Lunsford, the man disappointed of the Tower of London command. A collection of apprentices gathered and jeered, causing a fight with departing guests and palace servants; casualties resulted. Over in the City, two thousand apprentices then massed in Cheapside, armed with clubs, swords and home-made spears. Many were hard young nuts who lived for a fight. On Friday, the nervous King sent to the Tower for powder and ammunition, enough for five hundred soldiers. When this equipment reached Whitehall Palace, the House of Commons became equally nervous of what the King might do with the firepower, now concentrated a few hundred yards away. Members decamped to the Guildhall and Grocers' Hall.

Both Jukes brothers were now busy. While his brother printed news-sheets, Lambert was helping to make the streets safe against any armed men the King might send. Guards had been posted on the city gates. Bollards slung with chains to thwart cavalry were set up in critical locations; key streets were even bricked up. As the atmosphere became ever more tense, householders were told to arm themselves and stand by their doors, ready to defend their families and the community. Sturdy and willing, Lambert went from house to house giving instructions for resistance if the King sent troops.

The King offered a safe conduct if the Commons would return to Westminster; some members uneasily crept back. That night, rumours grew that Parliament intended to impeach the Queen, in response to the constant reports that she was involving herself in plots. The King became alarmed. Charles then took an unprecedented step: he went to the House of Commons in person, intending to arrest five particular troublemakers himself. He took four hundred soldiers, armed with halberds, swords and pistols. They shoved aside the doorkeepers, jostled members and their servants, and filled the corridors, making ominous threats about their marksmanship as they pointed their weapons into the chamber through its open doors. Bursting in uninvited, the King haughtily demanded the Five Members. The Speaker refused to reply. Forewarned, the five men had disappeared through a back door. The furious King stared around and accepted that 'the birds have flown'. He retreated ignominiously, pursued by angry cries of 'Privilege!' His armed guard waited around for orders to fall upon the members and cut all their throats, but then dispersed in disappointment.

The House of Commons declared the King's act to be a high breach of the rights and privilege of Parliament. Once again they adjourned to the Guildhall.

The Five Members, John Pym, John Hampden, Denzil Holles, Arthur Hazlerigg and William Strode, had also fled to the City. Gideon and his partner had a new apprentice, Amyas, who came running in excitedly. 'The Five Members are in Coleman Street!'

'At the Star Tavern?' Gideon guessed.

'That will be a secret then!' Robert reproved. 'Amyas, say nothing to anyone.'

'There could be spies,' the boy acknowledged, fired up by this exciting idea.

'Only if they are very stupid,' murmured Robert. 'An informant for the Duke of Buckingham was once chased out of Coleman Street and stoned to death.'

Theirs was one of the rumbling presses that worked through the night to give out news. Rumours flared of plots against members of Parliament, armed forces from the north gathering to attack London, dangerous new weapons that would stick in the body and could not be pulled out, sinister lists of citizens who would soon be rounded up . . .

Next morning tension remained high. City businesses stayed closed for safety. The King ventured in procession from Whitehall to Guildhall, where the Commons were sitting in committee. It was only two minutes from their shop. Gideon joined the mutinous crowd outside. Again King Charles demanded the Five Members; after a turbulent meeting, again he was refused. He had to leave Guildhall empty-handed and depart from the City, accompanied as was traditional by the Lord Mayor and aldermen. Now the crowds who had welcomed him home from Edinburgh were more sullen. When the ornate royal coach reached Temple Bar, obstreperous citizens banged on the King's coach, rocked it, peered rudely through the windows and even thrust copies of radical pamphlets inside.

Gideon had run though the streets, chasing after the King's coach. He followed it all the way beyond St Paul's, out of the city gates and as far as Temple Bar. Borne along by curiosity, he was among the angry crowd who surged forward and tried to rock the coach; he even stepped on the footboard, and pulled himself up. He looked in at the window. At the masque in the Banqueting House all those years before, Gideon had barely glimpsed the King and Queen. Now, for just a second, Gideon Jukes stared King Charles in his long face. They were barely two feet apart. Ignoring the apparition at the window, the King looked calm and aloof; it was the bravery of ignorance. He was convinced of a safe return to his palace, despite this noise and inconvenience. The wild appearance of his indignant young subject made no impression at all. Gideon was the more disturbed by the moment.

The carriage lurched. Gideon fell into the road, swinging by one hand for an instant, then landing on his back in the dust – from that moment a convinced republican.

The Lord Mayor and some aldermen were pulled from their horses. 'Not me,' Gideon assured Robert and Amyas on his return to the print shop. 'I would never dirty my hands on an alderman.'

Amyas chortled, though his gap-toothed grin did not linger. He was toiling at the press while Gideon and Robert stood by in their shirtsleeves, following the rule of all trades that juniors work while management loftily discuss the issues of the day.

The crisis grew more frightening. At dusk the next evening, shots were heard. Someone had accidentally discharged a carbine, and drunken courtiers were fighting a duel at an inn by the new Covent Garden piazza; it caused panic. In street after street, householders were roused by unseen fists banging their doors and urgent voices crying to be up in arms. Gideon went home to reassure his mother and was nearly shot by his father, who sat in a tall chair on guard, with a loaded musket. Families spent a sleepless night in fear.

Nothing happened.

* * *

In the next lull, petitioners from all over the country again flocked into London. Knights of the shire were joined by sailors, porters, fishwives and weavers.

A mass of poor women surrounded Parliament, to express the hardship they suffered due to '*the present distractions and distempers of state*'. They waylaid the Duke of Richmond in Palace Yard, threatening to dump their starving children at the House of Lords. They broke his ducal staff; he had to send peevishly for a replacement. A small group was allowed to present its grievances; when this produced no results, many swarmed around the House of Commons, exclaiming that where there was one woman today there would be five hundred tomorrow. Sergeant-Major Skippon of the City Militia was complimented by Parliament on the diplomatic way he then dispersed them.

'A fine shock to men, who believe we should stay at home, breed and knit stockings!' commented Parthenope Jukes. 'These women's poverty is brought about by the condition of the kingdom. But it seems unnatural – I would be afraid of being hurt in the crush.' Her younger, braver daughter-in-law, Anne, looked thoughtful.

Parliament doubled the night watch on the city and peevishly complained about the tumults.

Relations between the King and Parliament continued to deteriorate. The royal family became so anxious that they moved abruptly from Whitehall to Hampton Court. No preparations had been made to receive them; they had to sleep all together in one bed. This sudden flight from London was more significant than anyone immediately realised.

With the King gone, the Five Members left the Star Tavern, loudly applauded by locals. Jostled in the crowd, Robert and young Amyas could see very little, but Gideon was tall enough to glimpse their famous representatives, or at least the five black crowns of their five hats. The partners roared approval, then turned quietly back to their business. The members returned triumphantly to Westminster by water, with applause echoing along the embankment as their boats passed the now-deserted Whitehall Palace.

Disturbances continued. At the beginning of February a new deputation of tradesmen's wives, distressed women and widows, led by a brewer's wife, presented a petition. Invitations to join in had gone around the City. This time, Anne Jukes upped and took herself to

Westminster with them. Anne consulted nobody, but marched alone along Cheapside, joined the delegation and signed the petition; on her return that evening, she was flushed with achievement. 'There were very great numbers, mostly gentlewomen whose trade had been depressed, as our own has – all from London and the suburbs around. The Commons sent out Mr Pym and two other members, their chief men. They declared that the House had read the petition and was very apprehensive of the calamities we suffer, and will use all the best care they can for the preventing and remedying of them. Then they desired that we would continue our prayers for their endeavours.'

'And did they order out the militia against you?' enquired Lambert dryly.

'No,' scoffed Anne. 'They must have been mindful that we were genteel wives of men of substance – men from whom they are asking loans to protect the kingdom!'

From the moment the King fled London, his strategic aim was to struggle back. It was always apparent that to do so he would have to deal with the London Trained Bands.

On the 8th of January 1642, as relationships with the King finally broke down, Parliament had granted the freedom of the city to Sir Philip Skippon, an imperturbable veteran of the Dutch Wars. Two days later he was made commander of all the London Trained Bands. At that moment they comprised six thousand men, comparatively well trained and armed – and they supported Parliament.

Skippon blockaded the Tower, attempting to oust its governor, Sir John Byron, loyal to the King. Though Skippon failed, he was establishing his troops as the guardians of London. On the 10th of May, he paraded the Trained Bands, now fleshed out with eager new recruits and numbering ten thousand. Skippon reviewed them for members of Parliament and other worthies, in the shadow of the great windmills at Finsbury Fields. It was like a summer festival, with a large tented pavilion where the visitors were grandly entertained. As the brave ranks displayed themselves, the colonel of the Red Regiment, Alderman Atkins, had the misfortune to topple from his horse – being, according to a Royalist news-sheet, afflicted with a bowel problem.

Among new recruits in the Green Regiment, grinning, was Gideon Jukes.

Since his brother was a pikeman, Gideon had chosen to be a musketeer. Since Lambert was in the Blue Regiment, Gideon made sure he joined the Greens. Robert Allibone had paid for his musket, four feet long and twelve-bore. Gideon's father had joyfully set him up with other equipment: a forked barrel-rest, bandolier, sword, swordbelt and hangers. A leather coat and metal helmet completed the uniform. The first time he tried on his helmet, painted black against the rust, its heavy enclosing weight reminded him of the costume head he had worn years before as Third Dotterel. Like most of his comrades, he soon abandoned the helmet and was content with a much lighter Monmouth cap, made of soft felt. So far, none of them had witnessed the hideous results of being shot in the head.

Gideon saw little action at first. The Trained Bands reckoned only to defend London; they played no part in the inconclusive manoeuvres that went on elsewhere in 1642. For several months, Gideon received training only. A national Parliamentary army was commissioned in July, but the Trained Bands stayed separate. As a Londoner, Gideon believed this was correct. Possession of the capital, the seat of government since Roman times, with its strategic importance and its commercial connections, was a vital strength for Parliament. To hold London, while the King could only wander about the country ineffectually, gave Parliament a vital edge. The Trained Bands had to be here on guard.

In August, the King, who was visiting the north of England trying to generate support, formally raised his standard at Nottingham. It was a procedural move, a rallying point for recruits. It was also decisive: he had declared war upon his people.

At that point Parliament issued an order for London's protection. Ten thousand citizens were mobilised. The city closed down. Assembling by trade or guild, shouldering whatever tools they possessed, the people marched out to the surrounding fields and, week after week until autumn and winter brought freezing conditions, they toiled to construct road-blocks and earthworks. Women worked alongside men; Anne Jukes was there regularly, wielding a mattock and ferrying baskets of earth.

By the end of the year, all the city gates were locked with their portcullises down, streets were barred with mighty iron chains, every household had weapons at the ready and the Trained Bands were on day and night call-out. Supporters made loans and gifts to Parliament. There was regular recruitment; there were censuses of horses. Royalist sympathisers were targeted. Parliament issued decrees to summon known 'malignants', and to confiscate their horseflesh, weapons, money and plate. Those who were absent with the King had their homes broken open and possessions ransacked.

Everyone waited anxiously. They heard of skirmishes and sieges. In July the Earl of Essex had left London to take up overall command of the main Parliamentary army. The son of Queen Elizabeth's disgraced favourite, this heavy-jowled veteran had more military experience than any in the aristocracy and was a leading figure in the House of Lords. Famously touchy, he had survived his father's execution, his own divorce on grounds of impotence and then the flagrant adultery of his second wife. His fighting career had been undistinguished, though he had always been popular with his soldiers for his humane treatment of them, and they called him, affectionately, 'Old Robin'. Escorted by the Trained Bands, Essex mounted up at Temple Bar, and rode into the City, past St Paul's Cathedral and the Royal Exchange, then out through Moorgate on his way north through St Albans to Worcester.

The King eventually turned south, through the Midlands where he had a mixed reception. Up until that point there had been only manoeuvres. Then in October the King's army ran into Essex's forces near Kineton, at the foot of a ridge called Edgehill, and the first true battle of the civil war commenced.

The engagement was confused. Both sides claimed victory, though neither could capitalise on it. The two armies were traumatised by the confrontation, with their shocked commanders left temporarily at a loss. Essex withdrew to Warwick, the King to Oxford.

Exaggerating rumours in London claimed that Essex had won a great victory. Then it was said the King was racing south, with Essex in headlong pursuit. Their manoeuvres were more leisurely. But on the 6th of November, Essex and the Parliamentary army re-entered London, having marched straight down the old Roman highway of Watling Street. They were given a heroes' welcome and quartered out at Hammersmith, in preparation for an expected Royalist attack.

Meanwhile on leaving Oxford, the King ambled through Reading, besieging opponents' private houses more from spite than strategy.

Commissioners from Parliament rode out to try to negotiate peace. Despite their efforts, on the 12th of November the King's charismatic nephew Prince Rupert, a commander in the dashing Continental style, fell upon two Parliamentary regiments of foot that he encountered close to London at Brentford under cover of thick mist. Tales quickly arose of Prince Rupert's brutality. He was said to have massacred the garrison at Brentford; his men had tied prisoners head-to-toe and flung them into pigsties to endure the freezing night; the Royalists drove twenty Parliamentary supporters into the River Thames, forcing them into ever deeper water until they drowned. Whether true or not, such horrors reinforced opposition in London.

The Earl of Essex heard the guns from the House of Lords, where peers had been debating whether to order a cessation of hostilities. Essex galloped across Hyde Park to his army at Hammersmith. In the City a local deputation went to the Common Council, begging that the Trained Bands should now also be deployed.

Gideon Jukes was about to see his first military action.

Chapter Five

Turnham Green: 13 November 1642

Londoners loved a junket. Fairs and feasts had been part of city life since time immemorial. An excursion, with sightseeing, was bound to draw a crowd, especially if there might be gunfire. Parliament dispatched cheese, beer and bread to the army by road, with boats hauling munitions up the Thames. Mothers and wives of Trained Band members loaded carts with food and drink, while wiping away tears on their aprons as they waved off their men to protect the city. In case the defences failed, women boiled up cauldrons of hot water to pour down on attackers, and cluttered up the streets with empty barrels and old joint-stools, to get in the way of cavalry.

While drums beat to give them heart and to summon extra recruits, Skippon led out the Trained Bands, Gideon Jukes among them. From the east of the city particularly, where dirty and noisy processes were carried on, forges and foundries, dye works and tanneries fell silent and gave up their men. In the great markets, porters and stall-holders, fishmongers and slaughterers pulled on their boots and tightened their belts, then marched. From shops and from taverns came part-time pikemen and musketeers. Servants and their employers, apprentices and their masters poured forth until it seemed that all the males in London had been sucked from the streets, leaving behind an eerie quiet. Mothers with clenched jaws clutched their babies to their bodices, and listened to that stillness nervously. Only women, children and the old were left – the people that attackers would treat most cruelly.

Five of the six main regiments marched together westwards; one remained on guard. Sightseers who owned horses rode along with the departing troops. Girls pelted the soldiers with flowers, the boldest maidens running in among the ranks to press kisses upon them. The troops left the old city walls at Ludgate, moving from the workshop and commercial centre across the unsavoury valley of the Fleet river, past legal haunts at the Temple and the Inns of Court, then along the Strand with its grand noblemen's mansions. They passed the Banqueting House, the sole monument in a royal rebuilding project that would never now be completed, and then the crumbling old Whitehall Palace where Gideon saw in amazement that grass grew around the buildings, abandoned only a year ago when the King fled. Passing under the Holbein Gate, which was now manned by citizens instead of royal guards, they were cheered at the Houses of Parliament, then marched on beyond the turbulent suburbs, past the Westminster horse ferry, through the marshes and into the open countryside.

Many of the Trained Bands, including both Jukes brothers and Robert Allibone, had never been so far out of London in their lives. They tramped through fields and market gardens for nine miles, half a day's journey and far enough from home to make the inexperienced grow jumpy. The weather was clement, though chilly. With colours flying, drums rattling and wagons of armour and shot rumbling amongst them, they stepped out cheerfully. The old hands had drilled and marched regularly for years; new recruits fell in with spirit, though many were apprentices, and extremely young. To encourage them, Skippon rode from regiment to regiment calling, 'Come on, my boys, my brave boys! Let us pray heartily and fight heartily. I will run the same hazards with you . . . Come on, my boys!'

They found Essex's forces, drawn up in a defensive line at Turnham Green. As the Trained Bands marched through Hammersmith they saw an array of artillery, waiting in a lane. Gideon found the big guns ominous. When they reached the army, they passed a heavily guarded wagon-park. He began to feel part of a great, professional occasion.

Now he and his colleagues came among seasoned troops. Infantry survivors from the battle of Edgehill had been positioned across the approach to London, their flanks protected by blocks of cavalry. All had flags and pennants. Every company in every regiment was marked. The drums never stopped their insistent, tension-making beat; there would be much more noise and a blanket of smoke, if it came to a battle. The field marshal carefully interleaved Trained Band regiments among the more seasoned troops of the main army, some of whom wore the orange sashes that had become the recognised colours of Parliament.

By the time the new arrivals stood in their stations among the blockade, their excitement was becoming more muted. Some had been on parade many times and had fought sham fights for public amusement, but never before had they stood together in such numbers, drawn up in battle array for hours, waiting for real opponents to appear and try to kill them.

The Earl of Essex cantered along the line on his charger reviewing the regiments. As their general passed, soldiers threw up their caps and shouted 'Hey for Old Robin!'

'Come, my brave boys,' urged Skippon calmly again to the Trained Bands. 'Pray heartily, and fight heartily, and God will bless us.'

Glancing sideways for some reason, Gideon saw his partner tighten his mouth in a curious expression, and wondered unexpectedly whether Robert Allibone believed in God.

From the direction of Brentford came movement. Sightseers upped and scattered like a flock of uneasy pigeons.

Even the newest recruits now became aware of the presence of a large body of troops ahead of them. The King's army had arrived. From time to time the feeble winter sunlight glinted off weapons and helmets. Gideon, who was keen-sighted, could make out forests of tall pikes, a constant flicker of regimental colours, the restless shifting of cavalry, the occasional traverse of a commander on horseback and in full body armour. On both sides the cannon remained silent, the gunners beside them itching to test their range.

Gideon was beginning to feel the weight of his armoury. The heavy musket's four-foot barrel lay on the forked ash-wood rest he had plunged into the turf in front of him, but he had to remain in position, supporting the hard butt against his aching shoulder. Bullets were twelve to the pound; their pouch increasingly dragged. Retrieving shot from the pouch was so slow that he had learned the trick of carrying two bullets ready in his mouth; he was trying to ignore the taste of the lead. Each bullet needed half its weight in fine powder and two-thirds in coarse; he carried both, the fine in a flat flask with a nozzle and the common measured out into a dozen containers popularly called the twelve apostles. This added to his burden and made his every movement noisy. Around him sounded the incessant commotion of metal flasks, since each man carried his twelve powder containers on his bandolier, and all the bandoliers were rattling. They were using up hundreds of yards of match, the lengths of tow twisted into cord and soaked in vinegar to use as a fuse;

with the enemy so close they kept it lit ready for action, each holding a short length, which was burning at both ends. Going equipped with their cord alight would become second nature, in itself a cause of accidents as soldiers forgot they had match in their hands.

As the stand-off continued, they grew accustomed to the situation. They almost relaxed. Hours passed. Stomachs were rumbling. Some members of the Trained Bands slipped away in defiance of their officers and went home for supper and their own beds. The crowd of spectators thinned out too.

'What happens tonight?' quavered Amyas.

'We sleep in the fields.'

'On the ground?'

'On the cold ground, Amyas.' Gideon gave their apprentice an owly stare. 'Just as we are stood to in ranks here, we shall lie down in ranks, justified by our feet.' Justified was a printing joke; Amyas caught on, nervously. He had been complaining about his feet; he was unused to walking and had not yet worn in the new shoes issued to him as a recruit – two pairs, along with his cap, doublet, britches, two shirts and two pairs of stockings. He was in pain with his first wisdom tooth. Gideon wondered sombrely if he would live to complain about the rest, or even to wear his second new shirt.

'What if I need to piss?' Amyas demanded, with telling urgency.

'Don't piss on the rank in front.'

Amused, Gideon watched the boy working out that to be a soldier was to have no amenities and no privacy. Hardship already afflicted them. They received neither food nor water on the march or at battle stations. Armies fended for themselves. At least on this occasion Parliament had sent surgeons out to Hammersmith; those who had fought at Edgehill were saying that the wounded there had had to lie all night among the dead, without medical attention. Only the pity of local people had produced any succour.

Then as he stood in line of battle with nothing else to do, Gideon mused, if I die here today, what will my life have been? *I shall never have known a woman* . . . A strange panic gripped him. He determined to do something about it – if he lived.

He returned to the critical question of whether he should be bearded, and if so, in what style?

*   *   *

Causing muted catcalls, Lambert Jukes appeared and picked his way amongst their regiment. Lambert was always regarded as a good trooper, though known for his frisky attitude to discipline. He thought rules were for everyone else. Now, as the troops grew weary of waiting, Lambert had sneaked off from his own regiment. To Gideon's annoyance, he saw that his brother was sporting a full set of jawline whiskers coming to a jaunty point, with a neat chin stripe and a curled blond moustache.

That settled it. Gideon would shave.

Lambert lowered his pike casually. Pikes were supposed to be fifteen or even eighteen feet long, their main purpose being to nudge cavalry riders from their horses. Many soldiers trimmed the length, to make the unwieldy staves easier to manage. Lambert was no exception and had shortened his pike to little more than twelve feet. Gideon told him it was barely long enough to shove a milkmaid off a pony.

Lambert guffawed. 'What greeting is that, brother?'

'Should you not be at your station, soldier?' Robert Allibone resented association with this wandering fly-by-night.

Lambert soothed him: 'I'll be there when the shots fly. I see you brought your babe-in-arms?'

The big-eared, bandy-legged youngster Amyas raised his eyes to the heavens. He was grinning. This was all a big joke to him.

'He would not be left,' answered Gideon tersely. He and Robert thought their apprentice was too young, but it was out of their hands; Amyas had come anyway. Parliament had issued an order that all apprentices who joined up would be relieved of their obligations to complete their indentures. When this war ended, the commercial trades would be awash with half-trained young men who thought they owned the world – assuming they had not been killed first.

Gideon gazed at his brother, all wide shoulders and wise-boy jests, and he marvelled, not just that Lambert had bothered to come and make friendly contact at such a moment, but at his self-confidence. The Green Regiment's colonel, Alderman John Warner, was giving them a filthy look, but Lambert saluted the colonel as jauntily as if *he* were the officer, graciously noticing some junior.

A man had been following Lambert. It was unclear whether they knew one another and had arrived together, but while Lambert gossiped, the man spoke quietly to Colonel Warner, and he stayed when Lambert left.

He wore black and behaved as if he were freely allowed to saunter among the troops. Perhaps he was a preacher. If so, he did not preach. Someone suggested he was a scoutmaster, in charge of intelligence agents and terrain scouts.

Robert muttered under his breath that the prowling visitor looked like a grocer. Gideon dismissed him as a Stepney innkeeper's pudding-featured bung-puller. The middle-aged man was overweight, or gave that impression as he leaned back on his boot-heels slightly. He had dark jowls and intent black eyes, but otherwise cut a figure anyone might pass in an alley without glancing back. It was hard to know why he fascinated the two printers, except that they were both observant by nature, and found his presence odd.

Gideon was startled when this personage suddenly approached him. 'You are Gideon Jukes?'

Gideon altered his grip on his musket. 'I am Gideon Jukes, and I have work to do here, sir.'

'I am Mr Blakeby.'

'And what is *your* business?' demanded Robert, becoming defensive of Gideon.

Mr Blakeby kept up his peculiar scrutiny. 'I am told you are steadfast and have good judgement. Also that you have experience as an *actor*?' He barely lowered his voice, so heads turned. Gideon cringed.

'I once donned feathers in an entertainment, sir. I was a boy. It was a trifle. I was misguided.'

'But were you any *good*?' Mr Blakeby asked with a smile, keeping his gaze fixed upon him.

Gideon wondered with annoyance if his brother Lambert had given him this unwelcome character-reference, and whether his brother had brought the man here on purpose – perhaps to escape Blakeby's attentions himself. Lambert tended to attract notice because he was seen as a 'hearty lad', yet he was conservative. He would not want to be singled out. 'I am recruiting trusted men for special tasks,' offered Blakeby.

'Then please trouble yourself elsewhere.'

Though Gideon had answered back in such a forthright manner, Mr Blakeby was certain now that the scowling young man had a dark side that would suit his purposes. Jukes was too tall and his fair hair worked against him, but his intelligence and spirit showed.

The place was too public for argument. Mr Blakeby accepted the refusal, merely saying as he left, 'I should like to meet and talk again, Master Jukes.'

'What did that man want with you?' Amyas whispered.

'Whatever it was, Blakeby has *slipped up* with it,' muttered Robert. Slipping up was when lines of type shifted in the form and went askew.

The afternoon drew into evening, which came early as it was November. The men slowly realised there was unlikely to be an engagement. The Parliamentary regiments continued their stand, drums beating and colours flying. There were twenty-four thousand. It was a brave show, and the King had only half their numbers.

The Royalists havered in anguish, but the odds against them were too great. This was the King's one chance of taking London, and he had been out-faced. After hours of stand-off and hurried war councils, the Royalists accepted the situation. They withdrew, without a shot fired.

Essex's army and the Trained Bands heard the trumpeters' recall and watched the King's troops leaving. The Parliamentarians breathed and relaxed, but stayed fast. That night they remained at Turnham Green, where they spent their victory evening tucking into a great feast that the women of London sent out on carts for them. Holding a pie in one hand and bottled beer in the other, Gideon found himself reminiscing about that other feast he had once attended, after *The Triumph of Peace*. With a sense of rightness and victory, he was enjoying this far more.

A young woman approached, carrying a basket of bread and a board on which she cut slices from a huge hard cheese. She had contrived to hold the board against her apron-clad hip so her skirt was caught up to reveal a slim ankle in a pale knitted stocking. Her eye lighted on Gideon and she smiled at him. Robert and Amyas watched them frankly; Gideon felt his fair skin blush. 'A big slice of cheese for you, brave boy?'

'I'll have one!' Amyas reached for it annoyingly. She glanced at him: big teeth, big ears, about fourteen. Almost without seeming to do so, she summed up Robert Allibone too, sensing the widower's reticence with women, judging him to be beyond her reach. Her gaze returned to Gideon, who put down his beer carefully against a grass tussock, and quietly accepted her offering. The young woman looked willing to be detained for conversation.

Unluckily for Gideon, that was when his brother reappeared. 'Here's to a bloodless victory – and to a beautiful maiden, bearing bounty!' Cheese was immediately lavished upon Lambert, who received it as his birthright. He winked conspiratorially in Gideon's direction. 'Watch that one! He's a heart-breaker.'

'The quiet ones are the worst!' The young woman, who was not *quite* as young as Gideon had first supposed, looked unfazed by the warning. 'And you are another pretty hero,' she simpered at Lambert shamelessly.

'Oh, I am handy at push of pike!' he replied, with open innuendo, twirling the blond moustache against which Gideon had taken so badly.

'Your wife will hate to hear you have been flirting, Lambert!' As soon as Gideon spoke, he felt that this was mean-spirited. He noticed that Lambert hardly reacted. Nor did the cheese-bearer.

'*Lambert!*' she noted.

'And *Gideon!*' said Lambert, who had always been more generous than his brother deserved.

Lambert had left her free to choose between them, but the dynamics had changed. Two men in play was more than the woman wanted; she lost interest in both. The elder brother now seemed too cocky to tolerate, the younger too shy to educate. There were twenty-four thousand troops here and she let herself believe that her role was congratulating them. She moved off.

Lambert seemed disinclined to follow, though Gideon spotted that his brother watched which way she went. Had Gideon been older, more experienced, less inhibited by his companions, he might have gone along with her: offered to carry her basket, engaged in harmless conversation, waited to see what might happen. Inexperienced though he was, he felt it would have worked to his advantage.

He did not know how to manage this. He was not even sure that such an encounter was what he wanted. Gideon favoured what the *Grand Remonstrance* had called 'comfort and conversation' between men and women – even though his loins told him 'comfort' could have a wide meaning. With his partner, his apprentice and his brother all gawping like costermongers, it was easiest to remember he had been brought up in decent morality.

The pie in his hand was not as good as those his mother baked. He knew Parthenope would have sent provisions to the troops. Some other lucky bastard must be munching those. Like a true soldier already, he enjoyed the moment of repose and did not allow regret to linger.

The bloodless encounter at Turnham Green had saved London, though it solved nothing. The civil war had barely started yet.

Chapter Six

Oxford: September, 1642

When Edmund Treves was nearly killed by the head of the Virgin Mary, he took his first step towards marriage.

In truth his first step was very shaky. The soldiers' pot-shots had cracked into the stone Virgin, shearing off her veiled head. That smashed down on to the pavement, narrowly missing him. Oxford townspeople shouted with delight at the decapitation; their applause mingled with mutters of horror from robed university men. Treves saw in confusion that a stone shard from the statue had sliced across his wrist, causing blood to flow. Another shot rang out. It was his first time under fire. The familiar wide main street called the High, with its ancient university buildings, suddenly became a place of terror. As Treves realised the danger, his knees buckled and he nearly fainted.

Among the noisy onlookers, one man watched in silence. Orlando Lovell weighed up how the old feuds between town and gown festered with new complications. Freshly returned from the Continent after some years away, he saw with astonishment that tradesmen were openly jeering at frightened dons. Buff-coated troops had clustered in the gateway of Oriel College, threatening to manhandle gawping college servants and then firing at the University Church.

He knew it was the second wave of soldiers. These Parliamentarian hooligans had driven out a Royalist force only a few days previously, each group finding a welcome in some quarters but each fearing reprisals. Barely controlled by their officers, the newcomers were skittish. Already some had mutinied at a muster in the University Parks; dragoons had gone armed to church on Sunday, in fear of the townsmen's hostility; rival gangs had become drunk and caused chaos in running street-fights.

Today's soldiers were vandalising the ancient church of St Mary, to take out their spite against Archbishop William Laud. Authoritarian and ceremonial, he had enclosed altars with railings, repaired crucifixes, set up statues, imposed a uniform Prayer Book and, worst of all, insisted on the controlling power of bishops. Independent free thinkers were outraged. Now Laud languished in the Tower and these raucous London rebels were shooting at 'scandalous images', those hated statues with which Laud's chaplain had embellished a provocative new porch on St Mary's Church. To Lovell, as he stood watching, such scenes in England were astonishing. The anger Laud's measures had caused was distasteful, because it seemed pointless.

People in the crowd had told him one puritan alderman had claimed he witnessed people bowing to these statues: Nixon, a grocer. Nixon had interceded for All Souls College – to which he supplied figs and sugar – when the Puritans proposed to batter at religious images on the gate. Churches did not buy food in bulk, however, so at St Mary's the soldiers were doing what they liked. Lovell found their indiscipline a grave offence.

The endangered scholar was an idiot. With a curse, Lovell strode across the road, caught the swooning Treves roughly under the elbow and dragged him upright. Jeers came from the Parliamentary soldiers. The rescuer kicked Mary's head away, as he hauled the young scholar across the frontage of the church and the two of them stumbled out of danger. The troopers held fire, following their progress with aimed muskets, though the gesture was merely to intimidate; the football kick had pleased them – as had been intended.

'Take more care!' ordered a mounted officer crisply. Lovell assessed the rebel commander curiously: in his sixties, receding hair, thin, upswept moustache, tasselled baldric. This was Lord Saye and Sele himself, one of the leading Parliamentarians. He was a colonial financier, a campaigner against Ship Money, a plotter at his Broughton home with some prime enemies of the King. A man of great political skill, Saye and Sele had been nicknamed 'Old Subtlety' by King Charles.

Lovell passed muster, then Treves was waved away, assessed as a dreamy scholar who had ambled into the line of fire whilst in a world of his own.

'I could have been shot!' He nearly collapsed again.

Lovell walked him towards the Cornmarket, then wheeled him into an alehouse. He had taken command, setting the pattern of their future relationship. Pushed onto a straight-backed settle, Edmund first suspected the man was about to insist on some very strong beverage, yet Lovell quietly ordered small beer, the same watery brew that children drank.

He was sturdy and tanned. It was mid-September and still mild, but he kept a heavy black cloak close around him like a spy. He had been wearing a dark hat with a lowish crown and a long thin feather, which he now tossed aside on a table. He raised his tankard and held it steady. 'I'll drink to your health when I know your name.'

Ridiculously, Edmund felt tempted to supply a false one but he owned up to his identity. Lovell grunted. He enjoyed the fact he appeared threatening. He leached out danger with every move. Though a stranger to Oxford, yet he was at ease in his surroundings. He looked to Edmund as if he must smell of sweat and horseflesh, though in fact only a faint hint of old tobacco had smoked his dark garments, garments that were more serviceable than rich. He seemed liable to put up those well-travelled boots on a bench, while leaning back in a relaxed pose and calling for ripe cheese, clay pipes and available wenches . . .

Yet he remained sitting neatly. His light brown eyes gave nothing away, as he stated: 'Orlando Lovell.'

The tapster was glaring at them. Lovell ignored it. Treves had scrubbled up his gown and shoved it under the bench on their arrival; scholars were barred from alehouses. Since the colleges owned most of the inns in Oxford, there was a good chance that breaking the rule would be reported by an innkeeper anxious to preserve his lease.

'So you are a scholar!' said Lovell, smiling. It was perfectly obvious from the young man's sober dress. Having red hair and the pale colouring that goes with it, Edmund looked innocent as a child, though he was now made a little raffish by blood staining his linen cuff where the stone fragment had struck him.

Without seeming to do so, Orlando Lovell expertly drew out the scholar's history. He was a good-humoured youth from a family of minor gentry who would be hard pushed to secure him a position in life. In peacetime, his options were to become a country squire (difficult, with no estate of his own), a lawyer (though he lacked friends and family who could push for him as patrons) or a clergyman (not advisable while religion was causing such strife in the kingdom). His father had died some years before; his mother struggled. The family lacked sufficient funds or influence to send children into royal service at court. Edmund was too well born to undertake labour or trade, yet did not possess enough land to live off. Money had been scraped together to send him to the Merchant Taylors School, which his mother's brothers had attended. Somehow, with a smattering of the classics and the Merchant Taylors' influence, he had gained a place as an exhibitioner at St John's College in Oxford. If Oxford was not precisely educating him for a career, that was simply the way things had been through the centuries – and, cynics might say, how things would always be.

'Are you a university man, Master Lovell?'

'I never had that privilege.'

Lovell deduced Treves would probably leave without taking his degree. That was relatively common; he would be following many who had nonetheless become great men in political or literary life. 'It may be, dearest Ned,' wrote his mother in one of her weekly letters, seeking to console herself, 'that receiving education at a great university is a benefit in itself, and should you achieve something of note in your life to come, the record will state that you were once present at that seat of learning and none will think badly of you . . .' This feeble sentence whimpered to a close and Alice Treves snapped out her true feelings: 'Though in truth, I should be heartily glad to see you properly set up with a degree.'

Treves gloomily explained new regulations instituted by the all-controlling Archbishop Laud. To obtain a degree, it was no longer enough to attend a few lectures and hand in occasional written work. He must pass an examination.

'You have time to study harder.'

'Yes, but there is a war now!' Edmund burst out excitedly. Like most scholars, he paid as much attention to politics and religion as to his books – which meant, as little as he could get away with. He had been born the year before King Charles was crowned. He grew up in an England that was stable and prosperous, where he had been innocently unaware of trouble. The headmaster at his school and the dons he encountered at university were all loyal to the King; he took his lead from them. His college had benefited by an enormously expensive new quadrangle, paid for by Archbishop Laud, who had been President of St John's and also the university's Chancellor. Laud was impeached the first year Edmund went up to Oxford. At St John's, the threat of their

President being executed was a talking point even scholars could not ignore.

Lovell's interest focused. 'Your college is pricelessly endowed, I think?' he quizzed. 'There must be an excellent cellar. Do you enjoy a good kitchen?'

'Colleges are expecting to lose their treasures,' was the cautious reply. Even Treves could spot a chancer.

All over the kingdom, Lovell knew, men were seizing the initiative and taking control of weapon stores, town magazines, ships and money. In Cambridge a member of Parliament called Oliver Cromwell was adroitly removing the university silver for melting down. When Royalist forces had occupied Oxford under Sir John Byron, Byron afterwards thought it prudent to take away with him much of the Oxford university plate, 'lest it too fall into Parliament's hands'. The Christ Church plate was refused him, only to be discovered hidden behind wall-panelling. Whatever Byron left was now being tracked down by Lord Saye and Sele. But he, like Byron, had studied at Oxford and was diffident about looting his *alma mater*. He burned popish books and pictures in the streets, yet he had accepted the pleas of the Master of Trinity that the college pictures were not worth destroying – 'We esteem them no more than a dishcloth' – so those old masters were left, discreetly turned against the wall.

'Lectures are cancelled while all becomes muster, drill and fortify,' trilled Edmund.

'Don't you spend all hours swearing and gaming?' Lovell was teasing, to some extent.

'No, our statutes forbid gambling for money – more of Laud's reforms. We must keep our hair trim, dress plain, and not loiter in the streets in loathsome boots. There is to be no hunting with dogs or ferrets, and we may not carry weapons –'

'And what do you do for –' Lovell spoke in his usual polite timbre though the undertone was feral. Edmund looked alarmed. Lovell merely rubbed one cheekbone beneath his hooded eye, with the tip of a languid finger.

'For entertainment? We write Greek graces and solve Latin riddles,' Edmund replied solemnly.

*　　*　　*

The gentle jest puzzled Lovell. He reviewed it, considering how he should answer, or whether any answer was needed. Young Treves was accustomed to rapid banter, hurled to and fro by disrespectful students. Curious, he took it upon himself to ask what Lovell was doing in Oxford.

'I came with Byron.' Had Lovell been left behind here as a Royalist spy?

'Are you a professional soldier?'

'I have served in arms since I was younger than you.'

'How long is that?'

'A decade.' As Edmund looked impressed, Lovell turned the conversation. 'So, master scholar – no weapons! How does that suit in the present upsets?'

Then, while Lovell listened in amused silence, Edmund explained how many scholars and some dons had left Oxford, never to return; the normal new intake of students had dried up. Those who remained were drilling and helping to fortify the town.

As the risk of action increased, Edmund Treves had helped dig trenches, fortify Magdalen Bridge and carry stones to the top of Magdalen Tower to be thrown down upon any attackers. Lovell belched derisively. Treves pleaded with him for advice on how to join up in the King's service and Lovell agreed to help him.

Lovell set down his empty tankard and collected his hat. 'So what does your mother think of your warlike aims? Do you correspond?' Edmund admitted that his mother wrote to him very fondly every week. 'And you reply . . . ?'

'As often as seems advisable.' Edmund did reply every week, ornamenting his letters with phrases in Greek and Latin to prove that he was studying. However, he had enough about him to fudge the issue when talking to a sophisticated ex-mercenary, ten years his senior, whose expression verged on wry. 'Do you have family, Master Lovell?'

'None that trouble me,' replied Lovell briefly.

When this chance acquaintance between Lovell and Treves grew into an unlikely friendship – or what passed for friendship in an uncomfortable city, riven by faction – it was Lovell who recommended that Edmund Treves should try to marry an heiress he had heard about. Just as it was Lovell who advised Edmund on becoming a soldier, it was he who came up with Juliana Carlill.

In the autumn of 1642, in England, a gentleman of eighteen had two likely fates lying ahead of him: marriage and death. Many would achieve both very quickly. Few used their fear of a coffin as a reason to delay jumping into a marriage bed; it was commoner to hurry between the sheets, while the chance was there.

Sadly, it also became common for young married women to lose their new husbands while they were heavy with their first pregnancy. A proportion of widows would remarry, especially those were young, proven to be capable of child-bearing, and perhaps blessed with a legacy; some could hope for second chances. For others, life would be bleaker. Widows, especially widows on the losing side, could only expect to be shunted into corners of other people's parlours, often dogged by lawsuits and disappointed in their children. Despite this – luckily for men of eighteen – only in the most sensible families were young girls advised to be cautious about marriage.

For in the autumn of 1642, nobody supposed the civil war would last long. Most people were sure that some form of reconciliation would be negotiated between the King and Parliament. Anything else was unthinkable.

So Edmund Treves, who gave little thought to the possibility of dying until the Virgin Mary's head nearly killed him in the High, was soon presented with another dangerous fate. Edmund had not learned good judgement. He never considered that the war into which King and Parliament had stumbled was set to drag on pretty well for the rest of his life. He failed to understand that war should be approached not as an impromptu game of fives against a college wall, but with great caution. Love, too, needed long-term planning. This was a risky time to take major decisions – especially when they were prompted by a man whose reliability was untested.

Bearing a whole flowery nosegay of misapprehensions, therefore, Edmund Treves travelled cheerfully from Oxford to a house near Wallingford, in order to meet a young lady about whom he knew only what his new friend had told him – much of which would turn out to be wrong. Had he been older and worldlier, it was generally agreed, he would *not* have visited a prospective bride in company with Orlando Lovell.

Chapter Seven

Oxford: Autumn, 1642

Lovell always protested his innocence, but nobody who knew him and his already dark reputation really believed the protest.

Where had he come from? Where had he been? There were answers, and there were people who knew them. He saw no reason to volunteer the correct information, and if incorrect stories were circulating, that was how he liked it.

Lovell, who now styled himself captain, had come to England from genuine military service in Europe, arriving at about the same moment as one of the King's nephews. This was where his personal history first acquired an awkward kink. He let people assume that he had served under the eldest royal nephew: the Elector Palatine. Prince Charles Louis was a refugee. His father had been invited to take the crown of Bohemia, but was driven out ignominiously after less than a year; the 'Winter King' had then lost his own lands as well, and until he died he had campaigned to regain his position. His sons now carried on the hopeless quest. Charles Louis came to England to plead for assistance in 1641. He was also hoping to claim his promised bride, the King's eldest daughter Princess Mary, but found that she was to be married off more advantageously to Prince William of Orange.

It was a bad moment politically. King Charles had been bankrupted by the Bishops' Wars and his new Parliament was set on confrontation. Charles had nothing for his begging nephew. As English hostilities were breaking out, the threadbare prince spent some time in London, assuring friends in Parliamentary circles that his own allegiance was neutral. Whether this reflected his annoyance at losing Princess Mary, or his astute evaluation of his royal uncle's future, was unclear. He probably wanted to protect the pension that was paid to his mother Elizabeth. Her pension continued but, with polite expressions of regret, Parliament declined to help Charles Louis. He gave up on a bad situation and went back overseas. Lovell stayed.

At exactly the same time, the elector's dashing younger brother Prince Rupert turned up in England. Ostensibly, Rupert came to thank King Charles for helping to secure his release from an imperial prison after he had been captured while fighting. He had been to England before, when he made himself a favourite with the King and Queen. The young Palatine princes hailed from a very large family and had been homeless for most of their lives; as their own cause faltered in Europe, they were able to offer their military experience to any country that would give them an army or any relatives who needed them.

Born in Prague, Prince Rupert had been only a baby when his parents took flight from Bohemia; in the rush to leave, he was temporarily forgotten and only a quick-thinking nursemaid remembered at the last moment to fling the infant into a departing coach. He grew up abrupt, which was hardly surprising, but so good-looking he could usually carry off his rude manner. Now he was twenty-two and knew considerably more about war than his uncle, King Charles – though perhaps not quite enough.

'Over-valued,' growled Lovell, who thought himself a good judge. 'Over-valued mainly by himself, and nobody will take him down, because of his blood.' Then he chewed his pipe with a frank grimace which acknowledged both his envy of Prince Rupert and the irony that he, too, might in some respects over-value himself.

Both men were rootless, shiftless and penniless. Both also had a flagrant air of needing nothing and yet expecting all.

'This Prince Rupert is a St John's man,' mentioned Edmund Treves, also chewing a pipe stem. They were in St John's College at the time, feet up in his room. Edmund was mischievously tweaking his friend's lack of humour: 'Archbishop Laud inaugurated our new Canterbury Quadrangle – the King and Queen attended; they are honoured with elegant statues by the sculptor, Le Sueur.' He spent a moment tapping down his tobacco. Lovell waited impatiently. 'Prince Rupert must have been about sixteen; he came in the royal party and was admitted here as a scholar.'

'Is that so?'

'Truly.'

'Were you here then?'

'I fear not.'

'A pity. You might have shared a bench with His Highness, jogging his Palatine elbow as he slurped up his breakfast in the buttery.'

'Would that have been useful?'

'What, Edmund – calling the princeling "old colleague"? I believe it could have been!'

Edmund Treves smiled quietly. Even Lovell joined in.

Treves pondered his new friend's intentions and where Prince Rupert fitted into them.

When the civil war began, men who could fight were drawn to England. The native-born came from loyalty, foreigners descended for plunder. Experienced soldiers were pouring in from all quarters of Europe. Settlers, acting from conscience, were even returning from the Americas. Men with money began recruiting regiments. Orlando Lovell could not afford this. Volunteers of lesser means must inveigle themselves into any troop they could. That had to be his route. He must have earned hire-fees when abroad, and he had hoarded booty – but he always guarded his purse. The day they met, Treves had been right to sense himself being eyed up as prey. Only his poverty saved him.

Lovell had brought his talents home and declared allegiance to his King (he did appear to be English – or perhaps Irish or Welsh – though almost certainly not Scottish). He would be whole-hearted in his support, for he thought rebellion was madness and could only fail. Somehow, Lovell would eventually serve under Prince Rupert. He knew how to insert himself into the most charismatic position. Whatever his views on the prince's ability, he foresaw where useful friends could be procured and where reputations would be made. But to begin with, Prince Rupert was away again, escorting the Queen to Holland.

Impatient for action, Lovell had already looked at other positions. In May, the King had finally acknowledged that the upheaval in the country necessitated a Lifeguard of Horse to protect his royal person. Lovell at that time appeared briefly with Sir Thomas Byron, one of seven distinguished brothers on the Royalist side, who was the Lifeguards commander. The trial posting failed to please the fastidious Lovell. By August, he had attached himself to Sir *John* Byron, another of the brothers, who had ridden into Oxford on the 28th of the month with two hundred men.

This Byron was a chin-up commander with black brows and a moustache like a thick black ingot struck above his upper lip. He was famous for fighting even when there was no need; he survived being wounded in the face with a pole-axe and he would earn himself the nickname 'the Bloody Braggadocio'. His flamboyance failed to convince Lovell. Perhaps, for him, Sir John Byron was just too colourful. He burned so brightly he would overshadow subordinates, offering little to compensate. So when Sir John Byron rode away, Lovell stayed behind in Oxford.

'Was that permissible?' Edmund anxiously suspected that the high-handed Lovell had deserted Byron's colours.

'Never join the first troop you see,' snorted Lovell. Whenever he spoke as a soldier, with that experienced cynicism, the awed Treves accepted his words open-mouthed.

Lovell joked that there were still five other Byron brothers whose commands he could assess until he found one that suited him. But he knew what he wanted: service with Prince Rupert, working out of Oxford.

'Any fool can see this is the place,' Lovell barked. 'Hell's teeth, the King is wasting himself, struggling to capture Hull, just because it is supposed to be a good northern port and contains a mighty magazine –'

'A magazine?' asked Edmund.

'An arsenal. Left over from the Scottish Wars – but while King Charles has been faddling outside the gates like a butter maid, the magazine is whipped away and bundled down the road south to Parliament . . . What's left? Bristol is held by the rebels. Warwick is a hotbed of dissent. Nottingham and York are too remote to contemplate. *Oxford* is central, well disposed to the King, easy to supply, easy to access, defensible, and best of all, rich enough and gracious enough to host a royal court.'

'So . . . ?'

'So, let us sit here until the court arrives.'

Us, thought Edmund, feeling proud.

While they waited for the court to find them, Lovell's plan to marry Treves to Juliana Carlill flickered into life.

Lovell had heard of this heiress whose guardian wanted to find her a husband. Anyone more observant than Treves might have noticed the source of the tale was servants' gossip in an alehouse. Only a deep cynic would wonder whether the information had been deliberately planted among the potboys by the girl's associates, to snare some well-to-do scholar. Orlando Lovell, like many a passionate schemer, never supposed that anybody other than himself had the skill or the bravado to plot.

Once he had ascertained that the girl was young and alone in the world, supported only by an elderly bachelor guardian, Lovell declared that these people were innocents, waiting to be plucked. It was up to Edmund, Lovell urged, to snap up the unguarded prize before some quicker man stepped in ahead of him.

Orlando Lovell liked to make things complicated. He implied to Edmund that the proposal to find Juliana a husband had been initiated by the Queen. Henrietta Maria was then at her highest peak of influence. Given that the King was an indecisive cipher to his tenacious French wife, ambitious men would do well to respect her suggestions, Lovell said. Treves was too unworldly to doubt the Queen's involvement, let alone suspect Lovell of inventing it.

When, urged by his perturbed mother, Edmund did press for more details, Lovell just shrugged and said the Queen wanted to help the girl. That seemed reasonable. It seemed so to Edmund, anyway, though when she received his letter, Alice Treves smoothed her lace collar with an agitated gesture and her mouth tightened. For one thing, she knew that the Queen was abroad.

The Queen had gone to Holland, to convey her newly married ten-year-old daughter Princess Mary. Members of the House of Orange were eager to take custody of her. A substantial sum had been paid by the Dutch to secure the highly desirable Protestant bride, who should have been accompanied by a huge dowry, although because of the English political crisis this was threatened. Instead, the Queen vigorously sought to raise funds for her husband's war. Astutely, Henrietta Maria had taken many of the Crown Jewels – not hers to sell, protested Parliament – which she touted around continental moneylenders and arms dealers, raising cash and buying weapons. It was uncertain when she would return to England. Her absence affected the early course of the war in various ways. It caused the King great anxiety – and prevented any enquiry into Henrietta Maria's reported affection for Juliana Carlill.

The easy-going Treves had gained the impression (from whom? from Lovell?) that the girl's grandmother had been among the ladies-in-waiting who greeted the young queen on her arrival in England way back in 1625. In fact Roxanne Carlill was French herself, which should have made him wonder. He would probably have backed out, had he realised that Henrietta Maria had barely known, and certainly could not remember, her supposed maid-of-honour.

The Queen's interest in Juliana was his biggest misapprehension. There were others.

Juliana Carlill was reportedly heir to a property. Lovell believed it to be 'Kentish orchards', but he had allowed himself to be led up a very winding garden path in this respect, which Edmund failed to investigate. The men took it for granted that Juliana was educated (though not too much), chaste (though not frigid), beautiful, a good dancer, witty (they had not considered whatever they meant by *that*), and that she would allow her husband generous time to hunt, fish, see his male friends and go out to taverns. But it was to acquire the orchards that they pressed into action. They were cavaliers, with a romantic view of women, but they knew the value of money.

Edmund had good intentions towards Juliana herself, because by nature he was thoroughly decent. Nonetheless, he was a man of his time so he hoped that her property and her position in the Queen's favour would enable him to avoid work or worry. These were perfectly acceptable reasons for seeking to marry. Lovell assured him that if he managed to persuade the girl and her guardian to have him, his mother would forget she had been given no hand in the decision and would warmly welcome the bride, along with her apple (or cherry?) orchards – which grew ever more abundant in their imagination.

Lovell was constantly on hand to steer the plan. He himself lodged in a slightly unpleasant inn. Oxford inns, which had a constantly changing, disloyal clientele, were never sleepy havens for ancient regulars, but brisk businesses run by two-faced landlords who were barely polite and who wanted to take money. It seemed natural for Lovell to spend much free time at St John's.

There, Edmund had a historic room in the old quadrangle, a fair-sized chamber up an ancient stair, where he was looked after by a scout with skinny legs who could hardly mount the steps with a coal scuttle. Edmund's scout despised scholars, and he positively loathed the intruder Lovell. Lovell knew himself to be exposed. He showed no perturbation. He came most days, daring the scout to report them for smoking. In fairness, Lovell did supply the tobacco. However, that was because he deduced that Edmund had no idea how to buy a palatable leaf, while sending out the crabby scout to the tobacconist was never an option.

To his credit, Edmund did wrestle with a perceived problem. Education had not been wasted on him. 'I should much like to be a man securely enjoying his wife's estates, but I do not see, Lovell, why an heiress of this calibre should ever take me on.'

'Nothing to it,' said Lovell. 'You must carry yourself like a fellow who has much gallant farmland of his own − but it is all temporarily entailed on your Anabaptistical second cousin.'

'And how will I manage that?'

'With meekness,' laughed Lovell. Then he added as if he knew at first hand, 'And dismally.'

Juliana Carlill and her guardian were living at Wallingford in a house which the guardian, William Gadd, had borrowed. After a brief exchange of letters, Edmund Treves, supported by Lovell in the role of groomsman, travelled to see them there.

Wallingford was a spry market town, its moated castle decently held by Royalists, with lovers' walks along the river banks and a great bridge where William the Conqueror had forded the Thames on his way to be crowned. Wallingford went back in history longer than that. A fortified Saxon burgh founded by King Alfred, it had once been larger than Oxford; it was still strategic and remained very sure of itself. It was a typical English county town, which would soon be fought over bitterly.

Lovell and Treves were thrilled to learn from local intelligence that the house they had to visit was owned by a judge. This put Mr Gadd in a highly respectable context − just as Mr Gadd intended, had they known it.

Chapter Eight

Wallingford: October, 1642

One fine autumn afternoon in 1642, Juliana Carlill was summoned by her guardian's all-duties maid, Little Prue.

Juliana had custody of various heavy tomes which had belonged to her father, who spent more money than he should on books. She had been enjoying her reading, an accomplishment her father had taught her. He had collected 'utopias'; she was deep in one called *The Man in the Moon* by Francis Godwin, where a shipwrecked Spanish nobleman was towed to the moon in a chariot drawn by trained geese; there he discovered a benign social paradise, with fantastic, futuristic features.

> *'You shall then see men fly from place to place in the air. You shall be able to send messages in an instant many miles off, and receive answer again immediately. You shall be able to declare your mind presently unto your friend, being in some private and remote place of a populous city . . .'*

Lost to the real world, Juliana did not hear Little Prue knock at the bedchamber door, nor did she immediately notice her standing in the room. Little Prue, a vague, pale mite who came from a farming background, stared at the book as if its spellbinding hold on the young lady suggested Juliana was a witch. In seventeenth-century Europe, that could be a serious mistake. A spinster who wanted to avoid disaster never lived reclusively, nor kept a black cat, nor gave her neighbour — or her neighbour's cow — a lingering look. Otherwise, the next step was having voyeuristic men inspecting breasts and genitals for devil's teats. No witch-finder ever conceded he had made a mistake: invariably accusation led to a guilty verdict and the penalty was hanging.

Juliana smiled at Little Prue reassuringly.

*　　*　　*

On being informed that she was being visited by two strange gentlemen, Juliana went through all the sudden shifts of emotion that would overwhelm any young girl. She did not want to put down her book in mid-chapter, for one thing. Domingo Gonsales, the utopian voyager, was about to return to earth, where he landed in China . . . Yes, Juliana Carlill was a reader who peeked ahead.

Her next thoughts were for her appearance. Fortunately she was wearing a neat gown of pale yellow, sprigged with tiny flowers. Little Prue, whose memory was no bigger than a bluetit's, forgot her fears of witchcraft and took it upon herself to straighten Juliana's soft collar, with its falls of delicate lace from high in the throat then down across her shoulders. Juliana's lace was always good. It had been mended in many places, but the mends were invisible, she was entirely confident of that, having reworked the threads painstakingly herself. Her hair, too, was fashionable and smart. When a young lady is staying with an elderly bachelor guardian who refuses to hear of her assisting his all-duties maid in anything more than genteel gathering of herbs from the kitchen garden (which at Wallingford was not well stocked), she finds nothing much to do with herself except mope in her bedroom arranging her hair. So Juliana had a very neat flat bun on the crown of her head, with tendrils of curl framing her face and long loose ringlets at each side.

She stepped down the dog-leg staircase, pointing her toes as she took the wooden boards, so she would not trip on the long folds of her gown. This was a Tudor house, maybe a hundred years old, built in mixed materials, with some brick. Juliana descended into a small hall, with a low plaster ceiling rather than the great hammer-beamed caverns of earlier periods, though this one boasted a heavy rent table – too heavy to move easily, and so left to gather dust here while the house stood unoccupied.

Mr Gadd, shrunken but twinkling with excitement, waited for her outside the door to a withdrawing room or parlour. Skinny legs in old-fashioned black hose capered beneath a full-bottomed doublet in a style from the time of King James. He was mostly bald, but lengthy strands of grey hair dragged on his quaint outfit's tired brocade. With his elderly, watery eyes, this gave him an off-putting, slightly seedy impression. That was misleading.

He was, Juliana had discovered, extremely intelligent. At eighty years of age he had retired from the Inns of Court with a healthy pension; it was paid by several grateful lawyers whose careers he had burnished by steering clients their way, by discovering long-forgotten points of law, by tracing – or otherwise procuring – essential witnesses, and by knowing where to buy good malmsey. He had no formal qualifications; he was a pig-keeper's son. He knew more law than most judges, but he had not been born a gentleman so could not use this knowledge directly. Juliana's grandmother had pretended to think he was legally qualified, though in truth Roxanne recognised exactly what he was, just as *he* understood *her* position. They were outsiders. They had invaded a level of society that was theoretically closed to them – and they stuck there tenaciously. Roxanne had intended that something should be done about this for Juliana – and Mr Gadd concurred.

So here they were.

'What do we have, Master Gadd?'

'A pink-and-white mother's boy – manageable. And there's his supporter – who needs watching.'

Juliana and her guardian had had a sensible exchange of views on her future. They were prepared to deal with any wooers who came to call. 'If he looks sound husband material, we'll drop him!' chirruped Mr Gadd, pretending to level a firing piece at some unwary bird in a coppice. Juliana, who feared that shooting down a husband might be the only way to catch one, smiled as if she too were enjoying the chase.

Two gentlemen was more than they hoped for. Mr Gadd whispered quickly that it was only to be expected that the scholar-suitor would be nervous and would bring a friend. Juliana would have liked an encouraging friend of her own. But she had never had friends. Her grandmother had thought English children were nasty creatures.

All the same, she was not alone. She was lucky to have found herself placed in the care of a guardian with whom she could converse on a practical level. Their good humour together only increased her sense of obligation. She did not wish to burden Mr Gadd. Besides, Juliana might be only seventeen, but she had a keen sense of how the world worked; she preferred not to be alone in his care too long. So far, he was sheltering her with the gravest of good manners, but he was a man. Roxanne had been a man's woman – and Juliana knew what that meant. Her grandmother remained flirtatious right until she died;

Mr Gadd had been a conquest, undoubtedly. Mr Gadd on his stick-thin legs might yet launch some tottering sally against Juliana's honour. Girls who have other girls as friends give themselves courage against unwanted amorousness, but Juliana had no such confidante. Her chaperone was Little Prue, though she suspected instinctively that Little Prue *might* beat off an attacker with a warming pan − yet might as easily decide it was not her place to interfere.

So one reason Juliana welcomed marriage, marriage to anyone who seemed suitable, was that she wanted her own home, where she would have standing as the housewife and could enforce rules for her own protection.

Juliana and Mr Gadd knew in advance that Edmund Treves had a widowed mother, to whom he was close, and also siblings. This could entail married life with the Treves family. While Juliana might find herself immediate soulmates with her mother-in-law, she could equally end up in thrall to a harridan. She had been surprised when Mr Gadd discussed this. He actually warned her against life as a young bride in another, older, woman's home. His unfashionable attitude, which had a ring of experience, was her one glimpse of his personal background.

Until three months beforehand Juliana and her guardian had never met. He knew her grandmother only briefly in London, and although he prepared Roxanne's will on that occasion, nine years later when Roxanne died he was initially alarmed to find himself left in charge of Juliana. He took to the responsibility, however. Roxanne had foreseen this. Mr Gadd, who had never had dependants, was thoroughly enjoying himself as Juliana's guardian. Still, even though she knew Roxanne had vetted him, Juliana could not absolutely depend on him. When it came to accepting or rejecting the suitor, he would advise, but she had to decide.

Mr Gadd paused, with his hand on the latch, winked, then opened the door. Juliana took one hard look at the two men in the parlour, before she cast down her grey eyes modestly as a young girl was supposed to do.

Once she thought she could do so discreetly, naturally she then peeked.

Orlando Lovell − sombrely clad, heavy spurs, uptwirled moustache, pinched lips − had taken possession of one of the solid square wooden armchairs, whence he had been eyeing the room. Edmund Treves − shaved

−74−

until he bled and blushing pink — was standing. His gaze fluttered on her guardian but then came directly to Juliana. He wanted to know what was being offered to him. Juliana felt equally determined to assess her suitor: the younger, taller man, who wore a braided cherry suit slashed over silver satin (the main colour clashing with his red hair) and a billowing satin cloak wrapped over one arm. Mr Gadd had led her to expect someone wimpish, though in fact Treves's features were firm, with a forward-thrust chin, and his build was chunky. He appeared more athletic than scholarly. Juliana, who could not afford to make mistakes here, immediately assessed him as good-natured, but too young.

She felt more wary of the other man, who was so coolly assessing his surroundings. The room had linenfold oak panelling and contained only two monumental box chairs, plus a rather ugly fifty-year-old buffet, a long side table with two open levels, which currently displayed no plate, not even second-best pewter. There was an open hearth, where a modest log fire blazed, but it had made little encroachment on the chill that gripped the long-empty house. Nobody present, however, would have challenged the fact that a judge should own more houses than he could live in, and should be able to abandon a fine property, without tenants, for years at a time.

Juliana was introduced. For this, Lovell rose rather reluctantly; both visitors swept off their broad-brimmed beaver hats. Everyone uttered polite nonsense for the briefest time possible. Lovell returned to his great chair, leaving Mr Gadd to occupy the other, while Juliana and Edmund took separate window seats. It left both of them relegated to the sidelines, with a pillar between them. If Juliana had foreseen this, before the meeting she would have dragged in a couple of leather-backed dining chairs. She wanted to peer at the suitor, while the others talked.

Mr Gadd crisply enumerated Juliana's talents: chaste, sweet-natured, well read, religious, a good seamstress, able to manage a kitchen and a still. He called her fair, because 'beauty' was conventional. They could see for themselves that she had brown hair, grey eyes, straight teeth, a small nose (unlike her French grandmother), and a medium figure that could probably cope with child-bearing. Her manner seemed reserved. That was good. A woman had to accept her fate meekly.

'You have been at court, Mistress?' asked Treves, sounding hopeful as he leaned forward awkwardly from the other window seat. He was still flustered and blushing.

'She is far too young!' remonstrated Mr Gadd, with a friendly chuckle.

'You are French?' demanded Lovell. Nothing flustered him.

'My *grandmother* was French, Captain Lovell.'

'The French court is full of foppish men and filthy women.' He sounded as if his sneers were based on experience — though Juliana thought anyone could generalise in such a way.

'Perhaps,' Juliana countered, 'that was why Grand-mère was pleased to leave.'

Her retort was too strong. All three men blenched.

'The grandmother married a cloth merchant of Colchester, very well-to-do,' Mr Gadd said rapidly. It was true, although the cloth merchant was a haberdasher and he had vanished from the scene rather quickly. *'Drowned at sea — so sad!'* was how Roxanne had passed it off in her brisk manner. She always made it sound as though Mr Carlill was a bolter, who had left her in the lurch. Perhaps. Juliana had occasionally wondered disloyally whether he was dispatched by other means. For certain all his money and his stock-in-trade, while it lasted, remained with Roxanne.

He also left Roxanne pregnant — the only time the Frenchwoman was caught out. She thought her son Germain a British milksop, but brought him up diligently. She never complained, even when Germain spent most of his father's money (Roxanne kept some of it back in secret) and himself failed in business.

Germain Carlill survived childhood, grew up feckless and married a young woman called Mary, who was the antithesis of his mother, the simplicity of Mary's name and nature throwing her exotic foreign mother-in-law into high relief. Mary produced Juliana, miscarried, miscarried again, then died. Seeing there was no hope her dreamy son would take proper care of the little girl, Roxanne stepped in. Though never maternal previously, she and her granddaughter grew very close. Juliana was a sunny, self-reliant child. It helped.

None of that needed to be recounted to Treves and Lovell. The background and experiences which had formed Juliana's personality were irrelevant; only her paper assets counted.

'Are you able to supply a dowry list?' It was Lovell who asked.

'In preparation,' assured Mr Gadd. 'Her grandfather left a wealthy bequest and her grandmother was an excellent businesswoman. I was proud to have the acquaintance of Madame Carlill.' Mr Gadd saluted

Juliana who smiled gravely. She noted that nobody asked about her father. 'Captain Lovell, it would be helpful to hear whether your friend's landed estates would add the same level of material security? What jointure is being offered?' A jointure was money provided by a groom's family to support a wife if her husband predeceased her; it was generally similar to the dowry that a girl brought to the marriage.

Lovell bluffed: 'Mr Treves is a gentleman and a scholar, as you know. His family is well regarded in Northumberland – are they not, Edmund?'

'Staffordshire,' Edmund corrected, forgetting that Lovell had told him to say Northumberland as it was more remote, which would help flummox enquiries.

'He is a scholar,' repeated Mr Gadd thoughtfully. 'How can he marry whilst at the university?'

'Any gentleman may leave his studies to settle down. A degree is not in itself significant. The important thing is to have broadened his mind – then to seize the moment to establish himself wisely.' Lovell managed to suggest that acquiring a degree for career purposes was not only unnecessary, but even slightly sordid. Obtaining a rich bride was much more respectable.

'His estate will permit him to be immediately independent?' Mr Gadd was inspecting his skinny knees with a clerkish air.

'He is possessed of all the requisite rents to flourish.' Lovell remained polite, but implied Gadd had insulted them.

Mr Gadd had worked with lawyers, so he was impervious. He spoke as if he had made up his mind. 'It will be necessary to satisfy myself.' Juliana knew he was already making enquiries, a task he enjoyed, though the political upheaval meant answers were slow in coming.

The shrewd Gadd observed a passing shade of alarm in Treves – which gave him answer enough. The boy would not do.

Mr Gadd could have cut their losses immediately and withdrawn from negotiations, but there had been no other offers. The threat of war was a trial. Good families always liked to marry their offspring to their friends and relations. He knew it would be difficult to drum up interest.

Besides, rehearsing witnesses had been Mr Gadd's strength when he worked in the law; he wanted to give Juliana more practice with suitors.

The young redhead was mightily keen on obtaining the 'Kentish acres', which told its own story. Treves was no use. He needed to be dropped, but Mr Gadd was enjoying this race between impostors. He let Treves and Lovell run downhill with the cheese.

Chapter Nine

Wallingford: October, 1642

Treves and Lovell came daily for over a week. A phantom courtship was played out, with nobody learning much, nobody committing themselves. Mr Gadd had not yet warned Juliana he planned to refuse Edmund Treves.

So she donned her hat dutifully and went walking with the two gentlemen, chaperoned by Little Prue. They conversed politely of birdsong, the price of butter, the delights and pretensions of Wallingford. Juliana pressed Treves for stories of his family, ignored Lovell as much as possible and said nothing of her own background. She learned about Treves's widowed mother, Alice, his younger brothers and sisters, his two uncles who acted as interested patrons as far as they could afford. Through his private enquiries Mr Gadd had discovered that one of the uncles was supporting Parliament, although the keen Royalist Edmund seemed unaware of it. His mother must know, but had kept that back.

Juliana treated Edmund well. Unfortunately, he mistook her good manners for genuine interest in him. He had never had much contact with young women outside his own family. He found Juliana pleasant to look at; her intelligence impressed him without his noticing it. Even when he forgot to think about her apple orchards, he was falling in love with her.

Juliana had never had much contact with young men, but she had a practical streak, directly learned from her grandmother. She was certainly not falling in love with Edmund Treves.

Once or twice the men were invited to dine. On these occasions, it was natural that the conversation turned to the political situation. Juliana was glad, for it took attention away from Little Prue's indifferent efforts to pan-fry escalopes.

Juliana rarely spoke. She was supposed to remain silent. She knew these negotiations could just as well have been carried out without her presence. But she watched carefully.

'Are you for the King or Parliament?' It must have been Lovell who put the question to Mr Gadd; Treves innocently assumed that everyone he met was a Royalist.

'I am for King – and for Parliament, Captain.'

'A lawyer's answer!' Orlando Lovell quite rudely related how a country labourer had been asked the question by a troop of cavaliers; when he gave the same cautious reply as Gadd, they shot him dead. 'Many people would rather not choose,' Lovell acknowledged, 'but we shall all be forced to it.'

'So is it your opinion this armed conflict will rage long?' asked Mr Gadd – still slyly withholding his views, Juliana noticed.

Lovell answered at once. 'If there is a decisive battle this autumn and if the King wins – as he should – then all is over. If there is *no* decisive battle, or if Parliament prevails, then we are in for a long, hard-driven wrangle.'

'So you are for the King, even though it is a hopeless cause?' sniped Mr Gadd.

'Not hopeless,' returned Lovell. 'More ridiculous than I like. More ill-judged than it need be, longer, more bloody, more expensive, no doubt. But the King must win.'

Mr Gadd pursed his lips very slightly.

'Of course the King will win!' Edmund burst out immaturely.

While Juliana continued to observe in silence, the men reviewed the position. England had had no standing army. On both sides, gentlemen raised regiments, often composed of their own pressurised tenants, ill-equipped and mutinous. The King's call to arms was being only fitfully answered but in contrast, the Earl of Essex, Parliament's commanding general, was in charge of twenty thousand troops. Now, in October, the King was still trying to drum up support in the Midlands, with mixed success, his army still much inferior. At the time of Juliana's courtship, the King had moved to Shrewsbury.

'There he is well positioned for support to reach him from Wales, where several regiments are being raised for him,' said Mr Gadd.

'You speak like a strategist,' Edmund Treves commented.

'We shall all be strategists by winter,' replied Mr Gadd.

Lovell had previously worn a superior smile, but now spoke easily, as if he was enjoying the debate: 'The Earl of Essex prefers a waiting game; he wants the King to sue for peace.'

'You think the King will march on London?' Mr Gadd asked.

'What has your intelligence from London to say?'

'Oh my correspondence with London is all of demesnes and rents,' Gadd told Lovell softly.

'Of course it is.'

There was a small pause, as if contenders in a sparring match were taking breath.

Lovell reached for the wine flagon to refill his glass and that of Treves. Mr Gadd had already declined further liquor, on health grounds. Juliana's glass was empty, but she was a young girl, and Lovell no more considered replenishing her wineglass than he had deemed it proper to include her in the political conversation. She had a flashing vision of Roxanne, on rare occasions when there was wine at the Carlill table, grasping the flagon and pouring for everyone equally.

Edmund Treves caught Juliana's look and misinterpreted: 'Do not be alarmed by all our talk of war, madam. Neither side wishes this conflict to be a trouble for women.'

Juliana remembered what Mr Gadd had told her about Edmund's opposing uncles. 'Any woman connected to men who are fighting must find it a very deep trouble, Master Treves. Besides,' she added wickedly, 'perhaps if Captain Lovell had asked me, am *I* for King or Parliament, I might not give a lawyer's answer!'

Orlando Lovell looked amused. 'So let me ask you the question.'

For almost the first time in their acquaintance Juliana gazed straight at him. 'Oh I must ally myself with my husband – when I have a husband.' She let them feel smug, then added, 'However, if I did not like his views, that would be very difficult. I hope to have my husband's full confidence, and to share mine with him.'

'And if you could not?'

'Oh I should have to leave him of course, Captain Lovell.'

As they all laughed most merrily at this idea, it seemed that only Juliana Carlill recognised that she had not been joking.

By the time that they had this conversation, King Charles had made his move. He left Shrewsbury, to the relief of the townsfolk, who had been badly used by his bored and ill-provisioned soldiers, even after the royal Mint from Aberystwyth was brought to coin collected plate and pay the men. The Earl of Essex bestirred himself. Leaving Worcester, which had suffered from his billeted troops as badly as Shrewsbury from the King's, he set off to form a blockade between the King and London. So the two field armies moved slowly towards each other, with between fourteen and fifteen thousand men apiece, each strangely unaware of their converging paths. Poor physical communications and the indifference of the people in areas through which they passed combined to astonish them when they suddenly came within a few miles of each other, near Kineton in south Warwickshire. On the 23rd of October, the King decided to join battle, drawing up his troops on Edgehill ridge.

When news of the battle at Edgehill reached Wallingford, which happened quite swiftly despite the sleeting autumn weather, the courtship of Juliana faltered. Though reports were as confusing as the battle seemed to have been, Treves and Lovell were now eager to join the King's army. A polite note informed Mr Gadd they had left Wallingford to volunteer.

'We shall not see them again,' Juliana murmured, uncertain whether to be disappointed.

Six days after the battle, the King and his army marched into Oxford, where Lovell and Treves were waiting. Charles was welcomed by the university with great ceremony and with less warmth by the town. Four days later he set off again determined to capture London. This was his march to Turnham Green.

As the Royalist army travelled south, it passed Wallingford. Juliana and Mr Gadd were surprised to receive a new visit from Orlando Lovell. This time he came alone. He seemed depressed, which appeared to be his reaction to the battle; he had ascertained details which he shared with Mr Gadd, man to man, Juliana being permitted to listen in only because she sat so quiet in a corner the men forgot she was there.

According to Lovell, the fighting took place between three o'clock in the afternoon and darkness. He described sourly how Prince Rupert's cavalry thundered through one Parliamentary wing but then chased off the field in pursuit of their fleeing opponents instead of steadying. Against orders, the King's reserves followed Rupert, another episode that caused Lovell's displeasure. The Parliamentary centre held, he said, then their infantry and cavalry fought valiantly. Night fell upon widespread confusion. The exhausted armies gradually came to rest.

'Both sides claimed victory though neither could sustain the claim.' Lovell was speaking in a grim voice; Juliana saw that he knew about fighting like this. She heard undernotes of criticism. 'There was heroism, of course. There was futility. Seasoned soldiers are primed for both, but most men there had no past experience. They must have been terrified and shaken. Then after the guns and drums fell silent, the survivors spent the night on the battlefield. It was freezing cold. Under the gunsmoke, wounded men were moaning and dying. No medical aid came to them, though some were saved by the frost, which staunched their blood. It is said one of our men, stripped and left for dead, kept himself warm by pulling a corpse over him. Among the living, who had neither eaten nor drunk since the previous dawn, men shivered helplessly and tried to come to terms whilst in deep shock. Survivors of battle experience relief and also overwhelming guilt. Even their demoralised commanders sank into lethargy.'

'And where does this leave us?' Mr Gadd asked him.

'Hard to say. Parliament had the most dead, though they held the field. When dawn broke, there were arguments on both sides, but neither commander was willing to continue. Both withdrew. It achieved nothing and solved nothing. All it tells *me*, sir, is that there will be no fast resolution.'

Lovell then asked for a conversation in private with the lawyer, after which he wanted an interview with Juliana. While she waited, she found she was quite frightened by what she had heard. She did not know exactly where Edgehill or Kineton were, but Warwickshire was only the next county to Oxfordshire. If, as Orlando Lovell implied, the battle stalemate indicated that this war was to continue for a substantial period, Juliana felt suddenly more anxious about her own future.

When Lovell emerged, he suggested a walk in the garden. Mr Gadd pleaded age, so she found herself in an unexpected tête-à-tête.

The grounds of the judge's house ran down to the river, with green lawns that must be scythed by some hired labourer even though the judge never came here. The grass was too sodden to be walked on, at least in a young lady's delicate footwear. Lovell's boots might have done it, but he had no intention of sinking in up to his precious spurs. He led

Juliana to a raised terrace nearer the house, their feet crunching on wet pea-grain gravel.

'Forgive me,' said Lovell, speaking briskly, 'there does seem to be great haste in seeking a husband for you. I am struggling to understand it. Your guardian will barely take time to supply us with the documents about your orchards –' Juliana now believed Mr Gadd had decided not to pursue Treves's proposal, yet Lovell still spoke as if he had no suspicion his scheme might be rejected. 'There is nothing untoward, I hope?' His gaze dipped to Juliana's belly, making his suggestion unmistakable.

Juliana had an unpleasant moment, thinking that Lovell and Treves had been discussing her morals, though she knew men did so. Pulling her cloak tighter around her, she answered levelly, 'You think me *unchaste*, Captain Lovell?'

He seemed to back down. 'I am indelicate.'

'You are unforgivable!'

Lovell for once seemed alarmed. 'Forgive my bluntness. I am a soldier –'

'And soldiers have to be uncouth?'

Lovell looked rueful. 'Please listen. I have a pass "to visit friends", but I must make haste and who knows when I may visit Wallingford again . . . Treves and I are now attached to Prince Rupert's regiment. I must rejoin them immediately.'

Juliana did not relent. 'If there is urgency over my marriage, it is because my guardian is eighty years old, and I am otherwise alone in the world!' Still preoccupied and perturbed by Lovell's story of Edgehill, the thought of being alone oppressed her more than usual. She fought to regain her self-command and some control in the interview. 'It is best I am settled quickly. Especially in these troubled times.'

As she fixed her gaze on the lichen-coated balustrades and urns that surrounded the judge's parterre, she was aware that Lovell stared at her with a curiosity that verged on insolence. 'I am admiring your strength of character, Mistress Carlill. You have, if I may say so without annoying you again, a quality beyond your years.' She was too good for Treves, of course; Lovell saw that now. 'Too many difficulties while too young, I think?'

'Too much grief.' Juliana was equally blunt.

Lovell put a hand beneath her elbow and steered her to a stone bench.

He made a desultory attempt to brush it clean, the scatter of leaf litter catching on his hand. He was making it worse, and gave up. Juliana seated herself, her knees turned towards him so he could approach no closer, making space for herself, if not a barrier.

'So, madam. Tell me, what are your hopes in this negotiation? What are you seeking for yourself?'

The question was unexpected. For once Juliana felt uncertain. 'All the talk has been of "necessity".'

It always had been, for as long as she could remember. After her grandmother's long struggle to rise above poverty in a strange country, the need to survive had always driven her family. Her father's lack of business sense had destroyed any security they had. Her grandmother kept the family together and yearned for better things. Now, for Juliana to be respectable, better things could only come through a good marriage.

Her father had been a dreamer. Her grandmother despaired of him, could not believe she had raised a son who was so careless about his own future, or the future of them all. It was left to Grand-mère Roxanne to give Juliana any ambition she would have. Not enough, for Roxanne.

Yet Juliana's ambitions were fixed, and she enumerated them briskly to Lovell: 'A household of my own to run. A husband who values me as his true companion. To bear children but not bury them, nor to die myself while bearing them. Not to despair of how they shall turn out . . . A garden,' she added suddenly, glancing around. Most of the plants had withered, their few leaves hanging as brown rags. Frost had wreaked instant havoc.

'Well, this is a gloomy autumnal patch!' Lovell commented.

'A garden where the autumn die-back would not matter, because I would always see it bloom again next spring.'

Lovell had a sense that the Carlill family had moved about a great deal. He wondered why. However, the young woman did not look particularly hunted. These domestic hopes of hers were pretty conventional. 'There is always the blossom at your orchard in Kent.'

The situation was not as he thought. Juliana smiled again, in her gentle, non-committal way. 'Ah, my father's orchard!'

'So,' probed Lovell. 'Is Edmund Treves to be your life's companion?'

Juliana felt it was improper to give her answer to Edmund's friend. Although she acknowledged that Lovell had authority to hear it, the very fact that Edmund let his sponsor come alone dismayed her. Whatever the reason a man asked for her – and she did not by any means expect it to be love – Juliana wanted direct dealing. Her view of marriage demanded it. 'Edmund Treves has excellent qualities –'

To her surprise, Captain Lovell suddenly interrupted: 'Too young! Too untried, too unworldly, too poorly endowed to match your dowry –' He had *that* wrong, thought Juliana almost humorously. 'Altogether too damned milky white. No man for you.' As Lovell saw Juliana recoil at his frankness, his voice rasped. 'Do not make your decision from a sense of obligation, simply because young Treves has offered. You must defend yourself. No one else will. Think on that.'

He sounded like Mr Gadd. Juliana hardly paused. 'You are quite right. I will tell him –'

'*I* will tell him,' Lovell volunteered. 'I brought him to your door.'

'I would not wish Edmund to be hurt by this, Captain Lovell. I believe he may care for me –'

'He's in love. He'll recover. Edmund', explained Lovell brutally, 'has but one great idea in his head at any time. For the moment he is besotted with his new life as a soldier. However –' And for once Orlando Lovell favoured Juliana with an open grin, a grin of such enormous sincerity and charm that she felt her first abrupt awareness of him as a man. 'He badly needs your orchard!'

She looked downcast.

'Should you refuse young Treves, we are all left with the other problem,' Lovell mused. 'Your guardian, Mr Gadd, rightly wishes to procure a husband for *you*.'

Juliana's gaze slipped across the parterre. She saw the ancient climbing roses, their great stems bent to unseen wires, one with a last brave crimson flower, another with pale buds that would never now open fully since they were browned by frost. A cold breeze was twisting her ringlets and she had hunched her shoulders against the cold. The conversation could not last much longer; she would have to go indoors.

And then she heard Orlando Lovell suggest to her quietly, 'There is an answer. Marry me.'

Chapter Ten

Birmingham: October, 1642

'Why me?' wondered Kinchin Tew.

As the mad parson took hold of her, she felt indignant, resigned, desperate, bewildered. She was a fourteen-year-old girl, just an unattractive scavenger, born among masterless women and men. Kinchin was a nickname: never baptised, never enrolled in school, there were no records of her existence and her real given name was lost.

It was not the first time Mr Whitehall's watery gaze had lighted upon her expectantly. They were both daytime wanderers, so in a small town like Birmingham their paths were bound to cross. Skulking against walls or creeping up backstreets, Kinchin would sometimes startle him; more often, he would loom up from nowhere and cunningly trap her. Then she knew what was in store.

Why me? was a question she posed, yet never answered for herself. To others it would be obvious: she was vulnerable. Her parents and brothers generally left her to herself. She was a starveling, alone on the streets.

Kinchin never invited the man to accost her, but she endured what he did. Mr Whitehall was an adult, and as a churchman he carried authority even if he could no longer practise his calling because of his past. Everyone knew how he behaved to women. Even though Kinchin feared him, it was almost exciting that he chose her. These were the only occasions when she mattered to anyone.

If ever she had the advantage of surprise, she took herself out of his reach, but pride made her walk off unhurriedly as if continuing on some errand. The parson rarely followed if she had an escape route. For him the thrill lay in persuading women to give him kisses freely. Besides, he was sane enough to know that if he attempted pursuit and force, he could be brought before the church court, then the parish would send him back to Bedlam. Kinchin knew that he was recently released from the great London hospital for the insane, where he had been kept for twenty years. Now he had somehow found his way back to Birmingham, where new generations had ripened and Kinchin Tew was here to be preyed upon. Everyone knew his habits. A few women tolerated him. Generally he was thought to be safe, a mild nuisance who could be rebuffed quite easily. Many towns and villages harboured a similar pest, always had done, always would do.

'Ooh – has Mr Whitehall taken to Kinchin?' Her mother's speculative tone had been a shock. Kinchin heard the eager hope that someone of quality wanted something – and might pay for it. At once she saw that her family would never try to save her. Now she was fourteen, she had become useful. They would offer her wherever they could, to do whatever was asked. In their gruelling quest for survival, her parents wanted rewards for nurturing her. Doing whatever was necessary would be her duty. When she now tolerated Mr Whitehall touching and toying with her, she was aware that worse experiences lay ahead.

Life was harsh for the Tews. Kinchin remembered that it had not always been quite this bad. The family had once subsisted inefficiently on commonland at Lozells Heath. They were rag-pickers and tinkers, with harvest work every autumn, if they could be bothered to apply for it and if any farmers would put up with them. For generations they had scratched a living, inhabiting a decrepit hovel where scabby, tousled children snuffled five or six on the floor while their parents and associated adults squabbled over who would sleep in what passed for a bed. If it was winter and they were 'looking after' a cow, the cow took precedence in their shelter. Occasionally a handy Tew would concoct a lean-to byre in which to hide the stolen cow; then the children would have somewhere to skulk, plot, dream and, if the elder boys were obsessively curious that year, engage in mild incestuous activities. Pigs they claimed as their own roamed the scrubby heathland; chickens that answered their call pecked around outside the hovel. The Tews were masterless men. They were constantly at risk of being taken up for idleness, yet most were not completely idle and they all possessed a kind of freedom that was better to them than the bullied lives of servants or apprentices. As freedom went, it was dirty and cold, but for generations the Tews had managed to exist.

Then Sir Thomas Holte enclosed a third of Aston Manor to enlarge his park. The Tews were driven out.

The social gulf between the Tew family and that of 'Black Tom' Holte was vast. They had nothing. He had everything. Though his forebears had a long pedigree in the Midlands, his real social eminence developed with the Stuart kings. On the accession of King James, Holte had been knighted; later he pushed forward to be among the two hundred who paid a thousand pounds each for a baronetcy – a new rank, invented to create funds for the king. His red-handed badge then gave Sir Thomas Holte precedence over all except royalty and the peerage. He built himself a gem of Jacobean architecture, an ostentatious stately home to signify his importance. He sired sixteen well-fed children, by two wives. As lord of the manors of Aston, Duddeston and Nechells, Holte enjoyed an aristocratic idleness that was never made the subject of sermons or by-laws. He flourished, with the minimum of loyal service to the kingdom, while growing ever richer on the proceeds of brutal business methods. He hunted, quarrelled and counted his rents. He bought the extra manors of Lapworth and Bushwood; he acquired Erdington and Pipe. He became a Justice of the Peace for the county of Warwickshire and lay rector of Aston parish. With no opposition, or none that mattered, he then seized for himself the breezy open common. Some of it became his new deer park and the rest he parcelled out in tiny batches to local artisans. Their leases were short enough to keep the men craven, lest by displeasing their landlord they should lose their livelihoods.

With land in a commanding position astride the vital River Bourne, Holte controlled the necessary water supply for industry; he soon owned seven mills on the Bourne and two more on the River Rea, with dozens of one-man forges leased from him. Acquisitive, hot-tempered and vindictive, he had a reputation as well read and versed in languages, though this was not tested in Birmingham where the locals had their own curious intonation but only the Welsh drovers needed real interpreting. Velvet-suited Holte sons went to London as courtiers to the King. Pink-cheeked, pearl-bedecked Holte daughters played shuttlecock in the Long Gallery until they wed other landowners, their carefully negotiated marriages providing their father with more ample cash to adorn Aston Hall. The eldest son fell out with his father for twenty years and a daughter was reputedly locked up in a garret, but their father disdained to be called to account for either; he tried to ruin his son, who had married a girl with no dowry, even when pressed to forgive him by King Charles.

Aston lay a very short walk from Birmingham, where Sir Thomas Holte was disliked and insulted. Notoriously, he sued a local man for spreading rumours that Holte had struck his cook with a kitchen cleaver so violently that 'one part of the victim's head lay upon one shoulder and another part on the other'. Judges on appeal cleared the defendant of slander on the curious grounds that his claim did not say in so many words that the baronet had murdered the cook. The wry judgment stated, *'notwithstanding such wounding, the party may yet be living'*. This lawsuit led locally to open animosity that increased in the civil war. Sir Thomas Holte naturally supported the King; the rebellious people of Birmingham did not.

The Tews took neither side. The war would not be fought for them. They owned nothing worth fighting for. Following the land enclosure, they were homeless and destitute, without trade or other income. They gravitated to the town, but found little charity there; they were too strong-bodied to win places in guild almshouses and, if approached, the Birmingham churchwardens would only move the Tews on – back to their home parish of Aston, where Sir Thomas Holte was master. Their plight might be his fault, but he influenced the Aston churchwardens when they gave or withheld poor relief, so the Tews were convinced their chances were hopeless. 'If he cared, he would never have thrust us off the common,' moaned Kinchin's father, Emmett Tew, a shiftless, shabby laggard to whom complaining had always come easier than making the best of it. He had a point. Many aristocrats claimed that giving alms to the poor only encouraged them to remain idle and beg for more relief. This opinion allowed people of high birth and low cunning to avoid paying conscience money. It worked too. The number of paupers diminished, as they died from starvation and disease.

Kinchin's mother was pregnant yet again, though she looked too old for it; the new child would probably die but if it survived birth, it might have to be sneaked into a church porch and abandoned. Idealists in England would soon debate the principle that all men came into the world equal – yet the Tews knew that from birth to death they were less than the rest. Hounded from their toehold amid the gorse and wild-flowers, they joined the tinkers, pedlars, gypsies, vagabonds, cut-purses, thieves, actors, wounded soldiers and sailors, idiots and sturdy beggars who bedevilled better-off society. Many were begging through no fault of their own, though that never earned them kindness. Few refuges existed. There were houses of correction where destitute young boys could be taught trades, but few girls entered apprenticeships; their only legitimate option was to become servants. For Kinchin, that option was pretty well closed. No respectable housewife would take in a starved, scab-encrusted runt, who was bound to steal. So Sir Thomas Holte had his portrait painted in green silk, tulip-bottomed britches braided with gold and a silver jacket, his black-bearded personage hung about with rosettes, bows, baldrics and expensive lace-trimmed gauntlets. Kinchin Tew grew up wearing a mildewed skirt she had filched from washerwomen who had laid laundry to dry on thorny bushes. She never had shoes. Now although she looked a child still, she was fourteen, and a tribe of Tews was expecting her to earn for them – in what filthy manner no one had yet specified.

Some people who lost their livelihoods took to the road. As far back as memory would go, the Tews had had their fixed base in North Warwickshire; they clung on in their home district, except for one of Kinchin's brothers who left to try to be a sailor. Since they lived at the very centre of England, Nathaniel had a long walk to the sea in any direction and nobody expected to see him again. Little William was ordered into a charity apprenticeship but ran away after three weeks. Sukey found a position as a dairymaid, caught cowpox and died. Pen died of nothing in particular, as the poor did. Other Tews drifted into town and pleaded for jobs which rarely lasted more than a few days. Self-employed cutlers could not afford unskilled help, bigger businesses wanted workmen they could trust, and Tews tended to lose patience and barge off in a huff anyway.

Birmingham was sufficiently prosperous to offer them advantages. Just one of a multitude of small English towns, it stood at a crossroads of medieval pack-roads. A parish church dominated the old village green, which had been built around with little houses. Along the dog-leg curve of the single main street were several markets, chiefly for cattle which provided both meat sold by the butchers in the Shambles and hides for leather-working. There were sheep pens and a corn cheaping. The town boasted commercial cherry orchards, from which all the Tew children stole fruit, and a rabbit warren whose dozier coneys sometimes ended up in the Tews' cooking pot with bits of nettle and root. An old moated manor-house graced the pretty water-meadows of the River Rea, which was crossed by two stone bridges. The river here and its associated pools and springs had long supported cottage industries. Along the main stream were tanyards, steeping tanks, maltings and watermills. In recent decades Askrigge's corn mill had been converted by the entrepreneur Robert Porter to a steel mill, while numerous small open-fronted forges lined the side streets; they turned out every kind of metalwork, though mostly knives. Increasingly, the smiths made swordblades.

Because it had industry as well as its markets, Birmingham had been one of the most flourishing towns in Warwickshire for a hundred years. Although it still lacked borough status, self-made men had built handsome houses on the rising ground, surrounded by gardens and orchards. The local guild maintained almshouses for the few paupers of whom it approved. The guild financed market officials – the bailiffs, the ale and meat connors, the leather sealers and the constable, whose suspicious glare Tews of all ages tried to avoid. It supported the parish church-wardens, bellman, organist and caretaker; it also paid for a midwife. In the guildhall was housed the King Edward the Sixth Grammar School, where fortunate boys were given as good an education as Will Shakespeare had devoured at Stratford-upon-Avon – though lice-ridden, rude rascallions from the common were of course excluded, while girls had no perceived need of learning at all. Kinchin could neither read nor write. However, she knew the value of everything, especially its price as second-hand when second-hand meant stolen.

Throughout her childhood she had slunk through the commercial areas looking for opportunities. If she was shooed away from the Market Cross near the corn market, she moved on through the noisy beast market to the Welch Cross. She would beg openly or she would keep her eyes peeled for spillage and accidental loss. Small change dropped amongst the sordid straw of the cattle pens was often ignored by those who lost it; Kinchin would pounce and grab despite the dung and slime. Stray carrots and apples slipped into the tacked-on pocket of her tattered skirt however bruised they were. As evening fell, she would gaze long-ingly at unsold produce that the countryfolk might prefer not to carry home again. Clasping any trophies, she usually made her way to Dale End near the Old Priory or to Digbeth and Deritend, which was Dirty End, down by the river. Those places were where her adult relatives would most likely be lurking at the many taverns that supplied the forge-men's mighty thirsts. Tews sometimes earned a few pence for pot-washing; they could drain dregs while they were doing it.

If Kinchin had a friend, it was Thomas, an ostler at the Swan Inn in the High Street, a wiry, affable man who on stormy nights would let her sneak into the stable and bed down in the warmth with the horses. Recently she just kept the Swan in reserve, in case she was ever truly desperate. One day Thomas would want to be kept sweet, and she had a good idea how. Meanwhile her anxieties lay elsewhere.

Today, Mr Whitehall had come upon her while she dawdled in Moat Lane, near the manor-house. He whined the usual plea: 'Pray you, give but a comfortable kiss, Kinchin!' The old parson's tremulous, beseeching voice contrasted with the expert controlling grip in which he grasped her. She could feel his heart pounding through the black woollen clergyman's habit that he still wore, despite holding no position; no congregation would knowingly accept him. Even to Kinchin, herself unwashed, he had a rank smell that had nothing to do with mildewed Bibles. 'A cinnamon kiss, a kiss with some moistness –'

Why me? thought Kinchin drably.

A new indignity began. She felt Mr Whitehall's right hand pummelling between her legs. Her skirts were of thick and coarse worsted, which she had pulled around her clumsily; their heavy pleats were thwarting his entrance, yet he worked with bruising vigour. Confused, Kinchin wrestled and kicked, but in her agitation she had allowed his stinking wet mouth to fasten on hers. Disgusted by his excitement, the girl became angry; this time her ordeal was as painful as it was unwelcome.

He had lain long in Bedlam. What was a kiss to comfort a madman? *He might give me a penny* . . . A clawing hand that knew exactly how female dress would be arranged now tugged at her placket, thwarted only by the bunched folds of a garment that was several times too big for her.

'Let it be our secret, Kinchin, our special secret!'

Kinchin Tew wanted to be special in some way – *any* way – and Mr Whitehall knew it.

Chapter Eleven

Birmingham: October, 1642

'Oh Mr Whitehall, put it away!'

For a moment the new voice confused Kinchin. Although she knew the minister's cunning, she was surprised how rapidly he released his hold and slid apart from her. She glimpsed the offending prick, but it was sheathed away into his britches as soon as he heard the order.

With gratitude, Kinchin recognised Mistress Lucas, wife to a Birmingham forge-man. She was a quiet but forthright woman in a well-laundered white cap and apron over a modest oatmeal-coloured skirt and bodice, with a basket on one arm. She had chivvied the minister matter-of-factly, but the way her eyes lingered on Kinchin acknowledged that she knew this was a rescue. 'Come along with me and I'll give you some bread and butter, Kinchin.'

As soon as they emerged from Moat Lane, squeezing between small houses into the close below St Martin's Church, they met unusual bustle. All morning a cavalcade had been passing through town. The stream of mounted men and foot soldiers caused havoc in the markets, where there was always a squash of animals and people. It was the main Royalist army, coming down from the north, headed up by the King himself. The passing of the royal coach caused a particularly bad scrimmage and a humorous moment when a frightened goose landed on its roof.

There had been a stir in Birmingham for days. It was the middle of October, the first autumn of the war. It was, though nobody knew it yet, the week before the first true battle, which would be fought at Edgehill on the next Sunday. The King was travelling among the Midland shires, trying to out-manoeuvre the Parliamentary Earl of Essex, who had just mistakenly turned towards Worcester. Charles had come down on a slow route through Bridgnorth to Wolverhampton, where his usual appeals for funds and recruits were announced, while locals were plundered and a church chest broken open so that a man could tamper with title deeds relevant to a quarrel he had locally. A bronze statue, taken away to be cast into a gun, was rescued by the family of the Elizabethan dignitary it honoured. After summoning the people of Lichfield to send all their arms, plate and money to his standard – which most were disinclined to do – Charles had spent Tuesday night, yesterday, at Aston Hall, as the guest of Sir Thomas Holte. The irascible baronet had refused the King's entreaties to patch up the quarrel with his elder son, though as a keen business tycoon, Sir Thomas must have welcomed the visitation; it would enable his descendants to promote Aston Hall more commercially. Every stately home needs a royal bedchamber to show off to the paying public.

Mistress Lucas told Kinchin that this morning the King had addressed a scattering of new recruits nearby – including, Kinchin discovered later, her own brother Rowan, looking for adventure. Afterwards King Charles trundled his way through Birmingham and was believed to be heading to Kenilworth Castle.

Despite slow recruitment, the royal army had reached sixteen thousand. The soldiers took some time to force their passage down the narrow, curving main street of Birmingham, accompanied by traders' curses. Most people in town were unsympathetic and too occupied with their Wednesday morning's business to take much notice, though the goose that flew onto the carriage won laconic instructions to shit on the roof. These townspeople had a self-deprecating manner and a pessimistic drone to their voices, both of which they were proud of; they were all cocksure and bloody-minded. Bitterness seethed in Birmingham too. Eight years earlier the town had suffered particularly badly from plague. It happened just before the King tried to levy his notorious Ship-Money tax from inland counties, districts which thought naval matters were nothing to do with them. Times were already desperate. Many businesses had been forced to close during the plague. Birmingham was outraged to be assessed for Ship Money at a hundred pounds, the same as the county town of Warwick. Representations were made, unsuccessfully. The injustice had brought out the brooding side of the local character then, and still rankled. There were Royalists in Birmingham but they were a minority; the town would be decried by the tetchy royal historian, Clarendon, as *'of as great fame for hearty, wilful, affected disloyalty to the King as any place in England'*.

At first, the royal army passed through without incident. There had been looting earlier, but the King hanged two captains as an example; the Royalist version made much of this as a strict response after the captains had allegedly only taken trifles of small value from a house whose owner was away in the Parliamentary army. No one in Birmingham was impressed.

For Kinchin and her rescuer, the troops meant waiting at the corner of Well Street, until a gap in the ranks of foot soldiers enabled them to scamper hand in hand across the cobbles and arrive breathlessly in Little Park Street.

As they walked to the Lucas home, nothing was said about the mad minister. But Lucas's wife seemed to understand how troubling Kinchin found it. The man's perversions were becoming worse. Kinchin was increasingly enslaved to the minister's carefully wrought fiction that she was his special choice. She knew no way to escape.

After crossing Well Street with its many small forges, the two women continued down Little Park Street to a slightly larger house than some, in sight of the church steeple and within sound of Porter's steel mill. All the backstreets rang with one-man businesses. Some forges were in adapted huts and outhouses, some had been specially constructed to the purpose. Lucas was a good craftsman, with a reputation for sound work, and had done well for himself. He and his wife lived in four rooms, with his forge roaring separately behind their house; it was a few yards down a narrow garden that extended towards the pool from which he obtained water.

Kinchin had been indoors here before. From time to time she was allowed to enter the spotless kitchen and sit at the rectangular scrubbed table. When today Mistress Lucas gave her the promised bread and butter, she ate slowly. She wanted to prolong her time in the warmth of the kitchen fire – and to look around for goods to carry off. No fool, Lucas's wife kept a beady eye on her. The couple were of modest means yet their kitchen contained many portable, saleable items, from the fire irons to the pewter tankards and brass vessels and skimmers. It would be easy for Kinchin to seize upon tongs or a colander, a chafing dish, an iron candlestick, a kettle, a mortar or a fancy trivet. Like all homes in Birmingham, a town full of cutlers, this was well stocked with knives

– from sharp-pointed shredding knives to cleavers in several sizes . . .
Feeling the housewife's gaze upon her, Kinchin dropped the wicked
thought from her mind. She knew the rules: the food would stop if she
broke faith.

'This capon pie has come three times to table, Kinchin. Will you help
me to see it finished?' It was a delicate way to give Kinchin the last of
a deep and delectable cold pie, now well matured in its coffin of mutton-
broth paste. Seizing the dish, Kinchin let one side of her thin mouth
slide sideways in what passed for a swift smile.

Mistress Lucas watched curiously as Kinchin savoured the rare treat,
lingering as if it was to be her last meal before hanging. She did not
snatch and gobble; her small grubby fingers were picking apart the pie
with a strange delicacy, then she raised each mouthful at a dreamy pace.
Kinchin acted naturally, scarcely caring whether Mistress Lucas noticed
her delight. This seemed simply the best dinner of the starveling's life.

She was skin and bones, bulked out only by her bunched garments;
the girl was an insubstantial fairyweight. It was as well she ate so
slowly, or her stomach might have rebelled at the unaccustomed rich
fare. Her face looked blanched, her eyes hollow, with dark rings beneath.
Her tangled hair was greasy as an old sheep's wool, while bloody
scratches on Kinchin's forearms and forehead told their own story of
fleas and lice.

The housewife sighed. She had more compassion than many.
Birmingham was a puritan town, with a famously outspoken minister,
Francis Roberts. The inhabitants earned their livings by their skill and
enjoyed their independence while they did so, but they had imagination and knew good fortune was easily lost. Any accident in his forge
could render Lucas unable to work; then his penniless wife would have
no support for herself and the baby that was gnawing its rattle in the
wooden cradle. Another plague year, sooner or later, was inevitable
too. The last bad epidemic had struck when the Lucases were first
married. To be a young bride while trade was in the doldrums had
taught hard lessons. Pie had been a rarity. The couple had eaten not
even bread and butter, but bread and dripping if they ever had it, or
plain crusts otherwise.

Everyone was more prosperous now. Mistress Lucas could afford to
be charitable. Even so, she knew that to give more than occasional food
and friendship would risk bringing down a flock of Kinchin's feckless

relatives, all scrounging and whining for more than the housewife wanted to afford. She was wise enough to go warily, however much her heart pitied the pale waif.

She was preoccupied anyway. While she was out at market she had heard that the King's soldiers wanted to buy swords. 'Kinchin, lick up that dish and then run out the back and see if Lucas has anybody with him at the forge.'

Kinchin caught the troubled note in her voice. She scrambled to look outside, then squeaked excitedly that several men were arguing with Lucas. Seizing the girl by the wrist (still thinking of the danger to her pewter tankards and the firedogs if she left Kinchin indoors alone), Mistress Lucas rushed outside and approached nervously down the path. 'Oh no; I feared so. It is the King's men, wanting swords!'

Lucas had come out from the forge and was barring its wide door. Some of the soldiers had given up and were moving on, but a couple remained and were remonstrating with him.

'Tell them that you have none, Lucas!' called his wife.

He has some swords and has hidden them! thought Kinchin, in amazement, since resistance seemed so perilous. Wide-eyed, she assessed the strangers. Their court accents sounded ridiculous, as if they were exaggerating their voices as a jest. Not many such fanciful suits and boots crunched down the cinder paths to the backstreet forges. Unlike the stolid farmers who visited Birmingham, standing feet apart with their arms folded as they bought and sold cattle, these men positioned one foot in front of the other like dancing masters, while they leaned back in exaggerated poses; they had done it for so many years the stance was natural. They tilted their chins up to survey Lucas snootily, while he squarely blocked the entrance to his smithy and stared back. Beyond the group, Kinchin could see two tethered horses, expensive and glossy: wild-eyed, high-stepping beasts, too risky to be offered carrots.

'I will not sell to the King,' Lucas reiterated steadily. He was taking pig-headed pleasure in refusal. A strong man, red-faced from the fire and sure of his competence, Lucas normally conducted himself quietly. Blacksmiths had to be intelligent – and they had to be independent. He was unimpressed by the cavaliers' outrageous manners, and unafraid. He showed it.

'Five pounds the two dozen – we have offered the best price.' The

King's agent spoke with astonishment. They thought money was all. Having a tradesman talk back came as a shock too.

'Not enough to buy my conscience.'

'Then you are a rebel and a traitor!'

'So be it.'

'You will be sorry. Your whole damn traitorous town will regret this!'

Lucas merely shrugged. Mistress Lucas and Kinchin shrank together as the cavaliers strode off to their tall horses, cursing.

A while later, Kinchin left Little Park Street and made her way into Digbeth to search for relatives in the taverns. The streets were quiet; the unwanted troops had left.

It took some trouble to run her father to earth, for he was not at the Bull, the Crown, the Swan, the Peacock, the Talbot, the Old Leather Bottle, the White Hart or the Red Lion. When she found him, pretending to wash pots at the Old Tripe House – which rarely sold tripe now, since it was easier to offer ale only – he told her that one of her brothers had answered the King's call for local recruits. 'Our Rowan. He thinks they will pay him – he's a fool but so are they. If they don't use his head as a firing mark, he'll take anything he can grab and run away.'

'Shall we ever see him again?'

'Who cares? He's a mardy good-for-nothing, all mouth and snot. He's only gone for the rations and the plunder. Any army that takes him is piss-poor and ready for defeat.'

Suspecting that Rowan might really be quite clever to enlist, Emmett changed the subject. He had further news. Local men had ambushed a small group of Royalists who were tagging behind the main cavalcade with the baggage. Some of these guards had been killed; the rest were made prisoner and sent for safe keeping to Coventry, a better stronghold than Birmingham. The captors refused even to speak to their prisoners, thereby coining a new catchphrase: *sending to Coventry*. Correspondence, plate and jewels seized from the baggage train had been despatched to Warwick Castle.

'They should never have done it,' grumbled Tew. He was a thin wraith who hovered on the edges of taprooms, drawing suspicion to himself by the very furtive way he lurked. 'They will rue the day they set upon the King – and I'll tell you –' He was wagging his finger insistently. He must have found plenty of people to stand him a tankard to celebrate the very ambush he was deriding. 'It will never be the hotheads who suffer for it, but innocents like us.'

'The King stayed with Holte,' Kinchin muttered, knowing the effect it would have if she mentioned the man who had made the Tews homeless.

'Then the King is a whoreson bastard and I hate him!' yelled her father. He banged his tankard down so hard a great wash of ale slopped out. Kinchin sat quiet. Almost vindictively, Emmett turned on her. 'You have an admirer, my girl. Someone came looking for you, Kinchin! . . . Don't you want to know who he is and what he's after?'

'No.' Kinchin's tone was drab. She knew it could only have been Mr Whitehall, the mad minister, wanting what he always wanted.

Chapter Twelve

Birmingham: October, 1642

The sword Lucas was making had been hurriedly hidden from the cavaliers. He returned inside the smithy. It was purposely kept dark so he could evaluate the fire and judge from the colour of heated metal when it had reached the correct temperature – changing through a range of pale colours that did not show in the darkened forge, through dull red, sunrise red, cherry red, bright red, light red, orange, and yellow. Swords were forged at cherry red, then tempered at a lighter colour.

There were many stages to making a sword; that was why, apart from the metal they needed, they were never cheap. Birmingham was turning out weapons upon which soldiers could rely; there would be thousands of these sent to Parliament's armies eventually. They were workaday models that never carried makers' marks, short tough blades that the soldiers often abused. There were famous cutlers, many of them foreigners, who had worked in London and who would soon move to Oxford to follow royal patronage. These high-flown Swedes and Germans made long rapiers with polished gold- and silver-decoration and bijou daggers for gentlemen. They always sneered at the plain Birmingham blades, yet the King's men today had known what they were trying to buy. The war would be won using these unsigned, affordable, mass-produced weapons.

Purse-lipped, Lucas began work again. First he dragged open a large shutter with which he had closed off his workplace when the unwelcome purchasers came. To work in the heat and dust, he needed good ventilation. Still pensive, he added extra expensive charcoal to the forge. The brick-built hearth had its bellows permanently attached, with an air pipe that ended in an iron 'duck's nest' at the heart of the fire. Country forges allowed the smoke to wander upwards and find its own way out, but towns were more sophisticated and Lucas had a brick hood and a chimney to draw off smoke and fine ash. His anvil stood as near as possible to the fire to reduce the distance he must move when carrying hot metal.

The smithy interior was cluttered, both with items he had made or was still making, and with his tools. He was a true blacksmith; he worked with ferrous metals, never lead or tin. Nor did he use gold or silver, the jewellers' material, nor bronze, although for his own amusement very occasionally he would make a household item of brass, to prove he could do it and to please his wife with the gift. Although he could shoe horses, he hardly ever did so; that was a farrier's job. Nor did he like to mend wagons' iron rims, but would send would-be customers on to a wheelwright. He had originally specialised in knives, though to earn extra money he mended pots, farm tools and firedogs. Now he made swords.

The tools of his trade were cumbersome: the forge with its fuel buckets, riddles and rakes; the single-horned anvil, set into a heavy oak stump at the right height for his knuckles, with its variously shaped elements for different tasks; the bicks, fullers and swages that were the anvil's moveable accessories; the quenching bath and the slack tub, where worked metal cooled. On racks that Lucas had made for the purpose hung his hammers, especially the crowned peen hammers that he used most often, with their slightly rounded edges that would not mark a blade as it was worked; he had also a great sledge hammer and other hammers with large, flat heads. Beside the anvil stood the vice. Close to hand were tongs in various sizes, then chisels, punches, files, a treadle-operated grinder that he had devised himself, drills and presses. All around the workplace were racks for holding work-in-progress. The fuel hut was outside, along with water butts.

To make a regular sword, first iron would be drawn out: pulled to the required length and flattened. A small tang would be formed on one end, where eventually a pommel and protective hilt would be fixed. The edge would be dressed on the anvil with glancing hammer blows, finished, then polished by hand. Some swords tapered towards the point, which affected their balance. Bringing the weight back close to the soldier's fist would make a weapon easier to manoeuvre, though at the same time it reduced the killing power available at the point. Most of the swords Lucas made had very little tapering. The civil war armies generally used swords of almost equidistant width, with neat points, longer for cavalrymen who needed to sweep down from horseback, shorter for the close hacking of infantry.

There was a great deal of work in the early stage, when the metal was worked in sections of six or eight inches at a time, being continually turned over and worked from both sides, and frequently reheated. Carbon was added to the iron, forming steel and strengthening the blade. The whole piece would be completely heated in the forge and allowed to rest through cooling, to remove stresses. Once shaped, it would be reheated again and this time cooled down extremely slowly, for many hours and perhaps a whole day. This made it soft enough for grinding the edge. Then came more heating to harden the blade again, which had to be done evenly at the cherry-red temperature, during which process it was swiftly quenched in cold brine, maybe several times until the smith was satisfied. This rapid cooling created hardness, then tempering added toughness to the steel and ensured the blade was not too brittle. To temper a sword, Lucas would clean any scale from its blade, then take a solid iron bar as long as the sword itself. The sword was placed upon the bar, back down for a regular single-edged blade; it would heat up to a blue colour before being allowed to cool naturally in the air. The result would be a tough and springy body, with a hard edge.

Lucas was a worrier. He was distressed by the incident with the King's men, and he admitted it to himself. With his mind still in turmoil, he took the current half-finished blade and prepared to continue where he had left off. He was hardening the blade. His concentration was elsewhere. That was how this sword became, if not 'a Friday job', at least a Wednesday one. In his agitation, Lucas rushed the work.

After he resumed, he decided it would never be a good one. He had already worked on it for days. He was reluctant to dispose of it and start again. He was a sensitive, honest craftsman, so he knew when to give up and abandon a bad piece; yet there were some faults he could mend. That knowledge too was part of the skill he had built up over the years. He felt in his heart that this sword was beyond saving.

The fault, if there was one, could not be seen by eye. In time Lucas grudgingly completed the weapon, added metal guard, hilt and pommel, and finally sharpened the edge. But he hated it. The sword assumed abnormal significance, coloured by the sour incident with the cavaliers. They had caused him to make a bad piece. So long as he possessed this sword he would remember their visit, but he could not be rid of it because his instinct kept telling him it was not right. If he sent it to the army, he would never know what happened, but he feared it was too brittle and would shatter. That could be the death of the man using it.

Irritated with himself, Lucas kept it back from sale. He hung it in the rafters, out of the way. It would remain at the smithy for another six months, a perpetual reproach to him. Only when Prince Rupert of the Rhine came to Birmingham to exact revenge for anti-Royalist activities, would this sword be brought out and begin its travels.

Chapter Thirteen

Wallingford: November, 1642

Juliana Carlill and Orlando Lovell were married at the end of November.

To arrive at a wedding had involved a flurry of negotiation. Persuading Juliana to accept him had been relatively easy for Lovell. He was always persuasive. Although she was sensible and thoughtful, as soon as he broached the proposal, Juliana felt the allure. He was a mature man who posed a challenge, a challenge that the much younger and nicer Treves would never have matched. Though Lovell's interest was un-expected, he did seem serious. He had studied Juliana closely enough to express willingness to be her life's partner on equal terms. If he was not exactly befriending her – for his manner remained cool, rather than that of a besotted lover – at least he appeared to be offering kindness. No realistic woman could ask for more.

Initially Juliana suspected that Mr Gadd, as her cautious guardian, would resist this match. However, Gadd's enquiries about the two cavaliers had unearthed a pedigree for Orlando Lovell – a landed, county pedigree that would have been excellent, but for his quarrelling with his father and running away from home at the age of sixteen. To Lovell's ill-concealed annoyance, Mr Gadd had discovered that he was the second son of a gentleman in Hampshire; his father believed he had emigrated to the Americas eight years before, with no communica-tion since.

The Lovells were solid Independents and supporters of Parliament. The elder brother was now a captain in the Earl of Essex's army. How such a family would view this other son, if it became known he had been a mercenary soldier in Europe, was something Mr Gadd could guess. Lovell's current service with Prince Rupert would offend them even more. Was there was any chance of a reconciliation between Lovell and his father? Marriage could be the occasion for patching things up.

Mr Gadd had explored whether Lovell's mother might intercede, but discovered she was long dead.

When challenged, Lovell frankly confessed the quarrel's cause: 'I attempted an elopement with the dangerously young daughter of a wealthy neighbour. The girl, who was the sole heir to extensive property, was intercepted by family servants when already in a carriage with her favourite gowns, her jewellery and a picnic which consisted only of fresh pears.' He must have realised that the detail of the pears would make Juliana laugh, her first step towards forgiveness. Only much later did she guess he had invented the fruit.

The young heiress was whisked away to distant relatives. Lovell was flatly told he would never see her again. His parents, old friends of the girl's family, were horrified by the escapade. Orlando refused to admit any error; he claimed that a second son needed to find himself a future by whatever means he could. Worse, he refused to apologise.

'So you believed you were in love?' suggested William Gadd. He had no doubt Orlando Lovell was still finding himself a future – hence his interest in Juliana.

'I believed it,' said Lovell, looking pious. 'I was quite devoted.' Mr Gadd did not argue, though he was sure such a youthful infatuation would never have lasted.

'You have a romantic past,' commented Juliana who, because it affected her so directly, had been allowed to share their conversation. She managed not to sound as though a romantic past impressed her, although naturally it did. She already thought Lovell no better than he should be, so this did him no harm. 'What became of the poor young lady?'

'I do not know.' Lovell appeared to sound regretful. 'I dare say she has a whining husband, half a dozen children and gout.' Then he continued disarmingly: 'Inevitably people thought that I was in love only with her money – too foolish to realise that if the elopement had succeeded, the money would have been taken away from her.'

Mr Gadd surveyed him thoughtfully. He believed Lovell had never been foolish. The elopement would probably have worked: Gadd was wondering whether the sixteen-year-old had seen that the sole heiress of truly loving parents was unlikely to be stripped of her entire fortune, no matter what adventurer carried her off.

The question now was whether Lovell had prospects. Given his turbulent family history, his chances looked slim. He came up with an answer.

With an air of deep sorrow, Lovell explained why suddenly he could contemplate marriage: 'Tragedy has struck my family. At the battle of Edgehill last month, a ghastly incident occurred. Wearied beyond sense, a musketeer in the Earl of Essex's army clapped his hand into a wagon of gunpowder, forgetting that he still held a length of lighted match in his fingers. There was an enormous explosion, killing him and many comrades. One casualty, I grieve to tell it, was my elder brother Ralph.'

'This is a sad blow,' answered Mr Gadd with suitable solemnity. His legal mind at once assessed it: 'Did he have children?'

'I believe not.'

'A blessing . . . How distressed you must be to lose him.'

'Ralph was the finest fellow,' said Lovell in a perfunctory way he had. 'So here's the situation, Gadd: as soon as my father's first grief has abated, I shall attempt to mend matters. I would go to him at once, but I should look like a poxy opportunist . . .' Lovell spoke without irony.

'Do not besmirch your honest motives with such a suggestion,' chided Mr Gadd. He had nothing against poxy opportunists, if they fitted his own plans. With Ralph Lovell dead, and childless, Orlando was the heir.

So, on the basis that he was a gentleman, whose father was a gentleman of substance, Mr Gadd found Orlando Lovell's claim for Juliana acceptable. Documents were drawn up with the haste that comes in wartime. Lovell then rejoined the King's army on its journey to London and what would be the stand-off at Turnham Green.

Just before he mounted up and rode off, he turned back and kissed his new betrothed. Until that moment they had exchanged barely a handshake. Juliana received the kiss calmly, though a thrill shot through her and the warmth of his mouth pressing firmly on hers lingered in her memory for days.

She was not in love with Orlando Lovell, though she considered that she could be. She was smiling as the cavalier swung into the saddle and gave her a gallant wave of his black, feathered hat; from then on she looked for news of the King's campaign with a new interest and a new anxiety. The prospect of Lovell's return gave her the excitement every bride deserves to feel.

After the fiasco at Turnham Green, the King reversed his march and returned to Oxford, which was now destined to be his home and his military headquarters. Lovell did not revisit Wallingford en route, but he wrote: he and Juliana would go into lodgings in Oxford. He was busy finding somewhere, and would soon bring a marriage licence. Juliana must accompany him to Oxford; she had no other place of safety. Mr Gadd was anxious to return to Somerset where he would resume his quiet retirement, or as quiet as it could be during a civil war. Juliana had no other friends or relatives to give her a home. She could not expect to seek safety among the Lovell family, whose present feelings towards Orlando were untested. If he invited them to his wedding, they must have refused. Besides, Juliana was a bride of spirit, who wished to be beside her husband.

Lovell seemed pleased to take her to Oxford with him and he made the arrangements quickly. As the new royal headquarters, the town was crammed with more people than it could happily contain. Numbers increased daily. Even small houses were overflowing, sometimes with five or six soldiers billeted on reluctant civilians who had barely house room for their own families. The best Lovell could find was one room, though it was in the house of a glover so there would be no industrial or market smells.

'Will he charge us much rent?' Juliana asked nervously.

'He can charge what he likes; he won't be paid. I am a soldier, quartered upon him by the rules of war, and he must accept it.'

Lovell's quick-witted bride at once foresaw that she would receive a cold welcome. She grew perturbed about food, heating and laundry. From her past life, though she kept the reasons from Lovell, she knew that a landlord who was being paid no rent would refuse to provide meals, coals or clean bedding; he might loathe tenants coming and going; he was likely to be abusive . . . Lovell pinched her cheek affectionately and declared all would be well. Fortunately for him, he was marrying a girl whose past history had taught her resilience; perhaps he suspected it when he chose her. Juliana remembered her grandmother complaining of landlords' faults in more than one lodging house, as the Carlills had shifted from place to place; she only wished she could remember how Grand-mère had dealt with it.

Even before the church service she began to see that to be struggling among the gentry was no different from struggling at lower levels of society. Still, she was becoming a gentlewoman, as her grandmother had yearned for her to be. Juliana had faith in her new husband's obvious ambition. She and Lovell together would make a determined couple; they should be able to climb as high as they wanted.

The service took place at St Leonard's Church, Wallingford, which had a Royalist rector, Richard Pauling – a man who had told his congregation that the leaders of Parliament were *'men of broken fortunes who have spent their means lewdly'*. In accordance with the Book of Common Prayer, his wedding sermon emphasised that marriage was for the avoidance of fornication, dwelling less on its benefits for the mutual society, help and comfort of the partners. Eliding into the usual instructions to procreate, he expressed an enthusiastic hope that any children would be brought up in habits of 'obedience', where it was understood he meant obedience to the King. Since he assumed both parties were stalwart Royalists, he did not dwell on it.

During his duller passages, Juliana imagined how much havoc she could wreak if she jumped up and claimed to be an Antinomian by religion and a Pymite by politics . . .

Although her opinions were quiet and conservative, she was intellectually curious. She knew that John Pym was the arch rebel, and she understood why. In the public mind, Antinomianism was viewed as a particularly scandalous cult, since its devotees believed that they were under no obligation to obey any instructions from religious authorities. This would seriously distress the Reverend Pauling. Mr Gadd had explained to Juliana, one peaceful evening after dinner, that Antinomianists rejected the notion that obedience to a code of religious law was necessary for salvation. Gadd cheerily discussed why this doctrine was seen as leading inevitably to licentiousness: it was assumed that any Antinomian must have chosen his theology solely to justify unrestrained debauchery . . .

These whimsical thoughts kept Juliana sane during the lengthy service. Lovell, she thought, had simply braced himself. He appeared to be in a kind of coma.

Since neither bride nor groom had a local home parish, the union was by special licence, obtained from the Bishop of Oxford. Their witnesses were William Gadd and the ever-forgiving Edmund Treves. Still in love with Juliana, Treves was composing in his head a lyrical poem called 'On Juliana's Wedding'; at least the lopsided verses petered out quickly. No scholar emerged from Oxford University without knowing that a lyrical poem should be brief.

For female support, Juliana had only Little Prue, who saw no reason to cease gurning at the bride as if she thought Juliana was a witch.

No witch would be attired in a gown of deep peacock-blue satin over a silver petticoat, with cuffs and collar of antique Paris lace. These materials had been stored up among sheaves of dry lavender in a chest of her grandmother's for twenty years. Juliana only timidly believed herself worthy of the satin, yet she feared that in a time of war it would be lost altogether if it was not put into use. The chest, now hers, was her only dowry and trousseau. It contained finely embroidered household linen, much of it her grandmother's handiwork, in sufficient quantity to convince Lovell that the Carlills once possessed wealth and must still have it. When Juliana opened the chest and showed its contents, she could tell he had hoped to see money instead.

Lovell had looked absolutely ready to bolt when he noticed the chest contained exquisite baby-clothes. He had forgotten that marriage meant children. Still, any fine goods would have commercial value. A tactful bridegroom, he refrained from saying so.

They spent their wedding night at Wallingford, where the judge's house provided comfort, space and privacy. A supper was arranged, at which the officiating parson presented himself. After Juliana withdrew to the bridal chamber, Mr Gadd, Parson Pauling and Edmund Treves encouraged Lovell with the traditional bridegroom's toasts to put him in good heart for his duties, overdoing it by a good deal, as was also traditional.

Upstairs, Juliana was attended by Little Prue. The sombre maid helped her undress and brought her the finely embroidered nightdress that was her grandmother's last good piece of work. Nobody had supplied any lessons on what now awaited her; Juliana was reliant upon what she could remember of her grandmother's blunt descriptions of sexual exchanges. It was her good fortune that Roxanne had spoken out openly. No traumatic surprises would horrify Juliana. In fact, so detailed were her grandmother's stories that when she had lain waiting for some time in the exquisite bridal nightdress, and the bed had warmed, Juliana slipped from between the sheets, took off the nightdress, which she folded neatly on a country chair, and climbed back in bed to await her husband naked. This was not to seduce Lovell. She saw no point in having a beautiful garment damaged by passion.

Her wait was lengthy. Many brides fell asleep at this point. Instead,

Juliana lay quietly, in the judge's best bedroom with its dark panelled walls and a small fire flickering in the fireplace. She could still hear the faint voices of her wedding guests enjoying themselves in the parlour downstairs. A window seat looked over the garden; she could have knelt there and seen Edmund Treves revelling in his misery as her disappointed suitor, until he grew too cold in the November night air and went indoors, red-nosed, to get stupidly drunk. Even with the judge absent, it had been possible to find and hang the bed's robustly decorated woollen curtains. A narrow turkey rug lay beside the four-poster on the worn old floorboards. The room had been supplied with basic necessities: candlestick, chamberpot, warming pan and coals. There was a prayer book, though Juliana did not imagine her new husband would like to discover her at prayer.

For once, she was enjoying her sense of security in this spacious English room with its desirable, comfortable fittings. Already, she had forebodings about the future. Marriage might not be a haven. She knew, from what Lovell had told her about their rented room in the glover's house, that the first weeks would probably contain all the usual difficulties. At least now there would be two of them. She would not have to face the future alone.

Eventually voices came nearer, as the guests escorted the groom upstairs, all their feet stumbling tipsily on the staircase. Lovell was pushed into the room, but managed to slam shut the bedroom door behind him before anyone else entered. He waited, leaning against the door, until the others were heard retreating.

The fire had dimmed, but by its last faint light Juliana watched Lovell undress. Each masculine garment fell to the floor with a strangely heavy thud. When he turned towards the bed her heart was pounding. When he came to the bedside, she was pleasingly surprised that he paused, tilted his head a little to one side and looked down at her fondly. She was his. He had chosen her (she had chosen him).

'Here we are,' he said. 'Lovell and Lovell's wife . . .' Juliana gazed up at him with a dry throat. He smiled; he had a good smile, and he knew it. 'They have made me too tipsy to acquit myself resoundingly, but I shall do my best for you.'

His best on that occasion was brief. The experience left Juliana neither hurt nor shocked. Nor was she much moved, but she felt grateful for his attentions and for his polite thanks afterwards. When it was over, for one extravagantly emotional moment, she wanted to admit the truth: that her inherited 'fair orchards' in Kent on which he was laying such great store were nothing more than a modest house with, she had been told, a few undistinguished old apple trees. The house did not even yet belong to her.

Lovell had fallen asleep. By the next time they were speaking, her moment of would-be confession had passed.

When Juliana awoke in the morning, she heard Lovell relieving himself heartily by the pot-cupboard. Ruefully she recalled one of her grandmother's sarcastic comments on marriage: 'It is all pretending not to hear when they fart, and listening to them pissing in the pot!' She felt stiff, exhilarated that she was a wife, and badly in need of similar relief. As soon as Lovell returned to his side of the bed and fell back in, groaning, she slipped out on the opposite side and availed herself. Hot steam rising from the chamberpot after her husband's contribution gave her a start, but she brazened it out. They were together now. Every intimacy could be, would be, must be shared.

She had intended to rise and dress, but the air was so chilly, she scampered back to the warmth of the bed. As she shot under the coverlet, she landed with Lovell's arm around her. He had turned to her, shadowed eyes thoughtful.

'Well, madam!'

'Well, sir.'

Sweet nothings. Nothing indeed. *'Must I still call him Captain Lovell or may I say Orlando?'* They had exchanged vows and spent a night of love together, yet remained strangers.

Perhaps Lovell noticed the gust of loneliness that swept over his bride. Certainly he was gazing down at her from a close enough position to witness every flicker that passed across her normally candid grey eyes. 'We shall be comfortable soon enough,' he told Juliana in a low voice. *I must discover her pet name . . . no; find a name for her myself.* His free hand was caressing her throat, as if unaware he was doing it.

Sober now, he knew just what he was doing. Juliana would never ask him, but she thought it probable that the young girl he tried to elope with had been returned to her parents more experienced than she should have been. It was best not to speculate how many other women Lovell had bedded since, nor what quality they were. *'It will be better for you if he has done it!'* she heard her grandmother cackle. But it left Juliana feeling her inequality.

'I have been wondering' – she forced herself to converse – 'whether those who have been sweethearts from childhood find their wedding night easier . . .' It was ridiculous to be so shy with a man who had entered so closely into places she had never really believed others were intended to go.

Juliana closed her eyes. She was enjoying the pleasure Lovell's hands insidiously brought her. In small circling movements the light fingers of his right hand had come to her left breast, where the nipple reacted eagerly. Lovell bent his head to it. Juliana murmured with pleasure. Her back arched –

'Juliana, you are a man-lover!' She blushed hotly, horrified by the thought, ashamed that she had revealed too much of herself, frightening herself that her nature was improper. This was an impossible predicament; a respectable wife must not be prim, yet she could not be too forward either –

'I am as I always was –'

'Not *quite* the same, I hope!' Laughing, Lovell cut off her protest, his hand now sliding down her belly as the proprietor who had taken her maidenhead.

It could so easily all have gone wrong at that moment. Juliana was upset and wanted to flee from him. But Lovell only laughed with conspiratorial mockery then – fired by the exchange – he turned more urgently to the activities of a husband, which he this time fulfilled commendably. His bride was left shaken, exhilarated, and as they lay together spent, she heard once again her raucous grandmother: *'Let the man do sufficient that he can boast of it to himself . . .'*

Being Lovell, he would boast openly to everyone – if he chose to do it. Being Lovell, however, he might gain greater pleasure from keeping secrets. Juliana was already enough of his wife to know that.

Chapter Fourteen

Oxford: 1642–43

Juliana Lovell, still uneasy with her new name, arrived in the first month that Oxford was the King's permanent headquarters.

December was not the best time here. Low mist clung to the many country waterways. The hedgerows were dark, the sere trees gloomy of aspect. Houses on the city perimeter had been blown up for strategic reasons, leaving ugly gaps. Tentative efforts were being made to construct fortifications to replace the now-useless medieval city walls, but the hard frosted ground was resisting the tools wielded by thoroughly disgruntled citizens. This was a garrison, crammed to bursting point with soldiery and the great equipment of war. The once-pleasant, meadow-fringed River Cherwell, which formed the upper reaches of the Thames, was already oozing with pestilence as the raw sewage from impossible numbers of people mingled with dead horses and dogs that blocked the current, bobbing amidst oily bubbles under the willows that trailed their slender fingers into waters befouled by butchers' bloody rejects and fermenting horticultural garbage. Smoke from house-fires and minor industries curdled the atmosphere. A miasma of unease seeped through the cobbled streets, from the chilly castle to the Cornmarket where the lead roof had been stripped to make bullets.

Unwelcome to the townspeople, the King had ensconced himself in Christ Church College. Prince Rupert was at Magdalen. The Warden's Lodge at Merton had been earmarked for the absent Queen, should she ever arrive. The colleges sycophantically professed themselves honoured by their noble guests – except when unwanted new masters were dumped on them at royal command. In more humble areas there was frank resistance to billeting, as the domestic routine of the little people's little houses was brutally disrupted. Fear riffled through the winding backstreets. Bullying took over in the taverns. Needless to say, as stationers and booksellers braced themselves for bankruptcy, all the brewers were flourishing.

Her family had wandered about in search of trade, yet Juliana had never been in a university town before. Oxford colleges would have known quiet hours before this unending military crush but the peace of the cloisters had been lost. While the carriage Lovell had borrowed to fetch her from Wallingford forced its way through the cobbled streets, she flinched at the turmoil. Juliana saw that Lovell was excited by the bustle beyond the carriage's cloudy windows. Assuring her she would get used to the commotion, he rattled off a commentary: 'The perimeter defences are being thrown up by the townspeople; everyone between sixteen and sixty has to work one day a week. About one in a hundred actually turn up, of course. I shall not allow you to do it.' Juliana wondered how he would accomplish this autocratic refusal; already she guessed he would give his instructions to her, and leave her to address the authorities. 'Possibly the breastworks will never be complete, but if they are, this town will be the best defended in England so don't fret. There's a Dutchman, de Gomme, supervising the works. Supposed to be brilliant. Let us hope someone has told the herring-eating bastard we're not building dykes but battlements!'

They were now passing Christ Church, almost at their destination. 'Edmund was a scholar at this grand college?'

'Treves? No, St John's. Poxy place, never showed *me* much welcome, but if you say you are a cavalier's wife they may let you walk around the garden. Some colleges are quite taken over by the army, so watch yourself.'

Juliana felt perturbed. 'Soldiers are dangerous even to their own supporters?'

'Never take risks with soldiers,' replied Lovell in clipped tones. Was her husband a threat to women? Juliana dreaded to ask. 'Christ Church is where the King has found a perch, though its great quadrangle is being used to pasture oxen and sheep.'

'Why?'

Lovell stared at her, and she saw her mistake, one merely caused by inexperience, though he must think her stupid. 'Food, girl!' As Juliana shuddered at what it would mean to be trapped in a city under siege, Lovell continued his review undaunted: 'Gloucester Hall is being used for sword manufacture, there's another grinding-mill out at Wolvercote, gunpowder at Osney. New College holds the armoury and magazine. Magdalen Bridge has been converted into a drawbridge – you saw that –' Its significance had been lost on her. 'If the enemy come – *when* they come, I dare say – we can rattle it up cheerily. Magdalen Tower is a lookout and there are great guns in the grove. Their range is a mile and a half. All the schools are being turned over to warehouses for staples – cloth, cheese, coal and corn. It's out with dreamy scholars and in with tailors stitching uniforms . . .'

Listening, Juliana wondered if all the King's soldiers were this much aware of logistics; she suspected there would be many who merely took orders. Lovell was a complete professional; she was beginning to see how deeply he cared to be efficient and informed. He had made this his world. All over the country men like him who had served on the Continent would be bringing such expertise to bear, on both sides; it boded a long conflict. Orlando Lovell and others like him, who had had no future without a war to fight, were now digging in almost with enjoyment. He was eager to use his talent for organisation – and, presumably, his talents also for death and destruction.

I should have asked, thought Juliana, what his plans are when the civil war is ended. Will he return to fighting on the Continent? Shall I have to go with him, or be left here alone? She convinced herself that his marriage meant Lovell wished to settle to domestic life in England. He had, after all, spoken of mending matters with his family.

There were more pressing anxieties: 'Will you be paid by the King, sir?'

'When there is cash for the purpose. The order has gone out for metal to be brought in. We've taken down church bells for it, and the dear citizens are supposed to hand over their brass kitchenware –' How fortunate that we ourselves have none, Juliana thought. 'The Mint is coming down from Shrewsbury to produce coins, which will be made out of melted college plate – when the colleges can be pricked into collaborating.'

'"Pricked"? You mean, compelled to surrender their valuables?'

'The sneaky masters and fellows try to dodge, but His Majesty has quickly learned to be a beggar. He hardens his heart. St John's offered eight hundred pounds instead of its treasure. Charles thanked them heartily for the money – then took their precious plate as well. The county and the university must pay up over a thousand pounds a week for the upkeep of our cavalry – mind, most of the cash will be for bullets and hay for the horses.'

'So you *will* be paid, then.' Juliana was still doggedly worrying about rent, food and fuel.

The carriage had stopped, in a winding backstreet, but Lovell, caught up in his discourse, made no move. He gave his wife a wry look. 'One way or another, we'll be paid; depend on it!'

'How, "one way or another"? You cannot mean plunder?'

'A fact of war,' Lovell informed her.

Fortunately he then noticed they had arrived at their lodgings.

'All the allure of a rat-catcher's coat pocket,' Lovell admitted, as his young bride gazed around this depressing room that was to be their first married home. He helped the coachman deposit her great coffer alongside what must be his own campaign chest.

Juliana had seen worse – and she had seen her grandmother briskly refuse it. They had an upstairs chamber barely ten feet square, with a sagging mattress on a lop-sided bed behind stained and moth-eaten green curtains, a couple of spine-breaking bolt-upright chairs – not matching – and a pot-cupboard which, through one door with a broken hinge, was sending messages that the chamberpot had needed emptying for a fortnight. The stairs came up from the ground floor directly into their room, opposite the empty fireplace, then a narrower flight turned on up into the garret, whose occupants must trip to and fro via the Lovells' accommodation. Directly opposite the stairs she spotted a large mousehole in the wainscot.

She drew a deep, despondent breath and nearly choked on the malodorous air she had swallowed. 'Ah! Dearest, I was hoping for a sunlit closet where I could dry rose-petals and cook up lavender pastilles in a little brass pannikin!'

'Bear up, wife. I thought I had chosen someone more stalwart.' Lovell fielded her brave jest with the robust manner of a cavalier, though he sounded apologetic.

'Oh you will find me apt for the purpose,' Juliana assured him, though bitterness escaped in her voice. Lovell could not read just how grim her disappointment was, but he sensed hard times in the past. For him that was good. He was relying on the girl's resilience. A dainty maid, inexperienced, would be an encumbrance to him; even so, he felt sorry for Juliana's sad air of defeat.

Alerted by some stillness, Juliana looked at her husband. He held her under the chin. 'I hope you are not feeling betrayed. This is war; this is how it must be. At least,' he said, as if it did matter to him, 'we shall have our companionship.'

So Juliana smiled.

She could dispose of the chamberpot's half-gallon of stinking walnut-tinted urine. While she was pouring strangers' leavings into a gutter in the street, she encountered their landlord, a thin, sneering glove-maker with a bald head showing white through strands of greasy hair. Juliana greeted him politely but firmly; she was unconsciously mimicking her grandmother, who had been quick to despise others but knew when to conceal it. She begged him to provide a small table. He assured her she and Lovell were to 'table' with him, meaning he would provide a meal for them once a day; relieved to know they would have hot food, however indifferently cooked, Juliana insisted on having their own table even so, to do needlework.

She was making progress. She scrubbed, beat the mattress, tidied, made the window-catch work, sorted the rings that held up the bed-canopy. Lovell watched and approved. However, the mice always knew they had the mastery of her. They came out and warmed themselves whenever a small fire was in the grate.

'If we employ a servant he or she will have to sleep here, in our room.'

'So let us not have a servant yet!' Lovell chortled. 'I want no drip-nosed bootboy nor podgy maid listening from behind the bed-curtains when I come at your commodity.'

He was more fastidious than many. All over the country, servants in shared bedrooms overheard their employers' lovemaking. Juliana was glad Lovell wanted privacy. Besides, they could not afford servants. Nor would their financial situation improve, she now knew. Almost offhandedly, Lovell informed her, 'By the by. There was a mistake about the business with my brother. The wagon of powder that exploded at Edgehill was not on the Parliamentarian side. Ralph lives yet.'

'You must be rejoicing,' replied Juliana. His careless manner gave her the first hint that Lovell had always known the true facts. Shocked, she kept her anger hidden. Lovell shrugged and turned away quickly, unwilling to be quizzed. She wondered what Mr Gadd would say to this – then found herself hoping that he never heard of it. She had chosen her life. She would have to cope.

So now she was a wife. She had become loyal to her husband, protecting his reputation whatever he did, even when she suspected him of deliberate deceit.

They settled into a routine. Lovell was frequently out by day, but he returned for dinner every night. He had a streak of frugality; he rarely wasted funds on carousing. By day Juliana was lonely, but she could be content with her own company. When she did complain of her solitude, Lovell took her to view the King inspecting artillery in Magdalen Grove. The next time, they went to see the King playing tennis with Prince Rupert. Once, they watched the young Prince of Wales practise riding tricks.

That was about the limit of spectacles on offer, unless Juliana wished to be an observer when Parliament's negotiators argued for peace politely and pointlessly with the King and his circle in Christ Church quadrangle. 'Far too exciting, Orlando. I must be excused lest I disgrace myself with some hysterical outcry.' She was assured that prospects for enter- tainment would improve when the Queen arrived from Holland. Henrietta Maria had, after all, known her grandmother.

'It is unlikely Her Majesty will remember Grand-mère.' Juliana gave Lovell a straight look. She could gloss over invented history as blandly as he did. Soon she did it every quarter, as her husband asked when the rents from her apple orchards might arrive and she played dumb.

When they were discussing the peace commission she had called her husband by his first name. Orlando accepted this without comment. By now he called Juliana 'my sweet', which was conventional but he made it sound genuine. They were conducting their marriage with respect and affection.

Christmas was drear, though they did manage to obtain a presence at Christ Church where the King entertained in great splendour on Christmas Day. This dinner was hot, smoky and crowded, the musicians inaudible over the noise of the people, the service slow and the food cold by the time it reached them at the far end of the table.

By early February the Queen was known to have left Holland, with supplies and several thousand professional soldiers. She landed at

Bridlington, which the Earl of Newcastle, a great Royalist commander in the north, made as safe as possible for her reception. Not safe enough. Parliamentarian ships bombarded the house where she first lodged. Her Majesty accepted all with great spirit; when she was forced to take shelter outside in a ditch, Henrietta went back into the house for a lapdog that her fleeing maids-of-honour had left behind. This was widely seen as bravery. 'Damned stupid!' snarled Orlando Lovell. Juliana concurred.

The northern Parliamentarian army, commanded by Sir Thomas Fairfax, lay between the Queen and Oxford. The King was anxious to have Henrietta Maria with him, but conscious that if she were to fall into rebel hands she would become a fatal pawn. He was too devoted to risk it. For several weeks the Queen stayed with the Earl of Newcastle, revelling in her own courage and initiative, and dabbling merrily. Eventually a plan was hatched for Prince Rupert to advance from Oxford through the Midlands so he could clear a safe passage for his indomitable aunt. On the 29th of March, with Orlando Lovell among his retinue, the prince set out, planning to relieve the siege of Lichfield, and to secure a route for the Queen through Warwickshire. This would entail removing the threat posed by the rebel town of Birmingham. Not only were its fractious cutlers supplying arms to Parliament, they had set about strangers and imprisoned them on suspicion of being Royalists. King's messengers had been captured as spies too. Birmingham would have to be crushed. Lovell gave the impression the Oxford Royalists were looking forward to it.

This was a new spring offensive and obviously more important than anything Juliana had seen before. Lovell emptied his battered chest of a back-and-breastplate which he spent hours buffing. Their room stank with the reek of neat's-foot oil as he softened straps, belt and riding boots. A man she had never seen before, who seemed to be one of his soldiers, brought pistol bullets, dumping the heavy bag on her little work table with a dead thud that terrified her. Juliana sat nursing Lovell's rapier, a European blade with a cup hilt and a pommel encrusted with very worn silver. He was not its first owner, though he never told its history. Tired of the sick-looking thin feather in his beaver, Juliana had made him a new hatband from a piece of the peacock satin that had been left over when she cut out the bodice of her wedding-dress. Although he seemed to have no awareness that she had made the dress herself, Lovell appeared oddly touched by her ministrations to his hat.

'My will is in the chest. Your man Gadd insisted – you inherit everything, sweetest – though since I am worth nothing, spending the cash won't trouble you long. If I die, the first thing you'll need to do is sell my wedding suit. Then I'd advise you to remarry – take Treves; he's still writing poetry to the celestial bow of your eyebrow.' Lovell paused in the boisterous tirade. 'You'll think of me kindly, I hope.'

Men need to be loved. Juliana no longer had to rely on her grandmother for this motto; she could be cynical herself. 'Always, Orlando. May my devoted thoughts comfort you.'

He was a true cavalier. Every cavalier needed a woman to adore. Well, a woman to adore him.

Orlando strained Juliana to him, kissing her hard and making the embrace lascivious. She found herself memorising the faint scent of his tobacco, the rasp of his moustache against her cheek, the softness of his lips. Unexpectedly, tears tumbled down her cheeks. They gazed into each other's eyes, his chestnut brown, hers grey. They were bound to one another now; if it was not by love, it would pass as a near thing.

Juliana watched Prince Rupert's men ride out from Oxford by the North Gate. Try as she might, she failed to spot her husband in their midst. She knew that Edmund Treves was beside him, all jealousy forgotten. The young Prince Rupert rode at the head of the column, flourishing his commander's baton, handsome, confident and exquisitely dressed, with his favourite white poodle, Boy, looking around proudly from the saddle. A group of aristocratic officers accompanied the prince, all on excellent horses. Juliana guessed she had missed her husband because he must be closer to the prince in the cavalcade than she expected; he had bluffed his way forward. His boldness would not come amiss; Orlando Lovell would live up to any position, however deviously he acquired it.

The cavalry swept by in a continuous rattle of hoofbeats, with helmets and feathered hats bobbing, and colours flying impressively. Juliana could see there was a pattern to the pennants and tasselled flags that marked each officer and company, though she could not decipher it. Easier to distinguish were the foot regiments in their distinctive coloured coats of white, green, red, purple and blue, marching in blocks. Several cannon were dragged in the train, pulled by strings of heavy horses. Drums were beaten to time the march of the baggy-britches footmen, with their long muskets and even longer pikes. Many wore red sashes, the colours of the King.

Juliana was not fooled by the glamorous panoply. These glorious-looking companies streaming out of Oxford were ruthless raiders. They would seize anything they could from the country they passed through, to provide for themselves and to prevent the enemy's use of it, and she knew their intent was murderous. Though they fought for King Charles, many were foreigners, straightforward mercenaries. Even among the Englishmen were scarred veterans of the terrible wars on the Continent, whose cruel manners and methods Lovell had described to her. The lower ranks of armies on both sides of the conflict had been called loiterers and lewd livers, plucked from prisons, almshouses and inns, enticed into uniform with the crude lure of occasional pay and plentiful loot. Still, the cavalcade looked brave, bonny and businesslike; it took so long to pass that she grew chilled in the fresh March air.

When she returned to their lodging, she wept inconsolably. She had never been so totally alone. She had no idea how long she would have to wait in Oxford before the troops returned, what dangers Orlando would have to face while they were away, or what would happen to her if he never came back. By now, certain signs began to suggest to her that she was carrying a child. It was too early to have mentioned this to her husband, and she had been so wary of his reaction she would not attempt it in the bustle of his departure. He had left her three shillings. Otherwise, she was friendless and penniless.

So Juliana sat alone, watching motes drift by the window and listening to the stillness of their room. She wanted her husband to survive. Yet she understood clearly that even if he did, their life together would never be as she had hoped. For her, today might just be the beginning of many long periods of abandonment. If Lovell was wounded, captured or killed, her fate would be even worse.

Chapter Fifteen

Birmingham: Monday, 3 April 1643

They knew he was coming. Worse, they knew he was coming for *them*.
Somehow, word had passed along from the war council where the prince
laid his plan to ride to Lichfield. 'On the way, we'll take out Birmingham.'

Even before they heard the drums, some of those awaiting his army
must have known just how hopeless their situation was.

By now, Prince Rupert's habits of raiding for cattle, munitions and
money were notorious; they would earn him the nickname Prince Robber,
Duke of Plunderland. His attitude had been obvious since he first took
up his command as a general of horse. While raising troops in the
North Midlands he had written to the Mayor of Leicester, demanding
a large sum of money, or threatening roundly to devastate the town in
the brutal German manner. The King had reprimanded his nephew for
extortion — yet kept the money. As Orlando Lovell said, His Majesty
had learned to be a beggar. 'And precious Rupert gives not a fig for
rebuke. His uncle has neither taken away his hobby-horse, nor stopped
him going out to play.'

Few in the country districts of Warwickshire knew the full horrors
that were being acted out abroad. But despite decades of censorship,
news stories had reached England of European towns that were sacked
by first one army and then another amidst terrible violence; peasants
in forest and marketplace casually murdered by marauding mercenaries;
anguished victims tortured to make them reveal their valuables, then
killed in cold blood. Lurid details were regularly passed around: fat men
boiled down for candles, respectable burghers spit-roasted, priests
hanged in rows, widows grilled naked on griddles, babies ripped from
the bellies of their pregnant mothers, young girls raped while their
parents were forced to watch. Pamphlets with grisly pictures caused

revulsion – yet people were fascinated and the pamphlets were widely believed. Journalism was then very new.

This brutal theatre of war in which Prince Rupert had been schooled was recently condemned by Lord Brooke of Warwick:

In Germany they fought only for spoil, rapine and destruction. We must employ men who will fight merely for the cause's sake ... I had rather have a thousand or two thousand honest citizens that can only handle their arms, whose hearts go with their hands, than two thousand of mercenary soldiers that boast of their foreign experience.

An associate of Lord Saye and Sele, Brooke was one of Parliament's fervent supporters, an opponent of peace moves, an energetic raiser of regiments and finance. Commander of the Midlands Association, where he was highly popular, Lord Brooke was now charged with establishing a secure Parliamentarian base in the Midlands counties. In February he drove Royalists out of Stratford-upon-Avon, then set about besieging the cathedral town of Lichfield. Prince Rupert's main task that spring was to raise the siege. So the rigours of 'foreign experience' were about to be visited upon Lord Brooke's home territory.

The prince left Oxford and advanced through Chipping Norton, Shipston on Stour, Stratford-upon-Avon and Henley-in-Arden. It was Easter. The cavaliers stayed around Henley for four days, celebrating Holy Week by pillaging the countryside. Word of their presence, and their energetic plundering, quickly ran north.

Ten miles away, the inhabitants of Birmingham tried to believe the Royalists would pass them by. Henley was so near, they could almost hear the protests of outraged farmers being robbed of horses, poultry and beef. By Saturday, most people accepted that Prince Rupert would attack their town. They had time to send messages, begging for reinforcements, to the three main Parliamentary garrisons at Warwick, Kenilworth and Coventry. Only their desperate pleas to Coventry produced results, but Coventry was also threatened by Rupert's presence and could only spare one troop of light horse, dragoons under Captain Castledowne. In the end, the Coventry men withdrew from what was obviously a losing situation, three days before the prince arrived.

In Birmingham, a worried discussion took place. First Francis

Roberts, the puritan minister, pleaded with the militia captains and the chief men of the town to take the sensible course: with the odds so great against them, he said, they should march away, saving their arms and themselves even if it meant leaving behind their goods. That might avert Prince Rupert's wrath. It was like throwing raw meat to distract a vicious dog. The captains and chief men were eager, and Royalist sympathisers, of whom there were some among the wealthier townsmen, also spoke for appeasement. However, the crusty middle and lower classes, which included men who could afford their own arms, refused to abandon their town. This forced the captains and civil leaders to stay with them, rather than departing among curses and accusations of cowardice.

Preparations began. They created crude barricades to block streets. Arms were handed out to all who were capable and willing to bear them. At Deritend, they dug a trench to block the road from Henley and Stratford. On Easter Monday, scouts raced into town and reported that Prince Rupert was coming. By now it was known that he was bringing two thousand men, and cannon. Undeterred, into Birmingham's defensive trench climbed all the soldiers they had: a hundred musketeers.

It was a morning's march from Henley. The Royalist soldiers had been slow to move, many with hangovers, all encumbered with personal booty, besides the stolen cattle which they now drove up the muddy roads along with them as their general food supply. Hung about with dead ducks, household pots and cheeses, the foot soldiers cursed as they bestirred themselves at the drumbeat, dragging their pikes at a lacklustre angle, shouldering their muskets with a bad grace, and stumbling with curses down ill-maintained country roads through slurry churned up by the cavalry that had already gone ahead.

Henley-in-Arden was a hamlet. Few had found quarters under cover, so most had spent the last four nights sleeping out of doors on the hard ground. At the end of March the fields and coppices were cold, still bleak after winter, with thawing drips from trees and hedges making everywhere damp. Those who had bread or biscuit soon found it mouldy. Their campfires smoked and spluttered. The soldiers all stank of the smoke, along with a perpetual odour of unwashed clothes on unwashed bodies. Men rose in the mornings stiffly, their coats and britches clammy, their powder and match at risk.

Orlando Lovell and Edmund Treves had spent three days in an outhouse, which they shared with their horses. It showed. Mud and straw besmirched their once-gallant cloaks and boots. Their beards were ragged. Their tempers were short. As they made the journey to Birmingham, their mounts were fretful, only willing to move forwards because they were part of a group. When they reached the town's outskirts, the beasts stamped and steamed and dragged at the bit rebelliously. Treves soothed his horse, Faddle, a bounding brown mare bought with money his mother had sent him after accepting that her son could not be deterred from fighting. Lovell had stopped bothering to quieten his mount, an anonymous bay of very much superior quality, which he had borrowed – without mentioning it – from a higher officer in Oxford who was indisposed.

Quartermasters had been sent ahead, as was conventional. They were held up at the barricade. Arriving at the head of his small army, Prince Rupert quickly set up a military headquarters in the Ship Inn. He issued a message to the townspeople that if they provided shelter and received his men quietly, he would do them no injury. This was also conventional; he cannot have expected anyone would believe the offer. As Lovell and Treves rode up, the defenders raised their colours in the Deritend trench, then at once sallied forth and fired briskly.

Surprised, the Royalists pulled back.

'Madness!' scoffed Lovell, quietly counting them. He got to sixty, assessed the length of the trench, doubled his figure and was distressed by the pathetic opposition. From what he could see, the Birmingham musketeers confirmed the Royalist view that the rebels fighting against them were *'men without shirts'*: ships' deserters, runaway prisoners, beggars and broken-down serving men. 'They have no idea of their danger!'

'They have courage, Orlando.' Treves saw good where he could.

'The traitors will die for their bravado then.'

The location was bad, however. The prince – young, handsome, and in full body armour with his trademark pistol and poleaxe – took cover under the overhang of a building and consulted with advisers while his large white poodle, Boy, austerely sniffed the air. A signboard creaked with mournful insistence. High grey clouds moved slowly, shadowing the dreary scene. Rain was in the air, but would not fall.

The Royalists had approached on a badly maintained country road that crossed half-flooded, inhospitable water meadows and narrowed awkwardly between old half-timbered houses just before the bridge across the River Rea. They were overlooked by fourteenth-century inns, with steep roofs and crooked gables above the street. Although it seemed a meagre defence, the rebels' trench blocked a bottleneck and would serve its turn temporarily. Beyond it, on a shallow rise, a manor-house and church stood before a ribbon of almost medieval houses; it was a rural backwater, unprotected by walls or other fortifications. Word had it that there might be a few more musketeers hidden up; plus maybe a small troop of dragoons; maybe another troop of horse. No reinforcements from the Parliamentary garrisons were reported in the area.

Prince Rupert brought up his artillery, two sakers, which were heavy long-range field guns, and four lighter, more manoeuvrable drakes. He prepared to fire, using his own musketeers, though the defenders did not waver. An annoying barrage began, which the rebels managed somehow to sustain for over an hour. They yelled the usual shouts of 'Cursed dogs! Devilish cavaliers! Popish traitors!' The Royalists replied with desultory oaths of their own. Not taking the defenders seriously, they charged – and to their astonishment, were beaten back again by musketfire.

A second hour passed, before the Parliamentarians were inevitably forced out – only to take up another position in a second trench behind the first, at Digbeth. An untrained collection of smiths, nailmakers, labourers and cutlers was holding up a small army of professional soldiers. The rebels' boldness only increased the Royalists' bitterness against this town. Cannon could achieve little in such a tight situation. Eventually the prince ordered a thatched house to be fired, which spread to a couple more buildings, opening up an access route. This sent the right message.

Impatient to advance, a group of cavalry under the Earl of Denbigh set off across the water meadows to find other roads in. Lovell and Treves went along. They splashed through the shallows, managed to ford the river, and rode into the town through the back ways. Lord Denbigh led them, singing loudly as he went. Soon they were breaking through hedges, leaping garden walls, and bursting among the houses on the south side. Now Edmund Treves learned to be a cavalier, as the horsemen announced their presence by shooting at doors and windows whenever anyone showed a face. Enemy fire came sporadically from upper-storey windows. Barging along amongst his colleagues in the single winding main street, Edmund felt his heart pound. His right arm was up, bearing his sword, and he fired off his remaining pistol with his left hand, aiming badly as he held the reins, unaware whom he shot at, unable to determine friend or foe among the citizens who stared out in curiosity. Exhilarated, the cavaliers stormed at full tilt through the markets. Then at the north end where habitation petered out, quite suddenly they came upon a troop of rebel horse. These were local riders, raised and armed by a Mr Perkes of Birmingham and led by Captain Richard Greaves, who had already fought Prince Rupert once at King's Norton the previous year.

Greaves and his men took off at once down the road to Dudley, with the cavaliers flying at their heels. To have more room to ride, the cavaliers fanned out on either side of the highway. The chase had all the excitement and danger of a cross-country hunt − jumping into the unknown as they tackled hedges, palings and gates. Treves saw one rider fall, with such force he must have broken his neck. Though an anxious horseman himself, he took his own lead from Lovell, who saw foes and dashed straight at them. They galloped along furiously until they reached a place between two woods. There, at Shireland Road, Captain Greaves gave a signal and wheeled his men about. They fired, then charged the pursuing Royalists. In those first moments of surprise, the Earl of Denbigh was shot, knocked from his horse and left for dead. Instantly demoralised, his men scattered back across the fields. They were hotly chased by Greaves and his cheering troops; Greaves himself was streaming blood from several minor face wounds. The rout continued until the cavaliers had almost reached the prince and their own colours in Deritend. Unable to tackle Prince Rupert's whole force, Captain Greaves and his men retired.

Someone went to break the news to Rupert that Lord Denbigh, a close friend of his, had fallen. Lord Digby was thought to be missing too, along with another man of quality, reported as Sir William Ayres. While the riders shook themselves down and made light of the incident, they learned that progress had been made here. Under cover of the fracas and the smoke from the fired houses, the hundred Birmingham foot had abandoned the trench and made their escape. The prince ordered that the house-fires be quenched.

'They'll not be back.' Indicating Greaves's retreating horsemen, Lovell seemed unimpressed by the sharp little cavalry encounter, but he had advice for Treves. 'Edmund, if you are of a mind to prosper, take some of our men, ride back to where Denbigh fell and recover the corpse. He is much loved by Rupert. Do yourself some good by it.'

'And you, Orlando?'

Lovell cracked a grin that the rebels would rightly have called devilish. 'Business in town!'

'The Prince banned plunder,' warned Treves.

'Of course!' scoffed Lovell. 'He knows the rules of engagement. And *we* know how Rupert interprets them!'

Already sickened by the four days of looting at Henley-in-Arden, Treves wanted no part of whatever was to come here. He took the advice to search for Denbigh's corpse.

Beside the little River Rea, the situation changed. Opposition had finally ended; the rebel musketeers were scrambling off as fast as they could to hide their weapons and themselves. A Royalist signal was given: it was safe to advance across the bridge. The men collected themselves to ride in search of prey. Cavaliers streamed across the ancient stone bridge, galloping at any local people they saw, shooting wildly and cutting down anybody they caught in their path. They fanned out through gardens, orchards and back alleys. Soon Birmingham was theirs. They made brisk work of establishing their presence, then settled in for the night.

This was just the start. Birmingham was about to learn what it meant to be taken by Prince Rupert of the Rhine.

Chapter Sixteen

Birmingham: 3–4 April 1643

Kinchin Tew spent much of Monday morning out in the woods. She knew there had been arguments in parish meetings and in the taverns about whether Birmingham should defend itself or succumb. Her parents argued as hotly as anyone, though there was never any possibility her father or unenlisted brothers would fight; the Tews had decided to flee. None of them had much idea what to expect. That did not stop her father, Emmett, loudly asserting that Birmingham would be horribly punished for its acts of rebellion. 'And what poor devils will come off worst –?'

'Us,' grumbled Kinchin's mother. 'As always!'

The family built a smoky bonfire in the woods, made feeble efforts to put up a temporary shelter and hunched down glumly like a group of hibernating vermin to wait until it was over. They had no pity for the town's predicament. Only the fact that whatever livelihood they scraped together depended on Birmingham gave them any interest. If Birmingham people suffered, it would reduce available charity and for those Tews who occasionally accepted labouring jobs, serious trouble might end all possibility of work. However, they had seen the King and his army pass through in procession last autumn, so they did not imagine today's events would be much worse.

Around noon, Kinchin and some of her siblings grew bored and cold. They crept back to town, where they watched the handing out of arms. They noticed Francis Roberts, the minister, leaving; he knew he would be a target for reprisals after his many anti-Royalist sermons.

At that time, before Prince Rupert arrived, the streets were quiet, although many people stood in their open doorways. Small groups of neighbours huddled together, seeking reassurance. Kinchin visited her friend Thomas at the Swan Inn on the High Street. A short, pale, mild-mannered man in his thirties, the ostler's light wispy hair was balding back from his forehead and he had a limp where he had once been kicked by an unfriendly horse. 'I'll be working later. I won't see the carnival . . .'

Thomas took Kinchin down into Deritend and showed her the earthworks that had been thrown up across the road. Small groups of musketeers were standing about quietly, one or two drinking beer from pint pots brought out to them by sympathisers. Kinchin parted from Thomas and moved on to beg for bread and butter from Mistress Lucas. 'And can your good man spare a sword, so that my father may fight for us with the rest?' She knew Emmett would not fight. But he had trained her to try for anything available.

'We have no swords left, Kinchin. Every finished weapon has been given out to the men. Now take yourself to some safe place, girl.'

With a shrug, foreseeing no particular danger, Kinchin made her way sulkily back to her family. They would moan at her for coming empty-handed, the laziest of her work-shy brothers moaning the loudest. Shortly after she left Mistress Lucas, the dull reverberation of the prince's cannon nearby shook the smith's house, while loud salvoes of musket shot caused the housewife to catch her breath in panic. But as Kinchin crossed the fields, she heard that first gunfire, which out in the country-side seemed distant and innocuous.

She had almost reached the wood, homing in on the wispy smoke from the fire. Then, suddenly, thunderous hooves closed in behind her. So many horses were coming, the ground shook. After one scared glance back, the girl gathered her skirts and ran. It felt as if Captain Greaves and the pursuing cavaliers were furiously chasing her. Terrified, she stumbled into the wood, just as she realised the horses had stopped. Scratched by brambles and brushwood and shaking with panic, she turned back from cover. She heard shouts and pistol shots; creeping closer, she witnessed the fierce exchange between Greaves's and Denbigh's men. Abruptly the skirmish was over. The cavalry of both sides all rode away like furies, back towards Birmingham.

Several loose horses remained, milling in the road. Her father ran out instantly with a couple of other Tews, to round up any they could catch. These were gentlemen's horses, good quality and expensive, even though when sold without a provenance they would fetch far less than their true value. Emmett would move them fast, putting twenty miles between the place he found them and backstreet stables in other market towns where scoundrels as shady as he would be glad to take the beasts, no questions asked, then sell them back to one of the armies' buying agents.

Wounded men were crawling; dead ones lay on the ground. Kinchin's mother emerged from cover. Flinging her ragged shawl back over her shoulders, she grabbed her daughter's arm and headed for these casualties. The two women hovered cautiously, then grew bolder. Her mother poked the dead to see if that produced any movement, then eagerly began to strip them. She had a rusty knife, which she plunged into her victims, rather than take chances. It was the first time the Tews had plundered like this, but they needed no lessons. Boots, hats, breast-plates, jackets, belts and shirts were swiftly peeled from the bodies. Weapons, purses, finger rings, handkerchiefs, medallions, gloves, sashes and riding hose all followed. Kinchin and her mother worked fast and in silence, not stopping to waste time on cries of delight. Before her mother stripped off britches and coats, the girl's small fingers dug deep into pockets, knowing that gentlemen's pockets would probably have three interior divisions, and that she must not miss the smallest, which might be fastened with a button. Their gleanings were rushed away into the woods by other Tews who came running for armfuls of fine clothes and fistfuls of jewellery. One of the boys collected guns and bullets in a cloak, tied up the corners and dragged it away.

An elderly cavalier, heavily built and extremely well dressed, was seriously wounded in the head. Kinchin had ransacked his pockets, unaware that he was still alive until he groaned while her mother was dragging off his bloodied brocade britches. Kinchin jumped back in alarm. After landing a hard kick on the man's bare legs, her mother carried away his expensive suit in triumph. Kinchin lost her nerve. She moved away but later, after the rest of her family burrowed back into the woods to inspect their pickings, she went alone and squatted close to the old man, waiting for night and the cold to finish him off. She wanted his embroidered shirt. Kinchin had always been methodical, and very patient in her scavenging.

Stabbing him dead was beyond her. She had no knife anyway, though she wanted to do it. The Royalist was an aristocrat, like Sir Thomas Holte of Aston. Kinchin hated all his kind. So she crouched in silence, guarding her prey like a fox staring at a chicken house, until she could complete her search. She thought the man knew she was there. She thought he must know why.

As dusk fell, a new group of horsemen approached at a canter, thwarting her. Men dismounted and, looking over their shoulders in case of attack, they began hastily inspecting the now naked bodies. Kinchin Tew clung on there, but eventually a young red-haired cavalier came to the old man. She had lost her chance.

'Denbigh is over here – still breathing! Damme, he's been stripped; can somebody cover him? We must keep him warm. What are you up to, young savage?' Treves demanded of Kinchin sharply. His light blue eyes had summed up her filthy condition and her watchfulness. Suspicious, he dropped a heavy hand on her shoulder.

'I saw he was alive, sir. I wanted to help him.' Flagrantly pretending innocence, Kinchin in turn assessed this young fellow, a sharp-featured carrot-top who sounded too full of confidence. He lost interest in her, and was examining the earl's bloody head wounds, wincing. She eyed Edmund's clothes, which were plainer than those her family had dragged off to the woods, but still worth selling . . . He had too many men with him to risk it.

'Did you see who looted these bodies?'

'No, sir.'

'This is an important lord, a favourite of Prince Rupert's.' With a grunt of exertion, Treves was helping another man lift and put the badly injured earl over a horse's back. 'He needs attention urgently. Is there a surgeon in Birmingham?'

Reluctantly Kinchin nodded. 'Come up on Faddle.' Moments later, Treves had hoisted her up behind him on his own horse, where she clung on to his wide leather belt as he sped back into town. Adapting rapidly, she soon relaxed, as if riding on horseback behind Royalist gentlemen was her natural mode of travel. Her bare feet bounced against Faddle's hot flank and she now held Edmund round the waist with one skinny bare arm, fully confident she would not fall off.

As they rode into Birmingham, Kinchin squealed at what she saw. Cavaliers were breaking into all the houses. They were frightening the poor, threatening the rich, picking pockets and cursing, some in strange languages. Quartermasters pretended to arrange billets, an excuse for blackmail and bullying. Men were crashing about as they searched for concealed treasure or weapons – peering down wells and into pools, smashing roof tiles, running crazily through gardens. Carts and market trolleys were being piled high with stolen goods. A smell of smoke, different smoke from the normal hearth and forge fires, hung ominously in the damp April air.

Kinchin guided Treves to the surgeon's house and was put down to knock, but a maid came out looking flustered. The girl informed them that Mr Tillam had himself been shot, very seriously in the leg and thigh, as he stood at his house door, wanting to welcome the cavaliers. He was a Royalist supporter – or had been.

The surgeon's maid shot Kinchin a look of amazement. 'Get out of the road, Kinchin Tew, or the mad devils will shoot you too! I'm for hiding in the attic, me.'

Kinchin felt very frightened. Darkness had fallen. There was more noise than she ever remembered in Birmingham; the strange hubbub was clearly hazardous. Evening was for scavengers, but the Tews had lost their rights in Birmingham tonight. Louder, stronger, wickeder men had taken over.

After a brief debate with his fellow soldiers, Treves opted to carry the injured earl to the prince's headquarters; Rupert had bedded in at the Ship Inn. 'Where can I take you, mistress?' he enquired of Kinchin politely, leaning down from Faddle. The barefoot girl was still standing in the street, wondering what to do next. Having brought her as his guide, Edmund felt concerned; he knew what was likely to happen in this town tonight. But Denbigh was fading, so he was in a hurry.

Kinchin thought Treves was jesting. He must see her grimy condition. His genuine gallantry impressed her, however. She considered him an innocent; she even thought him stupid – yet she felt touched.

Her predicament was awkward. She could not ask to be taken back to her family, hiding up in the woods with their plunder. Instead, she assured Treves she had friends nearby. She convinced the cavalier the Swan Inn was a place of safety. So Kinchin watched her red-haired gallant move off through the chaos towards the Ship, where the prince was. She felt a sense of loss, and almost wished she had stayed with Treves, riding high on Faddle, to see out her adventure.

As soon as she was left alone, Kinchin panicked. Gunsmoke and the stench of burned houses made the air close. Many more soldiers were noisily pouring into town; they must have come up from Henley-in-Arden during the afternoon. All around her were sounds of assault.

Birmingham would normally be dark and still at this hour, with only a warm hum from tavern interiors; now it seemed alive with violence. Breaking window glass crashed and splintered. Men's harsh voices bellowed and swore. Women screamed. A group of prisoners were marched up to the Bull Ring, jostled and bullied by cavaliers who intended their racket to be heard and feared. Kinchin watched them searching the prisoners for money, amid threats and demands for large ransoms.

Nervously, she crept into the Swan's small courtyard, relieved that this dim area seemed comparatively quiet. A lantern swung beside the taproom. The door stood closed against the evening chill. A streak of faint light came from the stables. It was oddly still. She missed the normal buzz from regular drinkers. Even so, nothing seemed too badly amiss in those first moments.

Horses clattered up suddenly. As riders burst through the gateway, Kinchin froze. Alert for new customers, Thomas threw open a stable door and emerged from the warm stalls as he always did, ready to take the horses. He limped forwards obligingly, one hand outstretched to gather bridles, a smile of welcome blossoming.

Pistols shot. The ostler fell to the cobbles. Three cavaliers trotted right over him, and dismounted. They shouldered open the taproom door and entered, calling loudly for ale. None glanced back.

The flurry of noise over, there was silence. Kinchin stared. Thomas lay face down in the dark yard, one arm still outstretched. He must be dead. Who would do that? Why do it? He was not a threat. He was only doing his duty, coming to take their horses.

A new Royalist rode in. In a terrible miscalculation Kinchin believed this man brought help. Hard eyes took in the dead ostler, the dark pool of blood around Thomas, and the shaking girl. He levelled a gun. She had made a mistake.

He was covering her with the carbine. Faint light from the stable fell across him. Kinchin would never lose that image: the man ready to kill her, the huge horse, the filled moneybags tied to the saddlebow, the heavy spurred riding boots, the aimed gun in his gloved hand – and the reckless tilt to his curling brimmed black hat, with its bright turquoise band.

He chose not to shoot. The day was ending; he wanted rest and ale.

She felt the hot breath of his high-spirited horse as the rider pressed forwards to the taproom, then she clutched up her skirts, passed by him and ran like a rat, sliding out of the Swan gate in one long speechless streak, so secretly and swiftly the cavalier must have wondered if he ever really saw her.

Chapter Seventeen

Birmingham: Monday and Tuesday, 3–4 April 1643

With a thundering heart, Kinchin flung herself into a dark doorway, hoping to escape notice from the soldiers in the High Street. Shaking and petrified, she tried to breathe. Her lungs refused to expand. Her muscles seemed unable to bear her up.

'Where's your God Brooke now?' jeered raucous Royalists to their cowed prisoners, as they herded these beaten men into the Swan. 'Where's your Coventry now?'

Worn out and depressed, the Birmingham men in shirts and stockinged feet were holding up their britches; their coats, their belts and their boots had been stolen. They limped inside to the courtyard. Kinchin thought she spotted the smith Lucas among the wretched crowd. A baffled cavalier demanded of one prisoner, 'How can you take up arms against your oaths of allegiance and royal supremacy?'

The Birmingham man retorted, 'I never did and never would take any such oaths!'

A furious blow with a musket butt sent him flying — though he was not killed, because the Royalists were still hoping to make money from their captives. Kinchin heard grumbling that Prince Rupert would be annoyed that the ransoms from their impoverished opponents were only tuppence, eight pence, a shilling, and occasionally twenty shillings. More than one of the prisoners made indignant protests, claiming to be no soldier and no rebel but a faithful supporter of the King . . . a plea which earned only laughter. The soldiers declared that any forced ransom would be received as well by His Majesty as if it were a voluntary gift.

While Kinchin crouched in shadow, a familiar sight transfixed her: down the dark street, head in the air and eyes vague, sauntered Mr Whitehall. The crazy parson picked his way among the debris as if puzzled how so much clutter came to be littering the town. He sniffed the air, troubled by the smoke. He was walking about openly, either unafraid of the Royalists or unaware of danger. Kinchin now hardly knew which way to turn to avoid a mauling, yet Whitehall had not seen her so she clung to her dark space, still in shock after the brutal killing of Thomas.

Lit by flickers of candlelight through windows where the shutters had been flung open, the lunatic's long dark coat and white neckbands marked him out as clergy. Cavaliers quickly spotted him – and saw sport. They supposed he was Minister Roberts, whom they loathed. Despite all Mr Whitehall's past assaults, Kinchin almost shouted a warning. She dared not. Boisterous men surrounded him, shoving him to and fro, laughing at him, demanding whether he wanted quarter. Too crazy for caution, Mr Whitehall cried: 'I will have no quarter! I scorn quarter from popish armies! Your King is a perjured and papistical King! I would rather die than live under such a King! I would gladly fight against him –'

A poleaxe blow ended his rant. Cheering Royalists moved in and hacked him to death. They disembowelled him by twisting swords in his guts; then they quartered the body as if this were a formal execution. Searching his pockets, they found hand-written papers. Sordid stories of his attempts on local women were read out aloud gleefully, then came ribald promises to publish them to a wider audience. 'A comfortable kiss from one woman, a cinnamon kiss from another – and another from one of just fourteen –' Kinchin trembled, terrified she would be identified.

The cavaliers went up and down the town, exulting that they had killed Minister Roberts.

Only feet away from parts of the blood-soaked corpse, the distressed young girl still cowered. She felt no joy that Mr Whitehall's death had freed her. Worse dangers walked abroad; she felt as vulnerable tonight as she had ever been.

Once the killers moved off, the High Street emptied temporarily. Kinchin made a quick bolt for the only place that might offer her refuge. Shuddering and stumbling, she fled through the Corn Cheaping and around the houses by the church. Everywhere, doors stood wide open. From within the small houses came strangers' swearing and carousing. Little Park Street seemed darker and quieter, though a group of horses and carts should have told her that Royalists were close. Sure of kindness awaiting, she rushed in through the half-open door to the Lucases' kitchen, then realised her error.

A fug of tobacco smoke met her. Big men with loud voices had taken control of the smith's home. They were ransacking domestic cupboards, upsetting utensils, devouring food and drink, terrorising the family. As Kinchin ran in, two moustached cavaliers in open jerkins with their great boots astride the kitchen bench, raised overflowing tankards in a toast to Prince Rupert's dog: 'Here's a gallant health to Boy!' Another, with forward teeth and a wide mouth, was rocking the baby's cradle with the point of his sword. Across the room, Kinchin saw the terrified Mistress Lucas, gripped by a soldier who had his pistol at her breast. He kicked open a door that led to stairs up into the bedroom.

'Damme! A girl –' Kinchin's arrival caused brief delight – then disgust when they saw her condition. The men turned up their noses, just as she was repulsed by them; they reeked of horseflesh, stale ale and sour shirts. Their clothes and long hair were pickled in old smoke and sweat. 'A filthy monster –' The man's slurred accent was thick.

'What are you?' Her shocked whisper came out automatically.

'We are Frenchmen!' He was so drunk he could not boast and control a tankard simultaneously, but spilled ale over one flowing shirtsleeve. 'We have volunteered to save your miserable kingdom – we French, some Germans, Irish, Dutch, and Swedes.'

The baby was screaming. Now almost a year old, he was big enough to struggle upright in the cradle. Kinchin had never taken to this child; the chubby fellow in his knitted cap and embroidered bib was too clean, possessed too many home-made toys and was far too happy. He was always being given attention – kissed on the head as his mother passed his warm cradle, dandled by neighbours, fed little titbits, taken down to the forge to see his father . . .

The nearest soldier pricked at the child's jacket. His sword point caught in the wool; he planned to lift the little boy and drop him into the fire – but the sharp blade cut itself free and the red-faced infant sat back suddenly, with a renewed cry.

'Robert!' protested the mother faintly. The cavalier who held her gave her a vicious cuff across the face. She struggled wildly as he pulled at her waistcoat buttons. No stranger to beatings herself, Kinchin saw that such violence was completely new to the housewife, but Mistress Lucas only bit her lip, enduring whatever was done to her, out of terror for her child.

Kinchin tried to distract the men. 'The baby cries. Let me walk him.' She spoke with fake confidence, but scavenging had taught her how. She went quickly and picked up Robert, bringing his blanket with him to hide him in it. He clutched her, hampering her movements, and was heavy in her arms. Her eyes tried to reassure his mother. She never knew whether Mistress Lucas understood because the young terrified housewife was being dragged backwards out of the room.

Kinchin promenaded with Robert on her shoulder. Hushing him gave her some comfort. The soldiers now ignored them. One was rattling up the fire with a poker, then examining the poker to see if he would bother to steal it. From beyond the inner door came a loud thump, at which the man by the fire made an obscene gesture. Another signalled for Kinchin to pour him ale. She managed to do so one-handed, while Robert grabbed onto her. Nervously, she manoeuvred to keep all the men in view, in case they tried to jump her.

Mistress Lucas was being ravished. Kinchin heard it. She understood what this experience would mean to a chaste woman. It could be her turn next.

The Frenchman stomped back into the room, fastening the buttons of his britches. Without a word, another man stood up and pushed past his colleague, one hand at his belt. They were matter-of-fact. None discussed what they were doing. This was their routine. Enemies were killed; their houses stripped; their horses stolen; their women violated. The more blood shed and the more fear caused, the greater was the victory.

The nearest man had his back to her, shovelling firedogs and pots into a sack. Kinchin sneaked up her courage. Still carrying the Lucas infant, she slipped out of doors.

She crept away down the garden path, desperately trying to keep her steps quiet. Its cinders were painful under her cold, bare feet. She managed to drag open the forge's heavy shutter just enough to squeeze through with Robert. She had never been inside before, and was surprised that the high workplace seemed bigger than the house. It was dark, but dimly lit by the fire.

Warmth came from the hearth, even though Lucas could not have used it for two days; he would not have worked today because of the fighting and yesterday was Sunday. The cavaliers must have burst in here earlier. They had flung fuel on the hearth and blown up flames with the bellows while they turned everything upside down in their search for valuables. Kinchin squeezed through the strange scattered tools, knocking painfully into large items of equipment and gasping as her bare soles were gouged by pieces of metal on the floor. She crouched with the baby in her arms beside the brick hearth.

'Be safe, Robert – make no sound.' Away from the tumult and comforted by her steady voice, the child soon settled and slept.

For Kinchin there was no relaxation that long night. Hours stretched away. Holding Robert, with her cheek against his soft warm head, she stole to the doorway from time to time. It was no use. Throughout the town, cavaliers sat up drinking, blaspheming, tyrannising their prisoners, terrifying women, insolently boasting. With the outside air cold on her face, the miserable young girl wiped her nose on her sleeve, listening to the uproar. All night there was no let-up. Over and over again she slunk back miserably into the forge. She longed to help Mistress Lucas, but could not. If the cavaliers laid hands on her too, neither her youth nor her squalor would save her.

Dawn brought a temporary diminution in the terror. The character of the tumult changed. Carts and horses began clattering northwards in businesslike convoys. The sounds of organised companies of soldiers on the move under orders took over from rampage and riot. For Kinchin Tew some relief finally came.

A new silence lay on the house. Next time Kinchin ventured out of the forge, she made up her mind to go back to the kitchen. She collected the sleepy infant. By the grey light of early morn she spotted a single sword, hung on a rafter in the forge; climbing on a wooden trestle she managed to lift the weapon down and brought it out with her. It was the blade Lucas had made wrongly and kept back, though the heavy weapon seemed adequate to Kinchin.

Kinchin approached the open house door, carrying Robert in one arm with the sword, point down, in her other hand. The lack of noise indicated the soldiers had gone. Even so, she stayed outside, too scared to look.

After a long time watching, she stood the sword behind a barrel and crossed the threshold timidly. Indoors, she found a scene of despoliation.

The wrecked kitchen made her feel like a stranger. Once so neat, the room reeked of drink, smoke, and worse. The men had marked the house with their excrement, like wild animals claiming territory. Many domestic implements were missing. Objects that were too cumbersome to carry off, such as the bench and the baby's heavy oak cradle, had been crudely tossed and upended. Things of little value, or small items that male fingers made clumsy by drink had dropped, lay strewn all over the floor. Kicked ashes besmirched the slabbed floor. A worn cutlery box lay smashed on the table. The fire was dead in the grate, water buckets upset, heavy cauldrons bounced until they were dented beyond repair.

Dreadful stillness hung over the house. Kinchin found the wool-stuffed cradle-mattress, still usable though it had been singed in the fire; for safety she set Robert upon it in his cradle, which she righted and pushed to its normal position. He was hungry and started bawling; she ignored that. Then, bravely, she walked to the door opposite and ventured through.

She stopped. A body lay on the stairs.

Mistress Lucas had been repeatedly ravished right there on the steep, narrow wooden treads. At some time during the ordeal she had died. One hand gripped a banister rail; her head was turned far to one side, as if to avoid seeing her attackers. Her skirts were pushed up to her waist. Her buckled shoes were off. One stocking had wrinkled around her ankle in the struggle, though the other remained neatly over her knee, held by its knitted garter.

Whether she had died of the rapes, or shame, or shots, or suffocation Kinchin could not tell.

She stood at the foot of the stairs, wondering what to do. Noises in the kitchen alarmed her. She spun back there, perhaps to protect Robert or perhaps ready to run and save herself. The baby was now bound to her by their shared hours in the forge, but Kinchin had a loner's priorities.

An elderly woman had arrived from the house next door, anxious for Lucas and his family. She had a sharp, intelligent face and head of white hair, upon which sat a rather crooked coif. Automatically, she was righting the firejack, while gazing around in horror. Robert, blue-eyed and now silent, was watching. The old woman recognised Kinchin and asked after Mistress Lucas.

Kinchin sobbed, once.

The woman moved quietly past her. With a keening sound, she went to Mistress Lucas and pulled down her skirts decently. She loosened the dead woman's grip on the banister, and moved her arm. On returning to the kitchen, she found that Kinchin had sunk down amongst the devastation, lost in shock. 'A good woman. Cruelly used. Yet here's the poor baby all untouched –'

'I hid with him,' whispered Kinchin.

The neighbour nodded approval, though in the way of Birmingham people her reaction was restrained. She knew Mistress Lucas had given charity to this mite. Shaking her head and short of breath, the woman seated herself on a joint-stool. She had to right it first, and sat gently as if it might collapse; some of the pegs had been knocked out during the cavaliers' riot. 'They have killed Widow Collins, and fourteen or fifteen others. I heard that two coffins were made last night for men of quality of theirs.' She held her arms folded and rocked with grief. 'Many houses are stripped of goods and furnishings; people were forced to hand over all the money they had. Their own supporters have lost as much as anyone, but that is no help to the rest of us . . . Go to your people, Kinchin Tew. I will find women for what is needed. Here – she does not want this now –' The old neighbour jumped up, pulled a cloak from a peg on the door and wrapped it around Kinchin. Then she snatched a crust from the ground, blew the dust off and pushed it into the girl's hand. 'Have you seen Lucas? Some of our killed men were pushed into the trench and their bodies buried when the Royalists slighted the earthworks. They allowed nobody near to recover the dead.'

'Lucas was a prisoner. I saw him last night. I saw him at the Swan –' Remembering how Thomas was shot in cold blood, Kinchin retched. With nothing in her stomach, she controlled it. The old woman gazed at her; perhaps she had heard what had happened to the ostler.

'The prisoners are all ransomed and free to go. Leave this house now, girl, before Lucas comes home.'

Kinchin was not sure whether this was some warning that Lucas might suspect she had taken part in the theft of his goods, or that he might be angry to find such a starveling had survived while his poor decent wife was murdered. Kinchin had no place here. Women neighbours would attend to Mistress Lucas's laying-out. Jane This and Margery That, a Bess, an Alice, a Susanna . . . They had gossiped with the smith's wife, attended her churching after Robert was born, and they would now bury her, comfort Lucas and help the smith deal with nurturing the child alone. None of that was for Kinchin. She was an outsider, no matter how much grief she felt for the murdered woman.

She left the house without another word.

Clutching the cloak tightly around her and gnawing the hard bread, Kinchin wandered up through the markets, terrified of what she would find. She was carrying the sword from the forge. Under her cloak she held it with care, because there was no scabbard. A cart laden with half a dozen wounded Royalists trundled past, forcing her to press against the side of a house. Her feet stumbled with tiredness and terror. Groups of people, trembling bare-legged in their shirts and shifts, stood outside homes where open windows and doors revealed empty interiors. She saw people who had lost everything. Dazed and depressed, they simply collected in the streets.

Now Kinchin entered a scene that would have seemed to her like hell, had the Tews ever practised religion. As she passed the toll booth, heading into the Welsh End, many cavaliers were still at large. Prince Rupert had gone, but had left behind a group called an antiguard. These men were to protect his army in the rear and secure the route back to Oxford. They knew how to do this work. In every street, triumphal soldiers brandished drawn swords and pistols. They were making excited preparations to set fire to the town. Driving off householders, they used gunpowder, wisps of straw and matchcord. Some fired off special slugs which they said Lord Digby had invented: bullets wrapped in brown paper that they shot from pistols into stables and thatched roofs. Residents pleaded with them to stop, but the answer came back that each quartermaster had orders from the prince to fire his section of the town.

Legitimate arson was a wonderful game. In a market town full of forges, combustible material was easy to find. Laying the fires was easy. Anguished Birmingham people were complaining that they had paid out large sums of money to Prince Rupert, to buy protection for their homes. His men's response was cold and cruel. Anyone brave enough, who tried to save their goods or their premises, was fired at. Fresh blood ran over yesterday's dried blood on the cobbles.

Kinchin was frightened by the fire, more frightened by the soldiers' continuing violence. She pushed her way through to the High Cross, trying to leave town. But all the buildings ahead of her were ablaze. Their destitute owners stood weeping in the street; cavaliers only jeered as thick smoke gusted everywhere. Above Dale End and the Welch End, crackling flames leaped twice as high as the timber houses. To Kinchin's left, Moor Street was noisily burning, and when she ran into Chapel Street, a strong wind blew a great conflagration across the cherry orchards towards her.

At the Bull Inn, opposite the disused priory, with flames hot on her face, Kinchin stopped. A soldier barged past, carrying a pan of hot coals, on his way to start another fire somewhere. A man waved a besom broom at her, its bound twigs streaking the air with sparks. Too much terror finally overcame the girl. As she stood on the cobbles in confusion, she caught two riders' attention.

She recognised the red-haired cavalier and his horse: Faddle. A second rider loudly swore at people, 'The prince deals with you mercifully now! When we come back, with the Queen's army, you will know our true minds – no one will be left alive!'

Edmund Treves saw her. 'Get to safety!' He struggled to control his horse, disturbed by the fires. He could tell how the night's events had changed the girl. She had lost all her earlier trust of him. Of course she was right. Treves had stayed at the Ship Inn, on the outskirts, but he knew what had gone on in the town. Guilt sickened him – though he would not change his loyalty to the King.

Someone else spotted Kinchin. Her father, Emmett, had been loitering in the hope of grabbing property from open houses. Emmett dropped his robbery sack; with ghastly determination he grabbed his daughter and hauled her right under the cavaliers' horses. Gripped so fiercely, the nightmare of her encounters with Mr Whitehall returned to her. 'Here's a nice clean girl, sir!'

'Will you make her a doxy?' Treves retorted angrily.

'No, *you* may do that!' leered Emmett. 'She will know no other trade, sir,' he wheedled plaintively, as if this excused selling her. He sounded desperate. 'A kinchin mort – that's a girl, sir, who is brought to her full age and then –'

'*No!*' His daughter shrieked, now mortified.

Kinchin rebelled. The nickname she had always endured was suddenly hateful. She struggled wildly. Until now, she had accepted her family's intentions. They brought her up to sell. If she stayed with them, they would do it. The closest friends she had ever had were killed last night. Nobody cared for her now.

Unexpectedly, Kinchin wrenched free. In the fight with her father, she dropped the sword that she had taken from the forge. Then Treves's companion reined in his great horse above where it lay upon the ground.

She knew that man too. Kinchin looked up into those unblinking eyes. It was the man with the turquoise hatband. He was holding his carbine. Once again the idea of shooting this girl, the idea that had crossed Orlando Lovell's mind last night, returned to him.

This time, Kinchin picked up and held the sword so Lovell could see it. Lovell reached to hook it from her grasp. Kinchin scrambled backwards. Her father grabbed at her again but it was a feeble movement. She dodged Emmett and fled.

The fire roared all around her; she saw only one way to run. She beat a path back through the unburned part of the town, moving as fast as she could manage through the lamenting crowds. Slowing, she doubled back down the High Street past the Swan Inn where Thomas had been shot, back through the markets where Mr Whitehall had been mangled, around St Martin's Church and past Little Park Street where Mistress Lucas lay dead in her house. She ran down into Digbeth. The last cavaliers were leaving, over the stone bridge. Finding a gap in the procession, she went through Deritend where unknown numbers of killed defenders lay under the flattened earthworks. She passed the Ship Inn, where the elegant Prince Rupert had spent a civilised night, allegedly unaware of the deeds being perpetrated throughout Birmingham in his name.

When the distraught girl reached the end of the houses and taverns, she kept walking. The road she was on travelled out through the water meadows into open country. She went with it, sobbing. Once she was certain of her intent and sure that nobody was following, she paused, turned herself and looked back bleakly. Much of Birmingham was burning. Almost a hundred houses would be lost that day, with numerous barns and outbuildings. But the wind was changing; she could feel it on her tearstained face. The wind would eventually blow back upon itself, so the fire was contained and doused.

Hundreds of people were homeless and destitute, many more were shocked and grieving. They would cluster together and support one another. They would relate their troubles to the kingdom at large and perhaps be consoled by the telling. But this set-faced, lonely vagabond would gain no comfort, for she possessed no family and no community. Empty-handed, godless, friendless, hopeless and even nameless now, the young girl took one last look at the fiery desolation she had left behind. Then she turned her face to the south again and strode onwards in her sorrow.

Chapter Eighteen

London: May, 1643

Bad men bearing dubious offers always appear at the right time. So, once again, Bevan Bevan correctly chose his moment to manipulate his great-nephew, Gideon Jukes.

Bevan understood Gideon's situation. A young man of twenty-two, newly created a company freeman and recently cheered by military success, would be looking around for a woman. Unlike Lambert, a lively lad from puberty, the younger Jukes brother was a straightforward and still naïve bachelor. Despite his heritage as one of London's merchant class, Gideon did not canoodle with other men's wives or flirt with their daughters. He had never engaged with lewd women in back-alley taverns, let alone visited the notorious brothels that lay over the river in Southwark. Even if he secretly considered that, Gideon liked the easy life; he was too frightened of discovery. He still cringed at the fuss over his dotterel escapade. For him, marriage was the only solution.

Bevan knew, too, that Parthenope and John Jukes were leaving Gideon to find his own wife. The dangerous times made them cautious. They wanted him to be happy, but it seemed less urgent to push Gideon into marriage than when they had begged Lambert to wed Anne Tydeman after courting her for years. Anne and Lambert now lived in the family home; if Gideon married, it raised tricky questions about how far his parents should go in setting him up. The Jukes always claimed their sons were equal, but in families equality can be elastic.

Although it was a decade since Bevan regularly dined at the Jukes table, once in a while he still arrived on the doorstep. He expected his slice of roast beef and demanded more gravy with it, as if he were the family patriarch. Then when John Jukes angrily stomped out to the yard for a pipe, Bevan – who was less mobile with his gouty legs –

would push back his chair and pontificate on how Lambert and Gideon should manage their lives. Gideon was generally at home to hear it. Bevan seemed to have studied his pattern of behaviour.

'Don't leave it so long as I did! Marry while you have the spirit to manage your wife and brood.'

Startled by the idea of a brood, Gideon merely raised his eyebrows and scuttled off to join his father beside the burnt-out house-of-easement, where they gloomily enjoyed their tobacco and waited for the uncle to depart.

Undeterred, Bevan next brought his wife, Elizabeth, and her wide-eyed unmarried niece.

The niece, Lacy Keevil, was a relative through Elizabeth's previous marriage. 'Up from the country' – which only meant from Eltham – Lacy had been taken into the Bevan household to help with their rumbustious children. She seemed to know when to hang her head shyly among strangers. 'More to her than she shows!' Lambert muttered, conspiratorially. Gideon liked the sound of that.

He stared at Lacy Keevil. She looked too anxious to be dangerous. For her years – sixteen – she had a rounded, mature figure. Her rather ordinary face was a blank, with no signs of character to worry him, but she had exotic almond-shaped eyes that drew male attention, including his.

Proffered a paper of his mother's jumbles, Lacy treated Gideon as a special acquaintance. He fell for it. He knew he should be more wary; indeed, his previous lack of success with women made him wonder at his sudden popularity now. Still he let himself believe that Lacy had a sweet, shy personality to which he was keenly attracted, and that his looks and urbane charm had captured her heart. He decided he could handle the situation himself, so he confided in no one which meant nobody ever joshed him, 'What looks and charm?'

'Ask yourself what she wants,' Lambert's wife Anne alerted him, after she sensed tensions between the girl and her relatives. 'Why are Bevan and Elizabeth parading this puss about?' The hint came too late for Gideon.

A few days later Bevan turned up 'by chance' in Basinghall Street. Immediately his uncle broached marriage, Gideon threw himself at the idea. Already committed, he consulted Robert Allibone, who saw the case was hopeless so merely replied that he did not know the girl.

Because the match had been engineered by Bevan Bevan, Gideon's parents opposed it on principle, but their opposition spurred him on.

'He will never change,' wept his mother.

'He will never learn!' raved John.

Gideon would learn, and perhaps even change, though not yet.

Gideon Jukes and Lacy Keevil were married in early May, 1643. It was a large family wedding and differed little from such celebrations in peacetime. The bride was dainty and subdued. The groom felt racked with nerves. Killjoys grumbled into their handkerchiefs that the couple were making a mistake; the young fools should have waited until the war ended. Others retaliated that at a wedding in wartime, guests ought to make a special effort to be cheerful.

Despite the deprivations in trade, everyone flaunted finery. Money was available. Gideon had a new ash-coloured jacket with a subdued sheen, over full knee-britches, all fastened with gold buttons — several dozen of them in the suit. Lacy wore carnation taffeta which, as her Aunt Elizabeth said rather loudly, she *filled* extremely well. On the traditional walk to and from church, they were both sweetly excited and beaming with happiness. It was impossible to wish them anything but joy and long life together. That did not stop thin smiles among disparagers.

The feast took place at a neutral venue, chosen because neither family could agree who should host. It was the Talbot Inn, a large coaching inn in Talbot Court off Gracechurch Street, within smell of the Thames.

As the wedding party in their lustrous tissues went into the court-yard where long, laden tables waited, Gideon suddenly felt alien. The feast was for him, yet he observed the elegant procession as if he were no part of it.

Standing back in a gateway while guests chose their seats, his brother met an acquaintance, a younger man than Lambert, perhaps only a couple of years older than Gideon. Lambert introduced him: 'Edward Sexby, son of Marcus Sexby, gent — absolutely sharp and straight, and valiant for our cause. He was apprenticed to Edward Price, of the Grocers' Fraternity.' That was all the accreditation a man could need with the Jukes; Lambert in his jovial way invited Sexby to the wedding feast.

'It is not *his* party!' whispered Lacy crossly, the sweet new bride suddenly furious.

'Dear heart – your first quarrel with your in-laws!' Gideon was mildly pleased at how it smacked of domesticity. Lacy returned a cold stare, calculating that her new husband might be trickier to manage than the Bevans had promised her.

A buzz of rancour rose, as two very different families, intent on despising one another, took up positions over succulent chicken, pigeons and legs of roasted pork. The Jukes brooded over Bevan Bevan's past sins and his relatives' fecklessness, bitterly noting poor manners and shamelessly expensive gloves. The Bevans decried the sermon and the wedding breakfast, which the Jukes had provided. The Jukes led a large, loud contingent of cousins, friends, stockmen and errand boys, maids past and present, past maids' children, and present maids' sisters who were hopeful of becoming maids future. They also brought two tiny, extremely ancient ladies, hook-shouldered Aunt Susan and Good Mother Perslowe, who were no relation at all, but always attended family parties. By contrast, the Bevans and Keevils seemed oddly light on guests. Lacy's parents were absent, though presumably Elizabeth had invited them, and the journey from Eltham, at less than ten miles, should not have been prohibitive.

Parthenope Jukes seated herself in state at the head of the table squashed alongside Elizabeth Bevan (née Keevil), a large-boned, low-bosomed, florid-faced woman whose significance Gideon had missed when his great-uncle married her. He now understood: all tradesmen's widows in the City of London were well-to-do, for they inherited one-third of their husband's effects automatically, another third if they were childless as Elizabeth had been in her first marriage, and perhaps the final third too if they had persuaded their man to leave them everything. Beyond that, printers' widows had a special position: exceptionally, a print business passed from deceased husband to widow, together with prized membership of the Stationers' Company. When the late printer Keevil was carried off by illness, he left Elizabeth with attractive assets. Bevan had always 'lived on his wits' – or 'lived off his relatives' as John Jukes redefined it.

'Bevan must have employed fantastic footwork to displace her journey-man!' Gideon sneered to Robert Allibone. It was more or less traditional that a printer's widow continued the business through her husbands' apprentices – generally remarrying one of the journeymen. They had the right to be affronted if she chose elsewhere.

Allibone smiled wryly. 'Ah! You did not know that *I* served my time with Abraham Keevil?' Gideon swallowed, thinking he had committed some faux pas, but his friend gently ended his suffering: 'Oh, the dame had her eye on me, but I was always set on Margery!'

The matriarchs had drawn up battle lines, using fashion for weapons. Elizabeth Keevil made much of the fact that her olive-green satin had been bought at the Royal Exchange. Parthenope scoffed at the Exchange galleries as dangerously newfangled, while she cruelly noticed how the low-cut gown's pearl-bedecked elbow-sleeves hung so far off Elizabeth's shoulders they gripped her fleshy arms like a straitjacket, hampering her use of cutlery. Wielding her own fork daintily, Parthenope gazed on her family's resplendent outfits; in theory religious Independents shunned ornament, but a wedding was a matter of status and a wedding where they loathed the bride's family called for even more dash. Parthenope herself was in dark old-gold damask that had used up a year's profits from imported peppers. Anne wore a white petticoat, embroidered with maroon flowers and foliage, under a scalloped-edge gown that she had pinned back for easier movement; alone of the women she had put on a coif beneath her hat, which modestly hid most of her hair. Lambert and his father had let themselves be buttoned into their best black silks; John had become frail recently, but Lambert was as solid as a slab of slate.

Parthenope and Anne had acquired their finery not at the Exchange but in the traditional city way: knocking on doors to request special arrangements. This procedure for favours could be a fiction. When pleading gentlewomen called to negotiate bargains in grocery, Lambert would either charge the normal price or underweigh the goods. 'Putting a thumb on the scale is a usual grocers' trick!' Elizabeth whispered to the bride, managing to suggest that Lacy's marriage would be continually marred by such treacherous wiles.

Perhaps using the pennies he had saved, Lambert had hired two sackbut-players. The men were far from virtuosos; their primitive trombones were soon dreaded by everyone.

As the meal progressed, Bevan began talking politics. Covert signals failed to silence him. 'There is always an uncle who must cause trouble!' hissed Parthenope under cover of handing a vegetable tureen to Anne.

Gideon and Lacy had not exchanged wedding rings. Bevan denounced this as religious extremism, then latched onto Anne Jukes as a target. He referred scathingly to her foray into Westminster with the female petitioners. 'Shall we be seeing your wife as a she-preacher next, Lambert?' Lambert, moving around the company like a large benevolent lord, calmly raised a tankard to his great-uncle, oblivious of insult. Anne pretended not to hear, until Bevan's next jibe: 'I hear that rebel wives in the City are donating their jewels to Parliament's war chest!'

'I am glad to know,' snapped Anne. She was forthright and fearless, which offended Bevan all the more. 'They shall have my wedding ring tomorrow. Lambert and I need no pagan symbols.' In an undertone, she scoffed to her mother-in-law, 'He is not even drunk.'

'Not yet!'

Fortunately Elizabeth Bevan missed this, since she was frazzled at the separate table where her children were being fed. She purloined the bride to help her control them. In the decade of her marriage to Bevan, Elizabeth had been constantly pregnant. Although it had not stopped her parading bare breasts and forearms today like a decadent royal maid-of-honour, under her stays she was big-bellied again at nearly forty. There were five surviving offspring, all squealers and snivellers; Arthur, aged seven, was a particularly repugnant child.

Anne Jukes felt obliged to leave her food and assist. Childless throughout her own marriage, Anne knew herself to be an object of both pity and disapproval, as if the situation was her fault. The long wedding sermon, with its emphasis on marriage for procreation, had been torture. Now other people's insolent children would be dumped on her.

'Why thank you, my dear!' Elizabeth simpered. 'Do not let naughty Arthur throw syllabub on your good gown. Come, Lacy, resume your place of honour –'

The Keevil brood eyed her balefully. Anne Jukes, who came from a jolly, good-tempered brewing family, squared up to them. In their home these children ran amok like little princes, governed only with cajoling and bribes. But as the delinquent Arthur now raised his bowl to hurl it 'accidentally' over her embroidered skirts, Anne grasped his shoulders and lifted him right off the wooden bench; she dumped him down in front of her like a slop bucket. He was still small enough to be manhandled and Anne's kneading of her much-admired white manchet rolls had given her sturdy arms. 'Now, Arthur. We have thanked God for providing this fine feast. If you have no wish to eat, you may stand on a stool in a corner like a school dunce, and there wait for all the company to finish.'

Amazed, Arthur thought of screaming. Silently, she dared him. He thought better of it.

Anne reflected that before she took herself to Westminster with the female petitioners, this brat would have got the better of her. Since she began joining in demonstrations, she had acquired quiet resolution. For two pins she would have told Elizabeth just where she went wrong domestically . . . As she took charge of the young Bevans, who were lace-collared like miniature royalty, she thought with some pleasure of her new rebel character.

'Your daughter-in-law is *so* good with the little ones!' murmured Elizabeth Bevan, as the delinquent Arthur slunk back to his seat while Anne firmly tied napkins around his sulky siblings' necks. 'So good for one who is barren!'

Anne, who had the finest instincts in Cheapside, looked up and saw it said.

Then Anne Jukes let her surly gaze dwell speculatively upon the bride. Elizabeth Bevan understood; Lacy's aunt stilled, suddenly cold in her heart.

As the afternoon passed, the meal became less formal. People came and went around the inn courtyards. Gideon found it awkward to converse with his new wife while all eyes were upon them. He had been at enough weddings to know that soon relatives would start chivvying him with lewd advice. At his side, the inscrutable Lacy politely smiled at everything he said, and as the day continued, Gideon realised that had she been an ink-seller, he would have found her too meek to trust.

He noticed that the sackbut-players, with quarts of drink inside them, were slightly more tuneful.

He saw Robert Allibone saunter away towards the stable-yard, so made excuses and followed him. Always diffident in company, Robert was prone to sneaking off by himself to read. When Gideon first appeared, he had been studying a pamphlet, but he pushed the paper inside his doublet quickly. Side by side, they pissed on the dungheap.

'What's the news?'

'It will keep. I will not spoil your wedding day.'

Neither was in a hurry to rejoin the feast. Allibone addressed his friend with mock-solemnity: 'As your good groomsman, I should ask if you know what is expected of a husband?'

Gideon chuckled bravely. Few men who had been London apprentices needed an eve-of-wedding lecture. 'Lambert is threatening to lurk at the bedside with instructions . . . My father said: eat all that is set in front of you and always give your wife the victory in quarrels. My mother warned me not to spit in the hall, nor wear boots in the bedchamber, nor bring home a dozen ducks on laundry day – all needing to be plucked, glazed and roasted – not even though the purchase price was a great bargain.'

'Your father did that!' marvelled Robert, with admiration.

'And still lives,' Gideon confirmed.

It seemed a moment for confidences. Bevan and Elizabeth had set him wondering, so Gideon asked about the mysterious debt owed to Allibone by the Keevil estate. Robert's face clouded. 'It was an alphabetical debt.'

'Well, recite it.'

'Oh you know my distemper with stockholders . . .'

'Keevil held shares in the English Stock Company?'

During his apprenticeship, Gideon had absorbed the history of printing in London. He knew how William Caxton had first set up in the precincts of Westminster Abbey, producing legal and medical texts, then Caxton's successor, Wynkyn de Worde, moved to Fleet Street, to be close to his lawyer customers. From early days the principle applied that *authors* should not attempt to make a living from writing; their role was merely to keep printers and booksellers in business. Over time, the stationers who provided raw materials – vellum and paper, ink, skins for binding – had gained control of book production. Only their liverymen could print, bind and sell books. The Stationers' Company was self-governing, so entry to the trade was always tightly controlled by insiders. Allibone believed it led to abuse. Under Queen Elizabeth, censorship bit. New books had to be approved by Privy Counsellors and archbishops; the Stationers' Company kept a register of licensed books and allocated to its members the right to print them. This system could be benign, giving work to less prosperous printers – or it could be corrupt. Robert Allibone called it vile.

Stationers' Company involvement was formalised further in 1590, when the English Stock Company was created by the Crown. The money was provided by a hundred and five shareholders. Those shareholders accumulated copyrights in books, copyrights which they passed to their heirs, heirs who were not necessarily printers – and almost never authors. Increasingly, shares in the English Stock and possession of licences went into the hands of booksellers rather than printers.

By the time the civil war began, the Stationers' Company was officially joint-partner with the Crown in imposing censorship and that was Robert Allibone's main grievance. 'A monopoly,' he raged. 'As surely as those on beer and soap that we deplored when the King sold them. Our own company, which ought to have been the first to protect our livelihoods, was coerced and corrupted, cozened and cheated into doing the King's and Archbishop Laud's will for them. The vicious system stank then and it still does. The Stationers' Company did the dirty work of censorship for Star Chamber. When Star Chamber was abolished, we believed the mire was cleansed, but now Parliament has its own machinery, the *Committee for Printing* – oh Lord, how I hate them! – and the same old lackeys are attempting control. But they will not succeed. The people have tasted enjoyment of a free press. There is no going back.'

'Where in all this,' inserted Gideon quietly (he was dogged in discussion), 'was your quarrel with the late Keevil and my uncle Bevan?'

Allibone spoke tersely. 'Abraham Keevil was my master. He taught me well. He was, I rue it, a holder in the English Stock and as a benefit he acquired a licence for printing the ABC primer, which is compulsory in every school.'

'A very great bringer-in of cash, Robert.'

'Assuredly lucrative.'

'And *good work* – we want the people to read . . . So then?'

'Keevil caught some plague or pox. His lads, being barely supervised, lacked the capacity or the application for such a large commission. He and I struck a verbal agreement for me to print copies.'

'You were independent?'

'I had set up alone, having inherited a little money. Keevil knew I would produce the job in timely fashion and decently done. It was an important contract for me. I believe it was a relief to him, too, to share the work with a man he trusted – as he did, for he had trained me. Then his illness finished him.'

Gideon worked out what had happened: 'On Keevil's death, his widow reneged. She placed the job elsewhere.' He wondered whether Robert's preference for Margery was relevant to Elizabeth's action.

'She took it back; organised the staff herself; stole my profit. Perhaps in the chaos of grief,' Robert conceded dryly, though at the time, he had become so aggrieved he had threatened a complaint to the Stationers' Company. 'I had the right of it. Elizabeth knew that. So Bevan Bevan was sent waddling around to see me, silkily proposing we should settle the matter with a fifty pounds down-payment and seven years' use of an honest apprentice . . .'

'You were robbed there!' laughed Gideon.

'So true. At the time it seemed my only hope of compensation!'

Their privacy was at an end. Bevan Bevan staggered out to the courtyard, his white cambric shirt billowing through gaps between the buttons on his scarlet suit. He had grown larger than ever, so his vast thighs were close to splitting the grandiose spangled seams of his bright britches.

'Go in to your bride.' Robert encouraged Gideon with a light push. 'Leave me with the spouting leviathan.'

So Gideon slipped away while Bevan began another slurred tirade against Parliament. Afterwards, Gideon guiltily acknowledged that he had seen the angry glint in Robert's eye. He sensed that his friend was keen for something stronger than argument. Perhaps it had to do with the pamphlet he had put away.

But this was no time to linger. As soon as Gideon returned to the feast, he was gathered up, chivvied and badgered, for his bride was by now waiting in the wedding chamber and he must hasten to her. The quicker he went of his own accord, the less danger that he would be escorted by a throng of tipsy, titillated onlookers. His mother kissed him, shedding a tear. Lambert tagged after him, playing the wise older brother.

'Let me at it, Lambert; this is one thing I must do for myself –'

Lambert blearily cited the musketeer's drill: 'Just ram home and withdraw your scouring stick.'

What? Shivering inside his new shirt, Gideon walked upstairs, aware of every creak in the treads. Downstairs he could hear good-humoured cheers and knew his health was being drunk. Sackbuts hooted hoarsely. 'That is just the rude advice I would expect from a Blue Regiment pikeman.'

Leaning on the lowest baluster, Lambert continued, 'Draw forth your match, boy. Blow the ash from your coal and open your pan . . .'

'Plug your mouth, fool; you have the drill all arsy-versy.'

'Pray the weather be fair, so your weapon will fire – Nay, in the heat of engagement, brother, there is no more to it than this simple order: *prepare, present and give fire!*'

Groaning, Gideon quickly turned a corner out of sight. In his embarrassment, he opened the wrong door. Fortunately that room was empty.

Some kind soul had indicated the bridal bedroom with a wreath of flowers, hung on a nail outside. Still flustered, he grasped the handle and marched straight in. Lacy's almond eyes glared at him, above a dark coverlet. His new wife had just learned that husbands never knock. *'They cannot be changed!'* her aunt had scoffed. Elizabeth should know, thought Lacy, with a hardness that would have astonished her new husband.

Gideon crossed to a chest beneath a window where he sat to pull off his shoes and stockings. He was unknotting the thin, tangled ties of his shirt when a commotion below distracted him so much he opened the leaded casement and leaned out. The noise brought Lacy to his side and they hung over the sill together. Parthenope, weeping with laughter, looked up and waved them impatiently back to their bower, though not before Anne shouted: 'Bevan Bevan has been put in the horse-trough by your friend Allibone!'

Gideon barked with laughter. 'Well that has done for the scarlet suit at last!' Anne gazed up at him fondly. Lacy, she thought, would be well served in her wedding bed, whereas lovemaking with Lambert made his wife feel like a damp sheet being flattened in a mangle . . .

Gideon turned to his bride. She was behind him again, kneeling on the bed, pulling off her nightgown over her head with both arms. The only other naked woman Gideon had ever seen was Mother Eve in a picture. He had pored over the woodcut – yet it bore little relation to real anatomy.

Lacy glared at him. Her long chestnut hair went right down to her . . . She could sit on it. Gideon closed his eyes.

A man may look at his wife.

He opened his eyes again, now fully to attention for what he had to do.

Chapter Nineteen

London: May 1643

The next day, Gideon walked into the print shop with what he hoped was a debonair step. It was late to start work. He had already endured teasing quips about newly-weds lying abed, for he had come from home. It had been decreed, in the way families decide things, that Lacy and he would lodge with his parents temporarily, or 'until your first child comes'.

The notion of a child worried him. Gideon knew what really happened with babies but let himself envisage a small boy in a creased brown suit arriving on the doorstep, aged about five, with his belongings in a tidy snapsack. This imaginary child would 'come' as if ordered from abroad through a long-distance merchant, in the same way that Lambert and his father arranged imports of sultanas and allspice, not expecting word of the produce – or demands for full payment – for many months, if not a year . . .

The couple had money, though it needed careful management. Parthenope and John had given Gideon a generous wedding gift. For a second son he felt secure. Lacy brought a small marriage portion, which seemed to be largess from Bevan and Elizabeth rather than her own parents. With Gideon's printing income, even though it fluctuated crazily, the pair could have rented accommodation straightaway, but it was deemed better to save their shillings and let Lacy be taught house-wifery by Parthenope and Anne. 'Not just *better*, but *necessary!*' was Parthenope's tart verdict. According to Lacy, in Eltham nobody baked, while Elizabeth Bevan had mislaid her pudding bowl for the past two years.

Dumping Lacy at Bread Street, Gideon fled to work. Finding himself ravenous, he bought a muffin. In their tiny premises in Basinghall Street, he discovered Robert Allibone sunk in gloom. 'All well?'

'Aye. And with you?'

'Of course,' muttered Gideon through muffin crumbs.

Allibone gave him a benign nod. 'It gets easier.'

Gideon held back from grumpily demanding, *'What does?'* He flushed scarlet, remembering, then he cursed his fair complexion that so easily gave away his thoughts. Private unease struck him. As he walked through Cheapside and Ironmongers Lane that morning, accompanied by Lambert's terrible sackbuts whose belching valve music had stayed in his head, he had been troubled by memories: Lacy's anxiety, his uncertainty, their fumbled failures at union, his irritation and shame, then her patient suggestions: 'Will it perhaps go *here* more fittingly . . . ?'

He wanted to be a good husband; Lacy seemed more distant than he had hoped. Gideon feared it was due to his deficiencies as a lover. All the same, he was a man, and as he had transferred Lacy from the inn to his parents' house he had put on a show of equilibrium.

'Tell me about the horse-trough!' he instructed Robert briskly.

Allibone always opened up at his own pace. He busied himself with routine tasks, preparing the press for operation. He drew out from his doublet the pages Gideon had glimpsed yesterday. As the pamphlet lay on the flat bed of the press, Gideon saw the frontispiece bore a woodcut of a long-haired horseman, in full cavalry armour, a dog with a leonine mane cavorting at a rampant steed's heels.

'Your uncle picks his moments.' Robert's pamphlet looked lengthy for a news publication; Gideon rapidly assessed it was over thirty pages. 'Out he sailed, so full of incendiary disputatiousness he was fit to pop. He bearded me on the wrong day, Gideon. It was my journeyman's wedding. I desired to be in cheerful mood, but was already downcast. Bevan began boasting how *he* is contributing funds to a Royalist regiment and that with such help the King must return to his palace in the next twelvemonth . . . I was dodging these black bombardilloes, when your brother Lambert came out, with that stranger of his – Saxby? Sextant?'

'Sexby.' Lambert had talked of it with Gideon that morning – anything to avoid discussing his bridal night. 'Lambert knew him as an apprentice. He is going to East Anglia, where a kinsman has raised a troop of horse. Sexby was tempting Lambert to join him, but Anne fixed her cool eye upon my brother and that was the end of any elopement.'

'Well, Bevan set upon Lambert,' Robert growled. 'His new beef was the Lines of Communication: *"Oh, nephew, I hear that you and your mad hothead wife are excavating frozen earth, alongside a thousand oyster-women! You go digging fortifications with mattocks and picks, among confectioners and tailors, with those calumnious rogues from the Common Council, drums thundering and colours flying"* . . .'

After Turnham Green, Parliament had decided that the King's army would inevitably be back to attack London again. They had to increase their earlier hurried fortifications. Citizens rallied and turned out enthusiastically again. New barriers arose that were said to be eighteen Kentish miles long; Kentish miles were famously longer than the legal statute mile. The Lines of Communication surrounded much more of London than the ancient city walls ever had: from Constitution Hill to Whitechapel, going as far north as Islington, and taking in Southwark on the South Bank. The Houses of Parliament, the Tower, part of the River Thames and the docks at Wapping were all now safely enclosed in the citadel. Dutch engineers who were acknowledged experts in military earthworks had been summoned to advise. A complicated system of trenches, dykes and ramparts linked twenty-four substantial forts and redoubts. There were single and double ditches, then single or double palisades, the latter set with sharp pointed stakes facing outwards, a foot apart. The forts, shaped like four- and five-pointed stars for all-round vision, had heavy wooden platforms which bristled with cannon, protected under stone-tiled roofs. There were more than two hundred pieces of ordnance – from demi-culverins that hurled nine-pound balls and demi-cannons that threw twelve-pounders, right up to cannon royal that weighed over three tons and fired enormous missiles weighing sixty-four pounds.

Nobody could enter or leave the city without scrutiny from the sentinels. Companies from Trained Bands regiments were manning the fortifications day and night. It was far from an alarmist measure. Royalist strategy in that year of 1643 centred on a London attack. It was planned that Lord Newcastle in the north, Sir Ralph Hopton in the West Country and the King himself in the Midlands would defeat local opposition, then after meeting the King at Oxford all would surge towards the capital, set up a blockade by sea, and starve London into submission. If such a plan succeeded, which seemed quite likely as Royalist successes grew, Londoners could only hope the Lines of Communication would save them from the plight of so many desperate cities on the Continent.

'On the Continent, and here – as this grim pamphlet illustrates!'

Gideon reached for the pamphlet at last: *Prince Rupert's Burning Love to England, Discovered in Birmingham's Flames.* It was an eye-witness description of what had happened at Easter. *'Wherein is related how that famous and well affected Town of Birmingham was unworthily opposed, insolently invaded, notoriously robbed and plundered, and most cruelly fired in cold blood the next day . . .'* Gideon read it fast. Now he understood Robert's anger, shared it, saw why his colleague's outrage had simmered to a rolling boil with Bevan Bevan. When Bevan endlessly praised the King, whose unrestrained mercenaries had carried out the atrocities in Birmingham, Robert's frustration broke.

'I will not hold your wife's relatives against her, Gideon, but you must separate Lacy from any connection with the King's party. This is civil war. The conflict stalks in the parlour.'

Gideon was shaking his head in disbelief as he read: 'These were ordinary people, penalised – punished – robbed, raped, fired at in their houses, left naked in the street, terrorised with threats of more – a surgeon shot, a madman barbarised – their goods stolen and their homes burned.'

'If I had had my musket yesterday, I would have killed your uncle.'

Gideon looked up with a brief smile. 'That would have made a wedding to remember . . . Yet your nature is too sweet for it; you would have rued the business all your life. Robert, I can now see how you found the strength to tip so large a man into a horse-trough.'

Like Gideon, the printing press had made Robert tough, but he was of neat stature and not tall. 'I am proud of it. I pushed him hard against the trough; when the rim caught his gross thighs, he toppled backwards. A great wave washed over the brim. Then your brother Lambert helped, with that friend of his, who seized Bevan by the feet while Lambert fulcrumed him by his fat head. They spun him around, until he made a full-length fit. Lambert, being no featherweight, then leaned on his belly – I was hammering him flat – Bevan was soon so well wedged, he could not move. Then the sackbuts came and droned him a slow measure, so none could hear his pleas for help.'

'Lambert claims it took five men with a rope on a dray-horse to drag Bevan from his waterbed.'

'Traitors and reprobates,' Allibone declared. 'They should have drowned him.'

'It was impossible,' said Gideon. 'His bulk had swamped out all the water. The landlord begged to have my uncle's great carcass lifted, so he could refill the trough for waiting beasts –' *Thomas, the ostler at the Swan, pistolled, coming officiously to take their horses . . .* 'This news is terrible. What can we do?'

Robert gestured to the printing press. 'Print it. You are reading one of three pamphlets I have seen on the streets about Birmingham. Some scabrous apologist wrote a Royalist version, but there are two lucid rebuttals. This in your hand was published for the Parliamentary committee in Coventry: *"that the Kingdom may timely take notice of what is generally to be expected if the cavaliers' insolences be not speedily crushed".* Gideon, our task must be to gather the facts of this conflict and relate them truly. I have on the press the thoughts of Mr A.R., whom I find always a very considerate, trustworthy commentator.'

'Perhaps I shall meet the gentleman one day!' Gideon knew of several rousing pamphlets by this 'Mr A.R.'. He was sure Robert wrote them, hiding from censorship.

Robert smiled. 'Oh he comes to me bringing his work privately, late at night, and keeps his face hidden.'

'You are still responsible for what you print,' Gideon warned.

'I will answer for it, if challenged. He relates truth and his language is temperate. There are no "Turds shat from the devil's flaming arse" with Mr A.R.'

'And what is his next topic, Robert?'

Robert applied the oily ink to the composited letters with his lambs-wool swab. His freckled face was calm yet alight, as if he were engaged in holy work. 'That Birmingham will prove a disaster for the King. All the country is shocked by these monstrosities. The King hires the filthy foreign troops. His brigand nephew another glorified mercenary – leads them. Incidentally, Charles has been forced to berate Rupert, and to beg him in future to take his subjects' affections rather than their towns. It is scant consolation for the widows and orphans, and those left naked in the street when their homes burned. What may cheer them a little is that Lord Denbigh, a close confidant of the prince and much mourned by him, died from his wounds four days later at Cannock; the best of *that* is that Denbigh's son is staunch for Parliament. But a steel mill in Birmingham which had produced swords for Parliament has been pulled down by malignants – royal supporters lost more goods than anyone else, and they have claimed that the mill caused his anger against the town.'

Gideon was in a dark mood. 'The cavaliers' weapons are fire and fear – but we have our own. Words.'

'Never truer. Telling the news must become regular and accurate. It pains me to say, but the King has equipped himself for propaganda before our party even stirs.' King Charles had always taken a keen interest in what was printed; he had even written self-defensive pamphlets. Robert fumed, 'There is a printing press close to the King in Oxford – though I know of nobody there who belongs to our fraternity.'

'Is the printer a true Royalist', asked Gideon, 'or has he simply seen a way to profit?'

'Why, that would make him an opportunist!' laughed Robert. Neither thought it impossible. 'What's certain is that since January this astute toady has been printing a weekly news-sheet that speaks for the court. *Mercurius Aulicus* – dross, but we have nothing to compete. The King's version is the only version. It is not only produced at Oxford to edify the cavaliers, but it is carried to London in secret pouches and reprinted here in a larger format.'

Gideon straightened up. 'We need a Parliamentary answer – fast.'

'Why, that must be done by a *committee*!' Robert scoffed. Then he grew more serious. 'We must give weekly accounts of debates and events. The sheets must be cheap, no more than a penny or tuppence. They must be sold on every street corner in London, then carried to the provinces and made available at great highroad inns. We cannot have this present situation, where one or two interested parties procure the news from London haphazardly, but only if Honest Ned or the parson happens to be visiting town to sell eggs or see a cousin. Nor can we tolerate Royalist bleats or lies concocted by sloppy scriveners who print the most ridiculous rumours.'

'You must have honest intelligencers.' Gideon was ahead. 'Like those ambassadors to foreign courts, who write accounts of rulers, society and commerce overseas. Kings dispatch and merchants employ such people. Now, here at home, there must be trusted correspondents placed everywhere – in Parliament, close to the King, even on the battlefield.'

Robert nodded. 'And there must be a reliable network of carriers to take the truth every week from the press to the public.'

'Every *week*?'

'Every week,' stated Robert calmly. 'I am ready to work. I shall find scouts. There must be some cobbler in Westminster who can winkle me out information while he taps the members' boot-soles. I know of a victualler who has approval to run delivery carts through Clerkenwell; when he brings in cabbages he can carry out the news. He may need a false base building into his cart —' He realised the scope of this venture was worrying his younger colleague. 'The plan has some danger. You can be in, or out, Gideon.'

'Oh, I am in! What if we cannot discover enough news for the week?'

'We shall fill in with advertisements for ointments. Apothecaries' shillings will fund us.'

'Will it work?'

'Telling the news will be standard practice,' Robert assured Gideon airily. 'Parliament can grumble all it likes: this is the future, my friend.'

Chapter Twenty

London–Gloucester: autumn, 1643

Critics of the *Privileged Corranto* (a few scurrilous rival publications, all of little merit, according to the *Corranto*'s proprietors) would point out that although this journal sounded like a fast Italian courier, it had been named by mistake after a slightly seedy Spanish court dance. Robert and Gideon were unmoved. Printers of the civil war news were capricious, defiant, self-assured, non-compliant individualists. They were their own proprietors. Most wrote their own material. Some were vulgar, slanderous and obscene, though many were earnest moralists. A few wrote for money. That did not necessarily make their articles untrue.

'*"Privileged"* is weak though,' grumbled Gideon, who admired Robert, yet zealously picked on errors. 'It will frighten off the nervous.'

'People will judge from the content,' scoffed Robert.

'No, they won't judge unless they buy – and they will *buy* from the title. If it be lathered in Latin and pomposity, they will turn to some *True Diurnall* – especially if that shows a woodcut of pillaging soldiers roasting naked infants on a stolen spit.'

'Trust a grocer to know what makes people part with their money.'

'Dried prunes do well . . . Call ours the *Plain Speaking Corranto*.'

'The *Honest Corranto, Truthfully Intelligenced and without Lather*?'

'We alienate the soap-boilers then . . .' There was an enclave of soap-boilers only next door in Coleman Street. 'The *London Corranto*?'

'No; we want it to travel further. Why, it shall be the *Public Corranto* and all shall understand it is for them.'

So it was. Gideon never revealed to his partner that the Jukes family jocularly referred to the treasured news-sheet as *Robert's Raisin*. Even Lacy had picked up the habit of mockery, to Gideon's irritation. He bit it back. He did not like to quarrel with her, because she was expecting a child.

It was soon whispered that the producer of the king-congratulating *Mercurius Aulicus* was neither trained nor a licensed printer. 'Oxford University has a licence to print books, but no individual is so privileged.' Robert Allibone had heard gossip about the Royalist printer at his 'ordinary', the tavern which he used for economical daily dining now that Gideon was fed at home. 'This is some spangled parakeet who has been an *actor*.'

Gideon would never shake off his dotterelling. Used to it, he stayed calm. 'They say he is the son of a mayor of Oxford, one John Harris. Apparently the family are vintners and tavern-keepers.'

Robert shook his head. 'How can a wriggling alehouse maggot have got himself a press?'

'Who knows – but a brewer's dray would be heavy enough to carry it into town for him,' said Gideon, whose grocery background always made him consider logistics.

As that year of 1643 went forward, the *Public Corranto* took on Harris and *Mercurius Aulicus*, striving to give the Parliamentary view even though what happened in the war was often confusing. Every district had its sieges and skirmishes. Some actions were part of the overall battle-plan; many fights occurred willy-nilly, when troops unexpectedly happened upon their enemy or the enemy's provision trains. On the whole it was the King's year.

The *Corranto* tried to remain optimistic. But three important Parliamentary leaders were lost that year: first Lord Brooke of Warwick was shot through the eye at Lichfield, picked off by a sniper who had been positioned on the central spire of St Chad's Cathedral, the deaf-and-dumb younger son of local gentry. In June, John Hampden, the famous rebel against Ship Money, one of the Five Members and Pym's most able supporter for reform, received fatal wounds in an engagement at Chalgrove. Overloaded with powder, his pistol blew up; he died four days later, murmuring, 'O Lord! Save my country!' Meanwhile John Pym himself was falling victim to bowel cancer and would breathe his last in December.

Most military successes were on the King's side too. In the north, Lord Newcastle raised the siege of York, occupied Pontefract and Newark, locked in the Parliamentary arsenal at Hull, then heavily defeated Lord Fairfax and his son Sir Thomas at Adwalton Moor. In the south-west,

Sir Ralph Hopton cleared Cornwall and Devon, and moved on Wiltshire and Somerset. He was seriously injured when a careless tobacco pipe exploded a cart of gunpowder, but survived to annihilate Sir William Waller's Parliamentary army at Roundway Down. In July Prince Rupert stormed Bristol, England's second city and a vital port, although he took heavy casualties. The King's main army faced the Earl of Essex between Oxford and Reading, hoping for news that Newcastle and Hopton had overcome all opposition and were marching to join in a grand assault on London.

They never came. Their local levies were refusing to leave their home districts. In the west too, further advances were impossible while Gloucester and Plymouth held out for Parliament. Lord Newcastle was turned back by heavy Parliamentary resistance at Gainsborough, so diverted himself to a siege of Hull. But Royalists were cheered when the Queen at last reached Oxford.

So far there were no grand military sweeps or major battles. The area between the royal capital at Oxford and the King's constant goal of London saw endless manoeuvring. Towns were garrisoned, castles were fortified; they were abandoned for strategic reasons, or taken by the enemy; then they were reinvested or rescued; later, their fortunes often changed again. Small groups of soldiers moved in and then moved on, jostling for possession of local garrisons, farmhouses and market towns. Vital objectives changed hands repeatedly.

For Parliament, the Earl of Essex was criticised for indecision, although he was rarely free to take the initiative: if he moved away, he would leave London undefended. Essex successfully captured Reading, but while he occupied it his men were decimated by camp fever.

At that time the King was very close to recapturing his kingdom. The shifting boundary of Royalist control was little more than forty miles from London as the crow flew. A bird had the advantage. If they came, Royalist soldiers would have to advance on carriageways and byways which for years had been neglected or inconsistently maintained by their parishes and which, as well as being famous for broken bridges, flooded fords and missing signposts, were generally overgrown with trees and hedgerows, choked with mud, and carved up and criss-crossed with ruts like the face of a cheese-grater. Still, both sides kept careful watch on one another. Parliament issued an order that no one might travel from Oxford to London without a pass. Their own scouts and spies were active in the Royalist-held areas. Meanwhile, Royalist spies took detailed notes of the Lines of Communication around London; some were arrested as they scanned the fortifications.

With the King encouraged by his generals' successes and Parliament correspondingly depressed, this stalemate continued to late summer. Then Prince Rupert's capture of Bristol turned royal eyes to the west. Bristol surrendered in just three days, though the defenders under Nathaniel Fiennes were sufficiently brave for Rupert to allow them to march out with full honours. Parliament was angrier at Fiennes's conduct and court-martialled him for dereliction of duty; he was only spared through the intervention of the Earl of Essex.

Meanwhile the Parliamentary commander William Waller sustained a grave defeat. Waller's previous string of local victories had made him a hero to Parliament; perhaps fatally, he saw himself as a hero too. He made vainglorious boasts and even procured a wagon-load of leg-irons for anticipated Royalist prisoners. But at Roundway Down he failed to post scouts and fatally lost the advantage. Hopton's Royalists obtained reinforcements and charged gallantly uphill; they pushed some of the Parliamentary cavalry over a precipice and then bloodily routed the infantry. Waller fled to Bristol, unaware of the scale of the damage; his few surviving men were so dispirited they deserted. Waller then took himself to London where he was nonetheless welcomed as 'William the Conqueror'. Church bells rang and he made a stirring speech in Middle Temple Hall. The Earl of Essex, who loathed Waller – especially for having lost a fine army – was outraged. He fumed even more when Parliament decided it was now necessary to recruit a new national army – which Waller would lead.

Attempts to negotiate peace with the King in Oxford had failed. Essex's troops were broken by lack of resources and disease. He struggled to convince Parliament to give him financial aid but all available funds were about to be siphoned off to Waller. Then in August, before Waller's new army was ready, the King personally besieged the city of Gloucester. This was to prove a turning point.

Gloucester's position was perilous. Far up the River Severn, with the enemy now controlling the Bristol Channel on both sides, it was a puritan merchant city holding out alone in the heartland of Royalist control. It constantly threatened the King's recruiting operations in South Wales, his supply route by sea and his ironworks in the Forest of Dean. When Charles decided to remove this annoyance, he was full of confidence. He believed that his headquarters at Oxford and numerous Royalist garrisons in the surrounding area shielded him. It was inconceivable that the Earl of Essex could bring through any relief.

Gloucester seemed likely to fall as easily as Bristol. Charles was convinced its young military governor, Colonel Edward Massey, would capitulate. Even Royalist merchants in Gloucester viewed the coming Royalist army with such fear – in the light of events at Birmingham – they offered the King a fortune in return for reassurance that only supporters of Parliament would have their property ransacked. Charles promised a free pardon to everyone, if the town immediately gave up. He declared that Gloucester had no hope, for 'Waller is extinct and Essex cannot come'.

As the Royalist guns began to thunder and as siege engineers set about undermining the city walls, Gloucester sent desperate pleas for help from London.

Londoners were filled with fear and gloom. If Gloucester fell, London must soon be picked off too. Pamphleteers did their work; false rumours flew that the King was bringing an army of twenty thousand Irishmen. All suburban shops situated outside the Lines of Communication were ordered to close. The Common Council petitioned Parliament; Parliament instructed the lord mayor to take steps to quell the tumults that were once again disturbing the streets. A group of 'civilly disposed women' petitioned the Commons about their hardships and were put off with soothing words. A letter was sent to encourage Gloucester to hold out, while a Parliamentary committee ordered the Earl of Essex to prepare a relief force. Crucially, when Essex mustered his main army on Hounslow Heath, he knew he was to have nearly fifteen thousand men. To beef up his infantry, he would be supported by some of the London Trained Bands.

Chosen by lot were the Red Regiment, which recruited inside the city wall near the Tower, and the Blue Regiment, which drew its members from west of the Walbrook – Lambert Jukes's regiment. They sent a thousand men each. Also to go were three thousand auxiliaries, drawn from the Red, Blue and Orange regiments. On the first night of their march, they camped at Brentford; there some members' eagerness ebbed. They realised they faced weeks away from their homes and businesses, which many had never left before in their lives, not to mention deprivation, hard marching and possible death. They were permitted to find substitutes. Gideon Jukes, who was a member of the Green Regiment which would remain guarding London, received an urgent note from his brother to inform him of this opening. Urged on by Robert Allibone, who wanted him to write reports for the *Corranto*, Gideon volunteered to change places with a worried woollen draper from the Reds. So both Jukes brothers set out on their first adventure in the field.

The journey west was close on 150 miles. Choosing a long route to avoid the buzzing nest of Royalists at Oxford, the march took twelve days. The London Brigade formed up on the Artillery Ground and had marched for six days before they caught up with the regular army at Aylesford. Then they travelled with the main force, sometimes ahead, sometimes parallel, sometimes behind. Occasionally they sheltered in barns or were entertained at private houses, but mostly these supposedly soft city lads ate only what they could gather from the countryside, drinking brackish water, bivouacked out of doors, sleeping on the ground, lucky if they could make campfires with hedgerow branches or wooden palings and gates. They remained in good spirits, treating it as a duty and an adventure.

They safely bypassed Oxford to the north. As they passed Banbury, they were harried by Royalists under Lord Wilmot. When they entered Northamptonshire, Essex doubled the pace of their march. On the 2nd of September they were twenty-five miles from Gloucester. Royalist skirmishing increased. Prince Rupert met them with around four thousand cavalry at Stow-on-the-Wold. Great squadrons of Royalist horse began to surround the London Brigade, but were beaten off by the main force, using light cannon and dragoons. It was unsafe to halt at Stow so they marched on into the uplands until midnight, sleeping out in the fields where they dropped.

Gideon was anxious. By now they had no provisions. The countryside had been stripped by the enemy of all food, fuel and horse fodder. Everything Gideon had hastily packed in his snapsack had been used up days ago. Bread and beer were a dream; a sour windfall apple, scrounged from an orchard, was a luxury. Unwashed and with shirt and stockings unchanged, his skin was itching and uncomfortable; his own smell was offensive and his comrades repulsed him. Occasionally on the march he caught sight of his brother among the pikemen; set-faced, they conserved energy and exchanged no greeting. Both had learned to tramp ever onwards in a kind of daze, letting hours and miles pass unnumbered. In the damp wolds above Stow, as he lay down stiffly on bare ground with his stomach rumbling, Gideon wondered how much longer the men could continue in this fashion. For him, there was certainly no chance of sitting each evening with a rushlight and writing-slope, to pen a diary for the *Corranto*. A writer needs a good memory. But he was so weary and famished, he thought it unlikely he would ever remember details of the hardships he now experienced.

He had been sorely afraid when Prince Rupert's cavalry threatened to cut them off at Stow. Worse must lie ahead. By this time the Londoners all understood that, even if they were able to help Gloucester, their chances of returning home were slight.

On the evening of September the 5th, they marched over the Cotswolds and from a high point glimpsed Gloucester below. It lay too far off for the town garrison to hear the salvo of ordnance that Essex fired to announce that help had come. His troops had to spend the night up on the heights, famished, in tempestuous wind and rain, drenched and completely without shelter. When they descended the steep incline, wagons ran adrift, horses were fatally hurt and the men of the London Brigade found that by the time they reached level ground, all the houses where they had hoped to find refreshment were already filled up with other soldiers.

Rest and recuperation would be at hand, however. Alarming smoke turned out to be the enemy's quarters burning, set on fire as the King withdrew at their approach. After a month's siege, only sporadic fire came from the city, where stocks of ammunition had reached a critical low. Gloucester had survived only because incessant rain had flooded mines dug by the Royalists under walls and gates. The governor had sent out nightly raiding parties to sabotage the enemies' works; it was said he plied them with as much drink as they wanted to encourage their bravery, but there were many tales of energy and daring among those who volunteered for night-time missions. Bowmen had fired arrows from both sides, carrying written insults and threats. Fierce resistance by the city troops, together with the staunch mood of the townspeople, had helped Gloucester hold out, although by the time Essex and his army finally marched in, every commodity was stretched and they were down to their last three barrels of gunpowder.

The relief force found terrible scenes. Physical damage ran to thousands of pounds. Sixty-pound shot had torn up the ground. Fiery bombs with sizzling fuses had shot through the air at night like comets, only to whiz through stables too fast to set light to the straw and fall onto house-tops where they melted the lead and caused roofs to collapse. The city defences had been mined and counter-mined. The moat was partially blocked up with timber faggots and with the collapsed remains of experimental moving towers, modelled by some gentleman-scholar on ancient Roman siege-machines, for carrying parties of musketeers up to the city walls. The devastation particularly impressed itself on the Londoners, the Trained Band members, who were thinking hard of home.

The starving relief force was welcomed, fed and housed either in the city or surrounding parishes. They stayed for four days. Gloucester was reprovisioned, refortified, rearmed. The troops could rest and revive, but they knew the King was skulking close by, watching their moves, ready to cut them to pieces when they tried to make their journey home.

By now they were all experts. They knew their position.

'We're screwed!' muttered Lambert Jukes to his brother, picking up the old merchants' complaint about the injustice of the Ship-Money tax.

'Utterly screwed and wrung,' groaned Gideon in reply.

The relieving troops had done their duty, but were caught in a fatal trap.

Chapter Twenty-One

Gloucester, Newbury, London: 1643

The Earl of Essex, Old Robin, received insufficient credit for his cat-and-mouse Gloucester campaign. Getting there had caught the Royalists on the hop; extricating his army, if he could do it, would be an even greater feat.

First, leaving behind his artillery and baggage, he moved north to Tewkesbury. He ordered a classic bridge of boats over the River Severn. Villages on the west bank were scoured for food and fodder, while recalcitrant locals were swingeingly fined and the cash used to reprovision Gloucester. Then Essex sent across an advance unit as if he proposed to march on Worcester. The King immediately moved north, to block the way towards London via Evesham and Warwick.

Under cover of a dark night, Essex suddenly plunged his army south again. They travelled twenty miles across the Cotswolds and gained a day's advantage. Their rapid departure confused Royalist scouts and commanders, including Prince Rupert – though Rupert afterwards claimed he had warned what was happening but was disbelieved. At two o'clock in the morning, Essex reached Cirencester. There he captured forty wagon-loads of food intended for the King's troops and guarded only by newly raised recruits. These provisions crucially fortified his men for the perils ahead. Hunted by Prince Rupert's flying cavalry and pursued by the King with his infantry and ordnance, the Parliamentarians raced for home.

They almost made it. Prince Rupert had orders to find them and force them to make a stand at Newbury, where it was thought the superior numbers of Royalist cavalry could inflict mortal damage. He harried them at Aldbourne, trying to delay them while the main Royalist army caught up. The next day they slowed almost to a standstill as bad weather churned roads to a morass. They were hungry again, for although they had picked up a thousand sheep and sixty cattle as they marched, Londoners did not see themselves as shepherds so the animals had scattered while the soldiers gave their attention to an attack. By this night they were unsure where the enemy now was. As Essex's men approached Newbury, their quartermasters rode in to establish billets, only to discover that Prince Rupert had occupied the town ahead of them. Forced to flee, they abandoned all the food they had collected. So the Parliamentarians faced yet another wretched night in wet, frosty fields, with nothing to eat or drink. Prince Rupert blocked their passage at Newbury; he and his men settled into the town in comfort and waited for the King. The royal infantry arrived. Out in the countryside, the Parliamentarian troops were fatigued and full of anxiety. The King had put himself ahead of them. They had to fight their way through. It would be the first time that the London Trained Bands experienced a pitched battle.

Gideon Jukes's experience that night was of utter misery. They had seemed so near to home, yet now they were once again trapped in filthy conditions, knowing that they had to batter past the Royalist army — assuming they could. The enemy were relaxing in town, snug and warm in friendly houses, with full bellies and good supplies of beer. Gideon had only eaten a handful of maggoty blackberries all day. He was wet through, yet thirsty, trying to catch rain in a pannikin to drink. They had left behind the towering clouds that scudded up the Bristol Channel, bloated with heavy Atlantic rain, but here in the interior they were still being soaked by incessant showers and tonight they had to endure a hard frost. He could feel that frost beating up from the ground while the evening air chilled him to the bone.

He had marched for a month; he remembered how the first bad weather had run off his clothes, then eventually runnels had trickled inside his shirt and over his collarbones, water dripping from his hat onto his face, water making his shoes squelch, drips hanging permanently from his nose and ears. Once he became wet through, weeks ago, there had never been any way to dry off, even when temporary fine weather gave some respite. The insides of his britches and his buff coat remained soggy; the oil sealing his oxhide buff coat could no longer resist water. His stockings were perpetually damp and his shoes sodden. Whenever he stood still, he shifted from leg to leg, arms slightly akimbo, trying to keep free space between his heavy clothes and his skin, which was now sore, reddened and peeling. One night he had found his left shoe full of blood, from a huge blister which then refused to heal. He had pushed his powder flasks and matchcord inside his clothes to try to keep them dry, but he had so little warmth in his body this was probably achieving little. If he had to fight for his life, would his musket even fire?

So another dark, wild night passed in the open. Essex, Skippon and a few other officers found refuge in a thatched cottage near Enborne where they snatched rest and prayer and planned for the day to come. Out in the fields their men huddled under hedges, silent and apprehensive. Rain bucketed down incessantly. Winds bowled over the lonely Berkshire uplands in long, mournful gusts. Neither weasel nor water-vole was stirring, and the owls stayed in the barn.

The apprehensive troops rubbed the sleep from their sticky eyes early. Essex had to tell them that the enemy possessed all the advantages: 'the hill, the town, hedges, lane and river'. Inspired to defiance, his men roared back that they would take them all. They put greenery in their hats for recognition purposes.

Realistically, their options were nil. They had nowhere to retreat. Outflanking the Royalists looked impossible. Their way forward through Newbury was blocked. The Royalists held the crucial bridge over the River Kennet. The only alternative route entailed a detour south across various small field enclosures and hazardous open areas of common-land; it was rough country through which they would have to march and drag their artillery while the enemy constantly attacked them.

Essex chose this south passage. He disguised his intentions as long as possible with a 'forlorn hope' that pretended to be advancing on Newbury. In a landscape still marked by inhabitants from before the Romans, ancient tumuli would cover their real march to some extent. At seven in the morning, in a flat valley between Enborne and Newbury, the Parliamentarians drew up their line. They were positioned along a narrow country lane, intending to move through as a body, then up and over Wash Common which lay to their right. Skippon's brigade occupied the centre, the Trained Bands behind him, acting as reserves and guarding another overgrown and rutted lane which was the only way their artillery train could come up to move onto the common. The guns had to be dragged up a steep incline and even before that could begin, they took three hours to arrive on the scene. But Skippon took early control of a deceptive high point called Round Hill, which fooled the Royalists into believing the Parliamentarians were siting a battery there, with a plan to assault the bridge at Newbury.

The London Trained Bands had been desperately trying to gather nuts and berries from hedgerows as a meagre breakfast, when they heard the sounds of cavalry fighting; Royalist Welshmen had attacked the Parliamentary left flank. *'We were in despair,'* mused Gideon Jukes, in his head whimsically becoming the kind of correspondent Robert Allibone wanted, *'lest the enemy discovered we were so starved that if they but shouted "Toasted cheese!" we would straightway drop our weapons and rush to them, fainting . . .'* Instead, the Trained Bands arrived at a running march and in a great sweat, afraid they would miss the fight. There was no chance of that.

It had stopped raining.

The Red and Blue regiments spent most of the day on their army's right flank. They were facing eight Royalist guns and a large body of cavalry, barely the length of two musket shots apart. Prince Rupert himself was about to charge them.

The Red Regiment had been attacked before, at Stow-on-the-Wold and again at Aldbourne Chase. Gideon had fired off his musket, though never before in the thick of fighting, where he knew for sure his bullets were bringing wounds and death. Still, he found himself calm here. He understood that he and his colleagues were dismissed as inept, even by their own side. But critically the Trained Bands had practised, unlike more recently recruited troops. They were inexperienced under fire but had repeated their drill every fortnight until it was second nature; also now they had a month of hardship on the road bonding them. Drawn from shops, workshops and the Customs House, they were clerks, dyers, distillers, confectioners, printers, drapers, tailors, woodmongers and vinegar-sellers. Nothing was expected of them, so they had it all to prove. Labour and business had made them strong and self-willed. Besides, they were Londoners. They wanted to go home.

Throughout that long day, the infantry had very little idea what was happening elsewhere. Frequently it was a formless battle, with the attacking Royalists slight on strategy. Bodies of men locked together and pushed pointlessly for hour after hour, neither side making ground. Afterwards Gideon learned that on the left flank, up against the River

Kennet, Parliamentary cavalry fought back so hard they put their opponents to flight; in the centre Skippon's infantry brigade slogged it out for Round Hill against two of the Byron brothers' horse; on the right, Royalist cavalry tried to beat back the Parliamentarians from Wash Common, surrounding them in a desperate close struggle until many had died and the remainder were spent. The Trained Bands then bore the brunt of the enemy's attacks, holding their own as they fought furiously all day, to the astonishment of those who had previously disparaged them.

'No chance of missing,' murmured Gideon through the lead bullets he was holding in his teeth, as he set his musket on its rest. It was his last coherent thought all day.

The first time he fired, Gideon mentally followed all the twenty-four actions of musket drill. Just as Lambert had said to him on his wedding night, the motions often became reduced to: *prepare, present and fire!* Somehow – *open, clear, prime, shut* – he managed – *powder, bullet, scouring stick, rest, coal, match* – a smile at the old memory. *Give fire!*

For a very short time after the firing began, the white gunsmoke hanging low in the frost seemed no worse than a fine drift from an autumn bonfire. Soon Gideon's eyes were stinging. The powder smoke rapidly grew so thick it was impossible to see more than a few yards around, while the endless noise was wearying. A musket shot from the rank of men behind him was so loud against his head it temporarily deafened him, so he went through most of the battle in a weird world of his own. He could none the less hear the screams of wounded men and horses. He could see the terrible havoc wreaked when the Royalists fired their heavy guns. A whole file in the Red Regiment, six men deep, was beheaded together by a single cannon ball. Shocked soldiers wondered at dead men's bowels and brains flying up in their faces. Gideon smelled and was splattered by the organs and innards of men he had known. He gagged and fought on.

The fallen were left. Someone warned, 'If you're hurt, stay upright.' It was the best advice. As Gideon struggled forward or back, he stumbled and knew his feet were trampling the helpless. In the close fighting, wounded men and sometimes corpses were carried to and fro by the press of their colleagues.

They had learned that in the line of march, infantry were vulnerable to cavalry. They could be picked off into manageable groups.

They could be routed and scattered. But cavalry were vulnerable to cannon. And here, with two Trained Bands regiments steadfast in a body, cavalry could fail. When the Royalists temporarily silenced their great artillery and Prince Rupert led his cavaliers in their expensive coats on their fine horses against the Reds and Blues, at first the Trained Bands were terrified. They then learned just what the prince's famous 'thunderbolt charge' meant. They saw the dark massed lines of horsemen advancing towards them at a walk, which turned to a canter, which turned to a full gallop, then the cavaliers in the ranks all fired their first pistols at once from close range.

They only fired once, hoping for a devastating effect. But gunshot from horseback was problematic. Cavalrymen had two pistols each and could usually afford the best, but they kept their second gun in reserve. It was impossible to hold the reins and reload unless they withdrew from the mêlée. While they fired, their aim was spoiled by their horses' movements. Cavalry manuals suggested they should not fire until they rode right in among the enemy and could place a weapon point-blank against an opponent's breast. Prince Rupert preferred his men to rely on swords and poleaxes – but that required close contact.

At Newbury the cavaliers could not get close. The Trained Bands stood firm and stopped them. First a storm of small-shot from the musketeers took some heat from the charge, then at close range the pikes showed their power. Horsemen could do little against heavy-set men in breastplates who were used to manhandling bales and barrels; shoulder to shoulder, the Red and Blue regiments stood up to Rupert's legendary cavalry as cheerfully as if they were engaged in a tug-of-war among the roast pigs at Bartholomew Fair. Setting their right feet sideways, to give purchase for their staves, they showed what 'push of pike' could mean. Their long ash pikes, armed with vicious eighteen-inch steel barbs, held the horsemen off. Prince Rupert charged them once, and twice, then he gave up a bad business after suffering enormous losses.

Once a group of Royalist cavalry approached with green boughs in their hats crying 'Friends! Friends!'

'I don't *think* so!' muttered Gideon, as he and his colleagues rammed home more bullets, then swung their muskets at these conniving rogues and let off an unfriendly reply.

*   *   *

By seven o'clock in the evening, after a full twelve hours of fighting, the light had gone. In the dark, fighting came close to a lull. More ammunition had been spent than in any engagement so far. Powder and shot had run low. The King held a council of war. As an intermittent flare of shots still burst overhead in the smog and darkness, his casualties were assessed. There were about three and a half thousand dead on the field. The King had lost perhaps a quarter of his men, including twenty-five aristocratic officers, one of them his Secretary of State. It was clear that the wretched, starving and exhausted enemy would not surrender. Though Prince Rupert urged fighting on, as the prince generally did, all the Royalist artillery was towed from the field and the King retreated by night to Oxford. At ten o'clock, Essex's men found themselves alone on the field. They had been pushed back from the common, though no further, and were still standing in their ranks. In real terms, since they held their ground despite all that was thrown at them, the Parliamentarians had won.

Next morning was for counting and collecting the dead and wounded. The hard-hearted called this the butcher's bill. The King wrote to the Mayor of Newbury, ordering him to give medical attention to both sides. Only the lightly wounded, those with slashes and cuts, ever stood much chance of recovery. The terrible burns and internal injuries caused by shot and gunpowder were almost impossible to treat. Even those who survived temporarily were doomed if infection had been carried into their bodies by soil or clothing scraps. Gideon learned that a musket ball, his weapon, made a wound no wider than a sixpence on entry, but its exit was the size of a dinner-plate. Even pikemen, who wore breastplates and helmets, could be physically shredded if musket shots struck their ash staves into giant splinters. He saw devastating damage: shattered bones, spilling organs, missing faces, sheared skin, split skulls, suppurating powder burns that were unbearably painful and hideous to see.

And Gideon witnessed the dead. The London regiments suffered heavy losses: men he knew and strangers – he tried not to look. The Royalists reportedly collected thirty cartloads of dead and wounded on the night of the battle, then twenty more the next day. The Earl of Essex had no choice but to bury his lost troops under mighty mounds of earth. These new tumuli would stand as memorials at Newbury for centuries. On both sides the notables who had been killed were listed.

The rest, stripped and jumbled into mass graves, would be anonymous. Many were trampled beyond recognition. Their relatives could only deduce their fates from silence; their resting places would remain unknown.

The subdued Parliamentarians regrouped and marched over Wash Common, as they had originally intended. Close to Aldermaston, Prince Rupert came up and harried them hard but despite much panic, they beat him off and successfully reached safety at their own garrison at Reading. There at last, for three days, they rested and were fêted.

For Gideon Jukes, now suffering from deep shock as well as exhaustion, this period passed in a daze. Others succumbed to weakness, weariness, trauma and depression. Gideon at least stayed alive. His brother found him spent and dead-eyed, able only to sit with hunched shoulders, waiting for new orders. They both had red eyelids and choked lungs; their clothing was stiff with dried blood and other substances. They sat together in Reading, drinking ale. Neither spoke.

The London Brigade resumed its homeward march. Eight days after the battle of Newbury, the Trained Bands entered their home city via Southwark, crossing on London Bridge, that famous landmark lined with tight-packed old wooden houses where the mouldering heads of traitors were traditionally displayed. They marched through streets lined with cheering crowds and were welcomed by the Mayor and civic dignitaries at Temple Bar. They were led to Guildhall in triumph, but as the rest of London celebrated, gradually the shattered troops slipped away to their families.

Gideon and Lambert were brought to their parents' house by Robert Allibone. He had had the sense to commandeer a dray. First, to spare their family, he took them to the print shop, stripped off their disgusting outer clothes and ordered the apprentice Amyas to scrub Lambert's breastplate and burn whatever was too revolting to retrieve.

When the two soldiers limped indoors together, in their grey shirts and stockinged feet, they both managed smiles for their mother.

'Oh my heart, they are skin and bone!' gasped Parthenope faintly. Their father took one look at his boys' scarred and powder-burned faces and knew. Their faraway eyes told the story. They were home safe. But they had been among terror from which they would never entirely return to him. 'Gently,' murmured John Jukes, more to his squealing womenfolk than his silent sons, as Lambert and Gideon hung their heads and Parthenope and Anne fell upon them, weeping.

Gideon's wife Lacy entered the parlour. He was startled how much more pregnant she looked. He had been away just a month. It felt like a lifetime. His wife – he had almost forgotten he had one – looked equally vacant. Lacy was still musing on her day's lesson: there were four types of almond, some sweet and some bitter, of which she could never distinguish between Jordans and Valencians . . .

Lacy wrinkled her nose. Then she burst out in high annoyance: 'They stink!'

Neither Gideon nor Lambert cared. They were asleep on their feet.

Chapter Twenty-Two

Oxford: 1643

When her husband left her that April to go north with Prince Rupert towards Birmingham, Juliana Lovell's life as a wife properly began. This was how it would be during most of her marriage: he would go off, for increasingly long periods; she would be alone, struggling in poverty, not knowing if they would ever see one another again. Many shared this position, but most women who watched their husbands leave with the troops had friends and family to alleviate their loneliness and to help if they were widowed. She had no one.

She spent her eighteenth birthday alone, her first ever without any other family members. Now certain she was pregnant, Juliana wanted to make plans for herself and the child, if it lived. She found herself fretting helplessly over what they should do or where they could go if anything happened to Lovell, since Oxford held nothing for her without him. Ruefully she faced the possibility that marriage, that supposed safe haven for women, had only brought her the added burden of the child. Frustrated and sad, and more depressed as she mused on her life because of her anniversary, she went out for a walk. She would become very familiar with this city.

On her return to the house, she made the mistake of mentioning her birthday to their landlord. The glover at once presented her with a delicate pair of pale kidskin gloves. For an instant Juliana was grateful, then she stiffened and knew she had made a serious mistake. He must have been thinking up ways to ingratiate himself and she had handed him a fatal chance. She would pay a price for this gift – things she would never wear and could no longer bear to contemplate. The gloves were too small for her, anyway. They were probably too tight for anyone, which was why the man had parted with them. Now he thought she was his to claim; he was enjoying her discomfiture while he brooded on when and how to exact a show of gratitude. He could not believe his luck: the absent captain's wife was extremely young, bright-eyed and presentable. The glover, who had once bitterly resented having lodgers imposed on him, now salaciously saw the benefits.

He either did not know, or did not care, that she was breeding. Early pregnancy had its own allure, in any case – not least that a wife already pregnant by her husband held no risks of claims for fathering a bastard child.

His name was Wakelyn Smithers. He was one of the many townsmen who slyly endured the King's presence because it brought trading opportunities. By religion he was a lacklustre Independent, who served fowl instead of fish on Fridays in order to pinpoint his views for his lodgers, should any of them consider him guilty of popery. His real crimes were livid lechery and undercooking the small cuts on the turnspit. He supported Parliament, at least to the extent of voting for puritan town councillors, though he was allergic to giving money and if ever called upon to fight he would have added fifteen years to his age without a qualm and feigned a carbuncle that prevented marching. A physician was invited to dine once a month, which Juliana believed was to facilitate obtaining a medical note quickly.

Unmarried, Wakelyn Smithers gave the impression he had never had a wife. Juliana did not enquire, though she had spotted a meat charger so hideous that it had to be someone's wedding present. Taking meals here had been bad enough when Lovell was with her. Being forced to dine with Smithers alone would have been tortuous, though tabling with the landlord was her only choice; no respectable woman could go out unaccompanied to inns or ordinaries. Fortunately Juliana got through mealtimes at her lodgings because there were other people present: the silent cooper, his belly as round as the barrels he made, who lodged in the attic above her; the glover's depressed apprentice, Michael; Troth, the sniffing scullery maid who came in twice a day to wash dishes and mend fires; and the glover's overweight, permanently breathless sister. The sister was in her forties, a viciously pious widow whose marriage had been short and inharmonious. Her asthmatic condition was aggravated by the smoke if she sat too close to the fire, yet she hogged it relentlessly. She treated Juliana as a dangerous seductress; the beleaguered girl could never hope for assistance there. Complaint about the glover's behaviour would only confirm the sister's mean-eyed suspicion.

To escape Smithers's ominous friendliness (for he worked from a bench at home), Juliana increased her time out of doors by day, roaming endlessly around Oxford. The markets held limited interest for someone who had to watch every penny, while the butchers' shambles were sordid, with bloody bones and offcuts thrown into Queen Street, where there was no watercourse to carry the stinking flux away. Unaccompanied women were refused entry to the colleges, even now there were virtually no young scholars left here. To Juliana's regret, her sex barred her from the libraries. She would stroll in the Parks or by the river as long as she could, but it was dreary and perhaps foolhardy alone, while the spring weather soon chilled her. Buffeting through the streets was warmer, though equally tiring. Oxford was desperately crowded. The early years of the century had seen intensive building, with parks and orchards and any empty plots inside the city walls being covered over by new colleges and houses, to the detriment of the environment. Though not true slums, crowded lodgings and cottages had been crammed down entries and lanes, where they now filled up with Royalists. Shortage of space at ground level meant houses' upper storeys often hung over the streets, 'jettied out' as it was called, which increased the feeling of congestion. Most streets only had a gravel surface, with minimal or no drainage, a clutter of impeding signs and a ripe embroidery of dunghills. The broad main highways had frequently been encroached, with a line of shambles or cottages squeezed up their centre, narrowing the way and annoying those who lived in the finest houses by taking their light, spoiling their views, destroying their peace and their exclusivity.

Through the puddled thoroughfares tramped the teeming life of university and town, embellished now by a local garrison of over two thousand foot soldiers and three regiments of horse, plus the incomers of the royal court, from anxious lords and bored ladies to poulterers and pastry-makers, tennis teachers and dancing masters. All cursed their mud-splashed hems as they milled in a stew of brewers, builders and butter women, dons and college servants, priests and lawyers, along with the horses of cavalrymen and distributors who all thought they had right of way, fighting for space with protesting herds of raided cattle. Everyone was raucously abused by the traditional uncooperative low-life of lewd women and disorderly persons. Sometimes there were arrests. At Carfax, villains who committed lesser crimes were made to 'ride the wooden horse' as punishment, sitting painfully astride two planks to atone for theft or obscenity. Occasional hangings took place there. Some saw these as entertainment; Juliana had a gentler attitude to human life.

If there was no market, Juliana would sit to rest on Penniless Bench. This wooden seat, about a hundred years old, attached to the City Church of St Martin's, was where the butter girls sold their produce, citizens met, and the King had been welcomed on his first arrival with a gift of two hundred pounds – accompanied by the hopeful but futile hint that Oxford could afford no more. Once Juliana was moved on by a beadle who pronounced her a vagrant. Ruefully, she reflected that she was little better, though her habit of reading the news sheet *Mercurius Aulicus*, which was now produced for the King by a lively, satirical editor called John Berkenhead, should have identified her as literate gentry, merely troubled by lack of funds. Once she herself had to summon the beadle, when she found a dead soldier lying under the bench; the parish took away the corpse for burial.

When desperate for refuge from the crowds, she elected to become devout. While many Oxford worshippers liked short services, Juliana sought churches with verbose preachers where she could shelter for longer; a two-hour sermon suited her well and she learned to doze gently while sustaining an attentive expression. She would have been better provided for in the East End of London, where in the most Independent parishes lecturers were hired to give four-hour morning sermons, after which a new set of afternoon lecturers gave four hours more, speaking *ex tempore* with magnificent passion. In Oxford, worship was high; altars were ornately railed to protect the perfumed sanctity of God from persons with grubby consciences and muddy shoes. Sermons were intellectual, pre-written and dry; they were read by fleshy ministers with plummy voices who could spot a button slipped into the collection plate at twenty paces, or scrawnier men who used Latin like a flail to exclude their inferiors. Some churches were available to a pregnant woman seeking grace and respite for her weary feet, though not all: from time to time Royalist soldiers were billeted in St Michael's and St Peter-le-Bailey, until the despairing church-wardens paid them to find lodging out of town. Parliamentary prisoners were kept in St Giles, St Mary Magdalen and St Thomas, causing damage for which the King had had to pay compensation. Their lot was better than those who were locked up in the castle, who were said to have deplorable conditions.

In the hope of deterring the glover, Juliana made sure he knew of her churchgoing. It merely encouraged him. A girl with high morals was far more of a challenge – and clean goods, moreover.

Juliana would have liked to remain quietly in her room. She had been brought up to do embroidery, tatting, lace-making and sewing; among the gentry these were just about regarded as ladylike activities – though not so admirable as ornamental flower-painting, which shamed no one since it had no practical use. She had great talent in design herself, but also possessed many patterns created and drawn by her grandmother. These called to her as she filled in time with piety, and one cold day she became incensed that fear of her landlord was keeping her from home. From then on she spent more time in her lodgings, though she made sure when she sat working at her table she had a sharp array of needles and scissors displayed as a deterrent. She would slip into the house discreetly when she thought the glover was busy with customers. If he did accost her, she insisted on discussing sermons and scripture until his eyes glazed. Once she was in her room, she would remain still and quiet, hoping he might forget her presence.

It could not last. One night she awoke in her bed, horrified to feel a man lying on top of her. His great weight and beery gusts of breath confirmed it was not Lovell. While the fellow fumbled in the dark, Juliana screamed. Though he tried to silence her, she managed to avoid the fat hand scrabbling for her mouth. She kept screaming, even though she thought nobody would come to her aid – and was amazed when Smithers the glover rushed up the stairs and burst in with a candle, shouting.

In the dim light she saw that her assailant was the cooper who lodged upstairs. He rolled one way, spitting curses at her; she tumbled off the bed the other.

In the tiny house this coarse man had to pass right through her room on the staircase by the fireplace every time he came and went. Juliana hated it, though she had lived in similar situations with her grandmother. She had barely exchanged nods, preferring to keep a kind of privacy by pretending the barrel-cooper did not exist. He certainly knew that Lovell was away with Prince Rupert. This night, returning drunk from the Mitre or the Angel, he had seized his moment.

The cooper shambled off upstairs. The glover became nobly indignant, though it was hypocritical. Both men matter-of-factly assumed that any lone female was available to those who wanted her, whatever her own morals or her husband's potential jealousy. There was never a suggestion that the landlord might evict the culprit. Only his embarrassment at being seen stumbling over the hem of his ridiculously voluminous nightshirt made Smithers withdraw from Juliana's room.

She had been saved from rape, or whatever abuse the cooper could have managed in his drunken state. Juliana now found herself having to be grateful to Wakelyn Smithers. This was a nuisance to both of them, because for at least a week the glover felt obliged to maintain his role as honest pillar of respectability.

That did not last. Now the glover was aware of the cooper's interest and brooding over his permitted thoroughfare through the Lovells' room. Smithers became determined not to see another man get to Juliana before him.

The weeks were passing more slowly than the nervous girl could bear. Occasionally news filtered in of Prince Rupert's campaigns. Satisfaction greeted the sack of Birmingham, less joy when it was reported that Colonel Russell, the Parliamentary governor at Lichfield, had refused to surrender to Prince Rupert, on the grounds that his atrocities were 'not becoming a gentlemen, a Christian, or an Englishman, much less a prince'. About three weeks after the cavaliers first left Oxford, Juliana heard someone at market maintaining the King was at Wallingford (she noted it particularly, thinking fondly of her time there with her guardian, Mr Gadd) where it was said Prince Rupert was 'imminently expected'. She had already learned to distrust hearsay. It was not until the 21 of April that the prince took Lichfield, which he accomplished through undermining the Close, a novelty in warfare in England, the tunnels being dug by miners Rupert had summoned specially from Nottingham. A few days later he was indeed back in the neighbourhood of Oxford, but he and the King moved east in an attempt to relieve Reading. Reading was a key garrison between the King's headquarters and London. It had provided equipment to the Royalists, but its townsmen were of shifting allegiance and it was impossible to defend. Eventually the King retreated to Wallingford, where the castle could be well fortified, and Reading surrendered to the Earl of Essex and the Parliamentary army.

On the last day of April, the glover made his move. Everyone else was out of the house, but Juliana was seated at her table, frowning over some embroidery in the low afternoon light. On the pretence of pleading for rent money — which he knew he had no hope of getting — Wakelyn Smithers climbed the stairs to her room. Pretence then faded. Smithers meant business. He came straight across towards her, and when she jumped to her feet he took the opportunity to embrace her.

Although Juliana had dreaded this, she panicked and could summon up no strategy to deal with it. For a wild moment she struggled, leaning back to avoid the glover's bristly attempts at kissing. So far he was more bothersome than brutal; he was feigning love and she was managing to fend off that soiled commodity by vigorous use of knees and elbows.

Then he abruptly released her. She kept her feet with an effort.

'Why here is my husband, returned from the wars!' Juliana gasped.

Orlando Lovell had walked into the room. He had his usual casual air, as if he had left his wife only that morning on an errand to a tobacconist. In benign mood after a successful month of skirmishing and plundering, Lovell was taking the scene calmly. For a moment Juliana thought he would ignore her beseeching look; he seemed about to greet the glover as a friend. She was in a second danger: the two men could easily become drinking, dining, boasting, grumbling and gaming partners, which would leave her more than ever prey to the glover's advances whenever Lovell was absent. Smithers knew it too. He reckoned that the cavalier would overlook or even condone his overtures. She saw complacence settle on him — but then she saw it slide away. Orlando Lovell had decided to defend his own.

He swept off his hat. The peacock feather was bedraggled, but the silk band Juliana had made for him remained in place; Orlando's long fingers stroked the bright hatband as his eyes settled on the glover. He spoke quietly, but his voice was rich with menace: 'Master Smithers! What do I find? Are you perturbing my wife, sir?'

The glover scuttled from the room like a cellar rat.

Juliana closed her eyes, feeling faint. She turned away as she tried to recover, leaning on her table for support. Lovell came up behind her, put both arms around her, then as his hands played over her midriff he noticed her swollen body. 'You are with child!' She heard shock – and a fear of responsibility. 'Is it mine?' Spinning back towards him as he released her, Juliana bit back a furious retort. Orlando Lovell, ever the strategist, capitulated fast. 'Oh I am a dog! Of course it is – Come, come to me, sweetheart –'

Juliana fell into his arms, and allowed herself a rare moment of relief. As she shook with tears and he soothed her, Lovell seemed lost in thought. Perhaps he felt chastened by the trials his young wife had endured alone. Soon recovering her composure, Juliana observed that the lace-edged shirt collar she had wet with her tears was not one she recognised from her husband's previously meagre wardrobe – nor, she fancied, was this otherwise handsome garment very clean. His coat was new. He had a more expensive rapier, suspended in elaborate malmsey-red velvet carriers, and an enormous ruby finger-ring.

'This will not do,' said Lovell. 'I have a sword I shall give you.' Juliana was shaking her head but he overruled her. 'Nay, do not trouble your-self. I have no use for it; the thing sits in the hand poorly, but it will serve to protect yourself, should you be accosted.'

It was the weapon that Lovell had acquired in Birmingham from Kinchin Tew. He hung it on the wall by the window near Juliana's work table. She was to keep the sword dutifully for years, never used and always disliked. He offered to show her how to defend herself with it, but Juliana shrank from that idea.

Then, though he did nothing about it, Orlando promised to find them a better place to stay.

Chapter Twenty-Three

Oxford: 1643

The rest of the first year of her marriage, and her first pregnancy, passed in similar style for Juliana. Orlando came and went, as the princes came and went. Usually he was with Prince Rupert, though once, when Rupert went to the Midlands to escort the Queen to Oxford, Lovell despised that task and stayed behind on some excuse. When Prince Maurice then dashed into Oxford desperately calling for reinforcements for General Hopton, Lovell volunteered; as a result, he fought at the battle of Roundway Down when the Royalists trounced Waller, which gave him a violently low opinion of Waller and, being Lovell, a not particularly high one of Prince Maurice. He returned to Oxford, rode to the West Country and was with Rupert at the storming of Bristol, where he received a slight shoulder wound.

Lovell gave Juliana nothing to live on. The three shillings he left when he rode with Prince Rupert in April was apparently supposed to last her through her lying-in and into the next decade. He, by contrast, seemed to have some store of chattels. On his first return he had presented his bemused wife with a curious mixture of household goods, strings of sausage, a half-wheel of cheese, together with a fashionable necklet of large pearls which he said was a gift for her birthday. 'Don't look so surprised. Mr Gadd wrote and ordered me to remember your anniversary.'

'You knew when it was?' Juliana let him see her surprise.

'No. Gadd told me.' Orlando gave her a straight look. 'I shall know next year.'

'Will you remember?' Juliana asked, smiling.

'I have', Orlando Lovell said with stately self-composure, 'a very good memory.' He made it sound threatening. Juliana dismissed that as his inability to be teased.

The necklace was the most valuable thing they ever had. Juliana wore it on festive occasions, though she tried not to become fond of it in case one day their fortunes deteriorated and her pearls had to be sold. Besides, she was afraid of its history. Like everything Orlando brought her it was probably stolen. You could not tell with jewellery. Lovell was unlikely to have purchased this over the counter of a gold-smith's shop at a fair price. If he did, the fact was remarkable and he could only have been spending the profits of plunder. Juliana had real fears that her gift had been violently pulled from the pale neck of a previous owner. What might have happened to that owner next was too horrible to contemplate.

Lovell would never tell her.

No, that was wrong. He would tell her truthfully and brutally, if she was ever so foolish as to ask him. Juliana could prophesy his amuse-ment if the circumstances – and his part in them – then offended her.

During her times alone, which were many, she had plenty to read. Sometimes, on returning from military engagements, Lovell brought her books. She had to avoid thinking of him and his men bursting into some respectable puritan's home, then after the soldiers had stolen the cheese, the roasted chicken on its spit, the pewter and the bed-linen, the captain jauntily exclaiming 'Books! Damme, my wife will enjoy those . . .'

Life in Oxford had its stresses even when Lovell was with her. There was a bad atmosphere. People were oppressed by the constant talk of war, the never-ending fear of defeat, the loss of estates, the counting of the dead. The natural edginess between town and university had acquired an extra dimension, exacerbated by the King. After causing much dismay by his attitude to academic honours – on one occasion granting 140 of his supporters the title of Master of Arts – Charles had been forced to assure the university he would stop ordering up honorary degrees for courtiers. Oxford had to raise a garrison for its defence, due to the King's presence, and since the town was protesting at the costs of the court, at the end of July the Royalists announced that their troops were to be paid by taxing the scholars. That caused another outcry, especi-ally as there were now so few scholars. The colleges were constantly being asked for money. All the university and college buildings were being used for official purposes, and even private houses that had once been lodgings for students or their families now had soldiers billeted on them in large numbers. People of substance were prevailed upon to give way to high officials such as Privy Counsellors. The town clerk's house in the High was occupied by Princes Rupert and Maurice. The inns were chock-a-block with military personnel, curious foreign ambassadors, even on occasion peace-keeping legations from Parliament.

Numbers swelled to capacity in June, when Queen Henrietta Maria arrived. With peculiar symbolism, she and the King were reunited on the battlefield at Edgehill. Then Her Majesty was welcomed into Oxford with flowers strewn before her and given a purse of gold at Penniless Bench, Juliana's news-reading spot. The Queen brought four and a half thousand new troops from the north, which the Earl of Newcastle had raised and she had armed. Vibrant with her own success as a fund-raiser and her courageous adventures, Henrietta was ensconced in Merton College, with a covered way built to allow her to visit the King in Christ Church – a privilege the couple presumably enjoyed since a few weeks later the Queen was known to be pregnant. A Master of the Revels provided elegant entertainments, though even festive occasions were strained. There were complaints that the cramped colleges did not provide scope for the elaborate machinery of the theatrical masques Inigo Jones had once devised. The Queen found endless conversations about the war depressing.

August, when the King and all the army were away at the siege of Gloucester, was a difficult time. There had been suggestions that the Earl of Essex might attack Oxford in the King's absence, hoping to capture the Queen. News that Essex had in fact gone to relieve Gloucester only caused more anxiety, for that had previously been thought impossible. Meanwhile there was unrest because of the new, highly unpopular town governor, Sir Arthur Aston. A short-tempered Catholic disciplinarian who had been governor of Reading until Essex took that town, he was so loathed in Oxford that on his evening inspection rounds he had to be escorted by a special bodyguard of four red-coated halberdiers – despite which he was physically assaulted and wounded in the side during a scuffle in the street.

Trouble at night was regular, generally fuelled by drink. Once two men fought over possession of a horse; Prince Rupert emerged and parted the opponents with a poleaxe, though not before one had run the disputed horse through with his sword. With Lovell away throughout

August and September, Juliana lay awake at night listening to the street noises and hoping that the soldiers, whose pay was always uncertain, would not assault the glover's shop. She was frequently alarmed by cries, mysterious crashes or shattered glass. These were the common disturbances of a university town, a town filled with men, and sometimes women, who wrongly believed that they could hold their drink or who had lost the will to try. Nowadays the nightly riots had an extra edge of desperation brought on by the danger of the times. The women of the town were so busy they could be scornful and belligerent. Fights were more vicious, murmured couplings more desperate, sudden shrieks more alarming; the very silences filled with anxiety. Most streets were unlit. The darkness was ugly. Moonlight or starshine seemed incongruous.

So overcrowded was the town, and conditions everywhere so squalid, that summer inevitably brought an epidemic. It was called camp fever, and recognised as different from the regular bouts of plague that afflicted all towns. This was a new disease, which doctors insisted claimed fewer deaths than the regular plague, though as many as forty a week were recorded in July. It was known the Earl of Essex had had half his army stricken at Reading. Even Prince Maurice fell ill and was diagnosed with the fever, though he was strong and soon recovered.

Filth, excrement in the streets and college halls, unchanged clothes and bad diet all contributed. Over-population helped disease to spread. The wages of scavengers who collected rubbish from the streets were doubled, but the bad habits of courtiers and soldiery made it impossible to keep places sanitary. To be pregnant was dire. Still, Juliana somehow escaped the fever.

Orlando Lovell rode with the King to Gloucester. News of the terrible Royalist casualties at the first battle of Newbury in September reached Oxford at the same time as the King returned there. With no definite confirmation of her husband's safety, Juliana experienced her worst fears so far as she waited, by then seven months pregnant, alone at their lodgings.

It was Edmund Treves, still her admirer and still unmarried himself, who told her Orlando was safe. Lovell, Treves said, had asked him to dash to Juliana's side and comfort her. She suspected that Treves took this action on his own initiative. He was romantically devoted. Though modest, Juliana easily believed that Edmund still wrote poetry in her honour. Not that she supposed these lyrics had merit; Juliana had been brought up a reader, and possessed a clear literary judgement.

Some wives might have supposed Lovell had gone to a tavern instead of coming straight home, though Juliana did not see him as a drinker. She tried not to think of him as thoughtless, reckless, selfish and insensitive either. He was a man. Worse, he was a soldier. However, she knew there were plenty of cavaliers who were racked with anguish to be parted from their wives by war, men who would give their unborn children loving consideration. Still, Lovell had never promised her devotion. Juliana believed he was loyal and she hoped he was faithful, though if so it was in a brisk, unsentimental way. He relied on her to provide her own strength and to make her own domestic arrangements.

'Orlando will come when he can. I am glad to know he is safe, Edmund; it was so kind of you to think of me.'

She had done Lovell wrong, for Edmund then told her, 'Prince Rupert has stayed in the field, to harry Essex and his army on their homeward march. I had to return with the King and the infantry. My horse broke a leg.'

'Faddle?'

'I had to shoot her. Lord knows how I can get another. '

'There is no need for you to trouble over me, Edmund.'

'I am glad to do it!' declared the redhead, flushing scarlet under his light skin. Juliana sighed. She saw Treves as no threat – and yet that made him a greater responsibility.

Her fragile truce with Wakelyn Smithers would be at risk, if another man hung around her. Smithers would not understand that Edmund was genteel, kind-hearted, chivalrous to his friend Lovell – and unlikely ever to touch Juliana. After the odd beginning of their acquaintance, she and Lovell saw Edmund as a family friend, while ignoring the nature of his regard for Juliana. She never abused that. Nor did she underestimate it. She would not entirely trust him when drunk, or if Lovell imposed on him too thoughtlessly – as Lovell almost certainly would one day . . .

Smithers stayed at arm's length, but he still watched her. Fortunately she was now grown so large even the glover must be put off by it.

*　*　*

Lovell returned eventually. A royal council of war was held at Oriel College to re-examine strategy to finish the war. Soldiers were taken from local regiments and garrisons to be with Prince Rupert in the west; Lovell was bound to go too. More than ever, Juliana suspected that when her time came, she would be giving birth alone. She was terrified. Once at dinner, she even approached Wakelyn Smithers's hostile sister, pleading with her to attend at the birth. Most women, whatever their status, reckoned it a duty to rally when a neighbour was in labour, but Smithers's sister gave a vague answer and Juliana knew she would renege.

Being inexperienced and unsure of when to expect the birth, she was caught out. One morning while Lovell was still in Oxford, held there by terrible weather which prevented fighting, Juliana's contractions began unexpectedly. When her waters broke – a fright she was not prepared for – he was out of the house. She went through the first stages of labour alone, then in the afternoon began to fear she could not manage any longer. Eventually her husband came home. Relieved, she told him the situation and persuaded him to stay with her.

In his own way, Lovell disguised any reluctance to be involved. For an hour he sat in the room reading a news-sheet. Journalism had allowed the characteristic Englishman to become himself. Now, as the master of information, it was a husband's prerogative to seize the best chair in the room – which Lovell did, taking the one with wooden arms, the better to balance his elbows and control the broadsheet. The chair was normally graced with a plump cushion that Juliana had covered with stylish stumpwork embroidery; impatient of the cushion, Lovell tossed it to the floor. He flung his boots in two different directions. Then, while his wife sweated and gasped and bit the sheet behind the bed-curtain, not three yards away, Orlando Lovell applied himself to the Englishman's conviction that he could ride out any crisis by fixed study of the news.

'How do you fare, sweetheart?'

'Tolerably . . .'

'I am glad of it. Would I could be of assistance, dear girl, but this is woman's work.'

Lovell deemed it would help if he read out interesting passages from the news-sheet. He knew Juliana took an interest in the progress of the war. 'I see there has been a sharp exchange of fire at Winceby.

The Earl of Manchester – that old fool – with Sir Thomas Fairfax (he is the uppity one of the family), plus one Cromwell, have trounced a couple of northern cavaliers . . . This Cromwell is unknown to me. Have you encountered the name, my sweet?'

'No. Orlando, we have to hire a midwife . . . I was not sure of the timing and have not consulted her, but the licensed woman should come to us –'

'Oh I dare say we can save a shilling and manage without . . .'

'A shilling is in the brown crock on the mantelshelf – I have kept it particularly; there is no need to scrimp!' Writhing on the soiled sheets and drenched with sweat, Juliana could no longer silence herself. 'I shall die if this child be not taken out of me – and the child too, poor innocent thing that never asked for us two feckless souls as its parents!' As the most painful contraction yet seared through her, she let rip and screamed: *'Orlando, you must help me!'*

She heard the news-sheet fall. Lovell whipped aside the bed-curtains. He was a soldier. He could assess a situation. He went white. 'Do your best to endure it – I will fetch someone!'

His shock frightened Juliana even more. In all the years she was to know him, this was the only occasion Orlando Lovell showed plain terror. Well, I have wrought a wonder! she thought, with fatalistic pride. She reached for his hand, but he jumped back nervously.

At that moment she really thought she was dying. Given the nation-wide statistics for childbed mortality, any doctor would have nodded. From the desperate way he dragged on his bucket-topped boots and thundered headlong down the narrow stairs, Captain Orlando Lovell had been told about the dangers.

He went missing for ages. Juliana had heard him shout agitatedly for help from Smithers or his sister. The sister always came to the house in the late afternoon, but on this one day she had found some pressing reason to vanish. Smithers had scarpered too. Finding no one, Lovell himself must have left. Stillness fell downstairs.

Juliana sobbed. She feared that Lovell had abandoned her.

Finally through her pain came voices, one a woman's. Footsteps moved steadily upstairs. Juliana had a wild moment of horror. 'Dear heaven, he has brought me *an Irishwoman!'* She would come to be ashamed of that.

A large, middle-aged, unperturbed stranger in sensible black worsted swanned to her bedside. The lady assessed all, with benign disgust. Through tears of distress, Juliana saw a square face, enlivened by deep dimples and wise eyes. Lovell was nervously hanging back. 'My sweet, this is Major McIlwaine's good wife –'

Mistress McIlwaine cuffed him, rather hard. 'Get away, Captain Lovell! Are you a monster that this poor child has been provided with no single friend at such a time? Give me a knife; I need to pare my nails.'

Lovell looked bemused. Juliana understood. She somehow managed to laugh, then blurted out, *'Your midwife should be strong, quiet and calm, with clean hands and close-trimmed fingernails . . .'*

'And a stranger to drink!' returned the rescuer briskly. 'Though God alone knows, *that's* a rarity . . . The licensed bawd is stuck in St Clement's, tearing twins limb from limb. She will come to you by and by with her iron hooks and her ale bottle, but we can wing it by ourselves . . . I generally reckon to anoint the privities with sweet almond oil and violets, but I cannot suppose we shall find anything of that sort in a house of heathens. We must make do with goose fat, if this idle lump of a husband of yours can go down to the pantry . . . Just a cupful, Captain, if you please, and try not to bring too many nasty bits of burned meat in it. We want lubrication; we are not making gravy.'

Juliana was friendless no longer. Nerissa McIlwaine had arrived in her life.

'Get us some eggs, Lovell! And if you have any wine hidden about the place, surrender it now to me, if you please. I must make your lady and me a spiced caudle for relaxation.'

'Women's work,' muttered Lovell under his breath as he whisked off on these errands, grumbling and yet reassured. 'Women's rituals . . .'

Mistress McIlwaine had heard him. *'Eliminate the light, the air – and the men . . .* The last is good; the rest are old wives' tales . . . If you go out to buy the wine, Captain Lovell, do not linger above ten minutes! Then you may wait below until it is over. If I need a strong arm to pull one way while I haul the other, I shall call you up again.'

Amidst a continuing flow of this offhand commentary, Thomas Lovell was born. With the calming effects of caudle and the slitheriness of goose fat, there was no necessity for hauling. Mistress McIlwaine ensured the child was gently introduced to the world. He thrived from his first yell, while his tired young mother wept but survived. Even the father recovered his spirits enough to kiss both his wife and his red wrinkled son, then gravely salute the lady who had saved the day. After that Lovell felt free to forget the traditional duty of entertaining the godparents (since as yet there were none). He went out to get drunk on Juliana's shilling, the shilling he had saved by not employing the licensed midwife.

Chapter Twenty-Four

Oxford: 1644

Juliana discovered eventually that Orlando had had only a slight acquaintance with the Irish couple. A chance meeting in the street as he rushed about in despair had brought this happy result. For his wife, the accident was to be a double joy, for it initiated one of the main female friendships in her life.

As a consequence of inspecting their bleak room, Mistress McIlwaine subjected the landlord to inspection; she took his measure in one scathing bat of an eyelash, then berated Lovell for ever leaving Juliana alone in the beastly Smithers's vicinity. She suggested the Lovells should board with herself and Major Owen McIlwaine in St Aldate's. McIlwaine was a tall, lean man with a strong nose and large ears, who read widely and loved his wife. He was well liked by his soldiers and Lovell said he was a caring, efficient leader.

For the Lovells, this was a notable move up. Not only were they now well placed, directly opposite Christ Church where the King lodged, but the houses were large and splendid. At that time St Aldate's famously contained three earls, three barons, several baronets and various knights. Overcrowding was rife, with a census recording 408 'strangers' packed into seventy-four houses, along with original townspeople. Even so, the neighbourhood was coveted. The McIlwaines possessed resources; they rented a whole house and though periodically they shared it with other officers, who brought their wives, children and sometimes soldiers or servants, the Lovells nonetheless were given a good chamber of their own, where the small family eventually stayed for eighteen months. Now they lived in panelled rooms with ornamental plaster on the ceilings and decorated over-mantles above lofty fireplaces. From who-knew-what money, Lovell had made one flamboyant payment of rent, which he would probably not repeat, though it gave them a guilt-free start. Juliana felt able to use her grandmother's fine table- and bed-linen, as she dared to believe that she had her own establishment at last. In the great four-poster bed with its old embroidered drapes, her second child would be both conceived and born.

She was to know grief in that house as well as snatched happiness, but for a long time mainly pleasure – particularly the pleasure of living among congenial people, people who gladly extended their friendship. Although the McIlwaines were a quiet pair, who allowed Juliana plenty of privacy, they also had access to society. They were connected to the royal court because they worshipped at the Queen's Catholic chapel in Merton. There was music; there were plays and masques; for the men there was tennis and bowling. There was fine dining in the colleges as well as simple food and good company at home. For those who could bear its deprivations, Oxford even held a sense of excitement. It was inconceivable that the King would lose either the war or his crown; the city had the air of a temporary adventure which everyone would one day remember nostalgically.

Juliana, so young and completely inexperienced, had wise guidance as she learned motherhood with her first baby. Nerissa had borne children, though none was with her now. Juliana sensed that the McIlwaines had endured much tragedy, perhaps back in Ireland. At any rate, Nerissa helped with a light hand; perhaps she was reluctant to love the infant Tom Lovell too much. Despite developing a great fondness for Juliana herself, her warmth was tempered with restraint, as if nothing in life could be trusted to last.

Differences of religion only came between them with courtesy on both sides. Early in their acquaintance Nerissa did ask Juliana if she was a Catholic, since she was partly French. Roxanne Carlill had always maintained herself to be a Huguenot, though on her death-bed she had begged for a Catholic priest and Juliana, despite her distaste, had somehow found one. Whatever her grandmother's origins, Juliana herself had been brought up a general-duty Protestant. Her father had read aloud to her from a King James Bible. She shook off the question with a light laugh. 'I am but a quarter French. So I am a Catholic only on Mondays and Wednesday afternoons – and never on a Sunday, which prevents discovery.'

That first winter was bleak, with endless grim weather and heavy snow. It was good to be in an ordered house where roaring fires were built in the kitchen, and lodgers were welcome to drape their ice-stiffened cloaks over chair-backs and stuff their mud-splashed boots with old news-sheets to dry out near the hearth overnight. In January the Houses of Parliament at Westminster offered a pardon for all Royalists who submitted, took the Covenant – the Presbyterian oath – and paid a significant fine to compensate for their past delinquency. Despite their anxieties as the war continued, few at the King's headquarters paid much heed to the offer.

Besides, there were now two Parliaments. The King called for all loyal members of Parliament to assemble at Oxford, which already had lawcourts, a Mint and the royal presence. The Oxford Parliament met with considerable numbers present – forty-four Lords and, more surprisingly, over a hundred Commons, which was about a quarter of the lower house. It was not a success. Though these were the 'loyal' members, ironically the King found them no more compliant than the rebels in Westminster. He raved to his wife about 'the place of base and mutinous motions – that is to say, our mongrel Parliament here'. It was not in his nature to wonder why *neither* body was tractable.

In March 1644, as the weather cleared, Prince Rupert left for action in the North Midlands, Lovell with him. In April the pregnant Queen was sent away to Exeter by the King, who feared for her safety during her confinement. Once again came rumours that the Earl of Essex intended to lay siege to Oxford; at the end of May Essex and Waller made a determined effort to entrap the King. Essex marched through nearby Cowley and Bullingdon Green to Islip, and then advanced on Woodstock, which was a mere walking distance away; as an act of bravado the King spent a day hunting at Woodstock. Meanwhile Waller forced a crossing at Newbridge and came as close as Eynsham. Parliamentary soldiers strolled up to inspect the town defences, like spectators at a fair. Shots were fired. The King tricked Essex and quietly escaped with four and half thousand men by an all-night march. Lighted matchcord was left, hung on the hedgerows, to fool Essex that the royal army was still there. (This trick was used in so many engagements, it was surprising anyone was ever taken in by it.) The Parliamentary encirclement of Oxford ended, temporarily, though the panicky townsfolk only relaxed slowly.

Also at the end of May, Prince Rupert was ordered to the north. It was occasioned by a treaty John Pym had concluded with the Scots, just before he died in December 1643. Dismayed by the fact that three-quarters of the kingdom was then in Royalist hands, Pym had taken up the Scots' offer of help. They too were alarmed by the prospect of victory for the King, which would inevitably mean further attempts to overthrow their Presbyterian system. News that Charles was negotiating to bring over an Irish army for his own assistance, made them even keener.

By the Scots' treaty with Pym, religion in England was to be reformed. It would be a requirement for everyone to swear allegiance to the Covenant. In full, the oath ran to 1,252 words. Its salient clauses included:

> *calling to mind the treacherous and bloody plots, conspiracies, attempts, and practices of the enemies of God, against the true religion and professors thereof in all places . . . we have now at last (after other means of supplication, remonstrance, protestation, and sufferings), for the preservation of ourselves and our religion from utter ruin and destruction . . . resolved and determined to enter into a Mutual and Solemn League and Covenant, wherein we all subscribe, and each one of us for himself, with our hands lifted up to the Most High God, do swear . . . and shall endeavour to bring the Churches of God in the three kingdoms to the nearest conjunction and uniformity in religion, Confession of Faith, Form of Church Government, Directory for Worship and Catechising; that we, and our posterity after us, may, as brethren, live in faith and love, and the Lord may delight to dwell in the midst of us.*

In two words: no Popery.

Strong puritans would never wear it. At any mention of 'Form' and 'Directory', Independents leapt back, sucking their teeth. For them, the rigid and interfering rule of Presbyterianism was just as loathsome as the hierarchical Roman Catholic Church. There would be trouble. Members of Parliament and army officers at various levels were soon trying to duck the Covenant, even though taking the oath had become a requirement of public life. However, the first result suited them: an enormous army of Scots came marching over the border to support the Parliamentary cause in brotherhood.

This forced a change in the King's strategy. So far the flamboyantly rich and powerful Earl of Newcastle, recently created a marquis, had dominated the north despite all the strivings of Parliamentary commanders, notably Lord Fairfax and his son Sir Thomas. Now Newcastle was compelled to abandon marching south. The Fairfaxes were too dangerous and he had to manoeuvre frantically against the Scots.

In Yorkshire, the Scots joined Sir Thomas Fairfax, who was fresh from a stinging rout of Royalists at Nantwich. Caught suddenly on the hop, Newcastle was forced to take refuge in the important city of York. York was then systematically besieged. Meanwhile in the south, Waller had checked the Royalist forces under Hopton in an encounter at Alton, Prince Maurice was tied up in a long-drawn-out siege at Lyme and Essex had shown himself able to contain any moves by the King. Parliament's other main army was a force from the Eastern Association under the Earl of Manchester, together with his so far little-known deputy, Oliver Cromwell. Already successful, this army was therefore ordered north to co-operate with Fairfax and the Scots – a formidable liaison.

King Charles reckoned his crown depended on the fate of York. He sent Prince Rupert with all the men who could be spared. Both Orlando Lovell and Owen McIlwaine went, McIlwaine now raised to the rank of colonel. Their departure, one of so many that punctuated Juliana's life, entailed the usual intense activity that preceded a big expedition. Life revolved around kit and tack, with the men giving wholly un-necessary domestic instructions in a desperate last-minute wish to control their households, while the women concealed their real independence and disguised their fears.

After those men had ridden off again, when the whirlwind quietened, Juliana Lovell and Nerissa McIlwaine settled by the parlour fire. The baby fell asleep in his cradle; Tom was a placid child. They had bread and cheese for toasting, should the mood take them. A maid sang in the kitchen as she tended a cauldron of netted cabbage and a Dutch pudding. Mistress McIlwaine leaned forward and poked up the coals just enough to make a flame leap, without waste. Juliana pulled a shawl more cosily around her shoulders. As they relaxed together and enjoyed the peace that had settled on the empty house, each woman wore a slight smile, though they did not meet one another's eye. That would have been acknowledgement of their unspoken thought: *We are rid of the men. Now we shall be more comfortable!*

*   *   *

While they waited for news, or the men's return, they found suitable occupation for ladies of repute. They kept their diaries and wrote letters to their husbands. Juliana sewed and read. Nerissa strummed a lute in between organising her kitchen maid. Sometimes they went out and walked in college grounds, though this was fraught with problems. New College Grove, where grand cavalier madams in revealing gowns paraded to impress crass gallants, had acquired a louche reputation. Younger female Royalists, small-minded teases, had tormented the college dons with what they called playfulness and the elderly academics viewed as nuisance committed by hussies. For women who wanted to avoid being thought so wanton, it was best to avoid wandering in the colleges – which now stank of horses and worse – and instead apply themselves to good works: bringing baskets of salves and bandages, Juliana and Nerissa would nurse wounded soldiers.

Their great challenge was the castle, where Parliamentary prisoners were held. Ever since the first large group arrived, a thousand men brought in after the fall of Cirencester in the winter of 1642–3, the condition of prisoners at Oxford had been notorious. The Cirencester captives had been driven to a field for inspection by supercilious officers who threatened them with hanging; they were penned up in a cold church, stripped and starved for two days, then driven through snow, barefoot and hatless, some without even britches, their hands tied with matchcord. On arrival at Oxford they were paraded like cowed dogs before the King and his two gloating young sons. Lucky ones were put in churches. The most unfortunate were incarcerated at the castle, where deplorable treatment was doled out with the aim of persuading them to repent, change sides and join the King's army.

Originally, the castle had been run by a sadistic provost marshal called Smith, an appalling man who treated his prisoners with 'Turkish' cruelty. The elite, about forty gentlemen, were kept in one small room in Bridewell, the paupers' prison; they were beaten, tortured by burning with matchcord and kept up to their ankles in their own excrement. Some imprisoned puritan ministers were hounded with insults by Smith and made to sleep on the stone floor with not even foul straw beneath them. As for the common soldiers, Smith denied them medical attention and packed them so closely together, men had to sleep on top of each other. He allocated a penny-farthing a day to feed them, but no fresh water. They drank ablution water after Royalist soldiers had washed, they drank from muddy puddles in the yard, they even drank their own urine. Men died daily, either from this neglect or from the after-effects of torture; two had their fingers burned to the bone for trying to escape. The corpse of a hanged man was flung into an officer's cell where it putrefied for several days until a large bribe secured its removal.

Eventually forty prisoners broke out and escaped to safety, then told all. Smith became such a byword for brutality that even his own side disowned him. The London Parliament debated the issue and the Oxford Parliament had him imprisoned after three days in the pillory.

Now conditions in the castle were better, but still imprisonment was viewed as a just punishment for rebels, and a deterrent. Those who refused the option of changing sides might be lucky enough to be freed in a prisoner exchange, but that was rare; they could fester in cramped cells for years. For food, clothes and writing materials, they had to rely on friends outside; when held in enemy strongholds, this was impossible. Their lives passed from the humiliation of capture through malnutrition, depression and despair. Sores, diarrhoea and arthritis commonly afflicted survivors. With no exercise, no glimpse of outside light, and nothing to do but carve their names on prison walls, some would begin to hallucinate. Weakened, if they then caught jail fever, they soon perished. Many would die. All knew that death was the most likely end for them.

Nerissa McIlwaine and Juliana Lovell were willing to bring food and medicine to men held in the castle. The prisoners were allowed rare inspection visits from their own side, visits which cheered them, because they knew they were not entirely forgotten. But requests to bring charity were rebuffed. Nerissa and Juliana were turned away by an assistant jailer in the castle gateway on the Mound. 'Ladies, they are nothing but rebels and traitors. Execution is all they deserve.'

'If we abandon our civility and humanity,' Nerissa McIlwaine lectured him, 'we deny ourselves grace.'

When the two women were then asked scornfully why they should want to help the enemy, their answer was simple. Juliana explained: 'If our own husbands are ever captured, we hope some good woman among the enemy will show them kindness.'

It did not convince the jailer, who never did allow them in.

*　*　*

At the beginning of July, a crucial battle took place. It was known that Prince Rupert was blazing through the north at the head of a large army, which with reinforcements had reached over fourteen thousand horse and foot. Heading up through Cheshire and Lancashire, he had stormed Stockport and Bolton, met resistance at Liverpool, crossed the Pennines, reached Skipton Castle and surprised his opponents by bursting out at Knaresborough. On Rupert's sudden approach, the Parliamentarians raised the siege of York and began moving away south. Although Lord Newcastle wanted to rest his exhausted garrison and wait for the enemy's armies to disperse in their own time, Prince Rupert always preferred to fight. The Parliamentarian allies, who numbered between twenty and thirty thousand, far more than even his large array, heard of his eagerness and turned back to give battle. The Royalists, with the pick of the ground, drew up on Marston Moor. They had plenty of space on clear moorland, protected by a road and a significant ditch that would hamper enemy charges.

Word reached Oxford on the 9th of July that Prince Rupert had accomplished a great Royalist victory. It was reported that one of the Parliamentary leaders, the Earl of Manchester, was slain, and that Sir Thomas Fairfax and the Scots general David Leslie had been captured. General rejoicing broke out. Bonfires blazed. Ale flowed in the streets. Church bells rang.

Three days later the King, with his own troops in the west, received the Prince's dispatch telling the true story. Marston Moor was a disaster, a bloody defeat. The North was lost. York was lost. The intended march on London would never happen. The King's best troops were destroyed. Lord Newcastle's famous infantry, his Whitecoats, had stood and died to a man. Their bankrupt commander had fled to the Continent. Prince Rupert's fabulous reputation lay in shreds.

Parliament had found a new hope in Oliver Cromwell. For him the battle was a personal triumph; first his leadership of his 'Ironsides' had scattered Rupert's elite cavalry, then intelligence and discipline enabled him to rescue the situation elsewhere at the crucial time. Through Cromwell, Marston Moor could be a crucial turning point in the civil war.

Accurate accounts of the battle were quickly printed in London. Reality filtered up the Thames Valley to the Royalist headquarters. From Oxford's perspective, the battle in the north seemed far away and hard to appreciate. The false atmosphere of rejoicing died only slowly. For a long time no wounded men were brought south; few wives heard for certain whether they had been widowed; there were no eye-witness stories. It seemed unreal. The King, who had been pottering about on his endless manoeuvres against Essex and Waller, was currently penned in the West Country so his reaction was not witnessed. Prince Rupert was thought to have taken refuge at Chester with the rags of his cavalry but no one knew that for sure, or could say when, if ever, he might reappear in Oxford.

Life went on.

That Marston Moor was critical would slowly be accepted. The King, ever hopeful, ever sanguine when faced with losses, reassured despondent supporters that reverses would happen and that fortune might change in his favour again. Charles soon seemed justified when, after defeating William Waller at Cropredy Bridge, he was offered a great chance: the Earl of Essex wandered through Dorset and Devon, capturing Royalist houses and relieving Lyme and Plymouth, then calamitously continued on into the Cornwall peninsula. With Waller defeated, King Charles was safe to follow Essex. The Parliamentarians reached an area where the population was Royalist to a man. Eventually Essex was completely trapped at Lostwithiel. Though his cavalry cut their way out and Essex himself escaped by sea in a fishing smack, the infantry were starved into surrender. They laid down their arms and were allowed to march out, though every possible indignity, insult and hardship were inflicted on them by the King's men as they struggled to walk home across England.

While the King exulted, Parliament hastily summoned the Eastern Association troops back south. They were to join with the rags of Waller's army and prevent the King from sweeping to victory. A second battle was fought at Newbury. Weak deployment by the Earl of Manchester allowed the King to evade what should have been a decisive action. This was the occasion when Oliver Cromwell's exasperation with Lord Manchester brought him to argue for a new kind of army, which would be concentrated under one tried and determined commander. But while that idea was discussed in Parliament, the year ended with the same kind of stalemate as previously, Marston Moor almost seeming to count for nothing.

In Oxford one Sunday in early October a terrible fire occurred. For the garrison, the townspeople and those left behind by the field armies, this assumed much more importance than any aspect of the war. It began when a foot-soldier who had stolen a pig was roasting the beast in a cramped dwelling near the North Gate. The little house caught light. Fanned by a high north wind, flames spread rapidly. A frightening conflagration raced through much of the western area, from George Street south through St Ebbe's, destroying houses, stables, bakeries and brewhouses. As well as providing billets for soldiers, this was an area of labourers and artisans, who lived in cramped small cottages with too many thatched roofs and wooden chimneys. Oxford houses at the time tended to be built with timber rather than brick or stone. Their beams, bargeboards and decorative pargeting were grey with age and tinder-dry; the closeness of the buildings helped the flames to leap ferociously through entries and passageways.

Juliana had smelled smoke. Soon the McIlwaines' house was threatened. It survived, but not before Juliana and her friend had begun frantically gathering what they could – Juliana could carry little more than the baby. Outside, only half-hearted fire-fighting efforts were being attempted, for there was no good access to water. Ladders were brought to rescue trapped people – or to enable thieves to take advantage of abandoned houses – but the streets were full of fleeing, screaming inhabitants, who rushed in all directions not knowing where to take refuge. Some carried bundles of possessions, but most were just concerned to save their skins.

Feeling the approaching heatstorm and panicking, the women rushed out into the High. Nerissa pulled Juliana to safety in Christ Church, where the large quadrangle and heavy stonework would offer protection if the fire leapt across the street. Eventually the blaze was extinguished, however, and they were able to return home, finding the house still as they had left it, though every room and everything they owned was blackened with soot and smuts and stank of smoke. They coughed for days. The reek lasted weeks. Juliana found herself sniffing obsessively and peering through the windows in case a new fire had started. She slept badly and remained on edge.

Collections of money were started for homeless people, many of whom had lost their trades with their workshops. Relief was haphazard. The destitute would still be begging for assistance two decades later. Eighty houses were destroyed. Bread and beer were hard to find, since brew-houses, bakehouses and malthouses were destroyed. The butchers' stalls in Queen Street had also gone. There was food, however. Oxford always had a good supply of provisions. The King repeatedly ordered every household to lay in stocks to survive a siege.

At the end of the month, unexpectedly, Juliana came in from the market and saw boots warming by the fire, boots with enormous bucket-tops and butterfly-shaped leather patches on the insteps, which held mighty spurs. McIlwaine and Lovell had returned. Juliana found her husband in their room, face down, spread-eagled on the bed.

At first, Juliana convinced herself Lovell was unchanged. He and the colonel seemed more reticent and jaded, though neither had been badly wounded. They spoke only briefly of the battle of Marston Moor. McIlwaine had managed to get away with Prince Rupert, which saved his life; had he been captured, he would have been shot for being an Irishman. After hiding all night in a beanfield – a story loved by his enemies though rather played down by him – Rupert rendezvoused with his surviving men at York then refused an appeal from the Marquis of Montrose to fight in Scotland and instead rode back across the Pennines, picking up stragglers. Meanwhile Lovell had lost his horse and was captured by Roundheads after lying for hours in a damp gorse patch. Unlike most of the fifteen hundred prisoners taken after the battle, he somehow escaped. In subsequent weeks at home, he said little of what had happened to him.

The men's dark memories only slowly became apparent. When their husbands first reappeared, Juliana and Nerissa exchanged discreet glances, asking no questions. When Lovell came to the kitchen, where Colonel McIlwaine was tasting small pies as warily as if he had never seen a pie before, Juliana brought Tom to his father. It was six months since he had seen the child. Lovell responded with polite remarks on how Tom had developed. He held the boy; he held him close for a long time, staring at the fire. But he was not taking joy in his infant, merely using him as a comforter.

That night in bed, Juliana was shocked by the new force and urgency of Lovell's lovemaking. A foolish girl might have preened herself that he had missed her – which no doubt was true. Yet she realised that as he worked out his passion, he had locked himself away within some misery he might never share with her. The man was obliterating his disappointments through sexual effort. His ferociousness was a punishment – though hardly Juliana's punishment, for what had she done wrong? She provided wifely consolation, but she found it frightening and painful. In the end, Lovell's extreme passion roused her — she could not help herself — but after they fell back exhausted, they lay silent and uncommuning. Dry-eyed in the darkness, Juliana did not sleep.

She felt used like a whore. She could not help being angry.

As she surveyed her bruises the next day, while Lovell still lay in a dead sleep, she wondered if a similar scene had taken place in the McIlwaines' bed. Going downstairs, she almost believed that she heard a man weeping, though she could not believe it. Nerissa McIlwaine did not appear that morning and when Juliana did find her, quietly spreading herself damson jam on a crust of bread, it seemed impossible to ask intimate questions.

Some time before the end of that year, the Lovells' second child was conceived.

The King wintered at Oxford serenely. There was no sign that anything would ever change.

Chapter Twenty-Five

Oxford: 1645

Christmas brought an atmosphere closer to normality. The weeks before had been bleak, however. The men had been difficult ever since their return. Lovell was irritable and distant. Owen McIlwaine was drinking hard and uncharacteristically; Juliana noticed that his wife, who could be frankly outspoken, did not criticise. Nerissa must have seen this before. The men often took themselves off to be among other soldiers in taverns, close-bonding in hard knots over many tankards.

'They are sticking together, trying to forget,' Nerissa explained to Juliana.

'Omitting us from their confidence?'

'They were unprepared for such a bloody defeat. Their instinct is to protect their families from knowing what they endured. They will not speak in front of us – yet trust me, they need to. You must have noticed, they are both constantly on guard. They jump like cats at the slightest alarm.'

'Orlando is tormented by memories and night terrors.' Juliana had found out, when Lovell would never come to bed, that it was from fear of lurid nightmares. 'I can do nothing right; *he* has dropped three plates, yet *I* am blamed for clumsiness.'

'Many a woman has left her husband under these trials, Juley, and gone home to her mother. I am too far from home to do it –'

'And I have no mother alive.' Juliana had taken on Lovell as a challenge; she would not abandon him. 'What can we do, Nerissa?'

'Nothing. Live with it.'

Juliana made sure she talked to Lovell, asking gentle, general questions about Marston Moor. When he flared up initially, she backed off, yet she came back to it, until he let his guard drop. However bitter he might be, Orlando Lovell always stayed true to his intelligence. He lived with angry self-knowledge. He had applied honesty to their marriage; this was a courtesy he gave formally to Juliana as his wife. So, bit by bit, he allowed her probing and she drew from him a portrait of the great conflict.

He began with his usual disparagement of Rupert, then went on to blame Lord Newcastle. 'Yet, Orlando, he has spent his entire mighty fortune in the King's service?'

Lovell raved against the Duke's hedonistic lifestyle before the war – his legendary entertainments and twin passions of horse dressage and banqueting. 'Oh he is a great enthusiast. Horses, women, art, architecture – and, until now, the King's cause. But after Marston Moor, he fled to the Continent – he told Rupert he would not bear the laughter of courtiers.'

'Should *he* be blamed for the disaster?'

'When the rebels attacked, this piece of nobility Newcastle had retired to his coach to enjoy a pipe of tobacco.'

'That's bad, I agree. But Lord Goring commanded Newcastle's cavalry on the right wing, did he not?' Juliana asked.

'Goring drinks himself under the table nightly!' Lovell set off in rage again. 'No one has his capacity for sin. He is all wining, whoring and gaming. A legend for debauchery – and for failure to control his men. Sweetheart, the fool had Fairfax routed and beaten out of sight. If Goring had not chased from the field in search of Fairfax's baggage-train, our case would have been quite different. Their leaders – bumbling Manchester and that dour Scot, Leven – had given up. Leven ran scared for fourteen miles from the field before he stopped.'

'Better things are said of Sir Thomas Fairfax?'

Calmer, Lovell considered the question with some interest. 'A sickly, stubborn, crazily brave northerner. Armies have these characters, men who flare alight when action starts. We heard that Fairfax found himself alone, threw off his officer's sash and the field sign from his hat, then he passed right through Goring's men unrecognised. This was our undoing. Fairfax reached Cromwell and supplied him with full intelligence; Cromwell knew that you must be persistent, methodical, drive ever forwards, keep at it. So he took his troops looping around to eliminate Goring's men.'

'And what is known of Cromwell?'

'Nothing. Nothing, but that he broke us, then he held his men in check – as Rupert never can. Cromwell traversed the whole field and when he had mopped up Goring's cavalry, he turned on the centre and destroyed our infantry.'

'That was hard fighting?'

'Carnage. Slash and stab. Limbs flying, men with their faces ripped off, sides torn open, brains spilling from their heads –'

Lovell fell silent abruptly. It was time to stop. With her hand on his shoulder, Juliana saw the sweat shine on his face. She brought their son to him again, to remind him of life and hope and, perhaps, responsibility.

So they came to Christmas. With the onset of traditional festivities, the men did rally to accompany their wives. It was the year when, in response to that Covenant signed with the Scots, a Parliamentary committee was deciding just how the Church of England would be reformed. Christmas featured. The Covenant required the rooting-out of *'superstition, heresy, schism, profaneness, and whatsoever shall be found contrary to sound doctrine and the power of Godliness'.* Removing superstition provided a wreckers' charter. Not only would the clutter of idolatry be removed from churches – paintings, coloured windows, statues, crucifixes and those hated altar rails that Archbishop Laud had ordered – but the calendar would be cleansed too. Henceforth there would be no pagan festivals or saints' days. The only holy days would be Sundays and occasional national celebrations such as the 5th of November, Guy Fawkes Day – the day the great papist plot to blow up Parliament was prevented. But the celebration of Christmas would be banned.

In defiance, Royalists celebrated Christmas with gusto. The rich showed their generosity (within limits); the poor were welcomed (within limits), welcomed to warm halls that had been decorated with holly and ivy. Carols resounded, sometimes even in tune. Mince pies and plum pottage, which were popish fare to Presbyterians, became political emblems to Royalists, so gave double pleasure in the eating. There was beef and mutton; there were collars of brawn stuck with rosemary; there were capons, geese and turkeys.

Merry Old English indigestion followed, which the sensible worked off with country walks on starlit evenings. Streets in towns were alive with mummers, some of whom took the spirit of things dangerously far, demanding not merely traditional alms and Christmas boxes, but money with menaces. To refuse them because they were feckless and aggressive was disturbing to the refuser, who wanted to be generous. Traditions die hard, however. The civil jails were as full as the taverns, and as noisy. Only the prisons containing political prisoners were rank with despair.

The McIlwaines and Lovells dined in an Oxford college where a fragrant boar's head was carried into the warm hall in procession, while ancient carols were sung from the gallery by strong young voices of melting beauty. Silverware that had somehow escaped commandeering gleamed in the candlelight as they stuffed and sozzled cheerily. The women had titivated their best dresses with new braid, while the men had somehow acquired new suits in the latest fashion: short, decorated jackets beneath which billowed several inches of full shirt, then from the waist straight, open-kneed britches, with ribbon bunches cluttering their boot tops. It was meant as another affront to the godly. Juliana thought it a fanciful effeminate look, especially with long lovelocks and extremes of lace, though Lovell as always carried it off sardonically. With Orlando Lovell, one looked beyond the clothes to the man, and the man was not to be trifled with.

After the meal there was a masque and dancing, followed by extremely serious dicing and cards. Juliana, who did not play, was horrified by the heavy wagers and by the recklessness of those who took part. Even Nerissa joined in, proving herself a sharp, obsessive player with a demure face and a whiplash memory, who snapped down hand after winning hand. As Nerissa gathered money into her embroidered reticule with refined sweeps of beringed fingers, the colonel as quickly lost his wagers, until good sense made him excuse himself. Lovell was flinging large sums around, to Juliana's anguish. Noticing her dread, he winked and chivvied her, as men do who make out in public that their wives are social miseries – whereas they themselves are good fellows who must be allowed to carouse. Juliana was relieved and surprised when she learned afterwards that he had lost very little money, and perhaps even acquired winnings.

She should have realised. Orlando was bound to play well. He must have learned young, whilst in foreign service. Nor did it come as any surprise that luck attended him.

Disloyally, Juliana wondered if he cheated.

*　　*　　*

On return to their house, the festivity continued. Friends came by invitation, including Edmund Treves. Nerissa had left a wassail bowl standing – warm beer poured on sugar with spices, which she quickly reheated with a red-hot poker before floating on pieces of thinly toasted bread. It was obvious that more drink would be needed, so Juliana volunteered to make a favourite winter tipple called lambswool. She roasted apples until they burst, while Colonel McIlwaine tapped a barrel of strong old ale for her; she heated this in a pan with sugar, ginger and nutmeg, the traditional mulling flavours, before dropping in the apples. By now slightly tipsy and showing it, Lovell said it was called lambswool because it curled men's chest hair. Rather uncharacteristically, he offered to demonstrate, but nobody took him up on it.

He seemed in high spirits, yet Juliana felt anxious. When he disappeared, she followed and found him at a window, brooding. The nightly thick white frost was forming on the cold glass with its crazy patterns. He had rubbed a patch clear with his coat sleeve and was staring out into the street, whence came whoops and crashes. Troop numbers had increased that year, most of them the King's Welsh recruits. Disorder and pillaging were frequent. When the soldier roasting a stolen pig had started the October fire, his theft of the meat was a routine occurrence. Welsh and Irish women who travelled with these troops were much feared; they knew it, and created many a fracas with threatening behaviour.

Lovell watched a brief street fight. Juliana stood near, more intent on watching him. Melancholy had struck her; her spirits were even lower than his. With the approach of New Year, she was wondering yet again what life would hold, what life was for. They stood silently together, exhausted and anxious, listening to people in the street shouting raw abuse at each other. The last insult they overheard was a gloomy puritan townsman railing against Christmas and its excesses. Had he known he was outside a house that had been rented by a Catholic couple, he would have been even more virulent.

Lovell began to sing to himself: 'Leslie's March,' he said and paused, acknowledging Juliana's presence. Leslie was the general who had led the Scots Presbyterian army into England.

> *'When to the kirk we come,*
> *We'll purge it ilka room,*

Frae popish reliques, and a' sic innovation,
That a' the world may see,
There's nane in the right but we,
Of the auld Scottish nation . . .'

'"*Nane in the right but we*" – that's modest!' observed his wife, wincing at how terrible the verse was.

It made Lovell smile, as he gazed out through the misted window-pane. He was losing the demons. *'He has been among Scots!'* a voice said in Juliana's head. He had sung with a true accent. Slowly his lost weeks were coming together. *'Yes, and he did not enjoy the experience . . .'*

If she could have kept Orlando with her for a little longer then, she would have been sure of returning him to his old self. Of course that was impossible. With the turn of the year came not just Ploughing Sunday but another fighting season. Parliament had created a new standing army, a new and formidable weapon perhaps. Under command of the northerner Sir Thomas Fairfax, it was being put together with twenty-two thousand of the best men from existing armies, particularly the Eastern Association troops of Oliver Cromwell, those who had shown their fine mettle and discipline at Marston Moor. There had been negotiations for peace, at Uxbridge, but these were disrupted by Parliament's intransigence. In January, Archbishop Laud was put on trial; the examination took several months, all tending towards his certain execution.

The Royalist Marquis of Montrose raised the Highlands of Scotland against the Presbyterian Lowlands, fomenting old clan jealousies. His dramatic victories encouraged the King into 'new imaginings', as his critics called them. Charles replaced his old dream of three armies conjoining for a London assault with a wild new hope that the romantic Montrose would descend from Scotland to help devastate all the King's enemies. More prosaically, Prince Rupert was at his usual dogged work in the west and the Midlands, Lovell with him.

In April Parliament's New Model Army was formally instituted and the first result was that its commander, Sir Thomas Fairfax, took control of strategy in the Oxford area. The town was once again threatened with a siege.

On the 7th of May the King left Oxford – a timely exit. Fairfax continued to build siege works, east of the River Cherwell. As defensive measures by the Royalists, water meadows were flooded, buildings in the suburbs were burned and Wolvercote was garrisoned. There was worrying military activity. Real fighting came uncomfortably close. The Royalists lost an outpost at Gaunt House, but at the beginning of June the town garrison made a successful sally at Headington Hill. Then Fairfax left troops under Sir Richard Browne in the area, as he abandoned the siege to pursue the King.

Juliana had learned that her duty was to keep a brave face whatever happened. Nonetheless, she grew extremely fearful. Lovell had been away with Prince Rupert but, just before the King left, Rupert and his brother Maurice returned to Oxford for a rendezvous. Orlando came to her for two days, before the army moved out for their summer campaign. Juliana was then seven or eight months pregnant. They discussed sending her to a safe house, but had no friends or acquaintances who could offer such a refuge. She would have to remain in Oxford, where at least she was at home – in so far as they had ever had a home.

'Sweetheart, Fairfax will withdraw. He cannot keep his army tied up here while the King and the princes are out on the loose. Oxford is a nothing to them while it is empty of King Charles. You will be safe. Trust me.'

Juliana did trust him, on tactics. She was in such an advanced state of pregnancy she could no longer travel, especially since wherever she went she must take young Tom. One thing distressed her particularly: Nerissa McIlwaine would not be here with her when her time came.

The McIlwaines were planning to return soon to Ireland. There, the Irish Catholic Confederation, an alliance of upper-class Catholics and clergy, controlled two-thirds of the country and had formed an effective government. The confederation had concluded peace negotiations with the Marquis of Ormond, who represented the English Parliament and, confusingly, the King. It seemed a promising development.

Juliana finally asked openly why her friends had first left their country. She knew Colonel McIlwaine had gone to fight on the Catholic side in the Thirty Years War and had assumed it was caused by the intense English settlement of Ireland. 'Oh, there was a family quarrel,' Nerissa disabused her. 'Owen stormed off. He seems mild, but he's a hothead on occasion.' The colonel did indeed seem mild, though no milksop.

He spoke at least four languages, and occasionally talked with Juliana in French, when he wanted to annoy Lovell. Lovell, having fought on the Protestant side on the Continent, knew Flemish and German but had picked up only curses and insults in French.

After years in France, the McIlwaines had first come to England hoping to make a civilian life at the new Queen's court. They were in their sixties now; the colonel was looking for peace and retirement.

'What happened to your children?' Juliana blurted out. She had always feared some terrible, violent fate had befallen the family.

Nerissa shrugged. 'They never thrived. I lost every one, none older than six years. To some extent I blame our rootless life, our constant wanderings, our living in forts and garrisons. But we could have been on a country estate or in a neat town house and suffered the same.'

The women were silent for a while, thinking of life's fragility. Then Nerissa said slowly, 'So . . . Juliana, it is not from want of friendship towards you, but Owen will fight this year's campaign, then he and I will take our chance back in the old country.' Nerissa knew that losing her one close friend filled Juliana with deep foreboding. 'You must let me go and be of good heart. And when they leave Oxford, I shall be following my husband with the army.'

When the troops rode out, women always accompanied them. Yet camp followers were not all common wenches and whores, as their enemies suggested, but often respectable wives. For one thing, it kept the respectable husbands from the beds of prostitutes. The women cooked, made fires, guarded baggage, searched for the dead, nursed the wounded, provided encouragement and cheer.

'Of course, you must. I would come with you myself if I could.'

In her current condition, Juliana could not. She would have gone, to be with Orlando, to be with Nerissa, to taste adventure and to escape the claustrophobia of Oxford. But she was only weeks from delivery. A midwife was found therefore, examined, approved and appointed. In addition, Nerissa kindly left her maid, Grania. Juliana stayed in the St Aldate's house with her eighteen-month-old boy, Tom. Everyone else she knew went away to war without her.

Then, when Sir Thomas Fairfax lifted his siege preparations and chased after the King to the Midlands, everybody Juliana knew was at the battle of Naseby, where the King was defeated.

Chapter Twenty-Six

The Midlands: 1643–44

When Rowan Tew met his sister at Henley-in-Arden he decided the best way to avoid trouble was to rename her. So she became Joseph.

It was a few days after she fled alone from Birmingham, back after that terrible Easter. Her brother had recognised her instantly from the truculent set of her body and her pale, strained face as she approached, even though after nearly fifteen miles she was limping badly. Her bare feet were cut and bleeding. At the last hamlet where she begged for food, someone had given her rags for bandages but to little effect. She had found that in these tiny groups of cottages, shaken by Prince Rupert's passage a few days before, if she gave news of the greater assaults wreaked on Birmingham, people would provide her with food. She told her stories weeping; real tears came easily.

When the group of ragged cavalier soldiers rose from hedgerows either side of her, she thought her time was up.

'*Who are you for?*'

'Parliament and the King.'

'Wrong answer!' Although there was no glimmer of lit matchcord, she heard the click of a musket being cocked.

With the band of whiskery layabouts levelling swords and guns, her spirit faded too much for resistance. Once she would have yelled, thrown stones, punched and spat and bit, then run away faster than anyone would bother to pursue her. Fortunately, one of the louts turned out to be her brother.

Rowan was the young Tew who had volunteered for the royal army the year before, just after the war started, when King Charles passed through Birmingham. As their father had said at the time, Rowan wanted the rations and the plunder. He looked unchanged in the six months since his sister had last seen him: still wide-eyed with fake innocence, ready to whine about bad luck, always out for easy pickings. Thin as a pea-stick under a filthy, baggy shirt, he had a long fall of black hair and a new scrubby beard with a barely adequate moustache. His boots, which were too big and no doubt stolen, made him stagger with his legs apart, while sashes, sword-hangers and rattling bandoliers were slung in a carefree fashion over his bony shoulders.

The other soldiers cursed and dropped back into the damp hedges to resume their tobacco pipes. Rowan was eager to brag about his life: the free uniform, the daily food allowance, the drink, the access to weapons, the excitement, the untroubled life. He had instinctively fallen in with a bad crowd. In a disreputable army, the former vagabond had quickly found the most dissolute comrades among whom to burrow like a white maggot. A rascal from birth, he was now in his element, plundering and bullying. He and his fellows claimed to be an antiguard, men authorised by Prince Rupert to remain behind to control Henley-in-Arden; they were in effect deserters. No one had missed them – or if their absence was noticed, nothing had been done about it. To spend all day threatening farmers and robbing passers-by, then to drink the profits while singing cavalier ditties around a campfire every night, seemed a glorious life.

'Come and join us!'

'Do women become soldiers?'

'It happens.'

'In ballads.'

'More often than you think. You have to pass as a man.'

Rowan Tew realised that his sister would not make a camp-follower. She could neither cook nor launder nor nurse the wounded. She was no whore either, or not yet. He supposed she would come to it. To him, who had known her from childhood, she offered no prospects – otherwise he would have cleaned her up and organised a rapid sale on the spot to any man who was willing to give him sixpence for her. He gazed at the thin, undersized, immature figure, grey-faced from lack of nourishment, bunched in dirty old clothes. Though he was a lad with more imagination than sense, his sister was so unprepossessing he knew he could not pimp her. Family feeling was not dead, however. 'Damme! I shall hack off your hair this minute; you must play the boy and come along with me. I'll take care of you. You shall have britches and a buff coat and march bravely and swagger. What do you want to be called?'

'What girl's name was given to me when I was born?' demanded the former Kinchin with urgency. 'Do you remember?'

Rowan, the elder by about four years, thought of any girls' names he ever heard and then claimed expansively, 'Araminta!'

'It would be Mary or Joan, I think,' she corrected him severely.

'Maudie, maybe . . . well now you cannot have that. You shall be Joseph.'

So for a year and over, Joseph Tew served in the King's army.

The laggards skulked around Henley for a week, poaching deer and scaring milkmaids, then just when the milkmaids were starting to warm to them and flirt, along came a small party of Royalist cavalry from Dudley who rounded them up before the women of Warwickshire had managed to catch even half of their fleas and foul diseases. Most were ordered to march north to the siege of Lichfield; whether they would ever arrive was doubtful. Pasty-looking Rowan and his badly limping 'brother' were deemed unfit, so they were carried off westwards in a provender wagon to the garrison at Dudley Castle. There the governor was Colonel Thomas Leveson, a more active officer than they liked. Somehow they passed muster. They kept to themselves, and nobody enquired about them too closely. Many of the other soldiers were French or Irish, foreign-speakers, stuck in their own tight cliques. Officers noticed that the unit had acquired two rat-eyed, bone-idle, light-fingered tykes, but most common ranks in the Royalist army were scavengers and although the Tews hung back when action started, they never refused direct orders. So long as bodies marched where he needed them to be, the colonel was satisfied.

Castle life suited them. They had shelter, rations, company and instruction in the use of arms. The Royalist daily subsistence allowance was a luxury: two pounds of bread, one pound of meat and two bottles of beer. All their thinking was done for them. They even had leisure – so much leisure that among the rubbish which the soldiers in the Dudley Castle garrison threw down their latrines were gaming counters and animal-gut condoms. To have latrines at all was a novelty to the Tews; they had to learn how to use them. In their own minds, all they needed to do now was sit tight to the end of the war, when – if they could carry off their guns on disbandment – they would be equipped for life as highway robbers.

For Joseph, there *was* thinking to do. Women who passed themselves off as soldiers must stay endlessly alert. Their daily lives were geared to hiding their identities. Joseph had begun the fraud while grubby and gaunt enough not to seem too delicate; the other men at Dudley soon became used to their high-voiced, soft-cheeked, slightly built colleague. With regular food he grew taller and filled out; although breasts were a problem, they blossomed slowly. Breasts, especially adolescent ones, could be squashed flat beneath the firm heavy leather of a military buff coat. With care, monthly courses could be hidden and the necessary rags washed in private. A loner, who had always roamed independently, was able to cope with the intense secrecy of living in disguise. After a whole young life of solitude, keeping one's counsel came easily. Nature had issued one challenge, which from time to time became pressing: no woman could urinate in public and stay hidden. But like disguised drummer-boys and powder-monkeys throughout history, Joseph Tew found ways to manage.

Any street urchin knew how to bluff.

In December 1643, when the Tews had been living at Dudley Castle for six months, Colonel Leveson received a request for aid from a prominent Midlands landowner who believed Parliamentary sympathisers were planning an attack on his house. The colonel felt obliged to respond to an irascible local Justice of the Peace, a man with connections at court and who had entertained King Charles in that very house. Colonel Leveson reluctantly spared forty musketeers. They marched, grumbling, to the great hall in question; they were told it was five miles away though found it nearer ten. They were not surprised to be lied to, for that is how soldiers are generally cajoled.

On arrival, their discontent mellowed. It was a grand billet. While looking forward to an extremely comfortable Christmas in warm and grandiose surroundings, they began to fortify the place. Despite his danger, the haughty owner only reluctantly agreed to let them cut down trees to clear a line of fire from the house and dig protective earthworks in the deer park of which he was so proud. Like many landowners he was torn between trying to preserve ordinary life and standing up for his political beliefs.

The troops were quartered like bats in the attics, which were airy and luxurious, being barely ten years old; few ghosts and hardly any spiders had had time to take up residence. Though the ceilings sloped, there were fine views across the three hundred acres of parkland that surrounded the house. They would see the enemy coming.

The great house was built to the highest standards. It aimed to impress inferiors – and its scowling owner reckoned pretty well everyone around him was an inferior. For the Tews this was an ironic destination: they had come to Aston Hall near Birmingham. It was the home of black-browed Sir Thomas Holte, whose enclosure of local commons when he was creating this majestic house and its huge new park had dispossessed their family.

Once indoors, Rowan and Joseph were staggered by the size of the house, with its great hall, several parlours, dining room and withdrawing room, enormous long gallery, endless corridors and series of bed-chambers, cavernous kitchen with wet- and dry-larders, wine and beer cellars and endless stables and outbuildings. Aston Hall sat in lush park-land, created for hunting and for keeping the people at a distance; the house had high Jacobean gables and chimneys, elegant plaster strapwork ceilings, expensive fireplaces, fabulous carved woodwork and a profu-sion of expensive windows. The quantities of furniture and personal possessions were beyond anything the Tews had ever imagined. Even after large civil war losses, when Sir Thomas Holte died, his belongings would be inventoried on a scroll eleven feet long. The Tews wandered in amazement, sniggering at the Holte family behind their richly clad backs and pilfering small items whenever they could get away with it.

The Parliamentary forces arrived on Boxing Day. This was their reprisal for Prince Rupert's attack on Birmingham and they were hoping for revenge in the form of money and plate. They took up positions in the grounds, planted their standards, then in the language of war sent 'to demand the house for the use of the King and Parliament'.

Sieges had their own chivalry. Once the enemy turned up and formally 'summoned' a town or house – announced that they had come to take you over – it was vital to refuse surrender at least once, and in a robust fashion. To give up too easily meant disgrace and court martial. There was a fine knack to choosing the correct moment to submit with honour, in order to obtain 'terms'. Terms meant the defeated side would be allowed to lay down their weapons, march out and avoid cold-blooded slaughter. If they had fought tenaciously, they might be allowed to keep their arms and leave with their colours flying, though that was recognition of extreme courage. It was rare, and it took a merciful winning commander. More often, if the besieging commander had been seriously annoyed at any point, he would hang a few of his enemies just to relieve his feelings.

At Aston Hall, the Royalists answered the summons by defiantly retorting that they would not yield while they had a man alive. Sir Thomas Holte could be confident a man of his rank would be spared whatever happened.

It took three days for resistance to disintegrate. There were twelve hundred rebels, who had brought artillery. On the first day, Tuesday, the attackers made play with their cannon, doing serious damage to the house's interior, especially the fine dog-leg staircase with its bulbous carved balusters. The cannon-fire terrified the defenders. Amidst the smoke and noise and crashing shot, the Holtes, their servants and soldiers took refuge in the lower rooms. Next day, the attackers assailed the parish church, close to the house, where some of Colonel Leveson's Dudley troops had been out-stationed. Churches made very defensible strongholds, but it was quickly stormed. The Parliamentarians took French and Irish prisoners, including one female camp-follower who, in the enemy's tradition, was viciously abused as a whore.

The Tews heard the shouts and rattle of fire when the church fell. They were already quaking at cannon balls crashing through the house, and the smell of smoke and panic became too much for them. When enemy soldiers broke through the earthworks on the lawns, the young Tews passed their guns to servants and hid together under a great table in the entrance hall. Parliamentary troops soon burst into the house through its tall, elegant windows. As showers of broken glass fell inwards, large booted men swung through window cavities, shouting and brandishing swords. The defenders cried for quarter. It was granted.

Peering out from their hiding place, Rowan and Joseph then saw some trigger-happy Royalist soldiers kept firing anyway. Two rebels were shot in the face. At the sight of stricken comrades with blood pouring from their mouths, the Parliamentarians went mad. They killed and wounded twenty defenders before being brought under control by officers. Joseph and Rowan Tew cringed against the great carved table leg.

'Play dead Rowan!'

'Who needs to act it? We're done for!'

Eventually the shooting stopped. The attackers had better ways to enjoy themselves than wasting ammunition on a cowed foe. They were here to pillage goods and to capture anyone of quality who could be heavily fined and ransomed. Forty useful prisoners were rounded up. As soldiers rushed past their bolthole to stampede upstairs and search the house, the Tew brothers ventured out into the open, two disingenuous mites holding pieces of white cloth (they had sensibly equipped themselves with these tokens). 'Joseph' considered disclosure, but was deterred by how cruelly the woman previously taken was reviled as a whore. Royalist camp-followers risked mutilation and cold-blooded murder, especially if they were believed to be Irish. Women were hanged as rebels and spies almost as often as men. To be in disguise would not win favour.

The Tews instinctively knew how to pose with the typical hangdog relief of surrendering soldiers. They were stripped of weapons, hats, belts, boots, britches and coats – though not deprived of their verminous shirts, or Joseph would certainly have been discovered. While this was happening, they saw Sir Thomas Holte, a furious old man in his seventies, dragged from the house, bare-chested in the December cold as he had been stripped of even his fine cambric shirt. He and his family were taken away for special ransom. Lesser prisoners were strung together in a line, their hands bound behind them with matchcord, and marched to the church. There they were insulted, threatened and starved. Then the abject prisoners were offered the usual inducement: a dungeon in Warwick Castle, for ever – or repent of their Royalist delinquency, turn and fight for Parliament.

Some hung back, genuinely hating puritans. Joseph and Rowan Tew immediately swapped sides.

The new Roundheads were equipped with coats, shirts, stockings, shoes, britches and Monmouth caps, and allocated another daily allowance (threepence a day). Once they had been judged docile and trustworthy, they were armed with swords and guns made in Birmingham. They regarded these weapons as inferior, but for thruppence a day, plus a roof over their heads, they would put up with anything. Rowan could ride. Most horse thieves could stay safely on anything with four legs. He was given a mount, then appointed to be a light dragoon. His diminutive younger 'brother', who lacked the strength even to support a long musket properly, would be allotted camp duties. They were assigned to a new garrison which had recently been created for Parliament under Colonel John Fox.

Fox ran an irregular, roistering, free-ranging, unsupervised organisation that would eventually be disbanded under a cloud. Two guttersnipes could not have found themselves a more congenial position.

Warwickshire in the civil war was mostly held by Parliament, but a Royalist bloc lay to the west, including all of Wales; its rough boundary ran from Chester down through Shrewsbury and Worcester to Tewkesbury and on to the West Country. The district around Stratford-upon-Avon was Royalist, which provided a safe corridor when the King obtained Welsh recruits. The Midlands were constantly criss-crossed by Prince Rupert. His efforts early in 1643 had achieved their objective: the Queen's convoy of soldiers and ammunition wagons left York and passed safely south, bypassing Birmingham, though resting overnight nearby at the Saracen's Head in the Queen's personal manor of King's Norton. The next day Her Majesty arrived at Stratford-upon-Avon, where she was an overnight guest of Shakespeare's daughter, Susannah Hall, at New Place. There Henrietta Maria was joined by Rupert, and four days later met King Charles and progressed into Oxford.

The Royalist Lord Denbigh's death at Birmingham changed the balance of power in Warwickshire. Although Parliament then lost Lord Brooke at Lichfield, the new Lord Denbigh fought for Parliament. This Denbigh replaced Brooke in charge of the Midlands Association: Warwickshire, Worcestershire, Staffordshire and Shropshire. His Committee of Public Safety headquarters were at Coventry. He also had a large base at Warwick Castle, so strong that it was never besieged. Wherever there were suitable large houses he set out to take them from Royalists, fortify the buildings and establish garrisons which would control the countryside, raise money and recruit men to attack other Royalist strongholds.

Some of the rebels in these areas had curious origins. Most colourful were the 'Morelanders' in remote upland country in north-east Staffordshire. Armed only with birding-guns, cudgels and scythes, these shaggy turf-cutters had banded together, giving their leader the sinister title of 'the Grand Juryman'. Their boldest exploit was a doomed attempt to drive the Royalists from Stafford.

Equally seen as outsiders were Fox's men at Edgbaston. Lord Denbigh regarded this garrison as tricky and high-handed. Fox resented his commander's lack of warmth and his reluctance to send funds. If Denbigh's men trespassed into districts he regarded as his own, Fox complained. He wanted personal credit for his garrison's exploits. When *he* was summoned to Coventry on charges of plundering, and was compelled to cough up 'a goodly sum' to regain his position and his reputation, he made up the fine in further demands on local villages and individuals in the area he roamed.

Where exactly he came from and his true background were obscure. Enemies called him a tinker, yet he was literate, intelligent and effective. When civil war broke out, John Fox had found his role. He drew on his own resources. With him to Edgbaston he brought a brother and a brother-in-law, Major Reighnold Fox and Captain Humphrey Tudman. His core of sixteen men swelled to more than two hundred. Some he recruited for Edgbaston were locals. His clerk was called John Carter; a John Carter junior had been killed by Prince Rupert's men in Birmingham.

Denbigh formally granted Fox a colonel's commission in March 1644, to lead a regiment of six troops of horse and two of dragoons. Even so, it was three more months before Parliament allowed him financial support. Until the money came, he and his men fended for themselves. Robert Porter, the steel-mill magnate, assisted, though he and Fox were later to quarrel tiresomely over manor rents.

When the gentry established garrisons – stalwart knights of the shire with university educations and large landholdings – they were always admired for their energy, loyalty and honour. The real charge such people had against John Fox was that without social advantages and without being asked, he seized the initiative and set himself up at Edgbaston. Both Royalist and Parliamentarian leaders shunned him. Not only was he no gentleman, the job he decided to do for Parliament gave him a touch of the outlaw. His nickname, the 'Jovial Tinker', was because he rarely smiled, though if calling Fox a tinker was an insult, it never seemed to bother him.

Dressed in their latest uniforms, the Tew brothers were sent to serve 'Colonel Tinker' at Edgbaston Hall. This was nothing like the house where they had just been captured. Aston Hall, which lay immediately to the north-east of Birmingham, was brash and boastful, one man's symbol of his own new wealth and power. They found that Edgbaston, on the south-west side of Birmingham, was a moated medieval manor-house with a dovecote, typical of timeless English village life, surrounded by rickety watermills and weedy fishpools. Even when the Tews arrived they could see the idyll was deteriorating. The greens around the house were churned to mud and slime by soldiers' horses. No ducks swam in the moat; there were probably no fish left in the pools. The roof of the adjacent ancient church had been stripped and its bells removed; the lead was being melted down for bullets. The centuries-old Hall was treated with disrespect by Fox's soldiers; it already showed sad signs of wear and would in time be badly damaged, destroyed by fire and lost to posterity.

Brought before Fox for inspection, Rowan and Joseph cast their eyes down, though not too much. They knew the fine line between looking unobtrusive and looking suspiciously meek. Fox, a dour man in his mid-thirties, surveyed them with Midlands scepticism. He accepted them as turncoats; there were plenty of those on both sides. Still, he made it plain he expected nothing good from them and if they tried anything on, he would know about it. He gave them a sombre speech about the garrison, then handed them copies of 'The Soldier's Prayerbook', a religious publication for devout troops which was famous for the number of times its pages had stopped enemy bullets. 'Let the Word of the Lord be your breastplate!' Colonel Fox instructed – which covered up the fact that he could not afford to buy helmets or body armour.

He spoke with the deadbeat cadence of the area. Outsiders would assume he was slow-witted, but the Tews understood that language. Their colonel's dry tone hid intelligent qualities. John Fox lived by his wits. So did the Tews. They all thought themselves as good as anybody anywhere.

Rowan rode with the troopers. Joseph was left behind to scrub pots. The garrison had a brewer and a meat-salter who both allowed the skinny lad to help them with their work. Dripping snot, the so-called Joseph watched and learned. Service in an army teaches a bright spark skills for life.

The garrison's main task was the endless extraction of taxes. Fixed amounts were set, which towns and villages had to give in support of the war effort, whether or not those towns and villages supported Parliament. The King's side worked the same system. Some towns and villages therefore ended up paying twice; it was safer not to refuse. In addition, Parliament required that individuals whose land produced more than ten pounds a year or who had a hundred pounds in personal estate should make 'loans' of up to one-fifth of their revenue from land or a twentieth of their goods. Few expected repayment. Very few ever obtained it. Grumbling victims complained that Committees of Public Safety were making themselves rich; members of the committees protested that their own estates were plundered by soldiers, who often took them prisoner as well, in order to extract ransoms. Such was the chaos of war. Or so said Colonel Fox.

Outright plundering by local garrisons was rare because it made no sense. To ruin the countryside would leave troops and their horses starving, nor was it good practice to arouse too much hostility. Locals who felt they had nothing to lose might organise armed reprisals. But when they were out on the loose, Fox's men did seize horses 'for the service of Parliament'. If Fox knew, he turned a blind eye. They took free quarter where they could too – lodging for which they did not pay – and sometimes they made illegal promises to householders in order to obtain bribes. All over the country and regardless of affiliation, houses were being raided for food – oats, meat and cheese – for horse gear – bridles, saddles, spurs – and for weapons. Anything rideable or portable was at risk. Though the Tews took little interest in politics, as soon as they arrived they quickly grasped the attractive milieu into which they had been sent. For them, Edgbaston was a happy time.

Fox was a diligent scout. He made regular reports to Lord Denbigh, concentrating on the presence of Prince Rupert in the Midlands, sometimes noting manoeuvres of the King. It involved his men spying on troop movements; listening in on Royalist soldiers' conversations; writing detailed reports of intelligence gathered; and astutely interpreting the information. Messages were then sent considerable distances with speed. To achieve this required an established body of reliable scouts who had to be brave, sharp-eyed, able to call upon safe houses and a supply of fresh mounts both night and day. All the men had to be very familiar with a wide district. Scouts could not get lost. Messages must not be captured.

Sometimes Fox sent his reports much further afield: to Sir Samuel Luke, who was the Earl of Essex's scoutmaster.

For a couple of months after the Tews arrived, winter continued and there was little happening. In March 1644, Fox began a series of lightning activities. He captured Stourton Castle but was driven away by a massive Royalist response. He and his men fled headlong across Stourbridge Heath, pursued by the enemy who soon proclaimed that first to flee before them had been Fox himself. Undeterred, his men then besieged Hawkesley Farm on Clent Ridge, a strong Royalist outpost where the King had stayed on occasion; they drove out the owner, Mr Littlemore, and his family. But while they were away at Hawkesley, Prince Rupert and his brother Maurice rode into Birmingham and stole sheep and cattle from the markets.

In April, too, Fox organised a breath-taking night raid. Setting off one afternoon, he rode with sixty picked men to Bewdley, a pretty town on the River Severn which was famous for making Monmouth caps, the warm, easy-to-wear felt headgear worn by many soldiers instead of helmets. Bewdley was a Royalist stronghold and an inland port. Pottery and iron were taken there by packhorse, for onward shipping down to Bristol and beyond. King Charles several times stayed there at the grand comfortable house called Tickenhill which overlooked the town from high ground, surrounded by elegant woods and parks. It would be from Tickenhill that the King would write a very famous letter to Prince Rupert in June, saying that if York was lost he would reckon his kingdom lost too. However, in April the house was merely occupied by the Governor of Bewdley, Sir Thomas Lyttelton.

Fox and his men arrived in the dark, cheekily pretending to be some of Prince Rupert's men, who were lost. They quietly put the town guards out of action. They crept up to the house, where everyone was gently sleeping. The first the governor knew of this daring raid was when he woke up to find himself a prisoner. He and his retinue, with forty extremely good horses, were then sneaked out of Bewdley.

Eventually Royalists pursued Fox back to Edgbaston. They were too late. Fox had gone in triumph to Coventry. From the stronghold at Coventry, Lyttelton would be passed on under guard to London, where he would be held in the Tower for the rest of the war. 'Thanks be to

God,' murmured the Jovial Tinker piously of the Royalists to whom he had given the slip, 'they came a day after the fair!'

'Joseph' Tew had been terrified when angry cavaliers arrived at the Hall. Disappointed, they rode off soon enough, but fear jolted the brewster into action. Taking advantage of the colonel's absence at Coventry, the youngster slipped away.

There was a reason. Disguise would soon be impossible. Some comrade at Dudley Castle or Edgbaston Hall – or maybe more than one – had uncovered Joseph's secret. Discovery inevitably happened with women soldiers, because either they were following a sweetheart to the wars, or in their loneliness they found a confidant and broke their silence. The traditional fate had befallen young Tew. Secret couplings had led to the usual result. Soon everyone would know: the potboy 'Joseph' was to be the mother of a child.

Whether the father had refused to acknowledge his role, whether he already had a wife and children, or whether the right man could not even be identified, marriage was not an option. The young mother was, therefore, dealing with the problem in her own way. If she knew whom to blame, she had no wish to say so. Rather than be exposed, she deserted the garrison and fled. She dressed again in stolen female clothes. She dared not return to Birmingham, so she chose the route so many forlorn hopefuls took: she would go to London where, even if the streets turned out not to be paved with gold, those who wished to be anonymous had a chance to disappear.

So, once more, the sorry waif took to the road alone.

Chapter Twenty-Seven

London: autumn, 1643

When the two Jukes brothers had returned home from Gloucester and Newbury, they stood in the upstairs parlour of their parents' home, almost forlorn for a moment. Lambert was led away to be tended in private by his wife. Gideon passed a hand over his forehead as if the light hurt his eyes. Lacy took no interest. At first his parents were too polite to intervene but then as he shivered and swayed on his feet, Parthenope Jukes seized back her maternal rights. Soon she was gently washing her younger son as if he were still a small boy. Trying to shield him from her horror at his sores, she dispatched Lacy to the apothecary for stronger salves than were kept at home. Gideon, who was now clearly feverish, fretted as she touched him. He was crotchety in a way Parthenope found familiar. Just as when he caught chickenpox at the age of seven, Parthenope saw the moment when reddish-purple spots began to appear on his arms and chest.

His father came to inspect the rash. John pronounced the worst: Gideon had camp fever, probably caught at Reading. Conditions there had been crowded and lice-ridden; the lice were implicated. Essex's men had been put half out of action by this rampant sickness. 'Call it camp fever, ship fever, jail fever — it is all one. Our boy is in great danger!'

Gideon was gravely ill for weeks, sometimes with such wild delirium he could hardly be held down. Parthenope nursed him, since Lacy pleaded anxiety for her unborn child. Already weakened by hardship, Gideon was in no condition to resist the fever; headache, spasms of nausea and diarrhoea racked him. Although his mother produced broths and caudles, he could keep nothing down. He was so weak he could hardly climb out of bed to the chamberpot. He raged at his helplessness. His frustration and fear made him bad-tempered even with his mother as she cared for him.

Worse, Gideon began to relive the horrors he had experienced in the battle at Newbury. Hallucinations caused by fever danced wildly among traumatic flashbacks. He needed to rest; yet repetitions of the gunfire and visions of men being torn apart tormented him. Never a good patient, discomfort and mental anguish combined to make him a monster. Many a time his harassed mother left his room, leaned against the door-jamb and wept silently into her apron. She understood his behaviour and rarely snapped back. She was just terrified Gideon would die.

Parthenope Jukes was made of stern stuff, however. She had always been a scrupulous housewife. In her home, flies were swatted. Hands were washed before preparing food. Floors were mopped; tables scrubbed; dishcloths boiled. Cooking pots were cleaned to a sparkle with vinegar or lye. The well in the yard was kept sanitary.

A similarly strict regime was applied to her sick son. He was quarantined to a small, simply furnished room, where his bedding was changed daily. The lice were dealt with; Parthenope tenderly cut his hair short, combing out nits onto a piece of housewife-cloth which she burned. Once she realised the extent of the problem, his parents struggled to hold Gideon while a barber shaved him naked, including places where a seventeenth century man never dreamed of being shaved. His delirium was coloured by the constant smell of sulphur and lard from ointments to soothe his itching, an aroma that soon seemed to infest even his dreams.

Eventually came a worse odour: rotting flesh. When gangrenous sores appeared, a surgeon was called. Gideon lost three fingertips on his left hand and his right fourth fingertip.

Though frail, John Jukes played his part in tending his son. After close study of medical tracts, he had advanced views about airing sickrooms and even though it was winter, he insisted that a window was opened daily to allow the escape of dangerous 'miasmas'. John's more curious theories were rebuffed while Parthenope tackled the unpleasant day-to-day aspects of nursing. By some act of providence his parents managed not to catch the fever and slowly they restored Gideon's health. He moved from stupor into a clear mind. It took months, and even afterwards he clung to his room in a long depression.

At least he was rarely left alone with his terrors. Mostly his mother sat with him, studying her books of household management. It was years since she had had so many quiet moments and Parthenope came to enjoy the respite. Often Gideon emerged from restless sleep to find her, spectacles on nose, intent on putting her recipes in order – spreading the papers across his bed as she worked. Sometimes instead, a waft of tobacco smoke announced his father in attendance. Gideon felt bound to protect both from knowing what he had endured, but John was determined to find out. The days were long gone when John Jukes could parade with the Artillery Company, but he was full of curiosity about all that had happened to his sons. He plied Lambert with questions, unconsciously helping Lambert to unburden himself, then when Lambert lost patience John would turn to Gideon. In the early days, when Gideon was most dangerously ill, John took to dozing in a chair at the bedside overnight.

Gideon lost some of the distance from his parents that had built up while he was apprenticed. He was already much better friends with Lambert. So they all moved into a new family cycle. Whereas for some people the civil war damaged or destroyed stability, the Jukes were more fortunate. The parents were proud of the sons; the sons were encouraged by their parents' support. One son's wife was a fervent ally. Only Lacy held herself aloof, but that was never political.

Robert Allibone was of course another supporter. As soon as the invalid was adjudged out of danger and unlikely to be contagious, Robert hurried to help keep him cheery. For him, this meant bringing paper and ink to woo reminiscences that could be reconstructed into a diary. Like other memoirs by the Trained Bands, it was polished, edited and published. So the vivid, intrigued recollections of the ordinary soldier were brought to both contemporary and future readers in an unprecedented way. Gideon complained that the fever had made his mind hazy, but Robert persisted.

Robert brought news of how the London Trained Band regiments were continuing to serve in the field. Gideon listened, at first feeling out of it, but then relieved to be so.

Sir William Waller had now been made commander of various troops but was beset with problems. Particularly fraught was persuading his allocation from the London Trained Bands to do service outside the city. Some grumpy members of the Yellow Regiment were taken to Farnham Castle, Waller's headquarters. They met their new commander:

an intense West Countryman, with brows drawn anxiously down over wide-set eyes and a pursed mouth beneath a moustache that was swept up at the ends onto gaunt cheeks. He signalled his authority by hanging a clerk of his own regiment for mutiny. This failed to impress the disgruntled Londoners. Their relationship with Waller never gelled and he was frequently furious at their open cries of 'Home! Home!', which forced him to make unmilitary pleas for them to stay.

It was a bad time of year for manoeuvres. The troops marched towards Winchester but were turned back by extreme wet and snow. Waller swung them over to Basing House. This enormous Royalist stronghold dominated the area between Oxford and London, threatening both Essex's headquarters and Waller's base at Farnham. Once a staunch motte-and-bailey castle, it had been transformed by grandiose Tudor courtiers and now rivalled the Tower of London in size and strength. Over fourteen acres included the Old House, surrounded by still-viable Norman earthworks, and the palatial New House, which contained 380 rooms. Basing was garrisoned with two regiments of foot and extra cavalry, who were protected by star-shaped towers set into massive surrounding walls that were said to be eight feet thick, brick walls on an earth core that would withstand the heaviest cannon fire. The gate-house was a stupendous four storeys high.

Its position so close to London made the capture of Basing House imperative. But when Waller's men arrived and the cold fog dispersed to reveal this bastion, their hearts sank. The London regiments were wimpish besiegers, daunted by the task. Upon finding one of the build-ings in the grounds, Grange Farm, full of bread, beer, mild cheese, bacon, beef, milk and peas, the famished Trained Bands gorged them-selves, while the thatched roof blazed dangerously above them and shots rained all around. Ignoring their colleagues, who were struggling bravely elsewhere on the site, they threw themselves into looting and gluttony until the day's attack failed, with many men killed. Bad weather and lack of spirit caused two retreats from Basing, which would continue to hold out for three years.

Hopton approached. He was Waller's old friend and long-term Royalist rival; Waller had a vested interest in beating him. Waller kept the Trained Bands sweet by plying them with victuals. When he reviewed them on the 12th of December, he begged them to stay for one more task. They grudgingly remained until the following Monday. They marched towards

Basing again, then veered off to Alton; this important Royalist garrison was taken after a particularly vicious fight, which resulted in the Parliamentarians carrying away 875 prisoners, fifty officers, and various standards. Hopton was sore. Waller was satisfied. The Trained Bands' reputation had been saved – though they begged to be allowed to go home as promised, because it was nearly Christmas.

Gideon Jukes observed all this and convinced himself he was still a sick man.

Late on Christmas Day 1643, Lacy Jukes went into labour. A daughter was born to her on Boxing Day. Mother and child survived. The successful outcome was reported to Gideon by his own mother, with only the slightest puff of surprise that the birth had occurred so soon. Still, judging a pregnancy was an inexact science and, as Parthenope commented, many an innocent young woman giving birth prematurely had been accused of immorality. Being called to account by some interfering crone while racked in labour was a fear that dogged all women . . .

Parthenope was weary when she let slip this speculation; she regretted it afterwards. Luckily her son took her remarks very quietly so there appeared to be no harm done. She knew he was sensitive. She would not have wanted to perturb him.

The baby, in its long white gown and tiny lace cap, was shown to Gideon, briefly, from the doorway of his room. Everyone sent messages of the child's lustiness and its likeness to him. His wife said it was unthinkable that she should come near a sick man while nursing her daughter. Gideon made no objection.

He had a lot of time for private thought that winter. Too much, perhaps.

Both Jukes brothers were now reconsidering what they wanted from this conflict. Both had been deeply affected by their great adventure to Gloucester. They felt entitled to political reward for their contribution. Lambert fell back into domesticity, but Gideon became ever more restless.

By winter, Gideon had to accept that his physical recovery was assured. He continued to mope by himself in the sickroom. The loss of his finger ends gave him an excuse. He was a specimen: doctors came and went, writing up notes for their memoirs. Gangrene was not unknown in camp fever patients, but it was rare, and his father enjoyed parading Gideon as a singular case. Civil war doctors and surgeons wanted specialist reputations. Who could blame them, when a surgeon's pay was only five shillings a day, and each had to equip himself with a medical chest to the value of twenty-five pounds *at his own expense*. Most wounded soldiers died. Most, therefore, would pay no fees.

At least being a specimen was a two-way process. Gideon made it a condition that his doctors had their learned papers printed by Robert Allibone.

His wife had continued to occupy their bedchamber, apart from him. He had barely seen Lacy since he came home. In the New Year his mother decided to restore normality, so Parthenope stripped the sick-room bed, pulled up floor mats and beat them in clouds of dust, making so much bustle that Gideon capitulated. He shambled back to his old room, where Lacy received him with a brief shrug, perhaps of welcome, or perhaps indifference.

At the foot of their bed stood the cradle with the baby. Various scents that emanate from infants and breast-feeding mothers suffused the atmosphere. Many a father has felt an outsider on the arrival of a first baby. Gideon was no exception.

The child's existence forced him to face his predicament. His lack of pride and excitement at the birth was reprehensible, and he knew it. Coming from a good home, he had been brought up to do better. At least while his daughter remained a babe-in-arms, he could assign her to his womenfolk; many men, and more women than is generally acknowledged, do not care for babies. Once this infant became mobile, Gideon knew, he would be obliged to take on the full role of a cherishing father. He must pet her, praise her, instruct her in spiritual matters, consider her education, give her a puppy or a singing-bird, have a family portrait painted – and he must uncomplainingly provide her with siblings.

His own parents were already besotted with their first grandchild. This only emphasised Gideon's awkwardness.

Lacy, sloe-eyed and now lazily voluptuous, never asked him to coo over the cradle or pick up the tiny bundle. She and Gideon stalked around one another, never acknowledging that anything was wrong. They did not yet have the bitterness that seeps through many longer marriages, but their silences were deadly.

In due course, Lacy granted her favours in bed. She gave him his rights without resistance, yet Gideon was made aware that she had condescended to do this, when she could just as easily have rebuffed him. He did not enjoy their lovemaking and quite clearly Lacy could take it or leave it. Such occasions became infrequent.

All over the country soldiers were returning from campaigns to find themselves strangers in their marriages. Everywhere fathers were missing crucial moments in their children's lives. However, real difficulties rarely happened while campaigns were as short as the Gloucester and Newbury march. The estrangement between Gideon and Lacy Jukes was reckoned by others to be caused by the war, but they both knew it had more deep-seated origins. Gideon was starting to analyse his doubts.

Elizabeth and Bevan Bevan sent the child an extravagantly expensive silver bowl as a baptism gift.

'Return it,' snapped Gideon. 'We shall not dowse her in a font. I believe in adult baptism.'

His mother looked up over her spectacles at this revelation.

'What are you my son?' enquired John Jukes mildly. 'An Anabaptist, a General or a Particular Baptist? Do we harbour a Browneist? A Dutch Mennonite? Are you for full baptismal immersion, for sprinkling – or merely for careful pouring from a neat Delft jug?' Gideon looked truculent.

While Lacy sat at the dinner table deciding whether to put up a fight, Gideon stiffened into his new role as a domestic autocrat. Lacy gave way, surprisingly. 'As you wish.' She shot him one tart look, then cast down her eyes like a model of patience.

'I am sure my uncle and his good wife Elizabeth meant well,' murmured Parthenope, though playing the peacemaker went against her feelings. Everyone present knew she thought poorly of Elizabeth.

'They are hoping to be godparents,' sneered John.

'We shall have no papistical godparents!' thundered Gideon. *They are buying me off,* he thought bitterly, as he too brooded on the Bevans' motives.

He knew that other members of his own family were judging him, in the dark way families have. Lacy herself fell silent. Among the Jukes she had a sullen reserve, as if she was trapped – and knew they all understood exactly *how* she had been trapped.

Lacy had named her daughter. Without consulting Gideon, she had chosen her own mother's name, one of the only signs ever that Lacy cared for somebody other than herself. The tiny scrap was Harriet Jukes.

'She is an innocent,' Parthenope consoled herself. 'Her sweet soul is unblemished in the eyes of the Lord.'

'*She* is an innocent!' Gideon agreed tartly.

As Harriet lay in her cradle with her eyes tight shut, she emitted a softly bubbling burp as if practising to charm apocalyptic judges. Her mother went to her. Her father would not look her way.

Gideon grasped the monstrous bowl by its rim and strode with it from the house. It was almost the first time he had ventured out since his fever; anger gave his long legs strength, despite the enormous weight of silver he was carrying. He did not, in fact, return it to the Bevans, but carried the loathed object to the Guildhall where he handed it in ceremonially to be melted down for the Parliamentary war effort.

In this way he did for the first time exert himself to play the father, deciding his child's political allegiance and disposing of her property. It struck him guiltily that baby Harriet might grow into a spirited young lady who would take him to task. The bowl had been handsome and she would be a City girl who could correctly assess the value of ornamental metalware. Gideon supposed he might teach her his ways of thinking, but he would have to desire the task. So far, he saw the child in the cradle as little to do with him. Some men thought they were fighting the war for their children, but not he – or not yet.

The silver bowl discussion was the closest he ever came to confronting Lacy. She must see his growing suspicion that she and her infant had been foisted on him. He started looking for an escape, rather than to plunge them into discord. Divorce only existed for monarchs and the aristocracy. Even kings and earls were forced to cite reasons such as non-consummation of the marriage. For Gideon it was an impossibility. He was the wrong class. In any case, he felt squeamish about suggesting that Harriet might be a bastard. Whether she was his flesh and blood or not, his kind heart failed at the thought of condemning her.

When Gideon recovered his strength he rejoined his Trained Band regiment, though what he had heard about recent manoeuvres still demoralised him. He did not want to find himself among reluctant comrades under a general they all resented. Sooner or later, on rotation, the main Green Regiment would be deployed with Waller.

He was struggling physically. The loss of his fingertips hampered loading and firing his musket. His captain suspended him from active duty. Gideon went back to work full-time at the print shop. Having to relearn hand movements made him far from dexterous there too. There were worse disabilities, but he resented his fate.

The *Public Corranto* was still being turned out every week, so when Gideon was particularly grumpy Robert sent him out transporting copies. A system had been developed where bundles of pamphlets or news-sheets were taken beyond London, along the road to Oxford in particular, in order to satirise the enemy and depress them with their godly opponents' good spirits. Royalist publications were imported on the way back. Nobody was supposed to travel either way without a pass; realistically travellers needed two passes, one from each army, although to be in possession of two was in itself dangerous. Troops saw it as proof of treachery. In the previous November one of the King's messengers had been hanged as a spy.

A secret network of couriers had grown up. Women disguised as beggars did much of the work. Printed papers were dumped at a series of drops, to be picked up and discreetly passed along the network. Within the area close to London, controlled by the Trained Bands who knew him, Gideon could safely take copies to the first hideout. There were a few butchers and chandlers in the ranks who would always give a printer backchat, but in general his colleagues saw this as God's work. They would wave him through checkpoints without bothering to ask questions. He was rarely stopped.

Then one day early in 1644, instead of his normal trip west out of Hammersmith, Gideon happened to go with a carter north towards St Albans. As they were returning via Bushey, they were suddenly surrounded by a small group of armed men. At first Gideon feared this troop were cavaliers. They had a high-handed, aggressive demeanour and they meant business. They were light-armed dragoons, speedy horsemen who trotted under black banners which, when the heavy fringed cloth flapped open in the spring breeze, revealed emblems of Bibles. This was a banner of righteousness, yet even after Gideon ascertained that the troops came from a Parliamentary garrison, the situation remained tricky. The dragoons were so very completely righteous they were keen to arrest anyone, never mind if he claimed to be from their own side.

The carter behaved as if none of this concerned him. He was a lean Londoner from a family in Wapping, a wiry old worker with a dogged, equable mentality, often silent although Gideon had gained his confidence. He kept to decades-old routines, bringing his lunch with him in a battered basket, where every item had its place. The food was always in a threadbare square of housewife-cloth, well laundered. Every day he ate cheese with shallots and a thick wad of dark bread. Using a short-bladed, bone-handled penknife, he trimmed off the cheese in equal-sized pieces. The shallots were neatly topped, tailed and halved. He carried a beer bottle, from which he drank half before he ate and the rest once he finished. Since his ancient horse was placid, he generally drove along while doing this.

The cavalry had appeared while the daily routine was in progress. Benjamin Lucock remained placidly on his seat and carried on eating. The haughty men in buff coats barely noticed him. Crunching half a shallot was clearly a sign of innocence. That his occupation was innocent seemed to be confirmed by a load of winter vegetables from a market garden and a brace of trussed-together geese he was taking home to his daughter.

More sinister was the tall young man clad in a brown suit and jaunty beaver hat, unarmed, and apparently without trade or other decent excuse to be wandering. Gideon Jukes was ordered to descend from the cart in order to be pushed around.

Gideon now suffered because of his quiet demeanour, learned over the years from Robert Allibone. Anyone from the country areas, as these Eastern Association dragoons all were, knew that Londoners were mouthy. Gideon submitted far too demurely. His answers made things worse: he claimed he belonged to the Trained Bands and had been on the march to Gloucester. 'Which regiment?'

'The Greens.'

'Colonel Pennington's?'

It was a trap, Gideon reckoned. Isaac Pennington commanded the White Regiment. With his heart pounding, he answered as levelly as he could. 'Our colonel is Alderman John Warner.'

'In the Greens?' The soldiers were wary. 'The Reds and the Blues relieved Gloucester, that's well known.'

'I took a man's place –'

'Who? – Zebediah Nobody!'

Gideon could only smile weakly. It seemed a long time since he had offered himself as a replacement for the draper in the Red Regiment, and he really could not remember what the man had been called.

Gideon explained that today he had been delivering Parliamentary news-sheets. He had taken the precaution of keeping one in the cart. The man questioning him accepted this copy of the *Public Corranto*, glanced at it, then rolled it and slapped it dismissively against his thigh. The dragoons were anxious to go back to their quarters with some prize – *any* prize. They condemned all news-sheets as seditious and suggested that Gideon was a spy.

The usual way to extract information from spies was to hang them up over a barrel of gunpowder, before applying lighted match to their fingers. Only the bravest held out.

The dragoons produced lit matchcord to terrorise Gideon, but when they seized his fists to tie him up, they came upon his missing fingertips. To them, this implied he had already been given the burn-treatment in some previous arrest. Now they had an excuse to treat him as an escaped prisoner. They threw him across the back of a spare horse, tied his arms and feet under its belly, and began taking him across country for interrogation. They had let the carter go.

Gideon had told the truth about his mission. That would leave him nothing to confess once they began to torture him.

Chapter Twenty-Eight

> *When civil dudgeon first grew high,*
> *And men fell out they knew not why?*
> *When hard words, jealousies, and fears,*
> *Set folks together by the ears,*
> *And made them fight, like mad or drunk,*
> *For Dame Religion, as for punk;*
> *Whose honesty they all durst swear for,*
> *Though not a man of them knew wherefore:*
> *When Gospel-Trumpeter, surrounded*
> *With long-ear'd rout, to battle sounded,*
> *And pulpit, drum ecclesiastick,*
> *Was beat with fist, instead of a stick;*
> *Then did Sir Knight abandon dwelling,*
> *And out he rode a-colonelling . . .*

Sir Samuel Luke was a Bedfordshire knight of approximately forty years. That is to say, since he was very particular, in the early March of 1644 he was still forty, but by the end of the month he was forty-one. Gideon Jukes might have made a pocketbook note of the date, had he known he was to encounter a famous man, a man who was fingered many years later as the original of the lead figure in Samuel Butler's popular chivalric satire *Hudibras*. As a printer he had an interest in bestsellers.

However, Gideon knew what he liked in literature, and it was never mock-heroic poetry. Besides, Butler claimed that Hudibras was modelled on a Devon man.

Sweating with apprehension and struggling for breath as the horse painfully bounced him about, Gideon was taken a day and a half's ride, including a night when he lay trussed up on straw in stables at

Dunstable. He offered to give his parole but was told parole was only for officers; spies were hog-tied until they were hanged.

These dragoons were artists in causing apprehension. There was nothing like dangling upside down with his face against a hot, hairy horse to convince a prisoner to confess.

The ride ended at last at a walled market town in a part of the country unfamiliar to Gideon. They had travelled north-west, to where Bedfordshire met Northamptonshire. He regarded this as wilderness.

When the horses slowed to a stop, other beasts neighed greetings from close by. Gideon could hear the familiar unhurried noise of a musket-barrel being cleaned inside with a scouring tool. There were men's voices, leisurely and with occasional laughter, along with a faint waft of tobacco smoke. Their accents were English, though to a nervous Londoner they smacked discouragingly of marsh and fen. Gideon and Lambert reckoned that everyone in the Midlands had cowpox and no sense of humour, while all East Anglians had webbed feet and three ears.

Without warning, someone cut him free. He slid down off the horse. As he landed backwards and floundered to regain his balance on failing legs, he took sly note of his surroundings. He must be in a garrison town. They had arrived outside the gateway to an old castle, with colours planted before it – another black flag with those Bibles – head-quarters, no doubt.

Gideon was pushed indoors, and taken up stone steps to a quiet upstairs saloon. Magisterial oak armchairs stood around a long table. The room was cold and fireless. Gideon, who felt desperately hungry, had noticed a faint scent of roast fowl as he blundered upstairs, but nothing was offered to him. From beyond the leaded windows came sounds of groups of tired horsemen, clattering home in the late after-noon as the light faded. No attempt was made to steal his money, had he had any. Gideon had been searched for weapons when he was first arrested, but he was neither stripped of his clothes nor kept tied up. The castle was secure; the town was fortified. There was no point in trying to escape. Perhaps he did not want to. Adventure was already calling.

A servant in a long leather apron carried in a candlestick. The man stood this at the centre of the table, then fussily pushed in a couple of the chairs, emphasising that Gideon was not to sit.

He did have company. A drippy-nosed Bedfordshire bumpkin of about fifteen had been kicking his heels in the room. When they were left alone together Gideon ascertained that the heavy-jowled young scowler was a free person, who wished to enlist. His mother had died; his father had remarried only two months later. The unhappy teenager found this so intolerable he had run away from home.

'Are you a soldier?' asked the youth, hopefully.

'A printer.'

'What do you print?' Always a dangerous question.

'Words.' It came out as if Gideon too were still a boorish, obstinate adolescent giving silly answers. Some memory made him add, 'I print the words. I never take responsibility for ideas.' The boy who had quarrelled with his father was unimpressed.

In then walked a civilian, a man with a downturned mouth, clad in a grey suit with slightly effusive white shirtbands, carrying a satchel of documents, bearing a goblet of claret, and eating an apple. He seemed to have recently partaken of a good supper and was now ready to clear off extra business before the day ended. Hudibras, the gallivanting, truth-defending hero, would possess a constant companion in his loyal squire, Ralpho. This secretary may have made himself the model for witty, prescient, courageous, loyal, level-headed Ralph. However, he introduced himself plainly as Mr Butler, secretary to Sir Samuel Luke, MP.

Samuel Butler was around thirty years old, roughly ten years older than Gideon. The son of a minor landowner, educated at Cambridge University, his interests were history and poetry, music and painting. But he needed to earn his living. As an administrative assistant in a garrison he brought intellect and culture, not to mention legible handwriting for letters and lists.

Any future poet would regard a printer as a hireling, a mere ink-stained artisan. A printer deplored a poet as a dilettante dreamer, whose much-revised effusions were a devil to disentangle for type-setting and – more important – brought in no money. However, at their first meeting Gideon, with his stomach rumbling violently, was simply offended by the way the man chomped so thoughtlessly on his fruit. It looked like a pippin. A little rough-skinned. Juicy, crisp and sweet.

The young boy, who seemed edgy and liable to steal the firedogs, had to be tackled first. Mr Butler ascertained that he was able-bodied and just of serving age (fifteen years to sixty-five). He came from a small village called Elstow, where his father, though a freeholder, worked as a maker and mender of pots and pans.

'A *tinker*?' The secretary looked askance. Though this boy's humble, pot-fettling background might one day seem romantic, in 1644 at Newport it counted against him to be the barely schooled son of a Bedford kettle-mender. Parliament had struggled hard to shake off the Royalist slander that the Earl of Essex led a disreputable rabble of decayed tapsters, released prisoners – and tinkers. Moreover here, one sniffing boy was much like another: very young recruits were a nightmare. Lads played the fool with gunpowder, whined about long hours on duty, drank, stole food, were scared to be in open country in the dark, missed their mothers and were dangerously uncoordinated when first put on a horse.

'So you are a ragamuffin.'

'I have had schooling; I can read and write.'

'And curse and swear, lie and blaspheme against the Lord?' The boy nodded enthusiastically but Samuel Butler made preparations to admit him to Captain Ennis's company. A soldier was called to lead the recruit to the quartermaster.

'Robert Cox has come in,' the trooper mentioned to the secretary. 'News from Oxford.'

'I will take his report shortly – If the rabbits are ready to go up to Sir Samuel's father, there is correspondence too. The messenger must wait, though; I must copy it into the Letter Book. If Cox has acquired the latest *Mercurius Aulicus*, send it straight in to Sir Samuel. He will post it on to Sir Oliver, but he will want to read it first.'

Mr Butler's pen was dipped into an inkpot and applied with due formality in the regimental roll. He called after the tinker's lad, 'I forgot your name?'

'John Bunyan.'

Gideon Jukes had now met *two* notables of English literature. He had no idea. All he cared about was the secretary's apple. It had been reduced to a core, not tossed aside, but gently placed upon a sheet of used drafting paper. There it sat growing soft, while fuzziness spread about the nearest ink on the paper and the mouldings made by Samuel Butler's teeth started gently to go brown . . .

Having dispatched Bunyan, the secretary remembered his wine, sipped from the goblet, and immediately cheered up. 'And your name?'

'Gideon Jukes. Sir, I have not eaten for two days.'

'Well, well; credentials first . . . Age?'

'Twenty-three.'

'From?'

'The City of London.'

Butler was scowling. 'You were *brought in*.' That must be garrison code for an arrest.

Gideon let rip: 'I have been *brought* to misery. I was stopped in my honest business, insulted, kidnapped, threatened, starved, and joggled here on a cursed, mangy, thin-tailed, farting horse . . .' The future master of colourful tetrameters looked intrigued. 'Since your rob-dogs plucked me up, no one has even had the courtesy to tell me where I am, so I can put it in my petition of complaint!'

'Newport Pagnell.' It meant nothing. His friends and family would never think to look for Gideon here, even if they raised a ransom. 'Who are you for, Jukes?' It was a standard question, though Mr Butler had not asked it of the enlisting boy.

'For Parliament.'

'For Parliament *and the King*?'

'That rubric's a nonsense, a coward's refuge.'

Butler smiled slightly. 'So you say you are in the London Trained Bands?'

To Londoners there were no others worth mentioning. Gideon retorted proudly, 'I am in the Green Regiment, under Colonel John Warner, alderman and grocer. My troop is the third, that of Captain Robert Mainwaring. You may write to him to vouch for me, which he will do. He works at the Customs House, lives in Aldermanbury . . .'

At the secretary's silence, he realised a letter requesting validation had already been sent. They were hot on correspondence here.

'Why are you not at your work or with your regiment?'

Gideon held up his damaged fingers. 'Not safe with a musket. I need to practise dexterity.'

'So why were you brought here?' asked Mr Butler, looking away from the missing digits shyly. 'Did you have a ticket for the road?'

'No.'

'Why not?'

'I was doing loyal work.'

'There is an ordnance: you must be issued with a pass.'

'Apparently so,' replied Gideon. 'Hence I am deemed to be a spy.'

'That seems a reasonable deduction. Are you?' From a poet, this was refreshingly direct. Mr Samuel Butler had not yet settled into his future role. If he had a work in progress, he must be writing it secretly in his closet after his duties, scrawling couplets more as a refuge from the tedium of military life than in any hope yet of fortune and fame. '*Are you a spy, Master Jukes?*'

'No.' Gideon, the quiet man, stood his ground monosyllabically.

Then the secretary asked him in a mild tone: 'Would you like to be?'

For a Cheapside boy, the relocation offer was an insult. So was the way they had pressed him to enlist here. 'After your poxy horse ride from Hell?'

'Then go home to your family.'

Ah. It was an offer of distancing himself from his troubles. 'Oh I'll stay if I choose, sir!'

'Well, make up your mind, Master Jukes.'

'Very well, I shall try it.'

So, once London had vouched for him, Gideon took up a new career.

Newport Pagnell was, and is, a small English market town. Historically, it grew up beside the great North West Road, the old Roman military route across the Midlands towards North Wales. On the way to Northampton, it was fifty miles from London, fifteen from Bedford, thirty or more from Oxford. During the civil war Newport Pagnell was in the territory of the Eastern Association. Their committee regarded it as a hamlet on the road to somewhere else. But in the military context, to be within reach of those other centres justified Newport Pagnell's opinion that it was 'of considerable consequence'.

Gideon learned that the establishment of a Parliamentary garrison had been luck. At the end of 1643, the cavalier Sir Lewis Dyve had captured Newport Pagnell. Prince Rupert wanted to harry Parliament's Eastern Association; during the operation Royalists even briefly occupied Bedford and skirled around Northampton stealing cattle. However, less than three weeks later, Dyve evacuated Newport in haste as a result of an 'error': misunderstanding garbled instructions from the King.

As soon as Dyve decamped, his Parliamentarian neighbour, Sir Samuel

Luke, nipped in. Any Royalist plan to invade the Eastern Association was abandoned, permanently, as it turned out. Parliamentary cavalry, under Oliver Cromwell, was quartered around Newport that winter, for security. By the time Gideon arrived they had moved off, but connections with Cromwell persisted and he heard the name regularly.

Newport proved valuable, just beyond the King's reach from Oxford yet close enough for informants to report whatever the King was up to. From here, Sir Samuel Luke tenaciously kept watch on the enemy. His activities ranged over a fifty-mile radius in all directions and sometimes his contacts went further.

Gideon rarely had direct conversation with his colonel, but came to know him well by sight: a short man, broad of beam and bulbous-bellied, with a full jaw, fleshy face, long straggling hair and a brocaded neckerchief, who busied himself continuously. 'He knows who you are,' people said. Anyone who rode back to the garrison with information could feel confident that his debriefing, whether taken by Samuel Butler or by one of the officers, would be passed to the colonel himself; if relevant, it would be relayed by letter from him to the field generals or even to Parliament, probably the same day.

Luke was educated, energetic and obstinate. Like his father, Sir Oliver Luke, who was still active at Westminster, Samuel was a traditional English country squire. Hardly a day went by without his sending conies to his father or giving presents of deer or game pies to other gentlemen whose goodwill might be useful. To Gideon, this country life of sport and vigorous ingratiation came as a shock. He did not expect to see hunting hounds bustling through the garrison, or to make way for Sir Oliver Luke's falconer, bearing his hawk upon his arm as he went from wood to park. Gideon had always known there were favours done in the City, and although he only mildly disapproved of the weekly rabbits sent up to London for Sir Oliver Luke, he had much stronger feelings about the regular handouts to other landowners: the does, the red deer pies, the braces of partridge or pheasant, the teal and snipe. All the local estates were carefully protected by orders from Sir Samuel, whether owned by Parliamentarians or Royalists. It made the war, in which honest working men were dying, seem a mere game to the gentry.

There was more congenial bustle at Newport: the visits of Sir Samuel's agent, Mr Love, who brought funds from the Eastern Association counties – or with more frequency took anguished letters from Luke, trying to wring out arrears in order to feed and equip the garrison soldiers; the arrival of carts from Sir Samuel's quartermaster in London, carts bearing military equipment of all kinds – together with Sir Samuel's wine supply; and the constant flow in and out of cavalry.

The regime was unique. When other garrisons took prisoners – known Royalists or suspected spies – they sent them to Newport for examination. From Newport itself, regular parties of horsemen rode out to find and beat up Royalist soldiers, whom they cheerfully killed or took prisoner, then they carried off provisions and horses. They roamed through villages near Oxford – Burford, Bicester, Woodstock – harrying the King's main field army. Then individual scouts, colleagues Gideon came to know, travelled even longer distances – Banbury, Chard, even Salisbury – to discover information about enemy troop movements.

One of the first questions Gideon had been asked was 'Do you ride, Jukes?'

'I have sat on a horse.'

'Do you *ride*?'

'Not as a cavalryman would.'

'Then learn.'

The next time new horses were brought up from Smithfield, one was allocated to him. He would never be a safe infantry musketeer again; the complicated manoeuvres with bullets and powder were now too cumbersome for his poor fingers. So he happily became a dragoon, armed with a musket and a long sword, neither of which he used frequently, while he struggled to lure good service from his lacklustre nag. Mostly, as part of Luke's team, he had to master questioning and listening. Once he had learned his way around the districts, he became a valued independent scout.

Luke's scouts diligently watched Royalist regiments. They counted groups of the enemy, noted their arms and the quality of their horses, and tried to discover where they were going. They picked up Royalist news-sheets. They questioned people in local villages after the enemy had been there to demand taxes, weapons, food, or quarters. They knew all the inns. They stopped and searched travellers. They developed relationships with tradesmen and pedlars. A horse losing a shoe would give a good excuse to gossip with a farrier. Market days were good cover.

Sometimes they organised real spies who went in disguise into Royalist towns and garrisons. This included Oxford. Gideon volunteered himself but was too tall and too flaxen-haired. The task called for men who could pass inconspicuously – and women; they had a she-intelligencer called Parliament Jane in Oxford. The task was dangerous. Parliament Jane's husband was hanged by the King at Carfax. Undercover scouts had a short life.

Riding around by himself gave Gideon time to brood.

It was symptomatic of his failing relationship with his wife, that he wrote to tell his parents and Robert Allibone he had joined the Newport Pagnell regiment, but not Lacy. A month after his arrival, a letter from his father informed him sadly that both Lacy and the baby, Harriet, had been ill and had died.

Gideon tried to ignore his relief. His problems did not end. Now he felt guilty for leaving them.

Joining up at Newport Pagnell in order to forget his troubles now seemed pointless – even though Gideon knew he had an aptitude and a liking for his new work. At fifty miles' distance from London it could have been easy to put his bereavement from his mind. Yet as he rode around, often solitary, he had time and opportunity to wrestle all the more fiercely with his doubts.

Had Lacy Keevil been already with child – and had she known it – when he married her? Had he been singled out as a fool? Who was the child's father? What was the Bevans' involvement? Remembering how eagerly they had pressed for the union, they must have known the situation. So were Bevan and Elizabeth simply Lacy's keepers at the time of her disgrace, adults forced to scurry round to find a solution when a young girl in their household had behaved foolishly? Or was there a darker motive in their rush to find her a husband?

Gideon was not entirely pitiless. He saw that perhaps Lacy herself had been cruelly used. All of their lives had been soured by whatever his wife had done – or had had done to her. Now Lacy was dead, along with her four-month-old baby, and she left Gideon damaged. He might never really find the answers to his suspicions, but he had lost all faith in women.

He threw himself into scouting as if to court danger and seek oblivion. He went forwards, but he rode in a grim mood.

Chapter Twenty-Nine

Newport Pagnell and Stony Stratford: 1644

Gideon came to recognise many of the people who lived and worked in the districts through which he regularly rode. Some he knew well. Clergymen, innkeepers, market women and beggars were useful sources of information; after a season he recognised regular faces and exchanged greetings with many. He also took keen notice of strangers. Occasionally, he reported criminal activities to the authorities.

His remit covered the area towards Northampton. While looking out for Royalist fugitives after the battle of Marston Moor, he spotted a ragged young woman, lurking in a church porch. It was a medieval chapel-of-ease that lay alongside Watling Street on the west side of Stony Stratford. The waif was slightly built, her face hidden in a grubby shawl. Gideon watched her enter the ancient door to the square tower. A bundle in her arms aroused his immediate suspicions. He waited. As he had feared, when she emerged a few minutes later, she was carrying nothing.

She set off fast, heading away from the historic town. After a moment's consideration, Gideon urged his horse forward and overtook her. Dismounting, he stopped her.

'What are you doing?'

'Looking for horse mushrooms.'

'Too early! Don't lie or you'll be taken up for spying.' It was August. Gideon had been intently watching the hedgerows to which she clung, since that was where ambushes were laid; they were still overgrown and green. Nuts and berries had yet to ripen; spiders' webs did not yet glisten between the twigs; autumn mists had yet to bring up mushrooms, puffballs or fairy rings in wet fields and cowpats. Soldiers and scouts were still abroad. Battles yet lay ahead in the calendar.

Barely more than a child, the girl with the poor knowledge of nature was colourless, skinny and showed signs of perpetual hardship. She looked intensely agitated. She knew enough to control her truculence at being apprehended, however. Nor did she try to run away, although while she talked to Gideon she kept dodging out of arm's reach. She admitted to being a traveller; she claimed she earned her living by knocking on doors and begging for work.

'You mean knocking on doors and hoping to steal something! Where have you come from?'

'North . . .' She became vague, acting simple-minded.

'Don't play the loon,' Gideon snapped. 'I'll have to send you to Bedlam.' Mention of Bedlam chilled her, for reasons he could not imagine. 'Where are you going?'

'London!' exclaimed the vagrant, as if she thought herself on a highway to paradise.

'Ha!'

The girl stared. She saw a tall, fair-haired man in a well-filled buff coat, worsted britches and riding boots, a dragoon in his twenties who had an air of easy competence. Unperturbed by her attitude, he behaved as if he were in charge of this stretch of road. Unlike other soldiers she met, he made no move to threaten her, either with the sword in hangers from his belt or the musket which he had left beside his saddle. However, he kept himself between her and the horse, which was a grey mare, now stretching its neck after lush roadside grass, rather knock-kneed but well cared for.

There was no chance of stealing the gun, or the beaver hat which also hung on the saddle. The mare wasn't worth any risk. A three-shilling reject; good horses cost ten times that. The man noticed her looking at the gun. Having taken his measure, she decided not to try anything. His lips compressed slightly, as if he read her decision.

'Do you walk alone?' She nodded, almost too weary to speak. 'Always?'

'I met a pedlar woman, carrying a great pack of needles and threads, ribbons, peg dolls, shoelaces, buttons and buckles . . .' The wonders of the pack had held her in thrall. 'She took me along with her and talked of God and such –' Perhaps a Parliamentary soldier would be softened by mention of God, she thought, though he stood listening with the same quizzical look. He was in fact struggling to follow her sing-song whining accent. 'She told me of her life, selling to the rich then saving pennies of her profit. She swore she would one day be greatly rich herself, after this life of careful toil, and would leave all her money to the poor.'

Gideon reckoned the pedlar must have been a travelling Quaker or similar. 'Does she preach?'

'That would be shocking!'

'Perhaps not. The women who do it say they follow Hannah and Abigail.'

Biblical names meant nothing to the vagrant. 'She preaches, but I never heard her . . . She is a married woman, but left her husband to shift for himself while she takes the word of God along the roads. I wonder what her husband thinks!' For once the girl showed a trace of amusement. Gideon let himself grin back.

Now she acquired a more calculating expression, as she noticed he was good-looking when he relaxed. He ignored it. Women's wiles only hardened his heart now. He was a betrayed man; he knew all their tricks. 'So why did you leave this honest woman's company?' *And where is she? Has the vagabond murdered the preaching ribbon-seller? – No, or this scruff would be humping the pack of haberdashery herself and trying to sell me shoelaces* . . . When there came no answer, Gideon suggested, 'I suspect you bore a child.'

'You think I killed it!' flared the girl, denying nothing. That surprised him. Gideon was always unnerved by how much authority he carried, how readily people answered his questions.

'I believe you left it in the church.'

Infanticide was the last resort of single mothers. Abandoning a child for the parish was much more common. To a harassed churchwarden, stuck with finding a wet-nurse and paying for the child's upkeep at sixpence a week from scarce parish funds, that too was iniquitous, but Gideon could see this waif was barely able to keep herself alive. She stood no chance of bringing up a child; she ought to be in parish care herself. 'Maybe you put it in the safest place you could. Was it born in a barn?'

'It was born in a ditch.'

'You might both have died there.'

'Oh easily!' With a wry private smile, the girl reflected on how close they came. The baby had emerged tiny and blue. Although people of superior rank thought beggars gave birth easily, she had lain quite exhausted for a long time afterwards. She was revolted by the mess of the afterbirth and had to force herself somehow to cut the umbilical cord with a flint. When the snuffling child was free, she had then been severely tempted to leave it naked in the ditch-water and walk away. Instead, she sneaked into the church with it, because the baby had reminded her of carrying little Robert Lucas in her arms.

'Male or female?' asked the soldier, worming the truth out. 'Did you trouble to look?'

Very reluctantly, the young mother admitted, 'Male.'

'Who was the father?' It was the question unmarried mothers were pressed to answer – on their bed of labour, when possible – because the named father then had to pay to maintain the child. The girl lost patience with this inquisition. She squared her shoulders and quickly, fluently, contemptuously, summed up her past few months: in disguise as a boy in two different garrisons, then 'befriended' by men who obtained carnal knowledge of her frail body, seducing her in secret by offering apparent kindness. She had never known men's kindness before. She could not judge whether their overtures were genuine or false. So she had been coerced and betrayed – yet now she accepted her fate without rancour.

'You should be sent back to your home parish.' That did terrify her. Though she refused to name where she came from, she railed agitatedly against cavaliers on a killing spree, then plundering, raping and burning. Gideon guessed: 'Birmingham?'

Round-eyed, she gasped, 'You know?'

'From a news pamphlet.'

'Was *I* in that?' The thought both horrified and fascinated her.

'Only the dead were named.'

Patiently Gideon began to explain how news was gathered, written up and printed, why pamphlets were produced. He told her of his own part, then he tried to recruit her for Robert Allibone's network of news distributors.

She said she would do it; he had doubts. Small sums were paid to the beggars who moved the bundles of news-sheets from London to Oxford and elsewhere, but when he mentioned the figure he sensed that it was insufficient to tempt this free spirit. She would loathe the necessary supervision. So great was her anxiety to leave the vicinity where she had abandoned her baby, she was pretending to co-operate. But Gideon saw she was unreliable, so the conversation petered out.

Gideon also left the question of the baby. If the young mother was fifteen, as she told him, she would be only a year less than Lacy Keevil when she too found herself about to bear a child by a man she could not, or would not, name. He had bitter fellow-feeling for the waif's plight.

He might have ridden back to the church porch and looked for the whimpering bundle, but if he was discovered doing that he could be accused of fathering the infant himself. He had an informant to meet that afternoon; he was beginning to resent delays.

Before he left her, he asked her name. She gave him the defiantly straight stare that vagabonds used when they were lying. 'Dorothy Groome.'

'I think that was the pedlar woman's name,' Gideon rebuked her mildly.

'It is a good name!' The girl rounded on him defiantly. 'What is *your* name?'

'Gideon Jukes.' He was already mounting his three-shilling horse, routinely cursing as the idiotic beast tried to wander away from him.

'What place is this?' the waif called after him.

'Stony Stratford – Calverton parish, should you wish to reclaim your child.'

The girl dragged her tired feet, setting off on her long walk towards London. If she ever reached the city, Gideon thought, she would be sucked into the competing multitude. Among the starved masses on the hostile streets, her youth and her innocence could only tell against her. She would be lucky to last a week.

He did not see the waif in his area again. They had had a chance encounter. Neither expected to remember it.

By that time in late 1644, Gideon was greatly anxious about the progress of the war. After the great Parliamentary victory at Marston Moor the King achieved a personal triumph in shattering one of his opponents' armies, that of Sir William Waller at Cropredy Bridge, and outmanoeuvred the Earl of Essex in the pointless disaster of Lostwithiel. Charles spent the summer pottering, relieving garrisons that could well have been left to their own devices and languorously guesting in loyal gentlemen's houses as if the war could wait on his pleasure.

At Newport, Sir Samuel Luke was twitchy. The town's defences were in a bad way; he could obtain neither money, men nor tools for renewal works. His garrison muttered mutinously. Soldiers were unpaid. He was in poor health and feeling the cold; he sent to London for his fur coat.

Throughout that autumn, Gideon and the other scouts kept nervous watch on the area between Oxford and London. In October, the remnants of Essex's army and the relics of Waller's both joined Manchester in a blockade to prevent the King advancing to London. It was an unhappy merger. The Parliamentary commanders bickered. The troops were mutinous and demoralised. Essex was constantly sending to Parliament with recriminations against others; then he conveniently 'fell ill', when the Parliamentary forces, united in name though not in spirit, faced battle with the King at Newbury. Parliament's forces failed to co-operate. There was confusion and stalemate; after sundown, the King and his men were allowed to slip away through a gap and escape.

Charles would spend the winter of 1644–5 in Oxford, while his opponents reviewed their lacklustre efforts of the previous year. The baffling ineptitude at the second battle of Newbury achieved one useful result: men of energy, headed by Oliver Cromwell, urged Parliament to change their military affairs.

Now Sir Samuel Luke's scouts kept a closer than ever watch on Oxford. He had a paranoid fear that the King intended to strike at his garrison: *'There is some treacherous plot against us at present, for they never had that confidence and cheerfulness at Oxford as they have now . . .'* Luke's men were deserting; they knew the rival garrison at Aylesbury was better supported and more regularly paid than theirs. When Sir Samuel was recalled to sit in Parliament along with all the other members, he protested that he needed to stay at Newport or his unhappy soldiers would disband themselves.

None the less, he was forced to go up to Westminster. A new army was being proposed, in which no members of Parliament would hold commissions. At Newport Pagnell there was much troubled discussion of the impact this would have; Sir Samuel might never return.

He might be forced, as a member of Parliament, to 'volunteer' to give up his command. So it happened that during the lull in fighting at the end of the year, Gideon Jukes was given leave to visit his family. The vexed officers at Newport Pagnell had written Sir Samuel Luke a letter of support: *'Sir, we your poor and discontented officers are desirous you take notice how ready and cheerful we shall be to serve under you or any other body...'* Gideon thought it muddled and misguided, but he did not demur when his captain chose him to convey the letter. While Sir Samuel Luke was in London, he occupied a property that had been part of the King's Printing House at Blackfriars. 'You're a printer, Trooper Jukes; I can trust you to find the house.'

Gideon was told he could spend a week among his family. 'I'll try and bring back new britches!' he promised, for uniforms were in short supply.

'The devil with britches; we can fight the King bare-arsed. Bring bullets!' chortled a sergeant, sucking on an empty pipe as if the memory of old smoke that imbued the browned clay would bring him comfort. 'And remember, Cheapside boy, if you run into a great beast, square and bellowing, with a leg at each corner, it is a *cow*.'

Jokes about Londoners never having seen cattle gave endless entertainment to the country-born.

There were more jests about whether Gideon could find his way back to London, but thanks to the ancient Romans, it was a perfectly straight ride for two days down Watling Street until he passed under the shadow of Old St Paul's. He then simply had to turn off into Bread Street where his parents lived.

Approaching the city, when he came up to the Wardour Street Fort in the Lines of Communication, the sentries' cadences of London speech gave him a deep pang. 'Let him in, lads! It's Private Jukes, wandering home from market with a bag of magic beans...'

Gideon had adapted his City vowels while at Newport. The Northamptonshire turnips pretended they could not understand him otherwise. As he thanked the sentries, grinning at their badinage, he heard his natural accent return and felt he had become himself again after living in a kind of disguise for many months.

Homesickness swept over him. He realised how tired he was of riding around alone among woods, fields and beggarly villages. He turned in through the city gate. As he entered the metropolitan clamour and bustle, an enormous yearning to be back here struck. Encountering the smoke from thousands of chimneys in coal-burning homes and businesses, Gideon Jukes took the deepest breath he could and let the old familiar choking smog of London fill every cranny of his lungs.

Chapter Thirty

London and Newport Pagnell: 1644–45

Although he had given his word he would return to the garrison, and meant it, Gideon was surprised just how strongly home exerted its call. He could understand soldiers who deserted. If they chose to slink away, there would be little comeback; so grim was the manpower situation, apprehended deserters were simply returned to their colours and not punished.

As he sat at his mother's table, devotedly plied with pudding, Gideon was overwhelmed with yearning for ordinary life. 'I have to go back!' he warned, as much to remind himself. Parthenope pushed a wisp of greying hair under her cap, and nodded unconvincingly. He worried about her; ten months had wrought too many changes. She looked older, thinner, more anxious about his father. John had altered even more. He sat like a wraith at the fireside, hardly communing.

'He knows you!' Parthenope had exclaimed in delight when Gideon first entered. He realised there must be times when John Jukes no longer did know people. The old fellow beamed happily, aware that this was Gideon back. Shocked, his son saw that next time he came home − if there was a next time − either or both of his parents might be gone.

Others were already lost. Parthenope formally told Gideon how his wife and child sickened and died, how and where they were buried. He dutifully listened. 'I wrote to her mother, Gideon.' He was surprised. 'Oh, I am sure Elizabeth passed on the news. But we had taken Lacy into our family and I wanted to relate it in my own way . . . No answer came.' Parthenope sounded disappointed, and a little put out. 'Uncle Bevan and Elizabeth were at the funeral. They sat extremely quietly.' *Chastened!* thought Gideon bleakly.

When Parthenope fell silent he exclaimed, 'I should like to have known the truth.'

'Well, it is all finished.' His mother patted his shoulder vaguely. She was too good a woman to admit, even privately, that Gideon had had a fortunate escape. 'She was a strange girl, but she is gone, and so is the dear baby . . . It is all done with.'

He would never be free of it, however.

As if they knew Gideon was home, the Bevans came visiting like irritating ticks. Parthenope's mood towards her uncle must have softened enough for them to be sure of seats in the upstairs parlour for half an hour, but Gideon remained obdurate. Hearing Elizabeth's and Bevan's voices, he lit off through the back door, hid in the yard temporarily, then escaped over a fence, though it was bitter January and he was coatless and hatless.

He marched to Basinghall Street, where he was welcomed by Robert Allibone. On hearing that the Bevans had swanned into Cheapside, Robert winced and at once locked up the print shop; they headed for a tavern. The Star in Coleman Street lay nearest, and had enough reputation for hatching revolution to deter Bevan Bevan if he came on a search for Gideon. 'Being put into the horse-trough gave him an ague,' sighed Robert. 'I hear he is but a shadow of himself – yet it is an obnoxious shadow still.'

'Don't talk of him.'

'Then I shall order instead.' For all its political reputation, the Star had a quiet, almost dull atmosphere. It advertised a hearty beef roast, which the landlord was delighted to provide for Robert; devout revolutionaries rarely opened their purses for more than bread and butter, so the roast was close to expiry on the charger. After three days in his mother's kitchen, Gideon groaned and could not think of food.

By chance they met a group from the Trained Bands' Blue Regiment, Lambert's regiment, men whom Gideon remembered from the Gloucester march. The Blues normally congregated at alehouses in Bread Street or on Huggin Hill, but they had come north for a change of scenery. Christmas was little celebrated in the City; shops remained open, though it was a quiet time for trade. At New Year there was an allowed spirit of renewal. The men were in a mood to gather and gossip, reviewing the previous year and making prophecies for the next.

The Blues and the Reds had spent the past autumn in the

Parliamentary blockade, stationed at Reading and then in action at Newbury. Conversation inevitably turned on comparison between the two battles there. But first Gideon heard in more terrible detail what had happened at the defeat in Cornwall.

'We met the few lads who managed to struggle back. Those poor devils had a time of it. Getting penned up in Cornwall was folly by Old Robin. They ended at Lostwithiel, in a deep valley with a river to one side and steep hills around them, and only open sea ahead. It was a desperate place, with the local people violently hostile. Many only spoke a foreign language, and claimed to know no English. There was neither food nor any provisioning to be had. Our fellows were starved to the bone there for eight days, under constant attack. The cavalry cut their way out, by good management and luck, but for the rest it was hopeless. Then Essex left them, very suddenly, to save himself from capture, and was fetched off in a fishing smack. He had not even told Skippon what he intended.'

'This is a bad story!'

'True enough.' More wine was downed despondently. 'Skippon made the best surrender he could, and upon terms. Luckily the King was also hard pressed, too deprived of supplies to remain there himself. And so it was agreed that our infantry could march out, every man above corporal keeping his weapons, on a promise that they would not fight again until they came to Southampton. They marched through the enemy, who said they hung their heads like sheep. The very lice upon them were more alive than they. But the terms were broken. Our men were fallen upon, stripped, battered. The King and some of his officers tried to drive off troublemakers with the flats of their swords – but they did not try hard enough. Locals and disobedient Royalist soldiers tore the very shirts from our boys' backs, stole their weapons, reviled them, shoved them in the mire and kicked them, harried and taunted them. There was no food. The enemy went ever ahead of them, taking all from the villages. Our men shuffled through driving wind and rain, shivering, naked and unshod. Skippon had his coach, but to his credit he stayed right with them until he brought that miserable band safe into Southampton. Most never made it. They dropped in mid-stride, then they died where they dropped. We heard from those we met that only one in ten men came through their hardship alive. There are rotting bodies like milestones all along the roadside from Fowey to Southampton.'

Respectful silence fell. Eventually Robert prompted, 'When you met the survivors at Newbury . . . ?'

'Dismal as ghosts.'

The Blues were sombre. They hunched over their cups, each man turning into himself as he imagined what Essex's humiliated infantry had endured.

'Well, they were afforded some revenge –' Empty flagons and trenchers skidded swiftly across the worn oak taproom table to illustrate the battle at Newbury for Gideon and Robert. 'This is Shaw House . . . Donnington Castle . . . Speen village. The first encounter was at Shaw. The plan was for a double-pronged attack. In the hours of darkness Waller and Skippon, with a large contingent, had marched right around –' A sweep with goblets, scraping on the board, indicated a flanking move. 'They were to invade Speen, while Manchester was to charge on Shaw as soon as he heard their cannon. Waller duly did the business. That was when we saw the broken-hearted relics of Lostwithiel regain their manhood. They marched on, valiantly singing psalms, despite a hail of case-shot that ravaged the ranks. When they came to the very cannon that had been taken from them at Lostwithiel, their emotion was pitiful. Some embraced the gun-barrels with tears in their eyes. Prince Maurice had Cornishmen in his forces – they ran for it, shrieking. They knew what to expect. Our fellows raced after them and gave no quarter.'

No need to describe the Cornishmen's bloody end.

Though all had been confusion, these men who served at Newbury were certain what went wrong. 'Manchester failed to busy himself when he heard the guns. Men fought like furies at Speen, expecting Manchester's attack on Shaw to come at every moment; he did nothing. He took an hour to engage, and was then repulsed by Sir George Lisle –'

'Lisle, it was said, threw off his buff coat and fought in his white shirt, so his men could still see him in the gloom.' Robert had already read about this.

'Aye, while our dreary commanders dithered like blushing flower-girls . . . So the joint attack failed. Manchester would not bestir himself until half an hour from sunset. As soon as darkness came, the enemy reorganised and got safe away.'

'So where is the blame in this?' asked Robert, thoughtfully.

'Chaos at the top. We boys put our lives at hazard while the commanders niggle. *"He stole my toy!" "I'm the eldest!" "I hate him – I shan't play with him!"* The whole past season has been that way. And they were quarrelling days later, when the King came back. Reinforced by Prince Rupert, he danced in and carried his cannon out of Donnington, just as he had always intended. Our generals stood passive and refused battle.' Gideon knew this had annoyed Sir Samuel Luke. He related how Luke was livid when the King was allowed to retrieve his cannon from Donnington Castle, since they needed some great guns for Newport.

Disgusted, the Blues summoned another round of drinks. Robert Allibone tried to tell them lessons had been learned in Parliament. Oliver Cromwell, whose own role at Newbury had been less than stellar, had none the less been furiously lambasting the Earl of Manchester for 'backwardness', virtually accusing him of dereliction of duty. Even so, Cromwell now argued that it was pointless to assign blame; a remedy was needed. A committee was ordered to consider 'a frame or model of the whole militia'. All serving members of both Houses would voluntarily resign from army command and return to government, so the jealous earls and their fractious juniors would be removed at a stroke. The newly modelled army would be a national force, under one commander.

True soldiers, the Blues were happy to complain about their masters, but when theory cropped up, they lost interest.

In the course of the week, Gideon managed to hand over the Newport officers' letter to Sir Samuel Luke – along with two large veal pies baked by his mother. Parthenope had noted Gideon's stories of how country landowners liked presents. There was some coldness of reception for the letter, and Gideon was told he need not wait to take a reply. He had therefore to return next day to Newport. On his last evening, he went again to a tavern, this time with his brother Lambert. They took along their father, his role strangely changed so he seemed like a small boy being allowed out with adults. Lambert led them down Thames Street to the gracious area where once wealthy merchants had houses on the old road down to London Bridge.

Lambert knew a good tavern; Lambert always did. A hum of voices rose as the door was opened. It had a dark, noisy taproom, full of busy argument. Flagstone floors; dark panelled walls; two rows of old long tables; casement windows, set in deep embrasures, but barely visible through the smoke from pipes and the great log fire at the further end; waiting men and girls moving about rapidly, with trays borne aloft on their shoulders.

As soon as he entered, Gideon re-experienced his homesickness for London life. Lambert was subdued, regretful at losing him. As they ordered, Gideon looked around and listened to the flow of voices. He realised that he had been missing not only London, but the thrill of plotting. Although he liked his work as a scout, life at Newport Pagnell seemed empty by comparison. He had enjoyed the years leading up to war. He had been fired by political tension, excited by the hope of change. He loved being among men with opinions. These here were probably arguing about the rising price of haddock, but it could just as well be about freedom from tyranny.

That was why, sitting in Lambert's chosen inn off New Fish Street Hill, Gideon took a decision that if the army really was to be remodelled, he would try to be transferred to the new force. He told Lambert. The brothers' old wrangling had diminished. Partly it was the shift in their joint responsibility for their father, who now sat with them silently, wearing a sweet smile, far away in some world they could not enter. 'Lambert, I am sick of being stuck hungry in a backwater. To be honest, it is galling that we are pitifully equipped and never paid. We need our salaries so we can eat. Is it too much to ask?'

'*Spare the country and pinch the soldier, that's the way to thrive!*'

'Proverb?'

'Read it in a news-sheet.'

'Oh then it must be true! The new army will have regular monies, guaranteed by Parliament.'

'You believe that?' scoffed Lambert.

'No, but who wants his old-age memories to be of *Newport Pagnell?*' The two Londoners laughed.

Lambert confessed that he too wanted to move on from the Trained Bands. They both saw the problem for him. Who would run the grocery business? Who would, in the most literal sense, mind the family shop?

'The women!' It was their father who startlingly spoke up. 'If they were widowed,' declared John, emerging from frailty like some papery old prophet, 'they would set to and take it on.' True.

His sons reviewed this option. Women did run businesses when pressed. In the City there was a minor tradition of female business-management. Their mother was fading, yet still a hard worker. Parthenope knew the price of everything and could judge commodities perfectly. Anne Jukes was more than capable. Anne, who had once seemed just the prettiest girl in Bishopsgate when Lambert first squired her, nowadays displayed more independent traits. Lambert told Gideon how his wife took herself to Coleman Street where women preached –

'Notoriously!' interrupted Gideon with a grin. 'There was the famous Mrs Attaway from Bell Alley – the lace-maker – until she ran off with her paramour, both of them leaving behind young children.' It was an undeserving jibe but men were merciless with women who set themselves up as spiritual arbiters then broke the moral code.

Lambert smirked. 'Anne has quite lost her nervousness of petitioning Parliament. Now she regularly joins with women who are pleading for peace. She has met those whose husbands are in jail for producing seditious literature. Your Robert would know the men – John Lilburne, who has been pamphleteering for years, and that man Richard Overton, who lured you into the masque . . .' Gideon pretended not to remember *The Triumph of Peace*. 'Indeed, if it fell to my wife to organise our shop, I should heartily welcome it! Otherwise she will end up a she-controversialist, leading her sisterhood in prayer and tumults.'

'Would you trust Anne and Mother with your capital?' Gideon asked, giving his brother a sideways glance.

'They are honest women,' Lambert replied simply. He knew their talents too; wives of members of the great London trade associations could be powerful and respected. He made a grand resolution: 'By my life, I shall start showing them the ledgers and order books –'

'Save your breath,' chortled John, into the rim of his tankard. 'They know more about the books than you do, or than I ever did either.'

Gideon would treasure that evening all the rest of his life, for as well as refining his bond with his brother, it was the last time he ever saw his father. The three Jukes men enjoyed this rare excursion together, then both Gideon and Lambert kept the memory fondly in their hearts.

Next day, Gideon returned dutifully to Newport Pagnell, riding a good new horse bought for him by his parents. He was determined that garrison life would now be temporary. Sir Thomas Fairfax arrived in London from the north in February, and impressed the House of

Commons with his modest bearing. Parliament appointed Fairfax to be commander of the new army.

In February too, Sir Samuel came back to Newport. Still trying to drum up money or tools to repair Newport's defences, he complained that the area all around was becoming increasingly malignant. Gideon watched the situation deteriorating daily. That month a detachment of Manchester's army were quartered at Newport, causing such overcrowding Sir Samuel complained that soldiers were having to sleep 'three and three in a bed'. Since requests for money still failed, he claimed poignantly that his garrison was now so under-funded that two of his soldiers had only one pair of britches between them; when one soldier was on duty the other was compelled to remain in his quarters in bed. *'If the soldiers mutiny for want of pay, I cannot help it . . .'* The entire garrison was fractious and discontented.

Biding his time over asking for a transfer, Gideon assessed his commander's mood. Sir Samuel was a small man with a great spirit. He had thrown himself into his role as Scoutmaster-General with energy and application. *Mercurius Britannicus*, the official Parliamentary news-sheet, said of him: *'This noble commander watches the enemy so industri-ously that they eat, sleep, drink not, whisper not, but he can give us an account of their darkest proceedings.'* Sir Samuel stood for order in religion and society. While he struggled to control his men, he was anxiously attempting to rid the garrison of religious sectaries; he also feared that Newport Pagnell town was a hotbed of sexual licence, which would go the way of Sodom and Gomorrah. Such a sinful place clearly posed a terrible lure to his soldiers, whom he could not keep penned in the castle. He imposed a battery of approved chaplains, sermons three times a week and prayers and Bible-reading every morning at the changing of the guard.

Hunched at Newport, smarting at his impending loss of office, Sir Samuel knew his time was limited. Everyone could see it rankled. He was heard muttering of the new army, 'I should be glad to know who is what – and what pension we poor cast-off lads shall have!' Towards the end of March his anxieties about the King's intentions grew so severe he actually allowed a group under Major Ennis to pass them-selves off as cavaliers, in order to escape detection in deeply Royalist territory. However, he ordered them firmly that he wanted to hear of no cavalierish practices.

To break in upon Sir Samuel's worries would need care. Eventually, Gideon set up a discussion by enquiring whether Sir Samuel had enjoyed the veal pie his mother sent. The knight at once replied that it was the best veal pie he had ever had. 'Sir, she claims it is achieved by just management of orange peel and nutmeg.' Then he piped up and requested leave to enlist in the New Model Army.

As he feared, Sir Samuel became fretful. 'You want to be *moulded* in the new army's bread-trough – And just as I discovered you to be the source of an excellent pie!'

'Sir, I am of the party who believe the war now *must* be won.'

'That's a valiant belief.'

'Have I your leave to go then, sir? I had hopes of taking a recommendation – since they are being choosy.' Luke was glaring, but Gideon pressed on doggedly. 'I could beg your secretary Mr Butler to prepare an encomium. I would tell him not to varnish it too thickly with testimonials, or Sir Thomas Fairfax will suspect I am a half-baked, squint-eyed laggard who cannot shoot straight . . .'

Sir Samuel appeared to relax. But his answer was a blunt no.

England generally seemed to be declaring itself a land worth fighting for that spring. Gideon Jukes picked his way among the farms and hamlets, going about his duties according to orders, though at the same time hopefully searching for the New Model Army. Around him the fields were fresh and green. When he skirted great houses, avenues of imported horse-chestnut trees heaved and tossed pinkish-white candles of blossom in the frisky breeze; along the lanes and tangled hedges, the whiter starlets of may blossom draped small trees and bushes in dis-organised sprays from crown to floor. Willows flickered their bright young leaves beside the watercourses, which had swelled over their banks after April showers. Swans stretched their necks on the banks. Grey rabbits sat and stared. Occasionally a house showed its grey walls or tall red-brick chimneys, half glimpsed across the roll of the countryside. There were few visible cattle or horses; wise owners were hiding them in pits or secret shacks, lest they be rounded up and stolen by soldiers.

While Gideon gloomily patrolled, treasurers were appointed to secure eighty thousand pounds for maintaining the New Model Army. Fairfax was its commander-in-chief. Skippon commanded the infantry, Thomas Hammond the artillery, although the command of the cavalry was not at first granted. Skippon reviewed the foot at Reading, Fairfax the horse at St Albans. For much of April, as the new force was put together, it exercised at Windsor. Gideon received a letter to say his brother Lambert had been released from the Trained Bands and had joined up as a pikeman. Gideon became ever more frustrated at being trapped in Newport.

At the end of April Fairfax took the New Model Army to relieve Taunton, but when the King and his main army left Oxford on a new summer campaign, Fairfax was ordered to wheel about and besiege Oxford instead. A small detachment went to Taunton, where Robert Blake was holding out so valiantly he answered a summons to surrender by retorting that he would sooner eat his boots. On the approach of the relieving force, the Royalists withdrew, saving Blake the trouble.

Fairfax surrounded Oxford but could make little progress as he awaited his artillery train. Samuel Luke's troops still scouted in the area; as they mouldered in their crumbling castle, with their commander condemned to retirement, their pay in arrears, ill-equipped and hungry, their garrison saw its end-date. Relations between these run-down unhappy men and the buffed-up celebrities in the New Model Army became strained. Then Luke's personal troop, under Captain Evans, was reduced into the cavalry regiment of Colonel Greaves. His deputy, Samuel Bedford, was promoted away to be Scoutmaster General of the Committee of Both Kingdoms, Parliament's main war committee.

As the garrison was fragmenting, discipline began breaking down. In the middle of March, Major Ennis was given leave to attend to a family crisis; he left pay for his men with a lieutenant, who then ran away with the money. Lieutenant Carnaby used the cash to further his marriage to a surgeon's daughter.

On hearing that the reprobate was to be found at the Dog Tavern on Garlick Hill, Sir Samuel wrote in fury to London, demanding that a warrant be issued and the culprit clapped in irons. *'If officers be permitted to run up and down at their own wills, I fear we must not expect to see good days in England long . . .'* Four days later the scandal worsened when a London apothecary, disappointed by Carnaby's winning the surgeon's daughter, cut his own throat. His neck was said to be severed three-quarters through, though the wound was stitched up. Carnaby wrote to Sir Samuel and apologised. He did not return the money. The soldiers' arrears were not paid.

Sir Samuel was still obsessed that his garrison and the Eastern Association were a Royalist target. News that bridges over the River Cherwell close to Oxford were being repaired convinced him of imminent attack – even though he said wryly, *'This is a poor and beggarly town; here are nothing worthy of the enemy but fair maids and young lace-makers – which I intend to send out to them as a forlorn hope at their first approach.'*

At the end of May the crunch came. Prince Rupert besieged Leicester, clearly a distraction to compel Fairfax to abandon Oxford. It was the old story. The prince's men broke into Leicester amidst terrible atrocities. Soldiers and civilians were slaughtered; ruthless pillaging occurred.

Fairfax was instructed to leave Oxford, seek out the King and recover Leicester. On the 5th of June, Fairfax and the army arrived near Newport Pagnell. At this point, as an exceptional measure, Sir Samuel Luke's importance was recognised: Parliament granted him an extension as commander of Newport Pagnell for the next twenty days. Only one other member of the House of Commons had similar treatment: that was Oliver Cromwell.

The New Model Army quartered nearby for several days. Gideon knew this was his one chance to transfer. Sir Thomas Fairfax stayed at Sherington, a mile away, with his army at Brick Hill. Although Sir Samuel Luke was the most hospitable man and naturally good-mannered, he never invited the new general to visit. His father, Sir Oliver, wrote to him afterwards rebuking him for this lapse, saying it had caused comment.

Relations were proper, but strained. Sir Samuel loaned three hundred infantry to the New Model, but five days later Sir Thomas Fairfax wrote complaining that various New Model soldiers were known to have returned to Newport Pagnell, where they had served in the past. Fairfax growled that he could get no provisions from the Buckinghamshire Committee – an all too familiar plaint to Sir Samuel – and begged that provisions be sent from Newport, emphasising that these would be paid for. The reminder that the New Model was well supplied with money could only rankle.

Sir Samuel believed that if Fairfax's untried army should be beaten, his garrison could not hold out. He also feared there was a plan to remove soldiers from him on the advice of Sir Philip Skippon. He had only five hundred men left in the garrison, when in his opinion he needed two thousand. He observed the new moulded troops, as he called them, and was in two minds. He told his father they were extraordinarily personable, well armed and well paid, but he found the officers no better than common soldiers and he had never seen so many get so drunk and so quickly. But he also admitted: *'Sir Thomas Fairfax's army is the bravest I ever saw for bodies of men, both in number, arms, or other accoutrements . . .'*

For some it was an irresistible lure. Gideon Jukes found an excuse to ride out to Brick Hill and look at them. The new army had a buzz. To be of the 'Chosen' gives a lift. Any elite corps carries itself well. Despite raw recruits and pressed men in some numbers, levied from London and the county towns, the new army was generally formed from trained, experienced, highest-quality soldiers, who brought with them both certainty of purpose and optimism. They had high expectations. They knew that Sir Thomas Fairfax could assess what he needed, ask for it from Parliament – and get it too. In the month he had allowed himself for organisation, contracts had been arranged for pikes, pistols and muskets, saddles and horseshoes, back-and-breasts and helmets. The new general had five hundred pounds to spend on artillery and, tellingly, double that amount for intelligence.

His men were also equipped with religious fervour and political ideas. These they brought with them, at no cost to the war chest.

Gideon then skulked around Sherington and to his great excitement glimpsed Sir Thomas Fairfax. The tall commander-in-chief was light of step despite the serious wound from which he was recovering, one of four he was known to have taken in the war so far. At a little over thirty, Fairfax was twenty years younger than Essex, ten years less than Manchester, Skippon and Cromwell – though he was seven years older than his main opponent, Prince Rupert of the Rhine. Gideon's sighting of the spare figure in buff coat and fringed sash told him Fairfax had intelligent brown eyes set in a cheerful, chin-up Yorkshire face, generously framed by waving brown hair. Although he had a bodyguard, he strode off independently.

More and more stories emerged of Fairfax's dashing behaviour. At Bradford, it was said, he had ridden ahead of his men and found himself alone, facing a whole Royalist regiment; being mounted on a good horse, he had ridden straight at the fortifications, jumped right over them and escaped. Under siege at Wakefield with his family, when down to his last barrel of powder and completely out of matchcord, he had broken out of the town at the head of his men; after his wife was taken prisoner by Newcastle's troops, Fairfax rode for two days and nights, taking along his infant daughter and her redoubtable Daleswoman nursemaid. His wife was later returned to him with great chivalry in Lord Newcastle's coach.

Despite these and many other exploits, Sir Thomas Fairfax was a diffident man, who had a genuine air of surprise at his sudden elevation. The general's obvious charisma caused a flutter; after Fairfax disappeared indoors, Gideon was left feeling unsettled by expectation. His work for Luke had been essential at the time, but now it became his burning wish to join the new army.

Chapter Thirty-One

Newport Pagnell and Naseby: 1645

No open invitation had been issued for regular soldiers to transfer to the New Model. Unless Fairfax himself chose a particular troop or regiment, everyone was supposed to remain *in situ*. But among the public, agents were vocally calling for volunteers to present themselves at inns, while they rounded up the able-bodied from the streets, hauling in vagrants, sailors, prisoners, even captured Royalists who were willing to turn their coats. Some pressed men mutinied; others deserted. In this situation, Gideon hoped that the muster-master-general might look favourably on any trained man who presented himself. The army was supposed to reach twenty-one thousand strong, but so far was running at only two-thirds of that.

Gideon knew his way around at Brick Hill, which had been an old base used by the garrison's troops. He soon found a recruiting officer and begged for a place. He was welcomed, and assured that his transfer from the garrison would be squared with Sir Samuel Luke. He did not wait to find out.

He stood no chance of joining the cavalry; its standards would be those of Oliver Cromwell's rock-hard Ironsides, far above his capabilities as a rider. Since Gideon none the less owned his own horse – no longer the three-shilling Newport nag but the two-pounds mare his parents had bought him at New Year – he was instructed to present himself to Colonel John Okey, in command of the New Model's thousand dragoons. He would remain 'mounted infantry'.

'First into the hot spots and last out,' the recruiting officer jeered.

'Dogsbodies,' agreed Gideon.

'Your task', continued the officer, looking cool at the interruption, 'will be to secure bridges in advance of the infantry and hold those bridgeheads during a retreat, to contain enclosures, line hedges and guard artillery, then when required to dismount and beef up the regular footmen. While dismounted, one man in ten will hold the horses.'

'Scouts, pickets and sentinels. Dogsbodies!' Gideon repeated.

He was ordered to the regimental stores to collect his equipment issue. The 'stores' were less permanent than they sounded; since the army was now mobile, kit was being doled out from the backs of carts. His existing threadbare uniform was rejected; replacements were available, which he must pay for by deductions from the wages he had yet to receive. Uniform coats were of good, pre-shrunk English cloth in Venice red, with grey britches that he was pleased to find had leather pockets. They were all the same size – too short for him in the sleeve and the leg. 'One size fits all.'

'Fits nobody!' Gideon fretted over the length of the coat, which at twenty-nine-and-a-quarter inches was supposed to cover his backside but failed on a long-bodied lank like him.

'Tell that to the committee.' The storesman tugged down hard on the coat; he was a wiry, bandy-legged, square-jawed Kentishman who had lost an arm in some hedge skirmish and been relegated to the commissariat. 'Lengthen your tape-strings.'

'Thereby admitting a gale around the midriff –' Gideon fiddled half-heartedly with the flat tapes that were supposed to fasten his coat to his britches. Ever since the spurts of growth in his teens, he had had a problem with gaps; his wedding suit had been specially tailored. A long shirt would help, though it would billow through his clothes around his waist like a cavalier's fancy costume. 'It's a bum-starver . . . Do I not receive a buff jerkin?'

'Dragoons ride light.'

'Helmet?'

'Hat.' A grey Dutch felt was handed over, with a round crown and broad brim to keep off the weather.

Setting the hat at a jaunty angle, Gideon growled, 'I shall not even ask about armour.'

The storesman bared his teeth in a sickly grin.

A cheap dragoon saddle was offered, to Gideon's continued disgust, and he was told he could take a pair of two-and-threepenny shoes (sized ten, eleven, twelve or thirteen) or buy his own riding boots. He possessed his own buckskin gloves, bandolier with twelve powder apos-tles, and swordbelt for the long, cheap sword that was the best dragoons were thought to need. A new ninepenny snapsack was allowed him, a canvas bag in which he would stow rations, knife and spoon, handkerchief, fire-lighting kit, candle end, spare stockings and shirt, and his pocket Bible.

The storesman then turned to his assistant, a sleepy, small-eyed younger man with round ears like buttons, who looked as if he had trouble remembering his name. They held an intense conversation about exactly what firearm to issue. Gideon had honestly mentioned his lost fingertips. His hands were grabbed and pored over. His ability to manipulate the stricken fingers became the subject of surprisingly intelligent discussion. He posed a challenge. Gideon had learned that most men regarded any challenge as an excuse to say no, but these two seemed to welcome it positively, as a chance to devise a solution.

'He qualifies for a flintlock.' Gideon pricked up his ears.

No longer so dopey, the assistant eagerly agreed. 'Readier in use, and safer.'

From deep within the wagon, a brand-new flintlock musket, with a slightly shorter barrel than Gideon was used to, was placed gently in his grasp; he was encouraged to get the feel. Its light weight astonished him.

Flintlocks were much handier weapons than matchlocks, since although their mechanism was more complex they could be made ready to fire in one or two movements instead of the long sequence of actions required with lighted matchcord; flints were safer too. Flintlocks used no match, they were not at the mercy of the weather which, in the lightest shower, could render infantrymen's match unusable. Gideon *badly* wanted a flintlock.

'This is a *snaphance*!' announced the storesman, excitedly. 'We have two hundred, fresh in, just for the dragoons.'

Gideon brightened. He kept himself up-to-date. He knew that the snaphance musket had been developed from German fowling pieces. Hunters' guns were very fast to reload, and especially good for shooting while on the move; in theory, dragoons might have to fire from horseback.

The piece was whisked off him and its mechanism demonstrated. 'The flint is held in the jaws of your cock, which is fixed back by a sear. This engages on its tail, until you wish to fire. Your pan-cover will be slid out of the way automatically when the cock falls; as the flint strikes your frizzle, the cover is pushed aside, allowing a stream of sparks to fall in upon your powder.'

Gideon played the expert too. 'The frizzle is one piece with the cover pan?'

'No; separate. I need not explain a frizzle to you?'

Innuendo was second nature to anyone who grew up among City apprentices. 'I hope I seem like a man who knows what his frizzle is for.'

The storesman glanced at his deputy. He replied in a low, dangerous voice, 'Oh you do, Sergeant!'

'But can he tell a cow from a field-gate?' mused the younger man cheekily, half under his breath. From his hayrick burr, he must be a country boy, a thresher or general labourer; he knew how to irritate Londoners.

Gideon was suddenly startled. 'I am not a sergeant.'

The storesman made much of consulting the recruitment docket. 'Do I read this aright?' He flashed the paper in front of the assistant, who peered at it even though he was probably illiterate. They had honed their act as stooge and showman. '"*Sergeant* Jukes." Are you denying yourself, Sergeant?'

Gideon shrugged and shook his head. Perhaps a testimonial had been given for him by Sir Samuel Luke after all. He was amazed, not least because it was rumoured that some sergeants from the old regiments had volunteered to be reduced to privates, in order to serve in the New Model.

'Your halberd, *monsignor!*' sneered the storesman, handing the newly promoted Sergeant Jukes a staff weapon. The pole was eleven feet long, topped by a slim metal spike and a shaped flat blade like an axe-head or weathervane. In the English style, the blade was pierced by decorative heart-shaped holes. With this implement a sergeant would prise apart any of his men who were marching too close together and otherwise make much of himself. 'Do not lose this beauty.'

'No indeed,' replied Sergeant Jukes wholeheartedly. 'I can see it has exceptionally fine piercing on the flanges!'

Gideon found that John Okey, the dragoon commander, was to his liking: a fellow-Londoner, gaunt of cheek with a long nose and hair to his shoulders, parted centrally above a receding forehead. The colonel asked a few questions, concentrating on religious observance. He took the Baptist view that they were fighting for the Lord, who would give them victory if their righteousness was pleasing. Concealing any reservations on this point, Gideon was confirmed as a member of Okey's regiment. An enthusiastic conversation about the virtues of the snaphance musket may have been material. John Okey's God was a practical deity. The New Model Army contained plenty of Baptists; they were cheerful soldiers who prayed fervently and backed it up by shooting straight.

Gideon had already heard of this dragoon regiment. It was previously commanded by John Lilburne, the rabid pamphleteer whose wife Anne Jukes knew. Lilburne's place had fallen vacant because he declined to take the Covenant when that became compulsory.

Earlier, the Lilburne dragoons had been sent to protect the Isle of Ely against threats of invasion by Royalists from the north. Others with them there were infantry under Colonel Thomas Rainborough. Rainborough was tall and physically strapping; a man of great strength, he was a committed pikeman. By one of the quirks of war, when Gideon joined what was now Colonel Okey's regiment, he knew from a letter that his brother Lambert was already serving under Rainborough.

Their gifted colonels were to have a great influence on the Jukes brothers. The two commanders came from a similar milieu. Both their families had money, but had worked for it. Okey had been an East London ship's chandler with his own business. Rainborough came from a seagoing, shipowning family in Wapping. They were typical of the breed of officer Sir Thomas Fairfax had chosen for the new army: able, staunchly committed – in Rainborough's case almost too radical. Both men were to play significant parts in the war and its political aftermath.

While the New Model was waiting at Newport to go into action, Parliament gave Fairfax a free hand in military affairs. His council of war decided the primary object should be the destruction of the King's main army. That was wandering around the North Midlands. They also agreed to request urgently that command of the New Model cavalry should be given to Oliver Cromwell.

Fairfax moved out from Newport and just a day after Gideon joined them, the New Model Army came along the Great North Road to Stony Stratford. He had no time to remember the waif he once met here abandoning her baby. The King was at Daventry: only a few miles away.

After ransacking Leicester, the Royalists were in a high mood. They had been riding through the countryside, offending inhabitants with their fine clothes and the hordes of stolen cattle they were driving with them. When Fairfax caught up, they were taking their ease, foraging far and wide, with their horses out to grass, while the King himself casually hunted near Daventry. They had derided their opponents, calling Fairfax's army the New Noddle. When their complacent pickets were sent running helter-skelter by the Parliamentarian advance guard, it took the Royalists completely by surprise.

Relaxed as ever in the teeth of probable disaster, King Charles had written to his wife: 'My affairs were never in so fair or hopeful a way.' But that position had been jeopardised by wrangling over strategy: whether to attack the remnants of the Scots' Covenanters' army in an attempt to retake the North, or to tackle the New Model Army. Either was a good objective if pursued with vigour, but in a feeble compromise, a reduced royal army was pottering northwards, seriously outnumbered, especially in cavalry. This was because Charles had let the dilettante Lord Goring take away three thousand cavalry to the West Country. It was to prove fatal. Prince Rupert tried to recall Goring. Fairfax's scouts intercepted a letter from Goring making excuses to remain where he was. At fractious Royalist war councils, tension grew between Prince Rupert and the King's civilian advisers; in contrast, the New Model Army had been devised precisely to place all authority in one command. This was the moment to strike, and Fairfax had been given a free hand. He only had to await the arrival of his own cavalry commander.

Leaving nothing to chance, Fairfax rode around his sentry posts in the dark, to satisfy himself there was no chance of being caught by a surprise attack. A sentry challenged him; Fairfax, brooding, had forgotten the password. While the captain of the guard was called, the general was forced to stand to in the wet while the soldier threatened to blow his head off if he moved. Fairfax rewarded the sentry for diligence.

Royalist troop movements and campfires suggested the enemy might be pulling out. At Fairfax's dawn council on the morning of Friday the 13th of June, it was decided to pursue. In the middle of that meeting, Oliver Cromwell and three thousand extra cavalry arrived, to a great shout of acclaim. Battle was now fully anticipated. Sir Philip Skippon, as field marshal, had been ordered to devise a battle array a full six days before.

On a fair evening at the height of the English summer, the royal army convened on a long east-west ridge and seemed ready to make a stand. Next morning, when Royalist scouts were unable to confirm the New Model's movements, Rupert went out in person to reconnoitre. Fairfax did not need to; he knew where the enemy were: seven miles away, before the fine shoemaking market town of Market Harborough which lay just over the county boundary in Leicestershire.

The battle would take place slightly to the south, in the Northamptonshire uplands. This was not beautiful, but honest open country where ancient woodlands still slumbered darkly around villages deserted in the Black Death. By a neat quirk of geography, the place was a watershed; streams on one side flowed to the south and west to the Bristol Channel, while barely a few miles away they flowed north and east to the Wash. Undulating ridges would help disguise troop movements in the early manoeuvres. The area was mainly unenclosed, with irregular stands of cultivated grain among ragged patches of gorse. Between the armies lay a valley with areas of soft ground, called Broad Moor. Fairfax had taken the New Model Army as far as a large fallow field, close to the ancient Saxon village of Naseby. A strong double line of hedges crossed this field at right angles, to the Parliamentarians' left. On the right hand was Naseby Warren. This was significant for their cavalry; it meant much more than a few rabbit-holes to cause stumbles. An ancient warren would have many miles of tunnelling and large underground caverns that could possibly collapse.

Bringing two armies into battle array and then into close contact could take a long time. For the commanders, this required care, in order to prevent their soldiers losing heart, while having them ready when needed. At Marston Moor the initial uncertainty had lasted many hours, which was tiring and dispiriting for the enormous forces involved. Naseby would be brisk by comparison.

Prince Rupert, the King's commander-in-chief, had ordered a battle array with his own cavalry on the Royalist right wing while Sir Marmaduke Langdale took the Royalist left, leading the experienced Northern and Newark horse. Behind their infantry in the centre, the King, resplendent in full black body armour, watched among his Lifeguard, five hundred men who served as the Royalist reserve.

For Parliament, Skippon was arraying the infantry in the Swedish style, six deep, as Gideon and Lambert Jukes had seen them at the first battle of Newbury. Cromwell's cavalry, on the right flank, would be negotiating the rabbit-holes. The left flank, at Cromwell's request, was led by his fixer son-in-law-to-be, Henry Ireton. The left were therefore facing the dreaded Prince Rupert, but they had better ground and Cromwell was planning further protection from dragoons.

During the first hours after dawn, Prince Rupert came in sight of the van of the New Model Army. Signalling for the remainder of the King's army to follow him, he moved westwards, wanting to get upwind, so the Royalists would not be blinded by their opponents' gunsmoke. To the Parliamentarians, this looked like a flanking movement. It could mean Rupert had chosen not to give battle. He had, in fact, for once counselled against it, because of the enemy's superior numbers.

Fairfax finessed him. He moved his own men back a hundred paces from the higher ground they commanded. They could still see what the enemy were doing but while their dispositions for battle were being arranged, they were shielded by the crest of the ridge.

Thinking *Fairfax* might intend to withdraw, Prince Rupert was lured into action, even though his men would have to charge uphill against greater numbers. At about ten in the morning, even before his artillery had caught up, the prince ordered a general advance, while leading his cavalry into the start of a characteristic charge.

A Parliamentarian forlorn hope had been placed on the slope ahead of their army, to dissipate the force of the enemy's first attack. These musketeers fired off initial rounds. Classically, this was the signal that battle had been joined. The forlorn hope pulled back. The main body of the New Model Army then advanced in formation to the edge of their high ground, on what was named Mill Hill, and came into view of the Royalists.

The battle of which veterans would speak until their death-beds had begun.

Chapter Thirty-Two

Naseby: 14 June 1645

Gideon was queuing for powder at the regimental budge-wagon when it started. He felt exhausted and dirty. The army had been on the march for three days, with Colonel Okey's regiment responsible for mounting guard each night. No one had eaten the previous evening, in their regiment or others, because they barely paused in their search for the King. Gideon would be going into action not as starved as at Newbury, but still famished.

He was tired too. It was a week before the longest day. Last night had been light until barely two hours before midnight. Dawn came early. At three o'clock this morning they were ordered up. He had blundered to the prayer meeting, his chest tight while the chaplain asked the Lord's protection on what they all knew would be a day of battle. Since then the New Model had been on the move, edging towards the enemy. Eventually word came that Fairfax had called a halt, lest they stumble out of the thick ground mist and come upon the Royalists unexpectedly.

They were further north than Gideon ever remembered being; the general temperature seemed cooler than it would have been in London, maybe sixty miles away. Here on the uplands, chilly air made the men stiff, especially those who had old wounds to grumble about, as some of his soldiers did. All the dragoons were fretting because after rain showers in the night the going was very heavy for horses. While Gideon was waiting for his ammunition he could barely see three men in front of him through the fog. They spoke in low voices, when they spoke at all, lest the sound carry and reveal their presence to unseen opponents.

He wiped the side of his boot against a tussock of dewy meadow grass. Part of him wished, as always, that he were back at home, cleaning off dung deposited by some Cheapside dray-horse, and whistling on his way to work with Robert at the print-shop. Mostly he was glad to be here. Among his new colleagues as they patiently waited to fill their rattling flasks and apostles with coarse and fine gunpowder, the mood was cheerful. They had glints in their eyes and showed their teeth, in satisfaction that they would soon be fighting

Gideon remembered his responsibilities; he nodded encouragement. His men tolerated the attempt mildly. How he performed today would make the difference between whether or not they really accepted him. As the newest sergeant he had been assigned a slightly ramshackle group. One, Thomas Bentall, had been pressed straight from prison where he had been put for brawling; broken-nosed and toothless, he looked like it. A couple of others, thin-faced and gingery, gave every impression of having been horse-thieves and must have escaped jail only because they were too quick to be caught. He had a hatter, a farmer, two confectioners who were brothers-in-law and not speaking to each other, a docker who had been in the Westminster Trained Bands. After only three days, Gideon was still learning their names. Glory-to-God Parchment was easy enough; he was the one reading his pocket Bible while he queued, at the same time as picking his nose with his free hand. Walter Gummery was the oldest, certainly sixty, and had an un-acknowledged bladder problem; he was taking relief against the wheel of the budge wagon. All of them had seemed well disposed. Gideon's height, his modest manner, his scarred hands and his having side-stepped his commander's wishes at Newport Pagnell in order to be here combined to win their loyalty. Even the fact that his uniform coat and breeches failed to meet properly had helped; the men recognised him by the way he always tugged his coat down as he loped along on spidery legs. It made Sergeant Jukes look a bit of a character. His soldiers liked that – and the way he got on with things.

Colonel Okey had been supervising the share-out of powder and shot that morning in a large meadow. Between seven and eight o'clock, General Cromwell rode up and spoke to him. Gideon recognised the new commander of horse. Through yawns, he noticed the stout, armoured figure, clearly at one with his horse, a man who rode without haste and yet whose very presence signalled urgency. Cromwell passed within fifty feet, unaccompanied by any honour guard. Even through his 'triple-barred pot', a serviceable iron helmet with a lobster-tailed neck-guard and three simple face bars, he looked bright and confident.

It was the moment Cromwell himself would famously describe afterwards: 'when I saw the enemy draw up and march in gallant order towards us, and we a company of poor ignorant men, to seek how to order our battle . . . I could not, riding alone about my business, but smile out to God in praises, in assurance of victory . . .' As Cromwell approached Okey, Gideon wondered about this plain-featured countryman in his forties who three years ago had had no military training or experience at all, yet who was now acknowledged as one of the finest soldiers in the kingdom. He rode a damned good horse; all the men commented.

Wind was dispersing the mist. As the day cleared, Cromwell had observed the Royalist advance, its flickering standards, the light glinting off armour and precious metal braid, the blocks of pikemen and musketeers, the twinkles of matchcord, the shifting bodies of cavalry aching for the charge. He had already organised his own cavalry wings. His business now was to command the dragoons to protect the extreme left flank. Cromwell's words to Okey were inaudible, but Okey jumped to. Cromwell galloped off.

Gideon heard the regimental drums beating everyone to action. With his right hand steadying his musket butt, he went running back towards the horses which were gathered in a small spinney. Okey, with a straight back, was issuing rapid orders. Gideon saw his colleagues' hasty dismount. With a roar of jubilation, all those who were not to be left holding the horses scrambled on foot to line the great hedges that crossed Broad Moor from north to south. Gideon swerved off with them. They had barely time to prepare. Across in front of them, their ride contained by this natural boundary of the Sulby hedgerow, came Prince Rupert's cavaliers.

When musketeers fought cavalry, the instructions were to aim at the horses' legs. They wanted the mounts to fall. Unsaddling the cavaliers would do the most damage. Gideon tried to remember this, as he waited to give the first enfilading volley. Muskets had a long range but for full effect the dragoons were to delay shooting until the enemy were so close they could see the lines in their faces. It took nerve.

He loathed the new snaphance. With only a couple of days to practice, most of that time spent on the march, he had yet to master this strange weapon. It felt too light. He would never find its range. Loading was swift and easy but when the order came to fire, the short muzzle flew up so he knew that his shot went skywards. He had no musket-rest. Nobody had a rest. Rests were, as his new captain had scoffed, fine for monthly manoeuvres in the Artillery Yard, but no use in a fight. But using a rest for the long barrel of his matchlock was how Gideon Jukes had trained and as he struggled irritably with this new weapon, he wanted a musket-rest – desired it with a passion that was greater than any lust of man for woman, hated the captain who had spoken lightly of the way the Trained Bands trained and, of course, hated his own clumsiness.

He cursed the snaphance like a brewhouse stoker. Forcing open his pan and fumbling with fine powder, he primed, blew off residue, charged the barrel, spat a new ball from his mouth to his palm, jogged the bullet into the barrel so it sank into the powder, rammed, presented, and on the order fired again into the thundering lines of Rupert's charging men. These cavaliers were a grand sight as they galloped headlong in their fine clothes on glossy mounts, gloved and rapiered, with lace cuffs and ribboned boot-hose and deep lace collars rippling on their shoulders over polished cuirasses. Destroying the privileged bastards would be a pleasure.

With the second shot Gideon over-compensated. He knew the bullet must have struck the ground uselessly ahead of him. It was happening all over the field. Even artillery balls were burying themselves in bog, impotently casting up showers of mud. Not that he could hear much from anyone's artillery. Neither side seemed to be using their cannon to effect. At least he need not fear having his head ripped off.

Next time he got his shot right. He was not alone. To either side of him the dragoons were in high spirits, shooting, shouting and rejoicing. Gideon was swept by exhilaration, here among men who knew just what they were doing. Fear was displaced by assurance as they powered through routine musket moves. Amidst the low clatter of their powder canisters all around, he felt, rather than saw, the regiment moving in rhythm – nine hundred men loading charges of coarse powder, fine powder, lead bullets; raising their guns and then cocking the trigger; three hundred men waiting, then firing a volley in more-or-less unison; three hundred from the second rank firing; three hundred from the third.

The noise was appalling. Gunfire deafened everyone. Recoil from the hot musket would be bruising his shoulder. Other discomforts vaguely niggled. Ditchwater or dew was soaking the knees of his britches as he knelt in the hedge. Spiny twigs scratched the back of his neck, unsettling his hat. Someone in the crouching row of men behind, attempting second-rank fire over Gideon's shoulder, lost his balance and fell forwards right onto him. It could have been disastrous, though the soldier did his best to recover and keep his weight off. Gideon grunted. Others pulled the man back; Gideon's powder had spilled but he was already reaching for a new charge. There was no time for recrimination.

They saw Rupert's horse gain momentum. Ireton's Parliamentary wing was on the move too; the opposing cavalry surged together in heavy groups. Some Parliamentarian regiments, closest to the centre, survived the shock while the rest fought back bravely, causing severe Royalist casualties; but Rupert's charge and his skill enabled him to chase many right off the field. Ahead of Okey's regiment, after hard fighting, the Parliamentary left wing now milled in disarray.

Aware of damage from the dragoons' crossfire, enemy troops suddenly appeared by the hedge, hoping to dislodge them. It was dangerous. Footmen, with no armour, were in peril when attacked by cavalry and Prince Rupert customarily planted musketeers among his cavalry for extra sharp-shooting. Somehow, Okey's men repulsed them. How did not matter. It passed in a moment; they had other things to think about.

As the first waves of cavalry had made contact on the field, there was a prolonged bout of frantic cut and thrust until the Royalists broke through. Then they raced on, heading away too fast and too far. Okey's men watched the cavalier horse drive many of their own men from the field, yet the cavaliers fragmented into wild groups that streamed away almost to Naseby village. There they would find the Parliamentary baggage-train; Prince Rupert himself would be with them, absent from the battle for over an hour. He personally summoned the guards at the Parliamentary baggage to surrender, but they – an unregimented tawny-coated group of musketeers – first mistook him for Fairfax because he wore a similar crimson montero hat to one their general wore. Finally grasping Rupert's summons, they stood their ground and refused to yield. Realising belatedly that he was needed elsewhere, the prince left them.

Back on the field, in his absence a hallooing second rank of velvet-cloaked Royalist squierarchy had charged, stayed in position, and were carving up anything that remained of the Parliamentary left wing. Ireton had veered away to assist the infantry at the centre, where he was unhorsed, wounded in the thigh, wounded in the face with a halberd and then taken prisoner. Word whipped around his men, demoralising them. Their leaderless remnants milled in disorder. Next to Sulby Hedges, Colonel Butler's regiment was imperilled, until repeated rounds from Okey's dragoons saved them from certain extinction.

The dragoons had lost track of time but must have stayed by the hedges for an hour. Once most cavaliers had moved away, through the gunsmoke they could see pandemonium out among the infantry. The locked regiments at the centre swayed to and fro; glimpses showed that Skippon's desperate men, now no longer protected by cavalry on their left, were slogging it out at push of pike and butt of musket. Though they outnumbered the enemy, they had been over-mastered and had given ground. Skippon had had a bullet strike him in the ribs; it pushed part of his breastplate deep into his chest, but he refused to leave the field. Word that he was dangerously hurt was causing sections of the infantry to lose heart and fade.

For the New Model Army, the outcome looked grim for a period. They did have double the Royalist numbers, so Cromwell and Fairfax could deploy support to trouble-spots. But the Royalist infantry were as good as any. Had Prince Rupert's cavalry checked quickly enough after storming through, had they turned on Parliament's now-exposed centre, it would have been disastrous.

As the Parliamentary foot were pushed back across the moor and up the hill behind them by their tenacious opponents, they began to merge into the waiting reserve regiments under Colonels Hammond, Pride and Rainborough. Fairfax and other officers encouraged them to make a final stand. Somewhere in that mêlée was Lambert Jukes, cheerfully wielding his pike as the reserve regiments were called up and began to push heavily forwards.

The reserves were fresh and cheery. The mood at the centre altered.

On the far wing, matters went well from the start. Cromwell had led the Ironsides steadily across the broken ground, never creating the speed of Prince Rupert's men, but safely negotiating the treacherous rabbit-holes and various pits and waterholes they unexpectedly encountered. For an hour they fought it out hand-to-hand with the Royalist Langdale's unhappy and mutinous Northern Horse. Slowly at first, but then with greater momentum, Cromwell beat a way through. Watching from among his Lifeguards on the ridge, the King correctly assessed that Langdale's units were about to break. Once flight began, panic would rip through them, until men and horses chased from the field, wild with terror. Some at the rear of the Royalist left wing were already retreating, with groups of Parliamentary cavalry swooping in pursuit. The King prepared to lead a rescue mission. 'Face about once, and give one charge and save the day!' cried Charles with spirit.

His decision to ride into danger horrified his Lifeguards. The King might have saved the day in person. Equally, he might have perished, yet saved his cause heroically. Instead, a Scots nobleman grabbed at his horse's reins and turned its head, swearing at the King as he shouted: 'Will you go to your death?' Charles floundered. He let himself be dissuaded. Seeing his mount turning aside, the Royalist reserves were thrown into confusion. They lost heart. Control failed. Interpreting the movement as a sign that it was every man for himself, the Royalist reserves bolted from the field, without a shot fired.

Activity against Sulby Hedges was faltering. The dragoons now had no one in particular to shoot at. Colonel Okey perceived that on the far wing, some of the New Model cavalry were chasing Royalists. The rest, under Cromwell himself, had wheeled towards the centre, taking on the Royalist foot.

'Saddle up!'

His men raced for their horses. Defying standard practice, Okey then raised his sword and led out his dragoons in a charge.

Kicking up his mount with his short boots, Gideon was thrilled. Jostling uncomfortably knee-to-knee, the dragoons careered into battle on their reviled cheap nags, clods of earth kicking up behind them, their colours streaming. Gideon's mouth opened in a wordless yell that vanished in his wake as the regiment's surprised horses carried them in an unprecedented stampede right across their now deserted left wing and into action.

They bore down on the Royalist infantry just as Cromwell attacked from the opposite side. At the same time, blocks of Parliamentary infantry stormed the centre. The dragoons piled in cheerfully, raining blows from their musket butts and slashing with their long swords at the enemy's heads and shoulders. This threefold onslaught was too much.

There was no fight to the last man here, as there had been at Marston Moor; at Naseby, even the King's hardbitten Welsh footmen gave up en masse and miserably laid down their arms. From the royal infantry reserves, Prince Rupert's Bluecoats made a brief stand while the King's Lifeguards were sent against Okey's dragoons, but a cavalry charge led by Fairfax ended the last resistance. Fairfax, who had seemed like a dead man in the tension before battle, became a whirlwind once the action started. Fighting was said to make him 'raised, elevated, and transported'. Bare-headed after losing his helmet, his inspired presence rallied the faltering Parliamentary infantry. He personally killed a Royalist ensign, as colour upon colour from the surrendering infantry regiments was scooped up for Parliament. Almost the entire body of Royalist foot had been killed or were now taken prisoner.

Fairfax ordered a new line of battle to be drawn up. Gideon gathered his men into formation with the regiment. For Fairfax to achieve this – to reassemble his army under the gunsmoke in battle lines, ready to charge or be charged by the enemy – after two hours of hot fighting, was a measure of entrenched discipline, only forty-one days after the New Model was formed. They were proud, even before they saw the results.

Prince Rupert had finally rounded up some cavaliers and dragged them back. They came too late. He could not save the infantry. Langdale's cavalry had scattered. The royal reserves were out of hand. Rupert's own men, surly and discouraged by heavy losses, could not be put in order to face the controlled new line of battle that Fairfax had established. Nothing could be done. The Royalists gave in to defeat.

Okey's dragoons saw the enemy wavering at the last. One last resounding volley from them convinced the surviving Royalist cavalry to flee the field. The King, the prince and the poor remnants of their horse rode rapidly away towards Leicester. They must have known the royal cause was lost.

As the enemy straggled and fled, Gideon Jukes felt a huge flood of gratitude that he had managed to bring himself here, where he had seen this victory. Then, in almost the last moments of fighting, calamity struck. His mare was shot, perhaps by a stray bullet from his own side. So great had been his relief at this tremendous day, he was unaware what was happening. He heard one of his men shout a warning, but when the horse fell, he had no idea why she was depositing him groundwards.

He struck the bloody turf so hard he was seriously winded. Stars spun in his sight, then in sudden pain all over his body, he lay helpless while the regiment moved over him and passed on.

There were perhaps a thousand dead on the Royalist side. Their bodies lay thickest at the foot of the hill where their sovereign had watched his great defeat. Fairfax had lost not much more than a couple of hundred men. At the end of the day, despite the dragoons' significant service throughout, Okey had no fatalities at all, with only three wounded.

In the aftermath, it would take days to sort and count the prisoners, of whom there were nearly five thousand. The New Model had killed or captured all the King's experienced infantry. The list of Royalist officers who were taken ran to eight pages, while many more were dead – so many the King could never realistically re-create his army. All the Royalist bags and baggage were captured, with all their artillery, fifty-six standards, two hundred carriages, weapons, gunpowder and horses, carts laden with boats, royal servants, the Duke of York's Lifeguards, money and treasure and plunder the Royalists had with them, including some of the rich pickings from Leicester. Most important was a carriage containing the King's correspondence. It dealt him a devastating blow, because his letters revealed that Charles had been negotiating with Catholics and planning to bring an Irish Catholic army into the war on his side. This damning evidence of treasonous intentions would be published. Eventually, it would seal the King's fate.

Before the sad clear-up, the battlefield was filled with the terrible moans and screams of wounded and dying men, the wheezing death-throes of horses. The aftermath had the normal blood and terror. Royalists who escaped fled at least to Leicester, though Leicester was bound to be retaken by Parliament so some cavaliers kept going as far as their base at Newark, thirty miles distant. Fugitives were hunted and chopped down by cavalry, who rode up behind them and severed their necks with sword blows from above. A group of Royalist horse lost their way, were trapped by New Model pursuers in a dead end, butchered in a churchyard and their bodies tossed contemptuously into clay pits. One desperate fugitive ran for thirty miles, only to surprise a serving girl who was able to kill him with the dolly-stick she had been using to pound laundry.

Cromwell took his cavalry straight on to Leicester, Okey's dragoons with him. Much of the New Model had to stay at Naseby clearing up. The dead were stripped and buried; the wounded were collected. Prisoners were marched away. Various Royalist ladies of quality were found close to the battlefield and quietly returned to private life. Women of the lower orders fared much worse. A group of females were in an encampment, unaware of the battle's outcome. They were denounced as Irish, though they were more likely Welsh. Since they carried knives, whether for their own protection or merely for preparing dinner, they were violently attacked there among the smouldering campfires, denounced as whores, then mutilated by slashing their noses and faces. About a hundred, it was said, were murdered in cold blood.

Elsewhere, a large consignment of cheese and biscuit was discovered among the plunder. Parliament's weary soldiers devoured this, praising God.

Gideon Jukes did not know how long he lay semi-conscious. When he managed to crawl upright, he had been left behind by the dragoons. Now he was bemused. Standing among the littered carcases of men and horses, with his eyes still stinging from the sulphurous smoke of the gunpowder and every muscle aching, he wondered what he was supposed to do. He stumbled about, his booted feet unable to bear him straight. A little while later, he found himself close to where booty was being sorted. Someone handed him a share of the captured cheese and biscuit, which he ate mechanically. He was spent. He needed to be given orders. He felt lost without his regiment.

The field was said to be four miles broad, yet Gideon had a ridiculous chance encounter there. A familiar figure came along – wide-bodied, trailing a battered pike with its shaft bent, his blood-covered breastplate unbuckled so his tattered shirt hung out. It was unmistakably Lambert, who until that moment had had no inkling that Gideon was enlisted or present. His brother's helmet, his heavy iron pot, was missing, along with the soft Monmouth cap he usually wore under it. His tow-coloured hair was black with filth, his face streaked with blood and grime.

Coincidence never fazed Lambert. 'Trust you to sniff out the snap –'

Gideon tore in two the cheese he had been eating. Lambert took hold of the halves and measured them by eye, adjusting for fairness as if they were brothers squabbling at home; then both munched grimly in silence until they could take in no more.

'You join at Windsor?'

'Newport Pagnell.'

Lambert nodded. 'I tried to get and see you there. We were under orders not to mingle, in case the Newport garrison poked us in the eye for having better coats and guns.'

'No, it was because New Model Army soldiers kept trying to run off and join our rather fine garrison!' Gideon corrected his brother with a grin. 'I'm with Okey. Spent half the day on my knees in a ditch with a bramble cane in my ear.'

'We saw you crazy devils whooping and playing at cavaliers,' Lambert said, jealously.

'Going at it like heroes! . . . I have lost my father's horse.' Guilt was fixating Gideon.

'You have lost your father,' Lambert informed him in a grey voice, 'so there will be no comeback for the mare . . . He slipped away in his sleep at the end of March. Colonel Rainborough gave me home leave from Windsor for the funeral.'

'Our father would have wished to see this day . . .' Tears of grief mingled with tears of stress and fatigue as Gideon thought of John Jukes's delight if he had known of the victory. Then he imagined his mother, without John, to whom she had cleaved for nearly fifty years.

'God is our strength!' Lambert saluted the last crumbs of biscuit with the New Model's watchword of the day. Food had undone him. He looked down and saw that he was standing in a pool of blood. A wound to the foot which he had not felt in the heat of battle finally made its presence known. He passed out in a dead faint; Lambert could not stand the sight of blood. Gideon just about caught him and supported his substantial weight while others rushed to help lower the hefty pikeman to the ground.

A regimental surgeon's mate glanced at Lambert, cut off his shoe and stocking, and performed rapid cleaning. Gideon stood by, unable to move, suspended in lassitude. 'He'll live. Get him into one of the carriages going out to Northampton.' With two hundred captured vehicles, the Parliamentarian wounded were travelling in style.

'Find yourself another horse!' Lambert woozily commanded as he was lifted into his conveyance, still the elder brother, still trying to organise . . .

It was only early afternoon. Over Broad Moor, frantic plovers called and searched for fledglings they would never find again. The corn and even the prickly gorse were trampled flat. Smoke lay as thick as the mist that had hidden the armies from each other at daybreak. At least it hid some of the carnage.

Lambert would be tended at Northampton. Parliament sent doctors to attend the wounded there. Gideon helped collect other casualties until a riderless horse was given to him, so he set off to Leicester after his regiment. Along the road he witnessed the bloodied bodies of Royalists who had been chopped down as they tried to escape. Some still had in their hats the beanstalks that the King's men had worn as their field sign. The postures of the corpses and their wounds told its story of sword-blunting massacre. Flight gave a licence for a killing spree. Failure to surrender permitted bloody vengeance. The New Model Army had taken it.

'Honest men served you faithfully in this action,' Oliver Cromwell would write to the Speaker of the House of Commons. *'Sir, they are trusty. I beseech you in the name of God not to discourage them. I wish this action may beget thankfulness and humility in all that are concerned in it . . .'* It was natural for those honest men of faithful service to exult that the Lord had shown His favour by awarding them easy victory. Riding alone in search of the dragoons, however, Gideon Jukes experienced more melancholy feelings. He was all too aware how close the battle at Naseby came to being lost and how hard it had in fact been won. Then the mercy of God was not on any of the roads to Leicester that evening. The joy of the victor was tempered in Gideon's heart.

It was a clear evening with blackbirds singing from vantage points on stately trees and high barn roofs. He passed through the South Leicestershire hamlets, with their medieval churches, their elegant Tudor granges and halls owned by wealthy men who had taken over the church leases when the old monastic endowments were reformed. Sibbertoft, Husbands Bosworth, Shearsby and Peatling Magna . . . ridiculous British village names. Gideon had taken the westward road, because the eastern route through Market Harborough was clogged with conveys of guards and their dispirited, defeated prisoners. Children who should not have been allowed out stood on gates to watch his passing and to wave, thinking that today's procession of desperate fugitives and stern-faced pursuers was an exciting carnival. 'Who are you for, Mister?'

'I'm for freedom,' Gideon answered, deliberately puzzling the tousle-haired little scamps. He had fought for their future, though they neither knew it, nor cared.

He struggled to control the strange horse, which had been terrified in the fight and would not go easily under him. It was the tallest horse he had ever ridden, a beautiful creature that must have been the delight of its previous rider – some Royalist cavalryman who was now dead, in all probability. Maybe not even an English cavalier, but a Frenchman, or one of the King's Irish or German mercenaries. Now this horse was carrying one of the victorious New Modellers through the peaceful countryside, and neither of them much enjoyed the experience.

While the horse flicked its ears manically whenever he tried to soothe it, and pulled sideways across the roadway at every opportunity, Gideon kept his thoughts fixed on his dead father and his fears for his brother. He was utterly tired, mentally and physically, but he knew that he must keep awake. He had to find his regiment. He was bound to return to the colours. He could not allow himself to doze in the saddle; he dreaded the moment when exhaustion would claim him and force him to sleep.

Gideon's fear was the fear of remembered noise and terror: scenes of horror that he had barely taken in at the time, but which he knew from old experience would be etched in his memory. The battle of Naseby was now with him for ever; whenever he was particularly weak or weary, this day's work would come rampaging through his dreams.

Chapter Thirty-Three

Oxford: June 1645

Oxford always had violent noises at night. In the last month of her pregnancy, Juliana slept fitfully. When she realised there was knocking at the street door, she roused herself. Tipsy soldiers and ne'er-do-wells sometimes banged as they passed. Although it was intended to cause anxiety, the malefactors rarely kept it up but staggered on their way. Juliana longed to return to sleep, but she lay partly tensed for trouble.

When this noise became too insistent to ignore, she pulled a shawl around her shoulders. Stumbling and complaining, she blundered downstairs without lighting a candle. It was high summer and must be after midnight, judging by the dawn light which had already filtered through window curtains. The knocking continued. As she was about to unfasten the door onto St Aldate's, she became sufficiently alert to stop, laying her head against the wood and calling out, 'Who is it? Who goes there?'

'*Juliana!*'

She recognised Colonel McIlwaine's voice. In a flurry, she hastened to draw the bolts and open up. Sleepily laughing, she began to apologise for keeping him standing out on the doorstep of his own house.

'Juliana.' She stopped talking when she saw his face. 'Juliana.' The figure she admitted was spectral and abrupt. Seizing her shoulders, the colonel dropped a kiss upon her forehead with a kind of fervent despair. 'Lock the door – lock it tight!'

He strode past, making his way to the kitchen where faint warmth still came from the embers of the fire. He flung his muddy cloak on a chair, his hat – in which was a wizened wreath of vegetation – upon the table. He sank down on a bench. He laid his head in his hands, then shuddered long and hard.

Juliana hovered in the doorway behind him, stricken.

*   *   *

She recognised a man in trouble when she saw one. Lumbering to the hearth, fastening the loose ribbons on her nightgown for decency, she knelt and raddled up the coals, reaching for a pan to heat hot water. At the noise of utensils, McIlwaine raised his head. Always hook-shouldered and gaunt, his general appearance seemed unchanged, yet she noticed he was wearing his swordbelt but the hangers were empty. He had been waiting out of doors on foot; quickly she wondered where he had stabled his horse and what condition the beast was in.

'Let me find you food and drink.' She managed to keep her tone level. In response, the colonel breathed once rapidly, then he groaned. Juliana sat back on her heels and remained still. Moments passed, seeming long and extraordinary.

'Hot water to wash then,' she suggested gently.

'I want nothing . . . You are very kind.' Juliana read the worst into that heavy statement. This was a man in deep grief.

'You have come alone, sir?' Doggedly she began to prod for explanations: 'There have been rumours of fighting – but there are always rumours, usually wrong . . .' Only a slight lift of the colonel's chin, and maybe a shadow in his dark eyes, confirmed for her that battle had taken place. 'For the love of God, Owen, tell me what has happened.'

Then, because he was a professional soldier, Owen McIlwaine straightened up. In terse, bitter language, he explained what befell the King's army at Naseby. Written in a letter, it would have been only a paragraph. Fairfax and Cromwell took little more, when they reported their triumph to their masters in Parliament; for the defeated there was even less to say. The unembroidered facts were bleak. They had lost the battle. The royal cause had lost all hope. Victory, in the widest possible sense, belonged to Parliament.

This crisis was dire, but Juliana's preoccupations were different from those of the despondent Irishman. Struggling with good manners, she tried to drag out of him what she needed to know: 'You escaped with your life and I am heartily glad . . . What can you tell me of Orlando, please?'

As if she had overstepped good taste, the colonel rounded on her: 'When we rode from the field, I did not see him. He is gone, Juley!'

'*Gone?* What do you mean? Did you *see* what happened to him?' The colonel raised his shoulders a little, in a weary shrug. 'So you did not see him?'

He did not search, she thought. He was distancing himself from Lovell. This was hers to deal with. She was a woman alone, with one child to care for and another about to be born any day –

Sensing rebuke, McIlwaine flared, 'You must suppose him lost. There was a field of blood more than a mile long! Men dead and men not yet quite dead . . . Men who ought to be dead, but who refused to go to their God in timely fashion, groaning and twitching . . .'

'But if you did not *see* him,' Juliana insisted dully, 'there must be hope?'

McIlwaine gave her a cold look. Even with her mind racing about what would happen to her, her young son Tom, the baby that would be born in two weeks, Juliana realised there was some great matter he was not yet telling her. A still, terrifying voice warned her in advance. 'Why is Nerissa not with you? Did you lose her in the confusion?'

'I lost her,' agreed Owen. His voice was terrible.

There was a tortured silence as the man found himself devoid of speech. Then, quite suddenly, words broke from him. Juliana would always afterwards remember that moment and how the coals collapsed down so the fire blazed up suddenly, just when he told her. For the rest of her life she would remember the sudden heat and the crackle of the flames. She had to control the urge to lean back away from the heat on her face. She could not ply poker and brush in the normal hearth routine. A spark fell on her nightgown but she brushed it off discreetly.

'Nerissa was never one to seclude herself in a fine carriage. There were noblewomen who did that, and I suppose they were treated by the victors accordingly. Nerissa always saw it as her duty to guide the junior officers' and soldiers' wives.'

'So?'

'So, when the New Model Army troopers burst in among our women in their tranquil camp site, Nerissa stood among them. The Roundheads could not understand the women; they called them Irish papist whores. They began mutilating the poor creatures – slashing their noses as a sign they were supposed to be harlots, making them too ugly to ply such a trade . . . The bloodlust took hold; they callously slaughtered dozens. I am told that Nerissa marched forwards and stood up to the men indignantly. She cursed their blind morals and their cruelty – but not for long. Irish herself and not denying it, she quickly received punishment.'

Survivors, blood still pouring from their slit noses, had told Owen when he came to search. At his insistence, they showed him his wife's mangled body. He wept as he told Juliana.

'We were going home to Ireland. I shall go to Ireland still – in bitter sorrow that I must return alone. We thought if we were ever separated, Nerissa would bear that burden. This is not planned for, Juliana. Oh, how am I to deal with it?'

'Save yourself.' Not weeping herself yet, though tears were all too close, Juliana's throat had dried; her voice came as an angry croak. 'Leave this terrible, blood-soaked country. It is what she would want.'

Owen McIlwaine had had a long weary ride in which to think about his future. 'What is the point?' he asked, though it was a mere murmur of exhaustion. 'What is the point of anything?'

Women have their work. Juliana set aside her feelings. She kept going, temporarily, playing at housewife. She organised a bed, persuaded the colonel to take nourishment, saw him safe to his room. Then she roused Nerissa's servant and told her what had happened, so that Grania's first terrible torrent of distress could happen out of Owen's hearing and before little Tom awoke.

'The colonel will take you with him back to Ireland, Grania. He has come to Oxford to fetch you. He will take you safely home.'

He had come for the family valuables too, Juliana realised. Because of her friendship with his wife, she knew what the McIlwaines owned, and where they kept it. A discreet man, the colonel systematically gathered together the money, the papers and his wife's jewellery next day. There was silverware, off which they had all so often dined convivially – battered old Irish cutlery, chargers and dishes collected in France, ridiculously tall German goblets – and there were Venetian glasses, which were housed, wrapped in green velvet, in their own casket. Most precious and rare, there was a clock.

The colonel worked fast and miserably, and he worked alone. As a couple the McIlwaines had been generous with their energy, to the King they served and to their own friends, yet they had controlled their affairs with caution. They had lived, worked, fought, always with their eventual retirement in mind. Even Grania, the family retainer, had been kept in their household as someone who might tend them in old age. When Grania made a desultory offer to stay with Juliana until she gave birth, that was never a real option. 'No; you must go with the colonel. Mistress McIlwaine would expect you to look after him, now he is desolate. I have a midwife arranged for my lying-in; I shall do well enough.'

Juliana would never be able to afford to keep a servant. That was so evident, she barely considered the issue. So long as the colonel remained in the house, she was deferring any hard look at her future, but it could only be a life of poverty.

McIlwaine stayed two days. On the night before he left, he allowed Juliana to prepare a decent supper, set formally at table, instead of the hurried snacks he had taken in his own unhappy company. She dressed in the best gown she owned that would fit over her expanded belly; she wore the pearl necklace Lovell had brought back from campaign. Her son Tom and the servant Grania dined with them; little Tom, on what passed for his best behaviour, sat on a pile of cushions, tied with a sash to the tall chair-back. Afterwards Grania cleared the table, put the child to bed and retired to pray and weep for her lost mistress, leaving Juliana and the colonel to conduct dreary finalities.

McIlwaine now told Juliana the house had its rent paid up until December; she was welcome to have use of it for that period. He had listed various pieces of furniture that he could neither take with him nor sell; these were hers on permanent loan. He handed her one flat, velvet-lined jewel case containing an antique Irish gold-set sapphire necklace and earrings, which he said Nerissa had wanted her to have. Then he tried, as far as honesty would let him, to pretend that her husband might still return.

'We shall see.' Juliana quietly folded her hands and wished the conversation were over. For her there was no point in speculation. Either Orlando would turn up, completely out of the blue as was his habit, or in time she would have to accept he was not coming back. She might never discover what had happened to him. They had made no plans for this eventuality, so she must make the best of it. With resignation she saw that, back in Wallingford, Orlando had chosen her on a raffish presumption that, unlike women with more conventional upbringings, Juliana Carlill had enough spirit to fend for herself. If he was alive still, he would not be worrying about her.

It was a night for plain speaking. There in the twilight, Nerissa's widower and her young friend spent time talking about her. Owen and Juliana went through the difficult, necessary conversation bereaved people inflict upon themselves: they reviewed Nerissa's talents and reminisced over special events they had shared with her, as if they were fixing those dear past times in the memory.

'I shall never forget how, in the big fire here last October, we had scuttled for our lives over into Christ Church quadrangle and as we pushed in among the cattle some men ogled us – Nerissa gurgled with laughter and whispered to me, *"If we were not good wives, we should fill in the hour while the flames are doused, having liaisons with these gallants!"'*

'She was never a one for the gallants,' Owen congratulated himself.

'Oh do not be so sure, my dear! She would eye up a gallant astutely – you were safe because of her wisdom; those dark eyes of hers would twinkle as she knew them all for shallow idiots . . .'

Very carefully, avoiding too much emotion, they listed the qualities of loyalty and courage that had made Nerissa follow Owen and the army, and the sense of justice that made her denounce the New Model Army troopers who were savaging the other women.

The colonel had drunk deeper than usual. There were a few good bottles of wine in the cellar and this was his last chance to enjoy them. When he soldiered on the Continent, he and Nerissa had more than once moved on and left a life behind, but he had never had to do it alone. Nerissa had been there, ready to prepare some new home wherever they landed up. As he stretched his long legs and brooded, Juliana considered privately how relationships between families worked and sometimes shifted. Nerissa had been her friend; she took in the Lovells to be part of her household, yet it was her gift to Juliana specifically. The two couples had lived side by side, though theirs was never the timeless friendship that came from years of living in neighbouring villages or adjacent town houses, nor had they a history of working together as courtiers. Even though Juliana and Owen had just talked intimately about Nerissa, in truth she barely knew the man. She was not certain he understood why Nerissa had been so fond of her. Perhaps she and Owen were each a little jealous of Nerissa's closeness to the other . . . Now friendship would continue on the surface, but awkwardly. If Lovell had been here, that would have been worse.

Addressing the issue of Lovell more freely than usual, Juliana said abruptly: 'You do not like my husband, I suspect.'

The colonel started. 'He was a good soldier, madam.'

Juliana smiled dryly. 'You may be open – give me your opinion. I shall never see you again, nor you me – and anyway, he is probably dead.'

McIlwaine drew in breath, in the way he had of deferring difficulties. Juliana let him hesitate but she left a silence which needed to be filled. It was a night for closing accounts. Eventually he admitted: 'I did not like Lovell after Lichfield.'

'That was a siege Prince Rupert raised – what, two years ago? What happened?'

'Much desecration.' McIlwaine's brow darkened while Juliana watched him closely. 'When we relieved the town, it was already notorious for the sacrilegious behaviour of the Parliamentary troops who were there before us. Those Roundheads had been merciful to the people, but pitiless to the cathedral. They quartered the priests' copes and surplices, ripping them with swords as if the very vestments were being punished for treason. Destroyed the organ pipes. Stabled their horses in the nave, broke up the floors, shat in the quire. Every day they hunted a cat through the church, whooping as they raised an echo under the high vaulting. They brought a calf to the font, wrapped in linen, and baptised it, giving it a name, to express their scorn of the holy sacrament –'

Juliana interrupted. 'This was not my husband. This was the enemy.'

'You asked why I did not like him. Well, this is why: during their violations, the rebels had broken into the crypt. They tore open the ancient bishops' tombs, scattering the holy bones of those good men – and tearing the episcopal rings from their decaying fingers.'

Juliana now saw where the diatribe was heading. 'Orlando wears a great red-stoned ring. He had it off a prisoner.'

'So he says,' snapped Owen McIlwaine. 'I believe Lovell descended to the crypt himself, and he took that ring from some long-dead bishop's finger.'

Juliana could do nothing but nod gravely.

The conversation had opened sluices. Suddenly McIlwaine leaned forward earnestly. 'This is a stricken country. You have nothing here. Why don't you come away to Ireland?'

He could not know anything of Juliana's family background (Lovell never spoke of it), but McIlwaine must have seen enough to realise his wild question would not altogether startle this young woman. To up sticks and escape her troubled life held definite attractions. Juliana had the independence to do it. Her grandmother would have gone in a trice.

Juliana foresaw how it would end. At that moment, she was being offered nothing more than assistance and protection. But she knew enough of men to realise Owen McIlwaine had always until now had Nerissa to share his life; he would be unable to exist alone. He was a man in loss, already fumbling for simple solutions. If Juliana went to Ireland, it would eventually seem natural to him that she, Nerissa's friend, would take Nerissa's place. For Owen it would be a happy resolution.

For Juliana, it had a bad taste even while it was just an idea. She might have married Orlando Lovell, yet she was fastidious. *Do I think too much of myself?* she wondered. *Or just too little of men?* . . . This was war. She felt that social civilities were breaking down; she guessed at worse to come.

She thanked the colonel sweetly and said she had to stay in Oxford until her child was born. Before objections could be made, she added that Oxford was where Lovell would come to find her. She must remain here until she heard firm news. 'Whatever you think, I married him. It was my choice. He is my man, just as you were Nerissa's. He is the father of my children. Even if he is dead, when my children one day ask me about him, I must be able to tell them how he fared. Indeed, I must know it myself.'

'He does not deserve you,' said Owen. 'Though as my dearest Nerissa would say – what man is there alive who deserves the woman who puts up with him?'

They had spent their memories of Nerissa, however. The night was over. Next morning McIlwaine took his leave, Grania riding on a packhorse behind him. Men had appeared from nowhere to join him. A small party set off towards Wales, which had always been hot in support of the King. The colonel had once hoped to go north-west, if the roads were clear, and try to reach Holyhead where they could take a boat direct across the Irish Sea. Now it was thought too dangerous, so they were riding into South Wales and somehow onwards from there.

Juliana waved them off. She went indoors before the clatter of hooves had vanished, closing the door on a silent house. As soon as she was alone she remembered the sword Orlando had once given her to protect herself. She hated it and could have passed it on to the colonel to hang on his empty baldric. But she had lost her chance and was stuck with it. The weapon must remain under her mattress, where Orlando had insisted on placing it when they first came to St Aldate's.

Shortly she would break down in grief for Nerissa. After that, she must try to plan ahead.

For the time being she would only be weeping for her friend. She had no other sense of bereavement. She did not suppose for a moment that Orlando Lovell, her cavalier husband, had died at Naseby.

That would have been too easy.

Chapter Thirty-Four

Oxford: 1645

For almost a fortnight Juliana was stuck in the house, alone with a boisterous child not yet two years of age, coping with her fears of giving birth. She had warned the midwife who, being a decent woman, sent a maid to check on progress every day. On the 5th of July, three weeks after Naseby, the maid ran home to fetch the midwife who was fortunately free to attend. Under her supervision Juliana gave birth to her second son after a blessedly swift labour. The baby was small, which helped, despite which he seemed healthy. He looked like his father, much more than his brother Tom had done. The mother survived, without any infection setting in, though in the emotional aftermath of birth, she collapsed in wild torrents of tears. She refused to give the child a name, saying hysterically that his missing father must do that.

The concerned midwife stayed overnight, then took it upon herself to hire a nurse – 'As is so often necessary, not for the child, who thrives lustily, but the poor demented mother who is quite beside herself . . .'

The nurse was a fat, evil-smelling, elderly body who soon found what was left of Colonel McIlwaine's wine cellar. Thomas Lovell toddled to alert his mother that debauchery was taking place in the parlour. Aged twenty-one months and barely talking, Tom Lovell was, the nurse then swore, 'a spy and sneak as wicked as any Roundhead!'

'She whacked me!' accused Tom, who had until then known only gentle treatment and favouritism at the centre of the household. He already suspected that having a new little brother might threaten his position. However, he could still command attention. To preserve him from being beaten by a stranger, Juliana did what she had to: she stopped crying, wiped her wet face on a pillowcase, crawled out of bed, paid off the nurse and forced herself to take charge. Tom watched her avidly, looking after his own interests. Just as single-minded, the unnamed baby demanded milk voraciously. Nobody could doubt, Juliana thought bitterly, these two man-children were Lovell's.

When the midwife, Mrs Flewitt, learned the circumstances of the nurse's dismissal she was probably not surprised, yet rushed to apologise with her bonnet flapping. Mrs Flewitt was a good woman and better businesswoman. She did not know Nerissa McIlwaine had died, nor that Lovell was missing in action and Juliana facing penury. Juliana had lied by omission in keeping these details to herself; she glumly accepted that falsification must now become part of her lifestyle. Mrs Flewitt thought the handsome, pleasant-natured wife of a vigorous cavalier was a client to treasure since she might confidently be expected to become pregnant once a year, giving her midwife a secure income. She offered to lend Juliana her own maid, Mercy Tulk. No fool, Juliana snapped up the offer.

Inspecting Mercy Tulk, she found a short, undernourished young girl of perhaps sixteen, a horn-worker's daughter. She lived in a dream, unable to apply herself to any task without energetic encouragement, but she accepted direction. Soon she preferred helping Juliana to the more arduous existence she had had before, running errands and assisting Mrs Flewitt. Despite her other-worldly air, the wench knew enough to pipe up and suggest Juliana should poach her – which she claimed would be acceptable all round since her sister Alice 'had been taken on as a temporary in her old place and could easily become a permanent'. Juliana found herself suddenly ruthless. She brushed aside Mrs Flewitt's weak protestations of deserving more loyalty and having trained Mercy Tulk at her own expense. 'With less success than you may have supposed, Mrs Flewitt!' Juliana snatched Mercy Tulk for herself. So long as she could pretend there would be wages at the end of the year, she would now have someone to share domestic work and help care for the children.

She had scrutinised Mercy Tulk on the two counts a housewife most needed to check: whether the new maid would make doe-eyes at Lovell, if he ever reappeared, and whether Lovell himself would be susceptible to chasing Mercy up the back stairs. Juliana decided not.

It might be false confidence: 'Is Captain Lovell coming home soon?' asked Mercy Tulk, rather too hopefully.

'I doubt it!' snapped Juliana. 'Captain Lovell has to be found first.'

Her new maid assumed her husband had absconded with his mistress. Juliana let her think it.

There were procedures to follow and Juliana doggedly discovered what they were. She was a fast learner. That did not really help much, because most of the procedures were uncertain and all were extremely slow.

Finding out what had happened to her husband would have been easier if he had not fought on the losing side. As she nursed her baby, Juliana was racked with frustration and fear.

She scoured all the news-sheets she could get her hands on. There were wild reports at first, one even declaring that Prince Rupert had been captured. More reliable pamphlets informed her that when the battle at Naseby ended, four thousand Royalist prisoners had been taken overnight to Market Harborough. Then they were marched to London, via Newport Pagnell where Sir Samuel Luke was asked to assist with conveying them. In London, they were paraded through the streets as a spectacle for cheering crowds. Common soldiers were penned like sheep at market in the Artillery Ground or, depending on which story you read, in Tothill Fields. Either way, it was an outdoor billet, with no conveniences, where they were harangued with sermons and encouraged to transfer their allegiance to Parliament. Officers were initially lodged in Lord Peters's house in Aldersgate Street – presumably somewhat squashed, given the large number of prisoners. Since an officer was a gentleman and a gentleman's word was his bond, parole would be granted in due course and conditions meanwhile might be bearable. Colonels, lieutenant-colonels and majors would take precedence in the allocation of fair quarters. Captains came next, but once a published list of captured Royalist officers was printed, it included well over fifty captains, none called Lovell. Juliana supposed they would be jostling for good treatment. Extremely senior men were imprisoned in the Tower, or held in other grim London prisons; Lovell could not be regarded in that category. His survival strategy had always been to lie low, never looking dangerous.

For all these prisoners, the desirable route to freedom was through an exchange. Soldiers from the ranks would never achieve it; they must either become turncoats, enlisting in the New Model Army, or languish. Jail fever would carry them off rapidly; if they had been wounded in battle, they were probably dead already. Officers might feel more hopeful, so long as they had not come to Parliament's notice as particularly viru-lent Royalists. To arrange to be exchanged with Parliamentary officers held by the King, Royalists needed either parole passes, so they could go out and organise the matter themselves, or somebody on the outside working for them. For Orlando Lovell, that would have to be his wife.

First, he would have to tell her where he was.

Maybe she was wrong. Maybe Lovell had been killed.

If so, there was no sure way now to learn of it. Juliana had heard what happened after an action. Dead soldiers were quickly stripped. Cadavers on the field were piled into burial pits unceremoniously, prob-ably the same day as the battle, especially at Naseby, which only took a morning. Nobody would bother to identify them. Although she read that Oliver Cromwell had given orders afterwards that his pursuing cavalry were not to stop to plunder the men they cut down, there were always two versions. Reports from the Royalist side complained about the New Model Army taking as much plunder as they could – clothes and armour, weapons and money, lockets and finger rings. Afterwards, one naked man sprawled among the cow parsley in a hedge was little different from another.

Juliana could only wait. Silence from Lovell and silence about him from everyone else continued.

She still corresponded occasionally with her guardian Mr Gadd, if she could find a carrier going into Somerset where he lived in retirement. When she wrote with the good news that she was safely delivered of another healthy child, she mentioned that Lovell was missing. She put a brave face on it. Mr Gadd was now extremely old and frail; she thought there was nothing he could do to help and she did not want to cause him anxiety.

The New Model Army stormed across Royalist territory, bombarding castles and great houses into submission. Now essentially mopping up, Fairfax set out to subdue the West Country; on the 10th of July he and Cromwell defeated Lord Goring at the battle of Langport. On the same day, Archbishop Laud, whose recalcitrance had helped to cause the conflict, was executed on Tower Hill in London. Prince Rupert was attempting to rally Royalist spirits in the west; after Langport he was sent to Bristol. Was Lovell there? Fairfax took Bridgwater, acquiring Royalist provisions and ammunition. For the King, there was better news from Scotland where the brilliant campaign by the Marquis of Montrose continued so bravely that King Charles toyed with marching north to meet up with him.

Parliamentary troops were making so much headway in South Wales, Juliana feared for Colonel McIlwaine. He had promised to write to her once he reached Ireland. In an odd way, she hoped never to hear from him. She chided herself, but she was uneasy. The plain fact was that friendly correspondence from an Irish Catholic, if it were intercepted, might do her harm in a world ruled by Parliament. Owen McIlwaine would be a very dangerous friend.

While the New Model Army knocked out one Royalist base after another, the King hopped ahead of them as it was said 'like a hunted quail'. He spent three dreamy weeks at Raglan Castle, squandering precious time in entertainments and sports. Once Charles was shaken out of his inertia by news of Goring's defeat at Langport, he moved around indecisively until, at the end of August, he arrived for a brief visit to Oxford. Fairfax was preparing to besiege Prince Rupert at Bristol.

Juliana was astonished by the King's return, though it brought her hope. Lovell was not among the ragged band who limped back, though someone else she knew was: Edmund Treves. The sight of the familiar, red-haired figure, always a little more rugged physically than she expected and always so kindly disposed towards her, reduced Juliana to momentary tears.

Edmund was horrified. He chose to view Juliana as a lighthouse, firm-based on stalwart rocks in the storms of life (as one of his poems had it). He quickly discovered the source of her misery: 'Edmund, I do not know if Orlando is dead or alive!'

'God in heaven! You may assume he is alive. He was seen, Juliana, seen in the rout towards Leicester; his horse tripped and flipped him over its ears. He was last noticed being marched off as a prisoner.'

'I thought everyone was killed in the pursuit.'

Edmund was terse. 'Enough. Not all.'

'Did *you* see him taken?'

'No, but I had it from a man I trust. The Ironsides were champing at our heels. But you know Lovell . . .'

Edmund's ill-concealed shudder as he mentioned Cromwell's horsemen was felt by Juliana as she flung her arms around him gratefully. Thinner in the face now, and matured by defeat, her one-time suitor never had jealousy in his nature. He was simply thrilled to be of assistance.

'Oh but what of you, Edmund? My dear, how did you escape, and where have you been since the battle?'

'I rode from the field with Prince Rupert. The broken remnants of our army spent a despondent, sleepless night at Ashby-de-la-Zouch – Leicester was unsafe for us, and indeed Fairfax retook it only two days later. For us it was Lichfield, then on to Bewdley, where we were finally rested. I had been shot in the back of the neck and after I managed to be seen by a surgeon, his efforts to clean my wound of rags and dirt and powder made me so weak and infected, I had to be left behind.'

'Oh Edmund! You were lucky – wounds should be cleansed the first day they occur . . . Are you recovered now?'

'I am,' he claimed bravely, though Juliana noticed he was pale and held his shoulder awkwardly. 'I would be in Bristol with the prince, but now the gates are closed, I cannot ride up politely and ask the New Model Army to admit me! Besides, Bristol may be a very unsafe place. Everyone maintains Rupert will hold it, but I think Sir Thomas Fairfax is too determined – more important, he's too well-equipped with artillery. Rupert is losing heart. He will not hold out.'

Once it would have been Lovell who made that kind of assessment. Edmund had learned to think for himself. When Juliana asked if the King proposed a last stand, Edmund said baldly that he thought not. It would be unrealistic. 'I do not know how our affairs will end, but it has to be faced: we are on a downward spiral. The King ought to make terms – though he will not. In the meantime –' His face brightened again. 'In so far as I can be useful, I am at your service.'

So it was Edmund Treves who took upon himself the role of god-father to the new baby. It was Edmund, relishing this position, who ordained that the child must be baptised. 'Maybe I believe in Anabaptistical late immersion,' murmured Juliana. Her mischief was brushed aside. The baby was speedily dunked in a High Church font by a tall, thin, gobbler-necked, pinch-vowelled parish priest, while Edmund – after belatedly asking her permission – chose a name.

Being of a poetic nature, Edmund Treves called Juliana's baby Valentine.

Juliana had previously been urged by others to give her son his father's name (in case Lovell was dead), a proposal which offended her. At Edmund's florid choice she winced in private. She had only herself to blame. Lovell had nominated their firstborn. When made aware that he must perform that duty, Orlando selected Thomas, saying it was a good plain English iambic name that any honest man could bear. This was her one indication of what Lovell thought about his own literary appellation. She knew what he would say about Valentine. *'Damme, Juliana! You let that ginger wisp of whimsy give my boy a galloping three-syllable saint's designation? Odds doggerel, I disown him!' 'Who, my sweet – Edmund, or our dear little Val? . . .'*

Such was Juliana's yearning to see Orlando, she let Edmund's misnomer slip past her, too busy thinking how she longed to hear her husband's voice, even in a full flood of indignation.

The King only stayed three days at Oxford. Edmund rushed to tell her that they were leaving for Worcester, with the intention of relieving Hereford, a town currently under siege by the army of Scots Covenanters. Those tough troops – seven thousand of them, with four thousand wives and children as followers – had become a byword throughout the Midlands for their heavy-handed requisitioning; a Royalist news-sheet reported that after one night's acquaintance with the Scots' 'perfect plundering', Birmingham in Warwickshire even extolled Tinker Fox for moderation.

'Edmund, if you are leaving, tell me quickly, what must I do to find Orlando?'

'His name is now on our list of the missing, though he has not been heard of. But I must tell you, the more we lose garrisons, the fewer prisoners we possess for exchange. If he is a prisoner, he is in a tight spot, Juliana. The best thing is for you to begin writing letters to anyone who may help . . .' Treves had to go.

At the King's approach, the Covenanters lifted their siege and vanished away like the proverbial Scotch mist. It was the King's only success that year, but had deplorable results for him. Abandoning Hereford freed up the Scots for other business. By the time the Marquis of Montrose left Edinburgh to advance triumphantly into England to meet up with the King, the Covenanters' army was installed in the far north, waiting to prevent him.

At Bristol Sir Thomas Fairfax negotiated with Prince Rupert for terms, until Fairfax realised Rupert had no intention to surrender. The New Model Army began a full assault. Despite at first fiercely contesting the attack, Rupert decided his position was hopeless and after just one day he surrendered. Three days later the Covenanters utterly crushed the Marquis of Montrose at the battle of Philiphaugh, forty miles south of Edinburgh. Montrose had not even made it into England. Any last hope for the royal cause was gone.

The Parliamentarians gave Rupert a formal escort back to Oxford. No word came from Lovell afterwards, so Juliana decided he had not been at the siege.

The King never forgave his nephew for surrendering Bristol. He revoked all Rupert's commissions and spitefully ordered the arrest of Rupert's close friend, Will Legge, the governor of Oxford.

In September the Royalists pulled down all houses within three miles outside of the walls to prevent Parliament using them for billets in any coming siege. Fairfax was now expected back at any moment. Only self-deluding optimists thought the New Model would fail to take Oxford this time. Anyone with any sense was planning how to make it appear they had endured the King's presence out of necessity, but had really been Parliamentarians all along. Juliana just hoped women and children would be spared annoyance.

A new governor of Oxford, Thomas Glemham, was to replace the victimised Legge. This put an end to an enduring joke. A previous town governor, the highly unpopular Sir Arthur Aston, had fallen from his horse on Bullingdon Green while curvetting to impress a group of ladies; he broke his leg so badly it had to be amputated. The joke went: 'Who is governor of Oxford now?' 'One Legge.' 'A pox on him! Is he governor still?' Aston would have a cruel fate, beaten to death with his own wooden leg at the siege of Drogheda. Legge, who had been Owen McIlwaine's commander, had Irish connections. He had lodged in the largest house in St Aldate's, close by, so his departure added to Juliana's sense that the King's party were being squeezed out.

Prince Rupert insisted on his right to be heard. Against the King's orders he turned up at the great Royalist base in Newark, demanding a court martial. Though the Council of War acquitted him of any failure of duty, the King remained obdurate. Six days later Charles replaced another of Rupert's friends as governor of Newark. Furious quarrels ensued. The rift clearly would not be healed.

On the 5th of November, with few options left for winter quarters, the King returned to Oxford. Parliament issued passes for Rupert and named associates to leave for the Continent through specified exit ports. He did not immediately take advantage. Parliament warned him to go, or his concessions would be cancelled. However, Rupert and his brother Maurice came back again to Oxford with the King.

Lord Goring left England, officially citing health reasons. The King was urging the Prince of Wales to seek safety abroad. Berkeley Castle, Devizes and Winchester Castle surrendered to Parliament. Basing House, the enormous fortified manor which had held out under siege for three years, fell to Cromwell amid scenes of voracious plunder during which Inigo Jones, who had produced the iconic emblems of King Charles's theatrical reign, was carried out naked in a blanket. Newark was besieged by the Scots' Covenanters. Bolton Castle surrendered after its garrison was reduced to eating horseflesh. Beeston Castle fell. A small volunteer force of Parliamentarians made a surprise attack on Hereford and its dispirited Royalist governor fled. Chester was completely encircled.

At the very end of December, a little late in the day, King Charles decided to research other civil wars. A member of his staff instructed the Bodleian Library to send the King a volume on this subject. Since books from the university collection were never lent out, the warrant was refused.

In December, with the McIlwaines' lease on the St Aldate's house almost expired, Juliana received a letter from Mr Gadd. Like Edmund Treves, he advised her to take the dreary route to assistance: begging letters. Mr Gadd spelled out her options. If only she could learn where her husband was confined, she should demand to see him and maybe even share his prison quarters. If he had been offered no terms for release, she could petition Parliament, though to do that with any hope of success, she needed to go to Westminster and press her suit in person. Realistically, she would need a member of Parliament or a respected senior officer to negotiate for her. But first, there should be the straight-forward option: Royalists had been offered a chance of a Parliamentary pardon if they would compound for their release by paying a sum, to be assessed, which went to the public relief. Juliana had heard of this before; it had been roundly mocked by Lovell, though she tried to forget that. The offer had been renewed, said Mr Gadd, after the fall of Bristol. There was a committee, the Committee for Compounding, which sat in the Guildhall in London, to which Juliana should apply once she discovered Lovell's whereabouts.

If she still heard nothing, she must seek help from any influential friends on the Parliamentary side. Mr Gadd knew Juliana's position; she had no such friends. He realised her funds must be running out and she would soon be homeless. So he told her that if she became desperate then, whether Lovell would want this or not, she should make an attempt to contact his family.

That meant Juliana must go into Hampshire, introduce herself and beg for help from Orlando Lovell's long-estranged father.

'Take your little sons of course,' instructed Mr Gadd. He always saw how delicate negotiations might best be made to work.

Chapter Thirty-Five

Hampshire: 1646

It would always be daunting for a young woman of twenty, burdened by extremely young children, to meet her hostile in-laws for the first time, especially when all the parties were fully aware she had applied to them because she was desperate for money.

Still hoping to hear from Lovell, Juliana left her journey as late as she dared, but with the lease on the house nearly up, there was no longer a choice. At the turn of the year she left behind an Oxford which was full of distress and discord and, accompanied by Edmund Treves, set out for Hampshire. Her first act of begging had been to screw from the governor of Oxford travel passes for herself, one male escort, her infant children and a maid. Edmund had wanted to obtain a pass from the King, laden with royal seals, but Juliana suspected that in a Parliamentarian county she would meet a better reception if she arrived with a plain civil document and an apologetic manner. She needed a male bodyguard to prevent highway robbery. If Edmund was discovered to be a serving cavalier they would all be arrested. She planned to term him 'my son's godfather', to sound respectable. She managed to make him abandon his flowing shirt and beribboned suit, to dress down in a shabby coat. He refused to be disguised as a servant.

She had to decide whether to write ahead to explain herself, which might harden the family's attitude, or simply to arrive but perhaps spoil her chances by startling them. She compromised by sending a letter to say she was coming, immediately before she set out. They had no time to send a refusal.

Wrestling with such matters of judgement was new to her. It would be strange for most women. Juliana had a grim sense that this was just the start.

Inessential travel – which meant travel that was unconnected to trade or to military manoeuvres – was banned by both sides. Women with piteous stories could manage it, if they were lucky. The safest way was with carriers; they knew the routes and how to space their convoys and time their journeys to avoid being set upon by thieves. Some managed to obtain warrants to pass through military checks. In December the carriers were grumbling more than usual: roads were impassable for carts, horses had been stolen by the armies, everyone was too fearful to want to buy goods or dispatch letters . . .

Her party rode on two terrible pad horses – she did not want to be stranded, and better beasts might be stolen. Juliana sat behind Edmund on a pillion saddle, holding the baby, while Mercy Tulk followed with little Tom tied to her and a cloak bag bouncing on the nag's fat rump. Once they moved away from Oxford, Juliana knew they would be frequently stopped and questioned. She was disconcerted when they were subjected to searches as well. Fortunately the point was to discover arms, secret papers or items worth stealing. She had none of those. They had very quickly passed into areas that were controlled by enemy militia, but when the soldiers saw she had so little luggage of any kind they softened. When she claimed to be a Parliamentarian squire's daughter-in-law, urgently needing to visit him for family reasons, they lost interest and let her through.

Treves was impressed. He let Juliana do the talking. Although he was the man in the party, her status as a married woman sometimes won her respect. He noticed how she always made him slow the horse to a stop even before the soldiers signalled with their muskets, then how she spoke quietly and politely, however rude the men were.

Beyond the South Downs, they came to rolling country where narrow roads switchbacked between tiny villages with traditional thatched cottages that hid themselves among farmland hollows. Somehow they reached the small village beyond Salisbury that Mr Gadd had named. They took rooms at the only inn. Juliana sent a message to Squire Lovell, asking him to receive her the next day. Edmund strolled out a little before twilight to reconnoitre. He reported that Orlando's childhood home was a large house in the gabled Tudor style, glimpsed through a battlemented gatehouse, lying just outside the village among its own tenanted farmland. Locals had told him that the squire, his son and various sons-in-law were all passionate haters of bishops, anxious to reform the Church, severe men who had raised soldiers for Parliament from the beginning. Ralph Lovell, Orlando's elder brother, was now at home, rumoured to be almost dead of wounds.

Next morning a footman was sent to conduct her and Juliana walked to the manor-house.

The Lovell family had assembled in full force. Perhaps the younger members felt they should protect the father from weakening. That would be in their interests, thought Juliana grimly, though it seemed unlikely Squire Lovell would enfold her in his arms, forgiving Orlando and welcoming this new daughter-in-law and two more grandchildren among those whose toys and pets littered most of his home.

He was a balding old man in a dark suit and plain collar, who leaned with a quivering hand on a slim cane to help him walk; he had an austere expression, though that could be caused by joint pain. He was scrupulously courteous but, by making no distinction of persons, his absolute good manners also made it impossible to assess his true attitude.

The set-faced younger relations who clustered on upright chairs were introduced as two of Orlando's sisters, Mary and Aurora, the well-shod wives of Mr Francis Falconer and Sir Daniel Swayne, together with their brother Ralph's wife, Katherine. None looked like a strict religious bigot although Mrs Katherine Lovell, the most plainly dressed, appeared to be clutching a pocket Bible. The sisters were in the best fashions Hampshire could provide, which was nothing fancy, though they wore silk gowns, pinned on the low neck and flowing sleeve with small jewels; these they must have obtained from the same source, for although one gown was damson-coloured and the other oatmeal, Juliana noticed identical bodice shaping and pinked hems. She envied their tailoress her half-moon pinking tool.

All three young women appeared to be breeding. That increased Juliana's pessimism.

According to the landlady at her inn, there was a third Lovell sister, married to a New Englander called Bonalleck. They had returned to England from Massachusetts to help defy the King and at the moment were staying with the squire. They did not appear. Nor did Major Ralph Lovell, who was in bed upstairs, half dead from wounds he had received two months ago at the siege of Bristol. Aurora was at pains to tell Juliana that.

Juliana replied meekly. 'At least you have the comfort of knowing that he is alive and receiving care. You know where he is – which to me would be a luxury.' She thought a slight shock ran around the assembled Lovells. Perhaps they had not expected her to be robust.

It must be a curious situation for them. None had seen Orlando since he was sixteen, over ten years ago. He had been a forward, difficult boy, but they could only imagine what kind of man he had become. Now here was the woman he had married, turning up on their doorstep, undoubtedly seeming like an adventuress. But Juliana in person may not have matched their expectations. She was young, only just twenty. Since she married Lovell she had grown into her looks, partly through filling out with motherhood, but also gaining confidence from their life together, which had so much forced her to take responsibilities. Her face showed determination, her grey eyes were watchful and undeniably intelligent. True, she was anxious and weary. True, they may have detected discomfiture, though they might not guess the reason. That was purely her awareness that she was wearing her old yellow sprigged gown, so as not to appear well-to-do. She had realised it had grown too tight across the bodice; worse, like most mothers who nursed their children, Juliana possessed rather too many garments which she would never like again after unpleasant accidents. Both her boys had travelled badly yesterday. Now she was trying to win over relatives while not quite smelling of infant vomit, yet still vaguely aware of yesterday's mishaps.

At least she was not pregnant and queasy, though she almost felt sick with terror. *You are as good as them*, scoffed her grandmother's voice. *Ah, but they do not think so, Grand-mère* . . .

The stern old man, Orlando's father, took the lead in her interrogation. 'So what brings you to our neighbourhood?

'Sir, as I told you in my first letter, I have no relations, or none who can be of comfort, and that means my children have none. I need someone to give me advice.' Advice, Juliana had reckoned, was a better request than financial support. The squire would work out what she meant.

He gave her a long, straight, intimidating stare. 'And where are your children?'

'I left them in the care of my maid, an honest woman who came with me, at the Anchor —' *Where?* she could see the Lovells wondering. 'I believe it was previously the Crown. A diplomatic name-change.' All over England, signboards were being rapidly refreshed for political reasons.

'The ale has not changed!' muttered Mary's husband despondently.

Squire Lovell showed no amusement. 'Did my son send you?'

'No, sir. I am alone and without his guidance.'

'Would he be content that you came here?'

Never; he would be furious! 'I believe it would gladden his heart.'

'And why have you come?' broke in Mrs Katherine Lovell. She was bursting with anger towards Juliana. 'Intend you to show the squire his infant grandsons and soften his heart?'

'If that were my hope,' Juliana replied levelly, 'I should have carried them here with me today, the tiny baby at my breast, my boy running about impishly. I should have kept onion-skins hidden in my hand, to induce weeping, as actors did in plays. Since my purpose is honest' — she spaced it with a *very* small smile for the squire — 'I hope my tears will only flow naturally, where appropriate.'

'Surely you do not joke?' sneered Aurora.

'No, madam. I am desperate for my children. I was never so serious.'

'And do you weep for Orlando?' asked the squire, cocking an austere eyebrow.

'I do. He has been a good husband and a loving father.'

'If you intend to ask for money,' Mary Falconer spoke up frankly, 'then you must return disappointed.' Mary had seemed the least hostile, yet now she burst out with a list of crushing woes: 'My father and brother have given all they had to Parliament. We, like everyone, have been taxed and taxed again to support the war effort. Even so, we were invaded and plundered by soldiers — they took everything: the horses from the stables, my father's sheep and cattle, his draught oxen, the very coach we had — after which they burst indoors and violently broke open every cupboard and chest. They robbed us of all our household goods — sheets and bolsters, all our clothes, even my little babe's smocks and lace caps, and all our kitchen utensils, tubs, pots, pans, meat hooks and pot hooks, spits, bowls, plates, dishes, knives, spoons, the knifebox and my mother's silver fish servers, then pecks of wheat and oats, butter, cheese, bread, salt, bacon —'

I see you did the housewifely duty and compiled the complaints list . . . 'Were these of the King's party?' asked Juliana carefully.

'No – that is what we endured even from our own. Waller's soldiers, out of Farnham. Two men went to the gallows for it. All the candles I had just dipped! A full six dozen . . .' murmured Mary, biting back tears as she reminisced. 'And then we had the poor soldiers coming through from Southampton after Lostwithiel, and nothing left that we could give them – You, in your safe refuge in Oxford, cannot know how we in the country have suffered.'

Well, you are the victors now! 'Your trials may shortly be over.' Juliana kept her restraint. 'The King's cause wanes daily. His garrisons are captured, his armies destroyed, his commanders leaving for the Continent. Soon I shall have no refuge. Women and their helpless children should not be blamed for a husband's delinquency.' She sighed, pretending to hide it. 'I am a helpless supplicant, but I must consider my boys. They are innocents. I was hoping for a friendlier reception.'

There was a silence, perhaps slightly awkward.

Next it was Aurora's turn to raise objections. Juliana did not think these people had rehearsed their speeches, but they had all listened to Mary's outburst without surprise. She noticed Aurora nudge her husband with a dainty toe, embellished with a ribbon rosette.

Sir Daniel spoke for his wife pompously: 'We have no room for strangers. Squire Lovell's house is overflowing – my wife and I live over at the next parish, but Mary and Mr Falconer make their home here, so has Ralph always done, with Katherine and all their children. Then Mr and Mrs Bonalleck from Massachusetts are staying here at present – though Isaac Bonalleck is bound for the New Model Army to be a chaplain there, which means Bridget must remain with her father – and our sister Jane, whom we call Jenny, who has never married –' *So where is Jenny? Do they force their spinster daughters to stay out of sight beside the kitchen fire? If they take in widows or fugitives, must that be their fate too?* 'Jenny is sitting with poor Ralph, helping to nurse him.' Sir Daniel seemed to read Juliana's mind.

He was a heavy man, jowly, with a soft wet mouth, whose gaze lingered on Juliana momentarily. She saw how things were. Marrying a knight or baronet would have been a coup for Aurora, a squire's daughter. Before war put pressure on finances, the eldest Lovell girl would have had a good dowry. As Lady Swayne, Aurora had settled into her rank very comfortably, adding to the high-handed manner she must always have had. Her husband was probably satisfied that he had made a good match, as well as one where he could ply his courtship merely by strolling across a few fields, sparing himself any interruption to his hunting.

Juliana was sure if he and she had been alone in the room, Sir Daniel Swayne would have dropped some hint to the effect that *she* was too good to be penned up in a kitchen inglenook, meaning she should accept overtures from him. Even with his wife present, Juliana read insinuation in his eyes: one more problem that unprotected woman had to face. Some kinds of friendly reception were too unpleasant to contemplate.

Unable to face answering, Juliana waited patiently for the next onslaught.

It came unexpectedly. The parlour door crashed open. In burst a man in a long creased nightshirt, pale and distraught. Without doubt, Ralph Lovell.

Once, he must have looked very like his brother Orlando – a resemblance that gave Juliana a pang – yet he had recently been cruelly deprived of handsome features. A young woman who must be the spinster sister, Jane, scuttled in after him and attempted to place a blanket around his shoulders, only to be shaken off roughly.

The sight was horrific. Juliana had to force herself not to squeal with horror. Major Ralph Lovell's right arm had been shot off above the elbow and half his face blasted away. His life had been saved – at a terrible cost. A good surgeon must have done what he could to mend the damage; the results were still raw. Ralph's face was now twisted, with one eye socket dragged from its proper place – the eye missing – his burned flesh cobbled back together with terrible distortion and scars. When he struggled to speak it was evident he had lost pieces of his jaw and part of his tongue.

'Po-echt!' cried Ralph. It took Juliana a while to understand he was wanting to protest. She had already been struggling with the Hampshire accents of his relatives. Ralph could no longer form clear words, he had lost all ability to make tongued consonants, and was even hampered with his vowels.

Jane screwed her eyes shut and shook her head helplessly, telling her sisters she had not been able to prevent him coming downstairs. Probably they had instructed her to conceal Juliana's visit. Jane was still a girl. Now that the money had run out and taken her marriage chances with it, she was probably pushed around by everyone. Even her disabled brother bullied her while she dutifully nursed him.

'Ralph!' cried his father. 'Be easy. Do not trouble yourself.'

Ralph made more agitated, indecipherable sounds.

Mary leapt up and went to him. 'Oh this is not right. Never mind what Orlando did years ago – *though that was bad enough!* – His obstinate delinquency cannot be borne. We should not be asked to bear it!'

Ralph still forced out noises while gesticulating wildly. Jane, who must be used to it, interpreted. She spoke rather formally because it was so difficult: 'Orlando and Ralph can never be reconciled. Our brother's foolish adherence to the King must for ever cause grief to our father, and all of us. Fathers are fighting sons, brothers fighting brothers, cousin against cousin – men have sacrificed their lives in our cause. Ralph has shed his blood for the cause. He has endured grievous hardships and would have given his life. Orlando is resolute on his malignant course. Therefore he and those who belong to him must stay apart from us!'

Exhausted, Ralph collapsed on a chair brought to him by Sir Daniel. While Jane sank onto a footstool, their sister Mary wiped dribble from Ralph's chin with a handkerchief from her pocket. Her gesture was automatic; Ralph struggled with swallowing and would have to be mopped up for the rest of his life. Who knew what other intimate attentions he would require or how any of the parties would endure it.

Juliana assessed the damage that Ralph's terrible injuries had caused to his relatives. His wife, Katherine, was sitting silent and rigid; Juliana now recognised her complete devastation. Katherine had kept her husband, yet lost her marriage. She could not cope with what had happened and was barely hiding her disintegration. Juliana read the father's despair, the sisters' misery, the brothers-in-laws' discomfort. She could only imagine how children reacted. How the servants shuddered, the tenants whispered. How Ralph himself would alter, as pain and frustration embittered him.

All eyes turned to Juliana accusingly.

She was so shocked she had leapt to her feet. They would not want her sympathy, though they had it. Ralph's disfigurement and disablement were so dreadful they must have thought his death would be easier to bear. For him and for all of them. But no; he was going to struggle on and they were going to care for him. Nothing within this large, close family would ever be the same again.

Ralph's situation should make no difference. Her pleas on Orlando's behalf remained just as valid. Yet Juliana knew her suit was blown away.

Somehow she found words. 'I am appalled, Major Lovell, to see your suffering. You may not wish to hear this, but your brother will be heart-broken; he has always spoken most kindly of you —' *Well, except when he said you had died in an explosion, so he could masquerade as heir* . . . 'I plead with you only to remember this: just as you chose your cause according to your conscience, so did honest men on the other side. Both parties claim they fight to preserve the freedom and safety of the kingdom. That is the tragedy. Royalists' opposition to you was never ignoble; they serve the King because they believe it is the proper thing to do. They did not choose it as some path to wickedness. I know there are even those in the King's party who serve him out of ancient loyalty of subject to monarch, yet who still desire that Charles should yield to Parliament's demands. Some who always did wish it so, some who are even now pressing him to make a peace.'

This speech certainly was unexpected to the Lovells. Juliana had surprised herself.

'I do not take sides,' she added quickly. 'My coming here was for two earnest reasons. One was to give my boys an opportunity to know their grandfather – which is their right, as it is every child's right. The rest of you may decide how you regard them, but I beg you, do not interfere between the squire and Tom and Val.'

'Tom!' murmured Squire Lovell, his face irresistibly softening. Then Juliana realised for the first time that Orlando had named their elder boy after his own father. She knew at once: Orlando had done it deliberately.

'And I was hoping –' Unexpectedly, she stumbled. 'I hoped that since you have influence with Parliament and I do not, you might be willing to assist me. I have been told that my husband is a prisoner since Naseby. I am desperate to find out where he is.'

Again, there was that odd riffle of movement among the Lovells.

'Oh we know where the scoundrel is!' scoffed the squire. 'His first action on finding himself penned up in London was to write here and tell me!'

Chapter Thirty-Six

Hampshire: 1646

So shaken was Juliana that she was sent back to the Anchor under escort from Mary and Francis Falconer. During the walk, through the misty countryside and the quiet village, the couple explained to her in a fairly friendly fashion that there was a practical reason why Orlando wrote to his father and not to her. Paper and ink in jail were scarce. Orlando's most pressing concern involved his personal estate. When he first returned to England in 1642, Orlando must have brought home money he had earned – or acquired by other means, thought Juliana – during his service on the Continent. He had asked Squire Lovell's agent to buy land for him.

'You could say,' suggested Juliana slowly, 'the fact that he wished to invest close to his family home indicated that he was hoping to effect a reconciliation.'

'Or you could say,' returned Mr Falconer with spirit, 'the rogue just hoped to affront everyone!' Falconer was a sandy, unassuming man, with a sharp nose and long forward chin.

'My brother claimed,' Mary offered in a strained voice, 'he was newly arrived back in the country and Jack Jolley was the only agent he had ever known.'

'Have you seen Orlando?' Juliana queried in a tight voice. She was still finding it hard to accept that her husband had contacted the family he professed were bitterly at odds with him, while he had never written to her.

'Not since he first left us when he was sixteen. But now that we know where he is, I write to him weekly,' said Mary. She was unnervingly earnest: 'I constantly beseech him to abandon his delinquency.'

Juliana imagined Orlando's reaction. Mr Falconer caught her eye momentarily, clearly thinking as she did. In this tight-knit country community he must have known Orlando when they were boys. They had a similar background, yet ended up on different sides. Falconer must have fought; he had a healed sword slash on one wrist and even on a morning walk through his own village carried a sword as if he knew how to use it. Yet he was a quiet, ordinary countryman otherwise, more suited to smoking a pipe while he talked up the price of colts among his cronies.

The Falconers completed their explanation: Orlando had decided he wanted to obtain his release by paying his fine to the Committee for Compounding. Early in the war his land, known by everyone in the district as property of a hardened Royalist, had been confiscated, or as they called it sequestered, by the Hampshire Committee. To be assessed for his fine, Orlando needed a certificate of his estate's value, based on the income it brought in. The dilemma was that only the committee could know what his tenants had paid, since the committee received the rents now; they had no interest in providing the vital certificate to help a Royalist.

'So he is stuck!' said Francis Falconer, with enormous satisfaction.

Juliana was deposited at the Anchor, her head whirling.

She said little to Edmund Treves about her reception, though she briefly mentioned Ralph Lovell's wounds and the effect she believed his condition would have. 'Ralph's bitterness is all too understandable; his stricken family are bound to respect his feelings. There is no chance Squire Lovell will make peace with me.'

Despite that, to her surprise next morning, the squire arrived, inviting himself to meet his grandchildren. He first inspected Edmund, letting his cynical opinion show. On arrival, Edmund had changed from a plain coat into his normal clothes. Juliana cringed as the squire eyed up his burgundy brocade suit with its beribboned seams, his shirt belling out above his britches, his flounces of lace-trimmed boot-hose, his luminescent silk sash . . . Fortunately Edmund's innocent good heart was transparent. His position with Juliana could have looked dissolute, but her friend's very lack of awareness of that helped reassure the squire.

'*Valentine* . . .' mused the elder Lovell, clearly unimpressed. He did not take the baby in his arms, but let Juliana hold him. Valentine screwed up his little face like an ugly pink gargoyle, then wailed with gusto. Mercy Tulk scuttled up and carried him to another room.

'Who named Orlando?' murmured Juliana, fighting back.

'His mother wished that upon us.' The squire paused, unwilling to imply dissension. 'She was a good woman.'

Juliana deduced that the rift with Orlando had grieved his mother. 'You did not marry again?'

'She was the best of wives. I could never have matched her.'

Squire Lovell then met his namesake, who had been playing in the murky end of a stable, with inevitable results. As soon as Thomas sensed his mother praying he would behave well, it brought out his worst side. He clung to her skirts, continually whined for attention, then took off and raced noisily up and down the Anchor's endless narrow corridors like a two-year-old grenado. 'I expect his father was the same,' Juliana apologised, but it produced no thaw.

The squire had brought the children neither sweetmeats nor other presents, which he probably decided was as well. He made no offer to provide for the boys. He did not compliment Juliana on her motherhood.

Squire Lovell was startled when Juliana suddenly asked for an introduction to his land agent, John Jolley. Unsure of herself, she gave no reasons. Though curious, the squire subsequently arranged for the agent to visit her.

John Jolley was inevitably known behind his back as Jolly Jack, though it hardly fitted him. He was a man of plain habits who gave little away. His hair was too long as if he had better things to do than gossip with a barber; he wore a russet coat he was slightly bursting out of, over moleskin britches, with a great satchel slung around him. His broad belt and other leather accessories were all curled at the edges like objects of long service.

At first Jolley was diffident about dealing with a woman. Juliana squared up and convinced him that she was as reluctant as he was. But she must go forward. Wives had to undertake strange new roles, as a consequence of war. Chewing a long clay pipe, Jolley listened to her request. What she wanted was simple: a list of the tenants on the land her husband had bought for himself in 1642. John Jolley provided this within a few days, then as an extra courtesy took Juliana around to meet them. She would herself catalogue their rents so her husband could be fined and released.

Since she would have to stay in Hampshire for some time, Edmund left her and went back to Oxford, though he promised to return for her. Once her intentions were known — with the proviso that her stay must be temporary — the squire allowed her to move into a tiny cottage on his estate, adjacent to an elderly retired governess who had taught his daughters.

Initially all Orlando's tenants were hostile. When Juliana reassured them quietly that she was not asking for rents twice over, but merely hoped to compile a list of what they had paid, most of them changed. They scrabbled awkwardly in the backs of drawers for dirty receipts. Juliana was twenty years old, extremely well mannered and spoke of her personal situation with a brave, rather appealing smile. How useful this was, as the land agent dryly commented. Some tenants remained gruff, but that was the habit of farmers. Even the gruffest sent a lad running after her with a brace of dead rabbits.

She offered one of the rabbits to Jolley. He shook his head, saying she had more need of it. So she took both to simmer in a pot and share with the retired schoolteacher. These gifts were natural courtesies of life in the shires, where at some levels the civil war might not be taking place.

'The tenants think themselves hard men, but you will see them all dance to the tune of a pretty widow!' chortled John Jolley.

Juliana drew back. 'I am not quite a widow yet!'

'Oh but they think so, Mistress Lovell! They believe that your husband is locked up in the Tower of London and will never emerge. Do you know how to skin rabbits, by the by?'

'This will surprise you, but I do!' responded Juliana, a little coldly.

Lovell was not in the Tower. The squire had told Juliana he was held at Lambeth House, formerly the London palace of the Archbishop of Canterbury. In the new world of the Covenant-takers, it had been requisitioned by Parliament. Knowing where Orlando was fired Juliana; she made haste to present herself and her list before the local committee.

It could have been worse. She managed not to lose her temper. She claimed womanly reluctance to make pleadings and suits. The squire had declined any personal support at her hearing — though all the men on the committee must know him, know of his long-standing support for Parliament, know what had befallen Ralph. They were unfriendly to Juliana but would be reluctant to offend the Lovells.

Squire Lovell had given Juliana one piece of critical advice. The committee granted her a rent certificate, but then she requested more:

'I am deeply grateful. And I believe, sirs, as a wife, who is blameless of her husband's sins, I am entitled to up to a fifth of his income in order to provide for myself and my infant children. If you give me just a little to work with,' pleaded Juliana, 'I can manage it well – feed us and house us – eliminate debts – avoid becoming a charge upon the parish where we live –'

They humphed, but allowed her three pounds and six shillings as her statutory 'fifth'. Lovell's estate was meagre.

Juliana, who had been brought up to press to the limit in a shameless French manner, then asked for the 'fifths' from the preceding three years. It was indicated that she should think herself lucky already and take herself off. Which, with a pragmatic French shrug of her shoulders, Juliana did.

Had the committee ever realised that she had popish French blood, then her chance of squeezing concessions from them would have been nil.

The Hampshire certificate would now enable her to negotiate Lovell's pardon with the Committee for Compounding in London. Exhilarated by her success, she was preparing to go there when unexpected news came to the squire from a friend at Westminster. Bored with waiting, Orlando had escaped from prison.

Well, that convinced his family that he was an unrepentant reprobate.

Chapter Thirty-Seven

Oxford: 1646

Juliana knew Lovell would not present himself to his father as a refugee. She decided to return to Oxford.

The one person she was sorry to leave was the governess in the next-door cottage, whose lonely life on the estate had been brightened by Tom's antics and who loved to coo over the baby. When Juliana told her of her decision to leave, the two women shared yet another rabbit stew, sucking on the joints informally, with their bowls on their knees at the fireside.

'I confide in you, Mistress Lovell, whenever the squire is sent a carp pie it always comes from the house to me – they are very much full of fishbones so the squire will not attempt to eat them, and honestly they are not to my taste either, but I must be grateful . . .'

Juliana tried to lure the faded old lady into providing some picture of Orlando in his youth. 'I taught the girls; I never knew the boys . . .'

'Will you have a spoon for your gravy?'

Under the influence of a good rich gravy, discretion dissolved: 'Well, he was very much an inward, solitary youngster. Nobody was surprised at what he did, though it broke his mother's heart. He was a very pretty little man – much like your Tom – and she always made a great pet of him – which you, of course, have too much good sense to do with your boys – it may be why he gave himself expectations of an inheritance, despite not being the first-born. But then the squire set him straight in his delusions, telling him plainly that Ralph must have the estate, with dowries for the girls – of whom there are so many – you may think Jenny is not to have anything, but wrongly, for an allocation was set aside for her, and would be hers when she wanted, but her liking was for a young man who fights for the King; I believe he lives yet, but has married another, despairing of our squire's ever unbending – and that

(I mean, when the squire was so firm with Orlando) was when they fell to quarrelling, the squire and he. His late mother was a most kind, virtuous lady; her great passion was blackwork embroidery – if you saw Ralph in his nightshirt it is likely he wore a piece of his mother's stitchery.'

'Very fine on the high collar and in bands over the chest, patterned with meanders and carnations . . . Orlando caused a scandal, he told me?'

'Yes, he did. But we never talk of that.'

At the squire's house next day, news of Juliana's departure was a visible relief. Orlando's father took a small Venice glass of claret with her, to show his gratitude that she was making a quiet exit. Mary Falconer, who had been boiling sweet soap in the closet, rushed out in a long apron to give Juliana a wish for luck and a little lawn bag of rose-scented soap balls. More usefully, Lady Swayne parted with baby-clothes and cot-bedding, managing to do so like an empress condescending to a peasant. Although he had sworn against it, the squire in strict private pressed five pounds into Juliana's hand; he warned her off asking for any more ever, then advised her to keep the gift from her husband.

She had to bring it home safe first: in the time-honoured manner, that evening she sat up and she sewed her money into her petticoat.

To be rid of her faster, a travel pass had been obtained from the Hampshire Committee. She had planned to make her own way with the carriers, but the Lovells were anxious about danger from the clubmen – bands of armed countrymen who were wearied beyond endurance of being taxed and raided by soldiers. These vigilantes had declared themselves the enemies of both King and Parliament, and roamed about the counties frightening everyone. To avoid attack, Juliana was instructed that since the Reverend Isaac Bonalleck was going her way, he would take her safely to the outskirts of Oxford. 'Or indeed,' said Francis Falconer, hopefully, 'if the siege of that town has ended, he can escort you right to your house.'

Juliana feared she no longer had a house, although Edmund Treves had promised to try to intercede with the landlord.

She never met Isaac Bonalleck's wife. Orlando's sister Bridget was so determined not to be infected by Royalism, she had refused any introduction to Juliana. Bonalleck was a fervent preacher who read his Bible as he rode the dawdling pad horse. His suit was black, his linen devoid of ornament, his collar small, his mouth tight, his colour florid. He suffered hurricanes of flatulence. The surges of embarrassment which overwhelmed him after every blast from his stomach went some way towards giving him a fragile humanity.

It took them a week to forge a passage through the muddy lanes and pot-holed highways. Often the road was so impassable that carriers hacked down the hedges and crossed into neighbouring fields. Almost sanctioned in law because the landowners were supposed to maintain the roads, this was generally accepted; far-sighted travellers carried axes for the purpose. Where last week's carriers had churned up the fields too much, they moved over further and further, on one stretch travelling half a mile from the original road. During their slow progress Isaac Bonalleck never discussed meals, weather, the best routes, the state of the roads, prices, indigestion, bad carriers, good post runners, cheating wagoners, or any of the usual subjects travellers chewed over at stops by the wayside or around dining tables in inns.

Only when they reached the outskirts of Oxford, did Mr Bonalleck relax. A New Model Army regiment under Colonel Thomas Rainborough had set up an informal blockade, anticipating a full siege after the winter. Rainborough's brother-in-law was a Mr Winthrop from New England, a man known to Mr Bonalleck, who also shared with Rainborough friendship with a New England preacher called Hugh Peter. So Bonalleck felt he would now be among friends and privileged, whereas Juliana still had to persuade the soldiers to let her enter Oxford. She had arrived during the curfew, an unsuccessful measure against riotous behaviour, so she waited. There was no safety for a respectable woman on the dark streets full of noisy taverns where soldiers habitually sat up in all-night drinking bouts.

When they first arrived and prepared to wait, they were able to observe that Oxford's outlying districts had suffered badly during the war. Growing fields lay fallow. Pasture meadows had lost their turf, dug out to build fortifications. Houses were either badly damaged or completely pulled down. Trees had been felled. No cattle grazed.

Mercy Tulk had fallen asleep with the children. Juliana gritted her teeth for one last meal at the inn with Bonalleck.

Now it emerged that he had spent the whole week of their journey in trepidation, believing that he was escorting a Roman Catholic. 'Oh no. I would have tried to convert you!' exclaimed Juliana heartlessly. She gave up her meal after a few grim mites of tasteless bacon and carrots. Bonalleck was munching on; she told him how, when she was pregnant with Tom and had a bad landlord, she had attended sermons in High Anglican Oxford churches and found them too autocratic.

'Maybe you are a puritan,' commented Bonalleck, without much hope of it. He wiped his mouth with a fourpenny napkin fastidiously; the innkeeper's wife hovered close by, anxious to keep tally of her now very worn table-linen. Mr Bonalleck was already beginning to worry whether the bacon, or more likely the carrots, would give him his usual gales of wind but, encouraged by Juliana, he defined the term for her: 'A puritan yearns for the pure word of God, as revealed in Scripture and in his own prayers; that is, without any additions or falsifications from man – I mean, from diocesans – the Pope and his servants, or detestable bishops. A puritan declines all that is ceremonious in worship. They seek, therefore, a plain, convincing way of preaching which must be put before them in their familiar language. Natural speech, delivered as in a conversation, keeps the attention. Just as railing-off an altar puts separation between a congregation and God, so does the use of inexplicable language, drearily read by some highflown cleric who keeps his head down over his notes. Icons and pomp, statues and surplices, all create mystery, whereas the serious man of God in meek simplicity seeks, through days and hours of scriptural study and his own sober prayer, to see through darkness to the truth.' The need to contain wind forced Mr Bonalleck to a stop.

Juliana had swallowed a tankard of small ale, along with insufficient food; it made her reckless. 'You preach – men and women also? Does your wife preach, Mr Bonalleck, or is she content merely to be an ornament to her husband?'

Bonalleck stared at her. 'My wife has offended you.'

'Absolutely the contrary. Your wife has had *nothing* to do with me. I am married to her brother and she hates him – yet should she hate me too, without even seeing me? Where in this cold demeanour is "testing truth according to her conscience", which I have always been told is the Protestant ideal, or examining the "pure" evidence?'

'My wife,' said Bridget's husband heavily (he had drunk little; he was studiously godly), 'spent many hours in prayer, asking the Lord to show her a way to deal with you.'

Juliana scoffed angrily. 'If, after so much strict deliberation between the two of them, our Lord informs Mrs Bridget Bonalleck that I am not fit company, then I am as damned as a cockatrice and must take the straight path to hell. Your wife's worthy disapproval makes me feel like a court lady-in-waiting I once observed, making her presence felt in the pews by wearing transparent cobweb lawn.'

In Oxford, she had once seen two such young women float into church in low-cut white gowns, with their breasts barely concealed; among male Royalists they won themselves a reputation of dressing 'like angels', though Nerissa had been outraged. 'All the morals of a rag of old rope!'

Juliana eased herself wearily to her feet. Exhaustion made her disputatious. 'Here is an awkwardness, Mr Bonalleck. For while Mrs Bridget is informed I am so dangerous that merely to greet me politely would threaten her zealous soul, then the Lord comes tiptoeing from her chamber into my own where He tells *me* with His enduring compassion that I am an honest woman who has many troubles, yet who leads a decent life, with a true conscience. I bid you goodnight, Mr Bonalleck!'

Next morning Juliana, Mercy and the children were permitted to enter Oxford. There was never much difficulty getting into a beleaguered city; the enemy wanted the largest numbers possible inside, using up resources, in order to cause hardship and encourage surrender.

Nervously, Juliana went to the St Aldate's house. The key Nerissa had given her still worked. As soon as she entered, she knew Lovell was there. On his return, he had done what she ought to have done herself: sub-let. He had filled the spare rooms with lodgers, thus enabling himself both to pay the landlord and to obtain some weekly rents. With this income, he had bought new spurs and a brown corded suit, then hired a bootboy. Juliana found him in the parlour, his stockinged feet on the fender before a roaring fire, reading a news-sheet.

She gazed at him for a second before he became aware of her. Then he dropped the paper and spun to his feet. *He was a very pretty little man . . .* Oh yes. Under the sometimes-harsh exterior his attractiveness remained. When he smiled at a woman, it was clear he knew that perfectly.

Yet Juliana was *his* woman. His face lit. Her expression joyfully answered his. In an instant, the two were in each other's arms, clasped hard. Orlando felt very much leaner. Six months in prison had left him thin, weak and drained. 'Oh thank God!' he exclaimed as he held her, speaking with such force that Juliana believed he meant it honestly.

Next moment Tom burst in on them, screaming with delight at the father he must have only half remembered. Tom flung himself at Orlando; Orlando roared and tossed the child up to the smoke-stained kitchen ceiling while Juliana hung back, wincing in case her husband lost his grip and dropped her boy into the fire.

Various things emerged over the next days. Orlando now styled himself major. 'I had to bump myself up a rank to gain better quarters.' Even now he was back in Oxford, no one seemed to query it. He called himself a 'reformado', an officer whose regiment had been disbanded or merged into another, with no position left for him. 'First I was dumped in a hideous prison, the Compter in Southwark. But I managed to be moved to Lambeth Palace. The Archbishop of Canterbury's suites were excellent. Sir Roger Twysden's wife shared three rooms there with her husband, having a study and a fair chamber with a chimney. Not being a knight or baronet, I rated one room only – sometimes forced to share that with another prisoner,' Lovell added hastily, seeing that Juliana was wondering why she had not been allowed to come to him.

'And you had only enough ink to write to your father!' she sniffed.

Lovell gazed at her. 'Now you have met all the family, you are judging me as they do!'

'I am your wife. Judging you is my special privilege. So, dear heart, how did you escape from the ecclesiastical palace? Was there a crusty one-legged jailor with a beautiful unmarried daughter?'

'Of course!' teased Lovell.

'So you quickly won her confidence and unscrupulously seduced her?'

'Well, to be truthful, the dame was built like a woolsack with three bristly chins and she smelt of piss. Even the rats were scared of her. It took six months just to get her to let me out of a postern and I drew the line at the deed.'

'But she liked you?'

'*I* liked *her* more – for having a cousin who was a waterman. He rowed me all the way from Lambeth up to Richmond.'

'Then you walked home?'

'I found a horse.'

He stole the horse, undoubtedly.

* * *

He had *not* been captured after Naseby. He had not even fought at Naseby.

'But Edmund said you were seen!'

'Treves must have been so expecting to see me, he imagined me there . . . The sad truth is, sweetheart, some of Fairfax's damned new noddlers came into the village the evening before. Ireton and his boys, I think. They captured men of ours who were playing skittles in a tavern garden, then they burst in on us officers, as we sat eating our dinner. Instead of saying grace' – *Instead of what?* scoffed Juliana silently at this unlikely decoration – 'we were surprised and taken, before the fight ever began.'

'Well, you escaped being hurt,' Juliana replied, feeling her equilibrium falter. Would anything about this man ever be straightforward? Later, she would be relieved when Edmund visited and seemed as loyal to Lovell as always; he confirmed that the eve-of-battle arrests at Naseby village had happened.

Changing the subject, Juliana told Orlando about his brother's fate at Bristol. She spared him no details of Ralph's disfigurement, nor the lasting effects she thought it would have on his family. Orlando listened, with more respect than she had feared. He had seen men with such devastating wounds. He sat, head bowed for a long time, looking depressed.

'So . . .' he asked, after a suitable pause. 'How did my loving relatives receive you?'

'Badly.'

'That was hard for you.'

'You cannot blame them.' Juliana risked the tricky question: 'Was I right to go?'

Orlando flung up his hands. 'You were right to try. By heaven, you know I tried myself, truly. Anything a man could say to win them over, I threw at them as obsequiously as they could wish.'

That was not quite how the squire had described it. *I assume desperation made him peremptory. All he lacked was a demand that I myself should pay the fine for his delinquency . . .* 'What was your father's reply to you, Orlando?'

'Did he not tell you?'

'Only hints.'

'He wished no evil on me, but said he could do nothing with

Parliament. He sent me only one haughty letter, telling me to compound and beg for a pardon, then to mend my life.'

'Your sister Mary wrote more often, she told me.'

Orlando laughed briefly, suddenly himself again. 'Indeed! Endless sanctimonious instructions . . . After the first, I threw the letters in the fire unopened.'

'You had a fire then!' Juliana could be arch. '*I* would have been allowed to bring you food and comforts. Would you not have liked tidings of me and your boys?' She struggled against a catch in her voice.

'It would have broken my heart!' cried Orlando, like a true cavalier. 'The worst of being imprisoned was to be separated from you!' They were back on their old footing by that time, so Juliana received this gallantry without excitement.

She told Orlando about meeting his land agent and her forays among his tenants. He listened with astonishment. Then he declared he had always recognised her great spirit. He called her a queen among wives. 'Have the committee given you a certificate?'

'They have. But in view of your escape, my effort was wasted.'

'Oh I won't pay a fine now, but the certificate will be of good use if ever I am captured again.'

'You intend to go on fighting? You could still compound for your estates. Say you will live in peace. Thousands of Royalists are doing it. Comply, and you could be given all your land back.' Juliana was testing him. She was certain that he had escaped in order to avoid swearing an oath he could not keep. He would fight for the King again until every hope was gone. 'Did you give your parole to your captors?'

'I may have done . . .' Orlando looked vague. 'Did you get any funds from my father? He swore he would give me nothing.'

'And he was true to his word.'

The squire's five pounds was hidden in a pillow. Now Juliana was, as she had boasted to Isaac Bonalleck, an honest woman with a conscience. One who was lying, bare-faced, to her husband.

They had three and a half months together. For the rest of January, February, March, and almost all of April, they lived like a real family. Since the town was under siege, it was hardly normal life. Juliana felt she was permanently waiting to begin a proper domestic regime. Still, there were few deprivations. Three thousand cattle and cartloads of other provisions had been brought in during the previous autumn to prepare for the siege.

All the careful routines she had established for bringing up her children sensibly were upset by Lovell. He had no idea that infants should keep regular mealtimes and bedtimes. He would bring them expensive presents, splurging their meagre funds, while Juliana tried to scrimp. Tom, in particular, was like an intriguing pet to Orlando, who would disrupt their quiet lives with games and dangerous excursions 'to view the rebels over the walls'. A bad moment was when he made small firecrackers from gunpowder for Tom, throwing one in the fire unexpectedly to terrify Juliana. She could not remonstrate since Lovell used the excuse that he wanted to spend every possible moment with his sons, or at least with Tom, who was old enough to play. 'If we are enjoying ourselves, what can be the harm?'

'You buy Tom's love with a hobbyhorse, while you are teaching him to see his mother as a figure of fun – or a complaining ogre, which is worse. I see harm in that, Orlando! And I shall murder you, if he is stupidly burned by a firecracker.'

'I shall reform!' promised Orlando. He solemnly told his son, 'Thomas, your mother's word is law. Follow my example and do not make her grieve. And if ever I am not here, Tom, you must obey and cherish her.'

Tom, bright-eyed with shared mischief, covered his mouth to hide his enormous grin, then ran off in fits of silly giggling.

'He is three years old. And you are –'

'Twenty-eight!' admitted Lovell penitently, with that untrustworthy look in his eyes.

At the end of January Sir Thomas Fairfax began a siege of Exeter. The King's trusty general, Sir Ralph Hopton, lured away Fairfax and most of the New Model Army by digging in at Torrington, where Fairfax winkled him out after a fierce fight. Fairfax himself had a narrow escape from an enormous explosion when a desperate soldier fired a huge magazine in the church. Offered generous terms, Hopton accepted; he disbanded the King's army in the west and went abroad. The Prince of Wales gave up and sailed for the Scilly Isles. In March another old Royalist, Lord Astley, marched from Worcester to bring the King at

Oxford three thousand men. At Stow-on-the-Wold, he ran into a joint New Model Army force under Rainborough, Fleetwood and Brereton. After a heavy exchange of fire, Astley's force was overwhelmed and all made prisoners. This was the last remaining Royalist army in the field.

The King sought permission to go to Westminster, to negotiate in person, but was refused. A Frenchman began brokering terms for Charles secretly to join the Scottish Covenanters' army.

In April Sir Thomas Fairfax brought up the main body of the New Model Army from the West Country. The siege of Oxford began to bite. On the 26th the last Royalist garrison guarding the area, at Woodstock, fell. Next day the town governor, Sir Thomas Glemham, waved off a certain 'Harry', servant to a Mr Ashburnham. Harry and three companions successfully rode out over Magdalen Bridge. It was the King, disguised in rough clothes and with shorn hair, using a counterfeit warrant to get out through the Parliamentary lines.

Fairfax must have known the King had gone. He toughened up. At the end of the month he ordered his troops to allow no one to leave Oxford, except to negotiate terms. It had become a close siege.

Eight days after he left Oxford, the King turned up outside the long-standing Royalist base at Newark-on-Trent. It was still being besieged by the Covenanters and Charles placed himself in the Scots' control, hoping for better terms than he might expect from the English. He told Newark to surrender; three days later, the Scots took it. Immediately, they struck camp and transported themselves north to Newcastle, with the King in semi-captivity. In June, letters from him were intercepted, revealing his duplicitous secret negotiations with the Scots whilst at the same time, yet again, he requested armed support from the Irish and French. Parliament regarded this as treasonous.

In Oxford, neither side wanted a damaging siege. There was anxiety, though no desperate hardship. A magazine to supply provisions opened. A pronouncement was made that there would be a penalty of death for any soldier taking food from civilians. Cannon-fire was heard. Fairfax formally summoned the city, sending a trumpeter:

Sir, I do by these summon you to deliver up the City of Oxford into my hands for the use of the Parliament. I very much desire the

*preservation of that place (so famous for learning) from ruin, which
inevitably is like to fall upon it, unless you concur . . .*

There was a delay to save face. Artillery-fire was exchanged. A cannon
ball hit Christ Church. A shot from Oxford killed a New Model Army
colonel on Headington Hill. The Parliamentarians remained confident.
On June the 15th, outside Sir Thomas Fairfax's tented headquarters,
Oliver Cromwell's daughter Bridget was married to the dark-browed
manipulator, Henry Ireton.

The outcome of the siege had never been in doubt. There were
said to be six months' supplies of food remaining, but there was no
point holding out. The King sent Oxford his formal permission to
give up. The governor signed articles of surrender. Negotiations
dragged on, but on the 25th of June the keys of the city were formally
handed to Sir Thomas Fairfax. The garrison was allowed to march
out, each of the three thousand men with a safe conduct to travel
home. Princes Rupert and Maurice left, also with passes to leave the
country. However, James, Duke of York, was sent as Parliament's
prisoner to London.

Oxford filled up with New Model Army soldiers in their red coats.
Although he was a Cambridge man, Fairfax put a special guard on the
Bodleian Library. That preserved it from destruction, though the
Parliamentarians found many books had already had their chains cut
and been fraudulently sold.

By then, with his wife's foreknowledge, Orlando Lovell had quietly
disappeared. Juliana clung on in the house in St Aldate's, wondering
yet again when, if ever, she might next see her husband. He had promised to come back for her, once normality resumed. He said it was best
if she truthfully had no idea where he was. She feared he had gone with
Prince Rupert, and had left the country – not something Juliana wished
for herself, though she would follow him if he asked. She missed him
in the house and in her bed. She was hoping that this time he had not
left her pregnant.

'Well, little Tom. Now it is just you and me again, and baby
Valentine.'

Then Tom gazed up at her for a moment, as if to make sure she was
not actually weeping, before he returned to playing on the floor

extremely quietly. He had his father's eyes and his mother's swift intelligence. Tom could adapt to new situations fast. He had grasped, and amiably accepted, that times for revelry and noise were over. He had gained a hobbyhorse but knew he must take good care of it because there would not be another gift for a long while. The father he had only just come to know was gone again.

Chapter Thirty-Eight

On the Road: 1645

Some time in the aftermath of the battle of Naseby, a male traveller had ridden along the empty highway between Beaconsfield and Windsor. He looked well-to-do. His hat was velvet with half an ostrich plume, his cloak was scarlet, his britches had a rash of gold lacing, his boots were polished and lace cuffs dangled elegantly from his coat sleeves. His manner was jaunty and careless, despite the seriousness of the times. If he was a Royalist fugitive, he hid it well.

A mile or two before Slough, the rider came upon a young woman disconsolately leaning on a stile beside the road. In the cheerful way of any seventeenth-century gentleman who spied an unescorted female, he at once reined in his horse and bent down to offer her the courtesy of a lewd offer. As if she had been expecting this privilege, she straightened up and turned towards him. She was monumentally pregnant.

With the shameless good grace of the men of his time, he immediately apologised and – after a disappointed curse – changed the offer to one of general assistance. Clearly exhausted, the vulnerable damsel begged for a ride to the next town. He agreed. She climbed on the handy stile and mounted behind him side-saddle, surprisingly limber in her movements for one so near her time — though she groaned all too convincingly as she took her place.

They rode on. He whistled 'Greensleeves' to himself with the good humour any man would feel while doing a good deed for a pregnant woman. She clung to him, one slim arm around his waist rather charmingly. Since he had to presume she was a respectable wife, he refrained from conversation. She sat silent until he became used to her presence.

At a particularly deserted spot, with woods on either hand, the rider felt a sudden jarring movement behind him. As he half turned indignantly, he saw something drop behind the horse – a large cushion.

Next minute his head was pulled hard back by his flowing hair, then he was shoved off his mount sideways. His short sword flew from its scabbard and executed a spiral into a ditch. As he landed heavily on to the road, the woman jumped down after him. Practised hands slipped a noose of rope around his body, which tightened with a series of painful tugs, while his ruthless assailant pressed the hard, cold butt of a weapon meaningfully against his right ear. When he wriggled, she shoved his face in the mud with her foot, while she continued trussing him like a capon. Once he was helpless, she came rifling through his pockets, then she moved off to search his travel bags.

She obviously hoped for more than she found.

When she realised he had only threepence farthing, there was a thoughtful pause. The pauper victim risked rolling over to view her discomfiture. Any thought of escape was deterred by the carbine she brandished. 'Don't be a fool. I can use this. I served as a soldier in man's clothes.'

Even if the captive suspected she had no bullets, he was not keen to test it. Besides, he felt as much curiosity about her as she displayed towards him. 'Your bags are light, mister; are they to be filled with plunder, taken from travellers on the road?'

She was extremely thin, about seventeen. Now she had shed the false belly, her gown hung on her raggedly. Her hood had slipped back so her tangled hair showed, wound in a rough topknot.

She was fearless. The man on the ground waited to see what she would do. She flipped one of his lace cuffs with the butt of her gun, tugging away the fabric to reveal it was a sham; he had no shirt attached to it. 'Here's a turn-up. I came to rob you, but you would just as soon have robbed me!'

Her itchy red eyes went to his horse. She strolled across and managed to examine its long ear. 'I wonder – shall I find an army brand? Oh yes! I see you enlarged the letters, to disguise his origin – Newport Pagnell! Too close to be riding about on him; you should gallop him away at least thirty miles, and fence him to some trustworthy dealer . . . A false tail might keep you safe. Or you could give him a white blaze he was not foaled with.' She came back to her captive.

He produced a rueful grin. 'I am useless to you, madam. No point dragging me to a deep thicket for a strip-search,' he commiserated. 'Even if you were strong enough.'

'Leave you in a remote spot, tied to a post or tree?' She stared quickly up and down the road. 'Do you work alone?'

'Do you?' he shot back, pretending he had a crowd of lusty associates who would turn up any moment. She retorted that *she* had friends who would be along shortly. 'Of course!' he scoffed. 'Else how would you get away from here?'

She laughed easily. 'On your horse, I think. Though I shall be forced to ride him across country, in case some trooper under the Black Bible flag recognises him.' She walked over to the beast again, talking quietly. At first the horse shied away, head down, snatching at tussocks of long grass but watching her warily with one wild eye. She kept talking. Soon she had caught its reins and led it back.

While she was engaged in that, the supine man (who had been working on her rope surreptitiously) abruptly bucked and freed himself. As he squirmed and sat up, she swung the carbine in an easy movement and fired.

The gun *was* loaded. Just in time, he ducked, so all he lost was a small piece of ear. The blood was copious. The girl laughed heartlessly. She was tough. She was hard as a blacksmith's anvil. 'Stay where I put you next time.'

'Damned witch and whore!' He was mopping unsuccessfully with one of his fake lace cuffs. She left him to it, while she reloaded the carbine.

'Call me neither. True, I am a working woman, but I don't swive. I merely part those who have from what they have, that I may have it in their place.'

'How did you get your gun?'

'The usual way. Helped myself. A fine snaphance cavalry pistol with silver engraving, in its neat holder, powder in a flask and bullets in a darling little bag.'

'You could have sold it.'

'But I would rather use it!'

'Save your lead – I give you my parole.'

'Word of a gentleman?' scoffed the stylish gun-toter.

'Word of an honest rogue.'

'That's fair! Call me Eliza,' she offered. 'And what shall I call you?'

'Jem Starling.' He said it with some pride, waiting for her to recognise the name of a fairly well-known highway robber. Whether Eliza knew or not, she pretended his proudly born name was unfamiliar.

'And what are you, Jem Starling? Simply a licentious, devious cut-purse – or do you call yourself a knight of the road?' She pointed to his left hand, where a branded 'T', for 'Theft', at the base of his thumb showed how in the past he had been taken by the law officers. He had escaped hanging by pleading benefit of clergy; a man could be reprieved on his first offence if he showed he could read. 'Not very successful, are we, Jem?'

'An error when I was young and foolish,' admitted Starling, full of free and easy charm. He was still young, though more foolish than he thought. In his late twenties or early thirties, he looked fit, as a highway robber had to be. He reckoned himself handsome with it. He had voluminous brown-gold hair, through which he ran his fingers now his bloody ear was staunched. She let him sit up, rubbing his wrists ruefully where her rope had bitten in.

'We all make mistakes!' replied Eliza, surprisingly serious. 'What brought you to this life in the open air?'

'The same as many. I was apprenticed to a weaver in Shoreditch, but he was a bullying felon and I couldn't stick it. So being bold and cour-ageous, I took to the road. I have followed this genteel calling now for four years, and am held in high repute. Better bid travellers to stand than to be a pickpocket, a sneak-thief creeping in windows, or a cut-purse crawling around the fairs. I know all the inns where travellers may be assessed and their luggage weighed to detect valuables. I have studied the minds of those who make journeys; I can tell you which tall, hefty men will weep like babies if they are accosted and plead to have their rings and money stolen so long as they are not hurt in the process, or which mean wiry little men of affairs will put up a fight like mastiffs, then loudly call for constables and give chase all night, even though all I had off them was tuppence and a handkerchief. I know the cross-country lanes and byways by which to flee to a safe house. I have tickled up plenty of innkeepers who will deny ever seeing me – while letting me sup their best ale in a warm parlour overhead. In case of an unfortunate arrest, I know a good perjurer too, who will be my surety and have me out of jail in a trice, with a very small outlay necessary.'

The young woman pushed her carbine into her belt. She looked thoughtful again. 'We have both wasted an afternoon. To tell the truth, I am weary of the road alone, and it would be easier in company. I am as brave as you, and can help you gull fools – or hold them at my carbine's end while you soothe them and lift all their treasures. What do you say, Jem?'

The highwayman rocked to his feet in one long easy movement. He bowed like a courtier. 'I say, that is a handsome offer, and I accept it.'

'I will be no man's doxy!' Eliza warned. 'I will not bear a whining babe and leave it on the parish.' Nothing gave away the fact she spoke from bitter experience. 'We must be equal partners, and no cully-rumping.'

'Word of honour, milady!' Jem Starling assured her, with a flash of the eye and a twirl of the hand, gestures he had perfected for reassuring winsome lady travellers before he stole their necklaces, and fingered in their plackets too, if they looked ripe for it. He was thinking himself well capable of changing this one's mind. Eliza saw the thought form, but merely left him with it gently.

She had not wanted to trust anyone, but she foresaw hard times coming. If there was to be peace, now the big battle at Naseby had been fought, the road would be crowded with ragged, cast-off, starving soldiers, struggling homeward from their various armies, all desperate to cover their arrears by amateur theft. Professionals would need to band together to compete.

Chapter Thirty-Nine

The Dover Road and London: 1646–47

They robbed the rich; they robbed the poor. They robbed anyone who came along. They preferred the rich, for economy of effort, but if the poor sauntered past them off guard and had clothing, food or the proceeds of their own thefts, they set upon the poor without a qualm. Sometimes the poor struck back. Eliza lost her heart to a silver taffeta bodice she stole from a cloak bag, but had it snatched from her by a stranger before she had possessed it two hours; she spent the rest of her life hoping to find that bodice again or see one like it. Jem Starling was once beaten up at the back of a tavern so badly that he nearly lost an eye and for several months lacked his normal braggadocio.

It was a good time to be on the road. The hope of peace made people believe they could return to normal life. Projects that had been put into abeyance were revived. Bags of hidden gold were retrieved from thatched roofs and chimneys, then carried abroad to pay off outstanding debts, to pay fines, to fulfil legacies, to relieve suffering widows and succour the war's orphans. Delayed weddings were organised. Trade revived. All of these meant money would be on the move. Highway robbery flourished.

On the whole they were clever. Sometimes Jem Starling was accompanied by a 'boy' who held the horses; sometimes a woman was with him. They would dawdle around inns, never looking at each other. Since they were not lovers – or not often – Jem felt free to court serving wenches and innkeepers' wives like a virile single man, which concealed their partnership. They could ride for hours with other people, yet nobody suspected they knew each other. This enabled surprise when they attacked, but also they wanted their success kept secret. In their plan to own wild riches they gathered their 'earnings' as unobtrusively as possible. They hid away their money and any other treasures they had not yet exchanged for cash in safe houses across several counties. They had to pay a premium to the owners of the safe houses, but the repute they slowly earned for doing honest business (and for intolerance of treachery) helped make friends. Their willingness to shoot and stab to protect their capital was also known; this hint of danger about them did no harm.

In their first year they worked in the countryside. They moved gradually eastwards, in a wide loop around the capital, passing from one arterial road to the next as each location became too hot for them. Their methods were special but their aims were no different from those of honest business owners. They built up a reputation, earned goodwill, ruthlessly saw off competition and cautiously planned future expansion. They had treasurers who banked their capital. They used legal associates to bribe them out of trouble. Had their little empire's profits ever been subjected to unfair taxation, they would have fought that just as tenaciously as those tradesmen, merchants and landowners who went to war over the fiscal trickery of King Charles.

In due course Jem and Eliza gravitated closer to London. London was where all the big money was.

The year 1647 saw them reach Kent, working along the old Dover Road. During this period they found themselves at odds with the local criminals and highwaymen. Gadshill, Shooters Hill and the wilds of Blackheath were as busy with hold-ups as ever in their notorious history, but the nearby villagers believed that rich pickings from travellers were their hereditary right. The couple found that newcomers were resented and cold-shouldered. If newcomers failed to take the hint, locals turned nasty. As they took their ease at an inn, enjoying their spoils, others would barge in, bringing victims Jem and Eliza had robbed. The country bumpkins would point them out, even though Jem had by then pushed up his eye patch, while Eliza had set aside her pregnancy bump. They would have to buy off their victims, and perhaps a Justice's clerk as well, if one had been brought along. Inn staff were threatened with reprisals for giving them a welcome; fences and pawn merchants, who needed to live unobtrusively, were deterred with warnings. If all else failed, the locals resorted to bloody violence.

'Unfair practices are ruinous to us honest toilers. We must depart from these sheep-shagging parsnips,' Jem decided.

So they moved in even closer to London, where they thought the sophisticated business ethos might be more to their taste. They attached themselves to a party from Canterbury from whom, when they decamped in the night, they took two fat purses and a good saddle. Then they rode in through Greenwich and past Deptford, where there was a school for young ladies which they robbed of a sheet and pillowcase, a musical instrument and a freshly baked eel-pie, together with the dish it sat in. A man who claimed to be a royal park ranger offered to sell them a haunch of the King's venison, which he said his wife would cook for them. The King, they heard from the ranger (who presumably should know), had been sold by the Scots to the New Model Army. This news was of little interest to them, even if it meant His Majesty might be returned to London, wanting to eat his own venison. Since they had the eel-pie already, they declined the haunch politely; when dealing with other entrepreneurs, Jem Starling and Eliza were not greedy.

Their journey brought them down through the shipbuilding areas of Deptford and Rotherhithe, into the legendary stews of Southwark. The sour and seamy old rents of the bishopric of Winchester looked at their worst in the evening, when they managed to persuade guards to let them enter the Lines of Communication that enclosed even this grim old district within London's fortifications. On Bankside the bull- and bear-baiting pits still existed, though the famous theatres where Shakespeare and his contemporaries once made their names had been closed down. Other entertainments persisted. The Long Parliament's first wild rash of liberal acts had not just swept away censorship of printed material, but reduced prostitution from a felony to a nuisance. A felony was a hanging offence, as any professional thief had to know, but for a mere nuisance the penalty was just a whipping and a spell in a house of correction. In abolishing torture, too, Parliament had stopped whores being stripped to the waist and whipped at a cart-tail. But religious rectitude had forced the trade underground – where, as always, it flourished all the more.

Although prostitution migrated across the river to Cow Cross, Clerkenwell, Smithfield and most notoriously Turnmill Street and Pickthatch by Aldersgate, there were still blatant brothels on Bankside. Gone were the days of Holland's Leaguer, the elegant moated mansion in Old Paris Garden on Bankside, where gentlemen from King James downwards had been entertained to dancing, fine cuisine and expert fornication in luxurious surroundings run by the grand bawd Elizabeth Holland. The Leaguer, the epitome of a luxurious brothel, had been closed down by troops in the 1630s; its pleasant gardens now lay unkempt and its exquisite troupe of sexual specialists had fled through secret exits and dispersed. Yet the lowest women of the night still shrieked and caterwauled with their customers on the dark wharves, and drabs who had made themselves look attractive despite hard lives and the pox still clustered in doorways, beckoning gentlemen to come into Southwark's rotting houses for what passed as pleasure.

Regulations forbade Thames wherrymen from bringing their boats by night; it was supposedly to save young gentlemen from sin. Sin had gone north. Yet men in the city knew that on any South Bank street-corner cheap fornication with a woman desperate to buy food could be had. In these dark diocesan liberties where drunkenness and disorder had always flourished, nights were noisy and days were drear. Here beneath Winchester Palace, whose hypocritical bishops had raked in rents from the brothels for centuries, stood the Clink Prison, a miserable hole which regularly flooded, where heretics, debtors and those who ruined the doubtful peace were incarcerated. In local alleys used as lavatories and refuse dumps stood many rough dockside taverns where poor whores in white aprons (to make them visible on the dark streets) mingled with thieves, confidence tricksters, dubious surgeons and false astrologers. Above many a ship's chandlery were abortion premises. Into this slew of sad humanity slid Jem and Eliza as if it were their natural habitat.

For the greater part of a year they subsisted in Southwark. They robbed whores' clients while they were engaged in lust, and naive sailors so fresh off merchant ships they had not even found the whores. No longer on horseback, they took to luring victims up cul-de-sacs, hoping for an intrigue with Eliza but instead being beaten up by Jem. Sometimes Eliza would pretend to faint, with Jem leaping on any bystander who was foolish enough to try to help. Their simplest trick was to shout 'Stop, thief!', then watch where members of the public clapped their hands to make sure they still had their money safe – after which it was quickly removed by nimble hands. Despite ample profits, Eliza learned not to dress too richly, lest she be questioned by the authorities wanting to know how she could trick herself out in such finery. Jem learned little.

There comes a moment in many business partnerships where the more talented partner begins to regret hitching up with a lesser spirit. Since Eliza still refused to be Jem Starling's doxy, inevitably he found someone else. When he took up with a pockmarked bragging wanton called Sarah Straw, Eliza knew business would suffer.

When she was not 'conjugating' with Jem Starling, Straw was a procurer for a bawd called Mrs Flemming; she looked out for young girls who had just come up to London on a carrier's cart, seeking work. She befriended them, offered them somewhere to stay and lured them into prostitution. If these fresh-faced innocents were virgins, they fetched a premium at the brothel – and if they were *not* virgins, they could be 'restored' by a duplicitous physician called Doctor Lime for a modest fee. If they were pregnant, he would deal with that for a further shilling. If they were not pregnant, Mother Flemming's extremely fertile door-keeper, her hector, soon saw to the business.

Holding people up with firearms was too dangerous in London. Jem was now reliant on Eliza's skill to rob pockets. He had gone so soft he even relied on her aggression for his own protection. In Eliza's opinion, Jem Starling was nothing without her. His new ladyfriend was a demanding piece, and to keep Sarah sweet he began to diddle Eliza on the share-out from their work. Sarah Straw then made the mistake of attempting to recruit Eliza for Mrs Flemming's disorderly house by Blackfriars Stairs. 'After you have learned the hazards of your trade, you may seek promotion to be a bawd yourself. It requires very little outlay to set up in an establishment, and the profits are extreme. You are no beauty, but with a few tricks, you should pass for saleable . . .'

This ploy to get Eliza out of the way was Straw's mistake. She was left in no doubt of it, by the time Eliza finished beating her with a blackjack. Not only were Sarah Straw's physical attractions ruined, Jem Starling was soon in no position to lavish attention upon her. Eliza had informed on him to the Justices and he was thrown into jail. 'He works in company with a woman, one Straw, a bawd's baggage,' lied Eliza in her deposition. 'She will deny it, so do not heed her pleas . . .'

She knew Jem and Sarah were unlikely to make retaliatory accusations against her, because they needed her to remain on the outside, in order to fetch the money she and Jem had stashed away so they could bribe their way to freedom. Vowing herself innocent of their betrayal, she promised she would collect cash for a speedy rescue. She had no intention of doing it. Away she rode on a stolen horse, and she did indeed visit several of their old safe houses, removing what she considered her fair share of her savings with Jem. Then she kept riding north.

Suitably attired and with her old name of Dorothy Groome, she made her way to Stony Stratford. There she tracked down the parish authorities and with a humble confession made enquiries about the child she had abandoned. Sadly, she was told the records showed that, like most infants found in church porches, after it was put out to a wet-nurse her baby had died. Under pressure, she made a donation to parish funds, then cursed as she was forced to ride away in disappointment.

She had tried to do right. All it brought her were bad memories and financial loss.

Knowing no other life, she determined to return to Bankside. She thought she could make things straight with Jem. But during her long absence, Jem Starling and his doxy had found their own means of securing a release, though they needed to keep out of sight of the authorities and had vanished into the stews.

The day of her arrival back in Southwark was the 3rd of August 1647. Eliza gradually became aware that this whole area south of the river had a strange atmosphere. The streets were bare of whores, drunks and shady drifters. Foreign sailors risked walking about, staring around in curiosity. Some householders stood in their doorways, looking out. Otherwise, there were soldiers in red coats absolutely everywhere.

Her heart beat. Thinking about the baby had been bad enough. Now even older memories crowded upon her. However, there was no fighting, no looting, no burning of buildings Nobody screamed. Nobody was shot. None the less, living the life she did, Eliza preferred not to be stopped and subjected to military interrogation. She slipped into a tavern she knew, paid for a supper, ate it out of public view and discreetly bedded down.

Next morning she woke early and braced up to her need to find another new life. With all her possessions in a sagging snapsack, Eliza stood on the bank of the Thames and gazed over at the city, which lay shrouded in coal smoke. She was below London Bridge, the only crossing point. Opposite were Billingsgate and the Custom House, and beyond them the mighty bulk of the Tower, with its forbidding walls and array of turrets, ancient towers and pinnacles. A bridge had stood here for centuries, since Roman times; this one was medieval, built on twenty small arches, with a defensive gateway and a draw-bridge at the Southwark end. Along the bridge crowded houses and shops, some seven storeys high; only taverns were absent because there were no cellars for keeping liquor cool. At the centre stood the Chapel of St Thomas à Becket, grander than many parish churches, with steps at river level where fishermen and passenger boats landed. Landing was extremely difficult, as was sailing or rowing through the arches, which were so narrow they constricted the current and caused ferocious rapids. Most people preferred not to risk their lives; they disembarked at the Three Cranes, upstream, then walked along the north shore, past Nonesuch House, and took a different boat at Billingsgate. Watermills and grain mills at the northern end added to the fury of the current. Many people had drowned while 'shooting the bridge'. If they did pass through safely, they emerged into a more tranquil area; there, below the piers, where Eliza was standing dis-consolately, lay the calm waters of the Pool of London, which when it was not frozen over in winter was always packed with trading ships and busy with lighters like waterfleas. Now, in August, the warm weather meant the district was pervaded by the stink of waters so fetid they could rarely be cleansed by the tide.

As she pondered the fickleness of men and the perfidy of women, Eliza's attention was drawn by unusual sounds and sights. Drumbeats first attracted her notice – not a sombre, funereal beat, but the brisk tattoo that helped infantry to march in step and gave them heart. Turning, she witnessed the departure from Southwark of all the red-coated soldiers who had occupied the south bank yesterday. They were now moving across into London. Their red uniforms, she knew, meant the New Model Army. Amidst a clamour from within, they were given entrance onto the bridge by their supporters, who opened up the Stone Gateway to admit them. Rank after rank, in several regiments, marched over London Bridge. The city, which had taken such measures to protect itself from the enemy, was being invaded by its own troops.

Word on the streets said those soldiers had refused to be sent on service to Ireland and would not disband until Parliament paid money they were owed. 'Why have we fought,' they were supposed to have asked, 'if we are to be treated worse than slaves?'

Eliza waited until all the men had crossed the bridge, then she reached her decision. Although she had never served in such a large army, their military presence reminded her of the past at Dudley and Edgbaston, days which in a way she had enjoyed. That nostalgia emboldened her for the future. She did not need Jem Starling. She would go across and work alone in the city. Once the soldiers had passed, she quietly slipped after them. It was the first time she had set foot on London Bridge and her heart quavered as she negotiated the Stone Gateway, where sturdy poles carried the heads of long-dead traitors, dipped in tar to preserve them, though the relics were mouldering badly.

On the famous bridge, she passed between nearly two hundred tall buildings. Space was short, so houses had been built out over the river on strong wooden supports, projecting over the water as much as seven feet, and also sometimes joined to the opposite houses above the street. Eliza felt she had entered a long tunnel. Merchants lived on the upper storeys and displayed their goods in shop windows at pavement level. They signalled the nature of their businesses with signboards, and did their selling through the windows. This commerce added to the congestion in the two narrow lanes of traffic, which clogged the bridge so badly that someone could take an hour to get across its three hundred yards. But this was reckoned to be an extremely safe community, apart from the risks of fire and pickpockets. Every night there was a curfew, when the gates were closed.

At the far end, Eliza found a long gap in the houses, damage from a serious fire a decade earlier. She was able to stand at the side and gaze upon the great city she was entering. London stretched as far as she could see and would certainly enable her to vanish from Jem Starling's sight, if he discovered she was back here. She was wise enough to know she was a stranger in the city; being an outsider carried many dangers. This was nothing like the little market town of Birmingham, where she grew up and learned to scavenge. She told herself she had been a soldier and bold highway robber, and could carry off anything. All she ever needed to start afresh was a new alias, a different personality and her native tenacity. Emboldened, she set off across the last few yards and came at last past St Magnus Church onto New Fish Street.

People were marvelling that when the New Model Army soldiers had marched through, they were quiet and disciplined, and stole not so much as an apple.

More fool them! Eliza thought.

Chapter Forty

———◄◆►———

With the New Model Army: 1645–47

Since nobody had intended to start a civil war, inevitably no one knew how to finish it. Once Naseby had been fought and won, the Parliamentarians mopped up Royalist resistance. It took them ten months, through the winter of 1645–46. Conditions were dire. It was so cold the River Thames froze over in London, and in the West Country they were often battling through snow.

Gideon Jukes had found his regiment again, remaining with the dragoons as Sir Thomas Fairfax led the New Model Army through the West Country. They defeated Goring at the battle of Langport, during which picked bands of musketeers led by Lambert Jukes's colonel, Thomas Rainborough, crucially fought their way along the hedges to dislodge the Royalists. Lambert, with his foot wound healed, was back in the regiment. Subsequently, it was Gideon's turn for special action when a detachment under Colonel Okey left the main body of the army temporarily and captured Bath in a surprise dawn raid. They crept up so secretly, they were able to grab the barrels of the guards' muskets that stuck out of the loopholes; the guards fled, and after firing the gatehouse Okey's men took the town. Next the dragoons were at the siege of Bristol. Although they were facing Prince Rupert, he now had the difficulties that had beset Massey here two years before: insufficient troops, especially infantry, for the task of defending five miles of walled fortification. During Rupert's brief but fierce resistance, plague broke out, water ran low and expected orders from the King failed to arrive. None the less, he made good use of carefully positioned artillery, while his cavalry regularly dashed out to raid and harass. During one of these raids, Colonel Okey was taken prisoner, which depressed and unsettled his regiment.

Rupert delayed negotiations until Fairfax broke off discussion.

The ensuing assault was a dangerous and bloody action. The New Model breached the outer walls, then Rainborough's regiment took Prior's Hill Fort. First they climbed the walls in a hail of shot, then when their scaling ladders proved too short, they crept in at the portholes and after two hours' close combat the defenders were massacred. Rupert fell back towards Bristol Castle but when Cromwell's cavalry charged in, the prince realised his position was hopeless. The Royalists were granted terms, and Okey regained his liberty. The Parliamentarians could not know at the time, but Rupert's quarrel with the King over his surrender would soon rid them of the prince for good.

Fairfax then sent Colonel Rainborough to besiege Berkeley Castle, the only Royalist stronghold left between Bristol and Gloucester. He stormed it after a three-day bombardment. His regiment were deployed to Corfe Castle but, required for more important duties, they were pulled out. In December they went into quarters at Abingdon, on watch over the Oxford area as a preliminary to the city's siege. During the city blockade, Rainborough acquired a new sergeant.

Gideon Jukes had been having horse trouble. Never a natural rider, he was ill-suited to be a dragoon, much as he enjoyed it. After his first horse was shot under him at Naseby, the spirited remount he obtained was too strong and conscious of its own superiority. Gideon fought that horse all the way into the west but it finally threw him outside Bristol. His left spur caught, so for a couple of yards he was dragged along, head down. An alert colleague slashed the stirrup, cutting him free. He ended up sprawled in a bush with a dislocated shoulder while the horse galloped off. Ignominiously rescued, Gideon was taken up behind one of his men, as they all chaffed him and called him a dairymaid picked up for a ride to market because she looked good for a roll in a hayrick. An army surgeon took more delight than he thought necessary in wrenching his shoulder back into its socket.

A new horse was allocated by an agent.

A typical 'dragoon nag', this was a wry-nosed, sniffling creature that sickened and died after a day and a half. A horse doctor was summoned, far too late.

'What have you done to this bone-shaker, Sergeant?'

'He was snotty and hot on arrival.'

'You should have rejected him.'

'By the time I got a proper look, the agent was long gone. I hoped the sad beast was just spavined.'

The veterinarian stood up from the carcase and gave Gideon a straight look. He believed his equine expertise had given him acute understanding of human nature too. He was observant, certainly; he saw that Gideon was in his light-hearted mood. 'Have you any real idea what "spavined" means, Sergeant Jukes?'

'None at all. I gather he didn't have it?'

'Bastard strangles,' diagnosed the solemn expert. Gideon noticed the man was bandy-legged and knotted like a bunch of old rope – possibly the results of being thrown and kicked many times.

'Bastardy is more serious than honest strangles?' queried Gideon demurely.

'Goes around stables like a rat through shit. Mounts will be dropping all along the lines now. Keep your head down, or you'll cop the blame.'

'If I can get anyone to help drag him, I'll try to find a ditch upstream of a Royalist garrison to leave him in.' Gideon knew cavalrymen and dragoons felt little sentimentality towards their horses. In the midst of battle nobody could afford to stand weeping over the body of a faithful mount. But despite their short time together, he had taken responsibility for his animal. He felt driven to assert this: 'His name is Sir Rowland.'

'Rather extravagant?'

'Least I could do. He had nothing else going for him.'

Not only did Sir Rowland cause an epidemic, but since the horse had been supplied to him by the army, Gideon had to replace it at his own cost. Highly indignant, he pointed out that the army had been cheated by the two-timing agent, who had passed off on them a horse that was only fit to be fed to pigs. This happened so frequently no one got excited. Gideon then claimed that because of their pay arrears, he had no money for a new horse, 'even a new one of this piss-poor, rib-rattling quality'. He managed by borrowing other men's mounts, until February. When the next campaign season was about to start, the New Model battened down to finish the Oxford siege and his colonel reviewed the condition of his regiment. First he scrutinised the men's spiritual and political views; Okey was famous for weeding out anyone who failed to match his own beliefs. Next he inspected their horses. That was bad news for Gideon.

John Okey had come to view Sergeant Gideon Jukes as a slyly subversive character. This Jukes received pamphlets from London, which Okey suspected were seditious; the sergeant passed them on to others once he had read them. He seemed dangerously intrigued by *England's Birth-right Justified*, by John Lilburne, a man Gideon had heard of in the Eastern Association while he himself was working for Sir Samuel Luke. Colonel Lilburne, though then on good terms with Oliver Cromwell, had not joined the New Model Army but resigned from service because he refused to take the oath of the Covenant. He believed Presbyterianism, with its enforced suppression of all other beliefs, was just as terrible as imposed Catholicism or high Anglicanism.

Saturnine, highly intelligent and passionately argumentative, 'Freeborn John' Lilburne had become a prolific political author. He had a history of imprisonment for sedition. In 1637, after a pamphlet critical of bishops, he was pilloried, flogged — two hundred stripes — and imprisoned, becoming a popular hero, but was freed by the Long Parliament. Then early in the war, Royalists captured him; they took him to Oxford where they intended to hang him. Parliament threatened retaliation against its Royalist prisoners; in the nick of time Lilburne was saved when his pregnant wife Elizabeth carried a letter from the Speaker of the House of Commons to the King's headquarters. Subsequently he was freed in a prisoner-exchange. Now his quarrel was with Parliament.

Lilburne had embarked on a serious campaign for reform. Gideon had found his pamphlet startling. After a dry argument that Parliament's power should be limited in order to protect individual rights, it went on to denounce a curious mix of monopolies: preaching, as held by the established Church; wool and foreign trade, as controlled by the Merchant Adventurers; and printing. That was what caused Robert Allibone to send this pamphlet to Gideon; it echoed Robert's long-term loathing of the dead hand of the Stationers' Company.

Robert wrote that Lilburne had been sentenced by the House of Lords for publishing criticism of the Earl of Manchester; insulting a peer was a serious offence. Despite refusing to recognise the Lords' right to try him, Lilburne was sentenced to seven years' imprisonment, barred from holding civil or military office and fined two thousand pounds. The harsh penalty inspired mass marches, a petition signed by over two thousand citizens of London and a vocal lobby of Parliament.

It also led to the creation of the astonishing political organisation that would be called – by its opponents – the Leveller Party.

This began as a group of radical Londoners with headquarters at the Whalebone Tavern. Lilburne was their nominal head, with other pamphleteers: a master silk-weaver called William Walwyn and Richard Overton, the would-be actor Gideon remembered from *The Triumph of Peace*. Allibone had joined the group. Members paid a small subscription and met in taverns, the closest for Robert being the Nag's Head in Coleman Street. He spoke highly of Walwyn, a retiring family man, mainly self-taught, whose measured, lucid prose praising reason, toleration and love alarmed his opponents almost as much as it inspired devotees.

Robert said printers were well represented. The group elected officers and their executive committee met three times a week at the Whalebone, though others gathered regularly in various London parishes. Robert sent Gideon an anonymous tract which he reckoned was Walwyn's and Overton's collaboration, called *A Remonstrance of Many Thousand Citizens*. Addressed to the House of Commons, it reminded members that they were representatives of the people. Then its propositions were: absolute religious freedom, a completely free press, the end of monopolies and discriminating taxation, the reforming of unjust laws, and – astonishingly – abolition of the monarchy and the House of Lords. Robert Allibone found this exhilarating; Gideon did too, though not in front of his colonel.

Colonel Okey preferred to see his men at prayer meetings. Freedom of conscience is always regarded as a threat to military discipline. Okey viewed nervously the idea that instead of Parliament giving orders to the army, the army might make demands of Parliament.

Since men from the Newport Pagnell garrison were assisting at the siege of Oxford, Colonel Okey suggested the dangerous, horseless Jukes should reattach himself to his old colleagues.

'Once he takes a dislike, he never lets go. I am screwed and wrung!' complained Gideon to his brother.

'Stuff the Newports! Come to us,' suggested Lambert. 'Find a place in the sea-greens, Gideon.' The regiment referred to itself by its colonel's colours.

'In your rabble? I heard the governor of Abingdon wrote a distressed plea to Parliament to order your officers back to the regiment because it is so out of control.'

Lambert grinned. 'Six out of ten of our dear officers sloped off home during the winter break. Some of the lads have been too brisk with requests for provisions and, true, the town complained. Abingdon is of doubtful loyalty. But Rainborough has been empowered to have plunderers shot under martial law.'

'Articles of War. All commanders have that right.'

'Well, we are all being polite to Abingdon now, even when our stomachs are rumbling . . . I am with good lads, Gideon. You would like them, and they you.'

'Can I transfer between regiments?'

'It has been known! You went to Okey from Luke,' scoffed Lambert with his usual disrespect for rules. 'Remember Sexby? Edward Sexby, who was at your wedding?'

'Do not remind me of my wedding.'

'Oh I enjoyed it!' Lambert chortled. 'Sexby went off to serve under Oliver Cromwell – who was *he?* we innocently wondered at the time . . . Some relative of Sexby's, happily for him; they were, and are, extremely close and friendly. By cunning self-advancement, in the New Model, Sexby ended up in Fairfax's horse. If he can dodge around, so can you, my boy.' Lambert clapped his gloomy brother on the shoulder with a mighty paw, forgetting the shoulder had been dislocated. 'We are gaining new companies of foot. You can slip in among them – on my recommendation. Of course it means coming down to half pay!' In the New Model, dragoons were paid one shilling and sixpence a day but infantrymen only eightpence.

'Half pay hardly counts when pay never turns up.'

'Oh we shall fix that! Bring your seditious pamphlets,' instructed Lambert gleefully. 'Okey's a prim conservative, and your boys are dullards. *We* are known as the army's most devoted regiment for prayer, and our colonel is hot for freedom.'

'*Praying?*'

'And killing.'

Gideon remembered what he had heard about the bitter fighting for Prior's Hill Fort at Bristol, where Rainborough's men eventually slew all the defenders; he found it hard to reconcile his companionable, easy-going brother with such bloody slaughter.

'Well, if six out of ten of your officers have given themselves a home pass, that should ease a discreet transfer behind their backs.'

'They will return to us from soft beds and wifely succour, laden with puddings and bottled beer, and there you will be grinning in your short coat . . . Can't you get a coat that covers your buttocks, by the way? All will be well. You are not deserting the colours,' Lambert reassured his tall brother. 'Bring your snaphance.'

'It's a dragoon issue.'

'Just bring it!'

Arrears were still a problem. As 1646 progressed, the King remained evasive about a settlement, while Parliament viewed the army as redundant. Volunteers were wanted now to reconquer Ireland, but otherwise attempts were made to disband various regiments – if possible without paying them. It was a mean-spirited betrayal of the men who had risked their lives and livelihoods. It was also foolish.

When Parliament pressed for disbandment, the men realised they would lose all rights, and probably the pay they were owed. Those who had ended up far from home needed their money just to fund the return journey. The infantry were due eighteen weeks' pay, the cavalry forty-six. Faced with a debt of over three hundred thousand pounds, Parliament decreed that paying up for only six weeks would be sufficient discharge. Both officers and men stiffened their resistance.

The soldiers began to consider how far they would go in support of their grievances. Many started to think about the wider context – were they merely instruments of Parliament or men who had fought in their own right for issues of personal belief? If so, what sort of world had they fought for? Everyone in the army was also watching the issue of the kingdom's political settlement. There were concerns about indemnity for actions they might have taken in the war, which could in retrospect be called criminal. They wanted pensions for men who had been too badly wounded to work again and for the widows and orphans of those who had been killed. Some of the soldiers were beginning to demand far more than had ever been subjects' rights in the past. Contact began between the soldiers and the London radicals, the Levellers.

The King's personal fate had to be decided, together with how the state would be governed. Until now, most people had assumed the monarchy would survive. But the very questions that had caused a revolt remained undecided: how much authority was the King to have, and how far should the Houses of Parliament be allowed to restrict his actions, his choice of state servants, or his religious and monetary policies? An unforeseen complication was that the New Model Army required a voice – this threatening force of men who were bonded by two years of service together in the field and validated by the Lord's giving them victory.

The King's position in the debate was about to change. For six months Charles regarded his custody among the Scots as a temporary inconvenience; he continually tried to wriggle free by playing off his enemies against each other. Lambert and Gideon Jukes were scathing: 'In any fight, the loser has to capitulate. The man is like a foolish barrow-boy, who will not admit he has been knocked down. '

'And well kicked!'

The Scots always viewed the King as a negotiable hostage. With all the flaws in his personality, Charles failed to see this; he carried on as arrogant, shifty and unreliable as ever. He made offers to everyone: the Scots; Parliament as a body; the high Presbyterians who dominated Parliament; the City of London; the army. Lambert told Gideon divisive attempts had begun even before Charles fled from Oxford in 1646. 'During the blockade, he sent an approach to Rainborough personally, asking for a safe conduct so he could go to London and negotiate with Parliament. He claimed that in return for a guarantee that he would remain King, Woodstock and other garrisons would surrender.' It had failed to impress Rainborough, who notified Parliament.

While all the issues remained in flux, Rainborough – now possessing not one but two Jukes brothers in his regiment – was sent to the siege of Worcester. They captured the town, and he was made its governor, on the strength of the gracious way he obtained the surrender and Fairfax's praise that he was *very faithful, valiant and successful in many undertakings*. As Rainborough became a man of note, he was recruited as the member of Parliament for Droitwich, replacing Endymion Porter, a favourite courtier of the King's. Rainborough went up to Westminster, where he pleaded the soldiers' grievances. Word filtered back to the regiment that as he watched the political negotiations, he was unconvinced that the war was truly ended.

The Scots, too, became convinced that the King was too slippery. They reckoned Charles had no intention of keeping promises that he would install Presbyterianism in England – even though hopeful Presbyterians in the English Parliament still wanted to believe he would. In January 1647, the Covenanters cut their losses. They claimed that their military costs in supporting Parliament were two million pounds, but offered to settle for five hundred thousand. This was haggled down to four hundred thousand, with the King to be handed over to Parliament as if he were a receipt for the first instalment. Commissioners brought the first one hundred thousand pounds to Newcastle and the Scots passed King Charles to them.

He was conducted south to Holdenby House in Northamptonshire. His public reception convinced him all his royal authority remained. The gentry flocked to escort the procession; crowds lined the way; church bells were rung.

Charles arrived at Holdenby House in mid-February. A week later army officers refused to volunteer for Ireland without assurances; they presented Parliament with a respectful document called the *Moderate Petition*. Parliament declared it seditious. The MP Denzil Holles, who had once been a leading radical, one of the Five Members King Charles had tried to arrest, had turned into an intemperate loather of the New Model. He would sneer in his memoirs: '*most of the colonels were tradesmen, brewers, tailors, goldsmiths, shoemakers and the like – a notable dunghill*'. Now, in an astonishing tirade, he savaged the soldiers as violent mercenaries, enemies of the kingdom, only concerned about their arrears of pay:

> *The meanest of men, the basest and vilest of the nation, the lowest of the people have got the power in their hands; trampled upon the crown; baffled and misused the parliament; violated the laws, broke in sunder all bonds and ties of religion, conscience, duty, loyalty, faith, common honesty, and good manners.*

This eyebrow-raising vindictiveness came to be known wryly as '*The Declaration of Dislike*'. More followed. Parliament summoned Commissary-General Ireton (now Cromwell's son-in-law), and three colonels (one of them John Lilburne's brother) to answer charges that signatures for the officers' petition had been obtained by force. Tempers ran so high that Ireton and Holles had to be ordered not to fight a duel.

There were desperate divisions in English politics and religion. The Presbyterian majority in Parliament were determined to impose their will. They had taken over the London Trained Bands, replacing the Independent leadership with rigid Presbyterians. They were intent on disbanding the New Model and were thought to be planning to move its artillery away to the Tower of London. Worst, it was suspected that Presbyterians were entering into secret negotiations with the King.

In response, the New Model Army organised. The way it happened was extraordinary. No army had ever before discussed its aspirations and rights in the way that was about to happen.

Chapter Forty-One

The Agitators: 1647

Determination to achieve a good political solution ran through the ranks. Of their leaders, Fairfax yearned for the status quo, on just terms, but Cromwell was an unknown quantity, perhaps not yet certain himself what he sought. Others quickly decided. Radical soldiers and officers allied with radical civilians. Interesting links were forged, and not particularly in secret.

From the Tower of London John Lilburne created a roaring series of pamphlets under the title *Jonah's Cry out of the Whale's Belly*. He urged Oliver Cromwell to march to the city in peace, to deal with the King, to beware of untrustworthy members of the Commons and the army, but, most of all, to listen to petitions from the common soldiers. Lilburne wrote to Cromwell because he knew him well. He claimed insight into Cromwell's state of mind from *'a knowing man out of the army that came to me on purpose yesterday'*. This knowing man was reckoned to be Edward Sexby.

How often and how closely Sexby worked with Cromwell in that turbulent year neither would ever reveal. How intimately Sexby colluded with Lilburne was equally vague. How had he managed to travel to visit Lilburne in the Tower of London? Did he ride there on his cavalry horse, openly in uniform? Was Fairfax aware he absented himself from the regiment? How far did Sexby act alone in initiating the army movement which so quickly formed to 'agitate' for the soldiers' concerns? Following the officers' petition, he certainly took a major role in organising the rank and file. In April he masterminded *The Apology of the Common Soldiers of Sir Thomas Fairfax's Army*. This list of demands took the form of a letter to the commanders, Fairfax, Cromwell and Skippon, though it was always intended to be presented to Parliament. Initially it was put together by two representatives each from eight cavalry regiments. Cavalry were sufficiently mobile to communicate with each other, even though in theory it was mutiny. When Sexby and two colleagues, Allen and Shepherd, took the *Apology* to Westminster and were summoned for examination, they carefully insisted that the document was the work of all, not any individual, and that it had been produced by regiments acting independently.

Unnerved by the three troopers' steady resolve, Parliament promised to bring forward the measures sought, with payment of arrears. Cromwell, Skippon, Ireton and Fleetwood were made commissioners to restore calm. Meetings at Saffron Walden resulted in the appointment of agitators, or agents, for every regiment, no longer just the cavalry: two officers each and two from the ranks. They would meet in an army council to discuss anxieties. Cromwell would present Parliament with a new petition to give reassurances that the soldiers would remain loyal, provided they were fairly treated.

Parliament none the less proceeded with its intention to disband the troops. Promises to provide arrears of pay and redress of grievances would come into effect only *after* the disbandment. The regimental Agitators circulated letters, warning the soldiers to resist this.

Against this troubled background, Gideon Jukes once again met Edward Sexby.

Colonel Thomas Rainborough's regiment, Gideon had found, was articulate, fearless, and much more lively than he had expected from his brother's relaxed description of them as 'good lads'. These hefty musketeers and pikemen, many drawn from parishes in Rainborough's home area of Deptford and Wapping, accepted Gideon as one of their kind. They felt obliged to deride his eccentrically short uniform, but being tall was approved, since Rainborough himself was a notably big man. The soldiers welcomed Gideon into their conclaves. As Lambert's brother he was immediately trusted. Gideon found he had joined his new regiment at a significant moment: they were planning to mutiny.

Rainborough had been absent for some months at Westminster. Critics would claim afterwards that he kept away from his regiment deliberately, to distance himself as radicalism fomented. Gideon had learned more about him. Rainborough had a seafaring background; his father once rescued three hundred English prisoners of Algerian pirates, an event remembered in a Moor's head on the family badge. The Royalist press scornfully called him 'the Skipper's Boy', furthering an admiring myth that he rose to admiral from cabin boy. With this history, Rainborough had now won Parliamentary approval to make a seaborne expedition to Jersey, where the Prince of Wales had been living. So in May 1647, the regiment was moved to Hampshire, prior to embarkation for Jersey as soon as the order was given. They never went.

In only a few months, political organisation in the New Model had become busy, with the soldiers' enthusiastic support. For a meeting at Bury St Edmunds infantrymen contributed fourpence a head, which was half a day's pay; they wore red ribbon armbands on their left arms to signify solidarity to death. Not only was the main army involved, but messengers travelled to the navy and to detached forces in Wales and the North.

Incessant trips to plan were made between units, over long distances. Ciphers protected identities. It was a curious situation because, since the appointment of Agitators had been officially approved, their activity was sanctioned by the high command; more than fifteen hundred pounds was allocated from the army's contingency fund, authorised by Fairfax, for the Agitators' expenses. When Rainborough's regiment was quartered between Petersfield and Portsmouth, men on extremely high-quality horses came to inveigle the sea-greens into what the Agitators wanted.

Gideon and Lambert heard the Agitators' request and marvelled. Rainborough's men were being asked to defy their orders. No longer trusting either Parliament or any of their own Presbyterian officers, radical soldiers had identified two immediate aims: first, not to lose control of the King he was still confined at Holdenby House, although there were strong suspicions that the Presbyterians in Parliament intended to transfer him to Scotland; second, not to relinquish the New Model's artillery, which was currently at Oxford. If Parliament moved the artillery to the Tower of London, the Trained Bands, under new Presbyterian leadership, might turn the guns against Fairfax's men. The Agitators were hoping Rainborough's troops would help prevent that.

Gideon was chosen to take the regiment's reply. He went with a colleague; message-carriers rode in pairs, in case of accident. Because he had been a dragoon, the others assumed he was an assured rider and the Agitators produced a mount for him. Unlike the late Sir Rowland, this was a superb horse. His speed and stamina would be needed, for they had to reach the army's current headquarters in Chelmsford, an awkward trip of over a hundred miles. The Agitators' message had come from a man known as Cipher 102, whom they believed to be Lieutenant Chillenden of Colonel Whalley's regiment. But when they came to Chelmsford, the two saddle-sore messengers were taken to Edward Sexby.

Sexby was having the time of his life. Gideon, who recognised him at once, saw that the man had found his life's mission. When they were brought into his presence, Sexby was intently crouched over a letter he was writing. He was totally engrossed. Though the text was short and his pen-strokes controlled, the vigour with which he shook sand to dry the ink on the completed paper said everything. Gideon spotted that he had a cipher key by him, which he covered quickly.

Now thirty years old, all Sexby's waking moments were devoted to conspiracy. It seemed to Gideon that Sexby was so entirely taken up by this work that he almost loved the game more than the ideas. Gideon shook off his own curmudgeonly reaction to his colleague's intensity.

To establish his credentials, Gideon mentioned how Sexby had been at his wedding. Sexby took a moment to remember. Then he was all charm. 'Of course!' He did not ask after the fate of the marriage, the health of Gideon's bride, or whether they had been favoured with children.

Gideon never had any wish to discuss Lacy, yet he bridled a little. Years later, with hindsight, he thought Sexby was too self-centred. Perhaps at the time he was jealous of Sexby's success; if so, he rebuked himself. None the less, he reckoned that Parthenope, Sexby's hostess at the wedding breakfast, would disapprove. It was an odd moment for Gideon to be thinking of his mother but he knew she would have said a polite guest should at least have remembered the quantities of ale and the fine cuts of meat.

Still, revolutionaries are often bad at social relationships. Too many believe that all men are born equal – but that they themselves possess special talents which give them golden destinies.

'You helped my brother put my delinquent uncle in a horse-trough.'

'Ah Lambert Jukes!' The easy charm returned. 'Lambert – such a good fellow!'

'A stalwart of Rainborough's regiment. One of us,' said Gideon, where 'one of us' had particular resonance. 'True unto death.' The code-words brought them back to the reason for his visit.

He and his colleague reported their regiment's eagerness to be involved. Although Colonel Rainborough was still in London, Sexby seemed to have some private information that he would support the soldiers. *If Rainborough holds extreme radical views,* thought Gideon, *he is the only senior officer who does . . .* He saw that it left the colonel dangerously exposed.

They were given a letter to the regiment, a letter that Sexby rapidly prepared, explaining it to them carefully before it was sealed. 'There are those who would prevent us – Colonel Jackson, who is in the Presbyterians' pocket, may interfere; we are seeking a way to banish him from his regiment . . .'

'If we are captured,' said Gideon, almost the light-hearted bride-groom again, 'do we eat the instruction?'

Edward Sexby looked sour. He had passion and energy, but little sense of humour. '*Don't* get captured. Keep the terms clear: your boys are *invited* by the Agitators to join with other regiments.'

His fellow-soldier from Portsmouth dug Gideon in the ribs. 'We understand, sir.' *Sir?* Though he had the manner of an officer, Sexby was in fact a trooper still.

'We do understand,' Gideon reinforced it, close to an apology though he saw no reason to fawn on Sexby.

Sexby leaned back in his chair. 'You are a printer.'

'Was, before I came to the army.'

'Do you write?'

'Not for the public.'

'We are seeking able pen-men . . . We need a press,' Sexby growled fretfully. 'If a press is not got into the army, we are handicapped.'

While Sexby drummed his fingers in frustration, Gideon saw the point. 'We must be able to print documents speedily and safely. It needs a trusted printer, with his own press. That press must always travel with the army, so we can react fast to whatever happens. There are many loyal printers in London, but distance is a hindrance. Dangerous too – Parliament can, and will, shut down a press, then throw the printer into prison.'

'Walwyn's group have the means,' grumbled Sexby, 'but they are constantly under suspicion. Lilburne and Overton are stuck in the Tower –' He seemed to know a lot about the Levellers.

'Walwyn has issued a great petition, calling for their release.'

Sexby started, surprised that Gideon knew. Gideon let him wonder.

He considered suggesting Robert Allibone as the army printer. Robert behaved discreetly, but he was not entirely invisible from the authorities; besides, Robert was a stay-at-home. Gideon had a brainwave: 'I know of a press, now silent and ripe to be claimed. We would not need to bring it from London.'

Sexby became fully alert: 'Where?'

'Oxford.'

'Can we get it?'

'I will find it.' Smiling, Gideon gestured to the letter he and his colleague were taking back to Portsmouth. Sexby watched him, gangling and apparently so easy-going that he seemed slow-witted – yet, Sexby saw, this blond sergeant was deceptively sharp. 'Taking your *invitation*, our regiment will march to Oxford, Sexby. I have some knowledge of that city. Oxford was much under observation when I worked with Sir Samuel Luke.' Gideon was cheerfully exaggerating.

'What press is it?' Sexby's heart told him Gideon Jukes was reliable, yet he remembered the young man as a nervous bridegroom, destined for bamboozlement by that cold-eyed new wife . . . Never trust a man who thinks for himself, warned Sexby's head – Sexby, who also thought for himself.

'The press the Royalists used for their deceitful propaganda, *Mercurius Aulicus*,' said Gideon. 'John Harris owns it.' He stood his ground, keeping command of his idea: 'I volunteer to find Harris and his press. Then I would like to be our printer using it.'

'We shall have to pay him for it.' Sexby's thoughts raced. He ignored Gideon's request to become the printer. 'Promise Harris reimbursement. The officers will approve the money.' A true revolutionary, he was quick to speak for his masters' funding. 'Can you do this, Sergeant Jukes?'

'Trust me!' Their eyes met. Years later Gideon would remember how even at that moment, deep in conspiracy, he felt their interests faintly jarred.

On the 28th of May, Rainborough's regiment acted in breach of their orders. They formed themselves up and marched north away from

Portsmouth. As Sexby predicted, Colonel Jackson tried to intercept them at Braintree, but they refused to be stopped. Agitator 102 wrote to a colleague: *'Colonel Rainborough is to go to his Regiment, and it is by Oxford . . . Let two horsemen go presently to Colonel Rainborough to Oxford, and be very careful you be not overwitted. Now break the neck of this design, and you will doe well . . .'* The 'design' included another mission, even more secret and desperate: *'not to dally, but a good party of Horse of 1,000, and to have spies with them before to bring you intelligence, and to quarter your Horse overnight, and to march in the night . . . So God bless.'*

He did not sign it.

As soon as the mutiny was reported in London, Rainborough was despatched by Parliament to restore order among his men. He came across most of them at Culham, near Abingdon. Gideon and Lambert reckoned their colonel was sympathetic. They were sure Rainborough had known all about their mutinous march, in advance, and he supported it. He certainly issued no punishments.

He wrote telling Parliament of his troops' difficult temper, implying that their cramped quarters and problems with local provisioning caused it. While he hoped to prevent further trouble, he could not give undertakings for good behaviour. This was a very odd thing for a commander to say. Rainborough also failed to mention that three and a half thousand pounds intended to pay off and disband Colonel Ingoldsby's regiment had been commandeered. His regiment and Ingoldsby's had already seized the artillery and were guarding it at Oxford.

His disingenuous letter was read out in Parliament on the day that the secret horsemen achieved their object.

While Rainborough stayed at Culham, some of his men were deployed in Oxford guarding the artillery train. With them had gone Gideon Jukes, searching for John Harris. Harris came from a vintnering family, so Gideon began in the taverns.

He found Harris. He encouraged this slightly raffish character to see that a new career serving the revolution would be better for an ex-actor and failed wine merchant than no career at all. 'We are mere implementers of the word,' Gideon declared expansively. During the search, he had drunk more ale than he was used to.

'How much will they pay?' asked Harris, who was stone cold sober.

'We can commandeer the press if you do not co-operate.' Gideon invented this threat, fired up by what he had seen of Edward Sexby's certainty.

It worked. Harris seemed to think that if he volunteered, at least he might recover his equipment once the revolution was over. He knew the revolution would not last; he was, after all, a Royalist.

It was while he was supervising movement of the *Mercurius Aulicus* press on a brewery dray, that Gideon ran into the horsemen.

There were only five hundred, though Sexby and Chillenden had wanted a thousand. Leading this secret mission was an officer of Fairfax's Lifeguard called Cornet George Joyce. It was open knowledge that they had come to Oxford after a meeting at Oliver Cromwell's house in Drury Lane in London. Joyce consistently claimed he had Cromwell's approval – though Cromwell would keep his own counsel.

Joyce, a Durham man who was reputedly a tailor, held the most junior officer's rank in a cavalry regiment. Gideon viewed it cynically. Cornet Joyce was an unknown. An easy scapegoat if this expedition went bottom up. Expendable.

Once they had satisfied themselves that the cannon and ammunition were well guarded by Rainborough's men, the horsemen cantered out of Oxford on the second phase of their mission. Since Gideon still had possession of the good horse on which he went to Chelmsford, he had persuaded Cornet Joyce to take him along. He claimed he knew the best roads in Northamptonshire, and all the quiet byways, learned from his time with Sir Samuel Luke.

They rode for two nights. On the evening of the 3rd of June, this secret band arrived outside an enormous stately home. It had been built by Queen Elizabeth's Lord Chancellor, Sir Christopher Hatton, in order to entertain the Queen as extravagantly as she thought proper. It was said to be the largest house in England, built around two vast court-yards, with hundreds of windows, grandiose glass being the status symbol of the age.

Here, for the past four months, King Charles had been a prisoner. Holdenby House had passed to his father and remained royal property. These were civilised surroundings and he was barely restricted.

Though a small man who had had rickets in his childhood, the King had strode through the beautiful grounds at such a brisk pace that his keeper, the elderly Lord Pembroke, had trouble keeping up with him. From this fabulous house, Charles continued to negotiate with any party who approached him, his latest fragile promises being made to the Presbyterians in Parliament who were so set on dividing and disbanding the New Model Army.

Commissioners from Parliament were here with the King. As Joyce and his party reconnoitred the place, the commissioners' hostility was one of their worries. Another was the soldiers guarding the King, Colonel Richard Greaves's regiment. Greaves hailed from King's Norton in Warwickshire; he had led a troop that defended Birmingham against Prince Rupert's attack. The Agitators doubted his allegiance, because he was a known Presbyterian. They were reassured by learning that part of his regiment had been pulled out, under Major Adrian Scrope, and was away at a place called Papworth. Scrope was personally known to Joyce, who thought he might be a sympathiser, though this could not be relied upon.

On the night they arrived, they made discreet contact with the guards inside the house. Gideon knew some, men who had been in Sir Samuel Luke's regiment. They reported that Colonel Greaves had made a bolt for it earlier that night. It was bad news. He would undoubtedly bring a rescue party if he could.

At six o'clock, Joyce and his party drew up openly in front of the great main doorway and called for the King to be sent out. Most of the garrison had come over to them. The Parliamentary commissioners who were here to negotiate a settlement might cause problems, though with luck those gentlemen were not yet awake.

The five hundred riders remained on their horses. Gideon found he was clutching the reins in a cold sweat, his hands clammy inside his gauntlets. Three weeks before midsummer, it was already light, though with a weak sun that had yet to evaporate the dew. The dawn chorus had filled the chilly air for several hours, a little ragged at this point of the summer when many birds had established their territories and raised their first batches of young. All the great trees in the Holdenby park were heavy with leaf, unseen wafts of tree and grass pollen irritating the riders' throats as they waited. A few long-eared red squirrels perched on branches, inquisitively watching them.

The King kept them waiting. Eventually he walked out of doors. Still possessed of servants, the man who had made an art of iconic monarchy was handsomely dressed, his lace arranged, his beard and moustache trim. Even in captivity his brocaded suits were laid up in lavender and clove balls; his long hair was regularly treated with nourishing essences; he washed with warm water and exquisitely scented soap.

Cornet Joyce and his men had performed meagre ablutions in a coppice. They had ridden hard for two days without changing shirts. Most had three days of stubble. 'When we finally find quarters,' Gideon reflected ruefully, 'when five hundred tired and dirty men pull off a thousand riding boots, the whole neighbourhood will recoil!'

As he approached, Charles must have seen the curling breath of their lively horses and the steam off their flanks; he would have heard the restless chinks of harness and weaponry. The men looked anxious, yet determined. The sudden appearance of these heavily armed riders heralded change, but for the King, nothing would ever alter:

> *'I alone must answer to God for our exercise of the authority he has vested in me. It is for me to decide how our nation is to be governed, how my subjects are to be ruled, and above all how the Church shall be established under the rule of law. These are the Divine Rights of Kings and are ordained by the Almighty. It is not the place of the subject to question the royal prerogative . . .'*

Five hundred subjects were here because they did question it.

With a pounding heart, Gideon Jukes watched his sovereign's approach. This was the third time he had been in the King's presence. He remembered *The Triumph of Peace* and also how he had leapt onto the step of the royal coach as it came from Guildhall. The same aloof, fastidious figure was here now, viewing the guard party sardonically. If anything, he was more composed than they were. The horsemen were crushed together more raggedly than was elegant. None of them had ever dealt personally with anyone of such high rank.

Calmly, Charles asked to see their commission.

Whatever they had expected, it was not a request for paperwork. Of course they had no warrant. Everyone became embarrassed, until Joyce found the presence of mind to indicate the grim riders. 'Here is my commission.'

'Where?'

'Behind me.'

The King posed. 'It is as fair a commission, and as well written as I have seen a commission written in my life!' he agreed.

He was taken into custody, put on a horse and quickly carried away from Holdenby. The plan was to rush their royal prisoner to the army, which was gathering at Newmarket. It meant travelling east through uncertain country, with the risk that the King would be rescued. Now it was Cornet Joyce's turn to write feverish letters to anonymous friends:

We have secured the King. Greaves is run away; he got out about one o'clock in the morning and so went his way. It is suspected he is gone to London; you may imagine what he will do there. You must hasten an answer to us, and let us know what we shall do. We are resolved to obey no orders but the general's. I humbly entreat you to consider what is done and act accordingly with all the haste you can; we shall not rest night nor day till we hear from you . . .'

Chapter Forty-Two

From Holdenby to Putney: 1647

'I take my eyes off you for five minutes, you scallywag!' exclaimed Lambert Jukes. 'You step out on a simple errand, a walk to a vintner's, according to you — then suddenly men come rushing to tell me my rascal brother, Mother's pet, has *arrested the King*!' Bursting with admiration, Lambert was thrilled by this exciting connection. 'This is true? You were at Holdenby? *How* did you manage that?'

'I showed them where the house was,' stated Gideon. He smiled lazily. He knew how to jerk his brother's string.

Lambert gazed at the sky. They were side by side on a bench outside a barn, after Gideon was enfolded back into his regiment. Lambert indulged himself in sarcasm as if they were arguing at the dinner table in their parents' house. 'Providential. Oh truly, sir, it would not do to have Cornet Joyce stopping milkmaids to ask them for directions. You were riding by night, in any case — only unchaste, untrustworthy little milkmaids with soiled aprons would be wandering out of doors under the stars. Naturally Cornet Joyce needed Gideon Jukes, noted map-man and scout.'

They sat on together in a long silence.

'So,' Lambert addressed his brother quietly. 'Now you have seen him at close quarters, this monarch who has kept us in the field for five years. Did he praise you as the best dotterel that ever hopped before him?'

'Oh I kept in the background, lest acknowledging our past acquaintance should disconcert the others.'

'Such commendable modesty!'

'Besides, there was a chance my great performance might have slipped his memory. Brother, he is just a man.'

They were both silent again, wondering what would happen to that man now.

Others were wondering the same.

Cornet Joyce and his band had headed via Huntingdon and Cambridge towards Newmarket, where Fairfax had arranged for the army to rendezvous. Joyce was still writing urgent letters:

> *Read this enclosed, seal it up, and deliver it whatever you do, so we may not perish for want of your assistance. Let the Agitators know once more we have done nothing in our own name, but what we have done hath been in the name of the whole Army . . .'*

Oliver Cromwell arrived at Newmarket, having fled from Westminster in fear of impeachment by the Presbyterians for his presumed part in arranging the abduction.

Lord-General Fairfax, who had neither sanctioned the abduction nor even been aware it was happening, had sent Whalley's regiment to reinforce the guard on Holdenby House. Whalley intercepted the five hundred raiders and tried to conduct their hostage again to Holdenby. Contrary as ever, King Charles refused to go back. He asked to be taken to Fairfax. Fairfax responded as a gentleman and sent his own coach. Noblemen's coaches were pulled by fine horses but most were clumsy antique vehicles that still lacked springs. These bone-shakers had one advantage: quarantine. They kept the public at a distance. His Majesty could avoid communicating with Joyce and the desperadoes. They were relieved too.

Fairfax, Cromwell and other senior officers rode out to meet them near Cambridge. For unfathomable reasons, Charles asked to continue the journey to Newmarket. Fairfax allowed it, keeping control of him. When, over the following month or so, the army moved from place to place, coming closer to London, the King was taken with them. Generally they were able to lodge him in elegant houses of his own. It came as a shock to some, just how many royal properties there were.

Meanwhile, the army's confrontation with Parliament became ever more edgy. There were violent demonstrations at Westminster, some from the unemployed soldiers, the reformadoes, who had lost their regiments when the army was created. London apprentices were out on the streets too. Five years had brought a new generation of these excitable young men, whose demands now were that the King be restored and the New Model Army disbanded. Parliament had beefed up the London Trained Bands to oppose the New Model. Marching to St Albans, the army made Parliament a new declaration, claiming the right to speak for the people of England and demanding that members of Parliament who abused their power should be called to account. The Common Council of the City of London also urged that the soldiers' arrears should be paid.

The army called for the suspension of eleven specific members of the House of Commons, headed up by the vitriolic Denzil Holles; the troops were accused of attempting to overthrow liberty and justice. They moved headquarters again, this time to Uxbridge, which was ideally placed for cutting off supplies to London. The Commons refused to suspend the Eleven Members, but the Eleven thought it prudent to withdraw.

Proposals for peace were drawn up, primarily drafted by Henry Ireton, in the name of the New Model Army. Called *The Heads of the Proposals*, this had religious proposals which aimed to satisfy everyone: bishops would be retained, though with their power curbed; Laudian church rules repealed; the Covenant revoked. Biennial Parliaments would be called. A Council of State would conduct foreign policy. Parliament would control the appointment of state officials and military commanders for ten years. No Royalists would hold office for at least five years, though sequestration of their estates would end. An Act of Oblivion would ensure there were no recriminations for anyone's part in the civil war.

This was a generous, considered template for peace. More lenient than the proposals which had been put to the King while he was the Scots' prisoner at Newcastle, it could have created a lasting constitution. It was far too moderate for the Levellers, who responded with their own proposals, drafted by John Wildman and called *The Agreement of the People*.

The Heads of the Proposals was taken to the King by a large committee of officers. Charles rejected it. He was arrogant and contemptuous. Radicals hardened their hearts against the monarchy. Colonel Thomas Rainborough was so appalled by the King's attitude, he sneaked away and rode all night to inform the main army what was happening.

Even Fairfax was aroused, when a group of Independent members of the Houses of Commons and Lords were driven out of Westminster by the Presbyterians; they fled to the army. Fairfax took the New Model to Colnbrook, a few miles from London. Regiments were then sent around southwards to occupy historic Tilbury, where the fleet was based, and Deptford.

The King formally rejected *The Heads of the Proposals*. Army leaders published it.

In London clashes occurred between pro-Independent demonstrators and the Presbyterian militia. City leaders rode out and greeted Fairfax on Hounslow Heath. The army declared its intention to march on London to restore calm. Four regiments, under Colonel Rainborough, occupied Southwark on the night of August the 3rd.

Many of the soldiers were now in their home parishes. Others, like Lambert and Gideon Jukes, were only separated from home by the River Thames. They had not seen their family or home for two years. The last time they marched into the city was as the Trained Bands returned in triumph, after relieving Gloucester. Four years later, they came as invaders.

Few soldiers slept. At least they had decent quarters. As the last stopping place before the river crossing, the borough of Southwark was rich in great inns. Some old monastery and priory lodgings had been converted at the Reformation into multiple grim tenements frequented by criminals and prostitutes, or torn down and replaced with malodorous cottages. Many large and comfortable hostelries remained, often with famous medieval pedigrees, alongside two- and three-storeyed galleried taverns of Elizabethan and Jacobean design.

Southwark had a dual quality. Those who read, thought of Chaucer and Shakespeare. Others knew that the captain of the Pilgrim Fathers' ship, the *Mayflower*, came from Southwark, as did John Harvard, the benefactor of the first New World university. Historically this was an uncontrolled haven for illegitimate trades, but the district housed occupations of all kinds, not only prostitution, gambling and theft: amidst the famous stews were plenty of industrious craftsmen, often foreigners – Germans, Dutch or Flemings – who could not make or sell their wares across in the city because they were barred from the livery companies. There was a long-established, thriving leather industry, with tanneries stinking out the bankside air and its own market. There were cornmills, vinegar-makers and brewhouses. The river was lined with wharves. Though the theatres were closed, the baiting pits still existed; not only was the night split by the caterwauling of the legendary Southwark whores, but the soldiers could hear deep agitated barking from the mastiffs in their kennels and even occasional grunts from the unsettled bears behind their palisades.

The troops had been discouraged from walking out, but it was not forbidden. Earnest captains warned their men to avoid certain areas, particularly Paris Gardens, where the most notorious stews were concentrated. They had been told that 'bagnios' were by no means respectable bath-houses, but a cover for brothels. Nudity and exotic practices ran hand in hand. The men were ordered not to accept beckoning invitations from 'single women', who would certainly not be sweet preacheresses asking them in to a prayer meeting. They were lectured on the dangers of dark, derelict haunts, of the crowded cottages where the restless poor teemed like vermin, and of the shadowy gardens and mazes where once foreign ambassadors had met in secret to collude and trade state secrets.

Like the Londoners they were, on being advised against it, Lambert and Gideon Jukes went to have a look around.

It was a very quiet night in Southwark. The presence of several thousand red-coated soldiers of the Lord, presumed to be disapproving, had spoiled trade.

The Jukes were lodged at Lewes Inn, opposite St Olave's Church and close to St Thomas's Hospital. Strolling along Barms Street and Tooley Street, they passed St Augustine's Inn and Bridge House, a spacious collection of stores for wood, timber and other materials needed for the maintenance of London Bridge. There too were enormous ovens which could bake bread for the poor, and a large brewhouse which supplied much of the city. Continuing east, they crossed Battle Bridge over what called itself a stream but was an open sewer, then further along another odoriferous waterway beyond which lay the great Beer House once owned by Sir John Falstaffe. Turning towards the water, they came to a wharf right opposite the Tower.

They gazed across the Pool of London. Moored against the wharves, a multitude of ships showed faint lanterns. To their left, the bridge displayed its usual blaze of candles in a long illuminated line; across the dark water of the Thames, the lights in the City were more scattered and dim, but they were there like remote strings of stars. Directly across from them was Traitors' Gate, with its gloomy arched water-gate. Queens, princesses, royal favourites, and more lately Strafford and Laud had entered by that fatal door, with the dark water lapping over its slippery green steps. The Tower still housed unrepentant Royalists, penned up in friendly contiguity with more radical activists. Sir Lewis Dyve was there (the cavalier commander who had given up Newport Pagnell before Sir Samuel Luke took it); Dyve was currently spying on whomever visited John Lilburne to plot revolution. The brothers could make out the dark shapes of the towers, bastions and gateways of the ancient fortress, where pinpoints of light showed through high slit windows. Even in high summer, the air along the river valley was thick with coal-smoke. Occasionally a drunken man's maundering cry or a fishwife's coarse laughter came across the water from some night owl who had no idea that Rainborough's men on the other bank of the river overheard.

Somebody else had been watching the far shore. A burly man shouldered between them, dropping heavy gloved fists on one shoulder apiece. The Jukes brothers stiffened and stared straight ahead. Even in a radical regiment, soldiers became shy at direct notice from their colonel. 'Well, my lads!'

'Sir!'

'There it is.'

Gideon cleared his throat. 'Shall we have to fight our way across tomorrow?'

Thomas Rainborough half-turned, finding the tall Gideon one of the few of his men he looked straight in the eye. 'I believe not. I *hope* not! Arrangements have been made. We shall be all on our best behaviour and, I am assured, loyal friends will open the gates.' The Jukes brothers beamed with enthusiasm. 'So what do you think of our situation?' Rainborough asked, keen to test the feelings of his men.

'We think it awkward to be setting ourselves against those who first sent us forth,' replied Lambert, making his admission sombre. 'But we see that Parliament is nowadays full of men who will have peace on any terms, or men who hope that negotiations with the King may bring them personal advantage. Whereas we fought for sound reasons, which must now be answered.'

'The King will never accept our demands,' grumbled Gideon. 'And if Parliament will not either, then they must go the way of the King.'

'And what will that be, I wonder!' mused Rainborough. 'Tell me, lads, do either of you have a vote for Parliament?'

'I shall do, sir, now my father has died.' Lambert was a little awkward about it since he had never yet used his vote.

'I have no estate,' Gideon said ruefully. 'My partner and I run a print business, but we rent our premises, so neither of us can elect a representative.'

'Yet no one can deny that you have an interest in the country!' exclaimed Rainborough. It was a rare attitude in an officer. Gideon wondered what pamphlets his colonel had been reading.

Though night had drawn in, there was still just enough light in the sky for them to make out Rainborough's face. He had strong features, a pleasant expression, and long hair, pretty thin on top. He turned to Gideon, peering at his soldier's features. Perhaps the fair-haired lank with the short coat had been pointed out to him. 'You are the man of mine who went to Holmby House?'

'Sergeant Gideon Jukes, sir.'

'My brother.' At Lambert's proud declaration, Rainborough looked surprised, perhaps having presumed the gap in years between these two made them father and son. 'The man who found the press at Oxford,' put in Lambert again loyally.

'Was that not Sexby?'

'Sexby *wanted* a press,' Gideon conceded, staying polite. Then he laughed quietly. 'Truly I found it, however.'

'You had a busy time!' Rainborough commented. They all let the subject drop, which avoided any awkwardness over whether his soldiers' mutinous actions had had the colonel's sanction.

He asked where they were billeted. He began to walk them back that way, like a tolerant parent steering stay-out children home by twilight. They pooh-poohed the dangers of the area, although Rainborough told them about an obsession of his: children and servants who were snatched off the streets, kidnapped or 'spirited' away. These mites were collected by ship and transported to the New World.

'Are these not going to a better life?' asked Lambert in puzzlement.

'The waifs mostly find they are sent to work like slaves in the plantations,' growled Rainborough. He knew something of America; his sister had married the governor of Massachusetts' son and his brother William had lived there until he returned to England to fight in the civil war. His tone lightened. 'However, I have no fear the intrepid Jukes brothers will be nabbed!'

Thomas Rainborough's own brother was a fellow-radical. William was younger; he had shared Thomas's early life of seaborne adventure when they both put money into Ireland and later went there on an expedition to help quell rebellion. William would one day involve himself in dangerous activites, but Thomas had more to him now. Rainborough sensed it was the other way around with the two Jukes. Lambert was a true diamond, but Gideon had a sharper edge.

The unfairness in their position was not lost on Rainborough. Why should Lambert Jukes inherit the family home and business, and a vote for Parliament, simply because he was born first, whilst his brother was entitled to neither property nor representation? Their colonel detected no rancour between them. He knew they had both fought, both risked injury and death, both endured rain and snow, starvation and terror for the same cause. Now they deserved equal rewards. As his political ideals formed, this encounter could only strengthen Rainborough's audacious new opinions.

The next morning, Rainborough led the four regiments across London Bridge. The gates had indeed been opened from inside by supporters, so the troops were able to march into London steadily and peacefully. The citizens marvelled at their discipline.

As Rainborough occupied the eastern parishes and his men filed through the city towards Westminster, Fairfax and the remainder of the New Model were drawn up west of London. Parliament was trapped between this pincer movement, the purpose of which went unstated, though it must have been obvious.

The Lord Mayor and aldermen, always quick to ingratiate themselves, met Fairfax at Hyde Park; the Common Council of the City of London welcomed him at Charing Cross. Fairfax himself rode ceremonially into New Palace Yard at the Houses of Parliament. The fugitive Independents from the Commons and Lords were reinstated.

Fairfax was appointed Constable of the Tower of London. When he visited the Tower, he asked to see a copy of *Magna Carta* that was kept there. Taking off his hat, he observed, 'This is that we have fought for, and by God's help we must maintain.' Obsequiously wooing him, the City presented the Lord General with a gold bowl and ewer, valued at a thousand pounds and overflowing with gold coins. He was given a newly created Tower Guard.

London was under control. The army removed to new headquarters at Croydon. The Agitators called for a purge of Presbyterian MPs. Six of the hated Eleven fled abroad. Although Fairfax opposed purging Parliament, Cromwell went with an armed guard to oversee passage of a 'Null and Void Ordinance', which cancelled outright all legislation that had been passed while the Independent members were fugitives.

That August, the King was transferred to Hampton Court. Fairfax stationed the New Model Army at Putney, midway between Westminster and Hampton Court. Colonel Thomas Rainborough was living at his brother William's house in Fulham, convenient for the army. The King was still secretly negotiating with Presbyterians. Charles again rejected Ireton's liberal *Heads of the Proposals*. Parliament offered instead the sterner proposals that had been previously under discussion while the King was a prisoner in Newcastle; this would pacify the Scots, who devised them, and perhaps make the *Heads of the Proposals* seem less alarming. Everyone was becoming more Machiavellian.

In September, there was a pause to regroup. Oliver Cromwell visited John Lilburne in the Tower. The hot-headed Leveller refused to pledge he would cause no 'hurly-burlies' in the army if he was released, then he roundly denounced Cromwell as a hypocrite. Even so, there was official softening towards the Levellers and Richard Overton was unconditionally released from prison. But in the army, factions were strengthening. It was perceived that the libertarian Colonel Rainborough might become a rival to Cromwell. Cromwell was known to be visiting the King and was admittedly bedazzled; Rainborough paid no such court to Charles. Relations between Cromwell and Rainborough became so strained that at an Army Council meeting in the middle of the month Rainborough openly stormed at Cromwell, 'One of us must not live!'

Trying to ensure loyalty in the navy, Parliament appointed new Admiralty commissioners, including the radical MP Henry Marten, who was often seen as disreputable because he had a wife but lived openly with his mistress, and Thomas Rainborough. Vice-Admiral Batten, a pro-Royalist at heart, fled by sea to Holland, taking valuable ships with him. Rainborough was nominated as his replacement. In theory this meant Rainborough was no longer in charge of his army regiment, though in the crucial coming weeks, he and they took a relaxed attitude to that.

The Army Council decided *they* would negotiate directly with the King, instead of Parliament. Scottish lords were visiting Charles at Hampton Court, promising to help him regain his throne and urging him to escape. In Parliament, Oliver Cromwell made a speech in which he dissociated the army leadership from Leveller principles and advocated keeping the monarchy. But only eight days later, Cromwell was in the chair when the Council of the Army met at Putney for what was to become a debate not simply about the position of the soldiers who had won the civil war, but about much wider constitutional issues and the liberty of the individual.

Gideon Jukes was not a regimental Agitator but in the way that had become his trademark he turned up anyway, looking as if he had an invitation. On several days he managed to be present.

Chapter Forty-Three

The Putney Debates: 1647

Putney lay five miles outside London, on the south bank of the Thames. There was no bridge, though ferries carried people over the water. It was a pleasant, countrified outlying suburb full of market gardens, through which travellers and traders from many parts of the country passed on their journey to the capital. In the last days of October and the beginning of November 1647 it was chilly, though not too exposed.

The debates took place in St Mary's Church. A large medieval parish church with a square bell tower, it had a lofty chancel, which was borrowed for these unprecedented meetings. Several times consensus seemed so difficult to achieve that before afternoon debates the Army Council held morning prayer meetings to seek divine guidance. At Ireton's urging, those took place in private houses. His brother hosted one. The council might discuss civil issues in a 'steeple house' for convenience, but God would make his will felt in men's hearts.

The church was packed. Gideon Jukes stood, bare-headed, among the soldier Agitators while the officers sat down around a large table and kept on their hats. The distinctions struck him. As he waited for the first debate to start, Gideon even mused whether to put back his own hat defiantly. Rebel though he was, he would have felt too uncomfortable. He had grown up in a society that was riven by grades and privilege. Kings took precedence over princes and barons over earls. Scholars must not look or behave like gentlemen of leisure. Women must not dress too sumptuously. Artisans should never walk abroad without signs of their trade; apprentices must be marked by their aprons and short hair. But these rules were coming under scrutiny.

Gideon remembered hearing of a strange, tense meeting that had taken place in a garden in Cambridge. Fairfax and his senior officers had met the King, now their prisoner, for an all-day discussion. One peculiarity was that they produced Cornet Joyce to exonerate Fairfax from involvement in the Holdenby abduction. Joyce was an extremely junior officer, yet when he was let loose to explain himself he argued with his sovereign fearlessly. Another issue that aroused much comment was that when Fairfax and Cromwell came into the King's presence, neither knelt.

The council met for almost a fortnight. Fairfax was absent, ill, for the first week. As well as much physical damage caused by battle-wounds, he had a history of painful gout and kidney stones. It was not suggested he ducked out of the debates. There were two points on which Thomas Fairfax was resolute: he deplored the autocratic behaviour of King Charles and he demanded justice for his soldiers. Ultimately, it was Fairfax who summoned this council.

Cromwell took the chair instead. It was a forum to discuss the fate of the whole kingdom, so several civilian Levellers, foremost among them John Wildman, were allowed to join the meeting. Any officers who wished to do so could attend, together with the four Agitators from each regiment. Almost 150 men had congregated. Many did not speak, but all heard the discussions.

Pressed in behind several rows of spectators, Gideon could see mainly the backs of men's heads and only part of the conference table; the faces of those seated were often hidden from him by the high crowns and sweeping brims of their hats. How many great oak tables, he wondered, had army officers sat around gravely in conference? How many battered inn-boards had hosted radical leaders as they midwived revolutionary ideas? He was impressed by the lack of subservience here. The future of England had already been argued, chewed, wrested from tradition and superstition by countless groups of thoughtful people. He found it striking how many at this council spoke fearlessly as individuals and how genuinely those of all ranks struggled to find answers. Soldiers spoke for themselves, not cowed by even their most senior officers.

After three-hour prayer-meetings, the debates were long and intense, continuing into the night. Sometimes Gideon squeezed from the room to seek natural relief. Outside, he shook his long legs and stretched his back while he tried to clear his head. Other men smoked, though not many; that was a filthy cavalier habit. Nobody stayed out long. Everyone was eager not to miss anything important. Hardly anyone left Putney. Only once did Thomas Rainborough disappear, explaining the next afternoon that he had been ill and so had ridden to London overnight to see his doctor. It was thought he had really been consulting radical civilians.

Most members of the council came with fixed opinions, though they were willing to hear other points of view; occasionally someone retracted. The language was plain, but speakers thought on their feet and syntax sometimes suffered. They responded to what they heard. They struggled to develop their own ideas. There were quarrels and rebukes; there were brief apologies. Men spoke from their hearts. They grappled with concepts that went far beyond their original grievances. Their agenda was to decide what they had been fighting for and how they wanted to live in peacetime. That took them into fundamental questions about the rights of man.

Although Cromwell and Ireton tried to confine discussion to the points raised in *The Declaration of the Army* (which Ireton wrote), they were soon pressurised by Wildman and others into having *The Agreement of the People* (which Wildman wrote) read out and discussed. *The Agreement* was, by seventeenth-century standards, a terse paper, claiming in a few short clauses *'that as the laws ought to be equal, so they must be good, and not evidently destructive to the safety and well-being of the people'*. It ringingly concluded with *'These things we declare to be our native rights'*: the rights and rules for government for which the soldiers had fought, but which endless negotiation with the King threatened to deny them.

Henry Ireton thought the agreement's fundamental proposals were unrealistic, although he said so only carefully: 'I confess, there are plausible things in it, and there are things really good in it. There are those things that I do with my heart desire; and there are those things I would not oppose, that I should rejoice to see obtained.'

This was the first time Gideon had encountered Ireton and he took against him. He did not care for his neat-featured, cat-like face, his secretive temperament or his cool, clever, untrustworthy intellect. Ireton was Oxford-educated and a former lawyer at the Middle Temple, a man who worked so hard to create a workable constitution that he often wrote late into the night and forgot to eat. Every time Ireton twitched his whiskers and pronounced what his conscience would or would not accept, Gideon Jukes's hackles rose. This was despite Ireton's Puritanism and Gideon's approval of how Ireton had worked tirelessly as the army's theoretical pen-man.

*　*　*

Edward Sexby was there. Gideon exchanged no words with him. Sexby was too busy, demanding to widen the agenda. On the very first day he summed up the soldiers' dilemma. 'We sought to satisfy all men, and it was well; but in going about to do it, we have dissatisfied all men. We have laboured to please a king and I think, except we go about to cut all our throats, we shall not please him . . .'

God might be fighting with them, but time was against them. It was said − and was a genuine fear even in that victorious army − that if they delayed too long in discussion, they would lose the initiative so the King would have them all hanged. Many still saw themselves as rebels. Gideon Jukes, for one, ruefully remembered hearing how the Earl of Manchester had grumbled after the second battle of Newbury, 'The King need not care how oft he fights. If we fight a hundred times and beat him ninety-nine times, he will be King still. But if he beat us once . . . we shall be hanged; we shall lose our estates; our posterities be undone.' Even after Naseby, those words had a carrying power. At the time, Cromwell had stormed back, 'If this be so, why did we take up arms?' − which remained an active question.

Citing urgency, Colonel Rainborough argued that reaching a settlement for the future was more important than wasting effort trying to decide what 'engagement' they had had in the past. But Sexby kept plugging away that a contract had existed when they took up arms: 'We have engaged in this kingdom and ventured our lives, and it was all for this: to recover our birthrights and privileges as Englishmen.'

And what are my birthrights and privileges? wondered Gideon Jukes, only a little satirically.

As the Council of the Army deliberated it for him, Ireton clashed seriously with Rainborough and the radicals. What was the Englishman's birthright? As a lawyer Ireton tried rather clumsily to define it: 'their very being born in England − that we should not seclude them out of England, that we should not refuse to give them air and place and ground, and the freedom of the highways and other things, to live amongst us.' He conceded this applied to any man born in England, even though his status at birth gave him nothing of what Ireton called 'the permanent interest of this kingdom'.

'Permanent interest' could only be defined one way by men of Ireton's class. It really meant property, and that was a divisive area. At the conference, the gap between men of property and men with none became very apparent. To vote, a man had to own a freehold with an annual value of forty shillings. For Ireton, this qualification was essential. To earn the right to make decisions about the country, he believed a man should physically own a stake in it: ground, land, buildings, or at the very least membership of a trade guild. To this Colonel Rainborough passionately objected. 'I do hear nothing at all that can convince me, why *any* man that is born in England ought not to have his voice in election.' Rainborough's argument was that all Englishmen were subject to English laws, so therefore should have a say in what the law was. He snarled bluntly at Ireton: 'To the thing itself: property in the franchise: I would fain know how it comes to be the property of *some* men, and not of others.'

Gideon Jukes restrained a cheer.

There was much discussion of why the franchise had traditionally contained exclusions. It was agreed that servants, apprentices and beggars had been denied the vote because they were dependent on masters or givers of alms, who could exert influence. Nobody doubted the stubborn independence of the British workforce, but in that hierarchical society men in power believed they had the right to specify how people who depended upon them behaved. At the time elections were public; there was no secret ballot.

Ireton eventually won the argument for keeping a distinction, perhaps because even the humblest soldier needed someone to sneer at. Servants and beggars made good targets.

A man called Cowling, whom Gideon presumed to be a younger son, kept hammering at it: 'Whether the younger son have not as much right to the inheritance as the eldest? . . . There are men of substance in the country with no voice in elections. There is a tanner in Staines worth three thousand pounds, and another in Reading worth three horse-skins. The second has a voice; the first, none.'

As Henry Ireton bogged himself down trying to answer, Gideon rubbed his chin, stultified by the drone of his voice. With over a hundred men crammed in together, the chancel was extremely warm. Some shifted about, some cleared their throats. The style of the debates was conversational but that had drawbacks. Too many were poor at putting words together, even when their ideas were good. They came from all over the kingdom and all spoke with their local accents, each man distrusting anything that was said in other accents than his own. To a Londoner like Gideon, even other cities – York, Bristol, Warwick, Cambridge, Newcastle – were country huddles, and suspect.

Still a ramrod of self-belief, Ireton dragged to a stirring conclusion: 'A man ought to be subject to a law, that did not give his consent, but with this reservation, that if this man do think himself unsatisfied to be subject to this law, he may go into another kingdom!'

Many heads nodded. Telling foreigners where to go, thought Gideon, who had encountered his share of overseas traders in London, was sure to revive a sluggish audience. To stand firm against aliens' duplicity, their encroachments on trade and their unspeakable dress-sense was as much Englishmen's birthright (Englishmen felt) as air, space, or passage on the highways . . .

The subject widened to defining liberty. 'If we can agree where the liberty and freedom of the people lies, that will do all,' said Rainborough.

Sexby took the cue: 'There are many thousands of us soldiers that have ventured our lives. But it seems now, that except a man hath a fixed estate in this kingdom, he hath no right in this kingdom. I wonder we were so much deceived. If we had not a right to the kingdom, we were mere mercenary soldiers.' A murmur of support rose among the bare-headed soldier Agitators. 'I shall tell you my resolution: I am resolved to give my birthright to none.'

If there was any point in his knowledge of Edward Sexby when Gideon Jukes admired the man, this was it. There was one thing spoken to this effect: that if the poor and those in low condition were given their birthright, it would be the destruction of this kingdom. I do think the poor and meaner of this kingdom have been the means of the *preservation* of this kingdom. And now they demand the birthright for which they fought.'

That statement of Sexby's was reinforced by Thomas Rainborough, the most senior officer to support such ideas. He now made his own defining speech:

'I think that the poorest he that is in England hath a life to lead, as the greatest he. And therefore truly, sir, I think it's clear that every man that is to live under a government ought first by his own consent to put himself under that government. And I do think that the poorest

*man in England is not at all bound in a strict sense to that govern-
ment that he hath not had a voice to put himself under.'*

These were challenging principles, and they were too strong for the
army's leadership. In a military force, which relied on tight discipline,
allowing independence to all ranks was doubly dangerous. For the first
three days of the debates Gideon, as a printer, had particularly noticed
that William Clark, one of the civilian secretaries to Sir Thomas Fairfax,
was present in his robe and skullcap, furiously taking down verbatim
whatever was said. Subsequently, he took fewer notes and these were
only fragmentally published. In the end, news of the debates was censored
altogether. Gideon heard that Cromwell had the last transcripts formally
destroyed. At the same time, checks were tightened up and since Gideon
was not an Agitator, he felt it best to return to his regiment.

After the 5th of November, Fairfax, who had recovered from his
illness, took over the chair. A committee was formed to co-ordinate all
the papers under discussion, a committee which included both
Rainborough brothers, Sexby, Cromwell and Ireton. Thomas Rainborough
took time out to visit the Leveller John Lilburne in the Tower of London,
their first meeting. It supposedly lasted for two hours and led the
Royalist spy at the Tower, Sir Lewis Dyve, to inform the King that
Rainborough was likely to become head of an army faction that would
purge Parliament to further the Levellers' ideals. Thomas Rainborough
began to be seen as a dangerous man.

The committee, though drawn from all sides, produced a report which
was practical but made compromises. However, by then it was too late.
From the sidelines, anonymously, John Wildman counselled dolefully,
'Beware, that ye be not frightened by the word *anarchy*, unto a love of
monarchy, which is but the gilded name for *tyranny* . . .' The deep differences between the soldiers and the chief officers of the army had led
to the officers being nicknamed 'Grandees', a sneering title which implied
these select beings had got above themselves. The Agitators were writing
sadly to their comrades, complaining that 'we find many at the
Headquarters obstructing and opposing our proceedings'. Fairfax
decided that the Agitators were divisive and disorderly. He sent them
back to their regiments. The situation was diffused by appointing yet
another new committee, to draft a remonstrance which was to be
approved by the regiments at an army review.

So the Putney Debates were ended. For Gideon Jukes those discussions were more thorough than he had feared, although they achieved far less than he had hoped. Still, to the end of his days he would remain exhilarated simply to have been there, to have heard ideals of equality so openly and earnestly discussed.

Grandee or not, in a firm personal plea to Parliament, Fairfax repeated his many previous calls to redress the army's lawful grievances and those of the people. He offered ways in which it could be done. He suggested that church lands be sold to provide the soldiers' pay. Then he threatened that unless discipline was restored, he would give up his command. It was a serious threat, aimed as much at his men as at Parliament. The soldiers were genuinely devoted to Fairfax and Parliament respected him.

With mutiny imminent, for the promised army review, Fairfax and Cromwell insisted that the troops be divided into three manageable groups, instead of the mass rendezvous the Agitators wanted. At Corkbush Field, near Ware, Fairfax brought the first seven regiments together. The Levellers saw this as their moment to co-ordinate the army in support of their cause. The civilians John Wilding and Richard Overton were in Ware town, sweating with anxiety over the outcome. For them it went badly wrong.

At the start, Colonel Rainborough presented Fairfax formally with *The Agreement of the People*, together with a petition. Rainborough had hoped for a large civilian turn-out, including thousands of Spitalfield weavers. None appeared. Nor was there a mass revolt by the troops. Even his own Leveller colleagues let him down. Neither Sexby nor Rainborough's brother William lent him any assistance. Stranded, Rainborough became hesitant and was easily waved aside.

Fairfax took charge. Characteristically fearless, he rode around and addressed each regiment in turn. Commanding his men's loyalty was his special quality. They loved him and they trusted him. Promises from him to live and die with them in prosecution of their just demands were immediately believed. Discipline was restored.

Two further regiments did then appear uninvited, with copies of *The Agreement of the People* stuck in their hats defiantly. Fairfax soon won around one of these rebellious regiments, leaving only the most radical. This had been the regiment of Colonel Robert Lilburne (brother of the

Leveller John), though the men had been in open revolt for several weeks; they had driven away their officers, soldiers had been killed, an officer had lost a hand, and at Ware they stoned an officer of another regiment. Fairfax ordered these rowdies to remove the papers from their hats. They refused. Fairfax and senior officers, including Cromwell, then rode in among them, pulling out the papers. The regiment submitted.

Ringleaders were arrested. Eight soldiers were court-martialled on the spot, five were pardoned, three cast lots to survive and one was shot at the head of the regiment. The remainder were instructed to tear up their copies of *The Agreement*; they did it meekly, complaining that they had been 'misled by their officers'. Offending officers were to be court-martialled. Thomas Rainborough was packed off to Westminster to be dealt with by Parliament; he was ordered not to go to sea as vice-admiral until the matter had been investigated.

Two further army reviews, at St Albans and Kingston, passed off peacefully. Parliament thanked Fairfax and promised to uphold his requests for redress of grievances. Some regiments made declarations of loyalty to him, Colonel Okey's dragoon officers being particularly unctuous.

One reason the army capitulated was that the political situation changed. When the Agitators at Putney demanded to abolish the monarchy, King Charles took fright. Claiming that the Levellers intended to murder him, the King escaped from Hampton Court.

Chapter Forty-Four

Pelham Hall: 1646–47

Against her expectations, the ending of the siege of Oxford brought Juliana Lovell a period of happiness as a mother and wife. For a short time she feared that Orlando had left England. Prince Rupert sailed to France; his brother Maurice to the Netherlands. At this point, the contempt Lovell had always felt for Rupert's generalship, so often openly expressed, acted against him. He knew he had no chance of his name being put on the list of friends who received passports; he would be thanked for his service and told to save himself. Although Juliana did not immediately know it, Lovell decided to remain in England.

Being Lovell, he wasted no time on complaints. Without telling Juliana (though he did leave her a tender letter − albeit only a paragraph) he found an opportunity to escape from Oxford. After the New Model Army arrived, she had to submit to interrogation. She threw herself into the role of long-suffering wife, abandoned to her fate by a delinquent husband; she managed to bite her lip, while looking frightened but courageous. She did not need to weep; sensitive to upset, both her children were screaming so loudly in the kitchen that they were visibly disturbing the officer who questioned Juliana in the small parlour. 'And when did you last see your husband?'

She played simple. 'When he went out for a scuttle of logs and never came in again.'

'*When?*'

'Certainly last Thursday week. I had my blue gown on, with the rent in the hem, and I do remember the meat was overdone at dinner . . .'

Clearly this prattling woman posed no danger. Equally clearly, she could not be allowed to continue to occupy such a grand house.

'Oh! Will you turn me out on the streets with my little ones?'

'Have you no friends to go to?'

'I am an orphan. My foolish husband has been denounced by his good Parliamentarian family. I was married just as the war began and I have never known a settled life or the normal joys of peace.'

'Well, there will be peace now!' the captain assured her sanctimoniously, as he quartered a large number of his soldiers in her house.

Enduring the enemy in her home was a bad experience. Fortunately it did not last. To Juliana's amazement, Lovell reappeared in St Aldate's, without any explanation. She had to stop him losing his temper at the New Model Army soldiers, but by warning him he was on a wanted list, she managed to keep him hidden. She wondered how the subterfuge could continue; however that was not Lovell's plan. Wanting to use his family as a cover, he had come to fetch them. While the soldiers were out on duty, he produced a cart onto which with all-too-easy furtiveness he began to load their possessions. They owned more than when they arrived in Oxford as newlyweds. As well as purchases and the results of Lovell's plundering, they had the McIlwaines' Continental furniture.

'And damme, whose terrible tuck is this?' Lovell had discovered a sword under their bed. It was the blade he had picked up at Birmingham. 'Have you taken a half-baked forgetful lover I don't know about?'

'You yourself gave it me for my protection, dearest.' Juliana had been hoping to leave it behind. Whether or not he remembered the weapon, Orlando grunted and insisted that they bring it with them. He made a few feints with the blade, and shuddered fastidiously before packing it away.

'You must be curious about our sudden move,' Orlando then acknowledged to Juliana, as she and her maid Mercy Tulk manhandled a court cupboard out of the back door.

'Oh, I fully understand,' his wife murmured, controlling her breath and her sense of injustice as her husband merely busied himself counting dining chairs. The cupboard had bruised Mercy's hip and fallen on Juliana's foot. 'Were it night, this would be a moonlit flit.'

Lovell looked put out.

He had found them somewhere to live, a small farmhouse on the estate of a Royalist, Sir Lysander Pelham of Pelham Hall in Sussex. Mercy Tulk refused to go with them, preferring to stay in the town she knew; she would return to her old mistress, the midwife. Whatever happened to faithful servants who would travel with you anywhere? wondered Juliana, though she knew the answer.

They then lived in Sussex for over a year. Disillusioned by Royalist failure, or so he said, Lovell played no part in the last flares of resistance that Fairfax and the New Model mopped up in the West and Wales. The King was at Newcastle, then Holdenby House. So long as Charles toyed with agreeing to impose Presbyterianism, he only antagonised Lovell. Lovell hated any authoritarian government.

'Should you then join this new radical movement, dearest? Become a Leveller?'

He roared with indignation at that too.

Once the Levellers seemed to be holding sway in the Parliamentarian army, Juliana hardly dared bring a news-sheet into the house. Lovell procured them anyway at the nearest market town, winding himself into a fury over the numerous reports of Remonstrances and Declarations, like a man picking at a half-healed scab, unable to leave it alone. 'Damme, I know my father and my brother Ralph will go into ecstasies at this fantasy of birthrights.'

'I believe the Levellers claim we are all born equal under God. Would you not like to have natural parity with Ralph?' asked Juliana wickedly.

'Sweetheart, I am equal to Ralph any day!'

'You have not suffered like him.'

'Ah, Juliana, do not hold my luck in the field against me. Estates cannot be divided up; it would diminish them.' This was an intriguing glimpse of Lovell as the scion of landed gentry. He had no bitterness; he shrugged and made his own way. That he went off abroad at only sixteen to do it was simply precocious. The pity was that he broke with his family. Their differences were almost nothing to do with politics, though Lovell was becoming more and more the dedicated Royalist and the next phase of his career would confirm that.

Sir Lysander Pelham, their landlord and patron, looked like a barrel on legs, though some of it was due to enormous folds of clothing on a man with short thighs. He wore a huge hat with a sweeping brim, burgeoning with white ostrich feathers, and rough-hewn cavalry boots of enormous width, over which he was prone to tripping, especially when in sack. This was most of the time. Calling for a cup of sack was the noble Lysander's idea of conversation. When he wanted to sound cosmopolitan he roared for a *gobletto di sachietti* – a phrase he claimed as his own invention, proudly holding the opinion that the English knew more about foreign languages than the foolish foreigners who spoke them.

Among country squires, Sir Lysander did verge on sophistication; he possessed rags of Latin, Greek and several European tongues, knew a quarter of a treatise on mathematics and a glimmer of astronomy, was haunted by memories of books he had half-read twenty years ago, and had once met Sir Francis Bacon (who was by then extremely elderly and mistook him for a cook). Sir Lysander had a heart of gold – though, he claimed, very little money. Seven generations of Pelhams had spent their lives in royal service, adroitly dodging all changes of religion and monarch so that not one ever fell out of favour or was beheaded. By never entertaining any monarch at the Hall, they also managed not to go bankrupt, though since it never received extravagant modernisation to please royalty, their home did now look old-fashioned and rundown.

When the civil war began, Sir Lysander chose his side in the same spirit as Sir Ralph Verney, who had famously explained:

'. . . for my part I do not like the quarrel, and do heartily wish that the King would yield and consent to what they desire; so that my conscience is only concerned in honour and in gratitude to follow my master. I have eaten his bread and served him near thirty years, and will not do so base a thing as to forsake him.'

Lysander had devoted himself to the Royalist cause from the day King Charles set up his standard at Nottingham. When the royal standard fell down that stormy night and everyone else hid away in their lodgings, the Sussex knight had stood grappling with the pole and striving to hold the soaking wet flag upright for two hours, notwithstanding the rain and darkness and the fact that his cries for sack to sustain him went unheeded. Once he recovered from the ague he caught that dark night, he fought valiantly at every skirmish and battle that presented itself before his regiment – which Lovell described to Juliana as 'flybitten as any other farming tenants mounted on carthorses' – until his great faithful charger lay down exhausted at Naseby. Weeping, Sir Lysander then announced, 'If my dear Smudge can no longer bear me, it is a sign of God's will that I must retire from the fray. Henceforth I shall support my beloved sovereign only with my prayers.'

He was a widower. The Pelham line would die out. All four of Sir Lysander's sons – Phillip, Jeremy, Hengist and Little Barty, who was only fifteen – had perished fighting for the King. Juliana suspected that Lovell was hoping to ingratiate himself so he might be made the knight's heir. If so, he had reckoned without Sir Lysander's forthright daughters, Bessy and Susannah, not to mention their husbands. The girls arrived in carriages from different directions, each nursing an infant at the breast and towing a cowed spouse. 'Pulled by the nose!' muttered Sir Lysander to Lovell. 'I would get more spunk from Hercules and Ioleus.'

Hercules and Ioleus were his two white-faced bullocks, all he had left of a once-great herd after comprehensive plundering by one army and another. His trees were felled, his horses and cattle stolen, his palings broken down, his barns raided and his house robbed out, with even the pillows slit open and their feathers scattered over half the county. The two bullocks had been somehow left behind and became rather close friends. Sir Lysander explained to Juliana that they had lofty ancient Greek ideals and earthy ancient Greek habits. 'The love between males, which is unselfish, philosophical – and requires from the parties some adaptability in performance.'

Juliana cast her eyes down. 'I never heard of this before!'

'Then you never were in military quarters, madam.'

Untrue. Juliana thought back pensively to when Fairfax's New Model Army shared her house in Oxford. All she remembered were constant filth from muddy boots, queues day and night for the overflowing privy, endless demands for bread and butter and the men's tireless stares of disapproval for her and her little household. They kept Mercy and her out of the kitchen while they let the fire go out. When they wanted to make Juliana feel a sinful malignant, they piously sang psalms for hours, once trapping her son Tom in the room with them, until he bit a sergeant. The worst of it all had been the necessity to endure what was done. To complain risked more bad behaviour and uncertain official reprisals.

Now life was better. Although Orlando, who was ostensibly the knight's estate manager, often came in with his boots on after tramping through farmyards, Juliana only had to mop up after his one pair. She had trained the boys to sit on a bench and pull off their dirty shoes when they were called in for dinner. Tom and Val ran free in chicken-run and orchard, while as a family who lived in their own accommodation, generally they were left to their own devices.

Attempts at household regulation still foundered on Orlando's free-booting habits. Juliana did sometimes wonder how such a man could have been a competent soldier and whether he saw their life here only as some kind of game. He came and went in disorderly bursts. He continued to excite their sons at inappropriate moments, taking them from Juliana's lap when she was quietly reading to them, then when he remembered business of his own needing attention, he abruptly passed them back to her, stirred up and fractious.

Thomas was approaching four, Valentine had had his first birthday just after Oxford fell and was now unsteadily toddling. When Sir Lysander took Orlando on a trip to London (for reasons that were not quite clear), toys for which both boys were far too young were brought back. Given the warlike period, it was no surprise when Tom received a gun and even Val was given a flat-cast pewter cavalier, pressed out of metal. 'I won't have my boys play with dolls, Juliana!'

'Valentine is still in baby skirts, Orlando; he loves his doll.'

'Nonsense. Look at the exquisite detailing. I had a ship of the same type, with rigging and cannon and a wavy waterline —'

Val's soldier, on which he soon cut his lip, was one-dimensional, whereas Tom's copper toy musket was fully modelled, with imitation scroll motifs and a tiny trigger. It really fired. For a mother it was a nightmare. The harder Juliana tried to hide the hideous little weapon, the more Orlando conspired with Thomas and made her out to be a spoilsport. Fortunately when the toy misfired, it was Orlando who had it and was burned in the hand — after which he banned the gun and gave it away to an ostler's child. (Juliana found the ostler and warned him of the danger, but he had been in the Earl of Essex's infantry and told her he had spiked it and made all safe; his sneer was telling.) Tom cried for four days. Juliana was left to deal with that.

Life, however, was better than she had ever known before. Perhaps qualms made her suspect she was only playing at house, yet Juliana knew how to savour even a situation she distrusted. Since she married five years before, she had been accustomed to insecurity. Now here they were, all alive and together. She took what she could. Even to be wrangling with her husband over whether carrots should be glazed with parsley butter was a joy, infinitely preferable to wondering which battle he was in and whether he was dead or wounded. All the same, she wondered if she must spend the rest of her days feeling that every place they lived in was just a temporary stop on the way to a remote destination they would never reach.

Juliana was curious about how her husband had discovered Sir Lysander Pelham, and why Pelham had taken him up. She could not quite square the tale that Orlando was acting as an estate manager – when there must be plenty of men in the countryside who were better qualified. Sir Lysander certainly liked to share a drink with Orlando in the evening and would sometimes summon him to the hall for that purpose – a source of contention when Orlando came home the worse for wear. Juliana said little, because they needed the patronage.

Other men visited the hall, presumably friends of Sir Lysander. Juliana never met them.

Finding an occupation posed a problem for her husband. He was not suited to endure penurious exile at the royal court in Paris. There would be no pay, he spoke no French, and hanging about a cold château on the fringes of Queen Henrietta's retinue would be as boring for him as for his wife, assuming she went with him – which was never discussed. A professional soldier all his life, either Orlando now must find himself a new war, or he must buckle down to a civilian occupation, untrained and inexperienced. That he had fallen into this niche at Pelham Hall was as lucky as it was surprising – all the more so since England was awash with disbanded and retired soldiers, all desperate for employment. All claimed to be obedient to discipline, good at man-management, trained in horse-husbandry, loyal, hardened, healthy and, naturally, expert shots. Once the New Model Army was disbanded, this could only grow worse. Sussex was a Parliamentarian county and would have many returning soldiers.

In truth Sir Lysander seemed almost fonder of Juliana than Orlando. He was a kindly man and an appreciator of women. Telling her about Hercules and Ioleus, the bullock lovers, occurred because he could see Juliana had more sense of humour than her husband and indeed enjoyed curiosities, unlike the rather straight Orlando. Orlando thought himself a lively fellow with a racy past, but Juliana was more observant and had a better ear for an anecdote. If she baked an almond tart, Sir Lysander would willingly discuss its finer points with her. If one of her boys had a chill, he suggested remedies. He took her on walks, showing her how to identify edible plants and mushrooms. She rapidly learned on those walks not to dally to be helped through gates or over stiles, lest she be pinned to them and forced to notice a virile erection that advertised why English knights of the shire generally had long pedigrees. Juliana was taller than the knight and had faster legs, should running for home become necessary. But it never really came to that. She was never afraid of him.

He knew that she read. Orlando had always boasted that his Juliana was a great reader. She thought of herself more as a needlewoman, but her father had taught her a love of books. Sir Lysander presented her with his late wife's book of recipes and household management. 'Well, it will save Bessy and Susannah tearing it in half.' He then brought her a First Folio Shakespeare one day, simply because he thought she would enjoy it. 'A gift.' He shrugged. 'I never look at it, but you will gain pleasure from it.'

She did. In particular, she discovered Shakespearean heroines: their wisdom, wit, grounded good sense and intrepid bravery, their love for men in all their mastery, mystery and folly. Had he noticed, Orlando Lovell might have thought it ominous that Juliana admired Viola, Rosalind and Harry Hotspur's rumbustious wife, Kate Percy. The ladies in cavalier love lyrics were lofty objects of devotion, yet they were praised more for their clothes, especially fine silks and lawns that lay awry as if tumbled by lovers, than for their readiness to climb into britches, taunt men and take on fate. In the civil war, even the doughty matrons who defended castles were seen as handy to have, in order to preserve an absent husband's home, yet unnatural.

Like many extremely conservative men, once Sir Lysander Pelham found a girl he suspected was equal to anything, he soon developed an affectionate twinkle. He was even struck by Juliana's ability to tolerate and handle the sometimes tricky Orlando Lovell. Sir Lysander never commented on that; he was a gentleman, except in the vicinity of gates or stiles, where he believed a countryman had a blanket exemption from the rules of etiquette.

Eventually Juliana found out why her husband had been brought here. Orlando Lovell and Sir Lysander Pelham were in deep conspiracy.

Chapter Forty-Five

Carisbrooke, Isle of Wight: 1647–48

Juliana had become aware, almost subconsciously, that although the King's cause was waning, loyal supporters still worked tirelessly for him. Some of his private circle stayed close. After leaving Oxford, Sir John Ashburnham accompanied the fugitive King on his wanderings and his journey to the Scottish camp. When the New Model Army took possession of the King, they treated Charles respectfully and allowed him whichever royal servants he pleased; Ashburnham resumed attendance on his master at Hampton Court. Two other men assisted the King's flight. Sir John Berkeley was a great favourite of Queen Henrietta Maria and had been intermediary with Parliament. The third courtier, the most effective, was William Legge.

'Honest Will' was a close friend and confidant of Prince Rupert. He had played an energetic part in Royalist activities in Oxford and, despite the King's fury after Rupert's surrender of Bristol, Legge was quickly reinstated in favour. Parliament had allowed him to join the King at Holdenby House as Groom of the Bedchamber. At Oxford, Legge had lodged in one of the largest houses in St Aldate's, near the royal court and only a few doors away from the McIlwaines. Will Legge was known by sight to the Lovells. And as Juliana finally realised, Orlando Lovell must be known to him.

She began to understand what was going on in late November 1647. It was the evening of Tom's fourth birthday. Plans had been laid to cook pancakes, a great favourite with the little boy. Juliana had prepared batter, oranges and sugar, she was ready to heat up the frying pan and only waiting for her husband to join in the little celebration. At the crucial moment Orlando disappeared.

Tom was waiting, his face eagerly alight, though his lip was beginning to tremble on the verge of tears. As her child visibly prepared himself for the collapse of his birthday, Juliana grieved for the effect civil war had imposed on him. Tom was not surprised this had happened. A four-year-old should never be so ready for disappointment.

She discovered Orlando had gone to Pelham Hall. For once, she lost her temper. She stormed off there herself. She burst in on Lovell and Sir Lysander, ready to berate them like a sectarian zealot for their fecklessness and cruelty in arranging what she presumed was a drinking spree. Orlando was lucky she had not brought the heavy pancake pan to beat in his brains.

Curiously, there was no sack in sight. It gave Juliana pause. The two men were sitting together in the library: sober, serious, intent upon a letter. Lovell was reading it out aloud, because the knight's eyesight was poor even with spectacles. They sat either side of the fire, leaning forward intently on their carved, cane-backed chairs as they spoke in low voices. Lovell seemed to be consulting a cipher sheet.

His instant reaction was to push all the papers into his coat pocket. Then, for some reason, both men decided to include Juliana. Perhaps they simply could not bear to break off at that moment. Clearly there were secrets afoot, and possibly they could not remember how much or how little they had revealed before.

Lovell swiftly motioned her to sit. Thoroughly intrigued, Juliana dropped into a chair. She smoothed her skirts and glared at him. He muttered that they had a letter about the King; when she looked puzzled, he mentioned Will Legge. Whether Legge himself wrote this letter was never explained.

Juliana listened in amazement as she was told about the King's escape from Hampton Court. Using his sickly young daughter Elizabeth for cover, he had requested that his guards be moved further from his chamber, because the trampings of their heavy boots disturbed the child at night. Astoundingly, his jailors had agreed. 'Apparently the New Model Army's fighting hearts are tender towards pale, fair-haired little princesses!'

'That would be generous.' Juliana's mind was in turmoil. She was trying to grasp just what her husband's role was.

'Generous incompetence!' snarled Lovell.

Since it had been suggested that King Charles should try to find refuge in Essex, where Royalist support remained strong, in his wilful way he decided to make instead for the island of Jersey, in the opposite direction. Sir Lysander explained to Juliana, 'Ashburnham had also mentioned Sir John Oglander's house in the Isle of Wight. There the King could be concealed while the governor of the island was sounded out. If he was not sympathetic, our fugitive could take ship for France – although Ashburnham felt this might dismay supporters and encourage the enemy . . . But the Isle of Wight it is, and Lovell and I are sorry for it.'

With Will Legge, the King slipped away from Hampton Court, down a backstair and through the palace gardens. Arrangements began well; at Thames Ditton, a boat was waiting to row the escapees across the river. Ashburnham and Berkeley stood ready on the far bank with horses. The party galloped away in the night. No pursuit followed. Colonel Whalley, who had been in charge of the King, noticed that the bedchamber seemed too quiet, but its door was locked so the agitated Whalley strode through countless other rooms in the rambling old Tudor palace before he managed to reach the royal quarters and discovered the King had gone. Only a discarded cloak and the King's pet greyhound, whimpering pathetically, remained.

'But from then on,' growled Lovell to Juliana, 'a monkey could have arranged things better. They lost themselves for hours in Windsor Forest and took the wrong route past Farnham. At Bishop's Sutton they reached an inn where a servant was waiting with a change of horses – he came out to tell them that the local Parliamentarians were using the inn as a meeting place that night –'

'Debating the future of the monarchy?' Juliana scoffed. Her male companions bristled, then became sheepish. She forced herself to calm down. 'There is worse?'

'A debacle,' Lovell confessed. 'They made for the coast, where Ashburnham had allegedly arranged a ship for Jersey. They were so late, in the dark he could not find the ship. They panicked. The King was dumped –'

Sir Lysander grunted a protest.

'There were search parties out, and all the ports had been closed,' snarled Lovell, whose high opinion of himself as an organiser made him doubly scathing of this dangerous mess. 'His Majesty was *deposited* at a house of the Earl of Southampton at Titchfield, this side of the Solent.

I can hardly speak the next damned wickedness. That poltroon Berkeley goes across to the Isle of Wight, where the governor is a certain Hammond. The courtiers have convinced themselves Hammond will be sympathetic – why, in the name of God, should they think that? Hammond is John Hampden's cousin, fought under Essex, a fixed Cromwellian, a rabid puritan!'

'Calm yourself!' murmured Sir Lysander ineffectually.

'The ludicrous Berkeley excels himself. He blurts out to Hammond that he has somebody special secreted at the earl's house. *"Oh Governor Hammond! You will never guess who is nearby!"* Hammond not only guesses, he gallops straight to the house –'

'With soldiers?' asked Juliana.

'Of course! He swiftly took the King into custody. Whipped him across to Cowes and installed him in Carisbrooke Castle, which lies right in the heart of the island, terrifically defended. Even if His Majesty ever escapes the castle, he cannot get off the Isle of Wight. Anyone who tries to come to him will be spied upon as they make the crossing. Oh imagine how fast messengers rode to inform Parliament of this triumph!'

Juliana had rarely heard Orlando so angry. His voice squeaked like an old gate, hoarse with frustration. She could see the implications: 'At Hampton Court, confinement was comparatively civilised, but now the King will be securely barred up.' She gave Sir Lysander and Orlando a straight look. 'Ashburnham, Berkeley and Legge . . . And are *others* working for His Majesty?'

'It is best you do not know,' Sir Lysander told her with a kindly manner. She found it patronising. He could probably tell.

'Can I not be trusted?'

'Nobody can be trusted, sweetheart,' declared Orlando. Juliana froze him with a look. 'As soon as Colonel Hammond was brought to Titchfield, the King knew it was a fatal mistake – "Ah Jack, you have undone me!" he cried.' Lovell was skimming through the last sentences of their letter. 'He was dealing with idiots. Oh, listen! Ashburnham had a bright idea to put all to rights – he only offered to go downstairs to where Hammond was being given supper, and kill him! The King refused to countenance the deed.'

Sir Lysander pulled a face. 'One has to have standards.'

'It should never have come to that. It is *too serious!*' Lovell burst out, full of rage again. 'There should have been no risks, no mistakes, no compromises. Nothing left to chance. No thinking on the wing. No damned incompetence by pretty dancing-master courtiers of the Queen's! Will Legge should have been in charge of the escape, with a band of decent soldiers and a plan that allowed no slips.'

'The King was highly nervous,' Sir Lysander soothed him. 'He needed faces he knew. Even the jailors were more likely to relax their guard if they only saw familiar attendants.'

Lovell muttered something inaudible, clearly an obscenity.

After Lovell glanced through the letter one final time, he destroyed it. He flung it into the fire, but controlled his annoyance and carefully ensured with a poker that all the pages were consumed. In the light of the rising flames, Sir Lysander looked less tipsy and more adroit than Juliana had ever seen him; he announced that they must digest this news carefully. Tomorrow he and Lovell would speak further. Juliana now understood there was some much bigger conspiracy afoot.

Lovell returned with her to the farmhouse, saying no more. Juliana also remained silent, not trusting herself to talk.

Now the contrite father, Lovell threw himself into entertaining Tom. He tossed pancakes amidst much genuine merriment, slathering them with orange juice, feinting a near-miss with a flying crêpe. He played a full part in the birthday celebration. There was no sign that this was a disappointed plotter who had much to think about. Juliana realised that had she not gone to the Hall, she would never have learned Orlando was so close to the political crisis.

That night she tried to tackle him: 'You and I always believed in companionship, Orlando. A wife should share all her husband's secrets.'

'Were I able to speak freely, I should tell you all.' Begging had been fruitless. The need-to-know principle has caused many a domestic conflict. Safe people are excluded unnecessarily. Idiots and incompetents then break the confidence. 'They are not *my* secrets, sweetheart,' explained Orlando, disingenuously.

Juliana could not have watched him closer then, if she had suspected he had a mistress. When Lovell travelled to the Isle of Wight shortly afterwards, she was at least prepared. He, for once, did tell her he was going. She thought no better of him for that.

Juliana felt betrayed. It seemed their whole time at Pelham Hall had been arranged only to enable Lovell to work as a Royalist agent, close to his patron. He had had no real thought of giving her and the boys some family life, family life in which she had taken such delight but upon a false premise. Still, doggedly, she continued to pretend she and Lovell were as one. She offered to go to the Isle of Wight with him, taking the children, which might provide camouflage. Lovell made spurious excuses that his work for the King was too dangerous; he could not expose his dear family to risk. Juliana decided bleakly that he simply did not want them. She believed Orlando enjoyed the excitement and isolation. *He wants freedom to play on his own!*

Their year-long idyll abruptly ended. So too did Juliana Lovell's complaisance with her marriage, another casualty of the civil war.

Chapter Forty-Six

Carisbrooke to Goldsmiths Hall: 1648

Some stories of the King's captivity at Carisbrooke Castle were confided to Juliana by Sir Lysander Pelham. She knew that her husband was on the Isle of Wight at the end of 1647 and that he left in the early months of 1648. She was never told what part, if any, he played in the escape attempts. Not much, she thought. To give him credit, Lovell was competent. He would have managed better results.

The castle was a stalwart Norman motte-and-bailey affair, with stone walls, towers and a keep added to fortify it against possible invasion by the Spanish or the French. It made a strong prison but had never been used defensively. Nevertheless, it would be from here that King Charles launched the second civil war whilst, ironically, sanctioning a foreign invasion for his personal assistance.

At first the prison regime was lax, although his room did have barred windows, just as Royalist broadsheets depicted. They showed him looking out through the bars forlornly while wearing a full crown and a glimpse of ermine, which Juliana thought unlikely. The King's pursuits were those of a gentleman with endless leisure; she reckoned he would require smart, warm daywear which had plenty of room for movement, plus hat and gloves.

His carriage was brought over the Solent for taking the air; he went out sightseeing and even attended a funeral of a man he had never met. Colonel Hammond had a bowling green created in the castle for him. Reading material was available. As well as sermons, Latin for translation and Bacon's *Advancement of Learning*, Charles read Tasso and *The Faerie Queene*. Fiction should provide solace, but it was characteristic of the man to bury himself in romantic escapism just when he should have been most grounded in reality. Socially, his usher was busy. Political negotiators approached him gingerly. Isle of Wight gentry from time to time were permitted to kiss their sovereign's hand and, as Sir Lysander growled, 'piss themselves with the thrill of being in the same room as the blood royal'.

The courtiers who had assisted with the flight from Hampton Court stayed only briefly. Parliament ordered Will Legge's arrest. By January he had made his way to the Channel Islands though Juliana would learn later that he returned to the mainland to join Royalist activitists in Kent. Berkeley was again employed as a messenger from the Parliamentary generals to the King in April 1648, but he feared prosecution and thought it wise to retire abroad.

Royal servants of lower rank who had been left behind at Hampton Court faithfully followed what was now routine; they packed up trunks and traipsed after their master. He soon had his page, barber, tailor, coal-carrier and laundress; the laundress's assistant was one of several women who brought in letters from the Queen and supporters outside. Correspondence was passed to the King at dinner or hidden under carpets in his room. Royalist agents were everywhere – actually inside the castle or waiting ready to help in nearby towns, both on the Isle of Wight and the mainland. A flame-haired female devotee called Jane Whorwood, who had previously hung about Holdenby House, turned up in the Isle of Wight and affixed herself to the castle. The governor was too polite to send a woman packing – or preferred perhaps to keep her under observation.

Using guidance from the astrologer William Lilly, Jane Whorwood made numerous attempts to help the King escape. The stars proved unreliable on logistics: one plan was for the King to escape through the window bars, which Charles had tested for feasibility by poking his head out. The plan failed when his body would not follow (something he had not rehearsed) so, as the wind changed and his ship sailed away empty, he became ignominiously stuck. Jane Whorwood then fetched from London a consignment of aqua fortis, which was nitric acid; she spilled much of it on the long bumpy journey down to Hampshire though she managed to carry some, together with a file, as far as the King's stool-room. Her scheme was to weaken the window bars so they could be removed from their sockets. Unfortunately, the castle governor became aware what was going on and intervened. Other, wilder ideas were abandoned: to cut a hole in the ceiling of the King's bedroom; to fit him out in a crazy theatrical disguise; to set fire to a heap of charcoal stored near the royal chambers, as a diversion . . . As Colonel Hammond routinely uncovered these stratagems and routinely blocked them, he reduced the number of the King's attendants; after his barber was dismissed, Charles balked at having a Parliamentarian come anywhere near him with sharp implements, so he had to grow his hair.

Meanwhile in London a daring plan to free the King's second son, James, Duke of York, did come off. A woman called Anne Murray was enlisted by her lover, Colonel Bampfylde, to provide female clothing; after a convenient game of hide-and-seek, the young duke successfully bolted for freedom. Disguised in a dress with a crimson petticoat and fortified by Wood Street cake, he was whisked away to his mother in France, safe from being made a puppet-ruler in his father's stead.

As these ludicrous stories surfaced through Sir Lysander, Juliana became ever more annoyed with Lovell. *She* could have been just as willing, inventive and brave as those women. Her grandmother had worked for the court and although Juliana had never been compelled to declare formally whether or not she was a Royalist, she would certainly have made an indomitable partner. She shared Lovell's clear-eyed understanding of the King's faults and the limitations of the King's chosen advisers; her husband should have seen she could have done better. Juliana knew her own value; she thought Lovell knew it too. Being excluded left a chill in her heart.

Work was found for her, none the less. Early in 1648 Lovell wrote instructing her to go up to London, to face the notorious Committee for Compounding. Her task was to beg, plead, apologise, promise, rend hearts, screw favours and if needs be perjure herself in order to obtain the release of Lovell's property in Hampshire.

Sir Lysander sent her with a groom, and allowed her to live in his elegant London town house in Covent Garden. He had been a member of Parliament, though had ceased to take his seat at the Commons when the war began; as a result his London home was rather sparsely furnished and staffed – it had been ransacked in 1642 by Parliamentary officers. Juliana offered to organise an inventory of what survived and a list of work needed, in return for her keep.

Her departure for London was much approved by Bessy Sprott, née Pelham, who had recently come home to live at Pelham Hall because her husband died. The death of so young a man would once have been occasioned by pox or plague; nowadays, wounds were a more common cause. In fact Jack Sprott, the livelier of Sir Lysander's sons-in-law, died of an ague, caught on the malarial Essex marshes. It was a while before Juliana worked out what he had been doing there – Royalist plotting – and she reckoned his wife never did understand. The baffled Bessy returned to her childhood home, eager to annoy her sister by strengthening her hold over their father as gout and general bleariness took him towards the grave. Both sisters viewed Juliana's presence with jaundiced eyes. The more Sir Lysander admired Juliana, the more leery they became. Although entirely innocent, she was glad to leave.

She stayed in London for a month and a half, a time made the more tedious because she had left her children behind in Sussex. She had not realised how long this might take.

Delinquents had to present themselves at the Committee for Compounding of Malignants, which sat at Goldsmiths Hall. How appropriate! thought Juliana, as she became aware of how much money this committee was extorting. Successful appellants swore an oath not to bear arms against Parliament again, and they took the Covenant. They had to declare the full value of their estates; any misstatement or fudging rendered them liable to heavy fines. Juliana knew that the rates of assessment varied, depending on how strong a supporter of the King the victims were deemed to be. Sir Lysander, as an MP and a full colonel, had been fined half his estate. Lovell reckoned he might get away with the general rate, which was only a sixth.

Among Royalists there was much conferring about how to manage the committee. It was believed that sending a wife to plead was more likely to work than appearing in person. The more pregnant and sickly the wife looked, and the greater the number of her dependent children, the better. Lovell had written that he hoped he had left Juliana pregnant for this purpose; he had, but she suffered a miscarriage. 'Use your grief!' Bessy Sprott had advised her, which was cynical but sound.

Goldsmiths Hall was less than twenty years old, a large foursquare building with a lofty entrance, pillared and fanlighted in grandiose style. The monumental livery hall stood in the traditional heart of the City of London, occupying an enormous block between Foster Lane and Gresham Street. In close proximity to Guildhall and St Paul's, this was an area of great bustle and commerce, peopled by aldermen, clergymen, booksellers, jewellers and cut-purses. Juliana had lived in London for a while with her grandmother, though not since she was a child. The frenzy and noise now came as a shock.

Appellants had to mingle with goldsmiths and silversmiths bringing work to the Assay office, and the tough servants who acted as their bodyguards. When Juliana presented herself there was a queue, mainly of other women, most of them looking strained, some definitely viewing this occasion as beneath them. One extremely haughty lady in yards of black figured silk came stalking in, took a fraught look at the situation, then left again as if she could not demean herself. Juliana had been brought up to do whatever was necessary to survive. She quietly ascertained the system from a man she assumed to be a clerk, who nodded to the line of other supplicants. 'You will catch a strong whiff of lavender, for they have all dug into chests for finery, in order to seem more important . . . the sensible ones come looking as poor as possible.' His eyes lingered on Juliana; she had no finery to draw upon. 'You may present yourself first, madam.'

Despite this good start, the process was long and slow. The papers Juliana had obtained from the Hampshire committee the previous year were out of date; new enquiries had to be made about the rents. This was done by correspondence, but she needed to wait in London until answers came, and nobody seemed to hurry. Then there was a question whether, while he was a prisoner after Naseby, Lovell ever gave his parole, an officer's word that he would not try to escape. Records had gone missing. If he had not bound himself, escape was allowed and even admired; otherwise, Lovell had perjured himself fatally when he wriggled out of Lambeth Palace. Juliana stuck to her guns: 'My husband assured me particularly: he did *not* give his parole.' Did the committee read her thoughts as she wondered whether he had told her the truth?

'Where is your husband now, madam?'

Juliana saw she must fudge the fact that Lovell had been on the Isle of Wight. Fortunately, in news from Sussex she learned that Lovell had since transferred to 'an errand' in Kent. She could honestly deny any knowledge of what he was doing there, though she was starting to suspect. 'He works now; he is an estate manager for Sir Lysander Pelham, who has retired from all active support of His Majesty, due to old age, physical infirmity and heartbreak after losing all his sons in the late war.'

'Oh we know Sir Lysander Pelham!'

Not a good answer. After Sir Lysander was fined heavily, he refused to submit, but sued the tenants of his confiscated lands in the civil courts for rents they had paid to Parliament. He knew of other Royalists who had used the legal process in this way, some of whom won favourable rulings; this encouraged him. Both the courts and the members of Parliament who served on committees were so respectful of the law that they could be persuaded to uphold Royalists' claims. It was thwarting Parliament's plans to pay off the New Model Army using confiscated property – and it was embarrassing. Ruefully Juliana acknowledged that the situation worked against families like hers; Lovell had no resources to start risky lawsuits. If wealthier Royalists overturned decisions, larger fines would be levied on others.

As the weeks dawdled by, she began to fear that their request to compound would be refused. Then perhaps the question would be remitted to another, more shadowy body called the Treason Trustees, who met at Drury House. Lovell's chances there were nil. Juliana had been instructed not to court attention from that body. In her worst moments she dreaded finding out just why Lovell wished to be unobtrusive. His absences had always made her fearful, but now she grew more anxious about the consequences for her and the boys.

The Committee for Compounding liked to delay until they had made supplicants despairing and submissive. Juliana was now sick of looking humble. She was becoming resentful of the position in which Lovell had placed her. She had assumed he was comparatively unimportant but the degree of suspicion his name aroused was starting to alarm her. The committee seemed obsessed with where he was and why he was seeking to compound *now*. Thinking on her feet, Juliana fed them excuses about family needs and Orlando's desire to settle down. She managed to conceal her own despair at just how little he really wished for quietness and domesticity.

As she was constantly questioned about her husband's activities, Juliana scrutinised the news-sheets. Sir Lysander had told her, in strict confidence, that in December at Carisbrooke the King had formally signed an agreement with the Scots. Charles had committed to a promise that in return for an armed invasion to restore him to the throne, he would institute Presbyterianism for three years. He would then outlaw free-thinking sects, a colourful cliché collection of: *Anti-Trinitarians,*

Anabaptists, Antinomians, Arminians, Familists, Brownists, Separatists, Independents, Libertines and Seekers'. Although the 'Engagement' with the Scots had been secretly buried in a lead casket in the grounds of Carisbrooke Castle, Parliament discovered what had happened. They broke off all negotiations. Members passed a 'Vote of No Addresses', refusing any further contact. How the nation was settled would now be decided by Parliament alone – at least, it would be unless a new Royalist rebellion changed everything. Such a rebellion was in hand.

The King had been christened a Man of Blood by the New Model Army; he was proving it. The Scots began to prepare their invasion force. A countrywide new civil war was being co-ordinated by the King from Carisbrooke.

Dreading what it meant to her personally, Juliana noticed how even in London there was increasing Royalist support. Whether it was enough to achieve anything, she doubted. In a clampdown on troublemakers, John Lilburne and John Wildman had been arrested after addressing a large Leveller meeting in Smithfield, whilst a regiment of foot soldiers was now billeted in Whitehall to control Royalist demonstrations. By April the apprentices were rioting and the Lord Mayor took refuge in the Tower of London. As Juliana made her trips to Goldsmiths Hall, she was aware of the disturbed mood on the streets. Although she was missing her children, she was grateful she had left them in the security of Sussex. In mid-May she heard musket fire when pro-Royalist petitioners from Surrey and Essex tried to force their way into the House of Commons; guards who were pelted with missiles responded with bullets. Juliana heard that ten people were killed and a hundred more wounded.

Upheaval became country-wide. Rebellions began in Wales, where Parliamentary officers refused orders. In the north, the King's devoted supporter Sir Marmaduke Langdale took Berwick while Sir Philip Musgrove took Carlisle, in order to provide a clear invasion route for the Scots. They had been promised that the Prince of Wales would sail from Holland to join them. Rioting occurred in Norwich. Then throughout Kent – where Lovell was – a major uprising flared: Rochester, Sittingbourne, Faversham, Chatham, Dartford and Deptford were seized and the fleet was restive in the Downs, its anchorage off Kent. In May, nearby at Deal, a strange youth appeared, *on foot, and in an old black ragged suit, without any companions but lice'*. Keen locals welcomed this unlikely pretender, accepting his claim to be the Prince of Wales. Thomas Rainborough, then Parliamentary Vice-Admiral of the Fleet, rightly believed him to be an impostor, but the incident led to outright naval mutiny in which Rainborough was refused boarding of his own flagship. Although the sailors conceded he had been 'a loving and courteous colonel to them', they paid to send him (at the cost of sixpence) in a Dutch fly-boat, back to London with his wife and other relatives. The mutineers took nine warships and sailed to the Netherlands.

There were rumours that a large Royalist army, ten thousand men, had gathered in Kent. Juliana Lovell now believed Orlando was there, organising. If so, he probably wanted his estate back so he could sell or mortgage it to raise funds. He had deceived his wife, using her to achieve this for him, planning that if she succeeded, he would bankrupt them and destroy whatever inheritance their children might have had. Juliana seethed.

As the atmosphere in London became tumultuous, Juliana almost hoped the committee might refuse her plea. She wanted to return to Sussex. After a fruitless wait at Goldsmiths Hall one morning, she walked out for air and instead of taking her usual route to the bookshops around St Paul's, where she habitually window-shopped, her steps took her along Lothbury. It was a main thoroughfare, though notorious for its racket of metal-workers. She turned off for more peace into Basinghall Street, a narrow, winding cut-through that bent around Guildhall. From an overhead window, the measured notes of a tenor viol playing an air like a love song caught her attention. Attracted by the music, she entered a small print shop.

It was slightly dark and extremely busy. The great press dominated, with a tall desk for compositing. Papers were hung to dry on long wires. On the walls were large, faded publications, nailed up like posters, most of them about two years old as if someone had decorated the shop then: lists of two or three hundred victories ascribed to General Fairfax, surrounding large equestrian portraits of him or smaller busts of all the Parliamentary generals; memorials and elegies for the Earl of Essex, who had died in September 1646; she read: *Annals and most remarkable records of King Charles' reign . . . Wherein we may plainly see how the Popish, Jesuitical and Prelatical Malignant party have endeavoured the ruin of this*

church and kingdom but was by God's mercy most miraculously prevented . . .'
There could be no doubt where the printer's sympathies lay.

They were selling a news-sheet called *The Public Corranto*. Juliana
began to read the front page. The big-eared, buck-toothed apprentice
clearly thought her a time-waster. Deeply suspicious, he operated the
big press slowly as he watched her. He was eating slices of fruit pie
from a delft plate. In a corner, almost unnoticed at first, a good-looking,
dark-eyed woman in her late thirties was giving him a fractious look,
as if she wanted him to save the pie. She was stitching together
pamphlets; it was hard work, hardly a dainty thimble job. She had to
press down the eye of the needle on a piece of slate to force it through
the pages. Her fingers were red and sore, though she seemed to know
what she was doing.

Juliana approached and smiled. She preferred doing business with a
woman. They got into conversation, pleasantly enough, though both
were wary. Holding a copy of the *Corranto*, Juliana asked after the latest
news.

'Cromwell has been sent to Wales; the Lord General is taking men
to Kent. The Earl of Warwick has succeeded Rainborough as admiral
and gone to deal with the navy.'

'Do you think they will be successful?' Juliana asked, wondering what
would happen to Lovell. 'It sounds as if the King has very great support
now.'

'War will be short and brutal, so says Robert Allibone, the printer
here.'

'Your husband?'

'No, no!' The woman blushed, and seemed conscious of the apprentice listening in. Before she looked down quickly, she glanced up to the
ceiling, whence the sounds of the viol could still be heard, now playing
a fugue. 'My name is Anne Jukes.'

'You work here?'

'I run my husband's grocery business, while he is away.' *In the New
Model Army*, thought Juliana nervously. Then, looking at the woman,
and hearing that soulful music, she wondered on a whim, *Perhaps her
husband being away is convenient for her and she loves another . . .* 'I come
here to help with certain publications.'

Juliana nodded to the pamphlet Anne Jukes was now putting into
piles. 'Revolutionary publications?'

Anne had identified this customer as a Royalist. Long-faced, despondent women in faded gowns often came into the print shop alone, after they had taken a bruising in committees. 'In the City, women are allowed to think!' *And preach if we will, and make petitions, and pay our fees and join the Levellers . . .* 'This is a discussion of Leveller principles, for those who sympathise. Our new newspaper called *The Moderate* will start next month.'

Since it was so heavily implied that Juliana would not want a Leveller pamphlet, she bought it anyway, and also *The Public Corranto.* Surprised, the woman offered her a slice of pie; it was of her own making and extremely good. She told Juliana the recipe. As Juliana walked back to Goldsmiths Hall, she continued to wonder for whom at the print shop Anne Jukes had brought in the pie.

Astonishingly, right at that moment when it seemed as plain as day Lovell must be engaged in the Kent rebellion, the Committee for Compounding agreed a fine and gave him back his lands. Juliana had been authorised to arrange the fine through Sir Lysander's bank, so she spent the rest of the afternoon making arrangements; she obtained a certificate of exemption from sequestration and as dusk fell she left Goldsmiths Hall for the last time.

Approaching the town house, she was trying to remember Anne Jukes's recipe for sweet pastry until she had a chance to write it down. She became aware of a young woman keeping step with her, a little too close behind her shoulder. Juliana's purse was empty, though to lose the hard-won land certificate would have been tedious after months of work to get it, and she would have been even more annoyed to have *The Public Corranto* snatched before she had read it. She could see the front doorstep of Sir Lysander's house, which she knew was a dangerous position where many householders were mugged as they struggled with their keys. Abruptly, she turned round and stared out her shadower.

It was a thin, pale urchin, dressed in a ragged shawl over a dirty yellow petticoat. The creature affected innocence and walked off. A man who had been following *her* then caught up and spoke. Safe from the intended theft, Juliana lost interest.

Chapter Forty-Seven

Covent Garden: 1648

Her name was now . . . something new. Who needed a name? She worked alone these days, swooping about the arcades at twilight like a bat, hunting. She had made Covent Garden her roost, homing in on this grand place as ideal for her purposes.

The Italian piazza in the old convent kitchen garden of Westminster Abbey had been designed in 1632 by the King's surveyor, Inigo Jones, for the Earl of Bedford, one of the main conspiring aristocrats who organised the Long Parliament and the King's downfall. Despite growing antagonism between them, the King had been one of the chief supporters of this first experiment of town planning, with the creation of the first public square in London. The square was surrounded on two sides by tall terraced houses, intended for fashionable society – *'the habitations of Gentlemen and men of ability'*. To the west was the new church of St Paul, and to the south stood the existing mansion of the Bedford family, which faced onto the Strand, the major artery connecting the City of London with the court at Whitehall, or with Parliament at Westminster.

As with so many ambitious projects, money ran out. By the time Inigo was commissioned to build St Paul's Church, Lord Bedford ordered that he should make it no more expensive than a barn. The architect bravely responded, *'You shall have the handsomest barn in England!'*, but he had to endure further interference when William Laud, then Bishop of London, insisted that the church's altar should be on the east side, where an enormous Tuscan portico was designed as the main entrance. Two insignificant doors were added either side of it while a new entrance had to be made at the back, leading ignominiously from a small graveyard and a muddy field path.

Surrounding the piazza was a grid of straight roads, short but wide, quite unlike the winding lanes to which Londoners were accustomed:

King Street, Charles Street and Henrietta Street were named for royal patronage while Bedford Street, Russell Street, Southampton Street and Tavistock Street paid tribute to the earl's own family and connections.

People cannot be made to behave in accordance with a chart. The original grand plan failed in its lofty intentions. Despite the elegant housing for wealthy people, the square was a public area so undesirables rapidly colonised it. The presence of wealth was a lure for underworld skulkers of all sorts, who either provided the gentry with vice or simply robbed them. The famous vegetable and flower market began in a very minor way in the 1640s, before the Earl of Bedford capitalised on his investment with a full market permit; even the scatter of early stalls attracted both ordinary members of the public and criminals. The well-built new taverns in Inigo's beautiful streets instantly became a haunt of idlers, rakes and ne'er-do-wells. There were drunks. The drunks had fights. There were duels. At night the area had a noisy threatening quality which offended the refined householders beneath whose curtained sash-windows hubbubs took place. By 1648, the words 'Why do we pay our rents for this?' were uttered in strained aristocratic accents, and as soon as other, more peaceful private squares with greater security were built elsewhere, they superseded Covent Garden's attractions.

At the moment it still was a fine haven for a street urchin. She had unwary people to prey on and warm taverns to retreat to if she was in funds, which at first she was. Once her money ran out, the vegetable stalls reminded her of her upbringing; she knew how to chivvy or trick stall-holders into letting her have bruised or unsold wares. She went back to her childhood ways of looking out for dropped apples and carrots. To the huge piazza came strollers to jostle and steal from, with escape routes all over the place. She could leap the low wall that surrounded the central area, or dive away down uncluttered side streets. The noble arcades, with their round-topped Roman arches and sturdy brick pillars, provided opportunities to lurk. Designed to provide shade from the hot Italian sun, in England these Palladian corridors were shadowy and dank, with little street trade; unlit at night, they were full of menace.

Here the scavenger eked out her living, though with diminishing returns. She had soon wasted away all the funds she earned on the road with Jem Starling. She blew it on drink, or had her cash pilfered while she slept. Untutored in money-management, she was easily conned out of precious coins by street tricksters. Pawnbrokers diddled her when she turned in trinkets, then if she bought herself a fine jacket or a pair of gloves, they were ruined or stolen. Older now, she could not face going back to life as a highway robber, even if she could have found her way out of London to do it. So she stayed where she was, lurking in Covent Garden, where her descent into misery was rapid. Here, one day in summer 1648, she followed a young woman who appeared usefully preoccupied, until the mark turned around suddenly and stared straight at her. She had been spotted.

She walked on past. Then she realised, with annoyance, that while she tracked the young woman, a man was tailing *her*. As she turned to object and curse him, he accosted her: 'That gentlewoman saw you, and knew your intentions!'

She feigned innocence: 'She never did!'

'You know I am right.'

This man wore a brown suit several decades old, with stains down his jacket that were almost as old as the suit. She had seen him before in the area, though had no idea what trade he pursued or whether he lived locally. Not in these tall houses, unless he was some secretary or man of affairs. But he looked rougher, more like a press-gang leader, a pimp, or a justice's informer. He had the eyes of a loner, one who would not admit openly what filthy trade he followed. Perhaps he was just religious, some fanatical sectarian, she scoffed to herself.

She felt uncomfortable under his scrutiny. *He* was seeing a thin streak of tension and trouble, haggard-faced, hollow-eyed in the way only worn women on the London streets ever were. It was sometimes the result of drink. He could tell she was struggling. If this little thief had ever been prosperous, that was long past and she was heading for her destruction. She was ripe for him to take over. If he did not, she could be only a week away from being caught. Hanging then awaited. He would be doing her a service.

'I could turn you in – but I will not do it.'

'Oh I know what you want then!' she chided, rejecting his presumed advances with a sneer. Still, she wondered if she should give him his pleasure, just to gain a few pence in the hand.

'You know nothing. I can help you.'

'To what? To the stocks now and a sickly bastard in ten months' time?' Could he tell that she knew all about that?

'To a new life.'

'Oh you are a preacher!' The scavenger burst out laughing. Forget nurturing her soul. All she wanted was a bite to eat – and now she thought about it, she wanted that badly. She was so thin that even at the height of summer, she felt chilled to her fragile bones. Her weakness nowadays was dangerous; if a hue and cry started, she had no energy to run.

'I will not press religion on you,' promised the man. 'Not unless you choose that course. But those who do have faith and who have gone away to a new life in a better country, good honest people all of them, need healthy wenches of good character and spirit to serve them in their homes. I recruit for them. Were you wanting to escape your misery for a respectable career, in a land of hope and prosperity, I could show you the way to it.'

'Nobody would want me.'

'No one need know what you have been or where you come from.' He played his best card: 'I am walking now to an ordinary for a meal. Come, if you want. Eat with me at my expense and simply listen. Where will be the harm? No obligation. None at all.'

Of course she went. He knew what he was doing. A free meal would buy anyone. He knew how to time it, when they were desperate. Just as the light was fading and the evening chill set in, when they were tired after a long and useless day . . . Picking them up off the streets was his job, and he was unfailingly expert. Once he had lured her to the depot, in nearby St Giles-in-the-Fields, he would take his commission and vanish. Others would keep her secure. Fed, given a warm bed and safety, provided with a clean gown and cap, promised freedom and light work as a treasured servant in a respectable home in the colonies, she would be ripe for the bearers of contracts. Like many before her, she would 'sign indentures', make her mark on them voluntarily, listen while their importance was 'explained', not know she was being bamboozled and sold into something close to slavery . . .

It was no different from luring virgins into brothels, though it sounded better. He had done both, so he knew that both played on loneliness and fear, hope and misplaced ambition. The victims were young, most of them willingly entering into apprenticeships. By the time they saw they had been betrayed and were to labour in the plantations until they dropped, there were a thousand miles of ocean between them and home, with no chance of appeal. This one, along with so many others, had nobody to miss her.

She was his now. Her name hardly mattered. She was about to disappear, from Covent Garden, from London, even from England. She had been 'spirited'.

Chapter Forty-Eight

Colchester: 1648

The groom who had escorted Juliana to London was still hanging about the town house. He had taken up with the live-out maid so refused to return to Sussex, claiming to be afraid of soldiers on the road. Juliana could not persuade him. This was the problem with patronage. When it worked, life was easy; when it stopped working, dependants were trapped. She had no authority to give the servants orders. She did not want to lose the time it would take to write to Pelham Hall about it — and nor was she keen to travel with a hangdog, reluctant guard. Undaunted and longing to regain her children, she found a carrier who would take her. Luckily it was summer and there were plenty still working.

She reached Pelham Hall at the end of June. A good woman in the village had been caring for Tom and Valentine, who fell upon her in floods of tears, though she soon ascertained they were simply making her feel guilty. Now they at least were back together. There was no sign of Lovell, of course. Her sons kept asking where he was, as though he was their favourite parent.

There was bad news. While Juliana was away, Sir Lysander Pelham had been found dead in his bed. He had had no illness to speak of, though his daughters would claim he was broken-hearted by failure in the second civil war. With Sir Lysander gone, it was made plain the Lovells were no longer wanted. Although no efforts would be made to evict Juliana and her children while she was helpless, just as soon as her husband returned to her, the family would be expected to move on. It would be useful to start packing now.

Juliana accepted this precarious position calmly. She had tolerated Sir Lysander Pelham but never liked his relatives. She managed to remain polite to them through the month of June and into July, hoping her husband would reappear to claim her. Then, that wish was superseded. Reading news-sheets brought Juliana a great shock. Earlier than any of them might have hoped, she was able to oblige the hostile Pelham women.

The Royalist revolt's promising start had been systematically foiled. Oliver Cromwell had battened down in Wales, besieging rebel-held castles; once Tenby and Pembroke fell, he was free to go north and deal with the invading Scots. Juliana paid most attention to what happened in Kent, where her husband was supposed to be. There the Royalists had a large, well-organised army, support from the navy, towns and castles in their control, and a hoped-for welcome from the City of London. They had expected that Fairfax, now a lord after his father's death, would march the Parliamentary forces north, to block the Scots' army; they pinned their hopes on that army defeating him. Instead Fairfax took a small but highly experienced body of men to quell the insurrection in the south-east.

As he rode into Kent, Fairfax meant business. His reputation went before him; Royalist desertions began immediately. Although the rebels had recruited superior numbers, these were misguidedly divided between Maidstone, Dover and Rochester. There was a bloody fight at Maidstone, which Fairfax captured, street by street over the course of five hours. Elsewhere, Rich relieved Dover Castle and Ireton took Canterbury. On the promise of good treatment, many Royalists dispersed. Within weeks, the last pockets of rebellion were being mopped up.

Now came a change which was to horrify Juliana. The main Royalist army in Kent was commanded by the Earl of Norwich, Sir George Goring's elderly father. Lord Norwich moved towards London; he reached Blackheath on the outskirts, still full of confidence. However, when a fight seemed imminent the City lost heart; Norwich found the gates closed against him. Skippon was protecting London itself, while Whalley had ridden over London Bridge with some of the New Model Army men to take up a position in Essex. These were both reliable commanders. Harried by Parliamentary cavalry, Norwich moved down into Greenwich where he crossed the Thames northwards, with just five hundred desperate men either ferried in small boats or swimming their horses over. More than two thousand other Royalists had deserted and fled.

Away in eastern Kent, Fairfax deemed it safe to leave subordinates to finish restoring order. He crossed the estuary by boat from Gravesend to Tilbury. On the north side of the Thames in Essex, Royalist support at first snowballed, but just as quickly it spontaneously collapsed. Suddenly their situation looked desperate. Norwich sought refuge in Chelmsford from where, with Sir Charles Lucas and other leaders, he moved on to Colchester, which was Lucas's home town. Fairfax was dangerously close behind. Intending to stay only one night, the Royalists persuaded the Mayor of Colchester to admit them.

As soon as Fairfax arrived, he attempted to storm the town, but the defenders resisted. They could not escape because their men were mainly infantry and Parliamentary cavalry would cut them to pieces. Suffolk Trained Bands, supporting Fairfax, were blocking all the roads north. Royalist ships attempting to bring supplies up the River Colne were beaten back, then three Parliamentarian ships arrived from Harwich. Fairfax's troops seized the local harbour.

It began to rain. Fairfax sat down to starve out Colchester, in what would become a long, bitter and terrible siege. Juliana pored over the news as the town of her birth began to suffer. Fairfax had neither the men nor the equipment for a snap break-in. Grimly he encircled Colchester with ten forts, connected by rudimentary walls. The defenders fired the suburbs. Sallies out were made by the Royalists, which involved fierce fighting. The rain came down incessantly, until the countryside flooded. Conditions inside the town worsened.

Oliver Cromwell and John Lambert tailed the invading Scottish through the north of England. They defeated the Scots in a running rout near Preston over two days in August. When this was reported in Colchester, the Royalist leaders decided to break out and escape or perish; without horses the idea was hopeless and their soldiers mutinied. The town surrendered to Fairfax.

There were vivid news-sheets.

Juliana read them with mounting despair. Bread had run out. The imprisoned inhabitants had eaten horseflesh, then dogs and cats, and finally rats. Royalist leaders kept secret from the suffering townsfolk any favourable surrender terms Fairfax offered, until he had arrows shot over the walls, wrapped in papers that gave details. There was bad feeling as the people pleaded with Lord Norwich to surrender but he would not submit. Juliana thought of rats, envisaging all too clearly their size, their intelligent knowing eyes, and their frightful squeals if trapped . . . She had terrible dreams. She considered her options desperately, then made up her mind. The Pelham women were amazed when their unwelcome guest from Sir Lysander's farmhouse came in obvious agitation to tell them that she had to leave.

'I must urgently go to Colchester.'

'Why, madam, this cannot be sensible or safe – but do you think that your husband was there and has been captured?'

'I have to go. My family lived at Colchester. Someone of mine was in the town – someone who cannot have borne those conditions . . .'

For the first time, the Pelhams saw Juliana Lovell lose her serene control. Tears rushed into her eyes; her lip trembled. When Bessy felt moved to go to her, Juliana could not immediately speak but pressed one hand over her mouth and shook with distress. Years of absence and silence had finally become too much for her.

'Oh Mistress Lovell, whatever is it? Who do you know at Colchester?'

'Germain Carlill. A frail old man whose wits left him years ago, and the good woman who takes care of him.' Juliana took a breath and forced herself not to break down. 'He is my father,' she said.

Chapter Forty-Nine

Colchester: 1648

The New Model Army bitterly resented the second civil war. When the Leveller mutinies were overturned by Fairfax at Ware, the Jukes brothers, like most of their colleagues, grudgingly succumbed. They both admired the Lord General's personal courage and energy, and they wanted to trust his assurance that the army's grievances would be addressed. Whatever attractions new republican ideas held, they needed their back pay; mutiny was a sure way to lose it. The King's escape and the onset of the second civil war depressed them deeply. Both Jukes now burned with republican ideals, Gideon through Robert Allibone's influence and because of what he had heard at Putney, and Lambert because his wife Anne had become embroiled with the civilian Levellers. The new Royalist revolt put all their hopes on hold.

Levellers refrained from political activity during the uprising. If these revolts succeeded, five years of fighting and misery would have been in vain. There would be no chance of political reform. The King, who had learned nothing about compromise, would plunge them back into the same conditions that started the first civil war.

New Model soldiers were frustrated that they had to endure more fighting. For London soldiers, this was almost unbearable; their yearning for home had been exacerbated when Rainborough led their four regiments into the city. They had all worn laurel leaves in their hats that day as a sign of victory – yet it was no joyful homecoming. It was torture to be so near their houses and their loved ones, yet to be kept in arms in quarters. Even so, only a few men deserted. Most, like Gideon and Lambert, felt they had now risked too much to give up.

During that brief stay in London, friends and family made attempts to visit them. Seeing familiar faces was a joy, though deeply unsettling. The troops settled back into their military routine afterwards, wondering how much longer it would have to continue and feeling homesick with a new piquancy.

Robert Allibone had come looking for Gideon. He brought Anne to see Lambert. They all hoped that soon the brothers would be able to give up soldiering. They wanted a settlement, peace and the men's return. They managed several meetings, though Gideon felt that none went well. Rifts had opened. Lambert and he had always assumed that once they were discharged, they would quickly refamiliarise themselves with normality at home and work. Now doubts set in. Maybe civilian life held problems. People at home seemed to have changed. Of course they had changed themselves too, though they were mainly unaware of it.

Although Gideon and Robert had corresponded all along, Robert's behaviour seemed oddly remote when they met. Gideon suspected guilt. On one visit, the apprentice Amyas came. Amyas, whom Gideon remembered as a raw boy in his teens, was now a strapping young man and only a few months from finishing his apprenticeship. Nothing was said, but it was clear that if Gideon did not soon rejoin the business, Amyas would take his place as Robert's partner. Robert was embarrassed, but he was working hard for the Levellers and relied on Amyas's help. So long as nobody could guess when Gideon would leave the army, decisions might have to be taken without him.

Parthenope Jukes had died, without her sons even knowing. For Lambert, who had lived in their parents' house almost all his life, it was now *his* house, the shop and business his too – making his return so much more urgent. However, Lambert was in trouble with Anne. Gideon read the signs. They all managed to dine together one night, but he found it uncomfortable with Anne and Lambert quarrelsome. Afterwards, Lambert remained tetchy, as if he had had a shock. Anne had managed the grocery business for over three years without him. Like other women landed with businesses, she did it well. But when her husband asked for progress reports she seemed unwilling to discuss anything; it went down badly with the jealous Lambert. Gideon foresaw deep strife when his brother returned home and expected to take charge. He would be grateful for what Anne had done in his absence – but he would make no concessions. Anne probably realised already that her position would drastically alter. She could not relish being exiled back to the kitchen, not after her emergence as a woman with spending power, authority to enter into contracts and employer's rights over their servers in the shop.

It was no surprise to Gideon that his brother applied to transfer back to London. As Lieutenant of the Tower of London, Fairfax was forming his own Guard, a regiment of six companies, which would secure the Tower, its arsenal and its important political prisoners, using men Fairfax trusted. That was the original plan, although the Royalist uprising soon altered it.

Given his London associations and his service record, Lambert Jukes's request for a move was granted. He thought that he was going home. His hope was short-lived. The second civil war took the Tower Guard first on long marches into Kent, then to Colchester.

Gideon had remained behind in the New Model temporarily. Colonel Rainborough's regiment was, on Rainborough's appointment as vice-admiral, given to Richard Deane, a change Gideon did not welcome. All the regiment was hostile because Deane had been Oliver Cromwell's preferred candidate for vice-admiral; the men had heard that Cromwell actually made a surreptitious attempt to block Rainborough's appointment. Deane may have been innocent in this; he had served at sea under Rainborough's father and Thomas had been a witness at his wedding, so there was no bad feeling between them. Cromwell held political reservations about Rainborough. Rainborough was no man's protégé and open stress appeared between them.

While the Admiralty Committee were discussing the appointment, a captain in Rainborough's regiment overheard a furious quarrel behind closed doors. He came back full of indignation and gossip, so the awkwardness became common knowledge. Gideon already associated Cromwell with the Grandees' opposition to the Levellers. When Deane was given the regiment, he too asked for a transfer. Fairfax was still building up troop numbers in London, so it was allowed. Deane and the regiment went with Cromwell into Wales. Gideon followed his brother to London.

He caught up with the Tower Guard just as they went on forced marches into Kent. After the short, fierce campaign there, Gideon found himself besieging Colchester. The Parliamentarians were in a hard, angry mood. They were sick of war, exasperated that the King had stirred up further fighting while they were trying to make a decent settlement, determined to end the conflict once and for all.

*　　*　　*

This turned out to be the longest and most terrible siege ever conducted on English soil. It was necessary because Colchester was so close to London. Fairfax dared not leave such a substantial enemy force only two days' march away from the city. The Royalists, who were said to number 5,000, had seized and brought with them, as hostages, Parliament's entire Essex County Committee; the prisoners' fates also had to be considered.

The Royalists had superior numbers and at first they held genuine hopes that uprisings would flourish throughout the country, with the Scots bringing an invasion army south to join up with them. If the Royalists broke out and took London, they stood a good chance of obliterating Parliament, the New Model Army, the Levellers and all that had been won. Fairfax was stuck. He and his men were just as much prisoners of the situation as the rebels. So long as Lord Norwich, Lord Capel, Sir Charles Lucas and Sir George Lisle held them here, they were prevented from deploying their forces and their artillery anywhere else.

The local situation became deeply unhappy. The fugitives had been admitted to Colchester by the mayor because they swore they would only stay a few days. Besides, Sir Charles Lucas was a Colchester man; it still counted. They had ended up here on the urging of Lucas – a single-minded military man, who was generally thought so unpleasant that the civilians said enduring him was worse than enduring the siege. He had little sympathy with the townspeople, who had raided and plundered his house at the start of the war. Until now Colchester, a prosperous textile town, had loyally supported Parliament although it lay outside the main fields of action and avoided trouble. To have this siege wished upon them at this late stage was cruel. The townspeople were constantly at odds with their unwelcome, frequently boorish house guests.

Outside, the besiegers hated to be forced to impose terrible suffering on their own supporters. Deserting Royalist soldiers were promised an amnesty, yet civilians could not be permitted to leave. The essence of starving a garrison into surrender was to keep as many mouths as possible needing to be fed, to increase the pressure.

A siege was bad enough when hungry soldiers and civilians were on the same side; inside Colchester their antagonism worsened a fraught situation. The soldiers had first call on food, to keep them fit to fight;

civilians were just a drain on resources – though they could be a source of supplies. Colchester homes were stripped of thatch to feed military animals. Houses were roughly searched, their pantries and store cupboards stripped bare. As the siege progressed, people congregated outside the commanders' headquarters agitating to share the soldiers' food; to stall a riot, horsemeat had to be handed out to them, but it was clear the garrison took precedence and inflammatory stories circulated that the commanders were dining on beef washed down with good wine every night. Constant tension seethed as those commanders refused to surrender while the townsfolk were all the time begging them to accept Fairfax's terms. Week after week passed while Lord Norwich and the other commanders convinced themselves they would soon be relieved by the Scots or others.

Thomas Rainborough's career with the fleet had not lasted long. He was put off his flagship by navy mutineers and lost the admiral's post. Without a command, he in turn arrived at Colchester.

Fairfax's men believed Royalist snipers inside Colchester were shooting poisoned bullets, which killed both the colonel and lieutenant-colonel of the Tower Guard. The slugs were thought to have been either rolled in sand, which had fatal results in a wound, or else boiled in sulphate of iron, which was used in dyes and ink-making. It was contrary to the rules of war and in retaliation prisoners were killed. Rainborough, fortuitously on the spot, then became the Guards' replacement colonel. He and they were in the thick of events at Colchester. 'Fort Rainborough', on the north side of the city, was the final link built in the besiegers' encircling wall, a position the colonel ran, with his men's eager connivance, as an excitable, rather maverick outpost.

Hunkered down in Fort Rainborough, conditions were bad. Gideon thought he had never known a period when the weather was so terrible, so often, through year after year. The whole civil war had been fought in miserable conditions. Being out in rain, wind and snow would become his abiding memory of his military service. The soldiers, many used to town life, responded badly to lack of shelter. Then crops rotted in the fields and food shortages followed failed harvests. When they did have stints of fighting at Colchester, they had to contend with the River Colne, so swollen that its fords were generally impassable; two men who lost their footing close to Gideon were drowned during a skirmish.

The first few weeks were exhausting while they dug in. Depressingly, they could hear Royalists strengthening and repairing the town walls at the same time. As the rain kept coming, the besiegers' forts provided only meagre and part-time shelter. Their ten forts and fourteen redoubts formed a unique ribbon of earthworks which had to be manned constantly. This was trench warfare, with all its physical penalties. Those on duty did four- or six-hour stints, often in cold, stagnant water as the trenches flooded. They were soon battling vermin and disease. Keeping dry was nearly impossible. As the rain came down for week after week, their shoes and clothes became sodden; they acquired sores and trench-foot; tempers grew short. Sickness was troubling the town, worsening as the population became weaker, but there was serious sickness outside too: Fairfax had his painful gout, while his soldiers succumbed to agues and dysentery, which they vividly called 'running flux'. Morale began to fail. So dismal was the daily grind, some soldiers hired replacements to stand in for them; the going rate was ten shillings a week. Regular batches of Londoners marched out to grab the money. Gideon was tempted, but resisted.

He knew his brother, with an extra fifteen years and developing arthritis, did sometimes give in and hire a man to take his duties. Lambert was hauled before his captain, but once it emerged that he was suffering from the flux, he was designated sick and no more was said. He told Gideon he had applied for discharge.

Mistakes had been made. The town port at the Hythe was not secured by Fairfax quickly enough, enabling quantities of grain, wine, salt, fish, and worst of all gunpowder to be secretly carted into town. This lengthened the siege considerably. Early on, the Royalists were able to leave the town and cross no man's land – the dead ground that was called the leaguer – to forage for food. Later, the blockade was tightened both by land and sea, and Fairfax managed to secure the loyalty of the local militias in Surrey and Essex, with whose help he covered all possible escape routes, especially the roads to the north. By the end of June the trap was tight. Slowly it became clear to everyone that they still had a long way to go.

Through July the mood grew increasingly bitter. Fairfax brought in heavier guns to batter a Royalist observation post in the bell tower of St Mary's at the Wall, which stood on the highest point of the town.

This sniper's nest right against the town walls had been occupied by a brass demi-cannon which did much damage in the hands of a superior gunner known as 'One-eye'd Thompson'. Colonel Rainborough was given credit for taking out 'One-eye'd Thompson'. At any rate the man was shot and the top of the tower destroyed. The gun, which was locally called Humpty Dumpty, was sent crashing down in smithereens and Parliamentary movements were no longer spied upon.

A fierce sortie by the Royalists through the East Gate caused loss of life, though plainly the besieged were now suffering from shortage of ammunition. They still had too much food. On the 22nd of July, Rainborough led his men in an audacious raid. They crossed the swollen river at night to storm the last working cornmill, which until then had continued to provide the defenders with bread. To succeed in starving out the town it was vital to put the Middle Mill out of action. Gideon was among the group that tackled the sluice; frozen and soaked through, they managed to cut it, while comrades tried to fire the mill building. The Royalists fought back with a desperate counter-attack and put out the fire, using their hats to bale water from the river. Rainborough's men suffered losses and were compelled to withdraw, but they had done enough damage to stop the mill from working. However, they did not know then that the enemy had other, horse-powered, millstones. The Colchester garrison imposed strict rationing, though the mayor seemed unwilling or unable to give similar orders to civilians; they were suffering so badly that they were ready to mutiny.

The Parliamentarians squeezed closer. They battered the abbey gatehouse on the south side. After demolishing part of it, they managed to lob in grenades, which happened to hit the Royalists' main magazine. An enormous explosion killed many inside, destroyed the gatehouse, blew soldiers asunder and traumatised any defenders who struggled from the smoke and rubble. Close by was the private house of Sir Charles Lucas. The Parliamentarians broke in, under cover of the old walls, and when they found that the house had been stripped during riots some years previously, they wrecked the family tomb, committing foul acts of desecration on the bodies of the Lucas ancestors.

A month later they were still waiting for the town to surrender, even though they reckoned Royalist ammunition had now fallen to a dangerous low and starvation was close. Both the defenders and the attackers had fired houses to prevent their opponents using them for cover. Defenders had been killed when they slipped out at night to cut grass for their horses, which were now so weak that a cull was ordered of one in three. All remaining salt in town was used, to preserve as many lean carcases as possible. The rest were cooked up in a communal roast. Outside, Gideon and his colleagues were tantalised by the meat cooking as its scented smoke wafted over the leaguer. Later Gideon, who had a sensitive nose, noticed that spices discovered in house searches were now being boiled up with oil and starch.

He was already depressed. The puddingy wafts reminded him of his mother's warm, dry kitchen, always full of rich baking scents. It was a moment between guard duties; he was resting in limbo, as soldiers learn to do whenever action is not required of them. He had known about his mother's death for almost a year, but this was when it hit home. Grief for Parthenope overwhelmed him. He had never bidden her farewell; now Lambert and he would never enjoy her Dutch pudding or her caraway biscuits again. She would never make his favourite jumbles.

The effects of bereavement can be put off for a long time, then some jolt catches people off guard. Gideon had grown physically and mentally tired. The benefits of army service – travel, new skills, camaraderie – no longer mattered. He had all the normal troubles of a soldier; he was bored, fearful, hungry, run down, resentful of the enemy, suspicious of those who had ordered him here, worn out by constantly watching for danger. Grief and homesickness came together, one last blow.

Unbearably restless, he found a grey pony, a beast so small that when he mounted, his feet almost kicked into the turf. Colonel Rainborough spotted him. He knew his man, and perhaps noticed Gideon's unusual desolation.

'Leaving us, Sergeant Jukes?' It was forbidden to be more than a mile outside the leaguer. A formal headcount was taken twice a day.

'Taking a scout around, sir.'

'Be back by roll-call.'

'Yes sir. True unto death!'

'Very good.'

Whatever he had subconsciously intended, Gideon did not go far. He was shocked to find that in the fields around the town many wounded Parliamentarians were being tended under makeshift tents. He asked why they could not be taken to safety in London. He learned that casualty numbers were being concealed. Fairfax wanted to prevent the City money-men feeling nervous about his losses; he needed to deter ditherers from throwing in their lot with the Royalist rebels.

Somewhere among the sick and wounded lay Gideon's brother Lambert, groaning and disabled by the flux.

While he was out riding, Gideon found a weary messenger from Lancashire whom he led in to Fort Rainborough. The man was bringing news that in a three-day running victory near Preston, Cromwell and Lambert had defeated and destroyed the Covenanters' army. Both their infantry and cavalry had surrendered. At last there was hope.

By now, August, the Parliamentarians had pressed so close to the walls that opposing soldiers could speak to and throw stones at each other. Starvation, lack of clean water, and resultant epidemics had made conditions inside the town intolerable. The civilians' plight was grim. Poor people crowded outside the commander's lodgings, wailing for relief. The garrison had suffered desertion and high casualties; the soldiers were saving pieces of their bread ration to attract passing dogs, knocking in their skulls with musket butts and then eating them. Horses were stolen from stables almost every night, then their meat sold on the black market from the Shambles. Civilians ate rats. When the rat supply dwindled they gnawed on candle-ends and even soap, trying to suck nourishment from the mutton fat in them. As commotions increased, a Royalist officer was alleged to have brutally told a woman who begged for food for her starving baby that the child would make good eating, well boiled up.

It could not continue. Recriminations were ghastly on both sides. Parliamentary news-sheets denounced the Royalists for using the towns-folk as a human shield and for parading their County Committee hostages on the ramparts where they believed artillery fire was expected. Parliamentarians even muttered that the town had brought about its own misfortunes by admitting the Royalists, as if this loyal place had betrayed the cause, or had had any choice when faced with thousands of fully armed fugitive desperadoes. Fairfax's men were accused of using civilians for target practice; they did confess to burning the fingers of a fourteen-year-old messenger boy sent out to take a secret message to the Scots, though they had tried kinder tactics first, offering him a bribe to tell the truth. The Parliamentarians fired arrows and over the walls, carrying offers of amnesty to the rank and file; these were shot back bearing the message 'an answer from Colchester: as you may smell' and were discovered to be smeared with turds.

Astrologers arrived. This failed to help anyone.

Elsewhere the situation had moved on. There had been various reports of Royalist defeats. Wales was subdued, both south and north, and the outbursts of rebellion that had run through English counties like fire underground through peat were stamped out. But now came the final blow for the Royalists. News of Cromwell's complete massacre of the Scots' army was passed into Colchester by writing details on a paper kite; it was flown high over the town, then allowed to drop for civilians to pick up. Beset by pleading women and their screaming children, Lord Norwich agreed to open the gates and allow them to leave.

It had happened before. Wives of town worthies had requested Fairfax's permission to depart, and were refused, though word had it the resourceful madams then smuggled themselves out by boat. Fairfax's orders were clear: no concessions. Now five hundred starving women scrambled out through the gates and approached Rainborough's regiment. As they rushed across the leaguer, the colonel had his men first fire blanks over their heads. When the women kept coming, running right up to the mouths of cannon, he sent soldiers to threaten to strip them if they refused to budge. Four were stripped as an example, at which the wretched women finally fled back to the town. The Royalists refused to open the gates to readmit them. As the fugitives huddled between the town walls and the besiegers' fortifications all night, the Tower Guard hunched in their bleak quarters, hating the situation. Fairfax threatened to shoot every man in the Royalist garrison if the women and their wailing children were kept in the leaguer, so they were let back in.

Seventy-five days after the siege started, the Royalists made terms.

Rainborough's regiment was the first into Colchester. Gideon was profoundly shocked by how little of the town remained and by the weak, starving people who still fought one another for the last scraps of animal feed, begging from the soldiers piteously. Not a dog appeared. Houses had their roofs off; some were reduced to rubble; the elegant suburbs had been burned or dismantled; civic buildings had been battered and half destroyed. Fairfax had guaranteed that there would be no plundering, though in order to secure this promise the town had been forced to agree to pay a devastating fine of fourteen thousand pounds, the penalty for admitting the Royalists in the first place. It was unclear how the town would find the money. Colchester was ruined.

The New Model Army moved in and took control quietly. The fortifications, which Fairfax immediately inspected to see just how his efforts had been repulsed for so long, now stood denuded of soldiers though still strong and in good repair. The few surviving horses had been collected up; they stood, heads down and skeletal, in St Mary's Churchyard. Weapons, flags and drums were piled bleakly in St James's Church. Only one and half barrels of gunpowder were left.

Surrender of private soldiers and junior officers was taken at Fryer's Yard by the East Gate. They had been offered fair quarter, though lords, superior officers and gentlemen of distinction had assembled at the aptly named King's Head. Ireton argued fiercely for punitive treatment of the Royalist leaders.

Out of the Parliamentarians' bitterness at being forced to fight again came a long-lasting controversy. They believed the surrender terms were fair: ordinary soldiers and townspeople were granted quarter; when the Parliamentary infantry marched in, no harm was done to them, they were given warm clothing and food. Prisoners of war received miserable rations, but that was still more than the starving people of Colchester had lived on for weeks. In fact few prisoners would make it home safely; for them, they would learn, quarter entailed being shut up in churches, then marched long distances across the country. Many of the three thousand private soldiers would be shipped to the sugar plantations in Barbados or imprisoned in remote prisons from which few ever emerged; their officers were sent to the galleys until friends and relatives ransomed them.

The commanders were treated differently. Nobles were to be sent to be dealt with by Parliament; Lord Capel eventually went to the block, though Lord Norwich, the nominal leader of the revolt, was spared. Sir Charles Lucas, Sir George Lisle, the so-called Sir Bernard Gascoigne and Colonel Farre were put to the 'mercy' of their opposing general. This was a technical term which meant Fairfax could decide what to do with them. It gave no guarantees. He was famous for chivalry in such situations – though this time he was harder, because Sir Charles

Lucas had surrendered to him personally, and given his parole not to fight Parliament again, after the battle of Marston Moor.

An immediate Council of War was held in the Town Hall. Henry Ireton presided. Fairfax did not attend, but left the judgment to his officers. The four Royalist leaders were briskly condemned to death.

Farre escaped. 'Sir Bernard Gascoigne' was discovered to be an Italian citizen; rather than cause diplomatic offence, his life was spared. Lucas and Lisle were shot by firing squad. Fairfax's three most senior officers, Ireton, Whalley and Rainborough, formally witnessed this execution.

Gideon approved the verdict and the deaths of Lisle and Lucas. If assigned the task, he would willingly have been one of the firing squad. Like all the exhausted Parliamentarians, he wanted a brisk end to their trouble. They were tired of endangering their lives and frustrated by having to impose burdens on the civilian population, for whose rights to peace and prosperity they had fought. They hated the King and his supporters for stirring up a revolt when peace had been at hand.

There were military reasons for ordering these executions, reasons sanctioned by the rules of war: the Royalists had insisted on prolonging the siege, causing unnecessary hardship, especially to civilians. Lucas had broken his parole, and was also accused of executing enemy prisoners on more than one occasion; at the Council of War, ordinary soldiers gave evidence against him. Fairfax would always maintain that these men had put themselves in the position of soldiers of fortune. They earned their fate. The severity of their punishment warned others not to take up arms. That only Lucas and Lisle were shot seemed a display of restraint.

But Royalists regarded this execution as cold-blooded murder. It was to have tragic repercussions.

Chapter Fifty

Doncaster: October 1648

A month after Colchester fell, the Tower Guards were ordered north on a special mission. Their colonel initially remained in London, organising pay. Rainborough's regiment had been sent to attend to a last pocket of Royalist resistance: Pontefract Castle. This stronghold, known as 'the Key to the North', had been captured by a group of cavaliers who pretended to be delivering beds to the Parliamentary garrison. They had ensconced themselves with enough food to last twelve months. Since Colchester, the Royalists had no hope of mercy and were dug in for a long, desperate siege.

Their sojourn so far was not entirely miserable. Their besieger was Sir Henry Cholmeley, a snobbish, insular Yorkshire gentleman, an acquaintance of most of them and old friend to quite a few. Although he fought for Parliament, his brother fought for the King; they had remained on civil terms. He posed no serious threat to the Royalists in the castle. He knew them and they knew him. They were more loyal to one another as Yorkshiremen than to any outsiders. They therefore conducted activities like a local fête. They fraternised. They parleyed. They allowed each other to come and go at will. Cholmeley maintained a leaguer around the castle, but it was as loose as could be. It was said that he supplied the castle with mutton throughout the siege.

When Colonel Rainborough caught up with his regiment at Doncaster, he said that on the road between London and St Albans he had survived an ambush by three well-mounted Royalists. He fought them off. As sporadic outbursts of rebellion were put down, some Royalists were turning themselves into highwaymen. However, there was also talk of a death-list against senior Parliamentarians, and for his part in the execution of Lucas and Lisle, Rainborough could have been targeted.

The situation in Yorkshire was extremely tricky. The arrival of six companies of Londoners, led by a seafaring republican, all speaking in Thames-side accents (apart from a significant group from Massachusetts, where Rainborough had relatives), was never likely to go well. They might have felt out of place – had not Londoners believed everywhere belonged to them. In response, the locals adopted their own swagger. Though they should have worked as colleagues, the Tower Guards received no welcome from Sir Henry Cholmeley, who was outraged to find Rainborough appointed his superior – a much younger colonel, even though one who had a serious reputation. As a member of Parliament himself, Cholmeley refused to step aside and could not readily be sidelined. He had told his local County Committee he would accept no one less than Cromwell over him, and they had written to offer Cromwell the job. This undermined Rainborough locally, if not with his men.

The colonel could hardly take the regiment up to Pontefract Castle if Cholmeley was liable to start fisticuffs while rejoicing cavaliers smoked their pipes and gawped from the battlements. Rainborough's men were ready to knock seven bells out of Cholmeley's Yorkshire militia at break-fast, then deal with the cavaliers by dinner time – they regarded both with equal disdain – but for Parliamentarians to fight one another was unacceptable. It would give Rainborough's enemies yet another complaint. He had to tread carefully. His troops were 170 miles from London now and needed logistical support.

This was a wealthy part of South Yorkshire, full of rich men impressed with their own family histories, men who owned vast estates where their ancestors had built huge homes, far enough from London to think itself the centre of the world. It was an area of expensive horse-breeding, and horse-racing, which even then in its infancy was a royal sport. Pontefract was famous for its deep, soft loam, where for miles around sweet liquorice root grew and was made into medicinal cakes, good remedies for coughs and stomach diseases. Doncaster, where Rainborough made his tempor-ary headquarters, had been loyal to the King; the King had honoured the town and the inhabitants were not to be trusted.

The military situation was deplorable. The enemy ranged at will over a ten-mile area, merrily flouting Cholmeley's siege of Pontefract Castle. Cavaliers plundered the countryside; they took prisoners, whom they held to ransom, rounded up oxen and other booty, then rode back into the castle, happy as freebooters. At Scarborough on the coast, the Royalists captured a pinnace, a small two-masted ship used as an inshore tender, which provided quantities of supplies for them. Meanwhile, Cholmeley's Parliamentarians were levying demands on the reluctant local population, causing great hardship. Equally repressive were the cavaliers, whose vicious extortion reputedly brought in thirty thousand pounds a month.

After reconnaissance – Gideon rode around as one of the scouts – Rainborough wrote to Fairfax, dwelling lightly on his personal strife with Sir Henry Cholmeley, but asking to be excused this command. He offered to carry on only if he was provided with proper reinforcements and supplies. While he waited for an answer, he remained at Doncaster. He kept two companies with him in the town, billeting the rest, as was customary, in outside districts to spread the burden for the locals.

The cavaliers from the castle boldly continued their habit of raiding, or 'beating up' enemy quarters. At a village six miles from Pontefract they killed a Captain Layton and two others from Rainborough's regiment, with more men wounded or taken prisoner. Next day, Cholmeley's militia met the enemy at a horse-fair, drank with them, and gravely exchanged toasts: 'Here's to thee, Brother Roundhead!'

'I thank you, Brother Cavalier!'

On Captain Layton's death, Rainborough bumped up Gideon Jukes to officer level. It was a long jump to captain, but not without precedent. When he gave Gideon his commission, the colonel drew comparisons with the Leveller Edward Sexby. He had resigned from army service, but somehow turned up at the battle of Preston; he was still so trusted by Cromwell that he was employed as the official messenger to take news of the victory to Parliament – for which he received a hundred pounds' reward. Subsequently *he* was commissioned as a captain, then even made governor of Portland in Dorset.

Gideon's new troop was one of those quartered in outlying villages. He wondered afterwards whether, had he remained a scout, he might have spotted what was happening and things might have turned out differently. But on the night of the 28th of October, a Saturday, a terrible event occurred. Gideon was in Doncaster, conducting routine business with the regimental major. Major Wilkes was in gloomy mood, frustrated by Sir Henry Cholmeley's lackadaisical maintenance of the leaguer.

He confirmed that Rainborough was still waiting for orders from Fairfax or Cromwell, so the regiment would continue to keep its distance here, which was about ten miles from Pontefract.

Gideon nearly went back to his troop that night, but Wilkes had grumbled on at length and darkness fell early at the end of October in the north. He stayed at the house where Wilkes was quartered, though he went out by himself to obtain supper at an inn. He chose one called the Hinde, which he found in French Gate, not as gracious inside as it looked from the street, though he stuck with it rather than turn back out into the cold. A few of the regiment's soldiers were drinking there, fellows with whom he had never felt great affinity. His meal was indifferent; he had a feeling he was being watched; a woman kept trying to meet his eye in a way he did not like. Since Lacy, Gideon distrusted all women and of course he believed that for officers to deal with whores was reprehensible – it undermined discipline and failed to set a good moral standard (Gideon knew this was pompous but he had not been a field officer long enough to relax). When he was asked at the Hinde if he wanted a bedchamber, he thought he knew what that meant. He was glad to say he had lodgings elsewhere.

Back in the streets he met one of the files of men on guard duty, at that point patrolling without an officer. They said the town guard that night was commanded by Captain-Lieutenant John Smith, the senior captain, who led Rainborough's own company; Rainborough had inherited Smith from his predecessor, one of the officers who had been shot dead at Colchester with suspected poisoned bullets. Gideon knew little enough about Smith, though he seemed too ready to complain about others. He was a Maidstone man, which did not impress a Londoner.

Conscious of his responsibilities, Captain Jukes ordered the unsupervised soldiers to be careful in their watch. Still unsure of himself in command, it continued to surprise him that they stiffened up obediently. 'Captain Smith will be around to see all is well.'

'Oh he will!' the men assured Gideon, in the sardonic voices soldiers use to decry unpopular superiors. He had no reason to assume they meant Smith was dilatory. He assumed they just needed taking in hand. That was Smith's job.

The soldiers moved on. Gideon strode in the other direction, trying to walk like a man who knew where he was going. Of course he got lost. Mistakenly he found himself near St Sepulchre's Gate in the south of the town, where a man who was carrying a Bible rather ostentatiously told him his way back. 'Major Wilkes is at a house near Colonel Rainborough, who lodges opposite the Cross and the Shambles,' the man added knowingly.

'I believe he does.' Gideon played it down for security reasons. He said his thanks, walked back up St Sepulchre's to Barter Gate, crossed over, found the major's house, and stretched out on a settle in the warm kitchen. The household were asleep, Major Wilkes long since snoring in his chamber upstairs, which was a senior officer's entitlement. Gideon had a hard bed, but better than open country; he stewed happily in the close room with his boots off until morning.

Everything changed when Captain Smith arrived.

The first Gideon knew was waking to angry voices. He heard a rumpus upstairs. There must be an alarm.

He pulled on his boots and grabbed his weapons. As he ran to the upper floor, he detected real horror in the major's voice. Smith, whose whine Gideon recognised, was making self-righteous excuses. As Gideon tumbled into the room, Major Wilkes stormed accusingly, 'You are an accessory to it!' He was pulling on a boot, in his haste tangling his toes in mismanaged boot-hose. Seeing Gideon, he cried out despairingly, 'Colonel Rainborough is murdered! He lies dead in the street, basely betrayed by Cholmeley and this man!'

Captain Smith turned and told Gideon defensively, 'I was taken ill during the guard. I carried on as long as possible, but was urged by Master Watts and Corporal Flexney to seek a house with a fire –'

'At the Hinde? It's a damned whorehouse!' muttered Wilkes, struggling desperately into his coat.

Smith carried on justifying himself. 'Truly I knew it only as a travellers' rest. I saw nothing of any trouble until I heard a great noise of horses, the enemy leaving – at once I put the men on guard and came to you, sir –'

'Out of my way! Come with me, Jukes –'

It was just after sunrise. They tasted mist on the sharp autumn air. They ran to Rainborough's lodging. He lay out of doors, on the cobbles some yards from the house, with blood trails all along the street. They recognised his body instantly, that big, powerful man: unmistakable.

A small crowd had gathered, standing not too close. Their shocked murmurs stopped as Wilkes and Jukes approached. Beyond, a saddled horse stood, trembling, also covered in blood.

A second body lay somewhat apart. Major Wilkes walked over and turned the corpse, discovering their lieutenant. Neither Wilkes nor Gideon wanted to touch the colonel. The soldier who had been on guard as the colonel's sentinel was sitting on the kerb, badly shocked and woozy from a battering, saying over and over again, 'I had no match! I had been issued with no match!'

Rainborough had terrible sword thrusts through his torso, with defensive wounds on his arms. Gideon counted up: he had been slashed at least eight times. Under his jaw, his throat was cut.

The only witness to everything was a maid from the house.

'Get her story!' Major Wilkes ordered Gideon in an undertone. He was a hardened soldier, normally matter-of-fact but now badly shaken. Gideon saw the man's eyes darting as he assessed how much danger, if any, still threatened. Wilkes set about ordering a search of the town and drumming up the rest of the soldiers.

Gideon led the weeping woman back indoors where he seated her on a rush-bottomed chair. His heart pounded. He had witnessed terrible sights in the war, but Colonel Rainborough's savaged corpse would haunt his dreams for ever. He wanted to yell, but forced himself to address the maid reassuringly. 'Just say what happened.'

In their agitation, neither could well understand the other's accent, but Gideon had learned how to listen to a strange brogue and any northern woman knew how to tell a story. Up with the light, the maid had gone out for something – water? coal? She admitted she had temporarily left the door ajar. 'Three men came, dressed like gentry; they told the sentinel, proper like, they had brought a packet and letters from Oliver Cromwell. The lieutenant was there and he let them go up. The colonel was in his chamber – in his waistcoat, drawers and slippers!' whimpered the maid.

The image of those slippers would haunt Gideon. He had seen one in the gutter outside, completely drenched in blood. The other, moulded by long use to the exact shape of sole, toes and bunion, had stayed wedged on his colonel's foot. It was embroidered. A wife – Margaret Rainborough – would have bought those slippers as a loving gift, or even worked the tapestry herself. They were personal items, easy to pack, which Rainborough had carried with him everywhere, as soldiers did: a little piece of home, however far he travelled; comforting at the end of a hard day.

Gideon reddened and tersely corrected the maid: 'Say in his shirt. More decorous than drawers.'

She accepted the demure alteration. 'They claimed to have brought letters, but when he looked it was but a packet of blank paper. They made him come downstairs, dragged him in his shirt!'

'How do you know all this, if you had gone for water?'

'I was only gone with the pail a minute. I would not have left the door open, else.'

'All right. So you saw these men? Did you recognise them?'

'I never saw them before.'

'Did they sound local? Northerners?'

'Aye, they were not strangers.'

'Go on.'

Rainborough had been overpowered in his room before he could reach his sword and pistols. Ordering him to keep silent, the raiders forced him down to the hall. Unarmed, but thinking his sentinel would assist, Rainborough suddenly shook them off. The sentinel had no match for his musket and could do nothing to raise the alarm. (*Truly?* wondered Gideon, already alert for discrepancies and treachery. *Why did he not club them with his musket butt?*) The cavaliers then pushed Colonel Rainborough out to the street and tried to force him on to horseback. They had taken his lieutenant prisoner too but when Rainborough saw there were only four assailants, one of whom was holding the cavaliers' horses, he paused with his foot in the stirrup and roared a call to arms. He and his lieutenant put up a vigorous resistance. Rainborough snatched one man's sword, the lieutenant grabbed another's pistol. Rainborough was thrown down and thrust through the throat, his lieutenant was run through the body and killed.

'Are you telling me they wanted to carry off the colonel alive?'

'It seemed so. He refused to go.'

Gideon thought rapidly. This was a bungled kidnap? Perhaps the intention had been to make Rainborough a hostage, maybe exchange him for some prominent Royalist prisoner – Sir Marmaduke Langdale would be a prime candidate. After the battle of Preston, Cromwell's pursuing men had captured Langdale at an alehouse near Northampton, though in fact he had just escaped.

The struggle lasted, the maid thought, a quarter of an hour. *(And nobody else heard anything?)*

The maid kept going over it. The choreography seemed confused, but the picture was vivid enough. 'The colonel demanded a sword so he could die like a man. But they refused, then stabbed him through the body several times more. He nonetheless seized an assailant's sword, struggling for it with his bare hands, bending it right back on its pommel. I heard one man cry out to another to shoot him, but the pistol misfired. The shooter hurled the weapon, causing a great bruise on Rainborough's head that made him stagger.'

The lieutenant lay dead, the sentinel was out of action. No soldiers had answered the colonel's call to arms. The raiders began to move off. Rainborough staggered along the street after them.

'They noticed him, and cried out "The dog follows!" They turned back, even though the colonel had fainted. Then they ran him through again and again, and at last rode away crying "Farewell, Rainborough!" I heard him groan, before that, "I am betrayed! Oh I am betrayed!" Those were his last words on earth —' The maid collapsed.

Gideon slumped briefly in a country chair, covering his face.

Leaving the maid, he explored the house.

In the kitchen, he found the owner, sitting with other occupants, amazed and deeply shocked. There was a full water pail, abandoned. Gideon grew up in a house where working women were sternly controlled by his mother, but he had seen that other servants had their own ways. Some maids constantly vanished on little errands they dreamed up, to fetch water, wood, shopping, eggs from the henhouse, to borrow flour, to visit friends for gossip, to help at births. In some houses they took it as their right to come and go.

Accepting that the maid had not left the door open as part of the conspiracy, he continued his investigation. In the hall were signs of scuffle. On the stairs lay a dropped gauntlet. New marks disfigured the wall, white gouges in the simple panelling. He found his colonel's room by deduction; its door stood open. For a few moments he was able to stand there alone, hearing the silence, yearning to communicate with the dead man who had so recently stayed here.

The bed was turned back as if a sleeper had just left. One chair was a little askew, as if someone had stood up and turned to the doorway. There were few real signs of violence. A sword and sword belt, pistol and ammunition pouches were laid by on a chest of drawers, unreachable from the bed or the chair. Everything was as it ought to be: black cloak, scarlet coat, baldric and hat on door-pegs, britches folded over a chair-back, belt loosely coiled on the chair's seat, Bible at the bedside, papers on a small table with ink ready, small notebook for jottings (at Putney, Gideon remembered, the colonel had complained of a poor memory). Chests and saddlebags were neatly lined up along one wall. Everything was neat, as a sailor would have it.

A soldier entered quietly, with respect. The same maid had shown him in. 'Major Wilkes sent me, in case you need assistance.'

Gideon gave orders for securing the papers, which should be taken to the major. He explained that the room must be carefully locked up until Colonel Rainborough's property had been packed for his family. There would be no private sneakings up here to steal 'just a keepsake' – a handkerchief, falling bands, spectacles, prayer book – no stolen memorials appearing in seedy auctions later, with faked rusty blood-stains, *'as owned by the prominent Leveller Colonel Thomas Rainborough, and in his possession at Doncaster the same night he was treacherously slain . . .'*.

'Will they bring the corpse here?' The maid's eyes flickered to the bed. She could not help thinking of all the blood and how that blood, even congealing, would ruin good coverlets.

Gideon glanced at the soldier. 'If the body comes back to the house, let it lie on a table in some convenient room downstairs. A coffin will be ordered . . .' He and the soldier shared a brief silence, thinking of their great tall colonel. Rainborough would require a large coffin, specially made. Someone would have to organise that.

Tears wet the soldier's cheeks as he gazed miserably around the room. Like Gideon he was infected by melancholy as he viewed this place that Thomas Rainborough had used, in which he had spent his last moments. The doused candles in the sconces had been quenched by his fingers. The room still contained his smell and his spirit. His piss would be in the chamberpot, his clothes still carried hints of him. Those boots – which Gideon had just spotted with their crumpled boot-hose laid across their tops, ready to jump into again – would be intractably imprinted with his shape and sweat, permanently altered since they left the maker's last by the individual way he had walked and ridden.

'Never more!' uttered Gideon Jukes, despite himself. The reaction was private and unintentional. 'Farewell, Rainborough,' he added more formally, as he shepherded out his companions. They walked quietly on to the landing. Gideon himself found the key inside the chamber door, pulled it out and locked the room behind them. The housekeeper was staring up from downstairs.

After a second, Gideon unlocked the room again and reached behind the door for something which he carried downstairs on his arm. When he left the house, the body was still lying in the street, though Major Wilkes had set a guard until it could be taken up. He could hardly bear that terrible sight again, but Gideon Jukes walked steadily across to the corpse. The guards saw his intentions and allowed him through.

He knelt down on the cobbles, heedless of the wide pool of now-glutinous blood. There he gently covered Colonel Rainborough with his riding-cloak, for decency.

Chapter Fifty-One

Gideon Jukes escorted the coffin to London.

More details of the raid had emerged. Twenty-two Royalists had ridden out from Pontefract Castle, on Friday night. 'Eluding' Sir Henry Cholmeley's troops, a feat they achieved with ease, they crept south to Doncaster. They hid up in woods. At sunrise on Sunday morning, they emerged and met a spy from the town, carrying a Bible as identification – obviously the same man who directed Gideon. He passed on to the cavaliers details of how Doncaster was guarded and gave directions where to find Rainborough.

The horsemen presented themselves at St Sepulchre's Gate, on the south side. They claimed that they had brought dispatches from Cromwell. Since they appeared to have ridden up on the London road, the single sentinel on this approach believed it all too trustingly.

The raiders split up: six to fall on the guard at St Mary's Gate north of the town, through which they would make their eventual escape; six to tackle the main guard as it patrolled the middle of the town; six to cover the streets in case the alarm was raised. Four went to Rainborough's lodging, where they gained admittance by once again spinning the yarn about dispatches and were taken upstairs by the lieutenant.

After the murder, the cavaliers rode home in daylight to Pontefract. At two o'clock in the afternoon, in full view of Cholmeley and his several hundred cavalry, who made no attempt to interfere, they trotted back into the castle. A great shout was heard from within the garrison. It was said that the castle governor then sent a letter to Sir Henry Cholmeley to say that Rainborough was lying dead on the streets of Doncaster. Cholmeley was reported to have burst out laughing, and laughed for a quarter of an hour.

In Doncaster, recriminations flew. Captain John Smith was believed to have been with a whore at the Hinde Tavern. He fled, leaving a note for Major Wilkes, in which he claimed he intended to go to Fairfax at army headquarters to protest his innocence. He never got there; his money ran out halfway. Discovered and arrested, he was taken to London with a warrant to answer to both Houses of Parliament. While he was locked up at Ludgate, someone told him he had been convicted by a council of war and would be summarily shot. According to him, when he appealed to God for advice, God advised him to escape – so he took himself to the Netherlands, where in a feeble attempt to clear his name he issued a pamphlet, full of excuses for his own conduct and accusations of cowardice and grudge-bearing against Major Wilkes.

The rest of Rainborough's officers pleaded publicly for revenge for the murder. They took this chance to deplore the political situation, saying the King had deluded them 'into the hopes of a safe peace by the expectation of an unsafe Treaty'. Then they asked why, if the country was paying taxes, those taxes could not be used to pay the army? So the miserable quest for payment of arrears continued.

Sir Henry Cholmeley's collusion was taken for granted by both Royalist and Parliamentary news-sheets. Yet he was never examined or called to account.

Oliver Cromwell was ordered to end the siege at Pontefract. Although he sent for a formidable battery of guns, it took five more months. Cromwell was also instructed to conduct an enquiry into Rainborough's murder; nothing came of that. When the castle eventually surrendered to John Lambert, in March 1649, six officers would be exempted from mercy: men who were believed to have taken part in the murder, some of whom brazenly admitted it. They were given six days to escape if they could; the governor and one other made a getaway but were recaptured and executed. William Paulden, who had led the raid, had already died during the siege. Three others were hidden in the castle walls by their colleagues and evaded capture. By then, the Leveller John Lilburne was complaining bitterly in London that William Rainborough had been given no help to find his brother's killers.

The Tower Guards were moved back to St Albans. The House of Commons called for them to be disbanded, whether as a punishment for not protecting their colonel or because of fears that his radical spirit might linger dangerously among his men. The regiment, its name discontinued, was given to Colonel George Cook, a returned émigré from Massachusetts.

It took a fortnight to bring the body home. Even before he knew how negligently Parliament would treat his colonel's murder, Gideon Jukes was considering his position. With Rainborough gone, the Levellers had lost the most senior officer to support their cause – the *only* officer of note. With him departed any real hope of having their new ideas accepted. Gideon had two gloomy November weeks of slow travel with the hearse. As he rode, he decided to resign from the army. He had been selected for escort duty because he was the most junior captain but when he left, he warned Major Wilkes that he might stay in London. He felt bad, because the regiment was in disarray, with terrible morale.

Gideon told Wilkes that although he would always support Parliament, he was a volunteer and now wanted to be a volunteer no longer. The major merely reminded him wearily that if he kept the horse he was issued with for escort duties, he would have to pay for it.

On the 14th of November they reached the outskirts of London. Messages had gone ahead. As the cortège arrived at Tottenham High Cross, the escort found an astonishing crowd. Major William Rainborough, the colonel's brother, headed the mourners. Gideon had to tell him, as quickly as possible, what was now known about the circumstances of the murder. Although Gideon had prepared himself, he wept as he related it.

Opposition hacks would sneer snobbishly that 'Will the weaver, Tom the tapster, Kit the cobbler, Dick the door-sweeper' had turned out for their hero, and so they had, though the crowd also contained many people from the professions and from commerce. Thousands of City Levellers were waiting, for the first time wearing sea-green ribbons in sympathy with Rainborough's seafaring past.

The unprecedented procession wound through streets that were oddly silent. Even people who did not plan to follow the coffin, stood to watch it pass. Many cried. The cortège advanced slowly through Smithfield, past the cattle-pens and then the horse-market, always quieter on a Tuesday, than it would be at the main fair on Friday. Coming down along the western city wall, they passed the Old Bailey and the grim Fleet Prison, then approached Ludgate Hill. When they entered the old west gate, they were in London proper. Stationers' Hall was to their left and old St Paul's up ahead at the top of the short hill; Inigo Jones's columned portico was facing them and beyond it, the much more ancient square tower, blackened with generations of coal smoke, its tall lancet windows and dramatic flying buttresses familiar and unmistakable. As the procession made its way around the church, stationers and book-sellers closed their businesses and joined behind, all wearing the newfangled sea-green ribbons: Rainborough's colours, the Levellers' new symbol. At Cheapside, Gideon was in his home streets. By Bread Street he spotted Anne Jukes, with Robert and Amyas, who noticed with amazement that it was Gideon in charge of the honour guard, before they too began walking after the coffin.

The procession grew: forty coaches became fifty or sixty, followed by fifteen hundred horses. By the time they reached the commercial centre at Cornhill, passing close to Guildhall and right outside the flamboyant Royal Exchange, the perpetual creak and rumble of slowly moving wheels on the cobbles and the steady sounds of hooves from the multitude of gently ridden horses filled the air and would remain one of Gideon's clearest memories.

After Leadenhall, they reached the Tower of London. Since Thomas had been commander of the Tower Guards, as his coffin passed, deep-throated cannon boomed out in his honour. These guns, which had not been fired in anger during the civil war — all the guns that remained here after Fairfax's and Cromwell's requisitions for Colchester, Wales and the North — resounded mournfully across the Thames. In the enormous procession, startled horses dragged their reins and skittered nervously.

From the Tower it was a short distance through St Katharine's to the parish of Whitechapel and Wapping. Wapping High Street, close to the Thames, was a long street, off which ran numerous alleys filled with small tenements or cottages, built by sailors' victuallers, the stock from which the Rainborough family had originally come. Among the numerous shipping-related businesses were more than thirty taverns for the refreshment of sailors, from which the sailors now emerged, even the tipsiest managing to stand erect respectfully. The parish church itself, the Chapel of St John, Wapping, had a foreign look. Its belfry was no more than a gatehouse above a classically pedimented entrance door, with neither tower nor spire, which gave the chapel a plain, Dutch or Scandinavian appearance. Thomas Rainborough was buried there at St John's, alongside his father. There was a long wait while as many as possible packed in. It was an Independent funeral and the Royalist press sneered that 'the godly had their hands in their pockets' (despising religious formality). Thomas Brooks, the colonel's friend and colleague, who had served with him on water and land, preached the sermon. Appropriately he took his theme from St John:

'The whole world (saith he) lies in wickedness, in malignity; the world lies in troublesomeness. The greatest part of the great ones of this world do basely and wickedly against God! When may a man be said to do gloriously? – When he does things others have no heart for, or are afraid to do. When he holds on, notwithstanding discouragement, "blow high or blow low, rain or shine, let men smile or frown" ... I need not tell you what discouragements the noble Champion met with, but through all he was able to do God's work and to serve his generation ... It is nothing for a man to serve his generation when he hath wind and tide on his side.'

Colonel Rainborough had never had wind and tide on his side, thought Gideon rebelliously. He assessed the man for himself quietly, and decided Rainborough was perhaps never intended for the political greatness that was being put upon him now. But when the colonel's life was cut short, he was only thirty-eight years old, probably still finding his way. He was great enough to terrify his enemies and to give heart to his friends, through what he was and the thought of what he might have become. He was honest and fearless, worthy of the affection and respect that were shown to him that day at Wapping, worthy of the real grief that affected so many people. Gideon Jukes, for one, felt as if he had lost a father for the second time. It left him more disheartened than he had ever been since the war started seven years before.

Brooks was outspokenly critical of those who now held power:

'If Parliamentmen and men in the army, and in the City, and round the Kingdom did believe more gloriously, they would do more gloriously for God, in their relations and places than now they do ...
 'The more I think of the gallantry and worth of this Champion, the further off I am from discovering his worth. I think he was one of whom

this sinful Nation was not worthy; he was one of whom this declining Parliament was not worthy; he was one of whom these divided, formal, carnal Gospellers was not worthy. He served his Generation faithfully, though he died by the hands of treachery . . . They honoured him in life and they showed no small respect to him in death: He was a joy to the best, and a terror to the worst of men.'

Chapter Fifty-Two

St Katharine's and Newgate: 1648–50

The boom of the great guns had an unexpected benefit in the depot that housed the young people who had been 'spirited'. As soon as the cannonade began, all the keepers rushed to see what was going on. Most of their charges were too subdued or too youthful to take advantage. But for one troubled soul, the great funeral at Wapping provided an escape.

Her name was temporarily Alice Smith. She chose it to sound respectable on the indentures they had given her. Six months after she was taken from Covent Garden, she ended up in a holding-house, or depot, in St Katharine's-by-the-Tower, moved there from St Giles-in-the-Fields as the day for shipment to Virginia or the Indies grew closer. The second civil war, with the navy revolt and blockades downstream in the Thames estuary, had delayed transportation and given her a respite, but towards the end of the year the young people were told their boat would come soon.

During her captivity – though it was never openly called that – she had come to regret her agreement to emigrate. She was by nature more suspicious than the other kidnapped young people. She kept her ears open. Soon, the situation began to worry her. She overheard a pair of desperate parents begging to have their stolen child returned. She noted how the staff spoke among themselves of their kidnapped charges' fates. Always ready to believe she had been lied to for the gain of others, Alice Smith began to fear that once she reached her destination she would find that the 'service' she had signed up for was not mild house-work with respectable colonists but hard manual labour out of doors on plantations, in conditions close to slavery. Once she arrived overseas, it would be too late. She asked as many questions about conditions as she dared. When this was discouraged, she soon disbelieved all the glowing promises.

She stayed at the depot, because it was an easy life – so far. She had shelter and food. Even the meagre daily diet was better than she had been used to; her health and with it her inbuilt truculence began to revive. She kept alert for news of their ship, and was keyed up to abscond. When the matron and staff ran out to watch Rainborough's funeral procession, she decided to waste no more time. So she calmly filled an apron with whatever she could carry, then she slipped out of an unguarded door and made off.

St Katharine's was a forbidding area. It lay beyond the Tower, outside the city walls. Less than a hundred years before, this had been an empty quarter used only for drowning pirates on the foreshore; convicted pirates were by tradition chained to ramps until three tides had passed over them – a story that had been told to the spirited youngsters in the process of subduing them. Alice was not afraid of long-dead pirates – though she turned instinctively away from the river.

The main feature of this parish was a charitable foundation for the poor, the Royal Hospital or Free Chapel. Founded and supported by various queens of England, it had been a Catholic institution but was spared by Henry the Eighth during his dissolution of monastic orders, because it had belonged to his mother. The hospital was regarded with suspicion because, even when nominally Protestant, it was run by lay brethren and sisters. Like so many religious properties, it had attracted the poor and helpless until it became the centre of a rat's nest of lanes and mean streets, containing perhaps a thousand houses where stick-thin, dull-eyed paupers struggled against starvation and disease. As with all the liberties beyond London's walls, the area became a haven for illegal trades and the outsiders who practised them. The small, stinking cottages and dilapidated tenements housed a lawless English underclass and foreigners who were no better. The alleys had suggestive names: Dark Entry, Cat's Hole, Shovel Alley, Eagle and Child Alley, Axe Yard and Naked Boy Court. This grim district was a natural place to position the depot for stolen children: rough, unfriendly, secret and rarely visited by anyone respectable.

In some ways it was no worse an area than Southwark, across the river, where 'Eliza' and Jem Starling had holed up the previous year. There were just as many seamen on this side, with watermen of all types, especially the drunken, unemployed variety. Among the wrongdoers who had emerged like fleas at the funeral commotion were prostitutes looking for clients and vagabonds planning to pick pockets as the great procession of mourners wended up Wapping High Street. Astute ones had adorned their dishevelled coats with sea-green ribbons so they would blend in.

'Alice' picked her way through the tangle of unpaved lanes and alleys, stepping over piles of litter and runnels of nightsoil, while keeping an eye out for people throwing slops from the teetering tenements above. Nobody seemed to observe her. The dark, filthy courtyards seemed deserted, though she knew better than to feel secure here. Any unguarded moment could have pitched her into worse trouble than she had left behind. She pulled in her skirts and scurried past East Smithfield, where some of the most degraded brothels in London huddled, although the neat lines of little houses had once been pleasant dwellings occupied by hardworking hatters and shoemakers. Now the clothes they once made, so worn they barely held together by threads, were sold second, third or fourth hand in Rosemary Lane. That was where the public executioner lived, the man who had lopped off the heads of Strafford and Laud, or so turnkeys were wont to tell the children at the depot. 'And he will come for you too, if you give us any trouble!' It was a fetid little street crammed with sour taverns and totters' stalls, where 'Alice' managed to sell for a penny what she had stolen from the depot. Before leaving the lane, she carried out a swift piece of stall-robbery and fled with a tattered hood that would help to disguise her.

She went west. So she entered the City, by chance reversing the processional route which Thomas Rainborough's cortège had taken earlier that day. The streets remained subdued. Unsure where to turn, she began a long walk that would bring her back towards the Strand and Covent Garden where she had worked her way in misery before. This time she turned off, reluctant to be spotted again by the man who had lured her. Instead, she slipped into the disreputable alleys around Giltspur Street, north of the Old Bailey.

She survived there for six months. Time had no meaning for her, days, weeks and months slipping by as once again she deteriorated. She heard they beheaded the King, but the tentative start of the Commonwealth meant little at gutter level. Then, since the life of the dirt poor stayed unchanged by the absence of monarchy, one day she walked into a house where a maid had left a door open; she stole a silver charger, which was a felony. When she tried to fence the plate, a thief-taker informed on her; she was brought, spitting protests, before a particularly dyspeptic magistrate. It was her first mistake, so she hoped to get off with a fine and a whipping. Transportation to the colonies was a possibility that made her smile grimly, since she had escaped it once when she was spirited. But her manner was so defiant, she was despatched to Newgate Prison under sentence to be hanged.

She knew what to do; she 'pleaded her belly'. Examined physically by a 'jury of matrons', to check her story, she was pronounced genuinely pregnant. She was as surprised as they were. This would save her life until she came to term; she had no idea how long that would be, having no sure way to tell which of the casual couplings with lawyers' clerks and muffin boys that she had engaged in when particularly desperate for money had resulted in a baby.

It was born. It died. Still in prison, she disposed of the evidence secretly and for a while longer pretended she was still pregnant, mocking up a convincing bump as she had done in her short career of highway robbery. So she clung on in Newgate, a desperate jail where every staple of life, even a place near the fire, had to be paid for either with money or some base favour to the jailors. Prisoners were denuded of an entry fee on first arriving, then fees for food, for bedding, for clothes, even a release fee if they were pardoned or transported. Also, the longer she stayed, the greater the risk she would catch fatal jail fever.

Eventually she could no longer delay fate, but had to face her penalty. She made no attempt to bribe the jailor or his turnkeys, nor even to petition for the pardon that many obtained. Now friendless, she had nobody to bring in food or arrange an escape. Gone were the days when she could have sent for the proceeds of past robberies to pay her way out of trouble. She had no money to hire a 'knight of the post' to give false evidence and save her with an alibi. She sank into dreary acceptance that she was going the gallows. It was as if she no longer cared.

Then, at the last moment, she met Priscilla Fotheringham. Known in those days as a 'cat-eyed gipsy', Priss was a pockmarked, beaten-up Scot from the lowest scam of deprivation, already an experienced prostitute, who was about to become a bawd, keeping her own notorious house. 'Alice' overheard her cackling with two other whores who were inconvenienced by a spell in jail for robbery. They were laying plans to enliven the new Commonwealth with efficient and lucrative new pleasure-palaces. In years to come it would be said that Priss, and these two equally famous madams called Damaris Page and Elizabeth Cresswell, had shared a cell and plotted a Venetian-style courtesans' guild, with subscriptions. They planned to hire resident doctors to prescribe contraception, perform abortions, restore virginities and cure venereal disease. They would have scriveners to write letters and draft bonds, which were a bawd's main means of controlling her girls, since they imposed enforceable penalties for debt. As well as the normal battery of pimps and doorkeepers, or hectors, there would be specialist barbers to shave the girls' pubic commodities in the exotic Spanish style. A painter would draw erotic art to inspire patrons. And it was alleged that this prison council of working women also decided to link Priss Fotheringham's house to another legendary establishment: the Last and Lyon at Smithfield, otherwise known as Hammond's Prick Office, where the whores indulged clients with oral sex – another foreign innovation that raised eyebrows and therefore cost a great deal of money – each girl having first demonstrated her skills on Hammond's own readily available jockum.

Little of this heady future was apparent in those early days in Newgate. But even as a depressed prisoner in that hellish jail, Priss Fotheringham had manoeuvred access to the few comforts available. Despite her woeful appearance, she maintained links to the outside and could access funds. The usual grubby mystery attached to her background. She was listed as a spinster, though married perhaps twice, not bothering to wait until the first syphilitic husband died before taking a second. When one husband beat her up, she ran away with a halberdier from the Artillery Ground, until he spent all her money and abandoned her. She had been trained in her mother-in-law's brothel in Cowcross Street, a filthy area of Finsbury, where she became a hard-working exponent of the normal horizontal trade – though due to become famous for much more curious gymnastic skills.

She for her part immediately saw in 'Alice' a likely wench who was in need of kindly mentoring. Recruiting girls to the trade was a basic brothel skill. She fed the downcast mite a bowl of gruel, strengthened it with a slug of sack and quickly extracted her entire history. Discovering – with a dramatic cry of joy – that during her service in Tinker Fox's garrison this girl had been taught brewing, Priss Fotheringham revealed that her own release was imminent, expected any day; Priss had made arrangements of a traditional kind with the jailor. Upon regaining her freedom, she intended to open a refurbished alehouse called the Six Windmills by Finsbury Fields; it was previously known as Jack o' Newbury's, when according to her it had had a bad reputation that she intended to redeem. It was very well placed, alongside the Artillery Ground where the Trained Bands drilled.

'They work up a thirst?' asked the snivelling wench.

'Well, let's say they get up *something* . . .'

In no time Priss recruited 'Alice' to be sprung from prison for a new life – doing honest work with malt and hops in the brewhouse of an allegedly respectable travellers' rest.

It was in fact the unique retail establishment that would be known to history as Mother Fotheringham's Half Crown Chuck Office.

Chapter Fifty-Three

A Lane near Tottenham: October 1648

'A man!' exclaimed Valentine. After long hours of travel he had been hunched and silent, but what he saw made him excited.

'Oh, I think he is dead.' Tom, equally fascinated, scrambled to the side of the cart and stared ahead.

Until now they had both been extremely subdued. They were frightened that their mother, the only other person in their world, had been devastated by trouble which she avoided explaining. But children rapidly recover when given a new interest.

'Do not look!' instructed Juliana, though her words would make them do it. She tried to whip up the horse: useless. The beast, a cast-off of the Pelhams, had taken them to Colchester and was bringing them back, but it was pulling a cart laden with her possessions and what remained of her father's, a load it considered an outrageous imposition. It went only at its own pace.

'*Boys, don't look!*' She was prepared for them to see death. She meant, if he is alive, do not meet his eyes. Do not court trouble. Please, do not let us be drawn into a situation that I cannot manage . . .

As they passed, the horse took fright at the figure lying in the hedgerow. It dragged sideways with a pathetic whinny and crashed the cart against the bushes at the opposite roadside, so the only solution was to rein in. Fortunately when it slowed to a halt, they were yards beyond the man. All three looked back.

They were in a peaceful country lane. Like so many places, its hedges had not been tended for years. There were long gaps. To either side was English rough pasture, with tall clumps of rusty sorrel among the rank grass. Nothing grazed there. After the floods, it would be soggy underfoot; if she let the boys down to piss, they would come back with muddy shoes and kick slime over her skirt. Dead vegetation was caught among brambles. Great black rooks stalked around the pastureland as if they owned it.

'Stay here!' Too late. Three-year-old Val had already slid from the cart, legs straight, skidding on the seat of his britches. Once on the ground, he felt he had the better of his mother. He strolled back, slowly, showing only a little caution. Tom, who was older and more worldly wise, stayed at her side. The person in the hedge had not moved, yet Juliana felt reluctant to call Val, afraid to arouse the man's attention.

The horse became agitated in the traces. She could not entrust the reins to a child; handling this dreadful creature was almost beyond her own strength. 'I have to stay here. Thomas, fetch your brother.'

Tom jumped down like a cricket and was off down the lane. Wrong decision, Juliana decided wryly; now I have lost both of them. They were good children, but when they failed to see logic in her orders, they defied her with a casual ease that Tom for one had learned from their father. That was even though they hardly knew their father.

'He is not dead,' she heard Tom's clear voice, telling Val. How could he tell? Heavens, the man must have stirred, or looked at him. 'Though he is close to it. He has a red coat – he is one of *them*.' Val took his brother's hand as Tom addressed the man formally: 'Where are you going, sir?'

The figure spoke. He spoke so that even Juliana, struggling again with the recalcitrant horse, heard his destination.

'London? *We* are going to London!' Tom exclaimed. It was not an offer of assistance; he knew better, as his glance back to his mother confirmed. Thank you for the consultation, Juliana thought. The horse settled. She twisted in her seat, still clutching the reins as she half-stood so she could see over their mounded luggage.

'He might hurt us,' Val told his brother wisely.

'Not much!' Tom retaliated.

It seemed true. The man lay exhausted, obviously sick or wounded. She could see no bandages. Nor could she make out blood, or any of the terrible wounds soldiers suffered. Like the sick and exhausted people she had seen at Colchester, he must be simply failing from neglect and hunger. Colchester was a long way behind them now, but it was possible he too had come from there.

Juliana wanted the boys safely back with her. So much misery had crushed her lately, she was unable to abandon another sufferer. Like all people who have little, she was too close to thinking *What if this were me?* Therefore she heard herself call out grudgingly, 'You will experience a jolting, if you ride with us. But if you can climb in unaided, we will take you to the city gate.' She had set her conditions. Neither she nor her boys would touch him. He would stay well behind them, crammed among their baggage, where if he was as helpless as he seemed, he could not harm them.

'Tom, Val; come back here now.' Eager to see what would happen, they came scampering. She pulled them up in the front with her. They waited.

The man had roused himself. With difficulty, he stood upright. He wore, half unbuttoned, what had once been the uniform coat of the Parliamentary army, though the cloth was dark with use and the red colour had leached from its dye. He fumbled with a small bundle, his snapsack. One step at a time, he came to the cart. He had days' of matted beard-growth. The snaggles of hair sticking out from under his hat were filthy, though he was fair, apparently. Juliana cursed herself for not having considered whether he had weapons, though he appeared unarmed.

She had the sword! Annoyed, she remembered that old sword Lovell once gave her to protect herself; it was here in the cart with them. But too late. Always distasteful of it, she had hidden the thing right under their belongings, so she could not reach it now.

Tom wriggled free and jumped down again. In an instant he was at the tailboard, which he unleashed and dropped, very politely. As if afraid that they might still change their minds and leave him, the sick man forced himself forwards and up into the vehicle. He collapsed again, lying face down against their possessions, retreating into his sickness, yet not quite finished, for he made a desperate effort to pull in his legs so Tom could close up the tailboard. Just before he pushed it up, the well-mannered five-year-old introduced himself: 'My name is Tom Lovell, sir.' There was some mumbled reply.

The boy rushed back and climbed aboard. Gently, as if to spare their passenger, Juliana made the horse walk on. 'Watch behind,' she murmured. 'Val, Tom – if that man moves, tell me instantly.'

'His name is *Jukes*,' whispered Tom, as if he was reproving his mother for some discourtesy in speaking of him.

To Juliana it was familiar for some reason.

Chapter Fifty-Four

London and Lewisham: Autumn 1648

Anne Jukes was in her apron, with her hands all floury, when Robert Allibone's journeyman, as Amyas now was, urgently called her from her kitchen. Completely flustered, Anne gesticulated helplessly, not recognising Juliana among the strangers with Amyas. The tailboard was down. Amyas was shaking his head, almost as a warning, and then Anne saw the wasted, barely conscious soldier that this strange family had brought to her. 'Ah *Lambert!*'

Her husband slithered over the edge of the cart. He had grown so thin that Anne Jukes, a brewer's sturdy daughter, was strong enough to haul his arm over her shoulder and support his weight. She staggered with him indoors. 'Amyas, bring these people in and look after their things, please. I need to know what has happened . . .'

So the Lovells gazed up from their ramshackle flatbed at the gracious gables and sash windows of a substantial three-storey London merchant's house, then they were brought into a warm kitchen that glittered with burnished copper utensils, where they waited to be interviewed by Anne. Upstairs, it took her almost an hour to get Lambert undressed, washed and laid in a clean bed. A maid had been sent running out for a doctor. Downstairs, Juliana Lovell took it upon herself to find a cloth and remove Anne's nutmeg-scented bread pudding from the oven when it was obviously done. The boys stared with great hope at the pudding until they fell asleep against their mother, who was already dozing in exhaustion on a settle.

So Anne eventually found them, and realised she would have to take them in. She went quietly back upstairs and made up the guest bed. It was a high four-poster, a full tester, with fantastical tapestry hangings and swag ties so heavy they could have knocked a bullock unconscious. There her refugees all slept together that night, the most comfortable night they had had since they left Essex, or perhaps ever.

Next day, Anne took the little boys to the Jukes' shop, where Thomas solemnly helped to weigh things out while Valentine gorged himself on sweet raisins and almonds. Leaving them in safe hands, Anne hurried home. She found Juliana was ready to let her guard down, lulled by the unaccustomed luxury of knowing that her children were warm, fed and secure. It was weeks since she had freely spoken to another adult. It was three years since she last had a close woman friend and longer than that since she had openly discussed anything to do with her family.

Anne Jukes first wanted to find out what had happened to Lambert. All her normal housework was deferred. Upstairs, her husband slumbered and began his recovery. Anne was herself in a state of shock. She welcomed a morning when she could sit idle at the kitchen fireside while she prepared herself for having Lambert home. She was acutely curious about the Lovells too.

Juliana told how they came upon Lambert, some miles beyond Chelmsford. 'I managed to learn from him that carts were provided to bring the sick and wounded to London,' Anne said. 'He says they took a stop to rest and his cart accidentally went on without him – he could not run after it – yet the fool decided he would then walk home . . . I had been told he had a serious sickness that he could not shake off. Gideon wrote to me that Lambert had the bloody flux –'

Gideon? wondered Juliana, imagining some pinch-mouthed, fatalistic puritan. Clearly an idiot, if he had told poor Anne her faraway husband was gripped by the generally fatal epidemic.

Once she remembered that she had met a woman called Jukes at the printer's in Basinghall Street, Juliana had reasoned, rightly, that carrying in a sick New Model Army soldier might persuade the guards at Moorgate to admit her without too many questions. One had been detailed to accompany her to the print shop; he pushed her aside from the driving seat, as if a woman could not be trusted to control a horse, so she let him have the trouble of arguing with it. At the shop Amyas took over, intrigued to see how Anne would react to having Lambert home. Juliana remembered again her curiosity about this woman and the printer, Allibone. *He* had appeared briefly but merely gave Amyas instructions to escort the cart to Bread Street.

There Anne Jukes had greeted her husband's sudden return with simple surprise. She bounced automatically to wild panic at his dire condition, then she braced herself to tackle it. 'Well, so, so! I have him back . . . Now tell me, Mistress Lovell, how were you passing by at that lucky moment?'

Juliana was relieved to unburden herself. First she spoke of why she and the boys had been at Pelham Hall, and what she presumed her husband had been doing. Annoyed at being abandoned, she would not lie to Anne about either his politics or his activities. Then Juliana told how the Pelham family had been so relieved to see the back of her, they equipped her with horse, cart, a hamper for the journey and a travel-pass to Colchester that said, accurately, she was a distressed daughter looking for her invalid father.

'What was your father's situation?'

'As terrible as it could be.'

Germain Carlill, who had always been a misfit, had prematurely lost his wits like an old man. This was the sad secret Juliana and Mr Gadd had always kept. He began to fail in the 1630s, when Juliana was still a child. All the family were then living in Colchester, the original home of her vanished grandfather the haberdasher, a modest town house in the suburbs. As Germain became more and more vague and in need of constant care, he was placed with a young woman of the town; she was paid for nursing services with the rent from a property that Roxanne bought for the purpose. Germain had wasted most of their money but Roxanne earned some by making the costumes for a court masque. While doing that in London, she acquired the famous 'estate in Kent, with orchards' that Mr Gadd later touted as Juliana's dowry; it was little more than a small house with a market garden and few fruit trees near a village called Lewisham. The deeds were in Germain's name, for Roxanne wanted to ensure he would always be cared for. 'It was either that or put him in Bridewell. My father no longer knew us and could not be reasoned with.' Wiping away a tear, Juliana did not have to tell Anne Jukes that the Bridewell treatment of lunatics was to beat them with rods; it was supposed to drive out their demons and cure them, though it helped but few.

Once her grandmother could no longer bear Germain's decrepitude, being an intolerant woman who was angered by illness in others, she sold the Colchester house and took Juliana to London. There Roxanne died. Tottering himself, her guardian William Gadd saw his priority as settling Juliana; he never told Orlando Lovell that the 'Kentish orchards' were meagre and still belonged to Germain Carlill. Once she married, Juliana had frequently had to make excuses to Lovell for her non-receipt of the rents.

When Juliana went back to Colchester to look for her father after the siege, one of her trials was hearing from his keeper that no money had been received from the Lewisham tenants for some time. Juliana would have to discover why. None of the likely explanations was good.

Far worse news was waiting, however. By the time she arrived at Colchester and talked her way in through the victorious New Model Army soldiers, her father was dead. As she read the news-sheets, she had suspected this. He was too fragile to survive such a siege. His nurse's house had been lost to fire; the homeless had to shelter in a church. Before then, the poor old man – who was fifty, yet more like a man of ninety – had become utterly confused and terrified. Germain knew nothing of the civil war. He lived in his own world, no longer aware who he was, responding to his nurse out of habit. The noise of guns had appalled him; Juliana was told of one wild scene when he escaped to the town walls, half naked, and tried to instruct the soldiers to stop causing such a commotion. Starvation hit him hard. Already weak, he shrank to a wraith, refusing to eat even the unpalatable scraps that were available. His mind deteriorated further, very rapidly. He ranted uncontrollably and accused the poor woman who looked after him of trying to end his life. She had little to give him, and soon knew she could not save him.

'By the time I found her,' Juliana poured out to Anne Jukes through tears, 'she was herself desperately sick. She died, almost overcome by relief at telling me what had happened to Papa. She died apologising for his death – even though I was told by others afterwards that the woman had struggled to look after him long after most would have given up. She had not just shared her pitiful rations with him, but gave him the greater share because his pleas were so heartbreaking . . .'

Nobody left at Colchester could tell Juliana exactly when Germain Carlill died, or where he was buried. The dead had been disposed of by the fainting population in a random fashion, with no parish records kept. Nobody ever knew the full death toll among civilians.

Juliana had paid for the nurse to be buried. At the funeral, a woman who had probably intended to keep quiet suddenly came forward and told her where to find her father's remaining possessions. Juliana knew Germain had owned a watch and there had once been pewter, linen, colourful delft platters . . . she would never see any of those again. She did find sacks of haberdashery. She tracked down one great chair that her father had always sat in. In a chest, surviving because they must have seemed to have no value, were papers covered with her grandmother's patterns for lace and embroidery. Juliana piled all these onto her cart, with her own possessions.

She had one last task: to discover whether Orlando Lovell had been among the Royalists at Colchester. She was unable to find his name in the lists of prisoners and a few she was allowed to speak to had never heard of him. So she left Colchester, her last link with her own family, for ever.

Juliana confessed to Anne she was glad she never had to show her sons their grandfather without his wits and suffering. Eventually she would be able to tell Tom and Val about Germain, as she remembered him from her short but happy childhood – the affectionate father who had helped her learn her letters and given her a love of literature: gentle, always a little vague, unworldly, maddeningly untouched by common sense or commercial acumen, but also quite lacking in the greed, depravity and ambition that disfigured so many men's characters.

'Would he have been for Parliament or the King?' Anne Jukes asked curiously.

'I do not think he would have known how to decide.'

'Would he have wanted equality and liberty?'

Juliana smiled suddenly. She knew from their past meeting that Anne had a subscription to the Levellers. It would not have surprised her to hear that Anne attended meetings where she-preachers stood up. 'Oh, when he had his wits, my father could not have been for any other cause.'

'And you?' Anne wondered. She had learned enough from the episode yesterday when Juliana quietly removed the pudding from the oven during the crisis of Lambert's return – and then did not draw attention to her good deed. Anne was glad to have Juliana in her house for a few days. They understood one another, as some women do instinctively. 'So whom do you support?'

'I am a wife!' protested Juliana. The two women's eyes met.

'Oh you think as your husband does!' teased Anne Jukes. 'You think as your husband *tells* you to think – which is, you do not think at all.'

'He is the head of my household.' Juliana was smiling despite herself.

'You say he is never there.'

'So now Lambert has returned to you, will you do all he suggests – or will you wrangle?'

Anne smoothed down her apron. 'There will be fights ahead.' She let out the words like one who was just admitting it for the first time.

They sat in silence for a while, each pondering her own problems. When the moment came to rebuild the fire then develop a new subject, Juliana prodded, 'I do not suppose you have had much to do with Royalists?'

'Is there a family in England that does not have divided loyalties?' Anne was now in a gossipy mood. 'The Jukes had a terrible uncle, Bevan Bevan – a man who caused dissension every time he cleared his throat. He recently set himself on a horse and joined in the Kent rebellion. A more ridiculous cavalier the King could not muster; Bevan could hardly move for his weight and his gout, and he was far too old for adventuring. I am waiting to tell Lambert how the silly man advanced upon London with Lord Norwich's troops, and was with them when they swam their horses across the river by Greenwich. Bevan's horse managed to shed him and he was carried away by the current. Many were drowned; Bevan was among them. His body was washed ashore downriver. He was recognised by his belly – and his old red suit.'

'Your husband will rejoice at this?'

'My husband rejoices in no man's death,' Anne quickly replied. 'His uncle caused trouble all his life, but has left behind a wife nearly hysterical, with many children.' Anne paused. 'Elizabeth will marry again,' she confided, with certainty. 'There are women who always do.'

They smiled together, two natural survivors, deploring such women who could not live five minutes alone.

'Quite *how* many children?' Juliana queried meaningfully.

'Six or seven now, all badly behaved and snotty. You are right; it is enough to deter suitors – but the widow has ownership of a printing business . . .'

'Ah, just give her six months then!'

This time they both laughed gently.

*　　*　　*

Bereavement, loneliness and anxiety caught up with Juliana.

'Oh you have saddened me, Mistress Jukes,' she acknowledged. She had not gossiped by the fire with a woman friend since Nerissa died – she could not discuss Nerissa, both Irish and Roman Catholic, in this house of Independents. 'I am looking back and reassessing life. I have nobody now.' No one except a husband who was missing yet again and who would not thank her for enquiring after him. Even Mr Gadd had stopped answering her letters. He might be too frail to write; more likely he had died of old age. 'I see very clearly how these wars have taken everything from us. Orlando and I never enjoyed a life together. I find myself thinking of what I have had and lost – then I look forwards, only to see what I shall now never possess.'

'You are young,' Anne reminded her.

'And, you may say, madam, *you have your children*! My boys give me much – but they also cause me constant fear, fear for them, and for all of us. Sometimes, Mistress Jukes, I feel that I am yearning constantly . . . for I know not what.'

Anne Jukes smiled a small, intensely rueful smile. 'Ah *that*, Mistress Lovell! When you find whatever we women run after so blindly, let me know, I pray you, what it is.'

Once, Anne would have jumped up, to lose her emotion in making a beef broth to revive Lambert. Time and weariness had overtaken her too. So she sat on beside the fire, and merely thought about how she ought to be doing it.

A few days later Juliana set off with her sons on their travels again. This time, she was taking them to the house with the orchard, which was – though Juliana carefully did not excite the boys with this thought – a possibility of somewhere to call home. Anxieties over what she might find kept her silent. It was far-sighted.

The journey took longer than she had hoped; they were frequently stopped and questioned by soldiers. They crossed over London Bridge, then travelled through Southwark and Deptford, on the old Woolwich Road, which ran out through Greenwich, although they turned off just before the cobbled highway passed through the middle of the still-uncompleted Queen's House in the royal park. They went away from the river, following directions on a faint, tattered paper left by Juliana's grandmother. She at least had been here once; Roxanne Carlill was not a woman to buy property unseen. *She probably lay with the land agent*, thought Juliana, admitting the truth about her grandmother. Juliana understood now. Roxanne was a widow, and a widow in a foreign country, struggling to put bread on the table for her child – Germain, that wide-eyed innocent. The Levellers might say all men were born equal, yet Germain had been born both more affable and less able to help himself than most. Juliana's own children seemed to have escaped that – although she sometimes feared she saw a trace of her father in Valentine.

Perhaps not. It was Val who first spotted the overgrown path leading from the rutted lane where they had nearly bogged down. The day had been long enough for him; he jumped out of the cart and strutted off, announcing, 'I am going down there.' They had found the house, which was a large cottage with a collection of by now extremely gnarled mixed fruit trees. Immediately her heart failed, for she could see through the twilight that no lights showed and no smoke rose from the chimneys, yet the door was standing open.

The tenants must have left months before. Juliana never found out when, nor where they went. *Why* they left was obvious. The house had been vandalised. It could be by serving soldiers, disbanded troops, or local people who had decided that the property was owned by a Royalist. Plundering had taken place. Pointless plundering, mindless damage where fences were broken down, cupboard doors were wrenched off their hinges, firejacks were bent, mattresses and pillows were slit open and voided of their feathers, goods from the larder were not even stolen, but emptied upon the floor and kicked about.

The abandoned house had then reverted to nature. As damp entered the building, food remnants that were not taken by rats grew skeins and crowns of mould. Juliana found chairs where baby mice teemed squalidly in the seat-padding. Birds had hopped in through windows and nested in the upper rooms. Beetles of all types ran everywhere with the spiders. Wind and rain did their worst to the fabric.

Even then, the destruction continued. *Someone* had lived here, after the tenants' abandonment. Brutish people, with the lowest of standards, had occupied the dwelling not long ago; had caused more damage; strewn more rubbish; lit fires – not always in the hearths – and deposited human shit in room corners.

'I do not like it here,' mumbled Val nervously.

'*I* like it!' shouted Tom, running from room to filthy room like a true boy.

Juliana sat on a broken chair, thought better of it, then stood up again. In what had once been a tiny parlour, now with no door and all its shutters torn away, she gave way to despair and cried her eyes out.

Deciding that they would have to leave, she wrapped the boys in cloaks and blankets and sheltered with them beside their cart through a long, sleepless night in the open. Only in the pale light of next morning did she accept that they had nowhere else to go. Dispirited and almost broken, she began the task of clearing out her little house.

She had made one room just about habitable when, a few weeks after they arrived, they had a completely unexpected visitor. Juliana knew that she knew him, but out of context it took her a moment to remember who he was: he had ridden up on a squat pony, with a satchel slung around his body and a long birding gun, a solid man in a russet coat – 'Jolly Jack, mistress.' John Jolley! Squire Lovell's land agent.

Through her surprise, Juliana gasped questions about how he had known he might find her here – only to discover an offensive truth. Jolley had come to find *Orlando*, not her. Orlando had asked him to sell his Hampshire estates.

'So did you expect to find him here?'

'Not really. This was the only address I had.'

Juliana gritted her teeth. 'He wants to sell his land to finance revolt? Well, it is too late, Master Jolley. The uprising has failed.'

'That I know,' replied the agent calmly. 'But in conscience I wanted to explain to him face to face that I cannot sell. His activities –' John Jolley hesitated over his words. Jolley supported Parliament, Juliana knew without ever asking. 'What they call his malignancy has become well known. By going into Kent in arms against Parliament, he is adjudged to have broken his parole. The estate is absolutely taken from him. The lands will be sold to pay New Model Army soldiers.'

'No appeal?'

'None, you may believe it.'

The agent gave Juliana a small amount of money, which he had managed to wrest from the Hampshire Committee as her 'fifth' for the previous year. *Would he have given my fifth to Orlando, had Orlando been here . . . ?*

Jolley then stayed a few days, presumably out of loyalty to the Lovell family. He shot rabbits and birds to hang up for meat. Looking around at the conditions in which she was living, he himself made some basic repairs for her, then he found a local carpenter to help patch up doors, windows and the roof.

'I cannot afford to pay him,' Juliana protested frankly.

'I have squared him for two weeks' work for you.'

'With your own money?' She was horrified, yet she was desperate to have the work done.

'I shall mention it to the squire on my return. He will most likely see his way to reimbursing me.'

'Does he soften towards Orlando?'

'No, mistress. But the squire will be too proud to see me out of pocket for his son.'

For a blinding moment Juliana wondered if she was expected to make John Jolley an offer of payment in kind – she and Nerissa McIlwaine used to joke about women with loose morals who 'never had to pay a tradesman'. She felt hot. Setting her jaw against the very thought, she thanked the man sincerely but briefly. The moment passed.

'Has any word of my husband reached Hampshire?'

'None. And none has reached you, Mistress Lovell?'

'No.' Except that because of John Jolley's visit, Juliana now knew for sure Lovell had been here. Mr Gadd would have told him years ago where the house was. So it must have been Lovell and his Royalist associates who wrecked it. That smacked into her like a betrayal.

To have the house linked to Lovell was dangerous. Juliana inherited it when her father died but, as a wife, everything of hers legally belonged to her husband. Lovell could, now that she owned it, sell the house and land and leave her destitute. Even more simply, Parliament could remove it from her because her husband was a Royalist. Enquiry discovered that John Jolley had not mentioned this property to any committee, for which she was thankful.

After Jolley left, their living conditions improved. The carpenter made the house sound. Juliana swept, washed, even found one or two usable tools and utensils, hidden in outhouses or discarded in undergrowth. They lived frugally, but they survived. It was a hard winter for the poor. As she eked out their meagre funds, sometimes they had no dinner on the table. Eventually, though, they had a larder that would sustain them through the spring, because when Juliana wrote to confirm that she was settled, Anne Jukes sent one of the grocery carriers with a great quantity of goods, out of gratitude for saving Lambert. Now they had flour, sugar, butter, currants, almonds, even spices.

They still had to outwit the iron-cold English winter. They dressed in layers, sometimes wearing almost everything they owned. They slept some nights all huddled together, when even a hot brick wrapped in old rags would not keep the bed warm. Even on the mildest days, they woke to find a thick layer of frost on their one window with glass, and the frost would stay all day, never melting. When Juliana made the boys nightshirts, they would put them on beside the fire, then dive into bed shrieking; they soon learned how to dress in their day clothes next morning while huddled underneath the bedclothes. Laundry froze solid on the washing line. Milk came from the farm with lumps of ice in it. The boys paddled through slush in the lane, then scampered home with their fingers red-raw and their wet stockings stiff on their chilblained little feet.

When she could, Juliana followed the news. Apart from wanting information about Lovell's fate, she knew this was a momentous period. The New Model Army had called the King to account. Despairing of a peaceful settlement, they had brought him to trial at Westminster. So it was in the dead of that freezing winter, at the end of January, that she left her sons in the care of a friendly woman she had come to know on a farm locally. She considered taking them to London with her, so they could participate in the historic event, but she thought them too young so she went alone.

Juliana Lovell took a boat from Greenwich, travelled upriver and joined the crowds outside the Banqueting House in Whitehall on the 30th of January. There she watched the public execution of King Charles.

Chapter Fifty-Five

Westminster: January 1649

It came as a surprise to Gideon that when, back in London, he offered his services again to the Trained Bands' Green Regiment, they failed to welcome him with rapture. 'You can't just turn up! We are not a dump for cast-off New Modellers.'

'I am experienced.'

'And infected with fantastical, wild ideas, no doubt. All our officers are Presbyterians now. We don't have room for Baptists and Levellers and anti-monarchist firebrands with their bowels all on fire for giving potboys the vote.'

'I can use a snaphance musket.'

'Use it to shoot ducks then.'

'Is Colonel Warner still in charge?'

'No, he died in the summer.'

While Gideon was away, his old colonel, Sir John Warner, had been elected Lord Mayor of London. His obituaries took up almost as much newsprint as those for Thomas Rainborough, and in the conservative press more. Warner had been Lord Mayor during a contentious period. His predecessor, Sir John Gayre, had colluded with the Royalist rebels in Kent – to the extent that he was indicted for high treason. However, Warner was a puritanical Independent, who would be remembered longest for having abolished the traditional satirical puppets at Bartholomew's Fair. After he died, every puppeteer that August had a puppet playing Warner, making him a fool.

> *'Here lies my lord Mayor, under this stone,*
> *That last Bartholomew's Fair, no puppets would own,*

But next Bartholomew's Fair, who liveth to see,
Shall view my lord Mayor, a puppet to be!'

Reforms that would give the puppets much more to squeak about were coming to a head, and Gideon would find work. By remaining in London he witnessed December's and January's astonishing events.

Only three weeks after Rainborough's funeral, the move to bring the King to trial began. Up until then, peace negotiations had continued. Presbyterians, who still dominated Parliament, sent commissioners to the Isle of Wight, to speak to the King directly. He misinterpreted their eagerness to reach a settlement, which was really born out of deep fear of the radical republicans. The King took it for weakness, not grasping that even the Presbyterians now thought he was hopeless to deal with.

It was seven years since the war began, and one draft treaty after another had come to nothing. It was three and a half years since Naseby, after which the New Model Army thought there should be no further argument. Now, Henry Ireton was put in charge of steering their proposals with an iron hand. On behalf of the army Ireton drew up a remonstrance which demanded abandoning negotiations, dissolving the Long Parliament which had been sitting for almost a decade, reforming the franchise and putting the King to trial on a charge of high treason.

This was unacceptable to Parliament. Parliament, as it was then constituted, therefore had to go. A secret committee – three MPs and three senior army officers – gathered in a private room. They looked at the members, name by name, marking those who 'had continued faithfully to the public interest'. This meant specifically those who supported Ireton's latest remonstrance.

Next day, Colonel Pride's regiment appeared in Westminster and the rest, over 140 Members, were forcibly debarred from the House of Commons. Forty-one were taken prisoner and locked in an alehouse overnight – the alehouse adjoining Westminster Hall, which was ironically nicknamed 'Hell'. The eldest were offered parole, with permission to sleep at their own homes, but they refused, because they would not recognise the authority by which they were apprehended.

After Pride's Purge the tiny remainder came to be known derisively as the Rump Parliament (*'full of maggots'* jeered their enemies). These men put in hand the King's trial. Few were dedicated republicans, in fact, but they distrusted Charles and were exasperated by years of failing to reach a compromise. Even those who believed in monarchy as a principle were now prepared to remove the current office-holder.

The New Model Army transferred the King from Carisbrooke to the nearby mainland, a grim prison at Hurst Castle, cut off on all sides by sea except for a narrow pebbled causeway. In that cold bastion, the trappings of sovereignty were stripped from him. He lived in a dark cell where candles were needed even in daylight. It was said that only one servant was allowed him, though the House of Commons formally approved a daily allowance of ten pounds for his maintenance – ten pounds, when an infantry soldier was paid only eight pence a day. Charles also had a specified list of servants that started with two personal attendants and ran into: a carver, a cupbearer, a sewer, a master of the robes, a page of the back stairs, a paymaster, servants of the wood-yard, of the cellar and buttery, of the pantry and ewry, a page of the Presence, a groom of the chamber, a master cook and two undercooks. He was allowed to keep two pet dogs.

Those who had seen him reported that he was careless of dress and had let his hair grow long. It was all grey and his features had sunk, with pouchy eyes in a haggard face. At heart, he knew his fate. He spoke of it like a tragedian to any supporters who managed to visit him; he was gratified by their tears.

When the drastically reduced Parliament began setting up a High Court of Justice, the House of Lords refused to co-operate. The House of Commons pressed on, establishing the principle that the subjects of England had the right to pass judgment on their King: 'the Commons of England in Parliament assembled do declare that the people are, under God, the original of all just power'. Directly opposite to the Stuarts' belief in the Divine Right of Kings, this was the heart of why the civil war had been fought.

The trial was proclaimed by a sergeant at arms, who rode into Westminster Hall with the House of Commons mace upon his shoulder, attended by various officers and six trumpeters on horseback, while a guard of horse and foot beat up drums in New Palace Yard. The proclamation was made, then repeated later. Gideon heard it in Cheapside, Lambert at the Old Exchange. Orders were given for the practical management of the trial: provision of rooms and necessaries for the

King, a house for the lord president of the court, the supply of guards for the court, for the King's person, for all routes through which the King must pass, with extra guards on the roof and outside windows, security barriers to prevent crowd movements or rescue of the prisoner, even the blocking-up of tavern back doors which could give access to troublemakers.

No king of England had been tried for misdemeanours. There was no precedent; the very form of the court had to be worked out. Assassination, the tool of choice in previous history, was not to be allowed. There had to be a formal punishment for the kingdom's bloodshed. Retribution must be seen to occur. And although English subjects had no bill of rights, those who were struggling towards reform wanted to demonstrate that they made themselves subjects by an implied contract, a contract where they had an expectation of good government from their monarchs.

Appointed to the court as judges were 135 commissioners. Many found themselves suddenly unavailable for this privilege. More than half refused to appear, either doubting the legality of proceedings or terrified of the danger. Lord Fairfax, whose political opinions had always been kept very strictly private, excused himself. Others believed it their duty to God and the country to take part. A little-known judge agreed to preside: John Bradshaw, who had begun his career as an attorney's clerk at Congleton and progressed to Chief Justice of Chester; until then, he was unheard of outside Cheshire, which was viewed as a remote wilderness next to Wales. Even Bradshaw felt so petrified of being murdered for what he was doing, that he commissioned an armour-plated hat, which he clapped on for the trial's duration.

Now the King was brought closer to London, to Windsor Castle. He was in the custody of the Fifth-Monarchist Colonel Thomas Harrison, who had denounced him as 'that Man of Blood'. On the 19th of January, Charles was shifted again, to St James's Palace in Whitehall. Next morning, a Saturday, he was carried from St James's in a heavily curtained sedan chair, and then taken half a mile by water, escorted by boatloads of musketeers. They delivered him to Sir Robert Cotton's house, to await the opening of the first session of the trial. Cotton House had a superior position for a domestic building: right at the heart of the Parliamentary complex, between the Lobby and the Painted Hall.

Whenever the King was moved it happened discreetly, though people were aware of it. As always, a single cry of 'God save the King!' from a bystander would fill Charles with confidence, a bitter contrast, Parliamentarians thought, to his lack of reaction when hundreds of thousands of his subjects were so full of discontent they had been prepared to die fighting him. As he approached the trial, he seemed sure that his life was safe; he said that none of his enemies could possibly secure their interests unless they joined their fortunes to his.

He was not alone. Many people, in England and abroad, rejected any suggestion that the King might die. One practical reason was voiced: it would immediately pass his claim to the throne to his elder son, causing a new outbreak of war, with the advantage that the Prince of Wales would gain wide support as an object of pity, the innocent child of a martyr. Moreover, the army would be exchanging a King whose person they controlled for one who lay beyond their power abroad. The death of King Charles, it was presumed, would certainly not be the death of the monarchy.

Even the Levellers were divided. Richard Overton and the editors of *The Moderate* supported the trial. Overton had been campaigning openly against the monarchy; his 1647 pamphlet *Regal Tyranny Discovered* was the first to call for an execution. It had been roughly received by Parliament at the time: Anne Jukes told Gideon how Overton's wife Mary had been arrested while she was stitching together copies of that pamphlet. 'They called her a whore, and dragged her very violently through the dirt to Maiden Lane Prison, with her six-month-old baby wailing at the breast – after which they hauled her away to the hell of Bridewell. The poor babe died in jail not long after . . .'

A month before the trial there was a meeting in Whitehall between the army Grandees, Levellers and City Independents to discuss implementing a constitution. Overton and Lilburne walked out. John Lilburne later complained that the army officers had only played with them to keep them quiet like little children with rattles. Always a maverick, Lilburne actually opposed the King's trial on the basis that it was preferable to keep the monarchy as a balance against army tyranny.

From the moment of Pride's Purge, many soldiers and former soldiers, Gideon Jukes among them, gave whole-hearted support – not least because the members who were barred from the House had been responsible for denying them their pay. The current army was present in force during the trial. Officers and soldiers who no longer had garrisons or regiments also converged on London to see through what they had fought for.

It was clear that what was about to happen would be unparalleled. In setting up the High Court of Justice, the sovereignty of the people had been declared, taking precedence over the monarchy. This was revolutionary, courageous, and bound to create high drama.

Westminster Hall was the chosen venue. This stately Gothic monument was more than seven hundred years old. For its first five hundred years it had been a royal residence, a place of feasting and entertainment. Once the largest hall in Europe to have an unsupported roof, its magnificent hammer-beam interior dated from the reign of King Richard the Second. The hall's enormous size and spaciousness always made it ideal for ceremonious gatherings and in 1265 it had been the meeting place of the first true English Parliament, initiated by Simon de Montfort. Its existence had made Westminster the judicial and administrative centre of the kingdom. Various regular courts took place there: Common Pleas, Chancery, the Court of Wards, the King's Bench. Previous important trials held there had been those of Sir Thomas More and the Gunpowder Plot conspirators – so there was an established tradition of manipulating justice at Westminster for political reasons. This was where the Earl of Strafford was tried, and nearly argued himself into acquittal.

Ironically, it was also the traditional venue for coronation banquets, including that of King Charles.

Robert Allibone and Gideon turned up like sightseers on Saturday the 20th of January, then attended every day. Lambert was on the mend, but still too shaky on his legs, though his wife Anne put on a hooded cloak and came. Gideon noticed with mild amusement that Anne was now so independent that she detached herself without a word and went to inveigle herself in among important ladies who were allowed to sit in the upper gallery. At first other spectators were kept standing out in New Palace Yard.

The judges entered and were seated. The commissioners' names were called over and those who were present answered; there would never be any attempt to penalise those who absented themselves. In the gallery, Anne Jukes became a witness to an incident; when Lord Fairfax's name was called, a masked woman cried out, 'He has more wit than to be here!' People whispered that it was his wife, Lady Fairfax.

Silence was called for, then the mighty doors at the end of the hall were hauled open so that 'all persons desirous to see or hear (without exception) might enter'. There were *some* exceptions: all delinquents and papists had been barred from within ten miles of London (though not those who were trying to pay their fines . . .). Otherwise it was a scrum.

'Use your weight!' muttered Robert as the crowd surged through the entrance, rushing for good vantage points.

'Kick shins!' urged Gideon. They pressed forwards ruthlessly and planted themselves among many others, all cloaked, gloved and hatted against the icy cold, a cold which even the presence of so many people never alleviated. Gideon, who had never been there before, gazed around in wonder at the spectacular great hall.

The public seats and standing room filled up fast. Silence was once more ordered. Colonel Tomlinson, in charge of the King, was commanded to bring in his prisoner. Although Cotton House was the nextdoor building, with royal dallying this took a quarter of an hour. Then came twenty officers with specially ordered partisans, twelve-foot staves with gleaming sharp barbed heads. The sergeant at arms, resplendent with his Mace, received the King into the court's custody and conducted him straight to a crimson velvet chair. After a reproving glance around the court, the King took his place.

The judges refused to remove their hats to him. He refused to remove his hat to them.

'All men are born equal!' Robert Allibone snorted quietly.

Ever theatrical, the King had recovered his pride in his appearance. Maintaining a pose of great hauteur, he arrived in court in stunning black velvet, with the Order of the Garter resplendent on the left side of his cloak – a great, radiating circle of embroidered silver threads. This scintillating adornment, almost as long as his arm, was the oldest and highest English order of chivalry. It had been conceived to represent like-minded brotherhood – though a closed brotherhood of the sovereign with his elite private associates, not that of the sovereign and his subjects. The order's patron was St George, the dragon-slaying patron saint of England, who was depicted on a dramatic medal which Charles wore on a wide blue ribbon around his neck.

As Gideon sourly surveyed that Garter, its archaic symbolism seemed a serious error, grounded in exclusiveness. Taught by the authors of radical pamphlets, Gideon viewed *Honi Soi Qui Mal y Pense* as a mystic incantation in the language of the Normans, repressive foreign overlords who had seized power in England, then employed the barrier of ancient French to exclude the native population from government and the law. Chivalric this order might be, and comforting to the King, but for Gideon the black velvet and expensive embroidery were an attempt to shield the King, who lived so completely in this alien world, from the consequences of his own arrogance, deviousness, divisiveness, indifference, pettiness and vacillation, let alone (why be mealy-mouthed?) his misunderstanding of, distaste for and disloyalty to the common man.

Gideon felt the decorative trappings of monarchy had no relevance, not for any Parliamentary soldier who had marched until his feet were raw, his stomach gnawed by months of hunger, constantly tasting danger and terror amidst the smoke and din of battlefields where men were ripped apart, gouged open, shredded and knocked senseless. To those who had fought for Parliament, and to the women and children who shared their self-sacrifice, the charge that Charles Stuart had maintained a cruel war did matter; it mattered desperately.

Bradshaw, Lord President of the High Court of Justice, occupied a velvet throne, with a writing-desk before him. He was three steps up on a dais so spectators could see him. The King had his back to most of them; he was in a dock where the walls were so high that when he sat, only the crown of his hat was visible. From time to time he stood up and peered over at the audience disdainfully. Two clerks, the only people hatless, occupied a large square central table, covered with a deeply fringed turkey carpet in the traditional rich shades of red, black and green. They had to squeeze their pens and papers between the Mace and a ceremonial sword over which the Mace was crossed. Pikemen and musketeers lined all the seating areas. Since these heavily armed troops were standing, they had the best view. They were bitterly cold, and from time to time glumly stamped their booted feet. Their orders were to protect the court and its prisoner and to take into custody anyone who caused disturbances.

Bradshaw opened the unprecedented proceedings: 'Charles Stuart, King of England, the Commons of England assembled in Parliament, being deeply sensible of the calamities that have been brought upon this nation, which is fixed upon you as the principal author of it, have resolved to make inquisition for blood. And according to that debt and duty they owe to justice, to God, the Kingdom and themselves, they have resolved to bring you to trial and judgment, and for that purpose have constituted this High Court of Justice before which you are brought.'

The clerk of the court was commanded to read the formal charge. *'The Charge of the Commons of England against Charles Stuart, King of England, of High Treason and other high crimes.'* Gone now were the all-embracing lists of grievances that once featured in John Pym's *Grand Remonstrance.* Ship Money, monopolies, encroachments, Catholic plots, Laudian impositions, imprisoned pamphleteers, abuses of commerce, disagreements about religion, were mopped up as 'a wicked design to uphold to himself an unlimited and tyrannical power to rule according to his will' for which end the King had 'traitorously and maliciously levied war against the present Parliament and the people therein represented'. Key military engagements were listed, from initial manoeuvres in 1642 and the raising of the King's standard, through Edgehill, Reading, Gloucester, Newbury, Cropredy Bridge, Cornwall, Newbury again, Leicester, Naseby and the uprisings in Kent and elsewhere in 1648:

> *By which cruel and unnatural wars by him (the said Charles Stuart) levied, continued and renewed as aforesaid, much innocent blood of the free people of this nation hath been spilt, many families have been undone, the public treasury wasted and exhausted, trade obstructed and miserably decayed, vast expense and damage to the nation incurred, and many parts of the land spoiled, some of them even to desolation.*

When he heard himself accused of tyranny, the King laughed loudly. His arrogance shocked the commissioners who had come to sit in judgment, and it shocked spectators.

John Cook, Solicitor-General for the Commonwealth, was to prosecute. As Cook began, the King rapped him on the shoulder with his heavy silver cane, attempting to interrupt. Eventually, the head of the cane tumbled off. It rolled on the floor, noisily travelling to and fro. The King waited for someone to pick it up for him. Nobody moved. He was forced to stoop and retrieve the finial himself. He looked shaken.

Undaunted, Cook continued. The King assumed an insouciant expression, unaware that his contemptuous manner was losing him sympathy. He demanded to know by what lawful authority he had been brought there. He directly accused the court of having no more legality than thieves and highway robbers, who got their way by force. Bradshaw at first floundered nervously, saying that Charles was required to attend 'in the name of the people, of which you are elected king' – to which the King flashed back pedantically that England had not had an *elected* king in the past thousand years.

Bradshaw pressed on, repeatedly urging the King to give a plea, which he continually refused to do because he did not recognise the court. Finally Bradshaw gave up and adjourned proceedings. He ordered the soldiers to remove the prisoner.

Next day was Sunday. Bradshaw and the other commissioners sank themselves in prayer. Robert heard that Cromwell's chaplain Hugh Peter preached them a sermon based on Psalm 149: *To bind their kings with chains and their nobles with fetters of iron . . .*

When the court resumed on the Monday, the pattern was set. The King again refused to acknowledge the court's authority; the court doggedly insisted he must enter a plea, to no avail. Although dignified, the King's obstinacy became so frustrating that one of the army commanders, Colonel Hewson, rushed forwards, crying 'Justice!' and spat in his face. Charles wiped away the spittle, remarking, 'Well, sir, God has justice in store both for you and me.'

After three attempts, Bradshaw in exasperation ruled that the King's refusal to plead was contumacy. This was formally defined in the court minutes by the clerks at the turkey carpet table as: 'a standing mute, and tacit confession of the charge'.

'What does that mean?' whispered Gideon to Robert.

'A silent confession. It theoretically removes any need to bring witnesses.' Great care was taken to do so anyway. The record stated that the judges would have the witnesses examined, for their own satisfaction.

On the 24th of January, a subcommittee of the High Court, sitting in the Painted Chamber, examined thirty-three witnesses. Robert had discovered as much as possible about them. 'They have been meticulously assembled from the length and breadth of the country, from Cornwall to Northumberland, and even brought from Ireland. Many have fought as Royalists. They include nine gentlemen, five husbandmen, a painter, a smith, a butcher, a maltster, a ferryman, a barber-surgeon, a glover and a scrivener . . .'

The following day their depositions were read out in a public session. Gideon listened attentively. These witness statements would be much less famous than the angry exchanges between Charles and Bradshaw. Nonetheless, they confirmed the King's personal participation in battles, gave evidence of his close association with various atrocities – such as the tormenting of troops after Lostwithiel – and demonstrated his intention to stir up and continue war. The witnesses testified that they had seen the King on horseback in armour on battlefields; seventeen military actions, of various degrees, were mentioned by name:

> *This deponent saith that he did see the King at Edgehill in Warwickshire, where he (sitting on horseback while his army was drawn up before him) did speak to the colonel of every regiment that passed by him that he would have them speak to their soldiers to encourage them to stand it and to fight . . . And he did see many slain at the fight at Edgehill, and afterwards he did see a list brought in unto Oxford of the men which were slain in that fight, by which it was reported that there were slain 6,559 men.'*

Next, written evidence was put on record: namely the papers that had been taken from the King's cabinet after the battle of Naseby. In them he demonstrated his deviousness, his willingness to play off opponents against one another – and most damningly, his negotiations to bring in foreign armies to assist him against his subjects.

For the next two days, the commissioners sat in private. They came to their verdict and drafted the sentence. It condemned Charles Stuart as a 'tyrant, traitor, murderer and public enemy to the Commonwealth of England'. However, the King was still given one final chance to accept the jurisdiction of the court, and thus to have his defence heard. Some of the judges may have believed that the terror of death would at last induce him to compromise. Charles certainly did now retract his original position – but only so far as to offer to co-operate with a trial if it were held as a 'conference', jointly with the Houses of Lords and Commons.

Even at this stage the request was considered. Once more the King was removed while the court went into recess. Outside, Gideon Jukes and Robert Allibone paced about New Palace Yard, with Robert fuming, 'He has turned on his tail like a landed fish. This is just more prevarication!'

'By considering the proposal, they show they are fair-minded,' Gideon tried to pacify him. 'They will not agree it, yet they must be seen to consider all possibilities.'

The King's request was refused.

The trial ended on Saturday. The King was brought to court to hear the sentence. Lord President Bradshaw began his summing-up: 'Gentlemen, the Prisoner at the Bar hath been several times brought before the court to make answer to a charge of high treason in the name of the people of England . . .'

He was interrupted. From the same masked lady in the gallery came another shout: 'No! Not half nor a quarter of the people of England – Oliver Cromwell is a traitor!'

Colonel Axtell ordered his men to level their muskets at the gallery and cried, 'Down with the whore!'

The soldiers turned and aimed their guns. Women froze in their seats. There was, reported Anne Jukes afterwards, a terrible moment of stillness, until the soldiers refused to fire. The masked heckler, again thought to be Anne, Lady Fairfax, was hustled away by her friends.

Bradshaw now gave an address which lasted forty minutes. In it he stated that even a king was subject to the law, and that law originated with Parliament. Charles Stuart had broken the sacred bond between king and subject. By making war on his own people, he forfeited his right to their allegiance. 'There is a contract and a bargain made between a king and his people, and certainly the bond is reciprocal . . . Sir, if this bond be once broken, farewell sovereignty. Whether you have been – as by your office you ought to be – a Protector of England, or a Destroyer of England, let all England judge.'

Declaring Charles guilty of the charges against him, Bradshaw then ordered the sentence to be read out.

'Charles Stuart, as tyrant, traitor, murderer and public enemy to the good people of this nation shall be put to death by the severing of his head from his body.'

To his great dismay, Charles was not allowed to speak. Much was made of that by his supporters afterwards, but it was traditional. From the pronouncement of a death sentence a convicted man was legally dead.

Still protesting hopelessly, the prisoner was bustled away by soldiers with lighted matchcord, who contemptuously blew smoke in his face. Though it was said that Colonel Axtell beat them to make them do it, many of them shouted jubilantly, 'Justice!' and 'Execution!'

Chapter Fifty-Six

London: 27–30 January 1649

Gideon Jukes unexpectedly played a part in what happened next.

As he and Robert Allibone had reeled from Westminster Hall, dry-mouthed, waiting for the judge's final decision on the King's request to be heard by both Houses, Gideon had seen someone he recognised. He had already heard that Colonel Okey was in charge of security for the trial. At this last moment, John Okey was stamping the blood back into his numb feet in New Palace Yard, puffing his cheeks out and wearing a slightly stunned look.

The circumstances voided past differences, so the ex-dragoon felt sufficient loyalty to go up to his old commander and shake his hand. 'Gideon Jukes – I served under you, sir, at Naseby.'

'Sergeant Jukes – the tall one!'

Gideon accepted it ruefully. He had learned that courage, honesty and congeniality meant nothing if you were a lank in a memorable bum-starver coat. 'Captain now, sir. Colonel Rainborough honoured me.'

Okey, who had little sympathy with the Levellers, nonetheless looked solemn, acknowledging the filthiness of Rainborough's murder. He made no comment on Gideon's promotion, yet continued to talk with him. He seemed glad to share his thoughts with a man he trusted, but with whom he could omit the reserve he had to show troops under his command. After introducing Robert, Gideon volunteered that if he could assist, he was available. Okey nodded.

'Is the outcome certain?' Robert asked in a confidential tone.

'By no means. There are plenty who want to see his life preserved.'

Robert continued to press for publishable details. 'I heard that Oliver Cromwell said, "We will cut off the King's head, with the crown upon it."'

'Likely we will,' agreed Okey, 'but there shall be due form.'

As they hung about, Okey told them setting up the High Court of

Justice had been the work of a Dutch lawyer, one Dorislaus, who had drawn on the ancient Roman Praetorian Guard, who had authority to overturn tyrants. Taking notes, Robert asked about John Cook, the Solicitor-General and prosecutor. Okey was impressed by Cook, who had written a passionate pamphlet called *The Poor Man's Case*, in which he made direct associations between poverty and criminality, urging an end to imprisonment for debt and the offer of second chances for first-time offenders. Cook had advocated that all doctors and lawyers should give a tenth of their time to the poor, *pro bono*.

'No fees? *That* will never happen!' Gideon guffawed.

Robert murmured excuses and slipped away. 'He feels the cold,' Gideon said, although he knew Robert was going to write up his notes, to be printed later. He would probably try to find a copy of *The Poor Man's Case* too. Gideon would rather lazily let Robert hunt down the work, then snaffle it to read himself.

Gideon remained chatting to Okey for the rest of the hour it took for the judges formally to reach a decision. Okey gave him an insight into the behind-the-scenes organisation. Soldiers constantly came and went with messages, bearing out his description of endless activity.

'All must be scrupulous. Nothing is done without drafting and redrafting.' Okey's mild complaint was uttered with a certain pride; he showed the heightened excitement men acquired during busy planning. Gideon had seen Edward Sexby fired up like this. He had known the thrill himself. Soldiers in battle wore that look. Colonel Okey, who had shown when he led the dragoon charge at Naseby that he could be inspired by a heady moment, was full of his recent experience: 'Every document is framed many times. We were running to and fro for a week, wording the formal charge. Solicitor Cook wanted to go right back to the start of the reign, every niggle, rumour and false move for the past twenty years – even the possibility that the King had some duplicitous hand in his father's death –'

Gideon took a scathing view: 'King James died naturally. We would have looked like fools.'

Okey slapped his arm. 'That's my opinion. Still, every aspect has been chewed over like stale bread and dripping. How to style the King? – mere "Charles Stuart", or load him with his full paraphernalia of titles? Then we had to assemble witnesses, yet keep them safe from interference. The written evidence was held at the House of Lords – I had to squeeze the King's cabinet out of them when it was called for in evidence, and you know they won't co-operate . . . All the time, we must shift the King constantly and unexpectedly, for safety –'

Gideon's fair eyebrows shot up. 'Attempted escape? I heard that he refused to flee, after he left Carisbrooke.'

Okey glanced around nervously. Gideon took note of armed men lying on the leads at roof level, weapons covering the hall and New Palace Yard. 'Can't take any chance, Captain. Plenty of delinquents have slipped through and are hanging around London. Cotton House is convenient for the court, but it's a sieve, a glorified library, not built for defence. We built a barracks in the garden for two hundred men, but it is a nightmare. Whitehall Palace makes a good halfway-house, but he could gnaw his way out like a mouse through cheese if he was minded to. Hampton Court is safer – but it takes time to ferry him back again . . .'

There was movement near the hall doors. Gideon spotted Robert, gesticulating that the judges were returning. He and Okey began to move. 'Good to see you, Jukes!' exclaimed the colonel warmly – which surprised Gideon. 'Your offer of assistance is civil. Call on me at my house, if you will.'

That surprised him even more.

The King was declared guilty and sentence pronounced on Saturday. Sunday was the customary day of rest in theory, though not for some. Many were still negotiating to save the King's life, including Lord General Fairfax who attempted to persuade the Council of Officers to delay the execution; he was even rumoured to have been urged by friends to mount a rescue by force. Foreign ambassadors, the French and Dutch, beset Fairfax and Cromwell, pleading for the King's life. Some even approached Lady Fairfax, known as a firm Presbyterian. The Prince of Wales sent a direct appeal for mercy. All the time, Cromwell and the hardliners were working to steel the constancy of weak spirits who might wish to avoid regicide.

For Colonel Okey and the other organisers, Monday brought a race to finalise the death warrant. A draft with a blank space for details already existed, signed by some of the commissioners, but a full version with all its amendments filled in now had to be created or, in the language of legislation, engrossed. Two of the three officers originally named to supervise the execution refused to do it. The time and place needed to be fixed. As the clerks reworded these details, the parchment had to be carefully 'scraped' in places for amendments. This would inevitably look like tampering afterwards. Fears were that the commissioners who had already signed might back out if a clean new draft was drawn up.

Wild stories circulated of chaotic attempts to persuade more commissioners to sign. In the scramble to add signatures, Cromwell was said to have been almost hysterical, flicking ink at one, Henry Marten, like a manic schoolboy, and allegedly grasping another man's hand and forcing him to write. In fact more signatories came forward than had been allowed for, so later names had to be cramped inelegantly close together. Eventually the warrant was complete, the parchment engrossed, fifty-nine names courageously signed and sealed. The judges had given sentence. The army was to take over. The order for the execution was issued to Colonel Francis Hacker, Colonel Hunks and Colonel Phayre:

Whereas Charles Stuart, King of England, is and standeth convicted, attainted, and condemned of High Treason and other high crimes, and sentence upon Saturday last was pronounced against him by this court to be put to death by the severing of his head from his body, of which sentence execution yet remaineth to be done, these are therefore to will and require you to see the said sentence executed in the open street before Whitehall, upon the morrow, being the thirtieth day of this instant month of January, between the hours of ten in the morning and five in the afternoon of the same day, with full effect. And for so doing, this shall be your sufficient warrant. And these are to require all officers, soldiers, and others, the good people of this nation of England, to be assisting unto you in this service.

It was on the Monday evening that Gideon took himself to Colonel Okey's house.

Okey had a ship's-chandler's business near the Tower of London and his local church was St Giles in the Fields. He lived in Mare Street, Hackney, out on the eastern edges of London, at the opposite end from the enormous mansions of grander men who clustered near Westminster and Whitehall. Okey's chosen location, not far from London Fields, was a large, leased three-storeyed gabled house, called Barber's Barn. It stood among pasture and pleasant lanes, close enough to London to do business in the city, yet countrified. Gideon borrowed Robert's horse and rode out there, full of curiosity and as keen as always to be associated with any historic event.

'Yet another!' exclaimed Susanna Okey, the colonel's wife. She was soberly dressed in the Baptist style. She cannot have seen much of her husband during the latter years of their marriage. When Gideon introduced himself, she herself led him to Okey, as if to get him out from under her feet.

There were uniformed soldiers already in the house. In civilian dress, Gideon was taken past them, receiving odd glances. Okey was in tense conversation with a second man; they looked up sharply on Gideon's entrance to the room. A tray of bread and butter and beer, the staples of Parliamentarian housewives when they were suddenly called upon to feed committees, stood half-demolished on the table near to them. A jumble of papers covered the rest of the board.

'Come in, lad – this is Captain Jukes, who served under me. Colonel John Fox, commander of Bradshaw's guard in court.'

The man was a stranger to Gideon, unlike others congregated in London for the trial, familiar faces from the old campaigns. 'I held a garrison near Birmingham, in Warwickshire,' he said, perhaps rather stiffly.

'Edgbaston.' Gideon astonished the colonel, and was pleased by it. He gave no sign he knew Fox had been nicknamed the Jovial Tinker. 'I worked for Sir Samuel Luke, Essex's scoutmaster. We had your despatches often through our hands.'

'I tried to give good intelligence.'

'Your work was always valued, sir.'

'Would that the paymasters gave me some credit!'

Like Okey, Fox looked to be in his forties, though he could be younger. He was self-confident, bouncy and a little too open for Londoners to take him well, with an untuneful Midlands accent. Gideon found it whining. Someone had once told him that was how Shakespeare would have sounded – and if those were the terrible vowels of England's greatest playwright, he was glad to have abandoned any connection with the theatre.

The two colonels resumed their conversation. Gideon rapidly grasped its urgency. Richard Brandon, the public executioner, had refused to kill the King. He had cut off the heads of Strafford and Laud, but baulked at this.

'Does it have to be Brandon? Or does anybody else have the expertise?' Gideon asked, catching up with the implications. Once a mere captain would have stayed silent, but the war had changed that. He spoke the unthinkable. 'Must the King be beheaded?'

'Shortening it is!' Fox's grin confirmed that Midlanders had an odd sense of humour.

Okey shrugged restively. 'We cannot hang, draw and quarter a monarch, Captain Jukes. For the nobility, an axe is traditional. Besides,' he added glumly, with the bent logic of any man recently mired in bureaucracy, 'the death warrant is written now.'

Always realistical, Gideon accepted they could not swing King Charles on a gibbet like a horse-thief.

'We need surgical despatch. You ask about expertise,' Colonel Fox dropped his laconic derision and spoke as if he had looked into this rather practically. 'The prisoner's neck must be severed correctly, with a heavy, single blow through the fourth vertebra. When the Queen of Scots was beheaded at Fotheringhay Castle, it was terribly mangled – we cannot have such butchery tomorrow. The King of England will not run around the scaffold bleeding like a half-dead capon.'

'Any hitch will suggest that the deed is not well done,' Gideon agreed. 'This must not be botched.'

'We have a bright axe specially brought from the Tower,' Okey said anxiously, trying to reassure himself.

'Colonel Hewson has sworn his officers to secrecy and offered a hundred pounds to the man who will do the job.' Fox was calming Okey. Hewson was one of the officers charged with fulfilling the death warrant. 'He has identified two possibles, Hulet and Jackson. He says Sergeant Hulet is well-metalled.'

'If Hulet is up for the business,' Gideon suggested, 'he should be our fallback – call him an understudy – take the part of the axeman's assistant –'

'An assistant?' queried Fox.

'It is normal,' said Okey.

'It would be a lonely profession otherwise,' Gideon commented. 'This works to our advantage. A man we trust can be standing by, in case at the last moment Brandon fails. But the main man must be Brandon. He has practised a few times —' They all laughed, a little hoarsely.

There was a short silence.

'If he is afraid, he should be offered anonymity,' Gideon continued quietly. 'He could be masked, like an actor in the theatre. He can be assured that his name will never be revealed. Indeed, I think it right it should not be.'

'And he will be well paid,' added Fox, who had blunt standards. Gideon remembered Tinker Fox's reputation for extracting money by illegal methods.

'Well,' Okey decided, 'Colonel Axtell will take a troop to Brandon's house first thing in the morning and bring him.'

Gideon and Colonel Fox exchanged glances. They seemed to have formed an unlikely alliance. 'It must not look as if the executioner is our prisoner,' warned Fox. 'Besides, duress will make him unreliable.'

'Someone should first try patiently to win Brandon over.' After seeing how Axtell had run affairs at the King's trial, Gideon thought the man too brutal for this. Axtell was the coarse colonel with the straight-line moustache who had had muskets aimed at women in the gallery, then encouraged his men to blow smoke at the King and insult him.

Fox agreed. 'Not Daniel Axtell. He would lower the tone of a curate's breakfast . . . I suppose I shall volunteer!' he said, with the lugubrious world-weariness of his home district. 'Where does this Brandon live?'

'By the Tower of London.' Okey sounded unhappy. 'St Katharine's by the Tower . . . Rosemary Lane.' Gideon pulled a face.

'You know this street?' Fox turned and asked him.

'Rough!' exclaimed Gideon.

Again their eyes met. Colonel Fox nodded. 'Be here at first light, mounted. You shall be my guide, Captain Jukes.'

It was a bitterly cold morning. The strangely matched pair rode south from Hackney through mists and near darkness, down past the tenter-fields where newly dyed cloth was hung on endless parallel ropes. Robert's horse was a knock-kneed grey called Rumour, a city horse, puzzled by the sight of growing grass; he preferred to amble over cobbles, with time to look in shop windows. At one point he stopped dead unexpectedly. There had been nothing to cause him fear. In this weather most of the tenter-lines were empty. Nothing flapped at him; the few lengths of pegged-out cloth were frozen solid.

'Rumour flies . . . My partner, who is a whimsical spirit, named his horse in irony.' Fox looked on, while Gideon struggled. 'This curmudgeonly nag knows his way to a certain inn in King Street at Westminster, then he knows his way home to the stable even with his rider beery –' Drowsiness from overwork, Robert always claimed. 'But he despises me and he hates strange places.'

'He wants a carrot.'

'Well, he is not getting one!' snarled Gideon. Wishing he had worn a cloak against the cold, he kicked up the beast – though he did it warily because he knew that in the back yard behind the print shop Amyas had been naughtily training Rumour to rear up suddenly on his back legs and perform an upright *levade*, as if carrying a marquis in full armour, posing for Van Dyke. 'I am in the wrong suit for portraiture!' muttered Gideon in Rumour's ear, as the horse for no reason moved off and now trotted sedately.

He guided them on, through Brick Lane and into the airy pleasaunce of Spitalfield, where many small cottages with gardens occupied lanes beyond the city wall among the fields and bowling alleys around the great road that came in from Essex to Aldgate. At this hour, most roads were deserted. They saw maybe one milkmaid and a couple of men up to no good in an apple orchard; there was no one from whom to ask directions, had Fox come alone. But he was in good hands with Gideon.

As Captain Jukes found his way so confidently, Colonel Fox weighed him up. Gideon was in his once-red New Model Army coat. That meant his britches were too tight under the crotch and the usual gap was widening just above his belt, so his back was freezing. As well as his odd appearance, he was full of London swagger and with a dubious way of manoeuvring himself into positions of trust. Still, on the whole, the man from the Midlands accepted his motives were reliable. Fox would not have brought him on this delicate errand otherwise. Their association could go one of two ways during this ride – either they would take to one another fast, or a wall of dislike would rise up between them and perpetuate itself every time one of them spoke.

'I hear you were at Holmby, Captain.' Fox had made enquiries overnight. Had Okey told him? 'So – answer the question everybody wonders: *did* Cornet Joyce have direct orders from Oliver Cromwell?'

Gideon was terse. 'He never said.'

'You never asked?'

'None of us. Our commission was in our hearts.'

People would always be fascinated by that incident. Speculating happily, Fox filled in for himself: 'There was a meeting in a garden. At Cromwell's London house. Long June nights – minutes are not taken. No need for a secretary even to be there – so no chance of some disloyal clerk later making his reputation by spilling all . . . You all swore an oath of secrecy?'

'No, sir, we did not need to.' Gideon changed the subject curtly. 'So what brings you all the way from Warwickshire, Colonel Fox?'

'My garrison was closed down last May, despite my hearty resistance.' The man was disgruntled, on the verge of obsession about his lost command. He reminded Gideon of how Sir Samuel Luke, that other great passionate Parliamentary volunteer, had resented being told to resign. 'I have four thousand pounds in arrears to chase up – and I came to London for my wedding. My new wife is Lady Angelica Hasteville.' Fox sounded impressed by that himself. Gideon could not imagine how this rough-and-ready self-made soldier from the shires had encountered a lady on terms where they might ally in bed and board. Perhaps she possessed money. 'We were joined at St Bartholomew the Less in October.'

Then Colonel John Fox glanced down at his saddle pommel momentarily, as if embarrassed by his feelings. Gideon took back his scepticism. Even in the midst of war and trouble, he had glimpsed the human heart.

The dark bulk of the Tower of London suddenly lay ahead of them. With a grimace, Gideon brought them into Rosemary Lane. 'Now, sir, we must keep our wits about us.'

He heard Fox draw a sharp breath. He can have seen nothing like this in sleepy, rural Warwickshire. Gideon knew what to expect, though he never frequented such districts. This was the kind of sink, where unnumbered souls festered, that thin-faced Solicitor-General John Cook wanted to eliminate.

Rosemary Lane was a reeking little haven of abject poverty. It lay outside the city wall in the ward of Portsoken. It had sinister alleys, tiny cottages, dark taverns, and one forlorn old church. It teemed with totters and their tat, so in finer weather both sides of the muddy lane would be lined with barrows and mats, displaying for sale the meanest type of old clothes, holed shifts, crinkled left boots and chipped dishes. Suits, or half-suits, that had passed through nine generations of owner and were held together only by stiff grime and patches. Dented pots in metal so base it hurt Gideon's teeth to look upon them. Piles of crumpled linen, most of it stolen from washing lines, linen in curious shades of drab that were unknown to any fuller. Wardrobes of dead old ladies who had had no friends or family. Sheets that looked as if they had been stripped from week-old cadavers. Drowned sailors' hats.

Amidst this squalor wandered dazed-looking paupers. Drabs with diseased noses made vague offers that Fox and Gideon did not even acknowledge. The few people who were up and setting off for occupations laboured in sweatshops or as ballast-heavers and coal-haulers – bad, backbreaking, dirty work that would eventually kill them. Occasional sad men relieved themselves against a wall, looking as if they had been in the streets all night; dark humps in doorways showed where other vagrants were still sleeping – or had died of cold unnoticed. There were of course far too many taverns, of the lowest kind.

'The biggest cities have the highest dunghills!' muttered Fox.

Here, close by the Tower of London where he normally would carry out state executions, in a mean lodging among his frightened family, lurked Richard Brandon. He was a typical Rosemary Lane inhabitant, poor, feckless, aware of the need for secrecy, yet somehow reeking of unreliability. His calm acceptance of the grim trade he had inherited from his father was chilling. He relished its supposed mysteries but took the fact that he was employed to kill prisoners with a coldness and hardness that Gideon found troubling. His father, John, had once told him public hangmen were strange men. Lambert claimed to have met one, or an assistant, while drinking in a particularly frightful tavern. Gideon had never expected to encounter such a being. He decided to let Colonel Fox take the lead, but when Brandon proved unwilling to trust a Midlander, it became necessary to convince him in the language and custom of East London.

A conversation occurred. It was longer than they wanted, but short enough. They would meet their appointment. Clinging to a bag with unexplained tools of his trade, Brandon was taken to a meeting-point beside the Tower. Colonel Axtell was waiting with a cavalry escort and a spare horse.

They did not bother to root out Brandon's usual assistant, Richard Jones, a rag-and-bone man, although he lived on the same lane. Fox noticed Gideon's disappointed expression. 'I would think it neat,' Gideon murmured regretfully, 'if the King's head was severed from his body by a ragman.'

'You are a true Leveller, Captain Jukes!' Colonel John Fox laughed. It was impossible to deduce whether he was sympathetic.

In a rattle of urgent hoofbeats, the horsemen swept away from Tower Hill. Frost on the cobbles slowed them up later, but while London was still sleeping they rode through the City, past Temple Bar and St Paul's Cathedral, out through Ludgate, down the Strand to Charing Cross and into Whitehall. Everywhere was full of soldiers by the time they arrived. Shopkeepers were opening up — not all, but most. Like the puritans' Christmas, this was designated a working day, not special. Crowds were already gathering outside the Banqueting House. Heavy grey clouds lowered above them, the solemn sky of a freezing dawn in the dead of English winter.

They could hear the loudly beaten drums as Colonel Tomlinson came with the escort party at a fast walking pace across St James's Park, bringing his prisoner, the King.

Chapter Fifty-Seven

Whitehall: 30 January 1649

They went in through a back door and found the place packed. They nodded to the guards. So many soldiers were milling about, nobody paid any attention. There was no difficulty slipping through. The undercroft was seething. As usual in crowds, most noticed only their immediate neighbours. Surreptitiously, Gideon managed to locate a private room, where Fox and he stowed their charge. To keep Brandon occupied, they sent a soldier to find him breakfast. 'And some for us,' pleaded Fox, clearly not expecting it would happen.

Upon arrival, Brandon insisted he must be given a written order for today's work. It was the rule, and of course was for his protection. They had chosen him because he was professional.

Colonel Axtell bustled off to see Cromwell about it, leaving Gideon and Colonel Fox to ensure the hangman stayed put. A true printer, Gideon wondered whether the Brandon family owned a cache of tattered warrants for all the traitors and political misfits they had beheaded. Robert would have wondered whether a memoir could be made of it, but by tradition the public hangman led a life of secrecy. He was a non-person; his experiences were not for public consumption, however great the public's lust for lurid snippets from the block. Robert would claim public interest – always his excuse for printing's more soiled commerce – but Gideon remained sceptical about sensational tracts.

Colonel Hewson brought in two of his men. Gideon had seen John Hewson at the Putney Debates, where he opposed the Levellers. He also knew that in the second civil war Hewson was in Kent, where his regiment joined in the mopping-up of Dover, Sandwich, Deal and Walmer. Originally a shoemaker, he had worked his way up through the ranks until he became one of the signatories to the King's death warrant; a sermonising zealot, he called himself 'a Child of Wrath'.

Hewson had singled out a sergeant, a man he knew and trusted. This fellow was to stand in for the executioner's normal assistant. Brandon and his companion-to-be were provided with grey periwigs and false beards, the axeman's frizzled grey, the other of a lighter, tawnier shade.

'Now we'll frock you —'

The hangman looked alarmed. But he and the sergeant were merely provided with shapeless cover-alls. Gideon helped them arrange these, a necessary disguise when many people owned only one set of garments, by which they might be identified.

Then they waited. Like the King, now penned in his apartments in Whitehall Palace with Bishop Juxon, they had to sit out a three-hour delay. People in the streets outside were saying it was because Brandon had refused to come. In fact, the House of Commons had belatedly decided they must pass an order making it illegal to proclaim the Prince of Wales as King when his father was dead.

During this tedium, Colonel Fox opened up and told Gideon why there had been the moment of awkwardness at Okey's house, when Okey introduced him. While carrying out his duties as the commander of President Bradshaw's guard, Fox had been arrested for debt; it took a special order of the court to obtain his release. He uttered some choice comments, once again complaining that he was owed four thousand pounds in arrears. It seemed a large figure. Apparently a dispute with the treasurer of his garrison had complicated matters though, according to Fox, allegations of corruption were entirely erroneous . . . Gideon kept a non-committal face. The executioner and his temporary assistant listened in with great curiosity.

To while away more time, they took Brandon to check the scaffold. It had been erected outside a great window on the landing of the main staircase. He confirmed that arrangements were satisfactory. One Tench, a drum-maker in Houndsditch, had provided ropes, pulleys and hooks with which the King could be fastened down, in case he resisted.

The warrant finally came. It was passed to Brandon discreetly, though a whispered conversation took place outside the room. Gideon knew how to eavesdrop; he overheard that one of the three officers listed in the King's death warrant, the fabulously named Colonel Hercules Hunks, had refused to sign the order accepting his part in today's business. Colonel Axtell had burst out that he was ashamed of Hunks. 'The ship is coming into harbour – will you strike sail before we come to anchor?' Oliver Cromwell, infuriated, called Hunks a peevish fellow and scrawled out the necessary warrant himself. Gideon managed to peek at it and saw Cromwell had had it signed by Colonel Hacker, another of the officers in charge.

All that day, he never saw Cromwell. Afterwards he heard that Cromwell and Fairfax had been closeted together deep in prayer throughout: Fairfax, riven by doubts; Cromwell, bursting with certainty.

At two in the afternoon, a subtle change in atmosphere signalled developments.

The executioner and his assistant were led to a place on the landing, just inside the window. There Brandon would kneel and ask the King's forgiveness for what he had to do.

Numbers on the scaffold were strictly limited; there would be no place for Gideon. He paused, uncertain of his role now. After quickly shaking Brandon's hand – which seemed to startle everyone – he promised to see that the executioner got away safely and privately after the event.

The undercroft had emptied. Soldiers and members of the public were crowding on the stairs and pressing towards the hall, anxious for a glimpse of the King. As Gideon came down the stone steps, he felt colder air wafting upwards from some open door below. He remembered waiting here, in his feathered dotterel costume, just before *The Triumph of Peace.*

Someone was opening the double doors to the great room, just as they had when the masque started. Gideon went forwards and gazed in at the huge empty chamber. Its long windows were now boarded up, its once-thronged balconies deserted, its tall throne of state stripped of rich curtains and swags and barely visible across the gloom. Through this darkened room, he was told, Colonel Hacker and Colonel Tomlinson were about to bring the King.

When he saw them coming, Gideon slipped away. Down in the street outside, he forced a passage through the crowds and found a place by the Horse Guards opposite. He avoided soldiers he knew.

There were many familiar faces, men amongst whom he had fought, marched, ridden, struggled through torrential rain, wind, mud and floods, tangled in hedges, slept in frozen fields, endured clamour and flame and choking smoke, survived shit-making terror, buried the mangled dead. He reflected on these comrades, and the other, more senior names he knew – Hacker, Axtell, Tomlinson, Okey, and now Fox. The lawyers had done their work; it was the soldiers' turn to bring the business to completion. Cromwell was right. This was why they had done everything. There could be no turning back.

Gideon watched, unconsciously tugging down his bum-starver coat to keep his belly warm. After rising so early with no breakfast, he felt like a man in a dream. He had the benefit of height; even from the opposite side of Whitehall, he could look over heads and see.

Not long after he positioned himself, the King emerged. He was just visible, walking around the scaffold then talking to the Bishop of London and to the executioner. For ten or fifteen minutes, he attempted to speak to the crowd, but although nobody stopped him, the noise from thousands of onlookers was too great for anything to be heard. Allegedly a man took notes. As published afterwards, the King's speech was rambling. The phrases 'A subject and a sovereign are clean different things' and 'I am the Martyr of the People' would be plucked out of incoherent paragraphs and made famous. Gripped by tension, Gideon endured the pause while the King removed his cloak, his George medal, his outer coat. Charles passed the medal to the bishop for the Prince of Wales, saying 'Remember.' There was some business with a cap; long hair had to be pushed up under it. Another moment of gazing at the block.

The King knelt. Black swags now hid him completely from view. The wait seemed endless. Suddenly light flashed off the axe. It swung up and descended smoothly. Silence in the street. The assistant had stooped. Grasping the head by its long hair, Hewson's sergeant held it high for the crowd and cried out traditionally, 'Here is the head of a traitor!' Inexperience made him drop the severed head, which crashed on the boards. Through the crowd rippled that celebrated long groan of re-action. The body and head were carried off indoors. The tall window was closed.

Cavalry swept through the streets. The onlookers dispersed quickly. After twenty minutes, Whitehall lay completely empty. By then Gideon

Jukes had made his way quietly back into the Banqueting House, to fulfil his promise to Brandon.

The execution took place between two and three o'clock. Not long afterwards, with January darkness fast descending, a small file of Axtell's musketeers left the back of the Banqueting House and stamped down the narrow side streets to the River Thames. It took only a couple of minutes to reach Whitehall Stairs. Dark, icy cold water lapped menacingly against the mooring. The embankment seemed deserted.

'Where are the bargemen?'

They had all vanished. Thames watermen were a surly, tricky group, most of them deeply conservative. Only one boat was there, about to cast off with a woman passenger. She had fought hard to negotiate a trip downstream with a miserable and suspicious rower who did not want to take her or anybody else. He had finally agreed, though would not go below London Bridge because he claimed the Pool of London was frozen solid. A bitter wind across the water here seemed to confirm it.

The young woman was already sitting in the stern, hunched in her cloak, her hands buried in a muff, her face shadowed by a hood which she had pulled well forward to defy the wind-chill. She was cold, lonely and depressed, and as the twilight thickened into darkness, she was anxious that she was too late to make the journey to Greenwich, and on from there to reach her children. Her emotions were at their lowest ebb. The King's execution had forced her to face up to bitter truths about her own position, her sons' futures, her missing husband and her chances of ever knowing peace, prosperity or happiness. She had been weeping.

It was Juliana Lovell.

Her heart fell when she saw the soldiers. One of them directed a man to this solitary boat. The soldier indicated with an angry arm movement that she had to disembark.

With her Royalist connections, Juliana felt extremely nervous. Afraid of awkward questions, she did stumble to her feet. She actually climbed back onto the slimy green stairs. Her shoe slipped and slid a few inches. The soldier could have steadied her, but he stepped back instead. With only half his mind on it, he gesticulated irritably that she must move right out of the way.

There was no other boat to take her. She stayed put.

The soldier had turned away. He was tall, his face hidden by the shadow of his hat. Juliana could tell he had long service in the New Model Army, for the Venice Red dye in his coat had faded to a sickly yellow colour. As she waited for him to take notice of her plight, Juliana was surprised to see the escorted civilian hand the man in uniform a gold half-crown. 'Thanks, Captain.'

A soldier held a flaring torch. Juliana made out the unusual coin clearly, and she thought the boatman did so too.

Terrified of being stranded in London, on a night when safe beds would be difficult to find, Juliana stood her ground more fiercely. 'This is *my* boat! There are no others and I will not be put out of it.'

The tall captain interfered again. Now, in the torchlight, she could see that his hat was rammed down on short fair hair. His face looked weary. 'Stand aside, madam.'

He is not listening to me!

I take no interest in women, high-minded Captain Gideon Jukes told himself (taking an interest). She was young; she was spirited. She had inadvertently betrayed a glimpse of ankle as she scrambled to disembark.

In the shadow of her cloak hood, her face was washed-out and pale. She was definitely frightened of him. Gideon accepted that for the first time in his career, he was using the power of his uniform to domineer it over someone helpless. It was an emergency, but he was not proud. Naturally, he blamed the woman, as if her difficult behaviour made it necessary to bully her.

She had to get home. Abruptly, Juliana hopped back into the boat. The boatman neither helped nor prevented her. She took her seat again and defied them.

The escorted man was extremely agitated. The soldier reached a decision. He abandoned his tiff with Juliana, as if ignoring her would make her invisible. He grasped the man's arm and shoved him into the boat. 'Waterman, away with him – be gone quickly! To the Tower landing –'

The waterman had panicked but, fearing the soldiers, he made no protest. He launched off. After he had pulled out from the shore, however, he felt safer. Juliana heard him tackle the other passenger in a low, horrified tone, 'Who the devil have I got in my boat?'

'Why?'

Juliana sat extremely still. Fear and fascination gripped her equally. Now she was seriously wishing she had stayed behind on shore. She glanced back; the soldiers had all gone.

The boatman demanded angrily, 'Are you the hangman that cut off the King's head?'

'No, as I am a sinner to God – not I.'

The boatman trembled. It seemed to Juliana that the passenger also shook with anxiety. For a short time there was silence. The waterman rowed a little further, then he stopped again, rested his oars and examined the male passenger even more closely. 'Are you the hangman? I cannot carry you.'

Without saying his name, the man half confessed his identity, although he pleaded innocence: 'I was fetched with a troop of horse, and kept a close prisoner at Whitehall. Truly I did not do it. I was kept a close prisoner all the while, but they had my instruments.' Appalled, Juliana wondered just what was in that bag he clutched so tightly.

'I will sink the boat, if you do not tell me true!'

But Brandon continued to deny taking part. So they went on, all the way to London Bridge, where Richard Brandon was put off at Tower Pier. Carrying his bundle and a chinking purse, he went away fast in the direction of Whitechapel.

The waterman – his name was Abraham Smith, it turned out long afterwards – stood up in his boat and watched the man until he had gone right out of sight. Then, with some drama, Smith looked hard at the fare he had been given. It was another gold half-crown.

Afraid to disembark from the rocking craft without assistance, Juliana had sat tight. At last offering his arm for her to climb to land, Abraham Smith waved away her fare, then made it plain he intended to get very drunk in a tavern so if she was that sort of woman – as he clearly presumed she must be – she could join him. Juliana made the briefest of excuses. If the gates on London Bridge were still open, she would hasten over to the south bank in the hope of finding somebody who was travelling down the Dover Road.

With so much else to think about, her encounter on Whitehall Stairs was soon largely forgotten. She had wiped the Roundhead captain from her mind just as he had, almost, eradicated Juliana from his.

Chapter Fifty-Eight

London: 1649

The King's embalmed body, with the severed head ghoulishly stitched back on, lay in state in the royal apartments at St James's Palace for several days. It was then turned over to Bishop Juxon and other supporters for a private burial. When Westminster Abbey was refused them, as being too public, they settled on the Royal Chapel in Windsor. A vault was opened, which was found to contain the remains of King Henry VIII and Queen Jane Seymour. There, in a plain lead coffin, King Charles was buried. As the small cortège approached the chapel, the sky darkened and a furious snowstorm had started, turning the black velvet pall to white.

A book purporting to be the late King's prayers and meditations, *Eikon Basilike*, was printed to such an immense reception it ran into twenty-three editions within a year. Robert Allibone and Gideon Jukes despaired of the reading public.

Richard Brandon died in June. Some claimed it was a judgement.

In the months before he died, Brandon was said to have openly acknowledged, particularly when tipsy, that he was the King's executioner. He admitted he received thirty pounds for his day's work, paid to him in half-crowns within an hour of the deed. In Rosemary Lane, thirty pounds would keep a man in drink until he killed himself that way. The only problem was to find someone willing to give change for the half-crowns. The coins' face value was so large they were never currency among the poor.

Brandon also boasted of an orange stuck full of cloves and a handkerchief, which according to him were taken from the King's pocket after the headless corpse was carried off the scaffold. Brandon claimed he was offered twenty shillings for the orange by a gentleman in

Whitehall; he refused and then, lacking acumen, he sold it for only ten shillings in Rosemary Lane.

Later stories claimed he had suffered from a bad conscience. It was said that about six o'clock on the fateful day, he returned to his wife and gave her the money, saying it was the dearest money he ever earned in his life. Another version said Brandon used up the reward in stews and brothels, catching Naples scab which, along with the drink, then destroyed him. It was also maintained that he never again slept easily and was afraid to walk the streets or sleep without a candle. His successor was William Loe, a dust-carrier and cleaner of dungheaps.

Gideon Jukes, who felt permanent ties to Brandon, attended his funeral in Whitechapel. A noisy throng stood to see the corpse carried to the churchyard. Some heckled, 'Hang him, the rogue! Bury him in a dunghill.' Others battered the coffin, saying they would quarter him. Gideon later saw the burial register, which baldly pronounced: *'June 21st, Richard Brandon, a man out of Rosemary Lane. This R. Brandon is supposed to have cut off the head of Charles the First.'* Gideon wondered if the entry ought to be removed, but doing so would only draw more attention.

The sheriffs of the City of London sent large quantities of wine for the funeral.

Nobody came forward to validate Brandon's admission. The army remained resolutely silent. Although the axeman's identity seemed glaringly obvious, public speculation ran rife for years. Royalists theorised that the masked executioner had been Oliver Cromwell. Cromwell's chaplain, Hugh Peter, was named. Some claimed inside knowledge that it was Solicitor-General Cook. Years later Colonel Hewson's man, Sergeant Hulet, was formally charged with having been the axeman's assistant on that day, and was even found guilty by a jury, yet he was released unpunished, perhaps because of too many doubts. But Royalists' favourite bogeyman for the task was Colonel John Fox, Tinker Fox of Birmingham.

A year after the execution, Fox was sent on Parliament's business to Edinburgh, where the elders of the Kirk imprisoned him. By the time he was released in October 1650, he was so hugely in debt he was said to be ready to starve; his health collapsed and he died destitute at fifty, with his wife having to petition Parliament for ten pounds to pay for his funeral. Gideon Jukes could not attend that burial; he would by then be himself in Scotland.

Gideon had resumed normal life as a printer.

Immediately after the King's death, the mood in Basinghall Street was jubilant. Government was being reconstituted, with the King's Privy Council now replaced by a Council of State. Machinery was enacted daily to institute a Commonwealth. Robert printed a banner in a large font with the Parliamentary resolution: *'It hath been found by Experience that the Office of a King in this Nation is unnecessary, burdensome and dangerous to the Liberty, Safety and Public Interest of the People of this Nation; and therefore ought to be abolished.'* The House of Lords was done away with on even better grounds: that it was *'useless and dangerous'*.

One by one, the trappings of monarchy and the nobility were reviewed. The crown and sceptre had been secured and locked up. Other emblems and oaths were redesigned – among them the Great Seal, the Mace, the oaths of office for judges, the titles of public institutions, badges and coinage.

Gideon was living at his parents' house, now owned by Lambert and Anne. In part this was to save money until he decided whether he needed to set himself up in business separate from Robert. There was not enough work to keep both partners plus a journeyman, though Amyas would be leaving them. He was about to get married and was to be set up in his own workshop with his father-in-law's help. He had had his apprentice bond returned. In that he was more fortunate than Gideon, whose bond had been a debt repayment. Still, his father had bequeathed him a useful legacy out of affection and his mother had added to that when she died. He joked that even his army arrears might one day turn up.

Robert had taken on a new, fourteen-year-old apprentice called Miles, who spent a lot of time lusting after girls who would not look at him and the rest staring into space.

'This is a gormless, dawdling noodle of a lad, Robert!'

'Oh, just like my previous apprentices,' smiled Robert. Miles grinned vacantly before accidentally knocking over a pile of stitched pamphlets.

'You could pick those up, young man, and re-stack them tidily,' Gideon hinted. Miles gawped at him as if he could not believe the newly returned partner was so stiff and unreasonable. Gideon mimed taking a sight on him with a musket, holding the pose in concentrated silence as if covering some pernicious Royalist he intended to blast to smithereens. Very slowly, Miles stooped and retrieved the pamphlets. Robert hid a smile.

Another reason Gideon felt obliged to live with his brother was that relations between Lambert and Anne had become so strained he tried to be a peacemaker.

Lambert's health had never fully recovered after Colchester. He was now in his middle forties, with a limp in his foot from Naseby; he had the poor digestion and rheumatics of a much older man, and grumbled like one too. He seemed unlikely to achieve his parents' longevity. War had diminished his gusto; he was running to seed. Lumpish, touchy, dictatorial, and much given to seeking out old comrades for long nights of reminiscence, he ate and drank too much, with too little time spent at home. Gideon dared not imagine what happened in bed with his wife.

Anne still took the lead in running the grocery business. Lambert saw himself as the titular head, but let Anne get on with things as she had done while he was away. They did not tussle for supremacy; Lambert gave way as if he was too tired to care. Trade had suffered badly during the war. Lambert was given to pretending he thought this was Anne's bad management; she ceased taking criticism as a joke. They sniped at each other over business, but there was worse amiss.

Gideon realised that in some ways he had been lucky to be away soldiering. Life was simpler: you only struggled for food, sleep and survival. He had made the army his own refuge from domestic problems, and now he wondered how far Lambert did the same. Gideon had been away from home for over six years, Lambert for five. Returning was bound to take readjustment.

Slowly, they both settled. Perhaps because he was younger and a single man, Gideon found it easier. He slipped back without too much anxiety into the print shop, conveniently filling the place Amyas left. Robert welcomed him, welcomed his skill and reliability, and particularly his conversation. A year older than Lambert, Robert would have been penned up with only the dream-struck new apprentice had Gideon not come home.

* * *

Gideon picked up that other people thought in Lambert's absence something had been going on between Anne Jukes and Robert Allibone. He hated the idea. Robert was now forty-five, not too old for lust though surely too far gone for love (thought Gideon, at a mere twenty-eight), certainly Robert seemed fixed for ever as a widower. To Gideon, the man had aged noticeably; he was shocked at how the sandy hair had thinned and grown lank around Robert's nearly bald crown. Never one with much concern for good eating, Robert's diet at taverns had made him sallow and leather-skinned, with some of his freckles coarsening into liver spots. However, he remained lean and active, his mind sharp and his temperament kindly. As time went by, Gideon ignored other people sniggering; he convinced himself that if Robert did hanker after Anne, Anne safely ignored the infatuation.

The truth was that if Anne Jukes had ever had a soft spot for another man, it was not Robert but Gideon. Fortunately neither Gideon nor Lambert saw this.

Robert had guessed. Robert, trapped in unrequited and impossible heartache, was too great a spirit to speak of it. He had always been his own man, self-contained, emotionally reserved. He sought refuge in solitary evening journeys on his horse, Rumour; he dined several times a week at an inn in King Street, over in Westminster. Rumour had acquired a taste for buckets of ale, while Robert pecked for facts in the political undergrowth like a foraging blackbird tossing leaves. To those who knew him, Robert's nosing around Parliament seemed perfectly natural. Writing the *Public Corranto* was the work he loved best. Disappearing on his own to hunt down news let him hide his secret sorrow.

Gideon understood that he was unwelcome on these jaunts. He did not know why. It seemed to him only that Robert had established a routine he did not wish to break and that he had sources to protect. When Robert found news to report, he would be bright-eyed and enthusiastic as he set the text in the print shop the next day.

Arrangements for becoming a Commonwealth did not always run smoothly. When a proclamation went to sheriffs and mayors to promulgate the Act for Abolishing the Kingly Office, even the Lord Mayor of the City of London, Abraham Reynoldson, refused, because it went against his conscience; he was summoned to the bar of the House, stripped of his office and thrown in the Tower for a month. The City was ordered to elect a new lord mayor – and one with a compliant conscience was immediately produced.

The House of Commons was working hard. Some days Robert Allibone could hardly scribble down all the matters of note. On the same day, the 2nd of April, when Alderman Reynoldson's conscience was discussed, plenty of fascinating items vied for prominence.

'They gave an order for a committee looking into the affairs of Colonel Rainborough's widow,' Robert reported. 'She is to be given a grant of land from the confiscations from deans and chapters – three thousand pounds was mentioned to me by an informant. Then who turns up in the House of Commons but your friend Sexby!'

'*Sexby?*' Gideon experienced a pang.

'Quite the crawler, nowadays.' Robert distrusted Sexby, despite his Leveller links. 'There have been Scots commissioners lurking around since the attempt to make a Presbyterian peace. These dour souls are outraged by us lopping off a head that could have mouthed the Covenant. They scampered off, heading for The Hague, to make a devil's pact with the Prince of Wales, begging *him* to make us all slaves of the Kirk.'

'You must say, "Charles Stuart, eldest son of the late King"!' Gideon reproved Robert.

'Strip me naked, so I must.'

'So what of Sexby?'

'Honest Edward tells Parliament he has chased gallantly after the Scotch commissioners and has personally arrested them at Gravesend – with not a moment to spare (as he told it). He has tucked them up safe under guard in a fort – for which he has been awarded *twenty pounds*, not a penny less.'

'Handsome!'

Robert heard the edge in Gideon's tone. 'Did you obtain any benefit for that secret work of yours in January?'

'I was allowed to buy dinner for Colonel John Fox.'

'A *colonel*! Should he not have treated you?'

'He lacks his arrears,' replied Gideon dryly.

Robert was still niggled. 'I do not know how Sexby showed his face, preening himself, when that very day a petition was brought for the four Levellers who are languishing in the Tower.' John Wildman, John Lilburne, William Walwyn and Thomas Prince had been arrested on suspicion of promulgating republican pamphlets called *England's New Chains Discovered* and *The Second Part of England's New Chains Discovered*. 'There was no time for *them*,' snarled Robert. 'The petition got short shrift – the Commons had to rush to the day's most pressing business.'

'And what fine work was that?'

'"*Ordered*, That the Committee of the Revenue do take care, and give Order, That the Seats in the House be repaired".'

'*Seats*, Robert?' For a moment Gideon was flummoxed, then he sadly grinned. 'All you can expect from a *Rump*, I suppose.'

Of the civilian Levellers, William Walwyn was in some respects the most influential, yet the most discreet. Anne Jukes and Robert had a high opinion of him: a quiet, home-loving man who always said his favourite occupations were a good book and the conversation of friends. There was no evidence that Walwyn had contributed to the *England's Chains* pamphlets. His guiding principles were toleration and love. It was thought astonishing that he had been arrested, unlike Lilburne, who had spent so much time in the Tower of London that at least one of his children was born there and given the name Tower. 'The pathetic soul died,' said Anne Jukes. 'As you might expect!'

The critical pamphlets had been condemned in Parliament as scandalous and highly seditious, destructive to the present government, tending to division and mutiny in the army and to the raising of a new war. 'Somebody must have read them carefully,' scoffed Gideon.

The four Levellers were arrested by troops of horsemen, dragged from their beds in dawn raids. They were taken to Whitehall and charged with treason. During John Lilburne's examination by the Council of State, at one point he was sent into an adjoining room; he could hear Oliver Cromwell losing his temper and shouting at Lord Fairfax: 'I tell you, sir,' – thumping the table – 'you have no other way to deal with these men but to break them, or they will break you!'

The fear of army mutiny was justified: unhappiness homed in on impending service in Ireland. With England now settled, Cromwell was to make an expedition to end the long unrest there. Three hundred infantrymen in Colonel Hewson's regiment swore they would not leave for Ireland until the Levellers' programme had been introduced; they were cashiered without pay arrears. The next serious event, which caused

Gideon a desperate crisis of conscience, happened in London. This involved Robert Lockyer, a young Particular Baptist from Bishopsgate; Anne Jukes, whose family also came from Bishopsgate, had grown up with some of his relatives. Lockyer served in Whalley's regiment, which had incorporated some of Cromwell's original Ironsides; although Whalley himself was more or less a Presbyterian, there were radicals among his men. This regiment was guarding the King at Hampton Court when Charles escaped to Carisbrooke. They subsequently fought at Colchester. Whalley himself supported Pride's Purge, was a member of the High Court of Justice and signed the King's death warrant. He believed his regiment was governed by 'Reason, not Passion' – but he was wrong.

With the King dead, soldier Levellers as well as civilians had realised the execution merely gave the army grandees uncontrolled power. They had installed a republic, yet would ignore the Levellers' constitutional programme. Paying arrears, providing for the wounded and their dependants, and protecting soldiers from enforced service abroad also still remained a low priority.

Eight troopers had petitioned Fairfax to restore the original Council of the Army, with its regimental Agitators. The response was to court-martial five and subject them to the painful punishment called 'riding the wooden horse'. The civilian Richard Overton, who for once was not in prison, greeted this with a celebrated pamphlet likening the soldiers to foxes cruelly hunted down by beagles. Alone among the Leveller leaders, Overton approved the trial and execution of the King; he called it the finest piece of justice that was ever had in England.

A month later, part of Lockyer's troop was stationed in Bishopsgate. Radicals among them were already fired up, as the planned expedition to Ireland gave them a focus. The Levellers believed that the native Irish Catholics had the same right to their own land and to self-determination as the English – an opinion in which they were virtually isolated. Their ideals forbade travelling across international boundaries. Soldiers saw themselves as volunteers who could only be sent abroad with their own consent. Cromwell's intended expedition was gunpoint imperialism. The Levellers believed that any man might refuse to obey commands that were incompatible with his ideas of reason and justice.

When they were ordered to leave their quarters, thirty of Whalley's men seized their colours and barricaded themselves into the Bull Inn in Bishopsgate Street. When their captain tried to carry off the flag, Lockyer and others hung onto it. Colonel Whalley arrived on the scene to be told that the mutineers only wanted their arrears, to pay for their quarter before they left London. Money was promised, therefore, though not enough. A large crowd of civilians gathered and threatened a riot, but were dispersed by loyal soldiers. Next morning Fairfax and Cromwell turned up. Lockyer and fourteen others were arrested. In their subsequent trial, six were condemned to death, of whom Fairfax pardoned five. Lockyer was picked out as the ringleader.

A group of women with radical sympathies had petitioned for the release of the four civilian Levellers. 'We were instructed', said Anne Jukes, by now a veteran of such demonstrations, 'to go home and wash dishes.' Gideon heard the anger in her voice and saw Lambert cringing. 'We answered back that because of the war, we *have* no dishes!'

Robert Lockyer was brought to St Paul's Churchyard to face a regimental firing squad. Gideon went there in sympathy, though he could hardly bear to watch. If he had stayed in the army, this could so easily have been him.

Lockyer was twenty-three. His brave departure was deeply moving. He declared he was not afraid to look death in the face and regretted that he was to die for so small a thing as a dispute over pay, after fighting eight long years for the freedom and liberties of his country. As the firing party lined up, heckled by Lockyer's supporters, the grandees were terrified that this mutiny might lead to a popular uprising in the City.

Disdaining a blindfold, Lockyer stared out the six musketeers. He reminded them they had all fought together for a common aim. He willed them to spare him, as his brothers in arms, saying that their obedience to superior orders would not acquit them of murder. They shuffled with unease. Gideon saw with miserable sympathy that the troubled men could well refuse their duties. He remembered how he had thought at Colchester that, if chosen, he would cheerfully have joined the firing squad that shot Lucas and Lisle. Here, he was in agony for the musketeers. He knew this was wrong. But he saw, too, that the grandees had no other course. There was no solution to the impasse. The Leveller movement was unravelling.

Then Colonel Okey, who was said to have already lost his temper at the court martial, angrily distributed Lockyer's coat, boots and belt amongst the squad. Being soldiers, booty won them over. In his shirt, Lockyer prayed his last prayers and gave the appointed signal by raising both arms. Immediately he crumpled beneath the bullets.

At Lockyer's funeral, which Gideon attended, three thousand people followed the hearse, walking in total silence from Smithfield, through the City, to the New Church at Moorfields. On the coffin lay a naked sword and bunches of bloodstained rosemary. Sea-green ribbons were worn by mourners. Six trumpets sounded a knell. Lockyer's horse, draped in mourning, was led behind the coffin – a privilege normally reserved to a commander-in-chief. As the Leveller news-sheet, the *Moderate*, pointed out, this was a remarkable tribute for a private trooper.

A month later more trouble flared. Twelve hundred men, who had been assembled for Ireland, mutinied. As they camped at Burford in Oxfordshire, Fairfax and Cromwell mounted a surprise night attack. Resistance was brief. Several mutineers were killed. Most either surrendered or fled without much bloodshed, the rest being imprisoned in Burford Church for four days. Three ringleaders were shot against the church wall. For his part at Burford, Colonel Okey received a curious reward: he was made a Master of Arts of Oxford University.

Parliamentary forces crushed a further uprising which William Thompson, a friend and protégé of Lilburne, had inspired. Again the rebels were routed, with Cornet Thompson dying in a desperate action near Wellingborough. Military unrest then faded. By August Cromwell finally embarked for Ireland with the soldiers he needed. The civilian Levellers were still in jail, their enormous outpouring of pamphlets about to dribble to a close. Their supporters declined in disappointment.

Some took up more radical beliefs. As Lambert struggled to come to terms with life after the civil war, Anne sought refuge in a completely different community. She joined a group who were calling themselves True Levellers.

One day Gideon came home from the print shop and found his brother in a state of outraged hysteria. 'My wife has run off with some other man!'

'Calm yourself,' urged Gideon, relieved that he knew Robert Allibone had been working quietly at the shop all day. From conversations with Anne, Gideon realised where she had really gone and why. 'Your wife has a group of friends who say the world is a common treasury. They say that if the people band together in self-sufficient communities, the ruling class must either join in or starve because there will be no labourers for hire. Meanwhile the common people can support themselves and enjoy true liberty.'

'She has run away to anarchy!'

'No, she has run away to St George's Hill in Surrey,' snapped Gideon. 'She has gone to plant beans, carrots and parsnips.'

Lambert threw himself across the kitchen table, with his head in his hands. 'Then I would rather she was an adulteress!' he decided bitterly.

Chapter Fifty-Nine

Lewisham: 1649

To be a Royalist in the Commonwealth – whether by belief or because you were your husband's wife – had serious disadvantages. Sittings of the House of Commons were full of debates about Delinquents: how to secure their estates or extract their fines, and whether to execute, exile or pardon them. It was a time of retribution – but also a time when many Royalists came home and buckled down to living as best they could under the new Commonwealth. Not so Orlando Lovell. For the next six months after the King's execution, his wife never heard a word from him.

Then, at the beginning of June, Juliana was surprised by a visitor. As she returned home from a nearby farm, bearing the kitchen staples of milk, cream and eggs, she saw a lone horseman ride up to the house. He had bulky baggage packs strapped behind him, and was dressed in a plain suit buttoned to the neck like a respectable traveller, yet she could see he was heavily armed with a sword, pistols hung at his saddle, plus a poleaxe and what could be a musket-barrel protruding from his pack. Wide-topped riding boots and a broad-brimmed hat with an ostrich plume spoke of his being, not a wandering minister or land agent, but a cavalier. From his build and demeanour, it was not Lovell. Lovell never looked furtive either; this man kept looking back behind him anxiously.

Juliana felt extreme alarm. She had left Tom and Val playing in the orchard; she was afraid they would have heard hoofbeats and might run to investigate. As she approached cautiously, the rider noticed her; he dismounted, exclaiming, 'Juliana!'

When he swept off his hat and made a gallant bow, she saw his red hair. It was Edmund Treves. He seemed as startled as she was.

Juliana hurried him indoors. The boys came in and were greeted.

Tom thought he remembered Edmund from their trip to Hampshire. Val asked his usual question: 'Are you my father?'

They laughed it off. 'No, Valentine, this is your *god*father.'

Juliana sat Edmund down and produced food for everyone, reserving her curiosity until a quieter moment. The boys accepted her warning that Edmund was exhausted by travel, so eventually she persuaded them to go to bed. As she tucked the children in, both were highly excited, hoping that the arrival of a cavalier – any cavalier – meant their father might also come. Juliana had curiously mixed feelings.

She made preparations for her guest, moving her own things from her room. She would sleep with the boys, while Edmund could take her bed. She had no other space to give him.

When she went downstairs she could tell he had been weighing up how frugally she lived in this tiny dwelling: her lack of possessions, how carefully she had to measure out food, the cheap wooden bowls she served it in. More realistic than he would have been once, Edmund did not waste time on naïve expressions of horror, but simply asked curtly, 'Are you managing?'

'By the skin of my teeth.'

'Your lads look healthy.'

'They are thriving. They have never known any different, not that they can remember . . . They long to see Orlando. Any visitor raises their hopes.' Juliana let her despair show as she relaxed with Edmund at her kitchen hearth. 'I have a little parlour, or we can talk here with the pans bubbling. This is where I often sit once the light goes. The fire gives some comfort on lonely evenings.'

Edmund inclined his head and stayed put. Perhaps he realised that if they moved to the parlour they would have to carry their chairs with them.

Juliana quietly let herself enjoy the luxuries of adult company and old friendship. Edmund Treves must be in his late twenties now. It was seven years since he was a witness at her wedding and over three since Juliana last saw him, in the gloomy months after Naseby, before Lovell took her to Pelham Hall.

Had Edmund aged? After spotting only old scars, Juliana decided he had merely become much quieter. Had she? Edmund would be too polite to say.

She braced herself. 'Have you brought me bad news, Edmund?'

He looked surprised. Juliana now became certain that Edmund Treves had not expected to discover her here – and he was deep in some trouble of his own. In her usual frank way, she tackled her suspicions: 'I suspect you have been in this little house before, my friend. You lived here with my secretive husband, while he was stirring up rebellion in Kent. Tell me the truth, Edmund,' she said sternly. 'Was Lovell here, and were you with him?'

Edmund's brow cleared. He obediently confessed what she had already worked out: Lovell and a group of men had stayed there last year. Edmund was recruited to join them. Lovell had been made a colonel and, using Sir Lysander Pelham's money, raised a troop for the rebellion. 'You must have known!' marvelled Edmund, still something of an innocent. 'Lovell, of course, had the house as your dowry – I believe he found it somewhat smaller than we once supposed!'

'This house', Juliana returned crisply, 'was my *father*'s property. Still, Papa died at Colchester so Lovell can come back here and lord it as soon as he likes . . . If he still lives?' she tried out again on Edmund.

He gave her a swift, sweet smile, eager as always to dispel anxiety for her. 'Oh be sure he does. I saw him alive in January.'

'Tell me!' Juliana ordered. 'Go back to the beginning.'

In 1648, Lovell and his troop had assembled here. They took part in the Kent fighting, and were driven out of Maidstone by Fairfax. After reconnoitring at Rochester, where many men deserted them, a large group followed Lord Norwich towards London, but Lovell peeled off from the old commander. He had despised Norwich's son, the debauched Lord Goring, though Goring at least could fight when he was sober; the professional Lovell would not take orders from an ancient nobleman who had never engaged in war. He and Treves went with a group that captured the castles at Walmer, Sandwich and Deal, castles which guarded the naval anchorage called the Downs. Fairfax left a Parliamentary force to besiege them. Eventually, while Fairfax was on the other side of the Thames attempting to take Colchester, the Prince of Wales appeared off the coast with a little fleet. Prince Charles tried to relieve the castles, to build a bridgehead through which England could be invaded. His attempt at an amphibious landing with fifteen hundred men was repulsed by stiff enemy opposition. However, Lovell and Treves broke out and managed to get themselves aboard one of the ships.

'So the prince took us off, to our great relief. We drifted north to Yarmouth, which might have been taken but for loss of resolution – then we drifted south back to the Downs, where we might have destroyed the Parliamentary fleet but for a storm. Prince Rupert advised an attack on the Isle of Wight to carry off the King, who was then still there. But Rupert was talked down by doubters, so we ended up in Holland. We were pursued by the Parliamentary navy, which bottled up our ships in port until this January.'

'The exiled court moved to Holland.' Juliana had read it in a news-sheet.

'The Hague. The new King stays there while he assesses who will help him to regain the kingdom.'

'Edmund, do not refer to him as "the new King" while you are in England.'

'Damme –'

Juliana held up her hand firmly. 'Do not.'

Edmund, whose views had always been straightforward to the point of naïveté, resisted angrily. 'Are you a Commonwealther?'

'I choose to live a quiet life – in safety! Finish telling me about Orlando.'

'*He* won't accept this treason.'

'He will if he comes here. He will have to. Go on, I say.'

With a snort, Edmund continued. 'Prince Rupert took charge of the fleet. There was no money for fitting out and he had to put down mutinies; he suspended one ringleader over the side of the ship until the man capitulated . . . He bargained with merchants, raised credit on his mother's jewels, and plucked funds out of nowhere, as energetic and inspired as always. He and Prince Maurice found no attraction in the Prince of Wales's hopes for a Scottish alliance – Rupert is friendly with the Marquis of Montrose; he hates the Presbyterian Kirk.'

'So he found another way to use his energies?' Juliana asked.

'Ireland. The Marquis of Ormond has invited the young King to join him. Rupert and Maurice sailed with six warships and some lesser vessels to Kinsale. They have been raiding Commonwealth ships in the English Channel.'

'Indeed!' Juliana smiled ruefully. 'I read that they are so successful, marine insurance rates in London have increased by four hundred per cent!' Edmund laughed briefly. Juliana caught a nuance: 'Does this affect us?'

'Lovell went to sea with them.'

'He despises Prince Rupert.'

'He attached himself to Prince Maurice. They left in January, before we all knew, or could even believe, that the King would be executed.'

'So what of you, Edmund?'

'My mother is gravely ill; I am needed here.'

'Is your return dangerous?' Juliana was thinking of Parliament's measures against Delinquents.

'I have to take my chance.'

There was a pause, while Juliana thought about her own position. 'So now my heroic husband is a pirate at sea! Aye, and who knows when or where he may make land again.'

'Orlando wrote to you,' Edmund earnestly assured her. 'The letter must have gone astray.'

Juliana conceded that Lovell would not have known where she was, once she left Pelham Hall. She did not altogether trust Bessy and Susannah to redirect correspondence. Even if they would co-operate, there were many possible mishaps, from letters being dropped in the mud by careless carriers to Parliamentary spies seizing and opening suspect packets.

By now she felt certain that Edmund was obsessed by some dark trouble. As if satisfied with their discussion, she led him out of doors and walked him around her orchard. Chattering about the age and poor yield of her apple, pear and cherry trees, she enjoyed the long summer evening. The sky was still blue, a few bats flitted over an old pond, the country-side was peaceful, she had recovered an old friend . . .

They seated themselves on a mouldering wooden bench. Juliana spent all their time there in terror that this decayed rustic seat would collapse beneath them. She kept silent because the subject of their conversation changed abruptly – to one she could never have foreseen.

'You are strangely quiet. Has something gone wrong, Edmund?'

'Have you heard,' Edmund asked her slowly, 'of a man named Isaac Dorislaus?'

Because she read so many news-sheets, Juliana had. Dr Dorislaus was a Dutch lawyer and historian who had lived in England for many years. His academic interest was kingship, his thesis that regal authority had in ancient times been assigned to monarchs by the people, so that kings who abused their position were tyrants, from whom the rulership could be removed. This view had not won the doctor any favours during the early years of King Charles's personal rule, so his university career had foundered. After struggling in legal advocacy, he had supported Parliament, for whom he investigated Royalist plots and conducted diplomatic missions to the Netherlands. At the King's trial, he was one of the prosecuting counsels and although he did not speak, he had intended to do so if Charles had ever acknowledged the court and answered the charges.

What Juliana did not know was that after the King's execution Isaac Dorislaus was asked to perform a diplomatic mission for the new Council of State. He travelled to The Hague as a special envoy. His mission was to seek peace and reconciliation. Given that the princes of Orange had close marriage ties to the Stuart family, that they were giving the Prince of Wales refuge at their court, and that their ambassadors had besieged Parliament and Fairfax with pleas for the King's life, to send one of the King's prosecutors to Holland might seem ill-judged. However, Dorislaus had been a diplomat before, Holland was his country of birth, and he spoke the language.

'What is he to you, my dear?'

'The envoy died, Juley, the very night he first set foot in Holland.'

'Died?'

'Killed.' Juliana stared. Edmund leaned forwards, his elbows on his knees, his face in his hands. 'Killed at his inn, as he sat down for supper.'

Juliana spoke slowly: 'You know more about this, Edmund?' He remained silent, but she saw he must have been involved. 'You should tell me,' Juliana urged him. 'I can see you are affected. Were you there? Did you see? What happened to this man?'

Shaking his head, Edmund brought out the story: 'There are Royalists swarming everywhere in Holland, you understand. We were all outraged by the late King's martyrdom. To send Dorislaus was madness. About a dozen men, fully armoured, went to him that night.'

'Was this ordered officially?' prompted Juliana.

'I cannot tell you.'

'But you know!'

'Do not ask me . . . They entered the inn; the woman of the house cried out "Murder!" The man's servants closed his chamber door and held it, but they burst in. Doctor Dorislaus sat in his chair, facing the door, with his arms folded. He just seemed to be waiting . . . He was stabbed several times, his skull fractured, his heart and liver punctured, then his throat was cut – and all the time he never moved position. "Thus dies one of the King's judges!" cried the King's avengers, then they rode away.'

'He was a civilian. He was an *ambassador*!' Shocked, Juliana phrased her next question with care: 'Is it publicly known who did this?'

'No. The States General expressed horror, but may not want to identify the killers.' Edmund paused. 'Luckily!' he added, with feeling.

Juliana sat still, thoroughly disconcerted. She could see how the murder had happened, and why – but she could not approve of it. Edmund half turned to her. She was astonished to see tears on his face. 'I have seen terrible sights, Juley. I have done things that I can never tell you. This is what we have come to. Fighting is cruel. Men are hardened and brutalised. In this civil war we have learned to accept unholy occurrences, robberies and rapes and bloodshed . . . Now prisoners are executed, civilians are punished as if they were soldiers – do you know, the uprising here in Kent was fuelled by anger, simply when ordinary people rioted because the Mayor of Canterbury tried to abolish Christmas . . . The fighting at Maidstone was more vicious than ever. Then came the martyrdoms of Lucas and Lisle at Colchester. Then the King . . .'

Edmund fell silent, his face set. Juliana eventually murmured, 'You speak as if you were morally degenerate, but, dear man, if that were true you would not be so racked with conscience.'

Edmund hardly seemed aware of her. 'There was something ghastly about the death of a man in his fifties, a scholar on a courtly mission, tired by travel, eating his dinner in the presence of servants – herrings, shredded Dutch cabbage – a linen napkin tucked about his neck . . .'

His regret was dreadful to see. Juliana imagined the event – cavaliers, footloose and idle in Holland, frustrated by the news of the King's execution, encouraged by the Prince of Wales or those around him. News coming that Dr Dorislaus had landed as Parliament's ambassador. There would be a certain degree of pomp in his arrival; he represented a sovereign state. His disembarkation must have caused a flurry. People may have been on the lookout. Certainly word of his landing reached hard men who wanted retribution, men who welcomed a chance for derring-do. Juliana envisaged them riding rapidly to the inn. At the beginning of May, the evening would be light. Twelve on a noisy gallop would be exhilarated. The need for secrecy, the ritual bloodshed, the snatching of drink – for it took place in an inn, and Dutch drinking was notorious – then the wild, whooping ride away . . .

Afterwards, one of them was blasted by conscience.

Juliana was surprised how little shock she felt that Edmund Treves took part. It pained her that he had sunk so far from his nobler nature; he was experienced enough to have refused. She even wondered whether Orlando's departure with the fleet had left him vulnerable. Lovell had always seemed to be a bad influence – though when it came to it, he had often been there as Edmund's saviour.

She grieved for her friend. Edmund turned away from her, hiding his head, and wept openly. Juliana laid her arm gently across his back to comfort him.

She gazed up, into the deep indigo of midsummer twilight, lost in her own melancholy thoughts.

Chapter Sixty

Lewisham and London: 1649

Parliament retrieved the body of Dr Dorislaus and gave him a state funeral in Westminster Abbey.

The States General investigations were thought by the English to be cursory and ineffective; certainly no culprits were brought to justice. Various suspects were touted. Scots supporters of the Marquis of Montrose, perhaps. Montrose was appointed to negotiate with European states in the new King's name; he had sworn his loathing for those who killed Charles I and had threatened to write an epitaph in blood. Colonel Walter Whitford, a bishop's son, and Sir John Spottiswood were implicated. Sir Henry Bard, later Viscount Bellemount, was arrested but released. Montrose and also Lord Hopton were questioned. Later it seemed that others had organised the deed, with the new King's connivance. The murder became notorious and continued to rankle with the Commonwealth, being one of the excuses for trade wars with Holland. When other Parliamentary ambassadors were threatened or killed in foreign countries, it began to look like a campaign, not a spur-of-the-moment action by rogue cavaliers but a concerted plot that was approved by and directly linked to Charles II.

Juliana Lovell kept Edmund Treves's confidence. As far as she knew, he never spoke about Dorislaus to anyone again. Certainly she had warned him not to. Once he had unburdened himself that evening, his spirits visibly lifted. He returned to good humour, although the image of Dorislaus, sprawled on the inn table among his vinegar-soused herrings, would trouble Juliana herself for a long time.

The danger in which Edmund put himself by returning to England became clear, especially in Kent. Walter Breame, a Kentish cavalier, was arrested that month and sent to the Tower for possessing letters which referred to the ambassador's death. Ferdinand Storey was imprisoned in the Gatehouse the following year. There was a hue and cry for Captain Francis Murfield, who had been heard supporting the murder. A Captain Norwood was ordered to pay a bond of five hundred pounds a year to the Sheriff of Kent, against future good behaviour . . .

During Edmund's visit, there were more immediate concerns: he was travelling without a permit. Juliana knew this was far too dangerous. She herself would only risk it where she could claim to be going about ordinary business if soldiers stopped her; Royalists not allowed to travel beyond a five-mile radius of their homes.

Edmund was intending to throw himself upon the mercy of an uncle in London who had supported Parliament throughout the war. 'Merry Uncle Foulke; you will find him exceedingly pleasant'. Leaving Edmund to stay out of sight at her house, Juliana took a letter to the man, a member of the Merchant Taylors Company and brother of Edmund's ailing mother; he knew how urgently Alice Treves longed to see her 'dearest Ned' before she died.

The reception was friendly; promises were made for Edmund. Juliana was less taken with his uncle than her eager friend had foretold, but she found Foulke Adams apparently sympathetic to his Royalist nephew. He claimed numerous contacts who would ease Edmund's compounding and pardon, then help him obtain a pass to go to Staffordshire. It proved correct. Foulke Adams rode out to Lewisham in person, flourishing paperwork. He took Edmund away with him, then some time later Edmund wrote to say that he had satisfied the relevant committees, and was leaving straight for home.

Before he was removed, Juliana had urged good advice upon him. 'You have to accept the Commonwealth, Edmund. Do not waste your life with believing the popular song – "*All things will be well, when the King enjoys his own again*". Kings may never return to England. Build yourself a life, my dear. Bow to Parliament and button your tongue. You should marry. Marry for kindness, not money – though I admit, money will help.'

She wanted to add, do not write bad love lyrics to unobtainable women, but she knew Edmund saw poetry as the noble expression of his most romantic spirit.

After he had gone, Juliana considered her own future. If this Commonwealth continued, she wondered whether Orlando would ever return to England. How long would Prince Rupert keep the Royalist fleet at sea? Would Lovell one day settle in exile, in Holland or France? If so, would he send for her? Would it be her fate to uproot herself and her children? He husband's seafaring gave her some breathing space; she let herself defer worrying.

She went on with her isolated, quiet life, bringing up her sons. The countryside was ruined, bad harvests had increased the price of corn by half as much again and expensive fodder made meat go up twofold. Wood for fuel was in short supply. Work was scarce. But there was one great benefit: it was peacetime.

For some, however, peace was an imperfect state. Three months after Edmund left, Juliana was forced to learn exactly what her position was, as the wife of a known Royalist officer.

It was mid-morning. For an hour or two earlier, she had been sewing in her tiny parlour, lost in her work, though at that moment she had gone to prepare food. She was peeling a yellow carrot. This mundane action was brutally interrupted.

A commotion disturbed her. She walked to her door. Soldiers were throwing open outhouses and shouting at the boys. They pushed past her and began searching her house. Tom and Val were terrified; Juliana was too, though she had to hide it for their sakes. Before she grasped the situation properly, rude men were asking angry, noisy, sometimes stupid questions about her absent husband. They demanded his whereabouts; they wanted to know all his recent movements. They ordered her to name his associates. Finally they told her she had to go with them. With a sinking heart, Juliana realised that she was being arrested.

Given warning, she could have found a safe place for Thomas and Valentine. Alone with them at the cottage, she could not now send them running to the farm; she never let them go so far without her. So, given barely time to snatch cloaks, Tom and Val were taken up with her. Ruefully, Juliana hoped the presence of loudly crying children might help in whatever ordeal she faced.

They were all roughly put upon horses behind hard-faced cavalry. Nothing was said about their destination, though it became clear it was London. Trying to call out reassurance to her weeping boys, Juliana faced the terrible fear that she, and they, were about to be incarcerated in the Tower of London.

It had happened to others. Lady Carlisle had been shown the rack, when she was obdurate in refusing to give details of Royalist plots.

In the event, Juliana was not in penal custody. She was merely brought before the Committee for Investigations at Haberdashers Hall. This shadowy body, mainly composed of civilians, some of them members of Parliament, was much feared among Royalists. It dealt with hard cases – men whose delinquency was considered too serious to be left to local county committees. Men who were defined as soldiers of fortune, subject to firing squad if captured. Men with unforgivable war crimes listed against them. Men of stubborn and recalcitrant Royalist opinions. Men like Orlando Lovell.

'Has your husband, Colonel Lovell, compounded for pardon?'

'His particulars were accepted by the Committee at Goldsmiths Hall last year. I handed them his fine myself –'

"That is superseded. Has he presented himself for compounding since he took part in the revolt in Kent?'

'He is beyond the seas.'

Juliana knew from news-sheets that Parliament had laid down a timetable for Royalists to compound: the 20th of April for those who lived within eighty miles of London and the 3rd of May for those residing farther away. Delinquents living beyond the seas had to file their petitions by the 1st of June. After giving particulars, everyone had six weeks more to pay their fines. Keeping estates compelled returning to England. Anyone who neglected to render himself for compounding would lose his land to the Commonwealth. Juliana had taken particular note of that rule, because it was added that no further allowance would then be made for wives and children.

Even those whose estates had not been formally sequestered, but who merely suspected – or knew – they were liable, had to present themselves by the 1st of July. There was another rule, even worse for Juliana, that:

All who have or shall adhere to, or assist, Charles Stuart, Son of the late King, or any of the Forces in Ireland, against the Parliament of England; are, and be adjudged to be, Traitors and Rebels to the Commonwealth of England; and all their Estates shall be confiscated, and their Persons proceeded against as Traitors and Rebels.

Being on a ship with Prince Maurice, harrying Cromwell's supply lines to Ireland, certainly earned proceedings as a Traitor and Rebel.

At first when Juliana was marched in to be examined, Tom and Val were taken away to another room. Being separated from their mother traumatised them. She, and the committee, could hear them hysterically screaming. Horrified that her two very young children might themselves be asked questions – then even more frightened by what the little boys might innocently say – Juliana's own distress grew so dreadful, she was beyond answering anything. Not normally prone to collapse in a crisis, she was surprised how quickly she lost her calm and how violent her agitation became.

Permission was given for the children to be brought back. 'You must sit here very quietly,' she begged them, while they clung to her skirts and squirmed and wailed. 'When Mother speaks with the gentlemen, do not interrupt and do not cry.'

Tom was not quite six. Valentine was four. Neither of them could understand this.

Juliana had been allowed to bring nothing when she was dragged from home. She felt grubby. Such food as had been given to her had been tasteless and unappetising. She was empty and light-headed. Perhaps her everyday dress would help her. The soldiers who searched her had found nothing worse than the half-peeled carrot in her apron pocket; fortunately she had put down the paring knife on the kitchen table. When they found the carrot, she had snatched it back from them; there was good broth in it, she told them, before they had the grace to grin sheepishly, and even she forced a wan smile. They all had mothers. Some had wives. Juliana's preoccupation must seem all too familiar.

'I have nobody to speak for me,' Juliana told the committee through gritted teeth. 'I shall answer your questions as faithfully as possible. But I know very little.' She remembered how Lovell had said it was better if she knew nothing, and how angry she had been about that. Now she ought to be grateful. Being Juliana, she was in two minds. She was not sure how successful a dissembler she could be, but she would have liked a better idea of what she needed to say – or not say. 'My husband went abroad. I have not seen him, or had letters, for a year and a half. Before he left, he told me nothing of his plans.'

Silence greeted her declaration. Perhaps it sounded contrived. They must be used to wives denying contact with fugitive husbands. She let the men decide what to ask her.

She lost track of how long she was interrogated. Their questions were many, stern and remarkably detailed. Their response to her answers was often incredulity. Much of their interest was in whatever had been plotted from Pelham Hall.

'We lived there for a very short time only. My husband worked for Sir Lysander Pelham –'

'In what capacity?'

'An estate manager.'

'That was a subterfuge?'

'No; I believed it.'

'When did you leave Pelham Hall?'

'Around August last year.'

'*Why* did you leave?'

'Sir Lysander Pelham died very suddenly. We had so little connection with that place, that his daughters drove me out without compunction.'

'Now you live . . .' Papers were consulted. 'In Kent? At cottages owned by one, Carlill?'

'Of Colchester. A haberdasher. A town very strong for Parliament.'

Juliana managed to keep her face blank. She deduced that, in the manner of bureaucracy, the committee had imperfect information. They did not know that Germain Carlill was her father, nor that he had died. They must assume she was a tenant; how she found money for her rent, or whether she paid at all, was no concern of theirs. She took a chance and, since they did not ask her, remained silent about owning the cottage and orchard.

Questions about conspiracy continued. Juliana maintained she had never known who visited Pelham Hall, never guessed plots were being hatched, never knew her husband was involved. She sounded foolish to herself. Perhaps the men could see how perturbed she felt, as she realised the extent to which matters had been concealed from her. Perhaps they saw her starting to wonder how these things had become known to *them*, and why now?

'How close was Colonel Lovell's connection with Colonel William Legge?'

Will Legge? Juliana grew cold under her shift. 'Of course I heard of Colonel Legge; he was governor of Oxford when we lived there –'

'He lived close to you.'

'In the same street, that was well known. He was Prince Rupert's friend. We never moved in such circles.'

'When did your husband last see Colonel Legge?'

'*See* him?'

'Colonel Legge helped the late King escape from Hampton Court. He was then involved in the late rebellion in the county of Kent. He was reported to have been conferring with others, including his brother-in-law, Colonel Henry Washington, at Gravesend in Kent, as lately as this April.'

Juliana was truly astonished. 'This is nothing to do with us!'

'No, indeed,' one of the committee agreed, as if she had somehow incriminated herself. 'For according to you, your husband is beyond the seas.'

Another man said, 'Colonel Legge was sent by the late King's son, at the behest of the Marquis of Ormond, to join Prince Rupert's fleet. His ship was captured. Legge was taken prisoner at Plymouth in July and is currently in jail at Exeter, charged with high treason.'

Did that mean Lovell was a prisoner with Will Legge? Juliana stayed silent. In her heart she was raging at Lovell for never explaining anything.

There must have been no definitive connection between Lovell and Will Legge. The men let it drop. They held a discussion, almost among themselves, about the deputy lieutenants in Kent discharging Delinquents for only minor fines. Clearly it rankled. The powers given to the Kent Committee, the committee's recent actions and whether they had pursued the correct compounding rules had all been scrutinised by a Parliamentary subcommittee. Perhaps Juliana was only caught up in attempts to bring Kent into line . . .

When she felt so exhausted she thought she would faint, her interrogators lost interest. Then they revealed what had brought the soldiers to search her small house and garden, what had caused her to be carried here with her children and a wilting carrot in her pocket. One read out to her a resolution from the House of Commons:

The Question being put, For referring the Examination of Mr Orlando Lovell, being a Delinquent, to the Committee at Haberdashers Hall. It passed with the Affirmative.

Resolved, &c. That it be referred to the Committee to examine the Delinquency of Mr Orlando Lovell; and to proceed with him accordingly; the House having received Information, That he rode in Prince Rupert's Troop and has been involved in the late Rebellion in the County of Kent.

Someone had laid an information.

Now Juliana realised that a person, a person probably known to her, had deliberately and maliciously accused her husband.

Possibilities arose, each more upsetting. She hoped it was some anonymous soldier who had served with Orlando. She feared it was not. More likely, it was somebody she herself knew. Someone she had trusted, someone she had liked. Her circle of acquaintance was extremely small. Anne Jukes, or Anne's associates at the print shop? Anne's Roundhead husband, that man whose life Juliana had saved? Or one of the Lovell family in Hampshire? Someone closer – the farmer's wife in Lewisham? The Pelham sisters? Most terrible of all – she forced herself to consider it – was it Edmund Treves?

The timing pointed horribly to Edmund. Had he bartered this information in return for his own lenient treatment? Had Edmund, out of old jealousy over losing Juliana or old resentment of Orlando, done this appalling thing?

Juliana Lovell was released. 'Thank you – but I have no money and am a day's journey from home! You brought me here, and my little ones – either your soldiers must take us back, or you should give me the fare!'

She seemed naïve, she was exhausted, she had a shiny glaze of honesty. The committee men were so startled by her fierce request, they dipped into their contingency fund – which was replete with the proceeds of enemy estates and Crown and Church lands – to let her have enough coins to get back home. A clerk made her sign a receipt, for when they had to render accounts to Parliament.

As she struggled home with her whining children, Juliana faced the fact that from now on all relationships were dangerous. Her political predicament might never end. Suspicion and caution would sour her life. For her, as one of the defeated, whose husband would not concede defeat, living under the Commonwealth would be isolated, penalised, poisonous and devoid of all trust.

Only many weeks later did she realise that a likely candidate for giving the information against Lovell was Foulke Adams. He was a Parliamentarian. He knew who Juliana was and where she lived. Edmund's 'Merry Uncle Foulke' might have coerced Edmund to join with him (something she hated to believe), or he might independently have passed on facts he winkled from his unwary nephew. Juliana was able to convince herself that if Adams was the source, Edmund had just foolishly trusted an uncle he had never known well.

That helped. It helped a little, but not really enough.

When, eventually, Juliana heard that Orlando's sequestered estates in Hampshire had been put on the market and bought up cheaply by his own land agent, John Jolley, she then wondered if it was Jolley who had turned on him and reported his activities.

Her examination had brought home to her that it was best not to hope for Orlando's return to England. He was proscribed. He was, and he would remain, among a small group of hardened Royalists who were specifically exempted from pardon. His name was known to too many committees. Juliana could see this, long before Orlando Lovell's full status as a plotter became known.

Chapter Sixty-One

Cobham: 1649–50

Anne Jukes made her expedition into country living just before the worst winter anyone had ever known. To her husband's dismay, even this did not bring her running home.

'I would rather' – Lambert did not change his tune – 'she had run away with an Anabaptist hat-maker.'

'And took all your money,' Gideon added, to make the misery as bad as possible. In fact, Anne had taken few possessions and very little money – though she had left a note about her dowry that made Lambert sit up.

'She wants to distribute my investments among the world's beggars and idlers. I am screwed and wrung!'

'You are a gloomy ghoul around the house. I am not surprised she went.' Domestically, they were struggling like two bachelors. The maid had refused to live in and a cook whose name Anne had left them on the back of a linen list proved a grim disappointment. They were used to skilful English boiling and baking. The cook, on the other hand, was used to masters who ate her half-cooked puddings and burnt roasts; although she noticed that sometimes they did so in pinched silence, she put that down to people thinking about religion.

'I *cannot* understand it . . .'

Gideon sighed. Lambert ought to understand, because his brother had explained it often enough. Gideon had even produced a copy of *The True Levellers Standard Advanced*, the manifesto of the movement Anne had joined. The new group called themselves True Levellers to distinguish them from the originals. As soon as they set up their first establishment, at St George's Hill, near Weybridge in Surrey, the new community became known as the Diggers.

By April there were reputedly fifty. Their most vocal leader was

Gerard Winstanley, a former mercer whose business had been ruined in the civil wars. Forced to work as a cattle herdsman, he lived with his wife's relations at Walton-on-Thames.

'Bankrupt – and having to endure your in-laws' pity? – enough to make anybody have a vision of a better life!' chortled Gideon.

Winstanley claimed his inspiration for communal cultivation of the land arrived in a message he received while in a trance: *'Work together, Eat bread together'*. Nobody could object to that, but he was asking for trouble with his wider opinions: *'Was the earth made to preserve a few covetous, proud men to live at ease, and for them to bag and barn up the treasures of the Earth from others, that these may beg or starve in a fruitful land – or was it made to preserve all her children?'*

Winstanley's writings envisaged an ideal relationship between humans and nature. Like many radicals of the period, he promulgated the theory that a golden age had existed in England before the Norman Conquest, after which the common people had been robbed of their birthrights and exploited by a foreign ruling class.

With a view to overturning this centuries-old social injustice, Winstanley joined a community founded by a neighbouring idealist, William Everard, a former soldier and lay preacher. The Diggers occupied St George's Hill in April 1649, at a time when war, floods and bad harvests had pushed food prices to an all-time high. It seemed the right moment for a new democratic society established for the common man, instead of the existing pattern which was based on privilege and wealth. Winstanley deplored the plight of the people at the lowest levels of society, whose dismal existence was bemoaned and yet overlooked by most of the protagonists in the civil war – the poor, sick, hungry, and destitute. Some of them would join the Diggers. Other members, like Anne, were drawn there through having a conscience about their own good fortune.

The Diggers immediately aroused suspicion in the authorities. Lord Fairfax was instructed by the Council of State to remove this threat to public order. He sent a captain to inspect what they were up to, who said that they had invited *'all to come in and help them, and promise them meat, drink, and clothes'*. Captain Sanders reported darkly to Fairfax, *'It is feared they have some design in hand.'*

At the behest of furious local landowners, the lord general eventually arrived in person. Initially, Everard made himself the official spokesman. He described a vision telling him to plough the earth as an attempt to 'restore the Creation to its former condition'. However, it was now claimed that the Diggers did *not* intend to knock down enclosures or touch other men's property; they would simply till the common land until all men joined them. During the interview Winstanley and Everard refused to remove their hats, because to them, Lord Fairfax was 'but their fellow creature'.

As they were questioned there, Everard — who had been summed up by Fairfax's captain as a madman — decided that the Diggers were in serious trouble and evaporated away. Actually Fairfax viewed the Diggers as harmless, called this a civil dispute and advised the local landowners to use the courts for remedy. Gerard Winstanley stuck by his convictions, remained with the group and complained about the treatment they received.

Anne Jukes arrived at St George's Hill two months after the colony started. She could not have had a worse welcome, for the community was attacked by thugs hired by the local lord of the manor, the incongruously named Francis Drake. Scenes of chaos greeted her. In the systematic mistreatment and bullying meted out by the landowner, Diggers had been carried off as prisoners to Walton Church. Others were beaten up by local people, with the sheriff disdainfully looking on, then five were carried to the White Lion Prison for weeks. Goods were stolen from them. A young boy was attacked and had his clothes taken.

In this notorious attack, four Diggers had been battered by William Starr and John Taylor, with other men, who were all disguised as women. Anne heard from excited community members how Starr and Taylor set about their victims with long staves, leaving three badly beaten, a fourth in danger of death, so badly wounded he had to be brought home in a cart. As their wounds were tended, the bloodied survivors told how they had asked to be brought properly before the law, a suggestion ignored by the thugs. Afterwards, they were not vengeful, but issued a statement: *'Let the world take notice that we that do justify this cause of digging have obeyed the Lord, in setting forward this work of endeavouring to bring the earth into a Community, and we have peace and purposes to go on.'*

It was a frightening reception for Anne Jukes, who had gone there alone and who in any case was unused to the bone-hard grind of country life. She had, however, helped dig London's fortifications, the Lines of Communication. She could endure hard labour in biting wind if she had to.

Molestation continued. Digger houses were pulled down. Their tools were destroyed – spades and hoes cut to pieces or wrenched from them by force and never seen again. Cartwheels were damaged. Vegetables were uprooted. Growing corn was spoiled. They accepted these trials philosophically and, as they had promised, continued.

The landowners tried legal measures. Members of the community were arrested and charged with trespassing. Following a court case, in which the Diggers were forbidden to speak in their own defence, they were found guilty of being Ranters, an eccentric sect associated with free love. In fact Gerard Winstanley had reprimanded the Ranters' leader for his sexual practices.

'If, as I have heard, the Ranters run out into the streets naked to proclaim their visions, then to call us Ranters is madness,' Anne joked to her new comrades. 'Nobody would stand in the middle of a frozen field tending parsnips without clothes!'

This was not received with the humour she had enjoyed among the Jukes family. Her first pang of homesickness struck.

Once they lost the court case, the army could have been used to evict them, so the Diggers abandoned St George's Hill in August and set up again nearby at Cobham. There they repeated their efforts: tilling, planting and building shelters. Their reception was no better. In October, the local authorities tried to have them removed. In November, soldiers were dispatched to assist the local justices of peace. Members clung on, but their situation was worrying.

Despite this, Anne lived at Cobham for over six months, in one of the communal houses. Most of the other members were couples or families, although some were very elderly. Anne felt out of place. Forty years of age was a bad time to take up farming. Some male members naturally assumed that women members would be held in common – these were men who would have attempted liberties whatever society they lived in, Anne reckoned. Meanwhile, female members were suspicious of the motives of an unaccompanied woman. Married female members were certain Anne Jukes was after their husbands. Saying what she really thought of those husbands would only have caused friction.

There were disadvantages to communal life. Bursting with people, the houses were noisy. Occupants stayed up late, banging about while others were longing for rest after hard work in the fields. Idealistic principles made little impression on human nature. Food and belongings were shared, but bitterness sometimes festered over perceived hoarding, with dark suspicions about exactly how *equal* the sharing-out was.

Division of labour was fraught too. Some people were so overwhelmed and exhausted by their need to expound ecstatic visions, they left all the hard work to others. There had never in the world been a rota for wood-chopping that satisfied everyone named on it. Ideas varied widely on how full a fetched water-bucket should be. Born organisers do have to comment frankly on the deficiencies of lesser mortals, whereas, having taken courageous decisions on their way of life, some mortals are resistant to listening. Who, thought Anne Jukes irritably, having thrown off the Norman yoke of tyranny, then wants to be given instructions about chicken-feathers by a prissy confectioner who has clearly never plucked a fowl or stitched up a seam in linen in her life? A woman who does not even know the difference between a pillow- and a bolster-case?

Human endurance has limits. The Diggers were testing them.

That winter was bitter. Water froze in the pail. None the less, with the spring their crops flourished on Cobham Heath. Their hard-working community had eleven acres under cultivation and had built six or seven shelters. But local pressure against them continued relentlessly, and their situation became desperate. There was encouraging news that other Digger communities had developed and were doing well elsewhere, but they needed funds. A letter was sent out from Surrey requesting financial assistance from the other Diggers. Winstanley then discovered that impostors were going about soliciting donations with a forged letter which purportedly bore his signature.

The movement declined in early 1650. In March remnants were driven off St George's Hill. The government was becoming increasingly concerned. Throughout the spring the Diggers continued their work, despite harassment. Then, in April, the movement collapsed. The lord of the manor at Cobham was a Parson Platt. With several others he destroyed the Diggers' houses, burned their furniture and scattered their belongings. Platt threatened the Diggers with death if they continued their activity and hired guards to prevent their return.

With legal actions pending and dwindling financial resources, the Surrey Diggers quietly disbanded their community. Some were now in such reduced circumstances, they left their children to be cared for by parish welfare, which attracted much righteous criticism. By July, everything was over. It had been a brave experiment, but it had failed.

Anne Jukes had to find somewhere else to go. After three-quarters of a year away, she acknowledged to herself just how reluctant she was to slink back humbly to her no-doubt crowing husband.

Chapter Sixty-Two

Lewisham: 1650

One evening, Juliana Lovell opened her door at dusk and was startled by another visitor. Standing on the step with a bundle of possessions at her feet, which appeared to include large pieces of a demountable truckle bed, was Mistress Anne Jukes. Under a decent brown cloak and safeguard overskirt she wore a plain dress in a demure shade of grey, buttoned to her neat white collar, a coif over her hair and a broad-brimmed, high-crowned hat topping everything. She looked lean, fit and suntanned, yet quite exhausted. She tottered inside and kicked off her iron-soled country pattens. When she said she had tramped on foot all around the south of London to get here, the reason for her weariness was clear. It must be over twenty miles from Cobham in Surrey to Lewisham in Kent.

'Was there no kind person with a cart to give you a lift some of the way?'

Anne massaged her feet through extremely worn stockings. 'Would *you* take up a woman with her bed on her back and a sow on leading reins?'

'Oh! Where is the pig?' snapped Juliana, too poor to be polite.

'She collapsed by your gate. Your boys are cajoling her into a shelter.'

Juliana took in this runaway without question. Apart from their existing friendship, a result of war was that one woman without money or support instantly recognised the plight of another and opened her arms. They would struggle together. Moreover, Anne had brought a pig.

They shared what they had for several weeks, in an easy, companionable relationship. Once she had settled down and felt secure in this refuge, Anne decided she must write to tell Lambert where she was. She mentioned in passing that it would soon be her birthday.

*   *   *

In the Jukeses' house in London, the brothers were bereft. They had run through a period of complete anarchy, when nothing was cleaned or tidied up, but had grown tired of that, neither being a lad any more. Living on baker's pies and muffins had given Lambert indigestion on a monumental scale. They were now just about managing with a new hired cook and maid, though both women despised them, stole from the store cupboard, and let dishes and beakers slip through their clumsy fingers to shatter on the floor. The Jukes were subjected to a cuisine of boiled mutton and veal, with the scum never skimmed off even though Parthenope's graded set of brass skimmers hung right by the fire. Every day's grey and greasy dinner made the pair more despondent, especially since they were both aware how much their meticulous mother would have grieved over their sufferings.

This was not Lambert's only misery, however. He and Anne had married for true affection; they had been married for fifteen years, which was a long time in an age when death lurked at every wainscot corner. Though Lambert nostalgically remembered himself as a practised ladies' man, running through the sprightly Cheapside wenches with dash and just a hint of dishonour, Gideon suspected Anne was the only woman he had known – or ever wanted. She was good-looking, even-tempered, able to manage Lambert so he never minded being bossed; Lambert had genuinely admired her spirit when she began to take part in extreme religion and politics. His gratitude for the way she had run the grocery business for him was heartfelt. If he had known matters would come to this, he would have worked with her. He would have allowed her anything she wanted. He was accustomed to her being always there, and felt lost without her daily presence. If this was not love, it was as close to love as anything could be.

He would not say so. Lambert never denied his feelings, but he rarely mentioned them. Fortunately, his brother knew. Gideon was truly moved by Lambert's misery.

Their army experiences had left them with a bond, a greater tenderness for each other in time of trouble. When Anne wrote from her new home in Lewisham, Lambert let Gideon read the letter. It was couched in neutral language and could pass merely for what it said: information of her whereabouts. Nonetheless, Gideon suggested that although she had issued no specific invitation, Lambert should visit on her birthday – perhaps around luncheon time? – and try to persuade Anne to return to him. Lambert's enthusiasm was touching – but he wanted his brother to go with him in support.

Gideon cursed and said no. Then the ground was cut from under him. He received a deputation from a florid apparition: Elizabeth Bevan, his great-uncle's widow. Elizabeth believed God put men on earth for her personal assistance, and she had an unexpected request: she begged Gideon to visit the Keevils at Eltham – 'For I am certain they have another daughter, just the age to be brought to London to look after my piteous orphaned brood, even as poor dear Lacy cared for them, until you whisked her away from us.'

Gideon gazed out of the window, unsympathetically. He would never forget how Lacy had been placed in front of him like a piece of moist seed cake on a silver platter. He said coldly, 'That is not quite how I remember it, madam.'

He meant Elizabeth to see that he suspected her and Bevan of duplicity. Seated unflustered at the Jukeses' dining table, she rested her formidable low-slung bust upon the board. Age had bloated her. Though she was not breeding, since it was now two years after Bevan Bevan drowned in the Thames, she still exuded helplessness. She sighed with valiant self-pity. 'To say truth, he was never the same, after he was squashed into the horse-trough at your wedding, Gideon.'

'*I* was never the same after my wedding,' retorted Gideon frankly.

Elizabeth ignored that. She glossed over her desperate need for a new, cheap girl to bully in her tumultuous nursery; instead she claimed she was perturbed about the Keevil family's fortunes. 'We have heard nothing of them recently, and times being so hard, especially for country folk, I fear the worst . . . *I* cannot go, but it would surely be no burden for you to ride out to Eltham and see how they manage? Robert Allibone will lend you his horse.'

Gideon was impressed by how far she had thought this through. Still, Elizabeth and Bevan had always been great imposers.

He stood up, arms folded, and stared down at his bothersome great-uncle's untrustworthy wife.

'Lord, you are a long lad! I swear you were begot by a beanpole; you will have cost your dear mother some pain in bearing you . . .'

'I want to know the truth,' Gideon said.

'Why, whatever can you mean?'

'I mean this, madam. I say it without vindictiveness towards my late wife, for I believe she was abused just as much as me. I owned the child, and I would have set myself to be a good father all her days . . .'

'Yet Lacy said you never set the baby once upon your knee!' interposed Elizabeth waspishly.

'The more blame is mine!' Gideon believed himself older and more tolerant now. Perhaps he was. 'Is it any wonder though? I believed Lacy Keevil was fumbled by someone and got with child dishonestly, before I was ever introduced to her. I was duped. You know it – and you should now tell me how it happened.'

Elizabeth Bevan stood up too. Gathering herself together, which took some moments, she looked Gideon over just as disdainfully as he was surveying her. 'That is a terrible thing for anyone to think or say. May God forgive you for it, Gideon Jukes!'

She swept out. Gideon experienced one short moment of doubt – then apocalyptic certainty.

Which was why, when his brother was yearning to travel to Lewisham to plead with Anne, Gideon organised a cart to take them, then brought Robert's peculiar horse as well. Though he did not admit it to himself, and he certainly would not tell Elizabeth Bevan, he would be free, if the mood took him, to leave Lambert with Anne while he went off on his own to find Lacy's family in nearby Eltham.

'Write and warn Anne you are coming. Then you should take a gift for her birthday, Lambert.'

Lambert looked horrified. 'That has never been a tradition between Anne and me!'

'You great mutton-pasty! We live in a new world, brother,' argued Gideon, with great patience (he thought). 'Consider that we may therefore have a new situation between your wife and you.'

Lewisham was about to present Gideon Jukes with a much newer situation than he foresaw.

They turned up, trying not to look too stiff in their best suits. They were close-barbered, with well-brushed hats, cunningly arriving an hour before mealtime. Gideon sent his brother indoors alone, bearing the birthday present. He waited with the cart long enough to be sure Lambert was not to be sent packing. Then, since there was a paddock, he set about unharnessing the horses.

Two small boys walked out and stared through the hedge at him. They were lean-limbed, pleasant-featured, intelligent children. Their dark-haired locks curled on their collars – longer hair than Gideon approved of, though he was in a scratchy mood since he knew that the woman Anne lived with was a Royalist. These tidy little mother's boys had been dressed in two suits of the same ochre-coloured material, with brown braid trimming. The elder, about seven years old, looked a lad of spirit, the younger more withdrawn. They watched, as the ancient grey mare from Benjamin Lucock's cart rolled on her back on the grass, full of joy, then struggled herself upright to gallop around crazily. Rumour stood by the hedge looking sorry for himself. 'So much a city horse, he will not play,' commented Gideon to the older boy, who remained there watching, while Gideon followed the younger one indoors.

Nobody else was about. Gideon stood at a loss in the kitchen. He noticed hopefully a basket where Anne Jukes's famous manchet rolls were peeking from a napkin; he identified the delicious gammony scent of a fidget pie, still cooking. The boy watched him.

Gideon placed his hat beside Lambert's on a buffet and sat on a chair. There were three chairs, in wooden country style, all pushed back against the wall to leave more working space around a rectangular oak table. On it were signs of preparation for a celebration meal. Like a bored soldier awaiting action, Gideon put himself into a state of neutral suspense.

The small boy fetched himself a crockery jar, then squirmed up onto one of the other chairs, with his thin legs sticking out in front of him; he wrenched off a tight lid as if he had done it many times, dug in his fist and began eating biscuits.

In the tradition of boys, he could speak with his mouth full. 'Are you my father?'

'I believe not,' replied Gideon, nonplussed.

The child bore him no ill-will, but jumped down, came near and proffered the biscuit crock. 'You may have *one*!' he instructed.

'*Valentine!*' A woman came through an internal door. 'He has been taught good manners and he knows how to share.'

'But there are limits,' answered Gideon gravely, eating his single Shrewsbury cake with appropriate concentration and winking at Valentine.

He looked at the mother. Shock jarred on both sides, as they recognised each other. Immediately the woman looked away and went to the table, where she continued working.

What was she – twenty-five? Neat figure; uncovered dark hair in a flat bun on her crown; back of a long neck showing; small earrings hung from pretty ears; an air of wariness and caution.

She had carried in a large platter. Setting it before her, she placed an upturned pudding basin in the centre, then covered all the remaining plate with finely shredded lettuce that she had cut up and washed and swung dry in a clean cloth. She worked unhurriedly, with enjoyment and care.

The boy, Valentine, put back the biscuits on the shelf and stood beside the table to watch. By lolling against it and leaning his cheek on the board, he was able to swivel and stare at Gideon. Gideon stayed still and kept quiet. His light skin had flushed slightly red. At least the boy's presence acted as a distracting focus, making it unnecessary for the adults to converse.

Gideon thought hard. He decided to forget the scene on Whitehall Stairs, unless Richard Brandon was mentioned.

Juliana, for her part, would certainly not admit the conversation she had overheard with the executioner in the boat. She had immediately remembered this tall, fair-haired, clean-shaven man, though he looked different out of uniform – quite different, in fact, sitting demurely with his knees together and his hands clasped. The clothes he was wearing fitted better than the red New Model Army coat. It was not much of an improvement. He still looked, Juliana sneered to herself, like a glum piece of piety. She would not trust him with a kitchenmaid. Luckily she did not have one.

'What is this dish called?' demanded Valentine, nagging for her attention. He knew perfectly well.

'A salmagundi.'

'What is that?'

'A pretty mosaic of meat, fish and salad.'

Slices of cooked chicken had been laid around the outer perimeter of the platter, alternating neatly with a trimmed green bean between each. More beans made a second circle, then Juliana placed a third ring, this time pieces of boned anchovy mixed with nuts and silver onions. She painted salad oil on the pudding basin, a device of her own to help create a centrepiece by sticking on finely trimmed celery, transparent cut radishes, leaves of sorrel, berries and spinach. In a clean bowl she prepared chopped egg yolks, the diced leg-meat of the roasted chickens, capers, almonds and parsley, bonded with a salad dressing which she mixed up fresh. The whole grand display was decorated with nasturtium flowers and, on the top of the central bowl, a turnip cut into the shape of a flower, which Gideon Jukes knew of old must be his sister-in-law's handiwork.

Valentine lost interest and scampered outside. Juliana followed him to the door and called, 'Val – tell Thomas not to spy on people!' When she turned back to the kitchen, there was no choice but to speak.

'Anne Jukes and her husband are walking in the orchard, while they try to come to terms,' stated Juliana.

'I shall not disturb them.' Gideon reflected that this was the closest he had ever come to one of the enemy, except when he was killing them. It did kindle a frisson of excitement. The young woman had used an extremely sharp knife to slice the radishes. She had chopped those egg yolks, Gideon thought, as if she was imagining they were Roundheads' livers . . . Possibly he fantasised.

'So you are . . . ?' she asked pointedly. A woman had the right to know who was sitting in her kitchen, picking Shrewsbury cake off his doublet.

'Gideon Jukes.' He ate the crumbs. Orlando Lovell would have brushed them away. That was when Juliana spotted the missing ends to several of his fingertips.

He must be thirty; fair-skinned; boyish features. Although he and Lambert were of different builds, and must have many years between them, Juliana could now see a likeness. She noticed that Gideon Jukes did not use the title of Captain which she knew he had. When he said his name, with an effort she managed not to exclaim *Ah!* to let him know she had heard of him. Men should not be encouraged to think themselves famous, Grand-mère once said.

He was not what she had expected. Well, that was interesting.

For his part, Gideon identified from her manner and the shape of her face that this was definitely the boys' mother, though the children shared distinct looks from another source. He knew from Lambert that her absent husband, the Delinquent, was a Colonel Orlando Lovell. He knew something else too, which the woman might not herself have heard:

Robert – who had met Mistress Lovell when she brought Lambert home ill – had noticed in the Westminster reports that Colonel Lovell had levied war against Parliament last year, for which he had been labelled dangerous and voted unfit for pardon. Presumably the man was abroad. Presumably he would have to stay there.

Gideon Jukes felt curious. Mistress Juliana Lovell was not widowed, yet seemed condemned to a lonely life. Judging by her bare house, she lived close to poverty. How did she survive? Why did she not join her absent husband? She seemed too self-assured to be afraid of exile; besides, Anne Jukes had said Mistress Lovell was half-French.

Clearing his throat, he embarked on polite conversation, relating what Lambert had brought for Anne. 'It took us – two plain men, though with honest hearts – much ingenuity to find a suitable gift for a woman who believes that God made the world a treasury for the common man and woman, and that all wealth should be redistributed equally.'

'Since Mistress Jukes does not care for outward show, there was no point in a rushed trip to the nearest jewellers,' Juliana agreed. For some reason she thought of the great pearl necklace Lovell once brought her. It lay in its velvet-lined box, at the bottom of her linen chest. She could have worn it today, in honour of Anne.

She was wearing, however, beneath a long apron, the gown that had been her wedding dress. Its once-bright silk had faded until only the deepest gathers of the skirt still showed their original colour. It had a significantly low neckline, but she wore a decent linen gorget to cover her bosom. It seemed to her that Lambert Jukes's pious brother was concentrating too hard on the glimpses of flesh where the circular collar's vandyked lace edge did not altogether meet the top of her silk bodice . . .

Gideon would say his interest was purely mathematical. Being particularly observant, a fact he was proud of, he had also noted that when Mistress Juliana Lovell bent forwards – for instance, to place the glowing nasturtium flowers on her decorative solomongundi (as his mother had called them) – a narrow triangle of pale bare skin revealed itself intriguingly between the two fronts of the gorget, which was pinned at the neck with a pearl brooch and a bunch of blue ribbons. The ends of the ribbons spoiled the view sometimes – though that added to the challenge.

'Goldsmiths were barred to us,' he replied in a glum tone.

'*I* would have bought her a new Dutch hoe!' Juliana declared. The tall man eyed her in careful silence. This was hard work. 'So what did the pair of you settle on?' she asked, enticing the story from him as if he were one of her sons.

'Velvet house slippers.'

'With a fur trimming?'

'We did not think of that.' Gideon looked wistful about the lost opportunity. Still wearing that earnest expression, he appealed to Juliana for approval: 'The reasoning was thus: a frivolity – yet useful. Sufficiently expensive to indicate my brother's true repentance of his deficiencies as a husband – which are so many – yet soft on the feet after a hard day labouring in cold fields . . . In case our dear Anne was still partaking of the agricultural life.'

'Gracious heavens,' exploded Juliana. 'I hope you ninnies bought the right size!'

He shot her a look of reproof. 'This was not overlooked! An old shoe was found at the back of a cupboard, madam, and taken to be measured.'

You thought of that, thought Juliana, for some reason quite certain of it.

Then Gideon Jukes abruptly opened his true blue eyes wider and flashed a conspiratorial gleam. He knew Juliana realised how hard he had worked to bring Lambert here in a conciliatory frame of mind. Too late, she understood just how much mischief and amusement was being concealed. The man had been acting all along.

'And what,' asked Juliana, a little more coolly than she had intended, 'if Mistress Anne Jukes declines to be won over? If a bought gift will not do?'

'Horrors!' Lambert's brother propelled himself more upright. 'But in the failing of the first clause, the second clause at once comes into effect.'

'Which is?' Juliana fought off a smile.

'This, madam: my brother will tell his wife, Anne, of his unfailing devotion to her. His constancy and care of her. He will applaud her fine temperament and talents. Her personable features. Her devotion to God and to her meagre husband. Her gentleness, tolerance, honesty, good faith and bravery. Her wit, her skills, her conversation, her kindness.

He may – though of course I must blush to say this to a stranger – have some praising words for their pleasures in bed.' He did not blush, though Juliana felt somewhat heated. 'Above all,' Gideon went on, ticking off points on his damaged fingers, 'he will not forget to dwell avidly upon the splendour of her manchet rolls and how wondrously she can cut a turnip into the form of a delicate flower.'

'You are a wag, Captain Jukes. Do you also juggle with feather mops?'

'I am a true man. He will unburden his heart.'

It will work, thought Juliana. She felt wooed herself. That was dangerous.

Captain Jukes lowered his eyes. His voice was stripped of all comedy. 'Is it your opinion my poor brother will persuade his wife to return?'

'Will he live in the home, share her labours in their business, avoid the company of old soldiers, cease drinking in low taverns – and be grateful that he *has* a wife?'

'I can suggest this,' offered Gideon.

'*Anne* will suggest it!' returned Juliana fiercely. 'Well, sir; she must have told him her feelings by now, and they have not come in from the orchard, bitterly arguing. She has not called me out to help her bury his cadaver . . . Since you ask, I believe she will go back. She grew tired of the community at Cobham. The hard struggles and frequent danger. Tired of the cold fields, but also tired, she says, of people who were neither hers by blood nor chosen by her, tired of living in a noisy, crowded house, tired of never having anything to call her own. Besides –' Juliana took the baked pie out of the oven and allowed herself a moment to admire its golden, turned-back pastry. She kept the man in suspense deliberately. 'Besides, his faults are neither here nor there for Anne: she misses him.'

She gazed across the fidget pie at Gideon Jukes. He looked straight back – though had a visible temptation to scrutinise the gorgeous pie. He had a way of looking at Juliana as if they had been best friends for thirty years. There was approval in it, and certainty that they agreed with one another on all that was important. It gave Juliana a disconcerting tightness in her chest.

He was just an overgrown City of London apprentice, all cheeky eyes and an unwarranted opinion of his own worth. If she left him alone in the kitchen, he would cut the pie open and steal a slice, then pocket another and walk off whistling . . .

He was smiling very slightly. He knew everything she thought.

When Anne and Lambert walked in, they both saw it: Gideon was enjoying himself.

Chapter Sixty-Three

Lewisham: 1650

Anne and Lambert were reconciled. They drove off back to London together in Ben Lucock's cart, after a parting between Anne and Juliana which was tearful on both sides.

Before that, however, they had all enjoyed a luncheon where the mood was as happy as the food was resplendent. Lambert overcame self-consciousness by joshing Gideon; Juliana watched how Gideon accepted it. Lambert now needed to have a strong place in the family. Gideon relaxed from being his brother's stern organiser and good-humouredly allowed himself to be subordinate.

He watched her too. Gideon's instincts were entirely masculine.

He sensed it was a long time since she had entertained company. The boys, Tom seated on a barrel and Val on his mother's lap, due to the lack of chairs, were clearly unused to gatherings. Gideon thought that although Mistress Juliana Lovell enjoyed this little party, she was feeling a tug of melancholy. No doubt she was missing absent friends; that would be her husband in particular.

Lambert went out to the cart and returned with a wine bottle; even his brother had not known it was hidden there. French wines were illegal. But a master grocer could always obtain them, of course.

Juliana went into her parlour for decorated beakers she had brought away from Colchester; she did not own wineglasses. Gideon followed to help carry them. He saw her work table and her needlework every-where. He noticed too, a long shelf full of her father's books. 'May I look at what you have?' She stood watching as he examined them eagerly; she noticed that he always checked in the frontispiece for the printer's name, though he was interested in the subjects – and knowledgeable. 'A First Folio Shakespeare!'

'When I am next in want of money, it will have to be sold,' Juliana admitted quietly. She was on her knees, counting out the beakers from the back of a cupboard. Anne Jukes had paid for the feast today. The folio would already have been given up, but Lewisham to London was probably five miles in a straight line; Royalists were not supposed to go so far from home and Juliana would not risk visiting the book-sellers at St Paul's Churchyard until a trip to London was absolutely necessary.

'Offer it to me first! – Do you read these books?'

'I can read!' Juliana exclaimed haughtily. 'Yes, I read them, when I have time.' To prove it, she hauled herself to her feet, took the Shakespeare in her arms, found a place and read to him. It was from *The Tempest*, a speech of the courtier Gonzalo:

> 'Had I plantation of this isle, my lord,
> And were the king on't, what would I do?
> In the Commonwealth I would by contraries
> Execute all things. For no kind of traffic
> Would I admit; no name of magistrate;
> Letters should not be known; riches, poverty,
> And use of service, none; contract, succession,
> Bourn, bound of land, tilth, vineyard, none;
> No use of metal, corn, or wine, or oil;
> No occupation; all men idle, all;
> And women too, but innocent and pure;
> No sovereignty . . .
> All things in common nature should produce
> Without sweat or endeavour; treason, felony,
> Sword, pike, knife, gun, or need of any engine,
> Would I not have; But nature should bring forth,
> Of its own kind, all foison, all abundance,
> To feed my innocent people.

Well, sir. You have fought for ideal government. What think you?'

'A Utopia!' Gideon had noticed her father's Thomas More, his Plato, his Cicero, St Augustine, Bacon and Rabelais. (He had also seen a seventy-years-old Nuremburg almanac, in German, and shared a wince with her over it; Juliana prayed he did not guess it was plunder her husband had brought her.) 'I could listen to you reading it for many hours,' said the tall man, smiling and acting like a suitor. Juliana chose to think the lechery was a pose – though she was not entirely sure. Neither was Gideon.

'Beware, sir! It is from a play.'

For two pins Gideon would have admitted to this woman that he had acted in a masque once. 'Aye, the theatre is the devil's cockpit.'

Juliana laughed. 'Yes, I am aware of that. Such an attraction, is it not?'

From the other room, Lambert was bellowing for them to hurry with the cups. As Gideon came to take the heavy book from her and replace it, Juliana felt suddenly convinced he would trap her against the cupboard and kiss her. Indeed, the only reason Gideon did not, was that he felt so startled at how much he wanted to.

'Still, you are one of the New Model Army Saints, Captain Jukes, and if you ever saw a play you would forfeit your safe position in the new Millennium,' Juliana burbled, ushering him back to the kitchen.

'Madam,' Gideon rebuked her lazily, 'you are thinking of the Fifth Monarchists. Crazily deluded fellows. These people say the King's execution heralds a thousand years of Christ's personal rule upon the earth. One of the rascals told me that greed and power will be replaced by brotherly love! This, of course, is impossible heresy . . .'

Lambert had uncorked the wine. He shared it out, even giving small amounts to the excited children, while Anne filled up their cups with cold water. It was Gideon who asked Juliana quietly, 'Do you object?'

'My grandmother was French, Captain Jukes! I should object only if my boys were given wine from Italy or Portugal.'

So they batted humour lightly between them, as if they were laying on an entertainment formally for Anne and Lambert.

'Gideon and I do know a *Ranter*,' Lambert boasted.

'Do we?' asked Gideon, in some surprise.

'Major William Rainborough,' Lambert answered, lowering his voice, 'the brother of our poor murdered colonel. He paid for the pamphlet by one Laurence Clarkson, the Ranters' creed. It is all filthiness,' he informed Juliana furtively. 'They believe God is in every man, therefore all scripture is false and even the Bible cannot be the Word of God. They say there is no sin; sin was invented by the rulers of the earth to keep the poor in order. Therefore, *anything* is permitted!'

'*Anything?*' chuckled Juliana, raising her eyebrows. 'I have a good idea what that entails – and it is more than fidget pie!'

'Anything a *man* wants!' muttered Anne. 'With second helpings on the plate . . . To facilitate their freedoms, they throw off their clothes and run about the streets surprising people.'

'Ah, they are casting away their worldly goods! You did not go so far with the Diggers, dear Anne?'

Anne remained calm. 'At Cobham I found that a stout skirt and a broad hat to defend me against the weather made tending my seedlings more comfortable. I was too tired at the end of the day to rant – or to startle anyone with discarding my shift to preach.'

'I am glad to hear it!' growled Lambert with feeling. He still suspected that unspeakable numbers of lascivious male Diggers must have lain with his wife in the communal house at Cobham.

Anne's return would not go all smoothly, Juliana surmised. It may have shown in her expression. She found herself sharing a wise look with Lambert's younger brother. Acting in tandem, they moved the conversation along to less controversial subjects.

Soon after they had eaten, Gideon excused himself and left for Eltham. No explanation was offered for his errand.

A short time later, Lambert and Anne drove off as well. Tom and Val, released from their pledge of good behaviour while there were guests, rushed to see the sow, which Anne had left them, taking a bowl of scraps to feed it. They would be happy for hours scratching its head with a rake while the sow wheezed in delight. Juliana was left in the house alone.

She went into the parlour to sew, but soon put her work down and roamed about, feeling lost. She must be missing Anne's company. She could not settle.

Two hours later, Gideon Jukes came back.

Hearing a man's voice unexpectedly, Juliana feared an intruder. When he opened the door without knocking, the point of a sword right against his chest stopped him in his tracks.

Gideon went pale, but raised his blond eyebrows in a sarcastic gesture. 'You may put down your weapon, Mistress Lovell.' Juliana stayed put. 'Is this, "*Sword, pike, knife, gun, or need of any engine, Would*

I not have"? – Kill me if you must, but pray do *not* nick a hole in my best suit.'

Juliana lowered the sword-tip to the floor, yet kept both hands tight upon the hilt. 'Be calm, sir. I know it breaches the rules of war to kill an unarmed man – or harm his coat.'

'Thank the Lord you are so professional!'

Gideon eyed her weapon: a plain tuck, as basic infantry swords were called, probably made cheaply in the Midlands. It was the old sword that Lovell had brought away from Birmingham. Gideon had noticed this rusty beast earlier, skew-whiff on a nail behind the door. She would be safer not producing a weapon against intruders, but that was up to her. In case she had been taught how to run a man through, he stayed motionless and did not irritate her with advice.

'What do you want, Captain?'

'A favour, if you will.'

Juliana gave him a brusque nod to take a seat. She repositioned the sword on its nail.

'I have brought back with me,' said Gideon, more awkward now, 'a thirteen-year-old girl called Catherine Keevil, whom I found, with very great difficulty, living in the poorhouse, bereft of all friends and relatives. She is a sad creature. Her parents, John and Harriet Keevil, were good people in Eltham but both died in the last hard winter, as have all their other children.' Gideon did wonder now whether Elizabeth Bevan had known more about Catherine's situation than she told him. 'Thomas and Valentine have led her off to see their pig while I talk to you.'

'What is she to you?' asked Juliana, fascinated.

He showed a moment's hesitation, then stated, 'My wife's young sister.'

Juliana flashed a glance to his left hand and saw no wedding ring. A man of Independent religious beliefs would not wear one, however.

'Since my wife is dead,' explained Gideon quickly, after spotting her glance, 'I feel bound to take care of the wench. I have been asked to bring her to London to look after children where my wife was in service before we married, but –'

He faltered. Juliana interpreted: 'Some unhappy situation?'

She was quick! But Gideon ignored the question. 'Will you take her,

Mistress Lovell? Teach her to be a maidservant, or whatever you find she is suited for that will help her make her way in life. Keep her honest. Give her skills.'

Juliana was astonished. 'Explain yourself. Why are you doing this?'

In staccato sentences, he answered, 'Conscience. Obligation. Something befell my wife. I cannot be certain . . .' He had asked Catherine about Lacy, but the young girl could hardly remember her older sister – or so she claimed.

'You could take her to Anne, your sister-in-law,' suggested Juliana, looking at him oddly. *Keep her honest?* She made a rapid interpretation of that.

'Anne has her own servants. Anne does not need her. You do!' said Gideon forcefully.

'You are very forward! Why me – a stranger?'

'I trust you.' Juliana remained silent at this compliment. 'I have talked with her, Mistress Lovell. She seems sweet-natured, docile and willing. You have no servants – and it is not good for you to live here, out in the country, all alone.' When there was still no answer, Gideon used unfair pressure. It surprised Juliana, who had thought him a fair man. He dropped his voice. 'What if you fell ill? Who would take care of you? What would happen to your boys?'

'I have no servants,' Juliana admitted frankly, shuddering at the fears he had played on, 'because I cannot afford wages.'

Gideon thought about that. 'Tell me what it costs and I will pay the wages.'

'A maid earns two pounds a year, less for an untrained child –'

Gideon thought she was haggling, so offered, 'Also, I will pay you for her keep.' He was already on his feet, leaving. A widower had to protect himself from the wiles of married women. 'I will bring you the money in a few days.'

'Payment is made at the end of the twelvemonth,' argued Juliana weakly.

'To the servant. You need finances now, I think.'

Gideon Jukes bent over her hand and kissed it like a gallant. A gallant, full of etiquette, would take up a lady's right hand; he chose the left. He placed his kiss particularly on her middle finger, avoiding the fourth, where Juliana Lovell did, of course, wear her gold wedding ring. He tapped it. The roughened end of one of his lost digits rasped slightly.

'You could sell that!' he grinned. 'There would be a few good white puddings and Hackney turnips there!'

Captain Jukes had promised to return very soon. He did not come. That was annoying. Juliana felt cheated.

Still, the little maid was friendly, cheery, a good worker, excellent with children.

A carrier brought letters, three of them.

The first, clearly the oldest, was from Orlando. Juliana found herself almost leaving it to last, but dutifully opened it before the rest. As she expected, it had travelled around the country for many months before it found her. Orlando said very little. For reasons of safety, he used veiled language, omitting real details of where he had been and what doing. The letter's battered condition showed it had been opened by others, perhaps more than once, and it may have lain for long periods in some Parliamentary committee file. This had been written at The Hague, a year ago. He told her not to come to Holland, for reasons he failed to supply. She already knew Orlando was not there now, but gone to sea.

He sent love to her and to his sons. That was impeccable, and nicely put.

Following instructions that he had given her at Pelham Hall, Juliana burned the letter. She had no scope for sentimentality. A Royalist wife could not put her husband at risk.

The second letter looked mysterious. A stranger, whose name was Abdiel Impey, wrote to her from the Middle Temple with the news that William Gadd had died. She was invited to visit, should she be passing, when she would be given further information. Juliana shed tears for her guardian, even though she had long feared that he must have passed away. She had liked him, and knew he tried to do his best for her. He was a link with her grandmother; she had precious few family connections now.

The third letter was in a black, squiggledy hand which she did not recognise. Yet she guessed it. She held the document between her hands, almost afraid to break the untidy blob of sealing wax. She had saved it, like the juiciest plum in the basket. She had to admit that.

Madam.

> *What can I say to you?*
>
> *I promised to come shortly, but I dally here on urgent printing business, which I must attend to, for it is my livelihood. Probably you think yourself well rid of me — or would do, save I owe you money. That will make me welcome, naturally. Not that I think you mercenary — but a debt paid is a great relief between friends, obliterating any occasion for broody thoughts to fester in the creditor.*
>
> *I promised to come to you; come I shall. Pray you, send me a word of forgiveness and say if the little maid suits.*
>
> *Yr servant, GJ*

Juliana made up her mind not to answer it.

A day later she wrote back. Only to give him news of the maid, Catherine.

By return — it was difficult to tell, with the meanderings of carriers — Gideon Jukes scrawled off at her again.

> *Oh madam, madam, madam, madam!*
>
> *Now I have had your letter, the one which begins, 'Captain Jukes, we are obliged to you for remembering us.'*
>
> *Pish, what is this 'we'? Do you include yr children, yr household in general — cook, groom, bootboy, maid (lady's), maid (kitchen), maid (parlour, the one with the fabulously turned ankles), yr fat sow in the outhouse, and the little frowsty dog, Tousle, who lies by the hearth? Or, if he can climb up there unobserved, he lies in the good chair, with the leather back and brass studs, upon one of your fine stumpwork cushions.*
>
> *I did not write to them (though I cherish your children, for your sake, and am glad that the little maid does well with you).*
>
> *Now I have you. (I can hear you squealing 'But I have no dog — and if I did, I would not call him Tousle!') Fortunate for me, since that blackguard Tousle nips legs and rolls in all the muck that he can find, yet I would be compelled — were he yours, madam — to ingratiate myself by praising him.*
>
> *You have written too little. I am afraid that if I leave your black jot upon a table, I shall mistake it for a beetle and squash it with my thumb.*

I for my part have written too much. ('And a great nonsensical ramble!' niggles My Lady). You must think it was a lie, when I claimed my work detained me. Well, here I am in the print shop, where my apprentice Miles is turning the great press, while I must supervise in case he mis-orders the pages or nips his fingers. That can be done with harsh words and the occasional smart biff, in between the natural kindliness with which he is cajoled every five minutes. This leaves me four minutes now and then for correspondence. ('Faugh! Love letters!' cries Miles in disgust — 'Receipts for our ink and paper,' reply I, with noble patience. I have been fifteen, his age, with all its faults.)

Enough, fool! I shall come to you on Thursday.

Yr servant, GJ

Post script. Written two hours later. I am sending you by a separate package Golden Eye Ointment for Valentine, since you wrote that he was troubled with red eyes. This is the best ocular salve, according to regular advertisements in the Public Corranto, *the News Letter to Trust. The advertisements are extremely expensive, so you know these claims must be true. If the packet survives robbery and the pot survives shattering and the unction survives heat, cold, jolts upward, circular motions, and downward thrusts of the carrier's satchel, then if Val does not screw up his eyes and go blue when you advance on him bearing ointment upon your maternal finger, the medicament may do him some good.*

Juliana would burn this mad letter too. Well, she would once she had read it again and smiled over its foolishness a few more times. A wife should never keep letters that might annoy her husband.

That Thursday, Gideon Jukes came to her, true to his word.

The boys had been taken by Catherine Keevil over to the farm, where it was said that a foal had just been born. Juliana was alone in her parlour. She heard Gideon arrive, but did not run out eagerly. He came politely into the parlour, guessing where to find her.

'I have put your money on the table.'

Let us hope no foul-minded churchwarden hears that! 'Thank you.'

'No, I must thank you.' He seemed subdued. If it were Tom or Val, Juliana would be suspicious he was sickening. His face looked drawn.

He seemed like a man who had been thinking too much; Juliana recognised it, for so had she. 'This is a good solution, I am glad I thought of it. I am under a very great obligation . . .'

When he tailed off, Juliana provided a succinct report on how she found the girl, Catherine. 'She is bright, helpful, easy to instruct, without needing harsh words or biffs –' She had not meant to allude to his silly letter. She cast down her eyes. 'She sleeps on Mistress Anne's truckle bed in the garret; she eats and prays with us. I am happy to have her in my household; she is glad to have been given a home. Be easy in your mind, Captain. I shall treat her kindly.'

Gideon had remained standing. Now his chin came up. He looked at Juliana very directly, then asked without preamble, 'Will you be kind to *me*?'

She made no false pretence of misunderstanding. 'You know that cannot be.'

'When did you last see your husband?' Unbeknown to Gideon, the wording of that question took Juliana straight back to her unpleasant examination at Haberdashers Hall. It changed her willingness to answer. Automatically she was reduced to pinching her lips like a stubborn prisoner. 'Will he not come to you?' demanded Gideon, bitterly. 'Will he not summon you to him?'

Juliana stayed silent, caught in her need to protect Lovell and his whereabouts. This was the result of war: she could never risk anyone on the opposite side knowing too much and making further accusations against him.

'Nothing to say?'

It was hard enough to bear feeling forgotten and abandoned by Orlando; now she had an offer of friendship from a man to whom she was attracted, but she could not accept. Juliana's position was impossible. 'I am a married woman. Do not chastise me for my constancy.'

'Oh I can never do that.' Gideon flayed himself. 'Not when, if it were ever my place to deserve it, I should hope for the same constancy towards me.'

Juliana smiled sadly. 'I think that would not be hard to give.' Gideon huffed. She rose from her chair. They were extremely still now. 'You must not write to me.'

'No.' Gideon knew what he had been trying to do in his letters.

He feared what he had indeed done. He did not repent, though he would not repeat it.

'You must leave now, Captain Jukes.' Gideon looked rebellious. Juliana nearly panicked. 'You must! Merely to be here could cause comment. We live in a world of renewed morality. Indeed, I hear there is a new Act against Adultery, Incest and Fornication.'

'I am not planning incest!' snarled Gideon.

'Nor I adultery – it is a felony; the penalty is death!'

'For both parties.'

'I see you read it too.'

'I keep up with the news.'

'Ah, you are a good citizen.'

'You do not care for this putrid Act of Parliament, madam? Plenty of people ignore it.'

'And in doing so, they cause misery – to themselves and those around them. I have to take care for my children as well as myself – and since you will not, Captain Jukes, it seems I must care for you too.'

He seemed to accept this. With painful formality, they moved from the parlour and across the kitchen to the door. Juliana stepped outside first, looking for space in case an attempt was made to touch her. But Gideon left a clear yard of air between them.

'Is this what you want, Juliana?'

Despite the intimacy of their previous conversation, she felt oddly shocked. 'You may not call me Juliana!'

'*Oh I think I may!*' replied Gideon, his voice low with open recognition of their mutual yearning.

He turned from her. His horse was waiting. He threw himself into the saddle in one strong movement – a dragoon mount in time of crisis – kicked his heels and rode. He refused to look back.

Juliana stepped quickly into the house, closing the door fast, lest she accept temptation.

Gideon reached the road, then halted.

Rumour, Robert's eccentric horse, was always glad to stop and stand still. Gideon turned the beast, and sat for long minutes, staring at the house. Eventually, he could not help himself and he went back.

There was no answer when he knocked. He knocked and waited, knocked and waited.

At last, he accepted that his obsession with Colonel Lovell's wife had been rebuffed. He still believed she was stricken with as much attraction to him as he felt for her. He could only admire her resolution. He rode away. He knew his pain was permanent. He was a lost man.

He did *not* know that nobody had heard him knocking. No one was there. The house stood quite empty. In panic at her emotions, Juliana had slipped out by a back door which she rarely used, a door hidden behind a curtain in the parlour. Half blind with tears, she went striding along a field path to the farm where she would find her children.

Had she been at home and heard Gideon return, her strength of will would have certainly dissolved.

Chapter Sixty-Four

Ireland and Scotland: 1650

They would not see each other. That must help. They would recover. Each of them tried to believe that.

If they had been asked to analyse what had just happened to them, *she* would have blamed lust, and would not have supposed it could possibly be love, or if so, not lasting love, nor true. She lacked faith, he would have said. *He* would already have called it love – though at the same time honestly acknowledging his lust. In this, they would both have been right, and both wrong.

How it would grow or die, if they remained apart, time and circumstance must show them. For Gideon Jukes, now smitten and devastated, holding off from Juliana Lovell was so hard and his misery so great, that only one course seemed open: he must go back to the army. What was more, he must go quickly – and go far.

He had a choice of Ireland or Scotland.

This was the situation.

Immediately after the King's execution, Parliament urgently needed to impose order on Ireland and Scotland or see the union of Three Kingdoms disintegrate. (Wales had been sufficiently subdued by Cromwell to be no problem at this time.) The Scots' army had been wiped out at the battle of Preston, but the Prince of Wales was proclaimed in Edinburgh as King Charles II immediately after his father's death. To be accepted, however, he had to take the Covenant. While scruples delayed him, the Scots were recruiting a new army.

Meanwhile, Ireland deteriorated into confusion. The Royalist Marquis of Ormond had tried to unite all parties for the King. Catholics had been promised freedom of religion. Ulster Presbyterians loathed the new English republic with its tendency to dangerous free thought.

The native Irish hated the English settlers. Ormond now controlled most of the country and he invited Charles II to come to Ireland. To enable this, Prince Rupert was pirating from a base at Kinsale, attacking Commonwealth ships and keeping the seas open.

In England, Cromwell and Fairfax spent part of the summer hunting down various groups of Leveller-inspired mutineers but eventually Cromwell was free for Ireland. While he was there, Charles II landed in Scotland. It gave Cromwell's Irish mission greater urgency. Time was short. Troop numbers were inadequate. He had made careful preparations to have food and fodder shipped over, but his forces were cut off in hostile country. Mobility was hampered. General-at-Sea Robert Blake managed to pen up Prince Rupert's ships at Kinsale, but any problem with weather or Rupert breaking out would be fatal. Cromwell therefore undertook the reconquest of Ireland with speed and un-paralleled ferocity.

To Gideon Jukes in London, the full misery of what happened escaped him. Cromwell called the Irish barbarians, a denunciation Gideon did not share. But it was too far away. He read the news, and he had a tender conscience for the fate of other human beings, yet he was human himself. What was done in his name, beyond his reach, could be pushed to the back of his consciousness. However, he read enough to be deeply thankful that he had missed his chance to go on the Irish expedition.

Cities were taken. Garrisons were stormed amid bitter fighting and horrific scenes. At Drogheda and Wexford, the defending soldiers were all slaughtered, even after surrendering on the promise of their lives. The killing of prisoners continued long after any battle bloodlust ceased. Captured Catholic priests and friars were killed. The governor of Drogheda – the unpopular Royalist Sir Arthur Aston, one-time governor of Oxford – was beaten to death with his own wooden leg. Soldiers who took refuge in a church steeple were burned alive there. Civilians died too, which contravened the rules of war. Subsequently at Wexford the soldiers repeated this, even though Cromwell had given no orders for it. Two hundred refugees were drowned when their escape boat sank. The terrible scenes matched the barbarity of the Thirty Years War on the Continent – now, ironically, ended by the Treaty of Westphalia – the kind of brutality of which Parliamentary supporters had so bitterly complained when it was imposed upon English towns by Prince Rupert. Cromwell, however, saw his men as instruments of God.

The tussle for Ireland continued over the New Year. Sickness began to afflict Cromwell's troops. Every time an Irish army was destroyed, another soon sprang up in its place. A mistake at Clonmel cost the English nearly two thousand men – a rare disaster. But at the end of May the situation was sufficiently stable for Cromwell himself to sail back to England, leaving Henry Ireton to finish the job. Plague was sweeping the country and would claim Ireton. However, two years later, resistance finally petered out, allowing what became known as the Cromwellian Settlement.

Half a million people had already died of famine, fighting or disease and in the settlement hundreds of thousands would be dispossessed. Vast tracts of land were parcelled up for New Model Army soldiers, an easy solution to covering their pay arrears. Two-thirds of the country – two and a quarter million acres – were either given to the troops or awarded to those who had lost their own land in the old uprising of 1641. Most of the soldiers sold their land to speculators. The inhabitants of Leinster and Munster were expelled, 'to Hell or Connaught' – the far west of Ireland where the land was poor and living bleak. A third of them died of exposure. Many, especially children, were sent as slaves to the plantations of the West Indies. The legacy of loathing for Cromwell would last for centuries.

There was military necessity, caused by Irish geography and by the emergency in Scotland. But there were no grand concepts at stake; it was a simple struggle for power and vengeance, fuelled by religious bigotry. Rights of individual liberty, freedom of thought and conscience, rights which had been argued and fought for in England, received no recognition. Viewed as dispassionately as possible, the treatment of Ireland was the ultimate signal of how coarsened soldiers could become after too much war, especially when they went away from their own country and the oversight of their own people, and were instead among those they had been taught and encouraged to view as less than human. If civil war was terrible, war overseas – with its extra terrors and deprivations – could be even crueller. Moral responsibility was readily abandoned.

The Levellers had been right in wanting not to cross frontiers and, insofar as he considered Ireland, Gideon positioned himself with their view. But his personal motives were still pressing. Cromwell returned to England to address the Scottish problem. He should have been working alongside Fairfax, but Fairfax was reluctant to fight the Scots, with whom he had co-operated on so many important campaigns, and his conscience remained uneasy about the King's execution. Citing ill health, he resigned. Cromwell and other leaders pleaded with him, but he was adamant. Fairfax retired. Parliament gave the Lord Generalship to Oliver Cromwell so he would be going to Scotland as commander-in-chief.

Even though it meant travelling a great distance and crossing into another country, Gideon Jukes decided this fight was necessary. He felt bitterly depressed by the return of King Charles II. Even after so much hard effort, little had been achieved, the Commonwealth was under direct threat and everything was, once again, still to accomplish.

More than that, eight years after Gideon began fighting Royalists, his enemy had assumed a specific identity. His gloom was increased by the thought that Colonel Orlando Lovell, 'the Delinquent Lovell', that unknown, absent, yet unavoidable husband of the desirable Juliana, could be among the cavaliers who accompanied the new King Charles. With Charles, Lovell was coming closer. Well, that was one reason for Gideon Jukes to go to Scotland. Every time he aimed his musket, he stood a chance of picking off his man.

The King had hoped that the charismatic Marquis of Montrose would rally non-Presbyterian support in Scotland, so he could avoid a distasteful alliance with the Covenanters. But Montrose was speedily captured then hanged, drawn and quartered in Edinburgh just before Charles arrived. Held a virtual prisoner by the Covenanters, the young monarch was subjected to religious indoctrination, with sermons several times a day. He was systematically isolated from friends and supporters. Expediency, his personal trademark, convinced him that if he was to reclaim the English throne, he would have to take the Presbyterian Covenant.

The English Council of State decided to pre-empt an invasion by attacking Scotland. Cromwell took sixteen thousand troops, most of them experienced New Model Army men, though recruited anew for this task. Gideon Jukes was one of the volunteers.

Gideon had considered asking for a place again with Colonel Okey. He had heard on the veterans' grapevine that Okey had tried bitterly to rid his regiment of Captain Francis Freeman, a curious mystic. The dragoons had a reputation as religious fanatics, but their colonel wanted fanaticism that chimed with his own. He eventually court-martialled Freeman, who had been overheard playing music with his landlord, carolling what Freeman claimed were innocent traditional ditties, but Okey said were lewd songs. Neither would back down. To solve the impasse, Cromwell had instructed the captain to resign.

Gideon had been known to hum while he polished his boots, but did not flaunt it. He thought he was safe with Okey. But when he called at the Hackney house, he was informed that Okey had left for the north with Freeman's captaincy already filled. Undeterred – well, still desperate to escape from London – Gideon devised a new plan. At Derby House, where the committee in charge of military affairs sat, he asked to see Samuel Bedford. Gideon had known Bedford slightly as Sir Samuel Luke's trusted deputy at Newport Pagnell, subsequently poached to work in intelligence for the New Model Army.

On first approach, Gideon was merely asked to leave his personal details. Returning next day, he was informed that gentlemen of the committee would examine him.

An officer who never gave his name took charge, while a clerk took notes, and another man sat looking sombre: wearing a long black coat – late middle age, blue chin, beady eyes that gave the impression he knew more than he ought. Gideon repeated everything he had said the previous day. He did so quietly and patiently, for he knew how army bureaucracy worked. Eventually, the interviewer and the man in the black coat walked off together to the far end of the large room. They held a muttered discussion, sometimes glancing back at Gideon.

Black coat must have lost. He leaned back on his heels for a moment, surveying Gideon ruefully, then left in mild dudgeon. The interviewer recrossed the room. 'Well, Captain Jukes. Do you remember that gentleman? He met you once, and maintains if you are the man he thought, you will recall it.'

Turnham Green. Half a lifetime back. 'His name,' Gideon acknowledged, '– or the name he used then – is Mr Blakeby.'

The interviewer looked at him oddly, as if this long-stored memory marked out Gideon as a queer obsessive. Gideon sat quiet, managing to do so without looking smug. 'He tried to recruit you?'

'I turned him down, sir.'

'Well, he has lost you again. You volunteered yourself to the

scoutmaster. The army takes precedence over Blakeby's business —
though Sir Thomas Scott will never thank me for it.' At that time,
Gideon had no idea who Sir Thomas Scott might be, though when he
returned home later, Robert Allibone said the man had been placed in
charge of intelligence — political spying. 'You will go to Scotland.
Unregimented — you'll wear a tawny coat and answer to Scoutmaster-
General William Rowe, surveying the terrain.' Gideon did briefly wonder
how intelligencers were supposed to scout in a completely foreign
country where the locals were trying to kill them. Still, a Londoner
always had confidence.

The journey was three hundred miles. Gideon refused the chance to go
by sea, claiming he wanted to get used to his horse, a strong, speedy
pony which he had been promised could turn on a sixpence. When
pointed north, it seemed enthusiastic and cantered along day after day,
giving no trouble. This allowed him plenty of time for thought — and
for trying to avoid thought, where it was too painful.

The man who rode to Scotland at the end of July 1650 was now in
his full prime. He was almost thirty, as mature in character as he would
ever be, and by the end of that long trip physically hard again. He had
not lost his ideals, but he was beginning to see that he had spent much
of his life in a struggle that could have no straightforward resolution.

The dearest revolutionary principles of Gideon's life were already
lost. The Levellers had been destroyed. There had been Lockyer, Burford,
Wellingborough. John Wildman had given up and turned himself into
a land speculator, buying up the estates of disgraced and impecunious
Royalists. John Lilburne, 'Freeborn John', Cromwell's most implacable
antagonist, had been tried for treason to the Commonwealth; found not
guilty, he was nonetheless exiled to Bruges, whence he fulminated darkly.
Lilburne's Leveller associates were freed from prison; it was conditional
on their taking the oath of engagement to the new regime. Richard
Overton had done so with his usual grim wit, saying that he would be
as faithful to his oath as the Council of State had been to the Covenant
(that was, not at all). Sexby, Gideon's old Leveller colleague, had gone
ahead of him to Scotland. Sexby's Scottish service would go wrong and
he would react to the loss of their cause very differently from Gideon.

To the new, caustic, steely Gideon the world had been turned upside
down, but it had been turned into muddle and chaos. Conflict seemed

never-ending. His depression deepened on the long, solitary journey north; it held poignant memories, as he passed close to Holdenby, then Doncaster and Pontefract. He remembered past events, both stirring and disastrous, then brooded on the unexpected turn in his personal life, where he had charged in full of his usual cheerfulness and determination, but had been so knocked back. It made him think more forcefully about his own existence, his wishes and intentions.

The timing was cruel. He had spent years believing he felt no desire for women, blaming Lacy. Now he knew that he did want a woman, not just physically – although his great ache for Juliana Lovell was painfully physical – but emotionally and intellectually too. Yet it must not be any woman, only *that* woman. The speed of his falling for her shocked him; it also indicated the sureness of his devotion. He was even calm about knowing they must not meet again –

No; he was not calm. He would not be a hypocrite.

The journey took over. He had his work cut out now. Once he passed Doncaster, where he did not stop, and Pontefract, he was in unknown territory. His route took him via York, Durham, Newcastle and Berwick, where Cromwell had concentrated his forces before he crossed the border. After that, Gideon was in bandit country. He had to keep his wits about him. Even with regular rest-breaks he was tired, but the routine precautions of his craft came back and protected him. He began meeting soldiers in New Model uniform, who gave him directions, along with rations and companionship. Soon he found the main force, was brought to the scoutmaster general and introduced himself.

Naturally there were other scouts already here. Captain Jukes had to woo their respect, learn to work with them. He had done it before; he would do it now. He was kicking his heels for the first few days, before he wound his way in, making his place among them in his quiet way, as he always did. He found his role. He got to know the territory and even made a few contacts in the local population. He was first seen as gormless and harmless, then useful, then indispensable.

The Scots had been informed that the English Parliament did not intend any interference with their chosen way of government – provided they exercised respect for the Commonwealth. Cromwell, who shared much of their religious fervour, wrote to the Scottish clergy, begging them to reconsider whether Charles Stuart was a fit king for a godly people and famously pleading: *'I beseech you, in the bowels of Christ, think it possible you may be mistaken.'* To no avail.

The Covenanters urged their new King to issue a public statement attacking his mother's Catholicism and his father's bad counsellors. Charles refused to do that but the clergy dourly accepted his signed oath of allegiance to their Covenant. They remained uneasy with their new figurehead. Alarmed by his charisma and his suspected unreliability, they made Charles withdraw and wait across the Firth of Forth in Dunfermline while they faced Cromwell.

The Scottish forces were commanded by the tough David Leslie – no stranger to invading England under the Covenant banner. He was hampered by a Committee of the Kirk. They dogged his every move. Their first action was to purge his army of eighty good officers and more than three thousand experienced soldiers they suspected of loose morals or swearing in public. These valuable troops were replaced with raw recruits – *'nothing but useless clerks and ministers' sons, who have never seen a sword, much less used one'*. The committee then accompanied Leslie on his march.

Cromwell had fought alongside Leslie at the battle of Marston Moor and knew he would be a formidable foe. He was in his own territory. Like Ormond in Ireland, he avoided pitched battle, using classic guerrilla tactics. It gave Cromwell's scouts plenty to do, simply trying to find out where enemy pickets were hiding in the undergrowth. Gideon was busy; he almost enjoyed that. It was dangerous, however. By choosing to bring their campaign onto Leslie's own ground, where he knew every tussock on the inhospitable hills, the English had rashly exposed themselves. He stripped bare the country. Men vanished into the hills with their livestock, leaving only women, old men and children. Crops were taken from the fields. The bare hills were bad grazing for horses, so even fodder had to be imported. Meanwhile Leslie made excellent use of his forces, particularly his dragoons, who laid ambushes then melted away, leaving their opponents pointlessly wandering to and fro while their strength and their scant resources dwindled.

As in Ireland, supplies had to come by sea. Cromwell had made meticulous arrangements. Bread and Cheshire cheese were provided for the men. Beans and oats for the horses were ferried in too. The troops carried with them their own horseshoes, nails and portable ovens in order to bake unbreakable marching biscuit. But they lacked tents – only a hundred small ones for officers had been supplied – and as the weather closed in, this would severely hamper them.

Leslie had dug in to protect Edinburgh and its port at Leith; after abortive assaults it became clear that Cromwell's inferior numbers would never prevail there. Throughout August, the Scots skirmished endlessly, while their taunted foes became exhausted and demoralised. The Scots captured a cavalry patrol near Glasgow and sent tortured and mutilated bodies back to Cromwell. Sickness ran rife through the English ranks. In late August, they retreated to Musselburgh on the coast, from where hundreds of sick and wounded men were shipped home. The weather had turned foul and Leslie bothered the remainder mercilessly. They were tired, spent, hungry, apprehensive and harried. Far from home, with his army five thousand down, depleted and sinking, Cromwell retreated to the coast, where he hoped ships could bring supplies or even evacuate the troops.

After more pointless manoeuvring, driving rain and lack of rations drove the English to seek shelter at Dunbar. This could only be a temporary bolt-hole, but Gideon and the other scouts soon discovered the worst. The Scots had arrived ahead of them. They were blocking the route south to Berwick. In this narrow coastal strip, with the lowering sea to one side and the rain-drenched Lammermuir Hills above, they had been boxed in. Leslie marched his main regiments to the top of nearby Doon Hill, from where he dominated their fatal position.

As the rain beat down, Cromwell's men sought whatever shelter they could, in and around the tiny coastal town. Stationed above on a steep escarpment which was protected by a swollen, raging burn, the Scots poised for the kill. If the New Model chose to fight, they would have to charge uphill on precipitous ground, against superior numbers and into a blaze of artillery.

It was a dismal moment. For once, Cromwell had let himself be out-manoeuvred. His men were outnumbered two-to-one and a third of them were already out of action, with illness claiming more daily. The position looked hopeless. Communication with Berwick, the only possible retreat for the cavalry, had been cut. Evacuation of the infantry by sea, under the Scots' guns, would be a murderous exercise. There was no time to do it and they had too few ships in any case. Cromwell managed to send out an urgent dispatch to Sir Arthur Haselrigge, at Newcastle, pleading for reinforcements and urging him to keep the army's predicament a secret from Parliament. But the troops would be done for, long before reinforcements could arrive.

They were in a classic trap. All David Leslie had to do now was to stay where he was and starve them out.

Chapter Sixty-Five

Dunbar: 1650

1 O PRAISE the LORD, all ye nations; praise him, all ye people.
2 For his merciful kindness is great toward us: and the truth of the LORD
*   endureth for ever. Praise ye the LORD.*

Psalm 117

On the bleak dark night of the 2nd of September 1650, Captain Gideon
Jukes of the New Model Army lay on the ground on his belly at the
edge of a cornfield, soaked to the skin, believing he would die next day
and thinking about life. Life, Gideon believed, should be better than
this. He was hungry and freezing. His Monmouth cap was so sodden
with rainwater, it had stretched to almost twice its normal size –
unwearable, but he diligently kept it on because it was a dark colour
and camouflaged his light hair. Corn stubble had prickled his wet skin
like six-inch nails, adding to the insect bites that already tormented him.

Dunbar lay on a great curve of coastline that angled out, where the
Firth of Forth runs into the North Sea, dark and heaving water, often
dangerous to fishermen and sailors. The night was wild. Great curtains
of gale tore across the town, dragging sheets of vicious rain and hail.
Town was hardly the word, to a Londoner: just a line of hunched seaside
houses around a small harbour. On the east side, the army camped out
on a soggy, quagmired, fifty-year-old golf course. Camped was not strictly
accurate either. Most had no tents. The luckier ones who did could not
pitch them because the wind was too strong. Many men were too sick
and demoralised to care; disease was careering through the ranks by the
hour. A few found the energy to cheer themselves up by praying. There
was no point trying to sleep. The wailing wind and the battering rain
destroyed their rest. Besides, armies generally know when they are on
the verge of great endeavour. Especially when there is no hope for them.

Up on the high ground, Gideon could sense the enemy very close by. He was not surprised. It merely confirmed what they had seen happening all day: the Scots had moved down from the summit. The New Model did not know why; it would take the kind of spies they could not use – spies who could go right in among the Scots regiments and overhear what had compelled Leslie to this unnecessary decision when he had had it so easy. Gideon could guess one reason: the misery the English were suffering down on the shore was nothing to the buffeting that the Scottish troops must have endured, when they were exposed to all the elements threw at them, up high on the crest of Doon Hill. Battered to exhaustion, the men must have pleaded for respite.

Gideon would hardly have believed that David Leslie had been forced downhill by the Kirk Committee. But those dough-brained Presbyterian ministers wanted a fast solution. Since their cannon could not reach Cromwell's men from the hill and they wanted to see bombardment, they dumped Leslie's patient tactics. Fairfax and Cromwell had never been so overruled. Fairfax had made sure he was given a completely free hand as soon as the New Model Army was formed and the volatile Cromwell would have beaten up insufferable civilians who interfered.

On Sunday, when Cromwell's men first arrived, Leslie had wanted to attack before they could establish proper defences. Then, the ministers of the Kirk refused to let him fight on the Sabbath. Now that the New Model was properly positioned, Leslie preferred to leave disease and hunger to do his work. But on Monday, the Kirk worthies instructed him to move his men downhill, ready to do battle. After fruitless argument, he gave in. From four o'clock in the afternoon the English had been aware of this enormous army moving closer towards them – the shuffles of men and horses, the groan of wheels under gun carriages. The Scots descended the hill slowly, until they had formed a huge arc, hemming in their opponents against the coast. They were stretched out over almost two miles, intending to leave no exit for escape. That night they settled down in the cornfields along the far side of the Brox Burn; this was where Gideon was reconnoitring after dark. They had no tents at all. He could hear that they were extremely unhappy.

The Brox Burn was normally fordable, but after so much rain it now crashed down its forty-foot-deep chasm in furious torrents until it flowed into the sea. Gideon had just managed to cross at a lower place near the shore, where the banks dropped and the widened water calmed.

This place had been discovered earlier in the day, when Cromwell and his deputy, 'Honest John' Lambert, had ridden out to survey the enemy's movements. Leslie had deployed most of his cavalry opposite this area, his right wing, intending to prevent the English using any crossings near the shore.

Lambert, a sensible, dogged Yorkshireman, had spotted weaknesses in Leslie's deployment. The Scots' line spread too far towards the sea; it had them stretched and vulnerable on their right, while their left was cramped up, too close to Brox Burn to manoeuvre in support of their central infantry. Monck, the artillery commander, was consulted, a serious tactician; he agreed. A mounted council of war was held at nine o'clock that night, to demonstrate Lambert's observations and persuade the regimental officers that instead of waiting to be attacked and annihilated, the New Model should mount an unexpected offensive. Though many officers still favoured evacuation by sea, John Lambert won the argument.

With such heavy numbers arrayed against them, they relied on absolute surprise. In the dark, covered by the noise of the storm, men were discreetly moved to position. Cromwell, whose forte was careful placement of regiments in battle, rode around on a small pony to supervise. He was so intent, he bit his lip until the blood flowed. During that night, most of the English army slipped across the burn and formed up. John Lambert took three regiments of cavalry in a great loop, so they would not be noticed, aiming to attack the enemy's flank. All this was achieved while the Scots had no idea the English were on the move. For them that howling night, never was Cromwell's proverb more true: *'Praise the Lord — and keep your powder dry!'*

In his cornfield, Gideon twice heard an alarm raised among the Scots. He tensed, but then twice he heard them ordered to stand down again. Although they were drawn up in their regiments ready for battle, they were so confident of victory they did not stand on guard. The men lay down among the stooks, trying as best they could to escape the weather. Gideon crawled so close that when they snuggled back among the dripping, sodden sheaves, he could hear men's groans and snores. It seemed some of their officers had left them, retreating to local farms and barns for a good warm night's sleep. Unsaddled horses were left free to forage. Weapons were stacked. What Gideon could not see — and as a musketeer he looked for it — were many twinkles of lit matchcord.

'Alas poor Jocky!' he mouthed to himself, quoting a catchphrase from a London news-sheet. What he observed excited him. Some harebrained field officer had allowed the Scots infantry to extinguish their match, apart from just two men per company. They could be caught unprepared. Slowly Gideon began wriggling backwards to report and to join his comrades for the coming fight.

Just before dawn, at five in the morning, John Lambert suddenly attacked the Scots' right flank from the shore side. The New Model let out their famous exhilarated shouts. Drums beat. Trumpets sounded. The great guns they had brought from London began a powerful bombardment, as the bleary Scots scrambled to order, barely able to grasp what was happening. Lambert's cavalry and Monck's infantry crossed the burn and together attacked from the front. This large concentration soon made the Scots' right wing crumble, despite a furious downhill charge by lancers, who held up Lambert's advance temporarily. Cromwell and Lambert were using a tactic they had employed at Preston, when also faced with superior numbers; they were pinpointing one section of the enemy at a time, then rolling up the opposition systematically. They took few losses themselves but wreaked havoc.

The Scottish infantry roused themselves from sleep, at first unable to fire because their match was out. They recovered as fast as they could, but were disadvantaged from then on. Furious hand-to-hand fighting ensued: push of pike and butt of musket — the most brutal kind. The battle line swayed to and fro several times across the burn. Then Cromwell threw in his reserves at exactly the right moment. At six o'clock, the sun came up to sparkle off the now-calm sea. Cromwell famously quoted the 68th psalm: *Let God arise, let his enemies be scattered.* The Scottish right had failed. Unable to manoeuvre, their cavalry were driven back, trampling through their own infantry. Panic set in. Scots began to throw down their arms and run away. Their left wing fled without firing a shot. The indefatigable Ironsides slammed into the infantry and broke through the Scottish lines, according to Cromwell flying about the field like furies — or as another officer said colourfully, *'The Scots were driven out like turkeys.'*

Cromwell himself was so overcome by the relief of tension he laughed uncontrollably as if he was drunk. He had saved a disaster. It was his most perfect victory, a masterpiece of tactics, both in planning and execution. By seven o'clock in the morning it was all over. The English had lost only an estimated forty men, the Scots three thousand dead, with ten thousand more rounded up and taken prisoner. The New Model could not cope with such numbers. The wounded would be released, but half of the prisoners were taken to Durham in a terrible eight-day march, then held in revolting conditions. Between three and four thousand died of hunger and mistreatment, the rest being transported as slaves to New England.

As the English cavalry pursued fugitives, they paused to sing the 117th psalm: not a long delay, for it has only two verses. English booty included Leslie's entire baggage train, all of the Scottish artillery, armour and colours. Retreating to Stirling, Leslie had lost over half his army and although the war was not yet won, Cromwell would control Edinburgh and Leith. Edinburgh city surrendered at once and was occupied by Lambert; its strong castle followed by the end of the year.

When news of this victory reached London, the Rump Parliament ordered that a Dunbar medal should be struck for both officers and men. It was the first military medal celebrating a battle ever issued to British armed forces.

Captain Gideon Jukes fought in the savage mêlée at the centre. Hopping on his pony after he returned from reconnaissance, he joined himself to Okey's dragoons for old times' sake. They piled into the Scots' infantry from the shoreward end. At some point, he felt as if he had been punched hard; a bullet had gone into his body from the front, on the left side, though somehow bypassing his heart. Strangely exhilarated, he kept going. He took a sword thrust in his right thigh. He began losing blood from that. Unable to keep on his horse any longer, he reined in and slid off, landing on his right side so his pelvis moved, his ribs crunched and his shoulder came out of its socket, the same one he had dislocated four years before in the West Country.

In disappointment and surprise, Gideon tried to curl up for protection as the battle raged over and around him. He had no way to avoid being fatally trampled; he felt worse fear than ever in his life. He could do nothing for himself. Only when his loyal pony came and stood over him with its head down sadly, was he sheltered. He had not yet lost consciousness. In a dreamlike state, he experienced waves of blackness and devastating pain. He thought he saw visions. He wished it could be over.

Then he was kicked in the head — by man or horse he never knew — which solved that problem. The noise of guns and men shouting faded to a remote blur. The buffets his body was taking seemed no worse than being shaken by a companion in the night, who had heard a cat make suspicious noises on the roof. Believing himself in his own bed, Gideon Jukes smiled briefly, before he sank back dangerously into sleep and knew nothing for a long time.

Chapter Sixty-Six

Moorfields: 1650

Priss Fotheringham's scheme, as conceived in Newgate Prison, was that Alice Smith would be given a new virginity by the tame quack 'doctor', Hercules Pawlett. Daintily renamed as 'Mistress Pernelle', she would then join the Dutch 'girls' – some of whom were stretching that youthful definition beyond incredulity. To be foreign was to be exotic. One fraudulently passed herself off as Dutch even though she came from Clerkenwell. They worked at an old trade, in what was about to become London's most legendary brothel.

Mistress Pernelle had other ideas for herself. All along, the waif had understood more of what Priss was planning than she showed. In her life on the streets she had seen enough bawds to recognise exactly what Priss Fotheringham was, and to be wary. Although she herself had had connections with men from time to time, swindling was forced on her by desperation, either financially or because of an all-too-human need for comfort. A regular life of fornication was not for her. She feared the consequences. She had seen whores sink, in only a few months, through prettiness to coarseness then further into the vile ravages of syphilis, which rotted off their faces. She had known many who died, some of them going mad on the streets first.

The former Alice Smith did recognise the false promise of this life. A girl with a sweet visage, who managed to keep herself clean and nice just long enough to secure a rich patron, could live off her trade – in her own apartment with a lute and a French clock, if she was *extremely* well thought of – at least until the patron spent all his income on sack and gambling, or got himself married and retired to estates in the country, or simply found a newer mistress with a gayer laugh, a tighter commodity and perter breasts. Or until he died. Few of these women achieved a tolerable old age. There were, and there would be, mistresses of kings, long-term ones too, who died in abject poverty.

There was a different route to prosperity. A smart businesswoman, who kept out of debt to bawds and pimps, might begin as a whore but one day establish her own brothel, sit all day in a parlour beneath racks of delft plates, wearing a good gown, and retire from lying down with men herself. An organised bawd like this might make her fortune through her girls, at least until some man spent it for her. Some, and Priss Fotheringham was one, really enjoyed such entrepreneurship, which brought money and fame – though generally not enough money and sometimes the wrong kind of fame. It also carried a constant risk of fines and imprisonment.

In 1650, the Six Windmills was becoming known and had embarked on what would be a long period of secure notoriety. The place hummed with excitement. Priss was creaking with the pox, which could never quite be cured even by mercury, but in those days she remained full of energy and managed her girls in a grubby style that the shameless men who trekked out to Moorfields deemed to be a fine welcome. When they called her 'Mother' Fotheringham, it sounded as if she were some homely body who might offer tureens of nourishing soup and prayers before bedtime – although once her establishment became known as the Half-Crown Chuck Office, all suggestion of gentility was dropped. Anyone who knew that name knew into what moist and mysterious cavities the money was thrown.

Only men with a healthy disposable income, perhaps acquired illegally, could afford to throw away half a crown. Half-crowns – two shillings and sixpence – came in all shapes and sizes since the war started. Two-and-six would buy you a bedstead, a stack of bees, a hammer, a yard of kersey or a barrel of oysters, pretty well fresh. Half a crown was the going rate to place a high-class advertisement in a news sheet, or to buy a reading from the astrologer William Lilly.

At the Six Windmills, half a crown was what had to be tossed between the spread legs of Priss Fotheringham when she stood on her head with her feet wide apart, showing her bare belly and breech. The whooping culleyrumpers then *chucked* their coins into her vagina until the cavity was filled. It was reckoned there was space for sixteen standard half-crowns, which would pay a whole year's wages for a live-in household maid. French dollars or Spanish pistolles were an acceptable alternative if the customers were foreign. The sought-for coins were the various 'official' issues of the Tower Mint in London that was controlled by Parliament or from the now-defunct Royalist Mints of Shrewsbury and Oxford. Through having to assess more dubious offerings, Priss had become curiously expert in the irregular coins issued by besieged garrisons during the civil war – the triangles and rectangles showing castles and fortified gateways that had come into general circulation after being cut from donated tankards, trenchers, salts, bowls and apostle spoons in Beeston, near Chester, Scarborough and Colchester, the diamonds with jewelled crowns from the great Royalist cavalry station at Newark, the octagons from Pontefract. Since Cromwell's return from Ireland, she was familiar with coinage from Kilkenny, Inchquin, Cork; the Youghal copper farthing; the blacksmith's half-crown that was crudely executed yet bore an ambitious equestrian portrait of the King; the round coins issued by the Marquis of Ormond, with crowns, harps and beaded rims. Priss accepted them all if the metal in them was good, though for reasons of personal comfort, she preferred that diamonds and other parallelograms with sharp corners were not thrown at her privities in the Half-Crown Chuck.

At her best, Priss could do the chuck without assistance, and several times a night. As hours passed and she gulped aqua vitae – not easy, when you are upside down – she might need the whooping customers to hold her spread legs steady, but she kept going. On some occasions Rhenish wine or sack was poured in. Even the most athletic whore could not then drink the wine or sack herself – though others might, if they were not too squeamish. To imply that chucking came from a cultured tradition, it was always said to originate with the ancient Romans. 'Well, they were noble!' Priss would roar. 'Let's have an orgy in their memory . . .' Riotous roistering then ensued, with rudely skimpy costumes that no one bothered to check for classical authenticity. Inevitably, there were men who boasted they were experts at the chucking. The most intense of these dab hands would expound boringly on the best method to ensure insertion. Only complete rogues offered to sell their knowledge, even for the price of a cup of sack.

By those of a whimsical nature, the Half-Crown Chuck might be described as an early form of slot machine.

* * *

Friday the 15th of September 1650 was decreed by Parliament a Day of Public Thanksgiving. Such days had been regularly held throughout the previous decade, to celebrate military victories. This one was for the subjugating of Ireland by Oliver Cromwell, who was now subjugating the Scots too, in driving rain. Public thanksgiving took the form of sermons. Not many customers at the Six Windmills bothered to attend these sermons, or read them when Parliament subsequently had them printed – though some did, because, as in all walks of life, Ma Fotheringham's clientele included a number of hypocrites. Even by the management and generality such occasions were always marked, however. Celebrations were eagerly held in brothel premises. To enter into the spirit, extra drink was ordered to accompany a raucous performance of the famous Half-Crown Chuck ritual.

Parliament had in previous months passed a brisk sequence of reforming Acts and Ordinances: against Drunkenness; against Swearing and Cursing; against Immodest Dress, which specified the deplorable habits of painting, wearing black patches, and lewd dress in women; against the importation of French wines – unless captured by Oliver Cromwell as booty at Edinburgh, which was given a specific exclusion so he could sell it to pay soldiers; against the import of French silks and wool; against the import of foreign hats and hatbands. None of those Acts and Ordinances was observed at the Six Windmills. The men were blasphemous and drunk, the women were immodest. However, Priss coarsely conceded it was not obligatory to wear a foreign hat to fuck.

During the extremely noisy evening of the 15th of September, a group of sailors arrived from a ship called the *Emerald*. Sailors were always attended to kindly. Whores appreciated the danger of their adventurous lives at sea, not to mention their desperation for female company the minute they made land and the fact they would have just been paid, possibly with extra prize money. A sailor with a wooden leg posed a special challenge for a whore too.

Safe harbours for that evening's wind-blown matelots were at once provided. Only officers were permitted entry to the chuck, however, since it was understood that only officers would be in possession of the correct coins. The concept of having the right money ready, please, has older origins than may be supposed. Little interrogation was needed; experienced women could tell at a glance from a man's dress and attitude whether he was a basic pug-nosed seaman or an uglier, ruder specimen but of higher status with a heavier purse. The lower ranks were peeled off slickly to the basic booths, without offence being intended or taken.

Sailors were generally faithful to the King, but at least one crewman off the *Emerald* held libertarian ideals. Unimpressed with the elitist entry-rules Ma Fotheringham had imposed for her own performance, one toprigger loathed being excluded. He did not claim that the world was a treasury for the common man, he just shouted repeatedly that barring him from the chuck was unfair. During this unpleasantness he was threatened that the hector would be called from doorkeeping to expel him. His outrage continued, but he simmered down. The girls, who had heard blustering before, let him mooch off on his own; they had their hands full with other people anyway, for it was a busy night.

The grumbling sailor rambled about in quieter areas of the brothel, searching for a free girl, or a free supper, or at least a free drink. He passed various small cells where men who were more willing to spend money than he was were hard at it. He stepped over one or two who had collapsed in passageways, overcome by one kind of excitement or another. As he roamed and muttered, he saw another man emerge from what must be a privy. The landbird had a confident swagger, and looked as if he knew what he was about. The sailor followed him.

Appearances were deceptive, as is so often the case when much drink has been consumed. In the cavernous interior, the swaggerer soon lost his way. By accident, he lurched into the kitchen. The brothel might be mostly taken up with parlours and bedrooms but, once the long night ended, every tired whore liked to sit down with a slice of smoked gammon folded in a piece of bread and butter, then wash it down with a tankard of small beer while complaining about that day's customers. There was a kitchen, therefore, one remarkably well stocked with gleaming copper pans, bright slipware bowls and organised knife boxes. It had bunches of dried herbs, smoked meats hung over the hearth, even jelly moulds though they were rarely used. Clean wash-cloths and pan-holders hung neatly on a string on the mantel-beam. The fire was leaping cheerily. The mousetraps were all set.

This warm nook was the province of Mrs Mildmay – a perfectly respectable cook-housekeeper (or so she maintained) who came in from Moorfields on a daily basis, bringing a ten-year-old washer-up and a coal-scuttle boy. Like the brothel's doctor, wall-painter, scrivener and doorman, she was an expert professional. She could have worked in a duke's mansion, had dukes not preferred to use illegitimate offspring of their own and had the House of Lords not been abolished anyway the year before, on grounds of being useless and dangerous.

Of course the brothel doctor was a quack, but he was a *good* quack, one of the best fake physicians in London. Of course, too, the doorman was a pimp; he was the bawd's own pimp, hectors always were.

The point was that running a good brothel required high standards of domestic comfort. Men might as well remain at home, unless they were pampered, fed and entertained here decently. It was not enough that the girls knew their stuff – though if girls worked for Priss Fotheringham, they certainly did. Gentlemen expected that there would be meat pies in a choice of flavours, dishes of oysters, fine wines, foot-stools, someone who could play a flute, books of undemanding love poems, and up-to-date copies of news-sheets, with both Royalist and Parliamentarian points of view.

Expensive claret was available to be taken on silver (well, pewter) trays to the finest rooms – claret which was more overpriced than ever, now that imports had been banned. For the half-hour, pay-a-few-pennies booths where the antique hags and girls who were just learning their trade worked, there was beer. It was brewed on the premises, brewed in fabulously large quantities by a waiflike solitary brewster. She kept to herself. She never went with men, regarding men as trouble. She had stayed here in the brothel because she believed she owed Priss something for extracting her from prison. Anyway, it was a job.

That evening she was alone in the kitchen. While the house was busy but all the men and girls were concentrating on the Half-Crown Chuck, or on more straightforward entertainment, and after Mrs Mildmay had gone home, this became the brewster's kingdom. The banked fire flickered on the whitewashed walls and glittered on the copper pans. It was warm; it was peaceful. It reminded the young woman of a kitchen in Birmingham where she had once been shown kindness. For company, she could hear the low hum of distant voices, congenial thumps, occasional bursts of music, soaring cheers and laughter. She was surrounded by happy people, yet had no need to interact with any.

Until now.

The bastard in the green velvet coat and gold-laced boot-hose had an arrogant strut and was more than tipsy. He wore an eyepatch shoved askew up on his forehead and tossed his blond ringlets in a way that she instantly recognised. He was foolishly proud of his luxurious coiffure and so sure of himself she almost laughed out loud. He made a dramatic start. 'What have we here? A choice morsel!'

'Not for you, Jem Starling!' riposted the brewster instantly. She would have kept quiet, but she saw that through his befuddlement he realised he knew her.

'Eliza!'

'Mistress Pernelle now.'

'A good whore's name –' Jem lunged towards her, falling over a joint-stool. 'You owe me a thrust, for giving me up to the constable – I'll have my revenge this minute –'

'You will not.' She felt oddly calm. That had something to do with three pints of her own brewed beer inside her. Since she last saw him, she had come through many experiences. She was like a forged sword: hammered, quenched, tempered, sharpened and polished; brought through fire and water to great strength and perfect balance. When she spoke, it was to her ears like the whip of a good weapon through the air. 'Take yourself off and forget you saw me. I have my own life and will not be bothered.'

'Damme, you'll repay your debts!'

'I owe no debts to you,' answered Mistress Pernelle, jumping up from the settle where she had been so cosy. She lost her temper, which seemed a good reaction to the possibility of losing everything. Why could men never leave a woman quietly by herself? Why must their uncontrollable jockums always drive them to impose themselves?

She snatched up a spectacular brass bed-warmer that had been preparing on the fire. Five foot long in the handle, the implement was burning hot and heavy with live coals inside it. She put all the effort she could into a mighty swing, expelling all her years of grief in the action. The great implement cracked Jem Starling's skull. He fell down without a cry and did not move. The warmer clanged to the floor, badly dented.

Mistress Pernelle sat back down on the settle very suddenly, white as ash, with her heart pounding.

'Blow me, you've only killed the blighter!' commented a new voice from the passage doorway. More trouble. A man was already in the room, bending over Jem's boots. 'If I tow him out into the yard, do I get the fun he was asking for?'

'Don't even dream of it.'

'Always worth a try! I'll dispose of him for you anyway. Let's chuck him over the gunnels before anybody cops us –' A sailor. He was as good as his word, starting to pull the lifeless man to the back door. The girl rallied to help him, which speeded up the process. Beyond the door lay a lane, where Jem's body joined the drunks and riff-raff who were often found there, some clinging onto miserable life, some dead of cold or worse, all causing little public comment in this sordid area in the fields beyond the city walls. The sailor took coins from a pocket. 'Shall I save his boots?'

'I want nothing of his.'

'You knew him then.'

And I know you too, she thought to herself as they returned indoors. In the few moments while they removed the corpse, she had considered whether to say anything. One old acquaintance in a night was bad enough.

The sailor gazed at her. It was almost ten years since she had seen him. She had been about fourteen, and was now in her middle twenties, the age he must have been when he went away to sea. He was in his mid-thirties, a fit, lean man, dark-skinned from years of wind and weather, short, wiry, otherwise undistinguished-looking. One thing marked him out: he had the sing-song lilt of an ineradicable accent, one that came from as far inland as could be. She had noticed it immediately, feeling a pang of homesickness, and an urge to welcome him too. He had failed to spot that she spoke with the same intonation and vowels.

'Well, Mistress Pernelle!' The young sailor addressed her with the cocksure confidence of their home town. He had Midlands' goodheartedness too. He had known deprivation; he reacted kindly to her predicament. 'I covered him with leaves, nice and snug, but if he may be traced to you, you may like to think whether it is safe for you to remain here.'

She jumped up quickly, at that. With a pragmatic nod, she led the sailor down a passage to the brewhouse, where she normally slept on a mattress and kept her few belongings. Quickly putting together a bundle, she remarked that it had been in her mind to move on to a more respectable house. Brewing was a skill, she now realised; it could be marketed. The speed of her packing showed that her plans were already advanced. She turned her back and changed from her low-cut brothel gown into a plain skirt and jacket in unbleached linen, high on the neck, with a neat apron and white collar over it, clothes she must have hoarded ready for this day. She plumped a good hat on her head.

While he leaned on a malt shovel, waiting, the sailor revealed he too had dreams. He was carrying his savings and now planned to leave the sea, hoping to set up somewhere and earn his living on land.

'What can you do?'

'I can turn my hand to anything.'

'If you can work in a tavern,' suggested Mistress Pernelle, 'why don't you come along with me?'

'Do you have your own tavern, malt-masher?' chortled the sailor, with his easy grace.

'Not yet,' she quipped back, with the same wry humour. 'I shall have to begin in someone else's place, then persuade them to give it up to me.'

'Better bring your warming pan in case you need to bash heads.'

'No, that's Priss Fotheringham's own bed-warmer. I'll not be a thief – especially from her.'

'Well, it's true the pan got dinted badly. The next person who has it will be burned by the coals falling out. That should enliven the bawd's bed.'

'Say no more of bawds. My plan is to turn respectable.' She too had a few savings to bring to the venture, though she would not tell him so until she was sure that she trusted him not to drink or steal the money. 'We must go right across the city, where I am not known and the naval press-men will not look for you. Look out for purse-snatchers and pickpockets.'

They slipped out of doors and set off into the night. The sailor was intrigued. 'So why do you so suddenly trust your fortunes to a stranger?' At his side, the skinny brewster merely smiled, enjoying her mystery. 'My name is Nathaniel Tew – so who are you?'

'You will work it out eventually,' said the pale little wisp whom Nat Tew would in time recognise from long ago as one of his own raggle-taggle sisters: the one they had all called Kinchin.

Chapter Sixty-Seven

At sea: January 1649–September 1652

It was a small fleet that Prince Rupert took to Ireland: the *Constant Reformation* (his own command as admiral), the *Convertine* (under Prince Maurice as vice-admiral), plus the *Swallow, Charles, Thomas, James* and *Elizabeth* (the latter a hoy, or small sloop-rigged coastal vessel). On warships there were two commands; the captain and sailors operated the vessel whilst a separate complement of soldiers carried out the fighting. Prince Maurice's fighting troops included Orlando Lovell.

As colleagues they were polite but never close. Lovell grudgingly chose to attach himself to Maurice, Rupert's somewhat overshadowed younger brother, hoping he would be more congenial. Immensely tall, though not as striking as the daredevil Rupert, Prince Maurice had failed to get the measure of English politics and was thought unpersuasive in debate, so he was considered lightweight; it suited Lovell, who was as prone to jealousy of good commanders as to irritation with weak ones. The bravery, leadership and organisation that Maurice had shown in the war on land were beyond doubt; he was loved and respected by his immediate followers, and had provided Charles I with valuable officers. Serving under him at sea was not a retrograde step, or Lovell would never have done it.

Their first base was Kinsale in the south of County Cork, a perfect enclosed harbour, guarded by a narrow entrance that was almost invisible from the open sea, especially in rough weather – and the Irish Sea was notoriously rough. An attractive medieval town fringed the harbour bowl, long the centre of a thriving wine trade with Bordeaux, so Prince Rupert had something to drink when he fell ashore suffering from agonies of seasickness and Orlando Lovell had something to abstain from when he wanted to be fastidious. It was at St Multose Church that Rupert had his cousin immediately proclaimed King Charles II when, not long after they arrived, he heard of the execution of Charles I. The two princes had family reasons to be shocked, as well as feeling horror that an anointed monarch had been killed. For their men it was bad news too. Lovell, for one, took it to heart glumly. He had made the wrong choice, entirely his own fault, and was now consigned to serving as an adventurer among beaten men. He did not like it, but was in too deep to see any better options if he left.

They went to Ireland to prey on commercial shipping, and were resoundingly successful. Soon, as an adjunct to the land-based forces of the Marquis of Ormond, Rupert's ships also became a factor in the Commonwealth attempt to gain control of Ireland. He threatened Cromwell's supply line, forcing Admiral Robert Blake to patrol outside Kinsale whenever the foul weather was not interfering. The Royalists lurked in the mist like sea-wolves, threatening relief for the expeditionary force. But once they were penned up, the harbour became so full of shipping even neutral merchantmen could not enter. The Irish feared damage to their trade. Plots were fomented by supposed allies. Cromwell's galloping conquest of Ireland eventually made Kinsale untenable until, seizing his moment adroitly, Prince Rupert evaded Blake during a storm and sailed for Portugal.

They arrived at the mouth of the River Tagus in November. For almost a year Rupert made this an operational base. His initial reception from the King of Portugal was friendly; he sold prize goods, refitted and bought supplies. But Blake was on his heels, which unsettled Portuguese traders whose ships Blake threatened. Rupert issued an intemperate denunciation of Parliament; he became a liability. Blake several times prevented escape. Ingenuity was used on both sides. The English planned to ambush Rupert and Maurice while they were on land, hunting, but they galloped out of the trap. Rupert invented a booby-trap bomb disguised as a barrel of oil to blow up Blake's vice-admiral, but his agent gave himself away by swearing fluently in English. In August 1650, a French fleet arrived in a relief attempt, but their flagship sank and two others were taken, so the rest dispersed. Only in September, the month of the battle of Dunbar, did Rupert's ships slip out from the Tagus and bolt for the Mediterranean.

They were still being menaced. At the end of December, the little fleet was chased until five or six ships were 'defunct': two ran aground, one was set ablaze, two were captured. Rupert, temporarily separated from Maurice, escaped in a 'nimble sailor', the *Rainbow*. Maurice only caught up with him later at Toulon.

Intrepid piracy now became the way of life for the princes and their tattered band. They were outcasts, rarely permitted to land in European harbours and never again allowed to establish a base. Poverty-stricken and in constant danger, they were forced to hunt for prizes in shipping lanes where Blake patrolled and harried them.

They preyed not only on English merchantmen but on those of any country allied to the English Commonwealth. Only the Dutch saluted them as allies. Even countries that were hostile to the Commonwealth were nervous commercially, because the Rump Parliament was strengthening its navy, building new ships, appointing experienced New Model Army veterans to command and looking overseas for trade and position. The tiny Royalist flotilla made little impact and, apart from a general hope of seizing ships and treasure, their wanderings became troubled and aimless.

As they struggled, Lovell did not make a good pirate. There were intensely long periods when the ships were either moored or cruising on the lookout for prey, often pointlessly. While they were not fighting, he loathed the inactivity. Aboard ship or just as uncomfortable ashore in filthy taverns, he kept to himself, which made him unpopular, then he let it show that he despised people he had offended. He would not fawn on the princes; he would not cosy up to the men. Lovell could cope with deprivation; he prided himself on his hardness. But he regretted his decision to join this outlaw navy and he showed it. Always critical, he grumbled until he fell out of favour with Maurice. Though never as seasick as Rupert, he was frequently queasy, which did nothing to improve his sour mood. If he could have thought of anything better to do he would have left, but very few opportunities existed for landless cavaliers.

So, to his own surprise, he stayed with the princes for the three or four years they were at sea. As an existence it was hard and brutalising. Men ran a constant risk of being drowned or shot. Lovell lost colleagues he did respect to filthy weather, bad food and water, scurvy, other diseases and wounds. The group were denounced as common pirates. They had no letters of marque to validate them; no nation protected them under its flag; all ports offered an uncertain reception, so finding food and water was a constant anxiety. They committed brave acts of plunder, taking thirty-one prizes altogether, but were so hard pressed they never managed to sustain their good luck. Some of their ships were wrecked; some crews mutinied and deserted.

In November 1650 at Cartagena, Rupert managed to sell some valuable bronze cannon so was able to refit his little fleet, but the refurbished vessels still failed to prosper. Six months later, the French allowed him to berth at Toulon, where he bought stores, though on massive credit. He pinched together enough money to buy a ship he named the *Honest Seaman*; another they called the *Loyal Subject* joined them as they set off on travels that now took them through the Straits of Gibraltar and away from Europe. Rupert wanted to sail to the West Indies, where he believed there were Royalist supporters and rich pickings, but through 1651 was held off the west of Africa by endless wrangles among his men as they struggled to beat bad weather, the uncertainty of finding supplies and their own disagreements. Open plotting broke out among the officers on board.

Rupert's own ship, the *Constant Reformation*, had been leaking, and in a violent storm off the Azores the situation became desperate. His men were unable to plug the rift; they manned the pumps, heaved guns overboard to lighten the ship and used everything to hand to make a barrier against incoming water. Rupert even ordered them to force in 120 pieces of raw beef from their victuals but the storm battered through and poured in. The vessel was doomed – and so was the crew. Alerted by cannon-shots, Maurice brought the *Honest Seaman* as close as he dared, hoping to take people off. Rupert refused to leave the comrades who had been through so much with him, but a group of men jumped him and dragged him to the single lifeboat. They rowed him to safety. A couple more rescue trips were bravely made, Lovell supervising one, but the task was hopeless. The remnants of Rupert's crew kept their ship afloat until nightfall, but soon those with Prince Maurice watched the *Constant Reformation* go down, taking over three hundred men. Most of the treasure the fleet had acquired went to the bottom with her.

Limping to the Barbary Coast of Africa, they made repairs and tried to assemble supplies and water for an Atlantic crossing. During their refit they had various adventures with the local inhabitants. Sailors were killed or captured. Locals were taken as hostages. Peace overtures were misunderstood; there were pointless skirmishes. Rupert was struck by an arrow, which he cut out of his chest himself. At one point they made an incursion far up the Gambia river, where Prince Maurice captured two Spanish ships; one was broken up, the better vessel being taken by Maurice as his flagship, renamed the *Defiance*.

At last, in summer 1652, the tiny squadron crossed the Atlantic.

They had misjudged the moment. They found that the last Royalist enclave, in Barbados, had been extinguished by the Parliamentarian navy. The other islands and the American colonies saw where the future lay; they were coming to terms with the Commonwealth. There was no Caribbean safe haven. Instead of enjoying a tropical welcome, the Royalists found themselves isolated and at risk. Late summer was the season for heavy weather too, as fierce storms formed over the warm oceans. After sailing north past unfriendly islands, taking a few prizes, bartering glass beads for fruit and obtaining water – but no other supplies – at an anchorage controlled by the French, they sheltered in a bay called Dixon's Hole in the Virgin Islands. There they rationalised their motley collection of ships and prizes, while they prepared for the bad weather they knew was coming and considered their options. Provisions ran low, and there were many complaints about the local staple, cassava, a root for which they had to forage in dense undergrowth and which, even when they managed to find it, made unpalatable tapioca dumplings or a bitter bread; eating too much of it was poisonous.

Rupert had decided they were at risk of discovery by hostile Commonwealth patrols. He had set sail for Anguilla. Their situation worsened dramatically when, in the middle of September, a hurricane blew up. They were caught at sea; it was on them with frightening suddenness. They had seen enough bad weather, but this was far outside their experience. Apocalyptic winds howled in the sky. Enormous waves, fuelled by the great winds' passage over the mighty Atlantic, surged ever and ever higher. They had no chance to outrun the weather or to find shelter. Ships which had seemed perfectly substantial on a dockside now felt like fragile toys; they became unmanageable. Helpless, they slid down vast swells of water as if they were heading inevitably to the bottom, then when they somehow cheated death and were driven up again from terrifying troughs, unrelenting water swept across their decks so powerfully neither man nor gear could withstand its power. Anyone carried overboard was gone in seconds. Lifeboats, sails, masts and rigging were torn away. Loose barrels rumbled to and fro and crashed about dangerously in their flooded holds. Even with barely a shred of canvas, the waves forced ships to career sideways so steeply their spars seemed ready to touch the water and drag them under. Every rib and joint of their wooden hulls groaned in agony, as if the tormented timbers were being crushed in some giant ogre's paw. The soldiers cursed the sailors and the sailors, when they had breath to do it, cursed them back. Everyone was exhausted within hours, but they knew they would have days of this to endure.

Orlando Lovell played his part, as crews and troops fought heroically to survive. It was impossible to see from one end to the other of the small ship he was on. Dim figures loomed through spray, gesticulating wildly. Lovell worked now without complaint, soaked through to his shirt, long hair flying in wet strands as he fought to bail water, help reduce sail, clear spars, bolster holes. Now the men with him remembered why they had deemed him a good colleague. He lacked no courage in a disaster. Released from lethargy and ill-humour, he showed strong mental toughness. He bawled or signalled frantic orders above the howls of the wind, while he strove against their coming doom, using all his strength physically and encouraging others. They hardly heard a curse from him; he would not waste the energy. As the ship staggered and risked foundering, he was a desperate participant. Lovell was now a fierce man of action who fought strenuously, tirelessly, ingeniously for his own life and the lives of everybody with him.

The hurricane roared up to a climax. On the second day, the ships lost sight of one another. Unable to steer in the pitch darkness, they had to battle on, every ship independently, and every man for himself. Even the best captain in the sturdiest vessel could not help his craft survive the damage they were suffering. Rupert's ship was driven helplessly towards ferocious jagged rocks and his appalled men must all have perished, had not the wind then abruptly changed. They were flung into a safe harbour on an uninhabited island, where they made anchor in complete exhaustion.

When the hurricane finally passed over and made landfall far in the west, Rupert's battered vessel was alone. Somehow they crawled back to Dixon's Hole for repairs, intending to wait for any other survivors to reconnoitre at their last-known berth. As the last rags of storm blustered under grey skies, Rupert then searched desperately for his brother Maurice. One other ship of theirs was picked up, but of the *Defiance* no trace could be found.

Rupert was devastated. The *Defiance* and the other ships must have been wrecked on the treacherous reefs and rocks of the low-rising, sparsely populated Anegada, in the north of the Virgin Islands, or perhaps they came to grief on Sombrero Island, above Anguilla. Rupert hunted the region, fruitlessly seeking answers. Rumours would persist for years that Maurice was still alive, perhaps a prisoner of the Spanish, but eventually Rupert abandoned the search. He returned to Europe.

No word ever came. Only many years later did Sir Robert Holmes, who had served with Prince Maurice, learn from some Spaniards that shattered pipe-staves had been seen, washed ashore in great quantities on the beaches of Puerto Rico. Pipes were huge nautical barrels, the size of two hogsheads. These had been branded MP, which was the mark Prince Maurice used.

Long before that, early in 1653, just two ships crept back to France, with Prince Rupert. He was depressed, ill and exhausted. He lay sick for weeks, before his cousin Charles II sent a carriage and he rejoined the court. By then Rupert had accepted that his brother had perished. The *Defiance* was lost: utterly lost, with no survivors.

Chapter Sixty-Eight

The Middle Temple: 1653

In England, Juliana Lovell consulted a lawyer.

It came about by accident. Juliana did not go to the Middle Temple in order to enquire about her personal position. She thought she knew that all too well: a married woman, with two children to support, having no money – but a fixed intent to lead a life of the utmost simplicity. What else could she do? Since Edmund Treves first said her husband had sailed with Prince Maurice, she had had no news. The princes' movements were sporadically mentioned in news-sheets, so as the years passed, Juliana became familiar with foreign affairs as she scanned reports from France, Holland, Spain, Naples and anywhere else that might be relevant. Early in 1653 she saw mention that Prince Rupert and perhaps ten ships had been glimpsed carrying out repairs at Guadeloupe, then she read of a rumour he had been shipwrecked. In mid-February the *Weekly Intelligencer* gave her dark news:

> *It was this day confirmed by letters from Paris that Prince Rupert landing a few days before at Brest in Brittany, did take his journey from thence to Paris. Some letters make mention that he came only with two ships, some say three, the only relics of the storm. There is nothing yet certain of his brother Maurice, but some say that both he and his ship were devoured by the sea in the great tempest.*

Juliana went to the Middle Temple because she was invited. Mr Abdiel Impey, who had already informed her of her guardian's death, was searching for a document one day in spring 1653 and came upon the long-forgotten papers of Mr William Gadd, deceased – deceased, in fact, in 1649. Mr Impey kept an extremely cluttered office, where his rule was the good one that whenever he wrote a letter he placed a copy handy in a mountainous document tray; if nobody replied within two years, or when the pile grew so tall it toppled over, he dropped the copy into the basket of papers which his clerk was allowed to use to light the fire.

However, Mr Impey had known and liked William Gadd.

Extensive exploration among pleas, draft wills, receipts for embroidered waistcoats and vintners' price lists revealed that Mistress Juliana Lovell had answered his first letter with a polite acknowledgement; at the time she had said she would come to discuss matters as soon as it was convenient. This phrase either meant the party would turn up within three days, hoping money had been willed to them, or if they were frightened off by officialdom they would never come at all. Being in a kindly mood the day he found the papers, Mr Impey had his clerk dispatch a reminder.

This time, Juliana came. *She* worked on the principle that one invitation was mere etiquette, but two indicated something important.

Besides, she needed to cling to this last link with the people she had known during her marriage. Now Lovell was permanently missing. Mr Gadd was dead. So too, killed in 1651 at the battle of Worcester, was poor Edmund Treves. One of his sisters had sent Juliana a locket with his portrait, which apparently Edmund had wished her to have, and a jewelled watch for his godson Valentine; there was mention of a small legacy, though it had not arrived. Worcester had been the most desperate of battles. The young King's troops were outnumbered almost three to one and despite successful cavalry sallies in the early stages, they ended up bottled in, short of ammunition, lacking support from the Scots, and completely overwhelmed. It was thought that Edmund Treves had died below the castle during the last courageous struggle, when cover was being provided for the King's dramatic escape through the one city gate that remained open. True details of Treves's fate would never be known.

His sister railed bitterly in her letter about the waste of his life. He had spent the ten years when he could be called an adult fighting for the royal cause. He never finished university, never married nor had children. His family had barely seen him. When he finally went home in 1649, his mother was so ill she took no pleasure from his presence. She died, two years later, just before Edmund answered the call and went west to join Charles II's army as it marched down from Scotland to the Midlands. At least his mother never knew he was killed, though Juliana thought Alice Treves may have guessed what would happen.

Juliana herself was seriously depressed by losing him. His honest heart and unchanging affection had always given her comfort. He was her only real link to Lovell.

She had scanned the list of Royalists killed at Worcester, just in case, but found no Colonel Lovell named. A year later, in September 1652, came the hurricane. The following March she read that Prince Rupert had returned to France, depleted in spirit though more glamorous than ever: tall, handsome, honed, dark, weather-beaten, fashionably morose and tragic. He had lost eleven ships, including his brother's *Defiance*. Now thirty-three, Rupert had an exotic household of richly liveried Negro servants, parrots and monkeys – and exotic debts to match. Juliana would have liked to imagine Lovell in the same state, but she could not do it.

It seemed reasonable to suppose that any of Rupert's men who had families in England would, on returning to France, communicate with them. If no word came, presumably the man was dead. Juliana still heard nothing from Lovell, so had to face this thought. She hardly dared to address a letter to Prince Rupert and she knew no other Royalists from whom she could beg for news. Lovell congenitally managed without friends. Edmund Treves was the only one she ever knew him to have.

She presumed Lovell drowned with Prince Maurice. She became haunted by bad dreams in which the man she had married, and believed she loved, was a lost soul who spun helplessly in surging waves, caught up amidst a tangle of ropes, perhaps wounded by a fallen spar, until his strength failed and he drifted in the merciless cold water . . . She did not know if Orlando could even swim. She had heard that drowning was better – quicker and easier – for those who could not.

If this was what had happened, Juliana pitied Orlando and genuinely grieved. The only other alternative was bitter for her: that whatever had befallen him, he had now deliberately chosen to abandon his wife and children.

It happened. It had happened throughout history. However, Juliana knew there was a long tradition in European folklore of soldiers who had been away for decades returning unexpectedly to startled wives who barely recognised them . . . Losses like hers were in fact so frequent, the situation was recognised by Parliament in compassionate legislation. Juliana discovered this, during her visit to the lawyer.

Mr Impey inhabited a ramshackle first-storey chamber above Middle Temple Lane. He was of lizard-like appearance, completely bald, with a great nose and deep-cut lines to a receding chin. At first he appeared to have no idea who she was or what she wanted, but Juliana patiently accepted that lawyers were overwhelmed by the volume of business they had to remember (only privately thinking, the man was an idiot; the clerk had written his reminder, but Impey had himself signed it, and only last Wednesday . . .).

Once he recalled her circumstances, Impey became all kindness. He reminisced of Mr Gadd, so tellingly he caused Juliana to wipe away tears on the lace-edged handkerchief that she carried on formal occasions. To remedy her sadness, a glass of shrub was produced. Its bottle was kept handy on a long shelf, among the unused parchment. An opener hung on a piece of string Mr Impey could reach from his desk chair. Weeping women must be a regular hazard.

Juliana apologised for whimpering, swallowed a good slug of shrub – then belatedly remembered that shrub was composed by putting two quarts of brandy to the juice and peel of five lemons, with nutmeg, a pound and half of sugar and added white wine. It might seem like harmless sweet cordial for distressed ladies, but they needed to be ladies with hard heads. It had a kick like a dyspeptic dray-horse. The good thing was that by the time you realised how strong it was, you didn't care.

Mr Impey knuckled down to business. Mr Gadd had had two extremely elderly sisters to whom he bequeathed legacies, sufficient to see them kept in comfort for their remaining years. He left a large amount to charities, mostly in Somerset. 'You were his ward, I understand. He regarded you with immense affection.' Further touched, Juliana had more recourse to shrub. 'He has bequeathed you a London property.'

Without waiting to see how Juliana took it, Mr Impey poured her more shrub. Dispensing joy brought him so much satisfaction, he prepared a tot for himself too. It went without saying, the drinking vessels used by Middle Temple lawyers were gilded glass, of great beauty and considerable age. They were not small. A gift from a grateful client, Mr Impey hinted flagrantly. Juliana nodded non-committally.

'The house has been empty for a year – because we received no instructions from you as to tenanting –' He could have apologised for not actually asking her wishes, but did not wish recriminations to spoil the cheerful ambience. 'The shop was let until three weeks ago, when the tenant died – nothing infectious, I believe – and the premises have been cleared. A new tenant can be found as soon as convenient –'

'Let me think about that!' Bolstered by shrub, Juliana hardly needed to think. She had enough haberdashery, collected from Colchester, to start a shop herself.

Mr Impey delved in a drawer of his magnificent desk, managing to conceal an uneaten pie and a pair of holed stockings. After much huffing, he produced a large doorkey. 'There!'

Juliana did not immediately take it but asked him, 'As a married woman, I assume this property will belong to my husband?'

Abdiel Impey never gave an answer until he had ascertained full circumstances. Young wives who visited the Temple without their husbands were usually married to scamps; besides, Mr Gadd had left him private instructions which mentioned certain suspicions of Orlando Lovell. Mr Impey leaned forwards and posed potent questions. He learned from Juliana that Lovell, now a Delinquent colonel, had gone overseas several years ago and had not been heard of since. 'Apart from one letter I received in late 1649, though it was written earlier . . . I believed he sailed with Prince Maurice of the Palatine, supposed now to be lost in a tempest at sea.'

Gulping more shrub, Mr Impey made an expansive gesture that knocked law reports and almanacs to the floor. 'Count him dead, ma'am! Call the bounder defunct! Are you hoping to take a lover? You may do it with impunity.'

'Oh I cannot countenance adultery!' fluttered Juliana, with the heat of one who had once considered it extremely keenly. She too wished she had gone more slowly with the shrub. In fact, from that or some other cause, she was feeling slightly sick.

'Rush to it, my dear.'

'But the penalty is death!' Juliana knew adultery was a felony; both guilty parties would be condemned to death, death without benefit of clergy.

'Not in your case!'

Mr Impey took down from a shelf the Act of 10 May 1650 for

suppressing the detestable sins of Incest, Adultery and Fornication. It showed signs of frequent use. 'There are not *one* but *two* provisos, for the preservation of persons in your position: one! *"Provided, That this shall not extend to any man who, at the time of such Offence committed, is not knowing that such woman with whom such Offence is committed, is then married."* Many of my masculine clients have felt much relieved by *that!* "Oh no, sir! I had absolutely no idea!" And two! *"Proviso: Provided, That the said penalty in case of Adultery shall not extend to any woman whose Husband shall be continually remaining beyond the Seas by the space of three years"* — the Rumpers discussed five in committee, but they are charitable men — *"or shall by common fame be reputed to be dead; nor to any woman whose husband shall absent himself from his said wife by the space of three years together, so as the said wife shall not know her said husband to be living within that time".*'

'No one has informed me that Orlando is dead,' faltered Juliana.

'Pish! He was in Prince Maurice's ship; the *common fame* says it sank and vanished. Besides, you have not had a line from him for four years. Lamentable lady, this could be written just for you. You can lie gladly with your lover.'

'Oh, I do not have a lover!' Juliana believed Gideon Jukes was just a bothersome complication. She put him out of her mind. Generally.

'If you are of the inclination, madam, feel free to get one. Get him at your earliest convenience.'

Juliana Lovell showed the pinched look many women acquired when talking to lawyers about husbands who had caused them years of difficulty. Mr Impey glared sternly. He implied that obtaining this hypothetical lover was almost her duty; resistance was feeble.

So charged with enthusiasm for this glorious idea was Mr Impey that, but for the existence of Mrs Abigail Impey, he would have flung himself at Juliana's feet. Previous experience of Mrs Abigail's retribution when she suspected he wandered (or knew of it for certain from his back-stabbing colleagues) gently held him back.

'Of course I must warn you, Mistress Lovell, that *fornication* will be punished with three months' imprisonment without bail, for a first offence . . . So once you identify your lover, you are obliged to marry him.'

Let her enjoy herself, poor pretty little mite, he thought. If the man, Lovell, ever turned up again, there would be fees for someone in it.

It seemed kindest not to mention that in disputes when this happened, English courts always decreed *'that the woman should be given back to her first husband'*.

Accompanied by Mr Impey's mournful, knock-kneed clerk, a youth so devoid of any pretensions that he kept quiet and studied the gutter, Juliana tripped out to take possession of her property. The clerk was to show her the way, save her from falling down as the effect of the shrub took hold and help overcome any trepidation she felt about entering empty premises. Also, he was to check around surreptitiously, in case damage had occurred due to Mr Impey's neglect. Not that a lawyer would ever use the term 'neglect' apropos of his duty to a client.

It was not far. The house and shop were in the same ward as the Middle Temple, Farringdon Ward Without, off Shoe Lane, in one of several narrow alleyways in London that were called Fountain Court. Of course there was no fountain. It was not particularly courtly, though public scavengers had cleared away most recent rubbish and there were no beggars sleeping in doorways at that moment.

Juliana was led to an old door in a modest doorcase, beside a large square shop window with murky, cobwebbed glass. After passing through the shop, bare now of all but a long counter and a few battered racks, Juliana discovered a store for goods, then a scullery with a range, and a tiny paved yard outside. That had a pantry with stone shelves, a coal-store and an anonymous shed.

'Is there a privy?' The clerk nodded, too shy to show her. Juliana identified it herself. 'Does it work?'

'Most of the time.'

Indoors again, a steep little stair led up to three storeys of dusty domestic accommodation. First a well-lit best room and snug little parlour, then bedchambers. Under the eaves lay a low garret. There were adequate fireplaces. The floors were only slightly askew; the windows fitted decently. No rooms were furnished.

'There is no furniture, linen or crockery; the tenants were obliged to bring their own.'

'Tenants?'

'Mr Impey has the past rent waiting for you. You must pay him a fee for the managing of it though.'

'I imagined I would,' remarked Juliana gravely. She had no quibbles.

After her years of struggle, this wondrous bequest brought incredible relief. If there really was rent to come as well, that would help her equip the house.

Mr Impey had been unable to tell her whether her guardian ever lived here himself. Juliana wondered if possibly her grandmother visited this place with Mr Gadd . . . Delicacy made her content to respect their privacy.

Her first thought had been that she could sell this property and have enough money to survive in Lewisham for the foreseeable future. But why Lewisham? Mr Gadd had given her a wonderful gift, and its best feature was that she now possessed a bolt-hole. She decided Gadd probably knew that, and indeed intended it. She could vanish here. Nobody – meaning her husband – nobody would be aware she had this house. It gave Juliana a sense of independence that she found almost shocking.

She moved to London at once. She brought Tom, Val, and the little maid Catherine; she was able to hire a daily woman and occasional handyman too. She cleaned and aired the building, gradually providing simple furnishings and good utensils.

She did not lease out the shop. She had it fitted with drawers and cupboards, turning it into a haberdashery which she ran herself. She brought her own braids, ribbons and tassels, to which she soon added more – cords, silk and woollen threads for sewing and embroidery, needles, thimbles, darning mushrooms. She developed links with suppliers and weavers of what were called narrow wares – braid, bobbin lace, ribbon, tapes and gimps. She sold buttons, both fully finished and the wooden cores over which embroidery could be worked to match or contrast with particular material. Women of the gentrified classes learned of her shop, and although plain styles were worn by many nowadays, many others who could afford it wore decoration whatever their religion and politics. Everyone needed britches' hooks and apron strings. Juliana became known for her sound advice on dressmakers and hatters. She also sold patterns. Starting with her grandmother's traditional embroidery emblems, she went on to offer designs of her own, either on printed paper or ready sketched out on outfit pieces. She could prepare patterns to order.

Her natural talents were those necessary to a businesswoman: she was bright, energetic, courageous and dogged. She had a pleasant manner, but had learned to stand up for herself. Her buying mistakes were few; her debtors fewer. If her premises were the wrong end of the city for the Royal Exchange where grand silks, satins and velvets were sold, at least she had an untapped market. Lawyers, jewellers and their wives had money and the wish to deck themselves out. She did well.

It was hard work, and left her little time for herself in the first years, but as she became established and her boys grew older and less demanding, at last she was able to enjoy a quiet life, mostly free from anxiety. The boys went to school. Catherine Keevil assisted in the shop. Juliana had told Tom and Val that they had to assume that their father was dead. She did not remarry. She did not expect to. She was lonely, but she had been lonely ever since her marriage when she was seventeen. She made the best of it. At least she was free from anxiety, which brought her close to contentedness.

By the time she took possession of the Fountain Court premises, she had lost contact with her friend Anne Jukes. Anne had had wearing experiences with her husband, which Juliana heard about. She thought Anne might wish to remain private temporarily. Besides, Juliana felt a reluctance to be involved with that family. Of course she had been promised wages for her maid, Catherine Keevil, but after the first year which Gideon Jukes had paid for, Juliana found the money herself. She was proud to do so. It avoided obligation. It avoided awkwardness.

Some months after she set up in her new premises, Juliana did take herself nervously to Basinghall Street, however. She had a genuine commercial reason. She wanted to explore whether ready-designed embroidery patterns could be printed on paper sheets to sell. She believed there was a market, but was uncertain whether her idea was viable or how expensive it would be to have her drawings produced. To advise her, she wanted a printer, one who could be relied upon to deal fairly with a woman client.

She was dismayed to find that the print shop she knew, Robert Allibone's, was locked up. It looked deserted. When she tried again a few weeks later, still hopeful, it had become a confectionery shop. The new proprietors said the previous occupants had died or gone away. She felt her enquiries met with odd looks, so she wondered whether the shop had closed because of some problem with the authorities.

She could have asked Anne Jukes. After so long out of touch, she did not know how to make an approach. Then someone told her there was a new printer not far away from her house, just off Holborn. Hers was a business venture; with no moment for sentiment, Juliana packed up her designs and went there.

A young man was working the press. He had a vague air, but he was slowly doing the job, without supervision. A bell had tinkled briskly on Juliana's entry, but the apprentice or journeyman barely looked up. The shop seemed to stock mainly sermons and schoolbooks. Juliana, who could never resist new works, spotted on a shelf *A Treasury of English Wit*, nudging a Latin grammar and books on mathematics; against *Practical Remedies for Gout and Sciatica*, her eye lingered on a handbook of Women's Diseases . . .

There was a small pile of *Mercurius Politicus* – an edition Juliana had not seen; it would be published on Thursday – tomorrow.

'Can I buy this already?'

'Not supposed to,' answered the young man. He finally turned to talk to her. 'You can have it if you hide it.'

'How do you obtain them so early?'

'Our printer writes articles sometimes.'

This dismayed Juliana, who feared such a public man would not want her domestic commission. The youth assured her they undertook all work that was not obscene or seditious – though when Juliana began describing embroidery patterns, he looked affrighted. With her speech all prepared, she continued talking about her project until his eyes glazed. Stitchery patterns were something they had never attempted here; accepting strange jobs (which might have no profit) went beyond his authority . . . 'You should speak to my master.'

Juliana lost faith in her pitch and faltered. 'Maybe another day, when he is not too busy.'

'Suit yourself.' The young man turned back to the press, which was rude. Juliana had not quite finished speaking and she was aware from the bell behind her that another customer must have come into the shop. 'Of course,' added Miles, grinning oddly over his work, 'the correct way to commission a printer is to summon him to a tavern and ply him hard with drink – but my master is clean-living, so you may simply ask him . . .'

Annoyed now, Juliana crisply picked up her drawings and turned around, ready to share a disapproving frown with whoever stood behind her.

It was the printer himself. He was listening, quiet and serious, just inside the door. His tall height blocked part of the light through the glazing. She felt a shock: how blue his eyes were. He had been waiting a little wryly for her to notice him. Now that she had, he flushed faintly.

He stepped forward, offering his hand in conventional good manners. Juliana responded. As they clasped hands, he pulled hers in closer to him – an instinctive, momentary gesture. He may not have realised he did it.

The day was fine and he wore his coat fully unbuttoned. So although Gideon Jukes let go of her hand politely and her fingers slipped away through his in the same movement, Juliana had felt through his linen shirt the man's warmth and the strong beat of his heart.

Chapter Sixty-Nine

Dunbar and London: 1650–51

'We are in the hands of God.'

So pronounced a surgeon after the battle of Dunbar. He assumed this would spread well-being among his patients, those who had fought for the New Model Army and who had just been vouchsafed yet another glorious indication that God favoured them as His own. It carried extra force in Scotland, where the Covenanters were equally certain that God was all theirs. To worship the same God as your enemy, and to worship Him with exactly the same rigour, expecting the same signs of favour, might be unsettling. Thoughtful worshippers could be uneasy about placing God in a dilemma. But since Dunbar, the Kirkmen must know what God thought. Knowing it too, the New Model Army was once more cocksure and chipper.

Nevertheless, patients extracted from a battlefield view everything through the prism of pain. Disfigurement had already claimed casualties. Disease lay in wait. Death was smiling at the surgeon's shoulder, with his tally-stick ready to be notched. To a man lying on a blood-soaked pallet with his energy ebbing out of him, the words 'We are in the hands of God' spoken by a surgeon meant only one thing: there was no hope. To a surgeon, it was inconceivable that anyone else could be given credit for saving a patient, even God. God fought the battles, surgeons patched up the wreckage afterwards.

His name was Mr Nichols. He was short, stout and unspeakably abrupt. He was compassionate about his patients when addressing an audience, yet saw them as living experiments and rarely spoke directly *to* them. He thought explanations were wasted on woozy soldiers, who might not understand what he said, rarely answered his questions accurately, would not follow his orders and might die on him.

*   *   *

The blow to Gideon Jukes's cranium had only banged him uncon-scious temporarily. Time on the battlefield seemed to stretch out, increased by his terror. Among the carnage, he was found early. He was stretchered off rapidly. He reached the surgeon quicker than might have happened after a less tremendous victory. If there truly were only forty wounded on the English side, his turn for diagnosis and treatment would come fast. Even though surgeons were instructed to attend the victims from both sides, regimental commanders would insist that their own were looked after first.

Gideon woke up, pleased to find himself able to think disparaging thoughts. He heard Mr Nichols inform admiring bystanders that the patient's wakening was a blessing, because those who went into deep comas from their wounds, or the medical procedures that resulted, rarely woke up again. Gideon Jukes eyed the man balefully. He could see. He could scowl. It was a start. But he was a soldier and he knew when death was continuing to eye him up.

Gideon's mentality remained tough enough. He wanted to live. His body fought for it automatically, however weak he felt and however terrible the pain. When he first came round, the pain was worse than he thought anyone could stand. He imagined this would not soon improve.

Once Gideon Jukes caught the surgeon's eye, he warranted a lot of attention. He had so many wounds that were interesting – which he realised meant dangerous. He lay listening to a lecture on which of these wounds must be dealt with most urgently. Removal of the bullet in his body took priority, for leaving it in was likely to kill him. Removing it was just as likely to do that.

The surgeon enjoyed probing. He tried to find the bullet by asking where the pain felt worst and then fiddling just there; he was adept at causing more agony as a way to test if he was getting warm. When initial searches failed, he instructed that Gideon must be levered up into the exact position he had been in when he was shot – or as close as could be managed, given his frailty. Impressed onlookers murmured, while medical assistants sat Gideon up like a rider on a horse, for more probe-work.

Mr Nichols decided an incision would be made to his back – as if he was not already punctured enough. 'If the slug has pierced his lung, there is nothing to be done; such patients die . . .'

Gideon did not feel the cut too much. The bullet popped out rapidly and neatly, he gathered. There was mild applause. Too soon to relax – there had to be a further search down the track of the bullet to find all rags, dirt or bone splinters, otherwise infection would set in.

Four days. Gideon knew the situation: if you were going to die of infected wounds, it took four days. You just had to hope all bits and splinters would be found and taken out of you, all dirt cleansed. You prayed for a good bullet that had stayed intact. You hoped none of your own bones had shattered or, if so, that all fragments would be noticed and meticulously scraped away.

At Colchester, when ammunition ran low, bullets had been moulded from old waterpipes. They were full of impurities, which may have caused the story that the enemy had used poisoned bullets, deliberately rolled in sand. At Dunbar, Gideon was offered his bullet as a memento. It looked smooth and whole. It was lead. That was good. Lead did not rust in the body, unlike iron and brass.

The sword-cut in his thigh was examined, cleaned with cloths that had been moistened with oil of turpentine; to remove suppurating matter, the surgeon inserted a drain, or tent, made of absorbent white cloth – clean, if Gideon was lucky – to which a silk thread was attached, to prevent its being lost inside the body. Part of the wound was immediately sutured, using glover's stitch, a firm, even stitch that would not stretch out of shape in either direction. All Gideon's penetrating wounds were dressed with pads of medicated lint, then bandaged; Mr Nichols was proud of his bandage-rolling technique. He did it with panache.

Skeletal damage was dismissed as deep bruising. Surgeons were only interested in ribs if they stuck out through flesh or if there was evidence that they had punctured an organ. Gideon's coughing-up of blood caused mild concern, but apparently only time – or death – would cure that.

His head wound was reckoned more painful than dangerous. The blow had scraped along the scalp, without fracturing the skull or opening it up. Nichols was disappointed. He wanted the challenge of skinflaps, fractures, shattered bone and sight of brains. He liked to drill extra holes with his trepanning equipment. *Just to make sure the patient fails to thrive*, thought Gideon glumly.

Gideon had lost a lot of blood. He had lost so much, there was no question he could be further bled by the surgeon. Nichols was disappointed again.

The dislocated shoulder was to cause most trouble.

'It is a luxation, to be sure; I can feel the round bone lying out. His elbow hangs away from his side, and compared with the other, it is backwards . . .' It would not move forwards either. The man tried that. Gideon reacted badly. 'Bear up, Captain Jukes! Let us have no girlishness. Can you bring your hand to your mouth – no, see there is great pain! – or reach out to the wall beside you? No. A luxation – this is easy to cure in children, not so easy with grown men whose bodies have become muscular . . .'

Mr Nichols first tried manual replacement, pulling the bone forwards and upwards, while pressing Gideon's elbow to his side with one thigh. It failed. He tried again, using an assistant to press the elbow against Gideon's ribs, so the surgeon himself could apply full leverage higher up. It failed. A strongman was sent for. Gideon was suspended on this hunk's shoulder, so his own weight might correct the fault. It failed. Physical assistance was applied. A halter was made from bandage, incorporating a bolster which was fixed under Gideon's armpit while he sat on a low seat and the surgeon hauled on the bandage with all his might. No luck. Then the surgeon tried again, with Gideon lying on the ground; the surgeon sat behind him, the assistant lay alongside . . . Gideon was tiring badly, but they assured him this had been successful. 'It is knapt in, but must now be managed, to retain it.'

All this exertion had damaged his other wounds, which would have to be re-dressed. A cataplasm was prescribed; that sounded dismal, but turned out only to be a poultice based on breadcrumbs and herbs. Gideon coughed up more blood. No one took any notice. He was covered with good blankets and allowed to sleep.

Gideon remained ill for many weeks. The congestion in his lungs only very slowly reduced. His strength took even longer to recover and the penetrating wounds needed more weeks to heal. When Mr Nichols took out the drain, *that* left an ulcerated hole. Gideon became depressed. His shoulder still hurt, his arm was awkward and painful; he was convinced that the bone was imperfectly set. It was his right arm; he was right-handed.

He watched comrades die of wounds and disease. A clerk came around from time to time, to write letters home and take down wills. Gideon had a will written; at the time, he thought it wise. He left everything jointly to his brother Lambert and Robert Allibone. He declined to write home, however; why worry them? He had nobody else he could write to. It struck him that he had been fighting for years for the right to live as he wanted, yet had no household of his own, and might lose even his work if his arm never mended. He wanted a home and family, to work for them and to spend leisure time in their company. He would have to marry. A woman who could make his pulse rush with desire, while the thought of her made him laugh out loud, then quieten into deepest melancholy as he missed her . . . There were women like that. He had learned it. He could go back to London and look for one.

Perhaps at least his broken heart was mending.

At the turn of the year, which was a bad time for sailing, he was given a choice of being taken to Edinburgh or risking the long sea-voyage to London. He chose to go home. If he drowned on the way, it would solve everything.

He arrived safely, though he had been seasick and half starved because the food was dreadful; he had deteriorated while kept down in the half-flooded, rat-infested, permanently dark bilges. It was too cold and rough to lie on deck. Gideon was in a sorry state when he was carried to the soldiers' hospital at the Savoy. He was taken there after claiming he had nowhere to go and no one to look after him. He did not want to impose the burden of nursing him on Lambert's wife. Besides, the house in Bread Street would always be his parents' house; now they were gone, Gideon had stopped feeling it was home.

The Savoy had been a royal establishment for poor relief. Indigent locals who were neither too drunk nor too filthy to tolerate would be admitted by the master in the evening, set to pray for their royal founder, then offered a bed in a dormitory. Taken over for the Parliamentary sick and wounded, some of the rickety beds still had old blue counterpanes with red Tudor roses and gold portcullises. The governor and staff no longer wore red rose uniforms, but continued the old spirit of benevolent care, with a doctor and surgeon available but strict rules of behaviour: fines for missing church; pillory or cashiering for drunkenness and swearing; expulsion for marrying a nurse.

The nurses were mainly soldiers' widows. They were reputed all to be looking very keenly for new husbands. Some achieved it. The one

Gideon liked best was already spoken for. He could have persuaded her to ditch her betrothed, but he never thought to try.

The punishing journey from Scotland had aggravated his shoulder pain and Gideon saw his muscles were wasting too. The last thing he wanted was a withered arm. The Savoy surgeon admitted to insufficient expertise but sent him around London bone-setters one by one. All agreed that the dislocation looked cured, but was not; the stubborn round bone had remained out of place. New measures were attempted. A padded wooden staff was tried, to extend his arm and force back the joint. A rope suspended from a pulley was used to hang him up. Gideon was made to climb three steps of an upright ladder, during which ordeal, being too tall for the room, he banged his head badly. Finally, he went to a surgeon called Mr Elishak, who charged astronomical fees and who told him that since all else had failed, he must submit to the *glosso-comium.* 'We call it the Commander. It is of some use where the luxation has existed for long periods, in a strong man whose limbs are resistant to manual manipulation.'

'Why has nobody suggested this before?' asked Gideon.

'It must be used with great care. Accidents can happen.'

'Oh excellent news!'

'Face it, Captain Jukes: at this moment you cannot work, you cannot write or cut your meat, you cannot lie easy in your bed, you cannot hold your sweetheart on your knee. The pain has etched years upon you, and though you may have been once an even-tempered man, you have become fractious.'

'Damnation, not I!' raved the patient, irritably.

'Oh, Captain, I was warned that you are choleric. The Savoy matron, a woman of sense and experience, considers I should examine your skull, lest you have suffered untreated cranial damage . . .'

'There is nothing wrong with my head,' growled Gideon. 'Do your worst with the device!'

The Commander was a long wooden box, lined with padding, but fitted with a frightening array of pulleys. With this instrument of torture, the new surgeon applied swift traction of extreme severity. At least it was soon over.

Gideon thought he could feel a difference straightaway. Mr Elishak knew his stuff. He spent longer writing up Gideon's case-notes for his memoirs than he had spent fixing the joint. His enormous fee was enhanced by plagiarising patients' misery for his own glory: *'One GJ, a soldier wounded at the battle of Dunbar, I cured of a most stubborn luxation with apt practice of the* glossocomium, *where many others had had unsuccess even though the patient was co-operative . . .'*

Gideon lay speechless, listening to the scrawl of the quill pen. Afterwards, he was fastened in a plaster bandage made with oil, a variety of white lead, and what Mr Elishak called 'argillaceous earth', his own mixture of pungent wet clay. Gideon promised to be diligent in allowing the posture of the joint to be retrained. Anything to be rid of surgeons.

He was returned to the Savoy, where shortly afterwards Robert Allibone discovered his whereabouts and came to collect him. Now Gideon allowed himself to be carried to Bread Street. Anne Jukes hired a nurse for his intimate care. He saw little of Anne, and less of Lambert. He sensed trouble in the house. Unwilling to face whatever new crisis had befallen them, Gideon ignored the signs until he was able to emerge from his bedchamber to resume normal life.

One day soon afterwards when he entered the kitchen, he found a cold hearth beside which sat Anne, weeping. Gideon could not remember his mother ever letting her fire go out. He could no longer avoid the question: 'What has Lambert done?'

Whatever it was, Anne could not even bear to name the crime. She shook her head, sobbing louder; then she jumped up and turned to Gideon for comfort. She flung herself upon him, to his great embarrassment. He was an unmarried man, with normal masculine reactions; had this happened before he met Juliana Lovell, he would have been entirely vulnerable. Anne Jukes was more than ten years older than he but she had always been good-looking and Gideon had a soft heart.

Somehow, however, he recoiled from danger. Anne's old regard for him had increased, apparently, into a conviction that she had married the wrong brother. For a moment she clung to him but there were advantages in being tall; simply by standing straight, Gideon could choose who kissed him.

Anne sprang back before she made herself ridiculous by jumping up and down to get at him. She would not repeat her mistake. They passed it off as a moment of misery only.

When Gideon insisted on learning more about whatever turmoil his brother was in, Anne went to their chamber and returned with a piece of paper. Lambert had devoted himself to spiritual exploration of the most tortuous kind. He had written down a memo to himself:

1 *That you shall not acknowledge nor yield obedience to any other gods but me*
2 *That it is lawful to drink, swear and revel, and to lie with any woman whatsoever*
3 *That there is no Sabbath, no Heaven, no Hell, no Resurrection, and that both soul and body die together.*

'Well, now you see!' cried Anne bitterly.

Indeed, Gideon did. Number 3 was a dangerous dictum. Number 2 was a complete shocker. He groaned, while Anne told him the worst in a taut voice: 'These people whom *your brother* favours affirm that – in their words as said to me by *your brother* – "the man who tipples deepest, swears the frequentest, commits adultery, incest or buggers the oftenest" –'

'*Buggers?*'

'Do you know what it means?'

'Oh, I have an idea . . .'

Not Lambert. Definitely not Lambert. But to *lie with any woman whatsoever* would appeal to him.

Anne continued bitterly: 'They say, "Who blasphemes the impudent-est, and perpetrates the most notorious crimes, with the highest hand and rigidest resolution, is the dearest darling to be placed in the tribunal Throne of Heaven. Each Brother of their fellowship ought to take his Fellow-Female on his knee, saying, Let us lie down and multiply . . ." He wanted me to join with him, but I would not do it, Gideon. He boasts to me of wicked women in the sect who have let him have his way. He claims that these sinful brethren should not only make use of a man's wife, but of his estate, goods and chattels also, for all things are common . . . He asks what difference is there between this and what the Diggers believe – while in truth, there is a very great difference!'

'Oh indeed.' Gideon felt very ill now. 'Where is he?'

'*Your brother* is at a Christmas revel in the Horn Tavern in Fleet Street.'

'*Christmas?*'

'Free will is lawful. There is no sin. There are no laws.'

Sadly for Lambert that was untrue; there were laws directly forbidding this curious phase of his development. The sect he had joined was singled out for government disapproval.

'Do you know what takes place in this congregation?'

Anne railed bitterly, 'The men will make free with the women. They will be gambolling, dancing and revelling – I suppose, you and he being so close-knit, you are going there to join him?'

'No,' replied Gideon with a gloomy sigh. 'I am going there to try to fetch him back.'

Small chance, he thought. What grocer was going to turn up a chance to eat Christmas plum pudding and then to lie with everybody else's wife?

Whatever the Bible said, in respectable City of London society a man *was* his brother's keeper.

Although wobbly on his legs after so long as an invalid, Gideon walked to Fleet Street. The Horn Tavern was easy to find, due to a large crowd of fascinated onlookers who had congregated outside. Sounds of uninhibited celebration filled the street. Through a window Gideon saw wild dancing, with some participants dressed all in white and some of them only half dressed. One woman was walking on her hands upside down, with a man holding her legs like a wheelbarrow. Her skirts had fallen and she was bare from the waist down. Men had women sitting on their laps, whose bodies they were enthusiastically exploring while the women rejoiced and welcomed it.

As Gideon approached unsteadily, the tavern door was flung open. A man rushed out, stark naked. A beer-belly and the effects of the chilly December weather reduced any glimpse of his privates to the minimum, which was his only recourse to modesty – though Gideon saw he had sensibly retained his shoes.

The crowd shrieked with glee. 'Our Adam wants no figleaf – only a three-leaf clover!' When the hideously familiar apparition gesticulated, they pulled back nervously.

The capering figure had spotted Gideon. 'Brother! I cannot stop – I have the call!'

Gideon made a grab, but with his right arm still in plaster it was difficult. The wild nude shrugged him off and careered onwards, galloping away down Fleet Street. A cat-calling crowd ran in hot pursuit. Gideon leaned against the tavern wall, feeling weak and in despair.

Lambert Jukes had found a fine old way to punish his wife for her foray into Digging. He had become a Ranter.

Chapter Seventy

London: 1651–53

Lambert Jukes might have been discreetly plucked from Ranting, had he not thrown off his clothes before his dash through the streets. A stark naked, portly man in his forties, all flabby white flesh and ecstatic vision, made an easy target for parish constables. He attracted attention, as screaming women fled, mongrels barked, boys pointed and men gaped – men who were perhaps lost in the wish (Lambert suggested later, rather hopefully), that they too would have cut such an impressive figure.

'Or perhaps not,' muttered his baleful brother Gideon.

Lambert was cornered at the Fleet Conduit. Although he managed to floor three law officers in the process, they wrapped the flailing culprit in a blanket to avert public outrage and carried him to nearby Bridewell. His relatives could only hope that he would be diagnosed as crazy. Treatment of the insane was dire, but if Lambert was deemed accountable for his beliefs and actions, criminal law kicked in. He would be tried on a capital charge. Ranting was seen as so dangerous politically, there was no chance of bail.

Major William Rainborough sent expressions of concern. Anne and Gideon would have gladly done without this. Anne blamed the major for encouraging her husband's extreme views; he had paid for documents Lambert had read. Rainborough was an awkward connection; in view of his association with the Ranters, Parliament formally designated him dangerous. An ordinance forbade him from ever again acting as a justice of the peace in England. William Rainborough would make fruitless attempts to gain a navy post, only giving up when he abandoned England and emigrated to live among relatives in Massachusetts. He was protected to some extent by his late brother's eminence, or he would probably have been imprisoned. Rather than accept this kind of patronage, the Jukes family rallied to look after their own.

Gideon's visits to Lambert in prison horrified him. Once a royal palace and later used to lodge visiting foreign dignitaries, Bridewell was an enormous complex on the Thames at Blackfriars, rambling around three huge courtyards. Its glory days were long over. For a hundred years this had been a place of relief for the poor – but it was always a hard refuge. On arrival, both sexes were stripped and whipped, a spectacle that attracted so much salacious public attention that a special viewing gallery had been built. There was now a hospital for soldiers, where the grim conditions made Gideon delighted he had been taken to the Savoy instead. The general inmates included not only the indigent poor, but wilful beggars, rogues of all types and criminals from brutal organised gangs. It was also a standard prison for gutter prostitutes.

In this company, Lambert's insouciance was swiftly crushed. He soon cut an anxious, sorry figure. Gideon and Robert Allibone worked hard to have him transferred to the Gatehouse, a lock-up attached to Westminster Abbey that was used mainly to house Royalist officers. They chose to accept Parliament's view that Ranting was a political offence, an affront to the respectability of the Commonwealth. If they had been prepared to claim that Lambert was out of his wits, an alternative would have been Bedlam, but in that screeching madhouse they now feared he would go really insane. By contrast, Bridewell was the original house of correction, where inmates were made to work – either at carding and spinning, or, for intransigent cases, cleaning the sewers. Lambert submitted sweetly to being put in a sewer gang although later, when his health broke down in the filthy conditions, he gave in to his brother's entreaties and was transferred to a better cell in the quieter prison. By then he seemed almost sad to leave the new friends he had made among the gong-cleaners, as the sewermen were called. At the Gatehouse, Gideon assured him, all he would be required to do among the cavaliers was wear beribboned lovelocks and write lyric poetry. His brother greeted this idea with more horror than he had shown on shovelling ordure.

Being arrested naked had shocked Lambert. When he came to himself – 'When the drink wore off!' his wife muttered – he refused to recant, but ceased raving and dancing. They were fortunate. Others clung unrepentantly to their beliefs. One Ranter interred at Bridewell was a defiant shoemaker. Whenever he heard any mention of God, he would laugh and say, 'he believed money, good clothes, good meat, and drink, tobacco and merry company to be gods'. Anne heard that the wife had remonstrated, but the man retorted coldly that 'if she would give him any beer or tobacco he would take it, but as for her advice, she might keep it to herself'.

Scared that Lambert might be infected with these attitudes, Anne Jukes did not waste breath on nagging. She made a petition to Parliament. Mary Overton, wife of the Leveller, Richard, helped her write it. She pleaded Lambert's long military service and his dismal health since Colchester, then cited her own need for support and companionship. Lambert's own willingness to work meekly at a filthy job while in Bridewell may have helped convince the authorities that he was worth saving.

It took many months to work through the process, but at the end of summer Lambert was fined and pardoned. Gideon retrieved him from the Gatehouse and led his crushed, hangdog, enfeebled brother back home to Bread Street. Continuing to live with Lambert and Anne, Gideon then devoted himself to re-establishing normal family life.

It was not easy. Other mystic sects existed. In an effort to rebuild their marriage through shared interests, Anne and Lambert Jukes joined one together. They chose a visionary, Deist, anti-Trinitarian group called Reeveonians. Their sect had been established in February 1652 when John Reeve, a London tailor, received three visions which appointed him God's Prophet (he said), along with his cousin, Lodowick Muggleton. Their followers acclaimed them as the 'two witnesses' mentioned in the Book of Revelations, who would preach to an ungodly world in preparation for the beginning of the final days. Reeve and Muggleton honoured Reason and Faith. Gideon and Robert Allibone thought Reason had little to do with it, but they were known sceptics.

Confusingly, the group thought the soul was mortal, which meant all human existence died with the body and this sect looked for a heaven on earth rather than an afterlife. However, they also believed the Millennium was close at hand, so it was vital to prepare. Preparation took an amiable form. They met in taverns, where they held discreet Bible readings and sang godly tunes over a few rounds of drinks – during which they were generally viewed by other people only as a slightly eccentric private party.

Reeveonians, or Muggletonians as they became after John Reeve died, did not actively seek new members; they waited for those with an interest to approach. People who asked to receive the Revealed Word were welcomed; those who subsequently declined the Revealed Word were condemned. Perhaps as a result of this uncompromising outlook, they had a limited membership. That generally kept them below the sightlines of the authorities, though both Reeve and Muggleton were imprisoned in Bridewell for their beliefs in 1653, at which point Anne and Lambert Jukes let their membership slide. One spell in Bridewell was enough for Lambert. Besides, the grocery business was picking up.

Privately relieved, Gideon had kept quiet, because the Muggletonians had some likeable features: they supported toleration and avoided strict religious doctrines. A problem was that they attracted disheartened followers from crazier sects. Eventually Laurence Clarkson, the Ranters' founder, moved in on the group, which caused consternation; he quarrelled bitterly with Lodowick Muggleton and brazenly hijacked the leadership. Gideon cynically suggested Clarkson was attracted by the Muggletonians' female following; leaders of peculiar sects traditionally expect sickly adoration from female acolytes. By this time, fortunately, Anne and Lambert Jukes were long gone.

Lambert subsided as a religious fanatic. He lived quietly, hoping to avoid notice. Nothing was said by the Society of Grocers about his naked run, perhaps because it was known that Anne Jukes had been long-suffering. Livery companies tended to respect their members' wives, since most were formidable. Publicly forgiven, Lambert devoted himself to grocery and good works. From then on he occupied the traditional position of a City of London liveryman: under the thumb of his wronged wife.

Once a month or so, Lambert would courageously remind Anne that she too once had a revolutionary fling. They would excitedly discuss whether 'work together, eat together' was a more attractive doctrine than 'tippling, swearing, committing adultery, incest, buggery, dancing and gambolling, ranting naked in the street and sleeping with other men's wives'. Inevitably one thought one thing, one the other. If Gideon was at home, he sneaked out to the back yard to smoke a pipe of Virginia tobacco on the site of his father's aborted house-of-easement. Only occasionally did he throw in comments: how fortunate it was that disputatiousness filled awkward lulls in conversation, for instance. Irony was poorly received.

Yet, worn out by hard work in their business and by the encroachments of age, the couple gradually lost their inclination to wrangle.

Their arguments may have put Gideon off remarrying. Although he had thought of it on his return from Dunbar, somehow he never got around to it. Lambert and Anne occasionally paraded spinsters and widows in front of him (there were plenty to choose from while they were Muggletonians). Gideon would seem polite, but he would quickly disappear to the print shop. Lambert suggested Gideon did not know what he was looking for; Anne suspected he knew only too well.

Robert and Gideon ran the print shop together after Gideon's return to London. Despite their long friendship, it became an awkward fit. The reasons were practical. Robert had always been the master and, although they were nominally partners, he had run their business by himself ever since Gideon went to Newport Pagnell. That was nearly a decade ago. Now in his late forties, Robert was still fit and active. Gideon, though fifteen years younger, was limited in what he could do physically. His shoulder had eventually been righted by Mr Surgeon Elishak's sharp use of the Commander, but he had been warned he must not strain the joint with any heavy work. He had to be careful about turning the press or lifting bales of paper and piles of documents. He could set type, but that had never been his forte or his interest.

Ever affectionate and sympathetic, Robert suggested that Gideon should concentrate on building up a specialist list of copyrights. 'Just do not tell me we should cover poetry.' Gideon reckoned that with the coming of peace there would be new schools and a need for instructional material. He set about commissioning dictionaries, grammars and other textbooks. It was hard work for the compositor and at first sales were not brisk, but it kept him happy in a period when he was struggling at home and felt uncertain about his personal future.

Peace at last seemed a possibility. In 1651 Cromwell had lured the King and his Scots' allies into making a dash south; he imposed yet another set-piece crushing victory on them at Worcester. After some weeks on the run, including his famous night spent in the boughs of an oak tree, Charles II fled from England with a price on his head.

The Scots, meanwhile, had lost too many armies to continue; they were granted toleration of religion within their own country, but a powerful army under General Monck stayed in Scotland to ensure order.

There would be no more Presbyterian invasions. With all the three kingdoms quiescent at least temporarily, the new Commonwealth was sufficiently confident and free from home disturbances to turn its attention outward. Once Admiral Blake had driven away Prince Rupert, the navy was freed up to represent the Commonwealth's maritime interests. A Navigation Act was passed, which forbade the importation of goods into England or English colonies except in English ships or ships of the goods' country of origin. Aimed against Royalist-supporting Holland, it seriously affected the Dutch carrying trade, so after a three-year war at sea they capitulated. There would be setbacks, but this marked the establishment of Britain's maritime might.

In domestic policy, peace was welcome but nothing changed the fact that a way to govern the country had never been decided. The Rump Parliament was still sitting. By July 1652, the army was petitioning for new, free elections to end this moribund body, while Rump members were shamelessly attempting to thwart the proposed arrangements. In April 1653 came an upheaval. Oliver Cromwell heard that an Act was being passed in the Commons that would enable Rump members to continue in their seats without re-election. Informed of this by a series of breathless messengers, Cromwell strode to Parliament. He was dressed in black, with a tall black hat and grey woollen stockings, like an ordinary citizen, though he took troops.

At first he sat quietly listening. Then, just as the bill was about to be voted on, he rose in his place and, taking off his hat, began to speak. Initially, he addressed the House calmly, then – as he could do – he systematically wound himself into a towering rage. He informed the members they were useless, thinking only of themselves, that they had become tyrants and the supporters of tyrants. 'The Lord hath done with you,' he cried, 'and hath chosen other instruments for the carrying on of his work who are more worthy.' No plan had been laid as to who this should be.

Fully incandescent, Cromwell crushed his hat upon his head and strode on to the floor of the House. 'You are no Parliament,' he shouted, stamping his foot. 'I say you are no Parliament. Come, come, I will put an end to your prating. Call them in!' His soldiers grimly marched into the Chamber. The members scurried to leave, while Cromwell flung taunts, calling some drunkards, others unjust persons and evil-livers. Then came the most famous moment. Catching sight of the Mace as it lay upon the table, Oliver cried derisively, 'What shall we do with this bauble? – Here, take it away.'

The House was empty. Locking the door, Cromwell stomped off. So, after twelve monumental years, the Long Parliament ended.

Many people turned against Cromwell then. Amongst long-term radicals, feeling ran high. Edward Sexby changed his allegiance. So did John Wildman. John Lilburne was so incensed he returned from exile in Bruges, was thrown into Newgate Prison and between June and August was on trial, supported by Richard Overton. As a measure against subversion, John Thurloe, a member of the Council of State, was given sole charge of collecting intelligence. His role included oversight of press censorship. For him it was the start of a serious career as a spymaster, a career in which one day Gideon Jukes would work with him.

With the abolition of the Rump came further measures against printers. The press had been in difficulties politically for a long time. Almost as soon as the Star Chamber was abolished and freedom from censorship announced, Parliament had regretted it. Attempts to rein back began immediately and repression had continued ever since. Many of the news-sheets that had sprung up during the civil war had already been extinguished, though so far the *Public Corranto* struggled on. After the King was executed new laws had forced Robert to pay a bond of three hundred pounds, promising not to publish seditious or scandalous material.

Gideon knew that Robert Allibone was incensed. Robert saw Cromwell's expulsion of the Rump as new tyranny. The partners had had some arguments because Gideon was afraid that free elections would lead to a Presbyterian government. He shared the Army's exasperation with the Rump's attempts to self-perpetuate itself, yet he was anxious not to see the New Model Army's achievements thrown out. So Gideon did not entirely share Robert's anguish.

He was not *surprised* when Robert produced a new pamphlet under his old pseudonym, 'Mr A.R.', calling it *The Bauble-Botherer's Betrayal*. What was unusual was that for once Robert must have been careless. Gideon was astonished how fast the authorities reacted. Perhaps Robert had been under suspicion before. Perhaps this time an informant supplied an address. At any rate, early one morning, when Gideon and Lambert were having their breakfast in Bread Street, the printers' apprentice, Miles Gentry, burst in. Miles was hysterical, crying that the print shop had been trashed in a dawn raid. Robert had been dragged out of bed in his nightshirt and arrested.

Gideon ran to the shop. The weeping Miles stumbled at his heels. Everything was as he said: the print shop had been crudely turned over. Papers littered the street, but Gideon could tell that many printed items must have been removed. All copies of *The Bauble-Botherer's Betrayal* had been seized. Back editions of the *Public Corranto* were gone too. Metal letters had been tossed from their trays and strewn about the shop. Ink had been emptied out in the street gutters. Most extraordinary was that where the press had always stood was now an empty space.

Miles went down on his knees, fervently gathering up the scattered type, especially Robert's favourite, his Double Pica Roman, a clean and readable font he had used throughout his career after secretly smuggling the letter set from Flanders. Recent laws forbade the importation of printers' letters, implements or presses; replacements would be not only expensive but almost impossible to obtain.

Gideon stared at ink-stained floorboards, almost unable to believe his eyes. 'They took the press!'

'They brought a cart for the purpose, Gideon.'

'Robert has had that press as long as I have known him – we lugged it here from Fleet Alley, before the war!'

'It is confiscated. The men said they had orders to find all the obnoxious publications, seize the press and take Robert to the Tower.'

Word had run around the tight community. Other printers came from Coleman Street to commiserate. Witnesses were found. In that conspiratorial area, everyone was on constant alert for interference. A dawn raid might have an element of surprise for the victim but it could not be achieved without attracting a crowd. Miles was too distressed to describe the raid, but others came forward to tell how Robert had been subjected to a barrage of questions. He had with great spirit returned what seemed to be printers' standard answers:

'He was shown a pamphlet called *The Bauble-Botherer's Betrayal* and asked who the author of it was. Master Allibone stoutly replied, he was scarce able to say who was the author of it. About two weeks before, he had printed a book *like* the one he was being shown, but he could not say for certain whether that was the exact one or not. So he was then asked where was the original copy of the pamphlet, to which our Robert mildly returned that after we have printed and corrected works of that nature, the copies are thrown out as waste paper. "I expect," said he, with his whimsical smile, "it is being used as bum-fodder in the privy by some large-buttocked alderman." They pressed him again so, looking closely at the pamphlet, he claimed that there was some alteration from what he had printed; it might not be the same, and for all he knew it had been reprinted by others twenty times or more . . . He has answered interrogations before, of course –' It was news to Gideon. 'So they asked how many he had printed and he told them he had no idea, but the usual number would be one thousand. That was the grain of truth, you know, to make his other answers sound reasonable. Afterwards he protested, as we generally do, that unless the work is a matter of controversy, we never keep any spare copies.'

'Unfortunately,' said Miles miserably, 'the soldiers then found some hidden.'

'So they asked, who was "Mr A.R." and the good Allibone declared he had no idea, never having seen him before that day.'

As Gideon guffawed, another printer took up the story: 'Master Allibone was then informed that exceptions had been taken to the pamphlet. He was accused that the matters contained in it are erroneous, profane and highly scandalous.'

'He is never profane,' sniffed Gideon.

'True. But by then they were hauling out his press, which made him apoplectic. Thereupon he hit a soldier, who struck him in return with a musket-butt. And so they carried him away.'

Robert had been taken not to the Tower, it turned out, but to the Poultry Compter, a local civil prison, close by and reached down Ironmongers Lane. When Gideon rushed to this prison, again with Miles, he was at first told he could not see his friend. Then, a shamefaced jailor admitted that Robert had been brought here after he became unwell on the intended journey to the Tower. The man took Gideon to a cell. No one had explained, but as soon as Gideon knelt down beside his friend, he knew. Robert lay quite motionless. He was on his back, still in his nightshirt and bare feet, the nightshirt opened over the chest. He was dead.

Robert was still warm, as warm as if he lived. Gideon crouched with him, horrified. Miles could not accept the truth; he began rubbing Robert's hands, calling out to his master to revive.

'Miles, Miles, Miles! It is no use.'

A doctor was still talking to the staff. As Gideon held his old friend's lifeless body on his lap, this man came to the cell door, looking at them curiously.

'He is gone, sir. He was gone before I came. The shock of his arrest brought it on. His heart had a massive convulsion and he was taken from the world in a few minutes. He cannot have known what was happening.'

So Robert Allibone was lost, at two years short of fifty, as much a casualty of the civil war as if he had served in the army. His friends buried him with bunches of sea-green ribbons lying on the coffin. Copies of his most fervent pamphlets were hidden inside it with him, especially those that had been confiscated on the orders of the new, 'Barebones' Parliament – an act of defiance, which they deemed would have pleased him. Large numbers of the printing community attended the funeral, along with many civilian Levellers, foremost among them the estimable William Walwyn. Many tears were shed for Robert openly that day, others more privately. His partner Gideon Jukes and their apprentice Miles Gentry were inconsolable.

Chapter Seventy-One

Shoe Lane: Autumn 1653

When he walked into his print shop and found Juliana Lovell talking
to Miles, Gideon Jukes froze. He recognised the nape of her neck first,
then her voice, her figure, her determined way of speaking out even to
a youth who was annoying her . . . Gideon might have stepped backwards and fled, but Miles had seen him. As Juliana turned, there was
no escape. He had been a soldier, so he stood his ground.

Any other woman asking him to print embroidery designs would
have been out of luck. Forced into conversation about her request,
Gideon took refuge in his professional role. He outlined carefully what
would be involved in commissioning an engraver to draw illustrations. Even to his own ears his voice sounded colourless; he could see
Miles looking at him as if he thought Gideon was sickening. Since
Robert's death, Miles had taken obsessive care of him. The apprentice
had been shaken by the traumatic loss of his first master and was
anxious that he might be left alone in the world if anything happened
to the second. 'I accept there are precedents. Emblem books exist,
Mistress Lovell.'

'I have one!' snapped Juliana crisply. 'It is forty years out of date.
There are new fashions and I want to make them available.'

'I understand.' Ignoring the rebuke, Gideon continued to make her
aware of the complications.

Juliana interrupted irritably. 'I can pay you for this printing, Captain
Jukes. I am not begging for favours.'

Gideon was a good businessman, but acknowledged with a private
smile to himself – and to the wide-eyed Miles – that if there was one
customer who might persuade him to subsidise a commission, it would
be Juliana Lovell.

He confirmed that Miles was right; this was not a way to make large sums of money. Juliana set him straight: she wanted to offer designs mainly as a means to lure customers to her shop – 'You have a shop?'

'Haberdashery. I have returned to the trade of my grandfather.' She spoke with a mixture of defiance and pride. Grand-mère Roxanne would be horrified, but Juliana was happy with the life, and even happier to be earning a living. Gideon Jukes could see the change in her.

He thought he could find an engraver, and promised to make enquiries, perhaps ordering a sample design. Since he could not say how long this enquiry would take – both Miles and Juliana herself suspected he would conveniently 'forget' to do it – he had to ask where Juliana lived so he could find her to report. Her heart took an odd lurch, but she told him.

A few weeks later, as she was close to shutting up her business for the day, she felt slightly caught out when Gideon Jukes appeared, bearing a satchel. Catherine Keevil was with her in the shop, so Juliana left her downstairs and led Gideon up to her main room. He began laying out papers on the table, though first he put down a purse of money. Like any shopkeeper, Juliana assessed the weight of the purse by eye, without seeming to do so. He explained shamefacedly, 'I have been remiss. I promised you the wench's wages –'

'There is no need,' replied Juliana coolly – though he *had* promised and she might have been in difficulties. So when he waved aside her mild protest, she took up the money and put it away safely. She felt glad that her first good opinion of this man was now confirmed. Before Catherine reappeared they spoke of her quickly; Juliana acknowledged that she was a pleasant, willing worker who had become an essential part of her household. 'I have grown very fond of her. Indeed I could not manage without her.'

They broke off when Catherine came upstairs, now a slim, demure girl of almost twenty. She brought with her Thomas and Valentine, just home from the local petty school with their horn books. 'I taught them their letters myself,' said Juliana, 'but I think it is good for them to go out into the world now.' *Having no father*, she meant.

Gideon saw how much taller and more mature the boys were, Thomas now ten, Valentine two years younger. The hazel-eyed, brown-haired duo were not yet too big for a lone mother to keep in hand, but they had turned into real boys: slovenly, slow to move when asked, forgetful, obstreperous, prone to squabbling. Tom had something of his father's self-confidence, had Gideon known it. Val was sickly and given to whining, a mother's boy. Both stalked around, eyeing up the visitor like young dogs whose pack had been invaded by a stronger male. They parked themselves like guards either side of their mother, staring at Gideon in silence, although when the adults' conversation remained fixed on sewing and printing matters, they lost interest.

They needed to be fed, so Gideon was asked to join the family. He would not have stayed, but the printing discussion was unfinished; they were working through a draft booklet and Gideon wanted to take notes on all of the pages so he could have them set. Since the table was covered with papers, Juliana and Catherine organised a modest supper in the next-door parlour, with plates on their knees.

Over the meal, Gideon outlined how he had come to be working in Holborn. He explained Robert's death. It had taken months to get the press returned; he had had to pretend to the authorities he knew nothing about Robert's publications, but was a simple-minded dupe who only wanted to produce . . .

'Produce what, Captain?'

'Harmless poetry, I claimed.'

'Not true?'

'Not acceptable to my dear partner Robert. He was a man of great erudition, well read and the best conversationalist. But as a man of business, he despised the printing of verse and had banned me from any encouragement of poets.'

'Why was that?'

'No profit – but they expect the earth.'

'Ah! What would Master Allibone have thought of stitch patterns?'

Gideon pulled a face. 'What anyone thinks: I am out of my mind to dabble!' It was the closest he came to a joke. Mostly he spoke in the same level, subdued tone that Juliana found so disappointing. Whatever she had imagined if they chanced to meet again, it was not this.

He then told how, after he did retrieve the printing press, he decided revolutionary publishing was unsafe. The *Public Corranto* had been quashed when Robert was arrested. Gideon did not even attempt to revive it.

During his grief for his partner, he had reviewed his own ambitions. He decided to move premises. It was what Robert had done all those years before, when he shifted from Fleet Alley for a fresh start after his wife Margery died. So Gideon reversed the process. He came back to where they had worked when he was apprenticed and now he printed commercial books, school primers, spelling books, dictionaries and whatever was brought in to him by the professional men of the area. He had a growing trade with the American colonies, which had a big demand for school books.

'I noticed in your shop you deal in wit, gout and verse grammars.'

'All good lines – but my steadiest bestseller is on angling!'

Once he had told his own story, Gideon naturally asked Juliana what coincidence had brought her to the same quarter of London. She simply mentioned her guardian's legacy. With her sons present, she would not dwell on other matters.

After their meal, discussion of the proposed pattern book resumed. Catherine took away the boys, put them to bed and retired to her own room. If any tried to eavesdrop, they would only have heard polite voices as Juliana and Gideon continued to put together the draft pages.

Their work finally done, Gideon collected the drawings and Juliana's stitchery instructions into his satchel. From it he first removed a bundle of old news-sheets.

Perhaps for a second he looked uneasy. 'Customary printer's gift. Out-of-date editions. Useful for wrapping up fish heads and marrow bones. Clean your muddy heels and soles on them. People put them in the privy. As we printers say, let the nation wipe its arse on the news . . .' Juliana was slightly startled; this man had certainly not come to be romantic! Even Gideon had second thoughts. 'Bringing bum-fodder to a strange house? Apologies, madam; I must be mildly deranged . . .'

'No gift is turned away by tradespeople, Captain!'

She should have known that there was a point. Gideon lifted his hand, which had lain palm-down on the pile, apparently accidentally. Juliana read, upside down, that the top paper was called *The Moderate Intelligencer*. Gideon leafed through the first pages then read out, not looking at her: 'I thought you may not have seen this. *"By an express further from Holland, we hear that Prince Rupert is daily expected . . . he wrote letters not long since to his mother, intimating that as soon as he could hear of his brother Maurice, with those eleven ships that were carried away in the hurricano"* – he would go to his mother is intended, I presume, though this journal is too poorly edited to say so – *"His own letters say that he himself and one more"* – one more ship, it means – *"was not in it. What is become of the rest, the Lord knows."* This was at the end of March. Thinking of you, I made enquiries –'

Thinking of you? Juliana had once discussed Orlando with Anne Jukes;

Anne must have said her husband was at sea. 'Yes. There were other reports.' *Prince Rupert continues at the Palace Royal. There is no news yet of his brother Maurice . . .* A good mother, Juliana had kept news-sheets for her boys, if they were curious in future. 'Thank you. It was kind.' Her voice choked a little; she pressed her palm over her mouth. 'There was a rumour that Prince Maurice reappeared in the Mediterranean, but that was false . . . Even the two ships that survived were so worm-eaten they were quite unserviceable; I suppose in such a condition the rest were vulnerable to the storm . . .'

Gideon watched unexpected feelings rush upon Juliana. She had only ever discussed this with Mr Impey – a lawyer, with whom it had been neutral and professional. Otherwise, her deduction that Orlando must be lost had been borne in private, as she had always borne her troubles. Suddenly here was Gideon Jukes right at her dining table, agreeing: Lovell was gone. She was a widow. There would be no farewells, no explanations, nothing. Her married life was over.

Juliana had shed tears before, but her surging emotions now startled her. Gideon saw her face, just before she jumped up and swiftly left the room. She was trying to conceal the emergency, but her expression tore his heart.

He waited, uncertainly, then he followed and found her, in the little parlour next door, weeping uncontrollably. Gideon suppressed a curse, thinking he had made a bad mistake. He hardly dared approach, and Juliana held up a hand to stop him. He wanted to hold her, to console her, to let her cry at will onto his shoulder. Instead he could only stand silent in the doorway, offering at least his presence for comfort. *This grief is all for the malignant Lovell . . .* Yet he could not hate the man. Gradually he realised that he was witnessing more than straightforward torrents of grief. As Juliana wept herself into exhaustion, it was not just for love of her husband, for his suffering as he drowned, nor even for her sons' loss of their father. This was her release from years of introversion, struggle, loneliness and anxiety. It was necessary. It marked an end to that phase of her life.

When her sobs stopped, neither was embarrassed. Juliana turned away further, to begin the ghastly business of drying tears and nose-blowing.

'I am much to blame,' Gideon apologised, all humility. 'I bungled that. I did not know what to say for the best.'

Juliana still could not speak.

'Mistress Lovell, I will take my leave – do not disturb yourself; I will let myself out of the shop. Do not wait too long before you lock up properly.'

He went – not so hurriedly that he seemed to be afraid of a woman weeping, but more swiftly than she wanted. Feeling doubly bereft, Juliana slowly completed her mopping and snuffling, then she washed her hands and face. It had grown dark, so when she made her way downstairs to secure the premises she took a candle.

The shop door remained wide open. With his back to her, Gideon Jukes was leaning against the frame, disconsolately, gazing out. The street was dark and gusty. It was absolutely sheeting down with rain.

He had heard her, so Juliana went and stood in the doorway beside him. She stayed in the dry but let the weather cool her hot face. 'Come back in. You cannot go in that.' She knew she was glad. She hungered for more time with him.

Gideon did not stir. He seemed to be reminiscing. 'I was drenched often enough in the army – day after day, week after week, many a night lying out in the fields in filthy rain like this . . . You close yourself down, waiting for the misery to end – while you form dreams to take your mind away from it.' He half turned his head. His voice sharpened: 'Did you miss me?'

Convention got the better of Juliana. She fluttered uncharacteristically, 'Oh Captain Jukes, I hardly know you!'

'I believe you do.' Gideon was quieter than ever, yet no longer subdued. He had the air of a man who had reached a decision. 'I know you too,' he went on purposefully. 'Though not so well, because you hunch up in yourself. I shall have to winkle you out, when you allow me to do it. That could be good – it leaves more to discover at leisure . . . I missed you, I admit it. I carried your memory fast within me.'

He had lost the thin tone and careful formality he had used before. This was his normal voice, resonating as it had done in her reveries. Juliana luxuriated in its return. She asked him with her usual candour, 'What happened to the light lad who flirted?'

'Held in restraint.'

'I liked him!'

Gideon laughed quietly. 'I know you did.' They seemed able to speak together with astonishing honesty.

'And you liked *being* him.'

'Oh yes.' To himself, Gideon was confessing that he had never behaved before or since as he did the day of Anne Jukes's birthday and for that short time afterwards. He was not even behaving like that now; well, not yet. He could be working up to it. 'How did you like such an odd bubble of air?'

'Well, I thought him a sly-tongued rogue.' Now Juliana felt she was flirting. She had lost all her modesty, and did not care.

'Ever astute, madam! But you can trust him. Gideon Jukes: age thirty-three, height inconvenient, hair tow-coloured, eyes blue, journeyman printer, ten years fighting for liberty, some wounds but no loss of capacity' – soldiers always wanted to make *that* clear – 'clean and neat around the house. Favourite cake: gingerbread. Favourite pie: veal on a base of bacon. Favourite celebration dish: a salmagundi. True unto death.'

'True to what?'

'God, my cause, my city and family – the woman of my choice.'

Juliana let herself accept that the salmagundi in his manifesto was a heavy clue who *that* was.

The rain continued to pour incessantly. Anyone who walked outside would be soaked through at once.

'Move from the door and let me close it, Captain.'

Gideon stepped back, though he put up his hand on the edge of the door, preventing her from moving it. A gust of motion blew the candle out. It made little difference. The loss of its small light barely affected eyes that had grown used to the murk. All their senses were heightened and fixed on each other. 'Do you want me to leave you?'

'Do you want to go?'

'You know I do not.'

'*Do* I?'

There was a small, tense silence.

'You know my heart,' he said. Quiet people, Juliana thought, could be most single-minded. With this one, there was no vapid etiquette. Gideon Jukes came right out and declared himself, without prevarication or preamble. He shrugged. 'Let us be open with each other. You do not keep a strangers' lodging house; you never bid mere passers-by to shelter from the rain – nor do I linger on other women's doorsteps, hoping for an invitation.' He dropped his hand from the door, folding his arms tight across his chest. 'Here is the thing; I have to confess it – either I go now, and at once, or –' *Or I shall beg to stay with you.*

'Or?' *I will plead with you to do it.*

'We both know what will happen.' There was just enough light for Gideon to see Juliana gazing at him, questioning. Questioning not his motives, but his willingness to have those motives. She glimpsed a shadow of a smile from him that she might still doubt this. He spoke a little dryly, spelling out the situation much as he had earlier explained how drawings were printed: 'There will be kissing, and various matters that lead from it . . .'

'I am glad that you say so.' Juliana laid a hand on the door handle. 'Indeed, sir, I hope you will not think me forward – but I shall insist upon it.'

She felt extremely calm. She closed the door and turned the key in its lock. Gideon reached up and pushed a bolt home for her.

His arm dropped and came straight around Juliana, gathering her to him. She had thought she might have to stand on tiptoe, but they fitted together naturally. Gideon kissed her, gently and deferentially, though for a long time. She kissed him, making no bones about it. These were as honest and sweet as any kisses Juliana ever gave.

Soon, she took his hand to guide Gideon safely through the darkness of the haberdashery, where she knew her way around obstacles even without a candle. They came upstairs; she led him to her room. With children and a servant in the house, there was no place for turmoil, uncontrollable passion in stairwells or festoons of discarded clothes and cast-off shoes. That was not their way in any case. They had waited a long while for one another. They walked up through the house, closing doors and dousing lights almost as if it was their long-time nightly ritual. By one dim rush-light, they undressed as neatly as if they already had behind them a companionship of decades, each folding their clothes upon a chair. Only once naked, they did clasp one another, gazing together a little in wonder at their situation. Yet they were smiling and already bonded in trust and friendship, until suddenly they kissed again, this time harder and with greater urgency, no longer at all deferential though full of tenderness.

So, without any more words spoken, they came gladly to bed.

Chapter Seventy-Two

Shoe Lane: 1654

For Gideon Jukes, life under the Protectorate truly began on the morning he woke in the arms of his lover, drugged with spent passion, as he smiled into her smiling eyes. They lay together in silence, braving the risk that the door would burst open and they would be discovered. They heard the sounds of young boys scrambling for breakfast, petulant shouts, thrown shoes, mild scolding from Catherine Keevil. Either Catherine knew what had happened and shielded the couple from disturbance, or in the scramble to get ready for school there was no time for the boys even to think of plaguing their mother. They clattered downstairs. Catherine took the boys to school; on her return she would open the shop and remain there.

The house grew quiet. Juliana and Gideon were alone.

With some trepidation Juliana surveyed the man she had taken to her bed. 'Well, that's done!' he quipped callously. 'Time to be up and off!'

For a split second he deceived her.

Juliana responded with a languid stretch, tucking her hair behind her ears. She fought back: 'Bolt then. Always so convenient for everyone . . . So, Captain Jukes, you are a loose seducer who lies with a woman once, then thinks his wager over, and moves on, never to be seen again? No, I do not believe it – you *actor!*'

Gideon exploded into giggles. He kept laughing, lost in a helpless joke of his own, while Juliana gazed at him in amazement.

When he settled, she asked, 'What was that about?'

'A dotterel.'

'A *what?*'

'Oh I shall tell you one day, sweetheart . . . Now I must take you in hand. Milady Formal, let us dispense with this *Captain Jukes* of yours.

I shall have to compose a book of etiquette and print it for you. It will go thus: When a Lady hath lain the whole night with a Gentleman, making love together until they can no longer *move*, it is expected that the said Lady shall call the said Gentleman by his *name*!'

'Gideon.'

'Better.'

'Gideon . . .' Juliana rolled on her side – with a groan for he was right about movement being difficult. She kissed him on the forehead. 'Gideon . . .' She kissed him again, on the eyes, the nose, the chin, the lips, each time saying his name over. 'Gideon.'

'All this is good!'

'I believe I had called you so before.' She had indeed, while so desperate in passion that even the memory of it made her face colour up.

'Oh so you did!' chortled Gideon, lasciviously reminding her. Seriousness overcame him, however. His voice dropped into tenderness. So much had been left unspoken last night that delicate negotiation seemed required. 'Now shall I take myself off? Must I?' They were entwined like ancient ropes of bindweed and Gideon made no move to unravel himself. 'Then if I leave you, may I come again?'

'I hope you will.'

'When shall I come? When, dear heart?'

'Whenever you like,' Juliana answered, being completely honest. She had nothing to lose by it, she thought – and everything to gain. 'My house is yours,' she told Gideon then, more than ever full of gratitude to Mr Gadd that he had given her this gift, a house that was all hers, with no obligation to respect the feelings of anybody but herself. She could not have said it if this had ever been her family home with Lovell.

Gideon, too, had his moment of absolute truth: 'If you give me this freedom, I shall never leave. I love you and long for your company.'

'Death and disaster wait around every corner,' Juliana said. 'Let us not waste any of our lives.'

Gideon gave her a slow but cheeky London grin. 'I could court you,' he offered.

'You have done that.'

'Yes, it seems I have.'

'If formalities are needed, *I* could seduce *you*!'

'That too,' answered Gideon dryly, 'would appear to be superfluous.'

* * *

So they began their lives together. Gideon returned to the print shop later that day – *much* later – and gravely informed Miles that the business of the embroidery book would necessitate additional work with the client.

'How long?' asked Miles, a perfectly professional query. He was a romantic, and had already sensed the crackle of interest between his master and Mistress Juliana Lovell, yet from what he knew of Gideon he did not suppose anything had been done about it. Gideon's cheerful reply made his jaw drop.

'About forty years, God willing.' Gideon paused. 'Fifty, if she wants an index!'

Juliana did not wonder how she would explain this to her children or to Catherine. Catherine already had a personal debt to Gideon; she viewed him kindly. Tom and Val had been brought up with the kind of strict French discipline Juliana had known herself from her grandmother. Although she expected stressful moments, a lone mother did not beg for forgiveness that she had found new comfort for herself and a provider for her family. As soon as she knew for sure that she had lost her husband, Juliana would be expected to remarry. She was still not thirty. Supplying a stepfather was her social duty. Placing herself in the protection of another man was her proper role.

Both boys resisted reconciling themselves, none the less. They were used to being kingpins in a fatherless home. They viewed Gideon Jukes as an interloper and were sullen for some time. But sooner than they wanted to, they found they took to him. He made no fuss. His steadiness and likeability wore them down. Tom and Val responded well to having a happy mother; they were reassured by their new feeling of security.

Gideon's arrival expanded their horizons; they learned about printing, always had paper to write and draw on, got to know Miles – who owned a dog they liked; puppies were given to them and though they saw it as a bribe, they let themselves be suborned. They acquired relatives too. Once a week the family walked to Bread Street to dine with Anne and Lambert. Now Tom and Val not only had an aunt and uncle but childless ones, who loved children and generously spoiled them. They were always excited at going to the grocery shop, with its rich odours and endless supply of edible treats. Lambert took them to see the Trained

Bands exercise at the Artillery Ground. Lambert and Gideon together arranged male expeditions, fishing and shooting, or watching ships on the river.

To Gideon, the life they led now was what he had been fighting for. The regular pulse of work he enjoyed and a domestic life he loved hardly changed his character, yet settled him and rounded him. He came into contentment. He wished his parents could have seen him so happy. He wished Robert had known of it.

Juliana was slower to accept her good fortune. Life had taught her distrust. For some time she felt she was playing at house in a game, that this new wonder would be taken away from her. Yet gradually she relaxed. This existence became normal. To be sure that her man would return home every evening stopped feeling like a luxury and seemed like a right. To lie safe in his arms through the night, every night, became reliable and normal. She was allowed to see his weaknesses, to wrangle with him, to consult him, to care for his welfare. As well as Gideon's constant devotion to her, she had the delight of his physical lovemaking.

'I have ten years of extremely chaste life to make up —' Gideon declared.

'All *tonight?*'

'After ten years, it needs practice.'

'No, you remember how! — Enjoying it is a sin, you know.'

'Then both of us will go to the Devil!' answered Gideon with a gleam of glee that seemed both unexpected and delightful in a radical Independent.

To her joy, they read all the time. Juliana had not shared her love of books with anyone since her father's wits began to leave him. She and Gideon had every access to the printed word. Their shelves filled up with books. Rarely an evening passed without Gideon sitting with stockinged feet on the fender, reading aloud a news-sheet while Juliana plied some needlework. Separately and together they read books too.

Juliana accepted just how full her contentment was now. Sometimes she paused in her sewing to watch Gideon rebuild the sunken fire. It was one of his charms that he would do this — unlike Orlando Lovell, who deemed it his place to sprawl at leisure and have women tend the hearth, however black the evening when they must go out of doors to the coalshed, however steep the stairs up which they had to carry hods or scuttles. Gideon, by contrast, not only noticed when the embers were low but routinely fetched new fuel, without being asked, and he would automatically wash the coaldust off his hands afterwards to avoid black fingermarks. He was unquestionably the product of a mother who wanted him fit to live with; Juliana wished she could have known Parthenope Jukes. She wished she had Parthenope to advise on Tom and Val.

Of course, when he rinsed his hands Gideon always left the damp towel scrunched on a chair, but no man is perfect, despite the efforts of his mother. More often than not, he did remember *not* to leave the soap-ball sitting in a pool of water so it went slimy . . .

Whenever he caught Juliana watching him, Gideon cocked his head on one side like a speculating robin. They would survey one another in silence sometimes, wearing slight smiles. It was companionable, unde-manding, satisfied. He knew she was learning his habits, his ways of moving, all his thoughts. He looked for and found a new peacefulness in the gaze of her grey eyes. He had achieved that; he knew it. At such moments, Juliana would notice a sigh waft though him very faintly, not from trouble but in emotion that she knew he welcomed.

So, in December 1654, since they both thought it certain they would never desert one another, nor would anything ever come between them, they married. At that period of the Interregnum, the legal form of marriage was civil; weddings were performed with the Independents' belief in minimal noise and ceremony. It suited them both. They presented their particulars to their local parish registrar. Banns could be called in church or the market-place; Gideon and Juliana opted for the market-place. Once their banns had been cried, the registrar gave them their certificate of publication. A justice of the peace accepted their certificate, their decla-rations that they were over twenty-one, and their honest explanation of the continuing absence and presumed death of Juliana's first husband. The JP had met such situations before and did not quibble. So, with Anne, Lambert, Catherine and Miles as their credible witnesses, they were married in due Commonwealth form: *The man to be married, taking the woman to be married by the hand, shall plainly and distinctly pronounce these words:*

'I, Gideon Jukes, do here in the presence of God, the searcher of all hearts, take thee Juliana Lovell for my wedded wife; and do also in the presence of God, and before these witnesses, promise to be unto thee a loving and faithful husband.'

And then the woman, taking the man by the hand, shall plainly and distinctly pronounce these words:

'I, Juliana Lovell, do here in the presence of God, the searcher of all hearts, take thee Gideon Jukes for my wedded husband; and do also in the presence of God, and before these witnesses, promise to be unto thee a loving, faithful and obedient Wife.'

Juliana dropped her eyes a little at 'obedient' – while Gideon smiled at it.

Certain of themselves, they shared none of the qualms others had that the bare new marriage service lacked validity. Not for them fiddlers, white dresses, riotous games with bridesmaids and bridesmen, lewd fumbling with garters or terrible wedding jokes. Nor did they trouble to use a wedding ring, that diabolical circle for the devil to dance in. They would be bound by mutual loyalty. All the solemnity they needed had come to them with the admission of their love. To celebrate, they gave a dinner at home for a small circle of family and friends, then simply went on with the life together that by then they had firmly established.

Chapter Seventy-Three

Hampshire and London: 1653

Orlando Lovell came ashore in Hampshire, some time in early summer 1653, alone. He landed in a dapper cloak and an ash-grey suit, passing himself off as someone who travelled for education or business. He wore a sword like a gentleman. His baggage was compact and neat. He brought no horse, because Parliament imposed heavy customs duties on anyone importing horses into England unless they had obtained prior exemption from duty because they were diplomats. If Lovell thought of himself as a diplomat, it was not the kind who made formal addresses to the Lord Protector.

He bought a horse, finding it a good joke to cheat the man who sold it to him. Taking no trouble to hire a groom or other servant, he set about his personal business.

At this time, Lovell had not long been back in Europe. Earlier that year, a month before Oliver Cromwell lost his temper and dismissed the Rump Parliament, a disheartened Prince Rupert had returned to France from the West Indies, with Lovell in his company. While Rupert was devastated by the loss of his brother, Lovell's regret was a veneer. As he saw it, *he* had had a lucky escape, and not just from the hurricane. For the past three years he had led an adventurous life, but he had endured his fill of sailing.

Of course he had not died on the *Defiance*. That would have been the kind of bad planning Orlando Lovell deplored. During the storm, he was aboard one of their prize ships.

There was a disadvantage in capturing a ship: the victor had to reduce his own establishment by placing officers and men aboard, to sail her back to a home port. Prince Rupert had no home port, but if they were sound enough his prizes were attached to his slowly increasing squadron.

Lovell, a trusted officer, had sometimes been deployed elsewhere than on Maurice's flagship. Maurice, probably, had liked a break from him. Lovell, no admirer of commanders, had certainly liked a break from Maurice.

His vessel somehow survived, rendezvoused with Prince Rupert and limped back to France. At St Malo the bedraggled Lovell abandoned the rat-infested, rotten hulk on which he had floated back. He was ready to ditch Rupert too. He made his own journey to the court of King Charles II. Not many exiled cavaliers remembered him, but building up his reputation from scratch was nothing new. Orlando Lovell always had the air of a man they *ought* to remember. He could even persuade people to apologise for their forgetfulness, when in truth they had never met him before.

The young King's court and that of his widowed mother, Queen Henrietta Maria, moved between Paris and St Germain-en-Laye with their impoverished retinues. Lovell hated it. When, eventually, the French decided it was in their interests to begin making overtures to Cromwell and the English Commonwealth, the disgruntled Charles II moved to Holland. That had the advantage of placing him near the coast from which he would sail to invade his kingdom – if he ever did so. He had neither an army nor ships to transport it; there was no funding.

Throughout his exile, Charles would keep up the trappings of monarchy, dining in state formally to emphasise his privileged position – wasting money that Lovell thought would be better spent on men and arms. Throughout this time, too, Charles was the focus of continual scheming which, though it never came to much in real terms, served to unsettle and preoccupy the Commonwealth.

Lovell found that among the English Royalists, several groups were plotting. These exiles were by definition those who had done most tenacious service to the royal cause, men most virulently opposed to Parliament, men who would find it difficult or impossible to return home – men like Lovell himself, though he would not have acknowledged any likeness to most of them. Some had been denounced and banished. Whether in France, Germany or Holland, they had nothing else to do but drink, duel – and conspire.

Lovell was a modest drinker, preferring to spend his cash on himself rather than splash out on carousing with a feckless group. Guarded, he kept to himself, so avoided fights. As one of Rupert's privateers, Lovell was rather isolated at court, especially after Rupert quarrelled with everyone and left for Germany. But scheming always attracted him. Ever grimly practical, he surveyed the field. Turncoats and double agents were everywhere. Orlando Lovell enjoyed feeling that no man near him could be trusted. It absolved him from letting any man trust him.

What his Royalism still supplied was danger and a challenge. He had always been restless and risk-loving. So long as he had means to live, intriguing for the young King would suit Lovell. Like many men of shallow morals, he called himself a patriot. He had no romantic longings to restore the monarchy; he had fought for the Stuarts for more than a decade and knew their limitations. Still, he had made his choice, just before Edmund Treves first met him in Oxford. A proud man, he never went back on a decision. He would stay loyal. Always sure of his own worth, he thought this gave him nobility.

Among the exiles, he identified various conspirators. The Louvre Group tended to be Catholic and courted alliance with Scotland. The Old Royalists were Anglican and opposed a Scottish alliance. A set called the Swordsmen associated with Prince Rupert in Paris, men who had no particular policy, other than fighting. The Action Party were more militant but just as unsuccessful. Some time in 1653, the most famous and secretive group emerged, the Sealed Knot. They had hopes to attract backing from the Levellers. It was not completely crazy, because the Levellers had opposed the King's execution and disenchanted leaders of their party did come knocking at Royalist doors. They found them easily. That was how secret the secret plotters were.

Lovell made a scathing assessment of these cliques: their hopes were ridiculous, their disorder was dire. He despised them for working against one another, for their piss-poor judgement and lamentable lack of security. Typically, he attached himself to none of them. However, he did offer his services. Charles II always played the innocent, but from the start of his exile after the battle of Worcester he had used loyal friends to organise underhand designs. Lovell was told in confidence that Lord Cottingham and Sir Edward Hyde were behind the murders of two Commonwealth diplomats, Isaac Dorislaus at The Hague and Anthony Ascham in Madrid, with the King's connivance. He learned that his friend Edmund Treves was in the party that killed Dorislaus. He also heard Edmund later died at Worcester. He was surprised how much the waste of that good young life depressed him.

Hyde was very much still active in intrigue, though many cavaliers despised him as an over-ambitious careerist. Lovell hated Hyde. But also dabbling with secret work was Sir Marmaduke Langdale. Langdale had been one of Charles I's premier commanders. A long-faced, lean-figured, old-school cavalier, he had operated mainly in the north, a regular opponent of the Fairfaxes. He formed the Northern Horse from the relics of Lord Newcastle's broken troops after Marston Moor but they were defeated at Naseby. In the second civil war Langdale was crushed by Cromwell at the battle of Preston and captured; he escaped in various disguises, including that of a milkmaid. Now permanently excluded from England by Parliament, Sir Marmaduke Langdale was a member of Charles II's council in exile.

It was with Langdale that Orlando Lovell condescended to work. Langdale viewed him with fair regard. As a man of action, Lovell was experienced, physical, energetic, cool-headed and brave-hearted, a strong swordsman and an accurate shot. His mental skills included his ability to assess the enemy and, to a lesser extent, operational planning. Though a truculent follower, he made a terse but efficient leader. His supreme talent was to be devious. He was so good at that because he enjoyed it so much. Lovell would make a rabid plotter.

The plan hatched with Langdale was that Lovell would go across to England and resume normal life. He would pose as a penitent returning from exile; he would recover his estates, give false oaths of loyalty, establish himself somewhere convenient, recruit and report back on conditions. For this, his easiest disguise would be to live once again with his wife; he could use the regular Royalist claim, that he had come back to England 'to settle his family'.

At the moment when Lovell first landed in Hampshire, Juliana was still reluctant to believe he was dead. She was doggedly waiting to hear from him and would have taken up their old family life, wherever and however Lovell suggested. Had he found her, Lovell's plan would have worked.

So he landed in Hampshire. When he looked around his home county, he could see much damage but signs of recovery. True, war had had permanent effects. Large tracts of forest had been felled, stolen by locals for fuel or more recently commandeered by Parliament for shipbuilding; swathes of great trees, a whole generation, were lost for ever. Farms had decayed too, but they were now slowly being reclaimed for crops and livestock. Cattle and horses were now bred again. Prices were stabilising, fences were rebuilt, buildings that had been damaged beyond repair were pulled down for tidiness and to reuse their materials. Country-born, Orlando Lovell noticed these things. He had been born into the landowning class and was disgusted by the suffering imposed on the land by long years of war. His heart hardened against the rulers of the Commonwealth, whom he saw as responsible for the destruction.

In Hampshire, he was infuriated to find that his own meagre estates had never been returned to him after Juliana helped him compound for pardon. They were forfeited to Parliament. Worse, his property had been snapped up, at a knock-down price, by one of many astute speculators who were grabbing Royalist land: his own land agent, John Jolley. Lovell would never see the money; it went to pay Parliamentary soldiers.

When Jolley admitted this outrage, he only escaped injury because they were in a tavern with people watching – people who might report a trouble-making Royalist. Jolley informed the incensed Lovell that an information had been laid against him by somebody unknown. He had been proscribed by Parliament; designated 'dangerous and disaffected'; ordered into banishment. If caught, he would be imprisoned. He faced a firing-squad or the gallows.

Lovell disappeared fast, before he could be betrayed. In Hampshire he could trust no one. He had intended to try to see his father, but this was likely to go badly so he did not wait to do it. He had learned one other thing from John Jolley: Juliana and their two sons were at Lewisham. Lovell travelled there, but he found tenants in possession. He did not approach them. Had he done so, and had he tracked down Juliana to Shoe Lane, he would not have been too late. She would not – could not – have turned away her husband. She had not yet gone looking for a printer. So if Lovell lost her, it was due to his own inertia.

Fearing that trouble might follow him from Hampshire, Lovell burrowed into hiding in London. Much of the news there was of the trial of the Leveller, John Lilburne, who had returned to England from exile in Bruges; he claimed that Cromwell's dismissing the Rump had rendered his banishment invalid. His old ally Richard Overton tried to get him a good lawyer and attended daily. The jury would find Lilburne not guilty; he would try to obtain a writ of habeas corpus but would be put in the Tower again anyway.

During this highly charged trial, John Thurloe took over sole management of the intelligence service for Cromwell. Around the same time, intuition warned Colonel Orlando Lovell that he was being watched. Immediately he packed, changed his coat and his hairstyle, sold his horse for more than he had paid for it, left his lodging through an inconspicuous alley and escaped back to the Continent.

Chapter Seventy-Four

London and abroad: 1653–54

'If he be returned, it must be lately . . . I could learn nothing where he was,
but was assured he was upon dangerous designs . . .'
(From the State Papers of John Thurloe)

Not all plotters against the Commonwealth were Royalists. This was
the problem Thurloe had to face. If the Commonwealth failed, it was
likely to be because so much time and energy had to be given to counter-
ing dissent, both abroad and at home. At home the most dangerous
dissenter was Edward Sexby.

Orlando Lovell's ship back to France crossed one that was returning
to England with Sexby, whose history was becoming bizarre. He had
just spent months in Bordeaux, among elements of the Fronde rebellion against the French monarchy – a rebellion that had been more
farcical than fanatical, more striking for its in-fighting among aristocrats than for any serious reconsideration of social order. Sexby was at
the high point of a career that had bucketed through promotion, special
service, court-martial and cashiering, after which he was sent to France
with four associates, a thousand pounds and a special brief to *'find out*
things, prevent danger and create an interest'.

He took himself to Bordeaux as a self-appointed political adviser,
producing for the Frondeurs a document called *L'Accord du Peuple*,
crudely adapted from the Levellers' manifesto. Sexby had hopes of
Bordeaux where, unlike the general carnival elsewhere, craftsmen had
banded in a commune to declare a republic. The Fronde was really an
odd, half-hearted amalgam; fashionable loaves and hats had been created
in the shape of street-urchins' catapults or 'frondes', several beautiful
duchesses had intrigued with contemptible lovers and the usual misery
had been inflicted on the poor. Then this hotchpotch movement faded fast.

The commune in Bordeaux caved in. They opened their gates to royal troops. Threatened with arrest, Edward Sexby climbed out over the city walls by night.

His mission had undoubtedly been dangerous. One of his companions was captured and tortured to death. Sexby returned home, put in a stupendous expenses claim, then made a lofty attempt to set himself up as foreign policy adviser to Cromwell. He suggested a top-secret expedition to gain a British foothold in France, perhaps at La Rochelle. When Cromwell rejected this, Sexby turned bitterly against Cromwell. As Gideon Jukes had noted years before, being sidelined had never suited him.

The stage was now set for Edward Sexby's extraordinary career as Cromwell's implacable enemy.

Whether Oliver Cromwell was a hypocrite or simply pragmatic, in December 1653 he was forced to accept that, after the Rump departed, even its successor, the carefully vetted Barebones Parliament, did not work. Cromwell assumed the title of Lord Protector. He would be an absolute ruler, though he refused to consider the offer of the crown. His enemies mocked this rejection, though it was probably genuine. Many old allies were horrified. Old enemies saw this as their chance.

The Protectorate not only gave a focus for manic Royalist intrigue, it also led to opposition at home from religious and political radicals. Fifth Monarchists and Baptists fulminated. Levellers would bitterly oppose rule by one man, whether he called himself Protector or King. All of them sought Cromwell's removal. Sexby, too, was now busy at that work.

John Thurloe's intelligence service set about tracking every set of dissidents. To do so, the spymaster drew on any possible resources, encouraging turncoats and bribing double agents. In December 1653 as the Protectorate began, Richard Overton, the Leveller, who only a few months before had been stalwartly supporting John Lilburne at his trial, was paid twenty pounds by Thurloe. This substantial sum was an inducement to report on the activities of Edward Sexby.

It was suspected Overton might renege. An attempt was made, therefore, to recruit someone to monitor *his* activities – one candidate being Lambert Jukes, whose wife knew the wife of Overton. A doubt hung over Lambert, as a convicted Ranter. Even more likely to move in

Overton's circles, because he was a printer and Overton constantly wrote pamphlets, was Lambert's brother, Gideon Jukes. He had a sound New Model Army record, and sometimes wrote for the official Parliamentary publisher, Marchamont Nedham. Nedham had connections with Thurloe and it was he who made informal approaches to Gideon.

This Nedham had a mixed history as a publisher and editor, though Gideon found him fairly congenial. In the '40s, Nedham had published *Mercurius Britannicus*, the Parliamentary response to Royalist propaganda, and after Naseby he printed the King's incriminating papers. He changed sides dramatically over the execution – but while under sentence of death in Newgate, his old love for Parliament was reborn by magic. Ever since, he had championed the need for all parties to submit to the Commonwealth's government, in order to achieve social stability.

As the official propagandist, Nedham was paid a salary, though when he set up the state news-sheet *Mercurius Politicus*, he also supported it financially by taking in paid advertisements for a sister periodical called *The Public Adviser*; its regular news of houses and shops for sale, medical prescriptions and apprenticeships offered for gentlemen's sons seemed to Gideon a cheerful indication that life was getting back to normal after years of war. Nedham had a famously jocular style as editor, with superb contacts and correspondents. His official licenser was John Milton, also a contributor, who held a post with the Council of State, having oversight of foreign documents. Other collaborators were also poets, John Dryden and Andrew Marvell.

Gideon had been first introduced to Marchamont Nedham by Robert Allibone in 1651, when *Mercurius Politicus* was about a year old. He found Nedham a short, hawk-nosed, intense, lively character, whose long black hair and two earrings gave him a raffish appearance. Gideon liked him more than Robert did, so it was only after Robert's death that Gideon wrote occasional pieces for him. He approved of the man's belief in separation of church and state; his dedication to freedom of conscience; even his eagerness – so much despised by others – to make publishing pay. Gideon did not disapprove of that and, for him, Nedham's relationship with the secret service also held spice. He knew the editor worked very closely with John Thurloe. It was logical. They used each other's networks of correspondents. By drawing on Thurloe's intelligence,

Nedham obtained reports that were rightly seen as making *Mercurius Politicus* the only news worth reading.

Marchamont Nedham tried to recruit Gideon to spy on Richard Overton. Gideon wriggled, saying he had just become attached to a lady and was settling himself domestically. He smiled a little to think that the spymaster's office was unaware of his real acquaintance with Overton – the man who had once lured him into his dotterel suit in *The Triumph of Peace* . . .

Eventually he agreed the request. 'I shall need time to track him down –' Gideon rather hoped this would prove impossible.

'Covent Garden,' replied Nedham immediately. 'He lodges in Bedford Street with a Colonel Wetton.'

'Well, that will be helpful,' answered Gideon, a little primly, as his hopes of ducking the task were overturned. 'I may be able to find where he drinks –'

'The Cross Keys,' Nedham instructed firmly.

Now Sir Marmaduke Langdale had Orlando Lovell as his tool, and John Thurloe had Gideon Jukes. Nobody was aware of the ironies.

Thurloe did have Lovell on a list of Royalist activists. The spymaster used Royalist double agents on the Continent, one of whom had noticed Lovell. At this period Thurloe was cultivating a secret correspondent in France called Henry Manning, who was close to Charles II's court. He most usefully sent details of the Sealed Knot, so the supposedly secure group was corrupted from within pretty well as soon as it was formed. Thurloe knew of six founder members, Belasys, Loughborough, Compton, Villiers, Willys and Russell. Others were implicated, sometimes rightly, sometimes wrongly. A name that occasionally came up as an associate was 'Colonel Lovell', though the Duke of York's tutor was called Lovell, which at first confused the issue. Thurloe's agents had not fully latched on to Colonel *Orlando* Lovell, in cahoots with Sir Marmaduke Langdale. Nor were any of them yet aware of his awkward connection with their own informant, Gideon Jukes.

'We are here in great quiet under our new protector', wrote a Royalist from England, in a letter that was intercepted by Thurloe in January 1654. It was somewhat inaccurate.

Over winter and spring many upheavals occurred, though government espionage had success against them. Thurloe's organisation broke a curious plot directed by Cardinal Mazarin of France involving English Anabaptists. The codewords 'Mr Cross intends to visit Sweden' gave away the Earl of Glencairn's intended rebellion in Scotland which would have brought Charles II there. Imprisoned conspirators supplied long lists of names and haunts, such as the Windmill in Lothbury, where one man had met fellow-plotters under cover of his weekly trip to play billiards. The Gerard Plot was foiled and the two brothers who led it were executed.

Orlando Lovell took no part in these proliferating schemes; he derided all of them. However, in September 1654, when Charles II formally commissioned the Earl of Rochester to lead a new wave of risings in England, this seemed to be old-style action and Lovell deigned to assist. Over the next six months he was involved in the procurement and distribution of arms. The weapons were to furnish a countrywide rebellion, which would be led by long-time cavaliers and new recruits. Lord Rochester landed in Kent in mid-February 1655.

Lovell followed. After his involvement in the 1648 rebellion there, it was familiar territory. And Kent was a convenient base from which he could now seriously attempt to find his wife.

Chapter Seventy-Five

London, Gravesend, Kent: London, 1654–55

> *'Good God! What damned lick-arses are here!'*
> (Letter from a frustrated Royalist in exile,
> intercepted by Thurloe)

On the 6th of September 1654, Richard Overton penned a letter to Secretary Thurloe. Marchamont Nedham brought a copy to show Gideon, now deemed to be an expert on Overton:

> *I suppose I should not much mistake myself if I should more than suppose that there will be attempts and endeavours by persons of great ability and interest against the government, as it now is: but for my part I shall seek my own quiet and the public peace, and be glad I may be an instrument in the prevention of disturbance. I may happily be capable of doing some considerable service therein, and as may fall in my way; and I assure you, I shall be very ready to do it, if it may find but your acceptance. If it do, I humbly beg the favour of your notice, when and where I may best wait upon you, and have some discourse about the business, and to receive your directions and commands therein. Sir, craving your pardon for this presumption, and with all due acknowledgements of other favours I formerly received from you, I shall still remain,*
>   *Your honour's most humble servant to command,*
>   *Richard Overton.*

Gideon was fascinated. 'It is a wary piece of prose. I imagine that Secretary Thurloe enjoyed its deconstruction. The slithering clauses and two-faced humility are painful!'

'And most unlike the plain-speaking of the usual informants,' said

Nedham. ' *"Ruth Wiskin testifies that one Christopher Emerson called the Lord Protector a rogue and a rascal, and a bloodsucker, and said that he should have his throat cut ere long"* . . .'

Gideon considered Overton's note. 'Master Nedham, this phrase, "the government, as it now is", hints that he has lingering discomfort with the Protectorate. Is the man genuinely seeking public peace – or just strapped for cash?'

'He is an old pamphleteer, with no regular employment. The intelligence office has a large expenses fund, as Overton already knows.'

'This could be bluff – trying to find out what Thurloe knows. Will Thurloe meet him, as he asks?'

'Perhaps not, but there could be money. Last year Thurloe paid him twenty pounds for snitching on Sexby, whose behaviour was no secret anyway.'

'Sexby?'

'You know him too?' asked Nedham, pointedly noting it.

'I have met him,' responded Gideon, playing down their association.

'Would you care to go into the West Country to observe him?'

'Is that where Sexby is? My new wife would not welcome my leaving her, Master Nedham!'

Gideon was trying to back away from all this intrigue, but he was being pressed hard to help. When the first Protectorate Parliament assembled in the autumn of 1654, unrest assailed on all sides. The Fifth Monarchists' leader, Major-General Thomas Harrison, was a constant thorn in Cromwell's side. Three army colonels – Alured, Saunders and Gideon's old colonel, Okey – petitioned with claims that Cromwell had adopted greater powers than had been wielded by Charles I. John Wildman was accused of stirring an army plot in Scotland, put in the Tower and left to stew. The Scotland plot had thrown up a new participant. One of the Levellers that General Monck dismissed from the army, Miles Sindercombe, fled to Flanders. There he made dangerous contacts, one being Edward Sexby.

Notes which Thurloe prepared for the Council of State about these plots indicated the wide range of his espionage. Long witness statements gave names, places where meetings had been held, lists of regiments which might mutiny. Actual conversations were reported: *'Overton and Wildman spoke together of their dislike of things, but no design was laid . . .'* Thurloe knew far more than the various plotters ever seemed to realise. But he did not know enough.

Edward Sexby was openly intent on destroying Cromwell. Arresting Sexby became a priority. In February, a correspondent in the West Country reported that Sexby had been in Somerset, 'talking about a rising'. Two days later came a report from Exeter, addressed to the Protector, on efforts to preserve the peace: *'I also acquainted Your Highness that I had not been careless in making the most curious search after Sexby, having had parties out after him both in Devonshire and Dorsetshire . . .'*

The searches failed. Soon Sexby showed just how cunning and influential he was: in March he was thought to be staying with a Captain Arthur in Weymouth, *'a man esteemed of no good principle'*. Weymouth was close to Portland, where Sexby had been governor, and where he had used his charm to make firm friends throughout the community. He had acquired a mistress, Mrs Elizabeth Ford, a woman of quick wits and spirit. She became suspicious when a soldier came to the house, disguised as a yokel and pretending to have letters for Sexby. Mrs Ford raised the alarm; the mayor and the castle governor took into custody the very soldiers sent to arrest Sexby. Their spurious grounds were that the militiamen were attempting to deprive a freeborn Englishman of his liberty whilst they had no written warrant . . .

Sexby fled. He was next heard of in Antwerp.

Ports were watched. Customs officers carried out surveillance. They needed their wits. As Sexby escaped, other suspicious parties tried to enter England. Passengers in a ship bringing an ambassador from the King of Poland were a particular nightmare. One man not in the ambassador's accredited party loudly reviled the officers, saying they had no authority to question or seize him. As this troublemaker was secured, four shifty young Dutchmen queued to be interrogated.

'Gerrit Pauw, aged twenty-two; I am related to important Dutchmen and have come to England to see the country and learn English.'

A quiet man, waiting patiently, caught the customs officer's eye sympathetically. The officials were harassed by the diplomatic courtesies required for the Polish ambassador, bemused by the dozy Dutch boys, and desperate to keep pegs on a known Royalist – one Matthew Hutchin, also arrived in the same ship, who said he was carrying letters to Lord Newport at his house – a house to which Royalists in exile regularly sent correspondence – which Thurloe's agents routinely intercepted.

'Dirck Simonse, aged twenty. I am a gentleman living in the Hague. I have come to see fashions and learn English . . .'

The person still waiting was about thirty-six years, with a beard, quietly dressed. He tipped his black beaver hat with a nod, as if the busy officers knew him – an honest Englishman, the kind of diffident insider who can always pass through customs without paying duty.

'Cornelius Van Dyke, aged twenty, a chandler's son. I have come to see fashions, learn English – and to spend my money.'

The quiet man picked up his bag, as if gently moving forward in the queue. He and the officer exchanged weary smiles over these youthful travellers, who wanted fun without parental supervision, probably hoping English girls were easy . . .

'Jerit Johhes, a Frieslander, aged thirty-four . . .' Jerit wanted to see fashions and learn English, but he had complicated matters by bringing over two trunks of linen and apparel. The linen he intended to sell, he claimed, if he could get a market for it; otherwise he would carry it back again, or make use of it himself . . . This was an extreme nuisance because the trunks had to be tediously searched.

By the time that was over, the officers saw the quiet Englishman had slipped past them and made his way ashore without being questioned.

Once he left Gravesend, Orlando Lovell – for it was he – burrowed into anonymity in Kent. He was now increasingly trusted by Langdale and had been asked to assess the situation for the Earl of Rochester, who had entered the country to lead a revolt which they feared was compromised. Lovell found it all too true.

As a Hants man, Lovell placed much of the blame on Kent. Although some of its secret byways reminded him of Hampshire, he deplored this large, insular county where every man was more concerned with his own property first and, if pushed, Kent second, with no love for the kingdom in general at all. There were no great lords to provide leadership and the people did not even like each other. As well as the famous disputes between Men of Kent and Kentishmen, the High Weald hated the Low Weald, the marsh folk were thought peculiar by everybody, and the Isle of Thanet was so lawless some had proposed splitting it off as a tiny county by itself. Intermarried families in their agricultural manors had knuckled down under Parliament for much of the first civil war, only rising en masse in 1648 as a reaction to harsh penalties and interference. Lovell had been there then.

What Lovell remembered of those depressing weeks were desertions, separations, fouled-up actions in stinking old castles and endless angry conversations with mediocre men who could neither take nor give orders, all countrymen who were just longing to sneak away to check on their cows and their field boundaries.

Now he was back in Kent, and when he set about investigating the intended arms network, Lovell had a shock. He was amazed how extensively the Protector's agents had uncovered the arrangements. They had already seized weapons and apprehended collaborators. Lovell had to watch his step. Soon he discovered just how the expensively funded exercise had come to grief. He raged at the carelessness.

This time the Action Party had intended to arm troops all around the country, hoping that concerted risings in many places might stretch the Parliamentary army. Naturally they wanted surprise. 'And tossed it away!' growled Lovell, in despair. The idea had been ambitious – too ambitious for the fools into whose care it was placed.

Buying and distribution had been unsophisticated. Some weapons were to be imported, but correspondence revealed the ships and their landing places. Royalists had innocently written letters via the ordinary post service. They used ridiculous pseudonyms and labelled papers, *'Leave this at the post-house until called for'* – just begging for some under-occupied postmaster to start wondering.

Gunsmiths in London had been asked to supply large numbers of weapons, on flimsy excuses: *'Lord Willoughby has a plantation to the south-west of Barbados called Savannah, with six hundred men in it; and they are sending a ship with arms and other commodities'*. Lovell fumed; Willoughby of Parham, an old cavalier, must be just waiting for arrest after that fiasco. Other stories fed to gunsmiths were equally ludicrous: crackpot talk, for example, of buying commodities for a scheme to supply mulberry trees for silk-growing in Virginia . . . Worse, having established their cover, the Royalist agents had not even stuck to it, but confessed to the gunsmiths that they wanted false bills of lading in order to baffle government enquiries – and that all this was a tarradiddle because in reality there was a design to bring Charles II into England . . .

A gunsmith might drink the King's health as he took cavalier money, but once he was examined by Spymaster Thurloe, loyalty to Charles flew out of the window.

Transportation was bungled grotesquely. Ordinary county carriers were hired to take hampers and boxes to the homes of known cavaliers; these purported to contain wine bottles, saddles, or ladies' gowns. But the boxes were brand-new, specially constructed efforts in bright white deal, shrieking that they were the length and size of a bundle of muskets. They were incredibly heavy, sometimes too heavy for a carter's horses. The carriers, who were all under observation by Thurloe's agents, naturally swore they had no idea what was in the boxes. One, the Birmingham carrier, dodged interrogation as long he could, getting his brother to provide a list of items he had moved from London to the Midlands; this admitted to several hundredweight of mystery packages but tried to confuse the issue with *'Two firkins of soap for Mr Porter of Bromsgrove, and twenty-one fishes, fifteen whereof were for the informant, and six for the carrier's own use . . .'.* If the carriers refused to confess what they had been asked to do, maids or porters in the inns where goods were stored in London eagerly informed on them.

It was too late for Lord Rochester to retreat back to Holland; he convinced himself there was still hope and went north. Over on the Continent, King Charles had moved to Middelburg, ready to cross to England once support took hold. But Lovell felt the whole design was ruined.

He took himself to London. On the way, he went to Lewisham again. The old house standing in the orchard appeared empty, though efforts had been made to replace elderly cherry trees. A neighbour informed him that Mistress Juliana Lovell had sold the property, sold up to one Lambert Jukes, a grocer of the City of London. He rented out the orchard, but kept the house and stayed in it when he came to the area on business: the man was involved in the ships'-biscuit factory that had been set up in the old Tudor palace in Greenwich.

Greenwich was reputed to have more cavaliers than London so, mindful of recruitment, Lovell went to explore. He found the supposed Royalists were decayed court servants, mainly musicians and art collectors, who had hung around hoping that Parliament would give them their unpaid wages from the late King. They lived near the park, partly paid off with royal paintings, waiting glumly for the possible restoration of the monarchy. They might be loyal in theory, but flautists and lutenists were useless as soldiers. If this was the best Lovell could do, his mission would be a disaster. He knew other locals were even more unfriendly; when Lord Norwich camped in the park during the ill-fated uprising of 1648, his men had been jeered at and pelted by the Greenwich watermen.

Lovell sauntered past speculators' sheds and decaying riverside wharfs to look at the biscuit factory. When Parliament sold off other royal residences, the elderly Palace of Placentia had been retained – according to a cynical alehouse informant, because no buyer could be found for such a ramshackle monstrosity. It was now crisply called Greenwich House and assigned to the Lord Protector; Cromwell, satisfied with Hampton Court, never came here. The already decayed buildings had suffered. Various buildings and gardens had been parcelled up and sold off. Horses had been stabled in the palace where kings and queens were once born; ninety poor Greenwich families were installed in the state-rooms, before they were pushed out so the place could be a prison for captured sailors during the Dutch War. When the war ended last year, a venture making hardtack for the navy started up. Sneering, Lovell pictured Lambert Jukes as a puritan tradesman of the lowest quality.

Orlando Lovell had no real interest in grocers, though he was ready to demand that this tuppeny biscuit-maker give up details of Juliana's whereabouts – assuming he knew. There was no reason, on the face of it, why he should.

Lovell travelled by river to London, where he found a hot situation. In anticipation of Rochester's revolt, an order had been issued for the seizure of all horses in London and Westminster so they could not be commandeered by cavaliers. Horse-racing was banned, because race-meetings were a cover for conspiracy. Many known Action Party members were taken into custody. Security was tightened. A new City militia was organised. Extra troops were recruited for the Tower of London. Spies were out everywhere, watching Royalists.

The uprisings at the start of March failed to ignite. In Yorkshire, less than three hundred men came to a planned rendezvous with Lord Rochester. Other risings across the country were equally disappointing, even the most ambitious, that of Colonel Penruddock in Wiltshire. Leaders were captured, then executed or transported. Rochester was taken near Aylesbury, but bribed an innkeeper and escaped back to the

Continent. Within a fortnight, Cromwell felt confident enough to stand down the militia.

Orlando Lovell turned up a few weeks later in Flanders; his movements in the intervening period were, as usual, mysterious.

The seizure of London horses caused local upset. Gideon Jukes now owned Robert Allibone's old mount which, amidst much grumbling about costs, he kept at livery in an inn in Holborn. He was summoned one morning by an excited ostler, to find soldiers in the act of removing his horse.

'You want *Rumour?* An old, nervous irritating nag, who only cares to wend his way to taverns for a bucket of ale?'

'All serviceable horses –'

'Serviceable doesn't cover this one!'

'– have to be taken to the Tower of London.'

'Outrageous! Rumour is no traitor. He has given his oath of allegiance to the Protectorate.'

'Just doing my duty, Captain Jukes.' Gideon was using his rank today, in the hope it would give him some purchase on the argument.

Rumour added his twopennyworth. He bit the soldier who was trying to harness him.

'Look – we have nowhere to put all these animals. Colonel Barkstead is in a complete tizz; Tower Green looks like Smithfield horse-fair . . . There are two solutions, Captain –' The sergeant turned to Gideon, with a wild appeal. Every horse he tried to impound brought him new trouble from indignant citizens. 'Either we can put him down, which will waste a bullet – or you can hide him in a shed until it's all over.'

'Done!'

Hardly had Gideon reprieved the horse, for sentimental reasons, than he realised his error. His print shop had no outbuildings. If Rumour would agree to shift himself, he would have to be led from his familiar livery stable and taken to Shoe Lane. There, helpers must coax him to the shed in the back courtyard – which could only be reached by walking the horse right through Juliana's haberdashery shop. There would be neighing, horseshit, mud on the floor, breaking window-glass, leaning against fragile cabinets, flying ribbons and pin-packets, not to mention flabbergasted customers and a tense proprietor. Gideon knew before he asked her, Juliana would say this was not in her marriage contract.

His apprentice, Miles, refused to be involved. Gideon came up with two solutions. He did not *ask* his dear wife, he merely informed her, in the offhand manner of a head of household who is confident his every proposal reeks of common sense. (He realised he had become perilously like his father.) More astutely, he borrowed a bucket, which he filled with beer and carried ahead of Rumour to entice him to amble forwards, hopefully undistracted by baskets of bright haberdashery looking like treats to munch . . .

Other than this incident, they continued to live very quietly.

Chapter Seventy-Six

―◄◆►―

Antwerp and London: 1655–56

*'The Lord Protector should have great care of himself. There is still great
underhand labouring . . .'*
                                    (From the State Papers of John Thurloe)

In Holland, Edward Sexby lived in disguise in Antwerp. He was joined
for a time by Richard Overton, funded by Thurloe to spy on Sexby,
though Gideon Jukes had assessed Overton as disloyal. Sexby made
approaches to Sir Marmaduke Langdale, claiming that if protection was
given for popular liberties, he would happily see the King restored to
the throne. They could work together to achieve it.

Langdale had misgivings. 'What do you think, Lovell?'

'I would not trust this rebel to give a bowl of water to a dog.'

'He seems persuasive. He has wormed himself into the confidence of
Count Fuensaldanha.' That was the Spanish commander-in-chief in the
Netherlands, with whom Sexby somehow wangled a personal interview.
The unlikely liaison had serious consequences for Cromwell's govern-
ment, because Sexby betrayed to Spain the Western Design – the
Protectorate's ill-fated attempt to capture Cuba. He also offered to
organise a mutiny in the English fleet, which the Spanish seemed to
believe was attainable.

Surprisingly, Fuensaldanha sent Edward Sexby to Madrid. The uninhibited Sexby made formal requests for assistance to raise a rebellion
in England – a mission from which, astonishingly, he returned with
both promises and money. The Spanish government was notoriously
hard up, yet it was rumoured Sexby screwed a hundred thousand crowns
out of them; certainly eight hundred pounds that he sent to England
was seized by Thurloe.

'This Leveller has achieved greater success with the Spanish than the King!' marvelled Lovell. Lovell's opinion of Charles II's prospects with the Spanish matched doubts that had been voiced on that subject to John Thurloe by one of his trusted observers: *'This young man is grown close and wary, trusting very few with his secrets, managing his own business himself, whereby one may easily guess what is like to come of it. The Spanish ministers were wont to be too great an overmatch for a young man.'* Lovell, too, felt the young King Charles would go awry – though he thought no higher of Edward Sexby's capabilities. 'Sexby acts entirely on his own initiative, yet has become a dangerous international intriguer.'

Sexby's tortuous relations with the Royalists were almost foundering, mainly due to Langdale's suspicion. 'It sticks in my craw to ally with this extremist, Lovell.'

'But we are desperate.' Lovell still had a bad taste from what he had just seen in England. 'Rochester's rebellion was an expensive fiasco – and we have run out of resources. We must use Sexby to kill Cromwell for us. Then we may distance ourselves.'

The atmosphere was full of alarm. Thurloe's double agent at the young King's court, Henry Manning, had been exposed. Charles II had him immediately arrested. Manning was shot dead in a lonely wood outside Cologne. The incident emphasised that no one could be trusted. Orlando Lovell suggested himself to move in for a much more intimate watch on Sexby's intrigues.

The two men met. Sick of skulking in disguise, Sexby came across as peevish, morose and intractable. Lovell told Langdale the man was more interested in destroying Cromwell than in restoring the King. Despite this, Orlando Lovell had some time for Sexby. They were both loners, outsiders, aiming higher than somehow seemed proper.

Langdale had found Richard Overton a more sympathetic character, but at the end of the year Overton returned to England. He lodged with his previous landlord Colonel Wetton, where he came under observation again from Gideon Jukes. Gideon learned that Overton was now devoting himself to republishing a tract he had written ten years earlier called *Man's Mortalitie*. Dear to his Baptist heart throughout his life, this argued that the soul dies with the body. Since the soul's immortality was a fundamental Christian tenet, many Christians viewed the idea with horror. Gideon was enough of a sectarian to share Overton's opinion. Making no comment on the theology, he duly reported that as far as he could tell, Overton had turned away from political intrigue and was no longer working with Sexby.

Not until the middle of 1656 did Sexby's plans reach the point where he risked writing to his other old associate in England, the imprisoned John Wildman, hinting that his great enterprise was now afoot:

> *My Dear Friend,*
> *It's now about a year and two month since I left England, and longer since I writ to thee, and received any from thee. I pity thy condition, but prithee be of good comfort; all hopes of liberty is not utterly lost and gone. Nor I do not yet despair, but I shall see England again, and thee too, before I die . . .*
>
> *Oh! what would I give for an hour's discourse; but knowing that cannot be, let us converse this way, if possible. I understand thou art much dejected: you have as little cause so to be, as ever prisoner had; for though your unrighteous judge and his janissaries think they sit so sure there's no danger of falling; yet I tell thee, he will not be of that opinion long . . . That apostate thinks he knows me . . . Mark what I say to you . . . his soul (though as proud as Lucifer's) will fail within him.*
>
> *I am and for ever shall remain, my worthy friend,*
> *Thine to command till death,*
> *Thomas Brooke*
> *Antwerp, May 28, 1656*

'Thomas Brooke' had this risky letter intercepted by Thurloe. Only a few weeks later, John Wildman was abruptly released. *He* was now supposed to be acting as a double agent for Thurloe. However, it was Lockhart, the English ambassador in France, who wrote in July that Sexby had indeed gone to England: *'. . . I could learn nothing where he was, but was assured he was upon dangerous designs . . .'*

In fact Sexby was withdrawing from direct action and making himself a puppet-master. Just as he once masterminded the army Agitators, he now employed a virtual unknown, the man who had fled abroad from Scotland when General Monck was exposing the officers' plot: Miles Sindercombe.

Orlando Lovell had been introduced to Sindercombe.

Provided by Sexby with five hundred pounds, weapons and ammunition, Miles Sindercombe travelled to England in disguise to assemble a group of supporters. He took up old contacts with disgruntled soldiers, in particular a member of Cromwell's Lifeguards, who could pass on information about Cromwell's movements. Accompanying Sindercombe was a man called 'William Boyes', who used several disguises and names. The only thing certain about Boyes was that none of Sindercombe's group knew much about him. He had attached himself before they thought of asking questions. Somehow he put himself at the heart of their schemes. What made Boyes seem useful was a promise he made with great assurance that once Cromwell's death created a power vacuum in England, they were assured of support from Charles II. This suggested that he was a Royalist, one with intimate access to the King.

Sexby skilfully set up a network that included thirty or forty people. He arranged that not more than two ever knew the identities of the others. Though he himself remained a mystery, Boyes knew everyone.

The group hired a shop in King Street, in the ancient environs of Westminster, close to the abbey. From here, they hoped to assassinate the Protector as his coach passed by.

While they waited to make the attempt, the man they called Boyes took lodgings by himself. He first hired a room with the widow of a dead Royalist he had known in the Kent rebellion, a Mrs Elizabeth Bevan.

Chapter Seventy-Seven

London: 1656

'It is here credibly reported, the cavaliers have another design in hand. Surely they are madmen, that cannot discern the Lord hath blasted all their projects. I desire the Lord will settle us in peace, that we may get in our estates and be able to satisfy our creditors, and then, we may follow our employments quietly . . .'

(From the State Papers of John Thurloe)

For any family with aspirations, or at least a family containing boys, much time and effort had to be given to the issue of schools. In the country choice was limited, because only the great towns had grammar schools, but in London there were enough to occupy all the talk at dinner for months on end. For the Jukes of Shoe Lane the situation was precipitated by news of a legacy Juliana had been promised for her younger son from his godfather. Probate was finally granted and the money became available. Edmund Treves had stipulated it was to send Valentine to study for three years at Oxford University, hoping that Val would go to his own old college of St John's.

Long debates ensued. The boys, at twelve and ten, were sufficiently close in age for jealousy to be only a heartbeat away. It was already clear that Valentine was much more likely to benefit from this gift than Tom, yet Tom believed *he* ought to have been favoured because he was the firstborn. He appealed to Gideon, who was no help, because he had been a second son himself.

'Why don't *I* have godparents, Mother?'

'You did have. They were an Irish couple called McIlwaine, one of whom for certain is dead . . .'

'*Irish?*' demanded Gideon, slightly askance. He pretended this was a pose, though he felt genuine unease.

'Yes, dear heart, you have married an incorrigible Royalist with sinister connections. I thought you were aware of it!'

If their opinions were sought, both boys were young enough to fall either into silly behaviour or into secret deep anxiety. No child of that age is in a position to know his mind on his future. It had to be discussed, however. The legacy had caused more complications than it solved. If Valentine was to go to university he had to be prepared for it, starting now. Money for school must be found. With two incomes coming into the household, that was less a problem than it might once have been. But if Valentine was to be educated, Thomas must have the same opportunity – and so the discussions about schools began.

Juliana knew Edmund Treves had attended Merchant Taylors' School, but that was in St Lawrence Pountney, away in the City of London; since lessons started at six or seven in the morning, it would only be feasible if the boys boarded. Besides, Gideon heard the headmaster at Merchant Taylors' had been examined as a 'malignant schoolmaster' – thought to have Royalist tendencies; the man was a member of the Stationers' Company, who had recently been in trouble for publishing Roman Catholic material. Next, Juliana liked what she heard about Westminster, Ben Jonson's old school, until Gideon discovered that it still occupied abbey premises and the headmaster had locked in the boys during the King's execution to prevent their going to watch; Juliana was horrified to hear that boys sometimes climbed on the high roof to get a view of Parliament. They settled on St Paul's School, where all the teaching was done in Latin or Greek. To stand any chance of survival, the boys had first to be sent to a private tutor and given a grounding in the classics.

Marchamont Nedham, the editor, had given them a tract, *On Education*, by John Milton, the Secretary of Foreign Tongues. Milton, like Gideon and Lambert, had been brought up in Bread Street, where his father was a scrivener, highly musical, and a great believer in education. Milton had even kept a school himself, though primarily for his own nephews. Gideon took a look, then left Juliana to plough through his essay.

'Gideon, he recommends establishing an academy where the whole process can be undertaken, from the years of twelve to twenty-one. The day's work should be divided into study, exercise and diet. The study should begin with good grammar and clear enunciation, then: Latin, Greek, Arithmetic, Geometry, Religion in the evenings after dinner, authors on Agriculture, use of Globes and Maps, Geometry, Astronomy, Trigonometry, then Fortification, Architecture, Enginery and Navigation. To illuminate their studies they should be exposed to "the helpful experience of Hunters, Fowlers, Fishermen, Shepherds, Gardeners, Apothecaries, and in other sciences, Architects, Engineers, Mariners and Anatomists". Poetry. Ethics. The knowledge of virtue and the hatred of vice. Scripture, politics, law, Hebrew, then perhaps Chaldean and Syrian . . . I particularly like how he throws in, *"And either now, or before this, they may have learned at any odd hour the Italian tongue"* — I fail to see him mention French, however. That must be a fault.'

Gideon and Juliana gazed at one another in trepidation, as parents who read widely but neither of whom had had long formal schooling. 'It is a wondrous chance that Val has been given, though Tom may kick out against it.' Gideon's tone was almost humorous. 'Never fear, sweetheart. I dare say even Val will still want to sit with us sometimes for a dish of fricassee, while his dog Muff gently licks his fingers.'

Marchamont Nedham urged that the boys also be sent to a writing school to be taught a good hand; he spoke wistfully of a system called *'Zeiglographia, or a new art of short writing never before published, more easy, exact, speedy, and short than any heretofore. Invented and composed by Thomas Shalton, being his last 30 years' study.'*

The upshot was that the boys were taught the classics by a private tutor for a couple of years, until Thomas was enrolled at St Paul's when he was twelve. Valentine then made enormous strides while working solo under the tutor's care; he was an introverted bookworm, who absorbed knowledge like a sea sponge. Tom hated school, however. He was not a natural linguist. Classical literature failed to ignite him. Valentine's ease of learning only made Tom writhe the more. As he approached his thirteenth birthday at the end of 1656, Tom reminded Gideon all too much of his own unhappiness at that age.

One beam of sunlight in Tom's life was that he had expressed an interest in music. Anne and Lambert offered to pay for music lessons and Anne gave him Robert Allibone's two viols, which she had been bequeathed. Valentine refused to participate, so the music lessons were all Tom's. He grew in confidence every time he set off on his lone expeditions to his teacher, bowed under a viol case which he diligently humped on his back. He also grew closer to his benefactors. Juliana insisted that he regularly play to Lambert and Anne, to show them what he was learning. By now the boys had discovered that Lambert had been a Ranter; they viewed him as a highly exciting figure. Tom and Lambert got on particularly well. Occasionally, when there had been ructions at home, Tom would storm off and take his troubles to Lambert, who would wink to Anne, then lead off the boy to the grocery shop where they burrowed in among the spices together, taking a stock count until all unhappiness was forgotten.

From what she knew of Orlando Lovell's early life, Juliana was relieved that her son had found someone he would respond to, who would take a friendly interest. However, not even Lambert was able to prevent what happened that autumn to Thomas Lovell.

From what Juliana also knew of his father, the disaster came as no real surprise.

It was the period of elections to Oliver Cromwell's second Protectorate Parliament, the first with formal voting by the electorate, the first such voting since before the civil war. England was currently governed under the experimental Rule of the Major-Generals. A decision had been taken to reduce the numbers and cost of the standing army, but to reinforce it with local militias. In ten administrative districts, these forces were raised and led by Parliamentary major-generals, whose responsibilities included controlling Royalists and assisting the regular civil authorities in routine matters – or interfering, as it was seen by local justices and by the public at large. At least in providing an armed response to the Royalist risings of 1655 the unpopular system had worked. That partly explained why in the following year Sexby and Sindercombe took a different approach. They would concentrate first on the violent removal of Cromwell.

By the summer of 1656, the main preoccupation of the major-generals was vetting candidates for the Parliamentary elections and putting pressure on local selectors. All kinds of people were standing for Parliament. Royalists made a concerted effort to get elected, though they had to do it by subterfuge. Despite the major-generals' anxious scrutiny, almost a hundred new MPs were subsequently rejected by Cromwell's Council of State. This caused much discontent amongst those who were rejected – men whom Edward Sexby then busily courted from abroad. None the less, a kind of Parliament was put together and Cromwell was due to open it on the 17th of

September. It was understood that he was personally at risk.

In August, Will Lockhart, the Commonwealth ambassador to France, held up the post by bribery and beseeching so he could pen a desperate note to Thurloe:

> *I am certainly informed, that Colonel Sexby is returned into Flanders, and was for many hours together shut up in a room with him that was the Spanish ambassador in England. Tho' the particulars that passed betwixt them cannot be well known, yet this much I am assured of: that the Spaniards are very well satisfied with his negotiation, and promise themselves great advantages from it . . . He hath also given them hope, that upon their landing any forces in England, Ch. Stewart and his brother being upon their head, there will be several in the army declare for him . . . Sir, your enemies have many irons in the fire at this time: I wish, that not only some, but all of them may cool.*

Sexby re-emerged in Flanders after Miles Sindercombe's first idea was abandoned. Sindercombe had thought they could fire shots into Oliver Cromwell's coach as it passed through a very narrow part of King Street on his regular route to Parliament. The shop Sindercombe hired from a sempster, one Edward Hilton, had no decent escape route, however. The conspirators were not seeking to be martyrs; they always made sure they could flee after an attempt. That promising plan had been abandoned, leaving a large trunk of weapons behind in the house.

They did not give up. Sexby's obsession outlasted the setback. They were coming back when the new Parliament was officially opened in September. They dispersed temporarily. William Boyes, the mystery Royalist, was still lodging with a widow. Her husband, while participating in the second civil war, had drowned in the panic during Lord Norwich's desperate escape across the Thames from Greenwich. His name had been Bevan Bevan.

The widow's chattering drove Boyes to distraction. Her suggestiveness offended him. Her children were a noisy nightmare. He was planning a sudden flit. Before he left, Elizabeth Bevan had attempted to ingratiate herself by offering to have mended a tattered outfit she found hanging on the door-peg in his room. Boyes, who had arrived dressed respectably as a gentleman, hid a smile while he admitted that he used the ragged suit when he wanted to disguise himself as a struggling clergyman. He assumed, he murmured to Mistress Bevan with a rare flash of charm, he need not explain why . . .

Elizabeth dropped her voice. 'This is quite understood! Keep your tatters, Mr Boyes, and I wish you well in your designs.' She rearranged her mighty bosom and gave Boyes a narrow scrutiny. 'I would have taken your garments to a gentlewoman with whom I have a slight connection – she is esteemed an excellent needlewoman and keeps a notions shop. Indeed she has – or, I should say she previously *had* – the same name as a man my husband knew in the Kentish rebellion. He was a great cavalier, very sure of himself and a determined schemer, who had fought with Prince Rupert, it was said. His name was Lovell. I believe he was a colonel in your army. Do you know him, Master Boyes?'

'I believe I do,' drawled Boyes. 'And I should enjoy renewed acquaintance with his wife. Can you tell me the lady's whereabouts?'

'Indeed I can!' smiled Elizabeth Bevan, folding her arms across her chest and looking so helpful it could hardly be taken maliciously.

Rarely for him, 'Mr Boyes' then made a bad mistake: he left the widow's house without paying his rent.

After much thought, hoping to redeem some profit, Elizabeth upped and brought herself to Gideon Jukes. She confessed what she had told the cavalier. 'You know, Gideon, I am the loyallest woman in the Commonwealth and think it my duty to warn you of this dangerous renegade . . .'

Gideon's voice was clipped: 'Did you tell him Juliana remarried?'

'I was a widow alone in my house with a short-tempered, armed man! I quailed from it. I feared he would kill me.' Her quailing was true, though Gideon guessed she had dropped hints.

'You have been harbouring a Delinquent,' he growled. 'Best to get down to the intelligence office with your story, and hope you are not too severely questioned. That way you may save your skin.'

'And what will you do?' asked Elizabeth inquisitively.

'The man is disaffected – but no danger to me.' Still, Gideon's heart pounded.

Chapter Seventy-Eight

Shoe Lane: 1656

Orlando Lovell kept the shop under observation from a doorway for several hours. The building was narrow-fronted, one room wide, perhaps two deep, three storeys high, better maintained than those next door. It stood halfway down an alley off Shoe Lane, in a commercial district, more dingy than dangerous. There were worse stink-holes in London. A prostitute had accosted him in a desultory fashion as he turned the corner, but she made no move to follow him down the alley, nor did she curse him when he ignored her. Sparrows pecked in the gutter.

A succession of women in all shapes, sizes and qualities, some of them servants, called at the shop; most went away carrying little parcels. Through the bright crown-glass panes it appeared they were served by a young girl. Sometimes she came to the door when they left, curt-seying politely. About sixteen – far too young to be the shopkeeper, she seemed to be unsupervised today. She wore a brown unbleached apron over a saffron skirt and collared jacket, her hair hidden respectably by a white cap. Though her face was like a half-baked white muffin, she had eyes that a man who thought he had been chaste for too long could convince himself were lascivious. Lovell ogled her, as a cavalier was bound to, although the belief that she was employed by his wife acted as a natural deterrent.

About mid-afternoon he became bored. The young girl was no longer visible inside the shop. He walked across; he had already heard that a bell hung on the door but by opening it extremely slowly he managed to squeeze indoors with no alarm, only a faint quiver. The shop was neat, packed with products, thriving. He stood for a moment, contemplating the unpleasant fact (to him) that his wife, Juliana Lovell, was now engaged in *trade*. What bastard with no sense of the appropriate had put her up to *that*?

He walked quietly past the long counter, into a lobby at the foot of the stairs where he listened but heard nothing. He noticed an old sword, which he thought he recognised, hanging on a nail. Making his way along a slabbed corridor, he came to the back yard. He passed two bowls of cold water, presumably for dogs. His wife still had not acquired the garden she once hankered for, but barrel-halves stood in a line on the sunniest wall of this internal space, full of growing pot-herbs. An un-appealing horse huffed over a stable door at him. He discovered the privy and, being the man he was, blatantly made use of it.

When he emerged he heard movement. He walked back to the shop, expecting to surprise a woman; he saw nobody, passed into the room, then was startled as a tall fellow straightened up behind a counter, holding a plank. Apparently he was about to nail up an extra shelf. Orlando Lovell found himself being assessed as a potential snatch-thief by what he presumed was a hired workman.

The fellow was in shirtsleeves, his blond hair casually tousled. He had the kind of half-translucent fair skin that accompanied near-invisible eyelashes and blue eyes. There was nothing effeminate about him, however. His face was masculine, his build strong, his manner competent. He would be defined for the rest of his life by his past service in the Parliamentary army. There was far more to him than Lovell yet saw.

Some men can put up shelves. They know their superiority. Others merely stand about, pretending they *could* do this if they had to. Orlando Lovell, the interloper, was one of the latter. As a part-time joiner, Gideon Jukes knew what he was doing. He was the son of a man who had loved projects; John Jukes had had to equip himself with skills, or he would have been at the mercy of half-hearted craftsmen who promised to come on Thursday, then failed to show up.

With a mouth full of nails, Gideon did not bother to speak. Hammer in one hand, shelf in the other, he turned his back and more or less calmly continued his carpentry. Having tapped in a support at one end, he levelled the shelf by standing a saucer of water upon it, knocked in the other support lightly then made good with strong blows. Perhaps these blows were a little harder than necessary. Only when he had relieved his feelings did he turn and face Orlando Lovell.

Gideon knew who it was. Since Elizabeth Bevan's visit he had been waiting for this. Surprise was on his side, although he found that did not make the situation any easier.

Gideon surveyed his rival. Orlando Lovell, alias Boyes, looked like someone to be reckoned with. He was compact, small-boned, sanguine-complexioned, assured to the point of arrogance, with hooded eyes that saw too much and kept much hidden. He had long brown hair, sun-bleached at the ends where it curled down on his shoulders. He wore a beard, though Elizabeth Bevan had said she had seen him with it trimmed close. He was currently passing himself off as a gentleman. His suit was gunmetal, his cloak and hat black. A gloved hand lay easily on the basket-hilt of a sword. If he had brought pistols, they were not visible.

He seemed not much older than Gideon. A few years, maybe. Any appearance of other experience was due to their absolute difference in looking at the world. Nothing would change that. It was why they had fought their war.

'You must be Colonel Lovell.'

'And who the devil are you?' A well-bred accent. Haughty enough to rile a Londoner.

'Your wife's husband!' answered Gideon cheerfully. He allowed a tactful pause so the statement would sink in. 'This is awkward, for us both. I suggest we don't shake hands.'

Lovell stared. Gideon had the satisfaction of seeing the man grow hot under his weathered skin. But Lovell recovered; he knew how long it was since he contacted Juliana and he accepted that she might have made other arrangements. That did not mean he would allow it. 'You have stolen my wife! Where is she?'

'Not here. You will have to rampage at me.'

'You are a Roundhead!' Lovell accused him with disgust. He used Roundhead as a term of abuse; Gideon only squared up and was proud of it. 'I suppose it gives you satisfaction, to ravish one of the enemy –'

Gideon kept his temper. 'That's a cavalier trick! Besides, Juliana is no enemy of mine.'

'You dog! Who are you?'

'Captain Gideon Jukes, late of the New Model Army. Everything you fight against, everything you hate.'

That was certainly true, thought Lovell sourly. 'A rebel!'

'No, sir. A Commonwealthman. You are the rebel now.'

'I'll not take this from you.'

'Oh you will, Colonel. You are proscribed. The authorities know you are in London. You will be apprehended.'

Lovell was infuriated by the man's calmness. 'I have come for my wife.'

'Then you will go empty-handed.'

'We shall see.'

'You are a dead man to her.' Gideon Jukes pretended to explain: 'She thought you were drowned. You left her to think it, abandoned and destitute. The time allowed by law expired. She married me – she'll have none of you now.'

'You have made *my wife* a rebel!'

'Made her? Oh no.' Gideon rebuked him gently. 'Not Juliana! I liked her just as she came to me. I never sought to change her.'

Lovell's chin came up. He could hardly believe this outrage, yet controlled himself enough to say with mock politeness, 'Well, sir. I thank you for the care you have taken of my family. Your task is done. I retrieve them from you. I will have what is mine –'

'No, sir!' snapped Gideon crushingly. *'They are mine now!'*

He surprised himself. He surprised Lovell too.

Orlando Lovell gripped his sword, though the room was too narrow to employ the weapon. Gideon saw his thought. He bent swiftly, opening a low drawer where Juliana stored an expensive braid. The wound cards were bulky; a man's wedding suit could take a hundred yards of ornamental ribboning. But this was hideous, spangled purple stuff. Gideon had been confident Juliana would not look here. He was right and he found what he had hidden, preparing for this moment. Nestled among the cards of decorative braid, a weapon lay. When Gideon stood up, kicking the drawer shut, he held a carbine. Lovell had no way of knowing whether it was pre-loaded, but he saw it was set at half-cock. It was a good gun. It was new, bright, well cared for, not some rusted antique hidden under a bed for a decade. The tall, fair Roundhead handled it with confidence. He put the carbine at full cock with a smooth and confident movement, keeping his eyes fixed on Lovell. He knew guns.

'You were expecting me!' jeered the cavalier, still struggling to get the measure of the situation. 'But you will not fire.'

'Try me.'

Gideon released a safety catch. His calmness was close to contempt, his steadiness said everything. He was not some half-witted, rabbit-scared shopkeeper. Lovell saw that this man had indeed been a soldier, the kind who would never forget his training or his service mentality, a man who could kill without bothering to work up hatred, then justify it coldly.

Lovell took no risks. He had been a soldier too, a good one; he had outlived many desperate circumstances. He always used his head.

'Go now,' ordered the Roundhead. 'Take yourself off, do not come here again. Leave us in peace, Colonel Lovell.'

Lovell made one last try: 'I have come to visit my wife, to see my boys –'

Gideon knew this was a distraction. He raised the carbine from covering Lovell's heart to aiming steadily between his eyes. The weapon was heavy, but Lovell would not know how this strained his shoulder. They were ten feet apart; less than that, allowing for the length of his arm and the two-foot gun barrel. Gideon could not miss.

Orlando Lovell never lacked courage. He took a pace forwards. 'You cannot kill an unarmed man, Captain –'

Gideon pulled the trigger.

The carbine failed to go off.

Gideon hurriedly dragged open another drawer.

'Damme!' Lovell had gone pale; Gideon was too fair-skinned for any pallor to show. For an instant, despite themselves, they shared the fleeting grins of soldiers who had had a narrow escape. 'You have the pair?'

'Of course!' boasted Gideon. Carbines and pistols came boxed in twos. They were cavalry weapons, one for each saddle bow, one for each hand. Two shots. A man who loaded one would load them both. Any ex-soldier who fired one, would be prepared to fire two. The next shot could be good.

Lovell let out a *'tsk!'* of annoyance, shrugged, and while Gideon rummaged in the drawer noisily, the cavalier gave up. Turning on his boot-heel, Lovell flung open the door and, as the bell jangled, walked out of the shop. He made no threats; he knew absence of comment would feel more sinister. The bell stilled, the door closed. Gideon slowly pushed in a drawer of ruffle lace. He was sweating more than he liked; this had been a bluff; his second carbine was upstairs.

As soon as he recovered composure, he went to the door and looked out. There was no sign of Orlando Lovell in the alley. Gideon came in and locked the door. He unloaded the carbine for safety, cursing this new, useless gun. Rather than investigate immediately what had gone wrong, he hid it again, then ran quickly upstairs.

In their bedchamber, Juliana was asleep; so too was their tiny daughter, newborn only the evening before. Juliana looked peaceful, but was still exhausted. The baby was too small for her lace cap and gown, as yet insignificant in her deep cradle. Gideon checked them – even touched a knuckle gently to the babe's cheek – but woke neither. Unless he had to, he would not tell Juliana of today's encounter.

Colonel Orlando Lovell was no longer a shadowy figure who could be ignored. He was here. He was in London for a reason. It might not be primarily to find his deserted family, but he had said that he came for them.

The man had intelligence and courage; he exuded menace. He was also better-looking than Gideon had imagined. The haughty expression and rakish tilt of his hat would haunt Gideon annoyingly.

His decision to keep quiet was overturned. Gideon had to confess everything that very night. A disaster occurred. When Catherine Keevil went out to fetch Tom from his music lesson, she was followed. On Fleet Street, as they were passing Sergeants' Inn, a man approached them.

'Thomas Lovell! Well, my boy – do you remember me, I wonder?'

Tom stopped dead. Catherine saw the boy's young face light up. She tried to drag him on their way but he shook her off, crying with joy, 'It is my father, come home!'

The man embraced him, seeming to wipe away a tear of emotion. 'Why Tom! My dearest son, this is a lucky accident – now I have found you, come with me and I will tell you of adventures we can share –' He then turned to Catherine and, changing his manner, muttered with deadly earnest, 'Scamper off home, wench. Tell Mistress Juliana Lovell not to feel anxiety. Her son has come to his father, who will take the most loving care of him –' Then, as he caught Catherine by the arm with a grip that bruised her under his fingers, Lovell dropped his voice further so the boy could not hear. 'And tell that meddler Captain Jukes, not to do anything! He will understand.'

The last Catherine saw was the pair of them walking away towards Temple Bar. Tom was still bowed under the weight of his cased viol, which he wore slung on straps on his back. The man had his arm around Tom's shoulders and was carrying his music bag. To Catherine, the boy looked like a prisoner. To anyone else who noticed them, they were the picture of a happy father and his son.

Chapter Seventy-Nine

The Westminster Plot, 1656

At first, this was the most exciting thing that ever happened to Tom Lovell. He had achieved his troubled adolescent dream and run away from home.

He no longer had to go to school. He had dumped his tiresome younger brother and could avoid having to decide how he felt about his new baby sister.

He missed Hero, his dog. His father promised him another, though had not produced one.

Thomas now lived among men, who congregated in smoky taverns. They gave him beer, not troubling to water it, or ale, which was stronger, and sometimes even sack. They never went to church. Nobody said grace when they ate. They rarely sat down all together in any case, just took food individually when they felt like it. No one told him to change his shirt. If he needed a privy, they gestured where to find it and left him to go on his own.

He lived with his father in a rented room in an inn. His father was just as he remembered, careless and casual, the product of staggering adventures, bright-eyed with mischief, brimful of fascinating secrets. He had brought Tom amongst tough, tense, mismatched men who said little but, when they did, obsessively spoke of the day that was to come. They were planning a grand venture that would rescue the country from anarchy. This was all about as wonderful as a boy could want.

Orlando Lovell behaved like a loving father. He made sure there was food, he teased, joked, chased and scuffled; he even shared confidences – priceless ones. When the boy dropped from exhaustion, he tucked him up to sleep with unexpected tenderness. He never even poured blame on Juliana, but spoke to Tom of his mother with courteous gallantry. If Orlando expressed regret that she had chosen another man, he measured it with what appeared to be understanding of her predicament. If any of this was fake, the boy hardly saw it.

For Lovell the situation was perfect. He had been spared a decade of colic, vomit, shitty napkins, squalling, screaming, anxiety, the tedium of endlessly repeated infant's questions, the fractiousness, rashes and snot of childhood illnesses; instead, fate presented him with a fully formed loyal companion. Thomas came as a respectful schoolboy, ready for anything, yet still young enough to be obedient. Lovell romanticised his firstborn's birth and early years, in retrospect remembering his own role in Oxford and at Pelham Hall as much busier than it ever had been. Juliana was gradually washed out of the picture. Lovell behaved to Tom as if throughout the past twelve years they had been close comrades and best friends.

Tom wanted to write to tell his mother he was safe. Lovell let him prepare a letter, then secretly destroyed it. Tom never imagined his father would do that; indeed, he saw no reason why it should be necessary. When no answer came, he was troubled and unhappy. At first he blamed his mother for not caring, then, because he had her questioning intelligence, he wondered.

Thomas knew that Juliana would be heartbroken to have lost him. She had always encouraged Tom and Val to think affectionately of Lovell, yet Tom realised how much she would hate his going off to his father. He became very nervous of her anger; he knew he had behaved thoughtlessly and ungratefully. He wanted to be with Lovell, yet from the first he suspected that the reasons he had been taken up were not simple. His father seemed to want him here – yet Tom sometimes felt that he was being used. He disliked the pressure. He knew he was among people who had secrets, but he began to resent the faint sensation that there was more going on than he yet knew.

Thomas felt he must not be seen watching the conspirators too closely. But they fascinated him. Miles Sindercombe took the lead and controlled the funds, an ex-soldier – cashiered for plotting – and a Leveller. Sometimes they spoke of another man. Colonel Edward Sexby was providing them with weapons and ammunition. He was overseas, exiled, though they reckoned he still came to England, despite the spies looking for him. It was said Sexby might arrive here later. Until then, Sindercombe acted as their leader, Sindercombe devised the plans.

There was a man called John Sturgeon, who had prepared the way for their attempts by strewing copies of a pamphlet in the street. It was called *A Short Discourse of His Highness the Lord Protector's Intentions against the Anabaptists*, highly critical of Cromwell; the printer had been arrested and Sturgeon only narrowly escaped. (Tom said nothing, but he had already heard about this from Gideon; the printer's arrest had caused a sensation – more than the book itself.)

Others were on the fringes of the plot. A couple of times Lovell had supper with a Royalist called Major Wood, who was acting as go-between, travelling to London from the Continent. Tom noticed that his father talked to Major Wood in a completely different tone from that he used among the conspirators. Lovell and Wood had a natural ease together, speaking in catchphrases and laughing; their behaviour together was open and relaxed. If Sindercombe or one of the others arrived, Major Wood smoothly closed down this intimate conversation. In private, Wood and Lovell referred to the others sneeringly as Levellers. It was a term Tom knew from Gideon and Lambert, but he had never before heard used as an insult. Tom soon gained an impression there were two groups of plotters, the Royalists and the Levellers, cobbled together extremely awkwardly.

In closest cahoots with Sindercombe was another dissatisfied Parliamentary soldier, John Cecil. He was no longer in service, but still had army contacts, men whom they met from time to time in taverns. Loosely attached to the group, though vital, was John Toope, one of Cromwell's Lifeguards, who gave them information of when and where Oliver Cromwell would be. Miles Sindercombe had known him in the army too. He seemed extremely nervous. Every time Toope left them, the others would go into a huddle to discuss whether Toope was burdened by misgivings, whether they could trust him, how good his information was, whether he was liable to let them down.

Tom's father worked on John Toope, with Sindercombe. Tom saw them pass over coins. 'There's five pounds again, John, on top of the five we gave you before and when the tyrant is properly taken away, there will be fifteen hundred. You are sure to be made a colonel of horse, with your own troop, when the deed is done.' There was no idealistic talk of rights and liberty, only bleak bribery that promised money and honours.

The boy took a risk and asked about this plot they had. Miles

Sindercombe told him there was a design to alter the government, for which they were being paid by the King of Spain. He said it was better to have Charles Stuart rule here than the tyrant Cromwell. But, according to Sindercombe, it would never come to that. 'When the Protector is killed, there will be confusion. The King's men will never agree who should succeed, so they will fall together by the ears. Then the people will rise, and things will be brought to a true commonwealth again.'

Tom Lovell listened to Miles Sindercombe seriously. He showed no reaction to this wild information. His father was watching him. When they were alone, Orlando asked him outright what he thought; Tom only wriggled and played the bored twelve-year-old who had no opinions.

'Has the man Jukes ever spoken to you about the nation's affairs?'

Tom denied it, though when his father stopped questioning him, he thought much about past conversations he and Val had had, not only with Gideon but Lambert too. When out on expeditions, the boys had asked about when the Jukes brothers were soldiers, especially whether they had killed people. Both men had answered gravely, emphasising that to cause another's death – and to risk your own life – was not to be undertaken lightly. Asked about the King's execution, Gideon had said, 'He caused us to do it by not answering the charges. Always remember, King Charles was given a trial, where he could have defended himself. The court was established by Parliament, acting for all the free people of England. It was not assassination; that would be plain murder.'

'My mother went to see the King's head being cut off.'

'I know she did!' Gideon had given a little sweet smile. Thomas understood that smile; he believed it was good, which meant a shadow was now cast by his father upon what had been a sunny relationship. He saw that his mother was caught in the middle – and that so was he, Thomas.

'What are you thinking, boy?' demanded Lovell. 'Is it about that Jukes?'

'He is a good fellow, and always kind to us,' Tom replied steadily.

'Your good fellow tried to shoot me!' Lovell rounded on him. 'You keep away from him – in case he shoots you!'

To which Tom sensibly made no answer.

He was shocked, however. In his mind he had already built a picture of his mother's reaction to his leaving her; now he had another, more terrifying, image of Gideon full of wrath. Tom was not a prisoner; he could have gone home to Shoe Lane – but he became frightened to do it. Lovell knew that. Lovell used this fear to hold the boy.

Tom mulled things over often, for he was often left alone. His father kept them in lodgings privately, apart from the others. It was one reason he enjoyed having Tom with him, for company in the evenings. But the plotters were frequently active. On five or six occasions they lay in wait in ambushes but failed to assassinate Cromwell – when he made trips to Hampton Court, to Kensington, Hyde Park or Turnham Green. On those occasions Tom would be left to his own devices at the lodgings for hours. Lovell said he must not venture out, but must wait there in case something happened and they had to leave in a hurry.

Tom diligently played his viol.

Halfway through September the plotters hired a house beside Westminster Abbey, right by the east door. Sindercombe took out a lease, using the alias of 'John Fish'. Their landlord was Colonel James Midhouse, who knew nothing of their plot. He kept a couple of rooms in the house himself, so he was always likely to stumble upon them, which they found an inconvenience. They talked about making him a prisoner, so he could not inform on them.

Sindercombe, Cecil, Boyes and the lad went to the house together to check its suitability. There was a yard at the back, which overlooked the route the Lord Protector's coach would take as he travelled the short distance from hearing a sermon in Westminster Abbey to the House of Commons when he formally opened Parliament. Toope had said Cromwell would be escorted by his mounted Lifeguards, in their gleaming back-and-breasts, but the coach would travel so slowly that it would also be accompanied by his Lifeguard of Foot, who wore grey livery faced with black velvet and were popularly called Cromwell's magpies; the foot guarded him indoors, the horse went everywhere he travelled. In formal processions, the commander of the foot walked on one side of the coach and the commander of the horse on the other. Processions were unhurried.

'Time to get off a shot then!' gloated Sindercombe.

'But not to linger afterwards,' Toope warned him. 'The Lifeguards are chosen as the best cavalry – the most proper men on the best horses, and best governed. Once they start a chase –'

'Fear not. We shall be long gone.'

As a response to Royalist plots the previous winter, the Lifeguards had been purged of dissidents; this occasioned laughter amongst Sindercombe's group. Lifeguard numbers had been raised from 40 to 160 – significant, though still many less than Charles I had used as a bodyguard. The Protector's troopers were all carefully selected by Major-General Lambert. 'Toope got past Honest John somehow!' sniggered the plotters – though not when the turncoat Toope was present.

In the few days before the new Parliament was to be inaugurated, the conspirators began to erect scaffolding in the yard of their rented house. Having a lad in their company helped make them look like any normal party of labourers. Tom, who had had no haircut since his father found him and no change of clothes, looked sufficiently scruffy and desultory. He passed up poles, was sent out for beer, loafed in the yard looking bored.

They had a special gun to use. Cecil referred to it as an arquebus, but Orlando Lovell screwed up his face at that old-fashioned term. To Tom, he called it a blunderbuss. It had a short barrel, much wider than a pistol or carbine, slightly flared at the end; it could be loaded with twelve shots at once. There were special long bullets, with an extended range. 'Feel it –' Lovell let Tom handle the weapon. 'Light and handy. The range is inaccurate, but what we need is blasting power. The effect is as good as a mortar. It will shatter the Protector's coach and take him to oblivion.'

Thomas listened gravely, handing back the blunderbuss as quickly as he could. His father then prepared it. Although the gun had a ring, for attaching it to the spring-clip on a shoulder belt, Lovell explained that they could not walk through the streets openly armed in that way. Security would be tight. Suspicious characters were liable to be stopped by soldiers. The conspirators had thought of the perfect disguise for the gun, its ammunition and some spare loaded pistols; they would carry the weapons in the protective case from Tom's precious viol. He was not asked permission, but simply informed that he had to give it to them. Lovell saw the boy's unhappy face and was roughly contemptuous.

The day came. Thomas was made to wait behind at an inn. Sindercombe, Cecil and the so-called Boyes walked to the hired house, carrying Tom's viol case with the great gun inside it. Tom knew they had other weapons, pistols, and ammunition – lead shot and iron slugs.

Some time later, Lovell came back on his own, in more of a tizzy than Tom had ever seen. He moved their lodgings.

Gradually, the sorry tale came out. Toope, the Lifeguard, was supposed to come and tell them where Cromwell would be sitting in the coach, but he let them down. Cecil had remained the calmest, standing ready with his pistol. Sindercombe paced fretfully about the yard, steeling himself. As the hour approached, too many people crowded into the street to watch the Protector pass. Taking aim would be difficult. Innocent people would be hurt. The crush of bystanders would hinder their escape.

The plotters lost their nerve. 'Boyes' despaired and left the scene, quickly losing himself amongst the crowds. Sindercombe and Cecil abandoned the plan.

Major Wood, Boyes's colleague, wrote to the Royalists on the Continent that if Colonel Sexby had been there, he might have kept their courage up and carried it off. Sexby was only pulling strings from a distance. Even so, they felt his impatience. To pacify Sexby, another plot was swiftly put in hand.

Chapter Eighty

The Hyde Park Plot, 1656

By now they had attempted assassination from three different houses: the sempster's shop in King Street, the house by Westminster Abbey and another they had rented previously, which was out in Hammersmith. Lovell told Tom the Hammersmith location had been ideal as it was right on the road to Hampton Court, at a narrow dirty place where coaches were forced to slow down; there was a little banqueting house built on the garden wall, from where they had intended to shoot the Protector's coach to pieces using prepared splatter guns, armed with destructive shrapnel. The plan was good. The right opportunity never seemed to happen. Perhaps forewarned, Cromwell changed his habits.

They now hit on a way they could get close to Cromwell without attracting attention. He had given up his regular retreat to Hampton Court — a routine which had invented the English five-day week and leisured country weekend as, ever a countryman, he tried to escape the noise and smoke of London. While his Parliament was sitting, the Protector was too busy to leave Whitehall. Instead, he made it a habit to take the air in Kensington or Hyde Park. Hyde Park, once the great hunting ground of Henry VIII and Elizabeth I, had a large circular carriage track, created by Charles I so members of his court could drive around in fashionable style. It was surrounded by palings, to keep in the deer.

Once again the plotters tackled the problem with considerable ingenuity. As always, their main concern was how they could get away safely after their attack. They secretly made a gap in the palings. Since this could not be too large or it might be spotted, they also broke the hinges on the park gates. Tom had to go with them and act as a lookout while they were filing through the metal.

More importantly, they equipped themselves with the fastest horses they could buy. Thanks to Sexby, money was no object. At one time they talked of getting together a party of thirty or forty mounted men, so they wheeled and dealed with horse traders – Vanbrooke, Harvey, Cluff – surly men who carried surprising amounts of money in the vast pockets of shabby coats, men who gave off an odour of cheating, yet who surprisingly honoured any bargain they shook hands on. Eventually, assembling a large troop of horses in secret became too difficult; it would be obvious they were fitting up cavalry. They changed their plan. Only two superb getaway horses were now required. At a time when an ordinary cavalry trooper's horse cost five pounds, they lavished seventy-five pounds of Sexby's funding on a magnificent black beast they found in Carshalton and bought from a Mr Morgan. Then they gave another eighty pounds for a bay from Lord Salisbury's stable; Lord Salisbury lived in retirement at his family home, Hatfield House near St Albans, so he may not have known anything about the sale personally, but he had been elected to the new Parliament then barred from sitting, so the plotters knew he had a grouch against the government. Salisbury's horse was stabled at Cobham.

Obtaining these two horses needed much negotiation, but the conspirators now had mounts which would outstay any pursuit. Cecil claimed the black would go for a hundred miles without drawing bit, and would gallop the first ten miles so fast he would out-run any horse in England. Escape was vital to John Cecil, who intended to make his way over to the Continent; there, Miles Sindercombe had assured him, he would be well looked after by Colonel Sexby.

Tom saw this black horse and thought it beautiful, though to him a little frightening.

Toope, the Lifeguard, was still in theory providing them with details of Cromwell's movements. This time John Cecil was assigned to the killing, while Miles Sindercombe would wait anxiously outside the park, ready to assist the escape by pushing over the gates with their weakened hinges. On the day, Cromwell arrived for his regular airing; he came from Whitehall by coach but then would walk. Cecil had the black horse, Sindercombe the bay. They carried swords and pistols. Cecil, with his military contacts, was able to lurk on the fringes of the Protector's escort party, looking like part of the entourage.

The park had been designed for great people who believed they oozed style and charisma to display themselves ostentatiously to the jealous public. Even for the frugal Protector's appearances, members of the public hung about, ogling loyally. Lifeguards sometimes came prancing up on their great horses, moving the plebs back, but often they were more relaxed. It was meant to be a pleasant occasion. Oliver – as he was now familiarly known – saw himself as a simple servant of the Lord. When the public came to watch him, he responded with neither pretensions to grandeur nor paranoia.

Cecil's black mount screamed quality. It drew the eye, compact and refined in build, with strong limbs, an expressive face, a clean-cut head, well-defined withers, laid-back shoulders and a well-arched neck. It looked around eagerly with large, intelligent eyes. Clearly it would go superbly. Anyone who knew anything about horses could see this was an astounding animal. The Lord Protector, a cavalryman to the core, immediately noticed it.

Oliver descended from his coach. To the plotters' horror, he called John Cecil over, to ask who owned the horse.

Soldiers were everywhere, but Cecil now came as close as he could ever hope for. Face to face with Cromwell, he could have shot him point-blank. Here he was: the unmistakeable general. Now fifty-seven years old, sturdily built like the Huntingdon farmer he had started out; the florid complexion with the famous great wart under the centre of his lower lip; the high forehead from which lank hair straggled back, straight to ear level then slightly curled; the undistinguished grey moustache; the open face enlivened by that bright, hard stare.

As Cromwell talked about the horse admiringly, Cecil nearly collapsed. He had dressed in thin clothes that day, to make himself lighter in the getaway, so at the end of September he was very cold, which hampers courage. Cold-blooded murder was not for everyone. Most soldiers had killed opponents, but enemy troops were often indicated only by a puff of matchsmoke up ahead beside a hedge or by shadowy movement behind fortifications.

Now here was the Protector, once Cecil's commander. Cromwell's face was resoundingly famous from news-sheet, portrait and coinage. He had no royal hauteur; he was quite approachable. In the rhetoric of Sexby and Sindercombe he might be a tyrant, but for John Cecil at that moment Oliver Cromwell was flesh and blood, unarmed, out of uniform, completely vulnerable to unfair surprise.

Cecil could not do it. He excused himself later by saying that escape would have failed because the fabulous horse had a cold that day . . .

Cecil and Sindercombe slunk away like disappointed ferrets.

On the Continent, Sexby grew ever more agitated. Sindercombe and his group were taking too long. It reflected badly on Sexby, whose extravagant Spanish bankers expected results. His fragile accord with Charles II's Royalists was also at risk. Boyes and Major Wood reported back scathingly on the London bungles. Sindercombe and the others realised that Sexby harboured doubts about their competence. They set up a new plan, which had to be carried out quickly, to show that they were serious and not idle.

They were going to blow up Whitehall.

Chapter Eighty-One

Shoe Lane and Whitehall: 1656

The night her husband stole away her son was terrible. Juliana had been awake and feeding the baby when she heard Catherine return home, screaming. After a short exchange of words below, where Gideon – her *other* husband – was still minding the shop for her, he thundered up the stairs two at a time. He told her, as calmly as possible, everything that had happened.

Her mind in turmoil, Juliana tried to understand: first, that Orlando had been here – *here* – and second, that he had lured away Thomas. Terrifying Catherine, Orlando had made clear threats of what would happen if they tried to get Tom back. Juliana saw there could be no advantage in having a twelve-year-old boy at his heels. But he regarded Tom as his property. Snatching Tom was also a weapon against her. It showed that Orlando still governed her life; he could harm her just as easily and carelessly as he might have once done good.

Lovell had always treated her well, when he was present. Though he gave the impression he could be a wife-beater or otherwise dissolute, Juliana knew he wanted to look virtuous. He had chosen her in the first place because she had no means to threaten him – neither family, money, influence, nor even the kind of beauty that attracts attention – while he knew she was tenacious enough to stand up to life, with him or alone. In the King's court at Oxford, possessing a wife and family had made Lovell appear stable and reliable, better than a mercenary. Juliana's friendship with Nerissa provided an entrée to royal circles; later, his young family gave Orlando a lever with the Compounding Committee, even perhaps with his father. She guessed he might hope that she and the boys could be his cover now, in whatever schemes he had.

Until Sir Lysander Pelham sent him into Kent, Orlando had seemed generally content. Juliana knew, however, that there was another side.

Obtaining a wife's affection meant very little to him. He expected his dues, on his terms. Their contract was supposed to be for his advantage. Anyone who tried to get the better of him might find his reaction vicious.

'Thomas is in no danger. Tom is his own boy . . .' As Gideon tried to reassure her, Juliana only became even more anxious. She hoped that the charm Tom could deploy if he wanted to – especially with strangers – would help him gain his father's liking and so preserve him. But then Gideon was wrong; there *was* a danger: Tom might be won over to Lovell's ways and Lovell's thinking. Her boy would certainly be changed. Even if they ever managed to fetch him back, the Tom Juliana had loved and nurtured was permanently lost to her.

Gideon took Catherine out to show just where Tom went missing. 'Stay here – Juliana, *stay here*! Someone must be in the house, sweetheart –' Gideon dropped his voice. 'In case any word comes.'

There would be no word. Lovell would want her to suffer.

Catherine returned home alone eventually; Gideon, his apprentice and his brother stayed out searching.

Eventually Gideon came in, empty-handed. It was late, dark in the streets. Juliana had put Valentine to bed and cradled the new baby. Catherine had fled to her garret room, still weeping, and in fear that she would have the blame.

Gideon swallowed some of the food he found left out for him, then came stumbling to bed. Juliana was already lying rigid between the covers. He fell onto his side, turned away, two feet from her. He always slept on her right; he had chosen it to save pressure on his bad shoulder. It happened that Orlando had always lain to her left, so although Juliana had not consciously chosen to have a difference, it suited her. She and Gideon had never spent a night apart since the first time they were lovers. Quarrels between them were normally settled in the best way to end quarrels, by lovemaking. Tonight they were too exhausted, too shattered emotionally, and it would have been inappropriate.

Normally they slept close, always with a head or an arm touching, foot against shin or knee against knee. Often they fell asleep in each other's arms, or came together later. Always when they woke they turned to each other with tender greetings. Never had they been in bed like this, silent, for hour after hour, making no contact, each withdrawn into brooding and bitterness.

Juliana thought she had lost Gideon. She knew no way to break the impasse.

Only after many hours did she stop pretending that she was asleep. She moved a little. Then she heard Gideon turn towards her.

'What are we to do?' she whispered.

At first, Gideon only breathed a kind of rueful laugh. After longer reflection, he asked in a dead voice, 'Will you go back to him?'

Juliana was amazed. 'No!' It had come out firm and fast. 'Will you leave me?'

'Never.' Gideon rolled towards her. 'I will not leave you, nor will I let anyone take you from me against your will.'

He gathered Juliana into his arms, where she shed a few tears against his neck, though her weeping was brief, for she knew that too much lay ahead of them to take any solace yet.

After a while she confessed that she had never really believed Orlando had died. Then Gideon sighed and admitted he too had never relied on it. He even had a plan, that if Lovell ever reappeared, they would emigrate to Massachusetts. Gideon had obtained details of how to take a ship, long lists of the items that colonists should carry out to America, a secret savings chest . . .

They could not go while Thomas was missing. Juliana would never leave without him.

'Well, I, for sure,' Gideon declared, 'would not have had my life any other way than this. Nor will I change it now – so we must face out events.'

Juliana would not be the first woman who had left one husband to live with another, whatever the law said and however much the public enjoyed railing against such behaviour. 'I care nothing for my own notoriety, but I do not want our daughter to be stigmatised as a bastard.'

Gideon replied sadly, 'Celia will not be the first daughter of mine to have that distinction.' Celia was the name Juliana had given to the infant. Even after just one day, this puckered, red little creature exerted a greater tug on Gideon's heart than poor baby Harriet had ever managed.

That was when Juliana decided to say, 'Catherine told me once what happened to her sister.'

Gideon growled. 'Everybody knows but me!'

'Oh I think you do know, sweetheart . . . When she was working at Elizabeth Bevan's house, your great-uncle would follow the poor girl everywhere. He hung at her heels, so she could hardly do her work. Elizabeth his wife was very great with child and I suppose did not welcome her husband's attentions. So he threw the girl upon the bed one day and forcibly enjoyed her; when she cried out, he bade her hush, saying he was her master and paid her wages, so could do as he wished. Once Lacy fell pregnant, Elizabeth searched for signs, and questioned her.'

'I always suspected Bevan was the culprit. Perhaps it had happened before,' Gideon speculated. 'Perhaps he was known for meddling with the servants.'

'It seems likely. Catherine says the Bevans kept Lacy away from her family; they promised to arrange a marriage, saying it would prevent ruin – though it was for their own protection, clearly.'

Gideon nodded in the darkness. He was bitter. 'They concealed the scandal, saved Bevan's reputation – and saved themselves the costs, if Lacy had named him the father.'

He wanted to think he could have shown Lacy more tolerance, and her baby more love. But given a choice, with a young man's hard-heartedness, he would have spurned the marriage. Had he been certain that Lacy's child was not his own, he would have refused to rear her. Lacy must have always realised it.

Providence had granted him second chances. So despite all Orlando Lovell's threats, in deference to Juliana and in fear for her son, Gideon made up his mind *not* to inform against Lovell.

However, his brother intervened. Lambert had developed a special liking for Tom Lovell. He had even been mulling hopes to offer Tom an apprenticeship as a grocer. After he was called by Gideon to help in the search, Lambert marched to the Tower of London where he reported, to Sir John Barkstead, Colonel Orlando Lovell's presence in London, together with his probable designs against the city and the government.

Barkstead was one of the old-style London Parliamentarians. By background a goldsmith, he had joined up when the civil wars began. He was one of the Army officers who had sat in the court which tried the King, and he signed the death warrant. Recently appointed Lieutenant of the Tower, he worked closely with Secretary Thurloe and was guarding many political prisoners.

Sir John Barkstead took down Lambert Jukes's examination, which he sent within hours to Whitehall. Next day, Gideon was himself summoned. For the first time he was to meet Secretary John Thurloe.

The palace at Whitehall was a rambling conglomeration, built at various times. It contained between one and two thousand rooms, many in a state of dilapidation. The palace had been both royal home and formal seat of government since the time of King James, though it was much older, parts dating back to the thirteenth century. The Commonwealth Council had met there. When Cromwell was appointed Lord Protector, a number of royal palaces were assigned to him, to demonstrate publicly that he was the sovereign leader of a powerful state. This was his main London home.

Much had been stripped bare in the immediate aftermath of the King's execution, when royal possessions, the hated trappings of monarchy, were auctioned off. After great expense of time, money and embarrass-ment, several buildings and their auctioned adornments were bought back for Cromwell. Ancient royal pensioners in grace-and-favour quar-ters were kicked out. Apartments were opulently prepared; Cromwell moved from the Cockpit by the Tiltyard, where he had lived since he returned from Ireland, into Whitehall Palace proper, taking members of his family: his uneasy wife and his more eager children – except for his octogenarian mother. Madam Elizabeth was too suspicious to live in a palace and remained in a simpler house in King Street, near the Blue Boar Inn, until she died in 1654 and was – in defiance of her wishes – given a state funeral.

The Protector's household was equipped with all domestic equip-ment and ornaments: tapestries, carpets, suites of beds and chairs, feather mattresses, bedding and hangings, clocks, books, globes, pictures, garden fountains, household implements, table plate and a red-velvet-covered commode or close-stool, which was specially moved from Greenwich to be 'in His Highness's service'. Similar comforts were installed at Hampton Court, his weekend retreat, along with an organ from the chapel at Magdalen College, Oxford. Oliver also had the use of the Banqueting House to receive ambassadors.

As he applied for admission, Gideon reflected that this princely state demonstrated that the 'Lord Protector' was a monarch in all but name. It only differed from past royal display in that there were neither excesses nor sinecures. No favourites were given spurious titles and salaries; instead, the Commonwealth's courtiers and household servants had to do their jobs, without taking bribes. Whitehall appeared to be comfortable, though not visibly extravagant. Although Gideon knew that the palaces could and did host impressive functions, and although he himself was formally admitted by Lifeguards, daily life here seemed not to be ceremonious.

Some offices of state that previously occupied Whitehall had been moved away to other buildings. But Gideon knew from Marchamont Nedham that the intelligence office remained within the maze of old Tudor staterooms, as an adjunct to the quarters that Thurloe used as secretary to the Council of State and Cromwell's chief minister. Gideon was led there down ancient winding corridors, past rooms hung with recovered tapestries and furnished with suites of upholstered chairs. It was clear that many paintings from Charles I's enormous collection, which had once hung flamboyantly at least three-high on every wall, had gone. Madonnas, mythical nudes and unpleasantly martyred Roman Catholic saints had all been bought up cheap by soldiers and foreign ambassadors, astonished to be able to grab a Titian for a mere sixty pounds; even his brother Lambert had snaffled a rather dull Dutch watercolour, just for the say-so. At the refurbished palace, seemly pictures were retained, in discreet numbers. Fine hangings and furniture were acceptable comforts and in moderation they lent *gravitas* to the staterooms.

Thurloe worked in these handsome surroundings. It was said he was the only state servant who knew everything, and was never far from the Protector. However, he conducted much political business himself, judging the fine line between which papers must be shown directly to Oliver or what could be said and done without troubling him. On arrival, Gideon thought Thurloe's staff seemed content, always a good sign – and a sign, too, of an efficient office.

It was clear he would not be meeting Thurloe immediately. When he first arrived, Gideon was assigned to a secretary who pleasantly showed him around and explained what was done here. The main purpose of the office was legitimately diplomatic. In came long letters from private overseas correspondents and the official English Residents, accredited ambassadors, who reported from different courts of Europe and even wider afield almost weekly. They sent details of foreign wars, treaties and alliances, lists of ships, prices of goods, births, marriages and deaths of royalty. They reported the movement of known English Royalists, the location of Charles Stuart and his brothers, and what negotiations the princes had, or tried to have, with foreign governments. 'We have our own business abroad – with France, Spain, the Netherlands, Sweden, Poland, Russia, Constantinople, the Americas . . .'

'And you have spies?' Gideon asked bluntly.

His guide smiled and gestured to the salaried agents who were working at tables and desks – a small number, all relaxed in manner. Their pens moved unhurriedly. One read letters with the aid of spectacles, which he took off, then rubbed his eyes and massaged the pressure marks along his nose as if he had been reading with great concentration for a long time. 'The major-generals send the Protector statements about suspicious local characters.'

'You intercept letters.' Gideon spoke mildly. 'I imagine that is a curious science.' He had noticed that some of the clerks were not simply reading, but made notes on the documents in front of them.

The reply was equally frank. 'Many of the letters we receive have important names and places replaced with pseudonyms or number codes. A mathematician deciphers them if necessary. Some passages are written in white ink, which is supposed to be invisible.' Gideon noticed 'supposed'.

'Do people not spot it, when private letters you retrieve are not delivered?'

'Some must be aware of us, for they number their letters sequentially, so their correspondents can tell if one is missing. They may realise delays and omissions are not always the fault of letters being lost at sea or dumped in a ditch by a half-hearted carrier. But, Master Jukes, the letters we read generally *are* returned to the post office and sent on their way.'

'Yes, *concealing* that you have read them is the point – I see that!'

Gideon was no fool and it struck him that even this guided tour was deliberate. He was encouraged to feel at home. Everyone was pleasant; everyone seemed at ease in their work and welcoming to him. He guessed this was normal. Visitors were never treated confrontationally. All comers were coerced, if possible, whether they were supporters, Royalists or virulent republicans. The Commonwealth government – and Cromwell – hoped to be inclusive. Gideon was fascinated to observe how tolerance pervaded these staterooms. Enemies called the Protector a tyrant, yet what he was experiencing was not repressive.

Being Gideon, as they kept him kicking his heels, he asked openly about the Protector's attitude to his enemies.

'Oliver is as tender-hearted as a man could be. He yearns to make the nation godly, yet his wish is to allow all opinions freely. If he can, he will mercifully pardon horse-thieves and whores, equally with Royalists, Levellers and Fifth Monarchists.'

'Levellers?' Under the brim of his hat, which he had so far kept on, Gideon raised his eyebrows.

The secretary or agent or whatever he was, sighed. 'We are beset, Captain Jukes. I shall say no more.'

And neither will I! thought Gideon wryly.

Shortly afterwards, he was at last called in to meet John Thurloe. At this point, he voluntarily removed his hat.

Thurloe was an Essex man, just forty years of age, one of the regime's tireless, devoted workers. He had a legal background, a protégé of Oliver St John, who was a vague relative of Cromwell's and one of the original movers of Parliamentary resistance to King Charles, under John Pym. Thurloe had not served in the army. However, he had been a diplomat, secretary to the Council of State, clerk to the Committee for Foreign Affairs, Thomas Scott's successor as head of the intelligence and spying network, and Postmaster-General. When Cromwell dismissed the Barebones Parliament, Thurloe was closely involved in drafting *The Instrument of Government*, the constitutional document that legitimised the Protectorate; at that time he was co-opted to the Council of State.

He had a wide, square forehead and thrusting chin, with an eager, get-at-'em expression. His hair was abundant with heavy curls down to his plain collar, though he was clean-shaven. There was a precedent for his kind of intelligence work, in the spy network Sir Francis Walsingham once ran for Queen Elizabeth; however, Thurloe's firm-set mouth gave him the air of a man who might anyway have thought this up himself.

At first, questions about Gideon's career and where he lived passed easily like general conversation, even though Thurloe stared at him from under his brows as he evaluated every remark. Gideon had intended to put himself on guard as soon as the formal interrogation started, but he never saw that moment. Information was drawn from him before he was ready. Very soon he had listed the Trained Bands, Luke, Okey, Rainborough, scouting in Scotland . . . He had said he worked in Holborn, lived off Shoe Lane, had a wife (he did not say whose wife she had been), two stepsons, his wife newly delivered of a baby . . .

'Now let me show you this curiosity, Captain Jukes –' Secretary Thurloe led him around a table to see an object that lay upon a chair. It was an empty viol case.

Thurloe indicated that Gideon might examine it. It was for a bass viol, the largest standard size, the size Robert Allibone had played. In the pair he bequeathed to Anne Jukes was also an alto, suitable for a boy, learning, but Thomas Lovell had rejected that as a woman's instrument . . .

Gideon closed and reopened the viol case, which was of some age and fairly distinctive. He said nothing.

Coming close, Thurloe told him, 'This was found in a house near Westminster Abbey. It had been taken there as a means to conceal an exceptional weapon. It was intended for murder.' Gideon still kept his expression impassive, though he was horrified. 'A note was discovered, pushed down the lining –'

Thurloe put down a small square of paper where Gideon could read it. Not much bigger than a label, it said:

Thomas Lovell, his viol
If I am found, return me to the haberdashry by sign of the Bell in
Fountaine Court, Shoe Lane, and it shall undoubteddly bee to your advan-
tage. Ask there for Master Jukes

Gideon groaned. The childish handwriting, the misspelling, the trusting mention of his own name, wrenched his heart. 'I would hope that Your Honour has the viol that belongs in this case – but from my heart, sir, I would hope you have the boy who plays the viol.'

Thurloe shook his head, watching him closely. 'I presume he is with his father. One of Langdale's creatures. Probably entangled with the Sealed Knot, which is a secret Royalist group. Your brother has provided information that he is the man we are pursuing as William Boyes. *You* have said nothing, but I can understand that. Now I am hoping, Captain Jukes, I can enlist you to find Lovell.'

Gideon became agitated. 'I am the last person — indeed, I told the man never to show his face near me again —'

'You have *seen* him?' snapped Thurloe. 'Give me particulars — height, build, clothes, hair colouring!'

Calmer, Gideon described Lovell. For the first time, he saw Thurloe dashing down notes.

'So! Orlando Lovell — he uses other names and goes in different habits, though his intentions never vary . . . And you married his wife.'

Gideon felt his stomach clench. Thurloe knew more, much more, than he had thought. 'Lovell's return puts us in a nice predicament,' he conceded.

Thurloe made him squirm. 'Indeed! With reasonable cause to think her a widow, you and Lovell's wife were free to enjoy one another — I wonder, does your freedom continue, now that you know Lovell is alive? Is your lady a bigamist and an adulterer? Are you two committing the detestable sin of fornication? It would be fascinating to put this dilemma to the judgement of a court —'

Gideon felt threatened, even though Thurloe spoke as if genuinely curious about the legal issues. 'It is no intellectual quibble for *us*, sir. Our difficulty is painful.'

Thurloe stroked his chin. 'I imagine you want Colonel Lovell dead — though that wish is unchristian.'

'My conscience will live with it!' Gideon admitted, his back stiff as a ramrod.

'But he is here, alive —'

'And has seized from my custody the boy I love as my stepson, ward, call it what you will — a capture which Lovell is using wickedly. He sent messages that the boy is his hostage.'

'To prevent you assisting me? Will you succumb to blackmail?' This man cannot be married, Gideon thought. (He was wrong; Thurloe married twice and fathered children.) Thurloe continued to press him. 'Marchamont Nedham speaks well of you . . . I would pay you — we have funds — but I deduce you would not want money for this.' Thurloe spoke of payment matter-of-factly, as if many others did take it.

'For what? Why is Lovell so important?' asked Gideon.

'As "Boyes", he is engaged in dangerous business.' In four or five sentences, Thurloe listed the failed plots to shoot the Protector. At that time, they had not been publicised. 'Captain Jukes, do you know Edward Sexby?'

Gideon took a rapid decision to admit it: 'I met him. He was an Agitator then, and a private trooper.'

'When did you last see him?'

'Putney, where I heard him speak. We never were intimate.'

'Miles Sindercombe?'

'Unknown to me.'

'John Cecil?'

'No.'

'Sindercombe was a mischievous, very active army Leveller. He fomented the army plot in Scotland, if you heard about that – you never met him there?'

'I barely saw service in Scotland, sir. I was badly wounded at Dunbar. I can never wield a sword again to good purpose; I was shipped home.'

'I am sorry for your suffering . . . But you hold the Dunbar Medal?' After the compliment Thurloe asked, not altering his voice, 'Are *you* a Leveller?'

'True until death.' Gideon was not ashamed of his past. He reckoned the secretary of state would know his history, and that he had not been active recently. He refused to conceal his opinions.

'So what is your view of the present government, Captain Jukes?'

'I wish for elected representation – as I believe the Lord Protector does himself. When we risked all in the wars, we did it to secure free Parliaments. But I do understand how the present situation has come about. Every man thinks for himself – the fact that every man has such liberty is our great achievement – yet this makes for such contentious Parliaments, they cannot govern.'

'Do you believe His Highness the Lord Protector should be king?'

'I do not.'

That was a risk. Thurloe gazed at Gideon. It was a matter of record, Secretary Thurloe said the only political solution was to return the country into a formal monarchy – headed by King Oliver.

Gideon stuck his neck out as always: 'I believe Cromwell's refusal of the crown is his greatest quality. I trust his word that he accepts being Protector reluctantly, that he still hopes it can be temporary and that he never sought personal aggrandisement. Believing this, I support the present government. I will defend our Commonwealth with my life.'

'Then will you work with me, Captain?'

'I need to know what you are asking, sir.'

'One task: help me to arrest Colonel Lovell.'

Chapter Eighty-Two

The Whitehall Plot, January 1657

> *There is several practices in hand to cut off His Highness, and to make a diversion in the commonwealth of England . . .'*
>
> (The State Papers of John Thurloe)

Thomas Lovell saw the great fireworks being made. His father created them, on a table in their lodgings. Tom knew it was seriously dangerous. Orlando, who could airily take risks, even near his children, ordered him with great sternness not to touch any of the parts.

One explosive was built in a hand-basket. This was not just for concealment, but so the big sensitive bombarillo could be lifted and carried gently, without risk to those who handled it. It had not one but two slow fuses – lengths of match extending out on either side, each a yard long.

'Six hours,' said Lovell, groaning, as he gently massaged gunpowder into the matchcord to ensure that, once lit, it kept burning.

'That seems long.'

'Too long, Tom. Sindercombe's ridiculous instructions. To give these ninnies enough time for their terrified gallop to freedom!'

'If the explosion is to bring about a government that they want, why do they need to run away?'

'Good question!' Lovell laughed, proud of his son's intelligence, which he naturally saw as inherited from himself. On the other hand, curiosity was always discouraged.

'Where is it to be placed?'

'We shall see.'

'When will it be done?'

'We shall see that too.'

*   *   *

It was to be like Guy Fawkes's Gunpowder Plot. Lovell talked of that, while he was painstakingly putting together his own explosives. Fawkes's plan had been to blow up the King and Parliament all together at Westminster. Fawkes hired a vault under the Houses of Parliament, and the conspirators stuffed the vault full of gunpowder; the constant problem with gunpowder was that it deteriorated – and in a very short time, if it became at all damp. It had been said that Fawkes's decayed powder would have failed to ignite – although Lovell believed that was wrong; there had been so much powder in the confined vault – thirty-six barrels, say two and half tons – that once the burning match reached the hoarded barrels, they would have gone up in an enormous blast. All the powder would have activated. Not only would Parliament have disintegrated, blowing apart everyone inside, but the huge clouds of flying debris – large and small fragments of stone, glass, lead and rooftiles – would have wrought terrible damage throughout the village of Westminster, killing many others in the old medieval streets and narrow lanes.

'There would have been devastation, Tom. It would have caused terror then and there, plus fear throughout the land for many weeks afterwards. There would have been an ear-bursting, heart-stopping noise – then a terrible silence. After that, darkness, a heavy pall of smoke, acres of ruin.'

'And your devices will do the same in Whitehall?'

'Mine will be different.' Lovell continued to work the pitch and tar he was using. He was meticulous and methodical. Tom was sure these fireworks would behave properly; he could see why the other men viewed his father with respect. Lovell had made himself an expert. 'Vaults under government buildings are no longer hired out to the public, so that avenue is closed. We cannot carry large containers of gunpowder into Whitehall Palace. Some busybody would ask what we were doing. The Protector keeps a parsimonious household; every barrel of whelks is counted in. His office-holders refuse bribes too.'

'That is good?' piped up Tom.

'It is inconvenient for us!' answered Lovell, delighting his son with a fiendish grin.

'So what will you do?'

'This firebomb will be sneaked in and will explode, though not too vigorously. Its purpose is to start a fire, very hot and fast – an uncontrollable conflagration that will burn down those old buildings in spectacular style. There are wooden beams, floorboards, panelling that will take a spark in an instant, dry-as-dust old plastering, all the ancient hangings they have kept from the King's Wardrobe for the Protector's enjoyment, which will blaze from floor to ceiling. The buildings, too, are full of windings and turnings, where a fire can take hold and trap people. Miles Sindercombe calls it the fittest hole for a tyrant to live in —'

'Will young King Charles not need a palace? According to Master Sindercombe, he is coming back again.'

'In fact, Sindercombe hopes he will not.'

'They would cut off his head, if they caught him.'

'Ah Thomas, my boy, you worry me sometimes. I believe you have been infected with the rebels' ways of thought.'

'Well, I should like to see this almighty firework when it is set off!'

'You will see it go up, and so will all London.'

Lovell still kept the whereabouts of his lodgings secret from the others. In fact Sindercombe did the same, renting a room with a hatter, well away on London Bridge.

Lovell and Tom brought the first of the finished fireworks to an assignation with Sindercombe, then moved the device to John Toope's quarters. This was blatant, since the Lifeguards' barracks and stables were right in the Palace Mews.

Toope took Sindercombe and Boyes to reconnoitre and decide where best to plant their incendiary. They easily found their way into the ramshackle old building, unchecked by guards. They needed a central position, to create maximum damage with the initial blast, but a spot that was sufficiently isolated so the bomb would not be noticed while the long fuses burned. They would have to lay the device close to the Protector's lodgings, when he was sure to be in residence. Sindercombe had in his pocket a skeleton key, which he used to try to open rooms that might be suitable; it failed to work. Boyes was not amused. So they talked about laying the firework on the head of a staircase at the back of the chapel, but that seemed too public. Irritable and havering, they reached no decision.

Sindercombe and Boyes were afraid Toope was uneasy. He told the authorities later that he would have revealed the plan to the Protector, but could not gain private access to Oliver that day.

*   *   *

Sindercombe was so nervous about the Lifeguard's loyalty he recovered the device from Toope's quarters and took it for safety to where Cecil lodged, in King Street. This narrow old street was very close to the palace; it ran from St Margaret's, the Parliamentary church in Westminster, to one of the gates across Whitehall by St James's Park, where the palace buildings began.

The following Tuesday, Sindercombe met Toope at the Ben Jonson tavern in the Strand, at the opposite end of Whitehall. They had further intense conversation about the best way to proceed. Sindercombe gave assurances that he was expecting money from Sexby in Flanders by the next Monday – implying Toope would be given more cash if he continued to co-operate. Toope seemed more at ease. He volunteered to set the firework in the palace himself. Miles Sindercombe brushed aside that idea.

On Thursday, which was the 8th of January, Sindercombe, Cecil and Toope met at the Bear in King Street, where Sindercombe told Toope he and Cecil were now agreed that the device should be placed inside the palace chapel. A meeting was arranged for five o'clock that night when they would finally install the firebomb. Its match would burn until around about midnight, setting off the explosion while people were in bed. They could be confident the Protector would be in his private accommodation close by. He would perish in the initial fireball. The conflagration would be all the more dramatic for taking place at night.

Dusk had fallen when they met outside the chapel. They checked that everything in the area seemed to be as they wanted, then Miles Sindercombe and John Cecil went to fetch the great firework from King Street, lighting its match before they brought it. Being January, there was wintry darkness outside and they moved through the stone-slabbed palace corridors in eerie shadow, their nervous footsteps sounding far too loud. If they had stopped for a moment, they would have heard the faint fizzing of the slow matchcord in the hand-basket.

Cecil had crept here and cut a hole in the heavy chapel door, so he could unbolt it. Once he opened up, he and Toope kept guard to ensure nobody came by and noticed their activity. Sindercombe went in by himself and positioned the device. He nestled the fire-basket in one of the chairs. Afterwards, Cecil relocked the door. It was around six o'clock when they all went their separate ways, walking short distances through cold dark streets, their breath wreathing white in the January chill. In ten minutes they were mostly back in their individual lodgings. Only Sindercombe had farther to go.

What Sindercombe and Cecil failed to see was that despite their money and blandishments, John Toope had changed his mind.

At the chapel, guards had been secretly watching them. As soon as the plotters left, they quickly found the firework. They took it outside and tested it, causing a great flare of fire.

The troops went after the conspirators. Toope, who had revealed the plan to Thurloe earlier that day, handed himself over meekly. Cecil was also easily captured, giving up without a struggle; under interrogation he admitted everything. Only Miles Sindercombe, who took longer to find, put up a desperate fight; the soldiers only just managed to overpower him, after one of them cut off part of his nose. Covered with blood and still struggling wildly, Sindercombe followed Cecil to imprisonment in the Tower of London. He alone refused to answer any questions.

One of the group was not taken that night, nor was he traced in succeeding weeks. 'Boyes' had discreetly vanished.

Chapter Eighty-Three

London: 1657

I am persuaded to return this answer, That I cannot undertake this government with the title of king; and this is my answer to this weighty affair.

(The Protector's speech to Parliament at the
Banqueting House, May 1657)

John Cecil threw himself on the Protector's mercy and revealed everything about the plots. According to him, the others, Boyes in particular, were ruthless men of violence – *'not having the fear of God in their hearts, but moved and seduced by the instigation of the Devil'*. In giving their confessions and acting as witnesses against Sindercombe, Cecil and Toope escaped trial and punishment.

Miles Sindercombe stalwartly refused to admit anything. He was tried for treason on the 9th of February, a month after his arrest. Found guilty, he was sentenced to be hanged, drawn and quartered at Tyburn.

Whilst in the Tower of London, Sindercombe was visited by his widowed mother, his sister Elizabeth and an anonymous sweetheart. Somehow, he obtained an unknown toxic substance which he swallowed the night before his execution. Two hours later he was found in a coma, with a note that confirmed he intended to kill himself; he could not be restored to consciousness and very soon died. Before the civil war, Sindercombe had been apprenticed to a surgeon so it was presumed he had used his knowledge of poisons, though the substance was never identified, nor could his inquest decide how he had obtained it. Two post mortems had failed to ascertain anything certain. His suicide note declared, 'I do take this course because I would not have all the open shame of the world executed upon my body.' Though he could not be hanged as intended, as a suicide, his body was drawn to Tower Hill on a hurdle, naked; it was buried with an iron stake through the heart.

An unexpected result was renewed pressure on Cromwell to adopt the title of king. Although rumours of the failed fireball circulated almost immediately, Thurloe did not formally announce details of the plot to Parliament for ten days, after a frenzy of speculation had built up. Then he emphasised alarmingly how the assassination attempt had involved not only homegrown radical terrorists but designing foreign powers, all in alliance with the ever-treacherous Royalists. News-sheets relayed frightening stories of armies raised by these enemies, armies that were poised to sail to England at any moment in a flotilla of ships . . . This overlooked the known facts that Charles II had had a destructive quarrel with his brother the Duke of York; he had no money to pay for a fleet and his armies overseas were dwindling daily.

In the aura of panic, a day of thanksgiving for Cromwell's deliverance was held on Friday the 20th of February, with an enormous public feast in the Banqueting House. All the MPs were invited, as were foreign ambassadors. Four hundred luxurious dishes were served and the regal evening ended with a splendiferous musical entertainment. So great was the crush that a staircase collapsed, causing many injuries, particularly to Cromwell's eldest son Richard; he would eventually be known as Tumbledown Dick, supposedly from his indecisiveness, though perhaps also because in the accident he suffered several broken bones.

It had been assumed by many that the Protector would be offered the crown as he hosted this glittering occasion. This did not happen; perhaps the accident to Richard was an inhibiting factor. The formal request was made the following Monday, in the austere and appropriate environment of the House of Commons. It was stressed that a new monarchy, with a defined hereditary succession, might preserve Cromwell from further desperate attempts on his life. The offer specifically referred to the Sindercombe Plot: '*the continual danger your life is in from the bloody practices of the malignants and the discontented party . . . it being a received principle amongst them that nothing is wanted to bring us into blood and confusion and them to their desired ends, but the destruction of your person . . .*'

The first address to Cromwell was probably drafted by John Thurloe. It was repeated by Parliament in a modified form, but it was not universally welcomed; a hundred army officers appealed to Cromwell to reject the idea. Cromwell consistently maintained that kingship was unimportant to him; however, most people assumed he was attracted and would succumb eventually. It was believed that events were being stage-managed by Thurloe, with Cromwell's full approval.

After much private deliberation and prayer, however, Oliver Cromwell took an unexpected decision. After nearly two months' thought, he refused the crown. He conceded that those who had made the proposal were honourable, and that their purpose was to set the nation on a good footing. But he concluded that it would be sinful to take upon himself the title of king.

Cromwell made this surprise announcement to Parliament at a special meeting in the Banqueting House on the 7th of May. At the end of June Parliament would go into recess for six months and he was to be reproclaimed Protector, with much ceremony.

Then a pamphlet hit the streets – literally, for it was scattered there – entitled *Killing no Murder*. Authorship of *Killing no Murder* was ascribed to 'William Allen' – the genuine name of a New Model Army Leveller, an old associate of Sexby's. Allen denied involvement. Thurloe arrested John Sturgeon, another disaffected member of Cromwell's Lifeguards; whose connections with the Sindercombe plots were known. He had recently returned, secretly, from exile in Holland. *Killing no Murder* was printed in Holland.

Enough copies escaped into circulation. When Gideon Jukes read *Killing no Murder*, he laughed at its irony. Then he went hot-foot to visit Secretary of State Thurloe.

Thurloe saw him immediately. Gideon was taken to a small inner cabinet, where Thurloe had a copy of the pamphlet and a pile of witness examinations in front of him. 'This pernicious document has appeared all over the Continent – even published in *Dutch*! Royalists are crowing with delight, naturally . . .'

'But it is most certainly not by a Royalist,' Gideon murmured. He had brought his copy. It was a long tract, but he had read it carefully. As Thurloe brooded, Gideon quoted: *'"To Your Highness justly belongs the honour of dying for the people . . . Religion will be restored, Liberty asserted, and Parliaments have those Privileges they have fought for . . ."'*

Thurloe angrily took up the bile: *"In the Black Catalogue of High Malefactors, few can be found that have lived more to the affliction and disturbance of Mankind . . ."* This is slander and treason! It asks whether His Highness be a tyrant and if so, whether it be lawful – or profitable to the Commonwealth to do justice upon him? It means by killing him. It pretends that His Highness has put himself above the law, therefore should not have the law's protection.'

'Do you know where this has come from?' Gideon asked.

Thurloe summarised angrily: 'We were alerted to several Dutch vessels in the port of London. Colonel Barkstead learned that prohibited goods had been concealed in houses near the river. Barkstead ordered a search. At the house of Samuel Rogers, a distiller of strong-waters in St Katharine's Dock, he seized seven parcels of books, two hundred to each parcel. Rogers of course claimed no knowledge. When a watch was set secretly on his house, however, lo! There appears one Edward Wroughton – a man already known to us for distributing scandalous literature in Swan Alley.'

'Coleman Street?'

'You know it?'

'By reputation,' agreed Gideon, with a smile.

'Fifth Monarchy,' snarled Thurloe briefly. 'Venner's group. Your Okey is one –'

'Not *my* Okey!' Knowing that John Okey had recently only narrowly escaped a treason charge for involvement with the Fifth Monarchists, Gideon quickly distanced himself.

'Wroughton demanded to see an arrest warrant. These people are practised; he pointed out that the warrant specified *the assistance of a constable*. Barkstead's customs officer was compelled to send for one. Wroughton went along peacefully, but when they got him to the Tower Gate he suddenly broke free and they had to chase him all the way to Galley Quay.'

'Was Wroughton working for himself?'

'He was in league with John Sturgeon.'

'Arrested too?'

'Officers recognised Sturgeon in East Smithfield, carrying yet more bundles. They had paper wrapped about them, and were tied up with pack-thread, but the paper was loose and ruffled up, so the book titles were visible. The officers took from Sturgeon a pocket pistol' – Thurloe riffled through the examination papers – '*"which he had in a money-bag, a weapon with four barrels in the stock, being all charged and ready for execution."* He gave a false name, and has since refused to co-operate. *"Asked, whether or not he hath delivered any such books to Edward Wroughton? He saith, he will not answer to that, nor any other questions that shall be asked of him – though it be whether two and two make four" . . .'* Thurloe continued reading, with a startled expression, as if he had just noticed a postscript: 'Barkstead is so concerned he has asked for a back-dated warrant for Wroughton – lest he escape on a technicality!'

He looked up. He gazed for a moment at Gideon. 'And you have anxieties, Captain Jukes?'

This was Gideon's cue: 'I do not believe this well-penned piece, *Killing no Murder*, comes from William Allen. Edward Sexby wrote it.'

Thurloe started. 'It is Sexby's style?'

'Machiavelli peppering Scriptures and illustrations from the ancient Romans, like Jamaica spices mixed in a mortar. He cites not only Francis Bacon, but – cheekily – your own Secretary of Tongues, Mr John Milton! This is well-argued, thoughtful, sustained work. Twenty pages as good as anything Nedham produces for you –' Gideon noticed Thurloe looking put out. 'Well – I am a printer, as you know, and was told many years ago, never to take responsibility for ideas – but I can evaluate prose! See here, where he appeals to members of the army as his audience. The phrase he uses, *to all those Officers and soldiers of the Army that remember their engagements and dare to be honest* – "engagement" is a word beloved of Sexby; it is used again afterwards. And at the end he suddenly turns to the business of Miles Sindercombe, claiming his death was not suicide, but Colonel Barkstead smothered him with pillows. He equates Sindercombe with Brutus and Cassius – *"give him statues and monuments"* –'

'Wickedness!' snarled Thurloe.

'Persuasive wickedness: take it seriously. This has all Sexby's fervour. And the pamphlet is meant to introduce some new drama: *"Courteous reader, expect another sheet or two of this subject if I escape the tyrant's hands"* . . .' Thurloe shuddered. Gideon pressed on: 'Your arrest of Sindercombe and the rest lost Sexby his helpers. He will have to come to London himself.'

'Boyes too?' queried Thurloe. 'Your man Lovell?'

Gideon jumped on this instantly: 'If you think Lovell will *come*, then you know he has left England?'

Thurloe was almost tetchy. 'He went to Flanders.'

Gideon considered it, thinking of Thomas, now taken right abroad, to a strange country out of all reach of his family. 'Lovell *may* come here again – but Sexby will not send him. For Sexby, it is necessary that the Protector's life be taken by a man with the right credentials. A Royalist assassin will not do. The proclamation in June would seem an apt moment.' He and Thurloe both silently considered how the scene would be: trumpets, bells and bonfires, aldermen and soldiers, volleys of shot and huge crowds applauding them . . . a stupendous public occasion at which to cause terror with an assassination. Gideon then repeated, 'Sexby will come himself.'

Thurloe leaned back in his chair, his mouth compressed into an even tighter line than normal. He twirled a pen slowly between the fingers of his right hand. 'Reports come regularly that Sexby is here – we never see him to detain him . . .' He leaned forward to his papers again, looking tense. 'He somehow keeps the interest of both the Spanish and Charles Stuart . . . Here – from the end of January: *"It is not above five or six weeks since Sexby came last from England."* – So he was meddling, in December! Then he went back. Nothing changes!' Thurloe growled. 'Nothing, nothing, nothing . . .' He read again grimly: '*"You need to be very careful, that when His Highness should go forth to take the air, there be a special care had of the followers, that there be no strangers in company, but those who are known to be faithful . . ."* This came only in April.'

Gideon did not trust the April report. 'That sounds like some fool who has heard about the previous plots and reminds you to gain credibility. Did you pay money for that statement?'

'Cynic!' rebuked Thurloe good-humouredly. He plucked out another paper: '*"The sum of my intelligence from Flanders: Sexby did not go for England at the time formerly mentioned: want of money was the cause of his stay: he hath now received fourteen thousand pieces of eight, will be in England by the first of February. He expresses great regrets that the plot against His Highness's life did not take and gives out that he will lose his own, rather than fail to accomplish that design"* . . . Well, Sexby may come. Lovell may come. But I have a new concern.' Thurloe looked up and pierced Gideon with his fiercest gaze. 'Captain, when the Sindercombe plotters were examined, one – it was Toope – said Sindercombe had told him that a second great firework existed, in a box. He never knew where it was.'

'The gunpowder will be spent,' Gideon muttered at once, shaking his head. 'Even if he could have stored the bombarillo somewhere dry, it will be badly decayed.'

'Pitch and tar survive,' argued Thurloe. 'The spiteful thing could still do great damage. The first flamed up violently when it was tried. I want to find it, Captain. I would like *you* to find it.'

'Me? Surely the Lord Protector has his guards –'

'Toope was a Lifeguard!' Thurloe lifted yet another paper from his pile. 'Sturgeon is another such . . . Here I have an agent saying he shared a conversation in a tavern with some from His Highness's Lifeguard; they claimed one man in three of them is not to be trusted.'

Gideon knew enough history to be aware that great men surrounded by bodyguards were still at risk of assassination – most usually *by* their bodyguards. Not only did the soldiers have access, they lived close enough to see through their masters' charisma and to become disenchanted.

'Why trust me?' he demanded.

Thurloe smiled. 'I trust your desire to live in harmony with your wife, free of Colonel Lovell! Besides, you have an honest face.' He could be smooth. Flattery would not make Gideon co-operate; of course, John Thurloe knew that. He was both smooth and clever. He knew Gideon Jukes would assist for his own reasons.

Thurloe was right. Throughout the summer months, Gideon spent long hours searching. His mission was to find the explosive device, but he believed this would bring him close to Lovell.

He was given access to Cecil and Toope, whom he found less chastened than they should have been, in his opinion. They were as suspicious of him as he of them. Still, they helped him put together a list of places they had frequented with Miles Sindercombe. They also confirmed that the person they knew as Boyes had had a lad with him, a typical lad, who needed a wash and a haircut, who moped around taverns as they huddled at meetings or scuffled after his father looking bored. The lad had even helped Boyes carry the first firework, when it was brought in its hand-basket to Sindercombe.

'So *Boyes* made it?'

The second-hand glimpse of Thomas kept Gideon's interest from flagging. Hearing of it made Juliana tolerate his frequent absences from home and made Miles lenient when left to work in the print shop alone. Gideon did not mention Lovell's supposed second firework.

Cecil and Toope had never known where Boyes lodged. But they said he was easily able to come to assignations, so his room could not have been far away, certainly nearer than Sindercombe's room with Daniel Stockwell on London Bridge. Their regular haunts had been in the streets around Whitehall and Westminster. Gideon made house-to-house enquiries, undeterred by hostility from locals, who hated officialdom. Where he knew for certain that conspirators had stayed in particular houses or inns, he insisted on seeing the rooms they had occupied and searching for the missing firework. He went to all the drinking houses – and in King Street these were numerous. There he talked not only to landlords, but ostlers and tapsters. With Thurloe's approval, he promised money – either for details of the previous plots or reports about anyone suspicious who might turn up now.

The area where Gideon was searching had inns and ordinaries – the places where cheap meals could be bought – that he knew Robert Allibone had frequented when he winkled out subjects for his *Public Corranto*. Robert was always secretive, but Gideon used his name as an introduction. Once an ostler asked laughingly, 'Have you still got that silly old horse, Rumour? He liked his quart of ale!'

A landlord elsewhere rightly pointed out that Gideon was searching for ex-soldiers, but half the male population of London had fought in the civil wars at some time. They all knew how to swagger, and many had hoarded weapons since their time in service. The man Gideon was trying to track down would never stand out.

'You are asking us to remember a customer from January, and it is now high summer? Impossible. Besides, anyone who ever has a drink looks suspicious by the light of the wrong candle-end. We give him a stare, thinking he seems a bit odd, then he's guaranteed to glare back, looking even worse. You want to give up, Captain, before you're worn out!'

At yet another inn, Gideon met a bandy-legged landlord called Tew, an ex-sailor, now cultivating his beer belly. Like the rest, he denied any knowledge of Lovell; like the rest he gave the impression he knew something that he would not say. Tew ran the Swan, he said, with his sister. She was far too busy brewing to be called out for an interview, so Gideon did not meet her.

The Swan was a name-change; Robert would have known it as the Two Tuns. It seemed to thrive and had good ale. Gideon said so to the landlord. 'Well, pass on to your sister my praise — and what I said about the Delinquent, Lovell. If she ever does emerge into daylight from her brewhouse, she may see him.'

'Oh I'll tell her — but I give nowt for your chances, Captain,' answered Nat Tew in his lugubrious sing-song accent, enjoying the hopelessness. It made Gideon hunch his shoulders and move on. London landlords were bad enough; northerners, with their world-weary pessimism, made him truly depressed.

King Street had inns from end to end. These were all dark, unwelcoming holes, full of unhelpful, untrustworthy, dangerous-looking people, none of whom wanted to have anything to do with the government. At least Gideon knew they would have been the same, whatever government held power. They had all heard about Sindercombe's firework — the one placed in the palace chapel. A few even made vague claims, which rapidly collapsed under scrutiny, that they knew a man who knew someone else who had seen the device sitting on a tavern table . . . Nobody had ever heard of a second firework — or so they said.

In June, Thurloe received information that Sexby might be making one of his secret trips back to England.

There was no mention of Lovell. However, according to intelligence, Charles Stuart was sending his own would-be assassins. Gideon believed Lovell would be among them, perhaps the leading one. Everything he had learned about the man suggested he was too restless to hang around some hostile European town in a rundown regiment of the King's or Duke of York's, waiting to take part in a hypothetical invasion that might never happen. Lovell would be up to mischief. Lovell would return to England.

Lovell was indeed back. After the failure of the firework plot, he had fled to the Continent, taking Thomas. It was now almost a year since Tom had joined his father. He had had his thirteenth birthday, in November, and it was not lost on him that his father had been quite unaware of this anniversary. Tom knew his mother would have been thinking of him. In his heart, he knew she thought about him every day.

Being thirteen had made Tom wonder what his life would be. As Royalist exiles, he and his father were living on their uppers, with no real social place and no prospects. Tom loathed being in a foreign country, unable to speak the language, uncertain of his way around, frightened he might never see his home again. Other sons of cavaliers were sent back to England to live on their fathers' estates with their mothers; arrangements were made for these sons to have education and careers. Tom Lovell realised that no such life was planned for him. When he tried to talk to his father, Orlando merely said, 'We have to shift for ourselves, lad.' Tom mentioned cautiously how Lambert Jukes had once offered him an apprenticeship. His father's reaction was dramatic: 'Damme, I'd sooner have you dead in a ditch than a manufacturer of ships' biscuit!'

'Well, I never agreed to it,' Tom backed out hastily. 'Though Uncle Lambert did tell me, I could end up an alderman – or even Lord Mayor of London.'

Orlando Lovell became so distressed and annoyed, that although normally abstemious, he drank a whole bottle of Rhenish wine in half an hour before dinner, and then was ill after it.

He almost refused to bring Tom with him the next time he came back to England. But there was nowhere in unfriendly Flanders where a penniless English boy could be safely left. It was cheaper, and more secure, to bring Tom back. Travelling as a pair also made them less conspicuous.

Thomas seemed compliant. He never asked to return to his mother, never now even wanted to write to her. So father and son slipped ashore at Dover, which Royalists rightly believed was a slack port where unlawful immigrants could easily land. They made their way to London. After several moves to confuse observers, Lovell took them to an inn where they had stayed once before, the Swan in King Street. They had now slipped back into their old skulking life, looking anonymous and unremarkable.

But Thomas had his own ideas about that.

One evening, half an hour's walk away in Bread Street, Anne Jukes happened to glance out of a small window that overlooked the private yard at the back of her house. Lambert had recently completed his father's long-ago-planned house-of-easement, in memory of John. It was also to please his wife who, ever since the Ranting incident, believed it her right to exact work around the house at frequent intervals.

Glancing through the pane, Anne suppressed a startled squeak. She saw a boy she recognised, carrying a small bundle, slip into the house-of-easement. He did not come out.

Ten minutes later Anne walked quietly across the yard. She pulled open the door and remarked into the gloom, 'I made one of my walnut cakes this afternoon. I can bring you some out here – but you have no need to crouch in the dark. There is Gideon's old room in the house, just waiting to be occupied by somebody who needs a refuge, Thomas.'

Chapter Eighty-Four

The Tower of London: July 1657

The ceremonies for the Protector were held without incident. On July the 24th, a warrant was issued for the arrest of Edward Sexby. That same day, a man was plucked off a ship just as it was about to sail for Flanders. He was arrested and taken rapidly back to London. He looked like a countryman, in shabby clothes and with a rough beard; born in Suffolk, he managed a creditable country accent. But customs officers had seen through the disguise.

He was brought to the Tower. The welcoming party regarded him curiously. Following so many doomed world-movers and crown-chasers into that great fortress, was enough to make any heart quake. He showed no reaction as he was dwarfed by the stronghold, a city in itself, with its intimidating curtain walls, numerous towers – some so massive they had towers of their own – silent cannon, working portcullises, ancient chapels where implacable monarchs and governments had laid to rest queens, traitors, pretenders and misfits who offended them. He would know there were torture chambers. Deep in the bowels, out of earshot, was ferocious equipment, developed over centuries, in the keeping of heartless operators who enjoyed their work.

A tall, fair-haired man had been hurriedly sent by Thurloe. He identified the prisoner: 'Yes, this is Sexby.'

Sexby bore no malice. His self-confidence, always only a little short of arrogance, made him proud to be recognised. They were using the Beauchamp and Broad Arrow Towers for political prisoners these days, though there was plenty of choice. Sexby was taken to a cell, a grim lodging but at least it was a room, not a dungeon. Taking a chance, Gideon asked to be allowed time with him.

'Yes, settle him in – good notion. Soften him up . . .' No chance of that, not with Sexby.

It was nine years since Holdenby, eight from the Putney Debates. Gideon found Sexby older, more worn, yet more direct; probably he himself was the same. As a prisoner, Sexby looked tired, withdrawn, accepting. He made no excited protestations of innocence: all classic signs of guilt. Briefly questioned on arrival, he had given very little away. He would be like Sindercombe, never admitting anything. He would positively enjoy holding out. But Gideon did not believe Sexby would kill himself; he would force Cromwell to execute him, intending that Cromwell would look more tyrannical.

The two men stared around the bare, dark cell, with its barred windows, cold stone walls, empty fireplace. There was a narrow bed and an uneven little table. Through the thick stone walls crept sickness, damp, bedbugs and despair. There was a high risk of death.

'I would offer to bring in necessities, but . . .' Gideon was thinking of Sindercombe and the poison. Daring escapes had happened over the Tower's long history, but Colonel Barkstead was meticulous. He had caught one Royalist soaking his window bars with aqua fortis. He would not lose Sexby.

'Ink and paper?'

Gideon shook his head. 'Forbidden. I heard you are married – your wife and any other family will be allowed to visit.' Sexby gave a faint nod. Mrs Elizabeth Ford, the mistress who effected Sexby's escape from capture at Weymouth, now called herself Elizabeth Sexby; she had been with him in Flanders and had borne him children.

Gideon felt more demoralised than he had expected. Sexby half unbuttoned his coat, the best he could do to make himself at home. He turned and shared a fatalistic glance with Gideon. Though they had reached different positions, their shared past experiences gave them bonds. Both sighed. Neither blamed the other. The mutual dislike they had felt all those years ago became a matter of indifference.

'End of an era,' said Gideon in a grey voice. 'Walwyn is doctoring the poor, Wildman died of a seizure outside Eltham Jail as he returned from bail, Overton has turned to wild religion.' Lilburne, turning pragmatist, was still on the loose. Neither Gideon nor Sexby mentioned it. Gideon glanced at the door and lowered his voice as if his purpose was unofficial. 'My second wife was married to Orlando Lovell, the Royalist known as William Boyes. Will you tell me where to find him?'

Sexby looked at him more keenly. Gideon's legal quandary did not interest him; he was locked inside his personal predicament, weighing everything that was said to him against that. 'Have you been told to ask me?'

'My quest is personal.'

'I know nothing of him.' A standard answer. Gideon realised Sexby did not trust him. Even without knowing that Gideon had been ordered to look for the second firework, Sexby would protect Lovell.

'He has my wife's son.'

'*His* son, presumably.' Sexby shrugged. Elizabeth would have to bring up their children alone; Gideon wondered just how much – or how little – Sexby had invested in them emotionally.

Still, he tried again. 'Lambert wanted Thomas to be a grocer.'

Sexby, once a grocer's apprentice, finally laughed. 'And how is Lambert?'

'His health is broken.' He held up his own arm like a bird's broken wing. 'And I too am ruined.' Gloomily philosophical, Gideon opened up to Sexby, speaking his fears for the future as he would to no one else: 'We regret nothing. We would do it all again, and gladly. We recite to ourselves that miserable cliché, our fighting achieved so little, yet not to have fought would have been disastrous. It is, of course, no consolation. Failure has lain in wait all along and nothing changes that.'

Sexby was tensed to resist interrogation yet he too seemed prepared to forecast: 'Cromwell will die. The young Charles Stuart will return. Whatever promises he makes, monarchy restored under him will have a godless, dissolute core.' He spoke as one who had seen the man at close quarters. 'He will round up all those who brought his father to account. Liberty, which has died under Cromwell, will be permanently lost then . . . Well! I shall not see it.' Gideon could not argue with that bald conclusion. 'What will you do, Gideon Jukes?'

'As I must. Endure it. It has been fifteen years since we took up arms,' said Gideon. 'People are tired. Tired of fighting. We did our best, but we cannot continue. We want a normal life. A week of work, a Sunday sermon, a wife and children in the home, peace and prosperity. We want a settled commonwealth.'

'Your commonwealth is a lost cause,' Sexby told him. *No thanks to you*, thought Gideon.

He could bear no more and ended the interview. To his surprise, Sexby sent him off with the old Leveller salute: 'True unto death!'

Gideon could not bring himself to return the same.

It would take until November, four months of mental grind, for the authorities to persuade Edward Sexby to admit he was the author of *Killing no Murder.* Raving and shaking with an ague, he would confess everything – or so it would be said. Sexby would have no trial, but an inquest would decide he had been carried off by jail fever. That, he would have said, was extremely convenient for Cromwell.

His wife, recently delivered of a child, sent her maid with forty shillings to have him buried. Although she was given the opportunity to have his body taken outside, with her husband's kind of defiance, Elizabeth Sexby told them to inter him in the grounds of the Tower of London where he had died.

Gideon never saw Sexby again. Feeling exhausted and mournful, he had walked out that evening from a gatehouse, into the vast open interior spaces of the Tower of London, bathed in the last filtered twilight of a long July evening. Candles showed high in the constable's quarters. Military sounds came from the garrison. A breeze carried the smell of the stables; even its pungency failed to eradicate the stench of prison neglect he had absorbed. Chilled to the bone even after so short a visit, he felt his shoulder aching badly.

Somewhere here, Gideon remembered, was a copy of the Magna Carta. It had been shown to Lord Fairfax once, but Gideon Jukes did not request a viewing.

Chapter Eighty-Five

The Swan Tavern, King Street: July 1657

Mrs Maud Tew was well aware that her brother grew more and more to resemble their father. Red in the face, outstanding in the belly, complaining and work-shirking, Nat had happily adopted the traditions of his ancestors. He had become as useless as Emmett always was. Maud Tew squared up to her fate with resignation – a slight, pallid but pert figure, who had made herself formidable in her chosen domain. She looked as if a puff of wind would bowl her over, though she had the wiry strength of all working women who constantly heaved about heavy tubs and barrels. Nat allowed her to do it, unaware that she was perfectly capable of carrying out such work, whilst simultaneously plotting in her nowadays well-ordered mind how to be rid of him.

Her thin brown hair was tied in a tight little topknot, without a cap or headscarf, though she wore an oversized white collar on her tiny shoulders, above a more-or-less fitting grey gown. A capacious apron completed what would have been a respectable ensemble, had not the butt of her pistol been visible in her apron pocket where a lesser woman might carry a housewife-cloth to dust her mantel-shelves.

Mrs Tew had a reputation. Both her brother and her customers respected and admired it. She made no secret that she had been a soldier, in disguise; it was also reported that she had been a highway robber, like the infamous Molly out at the Black Dog Tavern on Blackheath. Maud kept her mouth shut about her history, but for a slightly built woman who kept an alehouse in a hard district, such rumours did no harm. It was one way to impress upon the public the Act against Drunkenness; when the Swan's customers had supped enough in her opinion, they were encouraged homewards by her gun.

It was, therefore, not sensible for anyone to cause a rumpus in her tavern's yard. When one of the occasional lodgers lost his temper with an ostler, he was asking for it. *Thomas, the ostler at the Swan, pistolled coming to take their horses* . . . Hearing the racket, Maud ran up from the brewhouse. She found a swank cove in a suit that annoyed her, yelling that his young son had been permitted to run off. He was attempting to take his horse from the ostler, who kept a good hold of the animal because the reckoning had not been paid.

'Now then!' cried Maud.

'You tell him, Maud,' encouraged Nat. Customers came out and jostled one another, eager to see the fun.

'So who is this?' demanded Maud like an actress, with her usual sarcasm, as if the cove were just a woodlouse that crawled under her broom as she swept out the taproom.

'Mr Boyes,' said her brother, pretending this situation was none of his fault.

'I think not!' rounded Maud, who still remembered the man from Birmingham. 'I know you,' she said, speaking directly to Lovell. She was no longer in the least afraid of him. She could not tell whether the cavalier who had once — twice — nearly killed her simply for being in his way now understood. 'This dodger's name is Lovell.'

'Oh!' piped up Nat. At last he spotted the connection. 'Would he be the dangerous cavalier the man Jukes was searching for so urgently?'

'Your head is as soft as a poached egg, Nat,' his sister informed him. 'None the less, it is true, and Master Jukes will pay us a fine ransom.'

Colonel Orlando Lovell cursed her to hell and back, very fluently like a true cavalier. Then he abandoned his horse — which was valuable — and his luggage — which was not. As he turned on his heel with a derogatory expression, ready to make his getaway without paying his bill, Maud did what she notoriously did to bolters. She advised him to stay where he was. To make sure he listened to her kind words, she drew out her pistol and threatened to shoot him.

When Orlando Lovell kept walking, she fired.

'That never happened before!' marvelled Nat. It was unlikely to be necessary again. Word would soon spread.

Lovell took her ball in the shoulder. He did not stop, but loped off into King Street. Keeping well back in case of trouble, Nat followed the blood spots all the way to the Cockpit Gate before the trail petered out.

Afraid to report he had lost the debtor, Nat drank ale at several other taverns, then crept home guiltily. Maud ticked him off on principle, then sold Lovell's horse, weapons and various disguises all within the next half-hour. She knew that unless Lovell found a surgeon very quickly, he was a dead man walking.

On the same morning, Lambert Jukes had gone to see his brother at the print shop. He sent Miles out to buy muffins. Then Lambert, broad as a gate and unusually sombre, seated himself on a joint-stool with his knees apart and his arms folded.

'Now listen to me, young Gideon, and do not interrupt. Tom Lovell is safe. We have him at home with us. You are not to visit, or let his mother visit, or do anything that will lead an observer to our house —' As the startled Gideon made to interject, Lambert held up his hand. 'Now, be calm in your spirits and thankful for this boy's intelligence. He came to us because his father will look for him — and the first place Lovell will come to is your house.'

Gideon was still resisting: 'Lambert, Thomas holds information. Enquiries must be made of him.'

Both brothers were silent, loathing the unpalatable thought of subjecting a child to formal interrogation.

'I will not allow it,' decided Lambert.

Gideon laid a hand on his brother's shoulder; Lambert shook him off. 'Lambert —'

'We shall lose him — he will run away back to his father.'

'Listen to me, Lambert. There may have been a second great firework for killing the Protector. Lovell made them. Thomas can tell us where they were living, where Lovell has perhaps left the device in a box —'

Lambert stood up. 'They stayed at the Swan, in King Street. Lovell brought them back again this week.' Gideon realised Lambert had in fact gently questioned the boy. 'Tom has mentioned no firework — but he is anxious because his viol, which Anne gave him, was left behind when they fled. His father told him not to ask after it.'

Gideon at once put on his coat. 'Go home, Lambert.'

'Not I!' Lambert scoffed. 'Do not argue. This is not Holdenby House. This time I am coming with you!'

* * *

They were too late. By the time they rolled up at the Swan, with Lambert puffing badly as Gideon hustled him, they were informed by the landlady that Lovell had left. Gideon swore. 'I talked about the gentleman before, with Master Tew —' He remembered Nat Tew as gloatingly unhelpful.

'I've sent that fool to buy meat pies for the ordinary. If you must speak, speak to me.' The sister eyed up Gideon with an attitude he could not place.

'I told your brother I was looking for a fugitive, William Boyes.'

'Lovell,' Mrs Tew agreed placidly. 'I knew him when he was a filthy cavalier in Prince Rupert's bloody army. I saw him at Birmingham. He never remembered me — but I knew him. Nat gave him the room, more fool him. I had not seen him myself until today, and I never saw the young boy. They were here for two days without any trouble. Then the boy vanished and the man caused a commotion. I shot him.'

'That must have surprised him,' said Gideon, feeling surprised himself.

'I know you too; you are Gideon Jukes,' said the woman coolly. 'Does that surprise *you?*'

She was pleased how astonished it made him. 'You know me from where?'

'On the road by Stony Stratford. Calverton — you wanted me to know the parish. I had another name then —'

'Dorothy Groome!'

'Well, I am Mrs Maud Tew now, and that's for real.'

'I am amazed she still remembers you,' commented Lambert to his brother.

'I remember the day I gave birth in a ditch!' asserted Maud Tew without embarrassment. 'Your brother was just a big stripling on a saggy-backed old horse — though he was spying for Sir Sam Luke then, and Nat says he's spying for John Thurloe now.'

Gideon was terse. 'I need to search Colonel Lovell's room.'

Maud Tew shrugged her narrow shoulders. 'Nothing there. As soon as he scarpered, I galloped to look. Just the usual full piss-pot and a smell of trouble.'

'Would that trouble smell like brimstone, pitch and tar?'

'What?'

'I must search your whole house. I apologise, but it may save you being blown up. While I am looking, please ask all your staff again: do they remember Lovell before? And when he went away then, did he leave behind a box?'

'He did not,' asserted Mrs Tew, jauntily. 'I would have looked in it.'

'A musical instrument?' asked Lambert.

'That would have been sold! But I would remember.'

'Could he have hidden something?'

'Where? Up the chimney with the jackdaw nests?'

'This would cause more than a soot-fire!' chortled Lambert.

'Cellars? Attic?' Gideon persisted.

'We are in and out of the cellars all the time, so no. The public never rummage in my attics; if he went up there, he's a cheeky beggar.'

'Oh Lovell is that!' Gideon confirmed. She knew he was right. 'Madam, take me to your garrets, if you will.'

In a low roof space at the Swan Tavern, Gideon and Lambert discovered Tom Lovell's missing viol. Its dead weight immediately revealed that it had been meddled with. When they lifted it down and found space and light in a low corridor to examine the thing, they could see its gut strings had been removed and the high bridge was missing. The silenced instrument was not one of the older designs that had a central sound hole; it resonated through two elegant F-shaped scrolls; they were too narrow to admit material in any quantity. So someone had spent time very skilfully removing the flat back of the viol's polished body, either prising it free or cutting it around the edge with a slim knife. The body, with its elegant waist, had been taken apart carefully, packed full and reassembled – glued and tied around with pack-thread, tightly in the first instance, though since it was done, the material inside had dried out the wood and made it gape slightly at the seams. 'Like an old powder barrel!' Lambert said meaningfully.

This size of viol was meant to be bowed by a seated performer, balancing it on the floor. Its neck would extend above the player's head. If such a large instrument was stuffed full of explosives, it was quite a bomb.

The Jukes brothers were both spirited. Gideon looked at Lambert; Lambert grinned back. Rather than wait for soldiers to remove the device officially, they each grabbed an end and lugged the viol downstairs between them, keeping it as horizontal as possible, which was how it had been stored. Outside, they put it down on its back in the middle of the small stable yard. A lad was sent to the Whitehall Mews for Lifeguards to take the device into custody.

Puffing out their cheeks with relief, Lambert and Gideon retired to a doorway; they calmed their nerves with pewter tankards of Maud Tew's excellent ale. Soon, she called them indoors for refills. While they were inside, one of Maud's more stupid customers wandered up to have a look. Detecting nothing of interest, he tapped out his pipe on the viol. Sparks fell through the sound-holes. Inside, a mass of combustible material was connected to gunpowder which was contained, for extra power, in a metal tube. Since the attic had been extremely dry, this still retained enough viability to produce a great flash and sheets of flame.

The mighty bang was not so large as the explosion of the magazine at Edgehill, into which a soldier put his hand while holding a lighted match. Nor so terrible as the eruption of eighty-four barrels of gunpowder at Torrington Church that nearly killed Sir Thomas Fairfax in a shower of blazing timbers, bricks and molten lead. Nor yet so enormous as the old gatehouse at Colchester that the two Jukes brothers had watched burst apart, showering severed limbs and shattered stone for many yards. But it was larger than anybody present ever wanted to experience.

The customer was killed outright. Fragments of him were flung across the yard. His clay pipe was seen later, stranded up on the thatch, mysteriously unbroken by its flight. Flames in the courtyard leapt as high as the second-floor balcony. Daubs of molten pitch flew in all directions, sticking to people and dribbling down walls, doors and windows. Small fires started where burning substances landed. Horses in the stables panicked. Women put aprons over their heads and ran away screaming. Men quickly sobered, picked themselves up and ran for water buckets. Mrs Tew flew among them, rapping out orders as she tried to save her tavern.

Lambert threw himself into fire-fighting. As if he had suddenly realised just what they were dealing with in Orlando Lovell, he roared at his brother to run, run home at once to where he might be sorely needed. So as the fire at the Swan came under control, Gideon Jukes raced off in pursuit of the man who had caused it. As fast as he could, Gideon set off back to Shoe Lane.

He was too late there too.

Chapter Eighty-Six

Shoe Lane: July 1657

No man takes a wife but there is an engagement, and I think that a man ought to keep it.

(Thomas Rainborough at the Putney Debates)

It was about three o'clock in the afternoon when Orlando Lovell walked into Juliana's shop. She looked up. Simply by standing silent in the doorway he had made her afraid. He came in and bolted the door behind him so they would not be interrupted.

Lovell had a burning pain in his left shoulder. He had dug out the slug himself, using a little quill-pen knife; he never lacked physical courage. He had buttoned up his coat tight to the collar, concealing the blood on his shirt. Some men swallowed aqua vitae in these circumstances, believing it would dull the pain. Lovell knew it did not work. Besides, he needed a clear head.

It was nearly ten years since he had seen his wife. Juliana had gone from a girl to a mature woman. Lovell found her queening it in her little shop, crisp and confident, fuller in the body, steelier in mind. But her face looked tired, and Lovell knew he had done that to her, by abducting Tom.

He told himself he was not, and never had been, a bad man. He had no real wish to hurt Juliana, not for hurt's sake. He just wanted what was his. He wanted it now, for most particular reasons. He had to get Tom back; Tom knew too much.

Lovell could see, even before he spoke to her, there was no chance of taking Juliana from that man, Jukes. He did not fool himself that he wanted her himself. He had lived without her happily enough for a long time. What did annoy him was the way she looked at him, as if she knew what he thought without his even having spoken. He resented being understood. He liked to be mysterious.

Naturally, he hated the fact Juliana preferred another man. 'Oh dear heart! What have you done to us?' Sighing heavily, he made his voice profound with sorrow, like an ageing tragedian throwing his all into a talismanic role for which he had been famous.

Jarred out of her trance, Juliana demanded, 'Where is Thomas?'

Lovell smiled sadly. 'I came here to ask you the same question.'

She panicked. 'What have you done with him?'

'He ran off. So, if he did not come here to you, the ungrateful brat could be anywhere.'

'He is just a child!' Juliana cried, as if father and son had just gone off together on a fishing trip and Lovell had lost sight of the boy accidentally. 'How could you let him go roaming the streets? Anyone may abduct him, for terrible purposes. How did you make him run away from you?'

Lovell immediately put the blame on her. 'Well, *you* brought him up disobedient and reckless!'

'Oh no! He inherited running away from you.' Juliana's voice hardened. They ought to have been strangers, but they fell into a quarrel like any married couple.

Lovell watched her, as she tried to gauge how to handle this situation. She was better-looking than he remembered. Her features had sharpened handsomely, while her new self-assurance made her shine. She dressed more prettily than she might have done as the wife of a Bible-scrutinising, psalm-singing, perjury-preaching puritan. Selling haberdashery demanded that she have fancies about her. Her skirt was glazed linen, over which she wore an unusual finely knitted jacket, patterned in shades of salmon and fern green; the silk came from Naples, but she had knitted the panels herself. Unadorned by jewellery – though Lovell was irritably sure he had given her plenty – she had tied up her dark hair in a neat bun, pulled straight back without a fringe nowadays, but still with bundles of side-ringlets like those she used to wear.

When he first walked in, Juliana had found that her mind cleared, the way soldiers must ignore everything except the immediate frightening emergency. She wanted to rid her premises of Lovell as quickly as possible, concentrating on that, even though she must learn what he had done with Tom and prevent his taking anything else she treasured . . .

'What happened to the little one?' Orlando's eyes bored into Juliana, as he instinctively sensed her anxiety.

'Valentine? His name is Valentine!' Juliana reprimanded him. 'I brought him up, as best I could, having no money or support from you. Sometimes we went hungry; often we were afraid; we were unwelcome where you had left us; and virtually homeless –'

'Don't dramatise. I know you lived in Lewisham.' Lovell glanced around, his lip curling. 'And now you have *this*! You have dwindled yourself into a seller of trifles –'

'*This*', Juliana informed him, stiffening, 'is what my father did, and my grandfather. *This* has put clothes on our backs and food on the table. Yesterday, for instance, we had scotch collops and tonight we shall have a chicken fricassee, which is Val's favourite.'

Wilfully missing the point, Lovell reminisced: 'Ah how I remember when you used to make us with your own hands a wonderful *quelquechose* –' A *quelquechose* was a mixed pan-fried dish with many ingredients – whatever a stretched housewife could cobble together by emptying her pantry. As a bride and young mother, Juliana had certainly been stretched and she remembered it bitterly. 'So dear little Val likes a fricassee, does he?' Juliana regretted mentioning Valentine. Lovell, who probably still thought of his younger son as a toddler, was playing on her fear again. 'So where is my little lordling?'

'He goes to school.' Juliana was hiding the truth. Valentine was here. He was upstairs, kept off school with an illness, probably feigned. Val's idea of a good life was lying in bed, wrapped in a quilt, surrounded by books and toys, with the dogs Muff and Hero snuggled alongside him, tended by sympathetic women who would bear him broths or fruit juices. Now eleven years old and a master-manipulator, Val had perfected a cough that sounded as if he had only two days left on earth. It had to be taken seriously. The one time Juliana had hardened her heart and sent him to school anyway, he had been brought home in an apple cart, semi-conscious, with the worst case of croup the doctor had ever seen . . . 'He is good at his books and is to go to Oxford University with a generous legacy from poor Edmund Treves.' She could not help a note of pride.

Lovell burst out in loud laughter. 'Well, thank the Lord! It is a gentlemanly future! I knew there was a reason for taking up with Edmund.' His voice dropped gravely, perhaps in memory of Treves. He and Juliana shared that moment, because Edmund had been a friend of their youth, a friend of their married life . . . 'Where else would Thomas go, if not here?'

'He is thirteen! Where has he to go?' snapped Juliana.

'Where does your printer work?'

'In Holborn.'

'He is there now? When will he return?'

'I have no idea.'

Lovell scoffed with sarcasm, not believing her. 'Well, suppose Thomas goes to him . . . Will not your fellow dash straight here, to bring your darling back to you?'

Juliana thought that Gideon might very well take Thomas straight to the intelligence office.

Lovell came closer. The pain from his bullet wound was bothering him; he lurched slightly against the counter. Unaware of the reason, Juliana even wondered if he might be tipsy; his eyes glittered with enlarged pupils and his cheeks were flushed.

Lovell assumed a soft expression, calculated to remind her of old moments of tenderness and lovemaking. 'You look as you did the day I first met you in Wallingford —' He reached out with one hand, as if to tweak her ringlets. Juliana jerked her head back, keeping away from him. '. . . Well, what do you think, Juley — will your man bring my boy home?'

She saw the dangers and hoped not. 'You assume Thomas can find his way to Holborn.'

'Oh he's bright.' Lovell made his tone suggest he now knew Tom better than she did.

'Tom would come to me.' Juliana, who never doubted her child's intelligence, desperately hoped he would work out that his father would come looking here.

Lovell fell silent. Once Thomas changed allegiance, he might successfully go into hiding. The past nine months had taught the boy about living undercover . . . 'I wonder — is that what you really think? You know how to wriggle when questioned!'

'I learned it', Juliana retorted, 'lying to the Committee for Compounding about your actions, then under interrogation from Parliament about your whereabouts!'

'Was it you who laid the information against me?'

The sudden question was crude. It shocked Juliana. 'How can you suggest it? I defended you, Orlando; I did it for years and against all comers —'

He at once became contrite. 'Oh I have been such a trouble to you! Sweetheart, I apologise –'

'You feel nothing. You never did.'

Lovell still had choices. Soon, with this wound, those choices would run out. Although he had done his best to cleanse the bullet hole and pack it, he was starting to feel drowsy. He decided that this was the best place to rest. The house was private enough. 'So Tom will come here ... Let us not stand in your shop, my dear. You and I will go upstairs and seat ourselves politely. Then we shall wait.'

Juliana flinched. She had managed to endure him in her shop, which was a public place, but letting him into her home, the home she shared with Gideon, would be hideous.

Lovell saw it. He grew angry, with an acid growl in the guts. He urged Juliana towards the lobby where he knew the stairs were, though he himself stayed and began flinging open the drawers where she kept her stock. He tossed out whatever he found there – ribbon, tape, needles, embroidery scissors, skeins of wool, buttons, bright silks wrapped in paper ...

'If you are searching for the carbine,' Juliana told him coldly, refusing to show her panic, 'Gideon took it away to Holborn, to find out why it did not fire.'

'He told you about that!'

She did not trouble to reply. Unable to bear the sight of her jumbled stock, she turned away and went quickly upstairs. Her mind whispered secretly, *If Gideon comes home, he will see the disturbance and know who is here ...*

Lovell followed her.

His presence was now an invasion. They were both aware of it.

Upstairs, he gazed around. He could see that this was the home Juliana had always said she wanted. She had made everywhere comfortable, in her own style. She and Jukes must have money. Their main room had had its walls painted with stencils of tendrilled flowers. Light monotone curtains hung at windows on fine brass rods, except where there were previously existing wooden shutters. Little of their furniture could be inherited; they had new sets of turned barley-twist chairs with long cane panels, small buffets, a large rectangular table that must have been a challenge for its hauliers to manipulate upstairs. Plain chimney boards stood across the grates since it was summer. There was an almanac nailed up in a corridor, with a couple of old maps. Conveniences were in good supply – hanging shelves and cupboards, joint-stools, rush-light holders, candle boxes, firedogs. Everywhere were cushions, embroidered in glorious colours.

Reconnoitring, Lovell flung open doors. Beyond the main room on the first floor he found a smart little parlour, with Juliana's needlework on a small round gateleg table; he also saw a teetering pile of news-sheets on the floor, beside a second chair. That annoyed him. Exploring on the second floor, his mood grew worse. The first room he looked in was the master bedroom. The bed had been made earlier; its coverlet was neutrally smoothed, hiding the side-by-side pillows. But beneath a square, rush-topped stool stood a pair of man's shoes, toes together and heels apart, tidy yet easy and casual. The householder's nightshirt, embroidered in self-colour linen thread, hung on a double hook, along with his wife's woollen shawl.

Deliberately offending Juliana, Orlando Lovell stretched out on her marital bed, in his boots. 'Comfortable!'

Too comforting: so tempting, he risked giving way to pain and losing his control. With a charmless invitation, he held open his arms to her. Sickened, Juliana turned away, on the verge of weeping.

Lovell swung upright. Sulkily, he sat on the edge of the bed. He looked around. Forcing himself to activity, he pulled open the door on the little pot-cupboard. He looked under the bed. The house was swept and spotless, so he was not surprised he found nothing; a man with an item to hide would know the maid would discover it there. Lovell stood, knocked chairs aside, filled the room with his violence.

'What do you want?' Juliana begged, trying to make him leave her bedroom.

'His other carbine.'

'Children live in the house – for heaven's sake! It is safe in its box, up on the top of the press cupboard.' This was a tall item for storing clothes, with deep drawers below an upper section that had doors.

'Get it for me.'

'Get it yourself!'

'Do as I say.' Lovell strode to Juliana, dragging her by one arm. Impatiently she pulled free, fetched a chair to climb on and lifted down the box.

Lovell snatched it. One-handed, he removed the gun, tucking it under his elbow as he took bullets and powder and charged it. Juliana was not altogether alarmed. Men regularly had weapons at home. She watched Lovell select spare bullets and powder. He shoved the gun through his belt.

There was no suggestion he would use the weapon to terrorise her. Why should he? To him, they still had their natural married relationship. He was giving orders which she obeyed. He expected her to be dutiful. She tried not to anger him. Only Juliana knew how much she was silently defying him.

He stared around the room once more, then stormed out, jerking his head for her to follow. He stomped back downstairs to the first floor. Juliana moved at his heels, pausing only to glance back tremulously in case Lovell had disturbed the other occupants of the house. No sound came from Valentine in his sickroom, or Catherine who was sitting with him. No sound came from the baby either, though that could never last.

In the main room on the first floor, Lovell eased himself into a large, ancient armchair with a carved scallop-shell back that stood beside the empty hearth. From the doorway, Juliana exclaimed faintly. 'You are in my father's chair!'

'It's damnably hard.'

'I should warn you, Father died in it.'

'When was that?'

'During the siege of Colchester.'

'He lived so long! You kept that from me. You kept a lot from me, I now suspect.'

'Nothing important,' replied Juliana matter-of-factly. 'I was true.'

'So true that you rushed into bigamy!' Obsessed, Lovell demanded in a low voice, 'Did you know this man Jukes while you knew me?'

'I met him long afterwards.'

'You were my wife, but he propositioned you?'

Tired of this, Juliana exclaimed, 'Oh be reasonable! You were long gone. I could see Gideon Jukes might love me. I could see I might love him. *You* were supposed to be in the ship lost with Prince Maurice —'

'That would have been convenient!'

A faint sheen on the forehead, combined with Lovell's hectic colour, now began to warn her he might be unwell. It made him unpredictable.

Deeper unease overcame her when he began abstractedly unbuttoning his coat so he could rub at his shoulder.

Lovell waved a hand around what he recognised was the most used room in the house. Shelves held books; he had seen books everywhere and he flattered himself some had been given to his wife by him. 'This is what you want? Your Commonwealth love-nest?' Juliana noticed warily that his tone became cajoling. 'Well, I see no objection to living this way. Come back to me, as you are meant to do. You shall have this in a house of ours, and I shall enjoy it with you.'

The request was so unreasonable, Juliana felt exhausted. 'This was what I always wanted. You and I *never* had it.'

'I gave you love.'

'And I to you – or so I tried, but I could not love the perpetually absent.' Juliana hated to engage with Lovell, but suddenly her anger came out strongly. 'You left me, Orlando, for year after year after year. You never told me your plans. You abandoned me and your children. You might never have come back to us at all, were it not for these plots I know you are tangled in. So now it is a convenience for you to say, "I am in England for my wife". But being a convenience is not enough for me. It is not marriage.'

From the high-backed, throne-like, Jacobean oak chair that had been her father's, Orlando Lovell gazed at his wife. She could see blood seeping through his shirt now, as he tried to ease his shoulder. 'I am wounded . . . Oh sweetheart, I am tired as well. Tired of constantly fighting . . . weary of squabbling with you.' He was lying. 'What would I give to have this domestic retreat? – Let us be sensible, Juliana. Protector Cromwell is elderly; he cannot last, even if he escapes murder. What will happen once he dies? He has no successor. There will be chaos. Then the King will be restored, to great rejoicing. All the King's supporters will return – I among them.' He leaned forwards. Juliana, still standing, went rigid. 'I want you back, dear heart. I want us to have the full and rich life that we have earned; I want that with you, the woman I chose, the woman who is bound to me before God and the law.'

'I will not come.'

'Must I beg you, my love?'

'I believe in divorce,' stated Juliana, without apology, regret or pity.

She had lived with a man of liberal ideals for so long, she was amazed at just how angry her declaration made Orlando Lovell. That devotee of traditional conservatism was in too much physical pain to berate her. He could only express his breath furiously, to show his disgust.

For a while Lovell closed his eyes, blotting her out, as he tried to deal with the pain in his shoulder. Juliana sat herself on a long form on one side of her dining table. Her left hand stroked the soft leather cloth that covered it in the daytime, where some people would use a turkey carpet to protect the wood from knocks. As Lovell fell silent, she considered what he had said about the political future.

Even in the dying days of the Protectorate, Juliana saw this as no moment to abandon Gideon Jukes. To return to Orlando Lovell simply because he would be among the victorious party held no appeal. She had invested her hopes too deeply elsewhere. She knew that in his heart, Gideon was preparing himself to lose all he had fought for. Her task, which she would enter into willingly and cheerfully, would be to support him as he tried to reconcile himself to whatever happened next.

A window was open, to air the room that sunny day. From somewhere below, came the cry of a very young child, calling for attention.

Juliana reacted, but stopped. Lovell saw it. He swung out of the chair and in three strides was at the window. With one hand gripping the sill, he stared down below into the small enclosed yard at the back of the property. On a rug in the sun he saw the baby playing: Celia Jukes, now nine months old, in a white dress to which were sewn long leading-reins, one of which she was devotedly chewing. She had become a beautiful baby, fair-haired, blue-eyed, bright-natured, the delight of both her parents.

Lovell realised at once whose child it was.

Juliana said nothing. There was nothing to say.

Resting in the chair had revived Lovell. He had enough energy to move. The enclosed yard reminded him that he had brought himself into a rat-trap, a cul-de-sac with no back exit. If anyone came in at the shop door, he had no escape.

He snapped into a plan. 'I shall leave your house. Do not look relieved too soon! I see you have that horse there.'

'Rumour? He was hidden when serviceable mounts were being seized to prevent rebel cavaliers taking them.'

Lovell laughed. 'Delicious! Well, a rebel cavalier is having him now! How is he brought out of your yard?'

'He has to be led through the shop –'

'You jest?'

'Unfortunately not.'

'Here is what will happen. You will saddle up your nag; I shall ride him. You will be up behind me –'

'I will not.'

'Oh, you will, my dear. Now –' On the table Lovell had found paper that Valentine been using earlier. He did not notice the significance of the boy's used juice beaker and the delft jug full of cooled friar's balsam. He still had no idea Valentine was upstairs. 'Write instructions. Tell Jukes, I will do a fair exchange – his golden child for my Tom.'

Juliana went cold. 'You are taking my baby?'

'You too. Jukes must bring Thomas to the Blue Boar in King Street at ten o'clock sharp tonight. He will be alone, unarmed, and give me no trouble. When he produces Tom, I shall return you and the pretty one. Write it.'

'No.'

Without thinking twice, Orlando Lovell put his boot on the back of a dining chair and kicked it over. As Juliana covered her mouth with her hand in horror, he pushed another sideways viciously, breaking a third. Destruction, noise and terror had arrived. *'Write!'*

Chairs are just things, thought Juliana weakly. Chairs can be mended, or replaced . . .

While she stood rooted to the spot, Lovell, despite his wound, lifted a stool one-handed and hurled it. It smashed against a wall, scarring the delicate painted plaster.

'Stop it! Be quiet and I will do it –'

Lovell behaved as cavaliers did. Pointlessly, he ripped the leather cloth from the table; everything on it cascaded to the floor. To pacify him, Juliana salvaged paper, quill and ink. Lovell kicked at the empty coal scuttle. Juliana began writing. Despite her submission, Lovell continued to destroy her home. Fired up by his personal enmity for Gideon, he wrenched the curtains from their pole, pulling the pole from the wall with them, then dragged the long strips of carpet off the hanging shelves, bringing down their contents. Plates and beakers crashed and shattered.

The result was inevitable. The commotion brought Catherine Keevil running down to investigate.

Lovell stilled. 'Oh she is a delight!' he announced, eyeing up Catherine with a leer. 'If you will not have me, madam, maybe your pretty maid will!'

'Leave her alone.' Juliana was still hastily writing.

She did not see Catherine's eyes dart to the stairs, as the girl decided to bolt for help. Then Catherine hesitated fatally. Lovell grabbed her. Juliana cried out a warning but Catherine's wild struggles became unmanageable. Lovell reacted professionally. He pulled out the carbine, cocked it, placed it to the young girl's forehead and shot her.

Frozen with horror, Juliana watched the slow slide floorwards of the lifeless Catherine Keevil. Blood and human tissue had spread on the door-frame and adjacent wall. The dead girl had joined all those other household servants who lost their lives accidentally and unfairly in the civil wars . . . Lovell dropped the corpse quite casually. 'Any other concealed helpers?'

Frantic and mute, Juliana shook her head. Lovell strode to the table, cast a glance at the written note, then grasped his trembling wife by the arm. As he pulled her with him, she had to step over Catherine, trying not to see what the bullet had done.

Lovell hauled Juliana down the steep stairs. Her skirts tangled in a dog-gate; Lovell impatiently dragged her free. He pushed her ahead, intending her to stumble and weep and plead with him, tyrannising her so she would obey him. In the sun-drenched yard, he shed Juliana roughly as he strode to the baby. He picked up the child, by her leading-reins; he swung her like a boy's top on a piece of rope. Many cavaliers had played ghastly games like this. If Celia's dress and the strings had been less robust, she would have fallen. Juliana screamed and reached out. Lovell grinned as he whirled the frightened child away from her. Terrified, Celia began to wail loudly.

Lovell slung the baby under one arm. He had to use his other forearm to shield himself from Juliana's pummelling fists. To defend himself from her furious rain of blows, Lovell swung his arm hard and felled her to the ground.

As she lay winded, she was vaguely aware of hammering at the shop door; farther away, dogs were yelping hysterically. Lovell lowered the wailing baby back onto the rug. He was almost exhausted. Restively, he unbuttoned his coat further, in order to rub at his bandaged shoulder. His savagery seemed to subside. With an expression of apology, he turned back towards Juliana, holding out a hand. She thought he intended to pull her to her feet, perhaps as a courtesy, perhaps so she could support him if he fainted.

Too late. There was a flash of white. A small figure, nightshirted and barefoot, burst upon them.

Juliana gasped. He had blood on his feet; he had run through Catherine's blood. Shock after what he had seen upstairs gave him impetus even before Orlando struck Juliana. The boy had witnessed that.

He was clutching a sword, the one the smith Lucas once rejected, that old weapon they had had for years. Recently, Gideon had sharpened it. The sword was heavy for a lad of twelve, even when held tightly in both hands. Barely able to manage, he kept the point up bravely, as he rushed forwards. He aimed where soldiers said you should, up and under the fifth rib; he guessed, but by chance he guessed correctly. Using all his strength, he ran the man through.

Gideon Jukes arrived moments later. He watched Lovell collapse. He saw Juliana, her head flung back, staring at the sky in despair; the way she was clutching the baby told him much. He saw the stricken boy, deep in shock. The sword had broken; its hilt and half the blade lay at his feet. Gideon's heart filled up with pity, though it was obvious no amount of compassion would help. The child had withdrawn into a horror that must last him all his life.

Like so many thousands of others, they were neither a cavalier nor a Roundhead family, neither wholly Royalist nor Parliamentarian. What had happened to them went beyond all matters of government. As Gideon started to grasp the events in his house today, he realised heavily how the civil war had claimed its newest victims. One more son and his brother had to live with the unthinkable. Another mother faced the endless effects of tragedy. Guilt, blame, recrimination, loneliness, misery and change lay ahead of them. They could move home, start again, seem to recover, but from this day they were all permanently damaged.

He knelt by the prone man, grasped him to provide human contact through his final moments, but his soul had ebbed out already. Nothing could be done. Not knowing who the stranger was, Valentine Lovell had just killed his father.